THE GIPSY BOY:

A ROMANCE

OF

THE WOODS AND THE WILDS.

BY THOMAS PREST,

AUTHOR OF "ELA, THE OUTCAST;" "ANGELINA;" "MARIETTE;" "OLD HOUSE OF WEST-STREET," ETC.

To hear thee speak might calm a madman's frenzy,
Till by attention he forgot his sorrow.

ROWE.

LONDON:

PRINTED AND PUBLISHED BY E. LLOYD, 12, SALISBURY-SQUARE,
FLEET-STREET.

THE RETURN OF THE LOST CHILD TO ITS MOTHER, AFTER ITS RESCUE FROM THE HANDS OF THE GIPSIES.

THE VILLAGE CONSTABLE AND THE POACHER BEFORE SQUIRE LESTER.

THE GIPSY BOY.

A ROMANCE OF THE WOODS AND THE WILDS.

BY THE AUTHOR OF "ELA, THE OUTCAST;" "OLD HOUSE OF WEST STREET;"
"MANIAC FATHER;" ETC., ETC.

See p. 10.

CHAPTER I.

THE TRAVELLERS.—THE ACCIDENT.—THE GIPSY BOY.—THE WANDERING TRIBE.
—THE FEARFUL MEETING.

LUXURIANT summer now showered its most bounteous blessings around—sweetest
season to the enraptured senses of the children of the earth, when nature displays
her richest foliage, and decorates the fields and meadows with myriads of indescribable gems, breathing the perfume of Heaven.

No.

Delightful, blushing summer! sweetly the birds attuned their throats to the wild melodies of love, and the face of creation glowed with exulting beauty.

Evening advanced. The grey shadows of twilight stole over the scenery around; while the bright monarch of the day, retiring to his western canopy, in clouds of purple and gold, cast a crimson lustre upon the summits of the lofty hills, and the luxuriant foliage of an adjacent wood. It was, in sooth, a peaceful hour, and such an one as is calculated to inspire the imagination with the most sublime thoughts. Even so calm and unclouded is the evening of age to a virtuous man; like the setting sun, adorned with tempered lustre, he sinks into the grave, directing his course to the goal from whence he may rise again with renovated splendour.

And now the bright moon burst forth with sweet and chastening effect. The heavens presented an appearance of one immeasurable ocean of silvery radiance, and the whole face of nature was bathed in the broad, mellow light.

The day had been sultry, but now the air was cool and refreshing, and came teeming to the grateful senses with the fragrance of innumerable flowers. It was an evening to tranquillize the ruffled emotions of the care-corroded breast; an evening for deep meditation, elevating the soul from the contemplation of the glories of nature, to wonder, love, and admiration of nature's God!

And what a charming scene was that upon which the pale moon now shed her lucid beams; so varied and so picturesque. At some distance was a beautiful wood, sheltered from the northern blasts by a long chain of hills, bordered with trees and shrubs, the growth of many centuries, whilst rising above a canopy of luxuriant foliage, the proud towers of an ancient edifice met the gaze of the far distant traveller, and the lofty turrets cast their long shadows across an extensive lake, that partly overspread the neighbouring valley.

The northern view was terminated by hills, grandly romantic; the valley beyond the lake led to a verdant opening of some miles in extent, revealing at once a thousand indescribable attractions.

At any time it was a scene of surpassing loveliness. The harmonious warblings of the feathered minstrels; the murmuring sound of intermingling streams; the lulling moans of the confined breezes, amidst the lofty trees, that waved their leafy heads; the verdant glades, here and there opening to the skies, and scattered over with sheep; the adjacent hills, hanging their dark brows over a vast sheet of quivering water, presented a combination of charms so magnificent, so abstracted from the busy world, that the beholder's heart thrilled with delicious transport, harmonized by the sublime sensations of enchanting melancholy.

No one would have thought, who gazed upon that fair scene, that there could have been anything like a sorrowing heart at that hour; for all nature seemed revelling in delight; yet even in that moment, serene and tranquil as the soft slumber of infancy, the dismal lamentations of anguish could be heard, so low that they might have been mistaken for the gentle sighing of the evening breeze among the exuberant foliage that everywhere abounded.

They proceeded apparently from the voice of a child, and were so soft, so plaintive, so heart-drawn, that they must have moved even the most insensible to pity.

By the roadside, before what appeared to be a natural mound, and which was covered with wild flowers, and overshadowed by the wide spreading branches of a venerable tree, knelt a boy, with clasped hands and upraised eyes, as if invoking the blessing of Heaven.

He did not seem to be more than ten or eleven years of age, and the ruddy, healthy glow of his sunburnt features strangely contrasted with the intensely melancholy expression of his countenance, a melancholy which apparently abstracted his thoughts entirely from all around.

It was sad, peculiarly impressive to behold so young a child a prey to the tortures of an anguished mind. But yet there was a tone of devotion in his attitude and looks, that could not fail to have created a feeling of melancholy admiration in the bosoms of all those who might have had an opportunity of contemplating him at that moment.

His attire was clean, but that of poverty, but as the bright moonbeams gleamed full upon him, what a countenance was there displayed! How would the skilful artist have exulted in such a subject on which to exercise his art! What would not the sculptor have given for such a model!

His features were formed in nature's most perfect mould; so regular, so nobly intelligent. His eyes were dark, full, and brilliant. No cap adorned his head, and his long silken hair, black as the plumage of the raven, flowed in picturesque luxuriance over his shoulders, gently fanned by the evening zephyrs that wafted around him.

And what did that boy at such an hour alone? Why knelt he before that flower decked mound to offer up his prayers and lamentations? Dreadful were the recollections which tortured his youthful mind in that peaceful hour. Strange and awful were the events of the past which riveted his very soul to that retired spot.

Hitherto his accents had been plaintive, melancholy, and indistinct. The large tears had glistened like pearls in the moonbeams upon his cheeks, and his small and graceful hands were clasped vehemently together in the intensity of the feelings which agitated his bosom; but suddenly he arose from his knees, and while his countenance assumed an expression of sternness, almost approaching to ferocity, that was truly awful and extraordinary in one so young, with fists clenched in the air, and every limb convulsed with the most powerful emotion, he exclaimed ;—

"Yes, by yon chaste moon that now shines so brightly upon me, and illumines the sad spot where an injured, deserted mother's cold arms encircled her poor child's neck in death, where her fond eyes closed for ever upon that child's unprotected innocence,—I swear to hate her heartless oppressor; remorse shall sting his guilty soul until he has rendered a fitting atonement for the many wrongs he has committed. Hear me, spirit of my mother, and as I keep my vow, so may happiness or misery befall me."

His handsome countenance was more than usually animated as he uttered these words; but he suddenly paused as a different feeling seemed to come over him, and looked anxiously around, as though he expected to be interrupted in his ruminations.

"They do not come," he said, "and yet I thought they would arrive before this. They will not surely chide me for having hastened on before them, so that I might have an opportunity of paying my solemn devotions here,—here at the death-bed of the unfortunate woman who gave me being. And yet their manners are at times so savage that they fill me with terror, and I have often thought of leaving them. But no, I must not be ungrateful; to them I am indebted for protection! They rescued me in helpless infancy from death, and never can I abandon my woodland life, where all are free as the fresh breeze of Heaven."

At this moment the loud rumbling of carriage wheels met the gipsy boy's ear, and immediately afterwards a piercing scream and a fearful crash followed, which awakened every echo. The sounds seemed to proceed from a romantic lane which opened on to the road, to the left of where he was standing; and instantly he hastened in that direction, and on entering the lane he perceived that one of the wheels of a travelling carriage had come off, and the postillions were disengaging the horses from the vehicle; while a gentleman of noble bearing was supporting a lady elegantly attired, and who seemed to be in a fainting condition. A beautiful little girl was clinging to the lady in a state of the greatest alarm.

The boy, prompted by curiosity and sympathy, hastened to the spot, in order that he might ascertain the extent of the accident, although it was not likely that he could render any assistance, and he then perceived that the lady was suffering more from fright than anything else, and that she was leaning apparently breathless on the shoulder of her supporter, who was a very handsome man, about five-and-thirty years of age.

"This is a most unfortunate accident, Amanda," said the gentleman; "but I trust that you are not hurt."

"No, my dear brother," answered the lady, in a faint voice; "thank Heaven it is only the violent shock that has so much alarmed me; but I am better now. My Angela!"

"Dear mamma," said the child, raising her lips to kiss her mother, who was extremely beautiful, "oh, how delighted I am that you are not hurt. I will offer up my prayers of thanksgiving to God night and morning, for having preserved my dear, dear mamma."

"My sweet, my affectionate child," said the lady, embracing the lovely little damsel with the most rapturous fondness; then turning to the gentleman, she said,—

"But this is indeed most unfortunate and vexatious; we are yet several miles from Branscombe House, and far away from any town or village. What is to be done in this dilemma?"

"I scarcely know," replied her brother; "however, we must exercise our patience. We cannot leave the vehicle in this place, and it is impossible for us to proceed in it until it is repaired. George," he continued, addressing one of the postillions, "mount one of the horses, and proceed with all possible despatch to the inn where we last put up, and bring with you some persons to repair the injury, or another vehicle to convey us the remainder of our journey. It is yet early, and as the evening is fine, we shall not be put to so much inconvenience as we otherwise should. Lose not a moment, George."

The man bowed, and instantly leaping upon the back of the horse, started off at full speed.

"Your pardon, sir," said the gipsy boy, advancing, and addressing the gentleman in accents of politeness, which it could not have been expected he was capable of, both from his youth and the poverty of his appearance, "there will be those here presently who may assist you in your present dilemma. Your carriage does not appear to have received much damage."

The gentleman turned hastily round as the boy thus spoke, for he had not before been aware of his presence, and as he fixed his eyes upon his handsome and intelligent countenance, he involuntarily started; his face became pale, and he otherwise evinced the most extraordinary emotion. The lady and her lovely daughter gazed upon him with the utmost astonishment and the deepest interest.

"Who are you, boy?" at length the gentleman faltered out, "and what brings you here?"

"I am the child of sorrow, but of freedom," replied the gipsy boy.

The emotion of the gentleman increased, and, drawing nearer to the boy, he gazed at him with greater intensity than ever.

"Your name, my lad, your name?" he eagerly demanded.

"Rosario," answered the boy; "but they call me the Fawn."

"They! whom do you mean, child?" asked the lady.

"They with whom I am associated, lady," answered the boy. "My home is in the woodlands, and the flowery dell; the green turf my bed; the bright, blue sky my canopy. Oh, it is a merry life to lead, though the proud and wealthy call us outcasts, vagrants, and frequently hunt our people from their doors, as they would beasts of prey, or send us to gaol for infringing upon what they call their vested rights; those rights which the great master of the human race sends in such abundance for the enjoyment of all his creatures."

"Poor lad, poor lad!" said the lady, compassionately. "I fear he has fallen into the hands of the base and abandoned. So young, so handsome, so intelligent, too!"

"The boy's language and appearance excite the most unaccountable sensations within my breast," said the gentleman, aside. "This spot, too, oh! what bitter, what painful recollections does it bring to my mind. Tell me, boy," he added, aloud, "who are your parents?"

"Parents!" repeated the gipsy boy, with the most extraordinary emotion, and his fine dark eyes sparkled with uncommon animation. "I have none!"

"An orphan!" ejaculated the lady, "unfortunate child!"

"Yes, yes," said the boy, after a pause, "I have one still living, I believe, whose name I know not, who should be to me a father, but whom I should ever, must ever hate."

"Hate, boy!" repeated the gentleman, with a look of astonishment, and in tremulous accents,—"hate the author of your being! Oh, why?"

"Because he is a villain."

"A villain!"

"Yes, the murderer of my poor mother," said the gypsy boy, while the big tears trembled in his eyes, and his bosom heaved with the intensity of his anguish. "Oh, I could tell you such a tale of horror, although I was so young when the dreadful event occurred which robbed me of my poor mother."

"And her name?" eagerly demanded the gentleman.

"My lips are forbidden to give utterance to it; it is buried with her in her lonely, unhallowed grave. I could tell you, how that wretched mother wandered with me, houseless, friendless, starving, when the cold blasts of winter howled around; until, worn out with want and suffering, she sank down to die not far from this place. A flowery mound marks the spot, and thither, this evening, have I been to pay my devotions, and offer up my vows. Relief came, when too late, relief from those outcast, vagrant wanderers, who are so much despised; my infant cheek received her dying caresses; her soul escaped in a blessing upon my head."

The poor boy's voice was choked with emotion, and the gentleman and his sister looked upon him with the deepest compassion, while the former evinced more than ordinary agitation, and again gazed upon the features of the gipsy boy, with the most trembling earnestness.

"But what are those persons with whom you have said you are associated, my poor boy?" asked Amanda.

"I have told you before, lady; they are wanderers, they boast the wide world for their home, and, in their lowly tents, are seen happier than those who dwell in princely halls, and roll in luxury and affluence."

"Gipsies?"

"Ay, so they are commonly called," answered the boy; "they are even now on their way to a place where they intend for awhile to encamp, and where the wealthy have never yet interfered with them. I rambled on before them in order to kneel upon the spot where my mother breathed her last sigh, and,—but, hark!—they come —I hear their voices on the evening air. Think you that hearts so light and joyous can be loaded with the many crimes that are attributed to them? Hark!"

The lady and gentleman did listen attentively, wound up as they were to a pitch of the greatest curiosity and amazement, and the wild but melodious tones of several voices, at a distance, smote their ears. Nearer, and nearer they came, and at length they were enabled to distinguish the following words:

> " By the light of the bright and bonny moon,
>   We merrily bend our way
> Far from the haunts of man, and soon
>   To our woodland home we'll stray.
>
> "Oh, what a world of joy is ours,
>   To whatever place we roam;
> No care upon our fortune lours,
>   In our happy greenwood home.
>   "Away! away!
>   To our greenwood home away!"

This simple chorus, borne as it was gradually louder upon the calm night air, had a peculiarly pleasing and romantic effect; still the lady could not help evincing some signs of fear, which the gipsy boy immediately noticed.

"Do not alarm yourself, lady," he said; "rude they be and simple in their manners, but they have hearts that throb with feelings warm within their breasts, and will not harm you. Hark! they approach nearer."

Again the voices of the wandering tribe smote the ears of the travellers, in more distinct tones than before, and they heard them sing the following additional stanza:—

> " Oh! what is a life of fine parade,—
>   What is a life of state?
> There's peace to be found in the woodland shade;
>   No pleasure is half so great.
>
> " Then, by the light of the bright bonny moon,
>   We merrily bend our way
> Far from the haunts of man, and soon
>   To our woodland home we'll stray.
>
>   "Away! away!
>   To our greenwood home away!"

"They are close at hand," said the gipsy boy, "and I must hasten to meet them. Do not fear, my lady, you will find them kind and ready to assist you."

Thus saying the boy waved his hand to them, and bounded off with the rapidity of lightning. The voices now ceased, and the travellers awaited with impatience, but not without some trepidation, the result of this adventure.

"You look dull and thoughtful, my dear brother," said Amanda, when the gipsy boy had left them.

"No, no, Amanda," replied the gentleman, with some confusion and hesitation in his manner, "though, I confess, the words of this strange boy have made a considerable impression on me."

"He is certainly a most mysterious lad, and his destiny seems to have been a cruel one," said Amanda; "from my very soul I pity him. And then he is so handsome, and so intelligent, too!"

"His features," said the gentleman, in an under tone, as if speaking to himself, and not wishing his sister to overhear him, but she did,—"his features so closely resembling one——"

He paused, when he perceived that Amanda was listening to him attentively, and he seemed vexed and confused that he should have betrayed himself into such expressions. Amanda guessed his thoughts, for she was partially acquainted with the early misfortunes of his life, and she, therefore, forbore to put any farther questions to him, for she knew it was a theme that always caused him the greatest emotion, and she had too great a regard for him to wish to give him a single pang.

They had, however, not much time given them for reflection, for, presently, they beheld the gipsies entering the lane, with a couple of carts, to carry their tents, and the women and children, while several men were on foot, whose rude and uncouth appearance filled the bosoms of Amanda and her child with dread. The gipsy boy led them on, running some distance before them, and pointing to the place where the travellers stood. Amanda and her child clung fearfully to their companion.

The boy soon arrived at the spot, and was quickly followed by the remainder of the gipsies, all of whom stopped at a short distance off, except Rosario, and one man, who advanced towards them.

This man was of a tall and athletic person, and, as far as they could distinguish his features by the light of the moon, they were dark, coarse, stern, and forbidding. His black hair hung in long tresses around his neck, and his piercing eyes peered up from beneath their shaggy brows, with an expression that was very disagreeable. He appeared to be a man verging upon fifty years of age; but, in all probability, he was not so old.

The brother of Amanda, although he was a stranger to fear, felt himself far from easy at the appearance of this man and his companions, and Amanda clung still closer to him, with an apprehension of approaching danger, which she tried but could not subdue.

"You have met with an accident, the boy tells me," said the gipsy, addressing himself to the gentleman, without appearing to take any particular notice of him.

"I have," answered the latter; "and ——"

But, before he could finish the sentence, the gipsy uttered an exclamation of mingled rage and astonishment, and, fixing his keen, black eyes upon the countenance of the gentleman, cried, in a hoarse voice, that was enough to inspire any one with terror,—

"Ah, villain! do I again encounter thee? By all the stars of evil destiny—by all the powers of revenge, it is Laurence Cleveland!"

Amanda and her daughter screamed, and even Sir Laurence Cleveland (for such was the name of the gentleman) started back aghast at the ferocious looks of the man, although he had not the least recollection of his features, and knew not for what reason he should entertain any fear of him.

"How know you my name?" he demanded, "and why do you fix such looks of deadly malice upon me?"

"How do I know your name!" repeated the gipsy, with a hollow laugh. "Can anything obliterate from my memory the hated name of Laurence Cleveland? Is it not imprinted on my brain in characters of fire? It never rises to my lips without a bitter curse."

"Oh, Heaven!" shrieked Amanda, fixing upon the gipsy a look of horror and supplication. "Man! man! why this furious rage? What do you mean?"

"Fear not, lady," replied the gipsy; "I will not harm you or your child, although you are the kindred of the hated miscreant who now stands trembling before me. But for your presence, he should never more quit this spot alive!"

"Ruffian! villain!" exclaimed Sir Laurence, erecting his form, and his eyes flashing with indignation.

"Villain!" shouted the gipsy, in terrible tones, as he drew forth a long-bladed knife from his belt, and rushed upon Sir Laurence; "by all the infernal host, if thou dost not recall that word, I will cut the lying tongue that uttered it from thy throat."

"Mercy! mercy! mercy!" shrieked the horror-struck Amanda, sinking on her knees.

"Hold, Harold!" exclaimed the gipsy boy, rushing in between Sir Laurence and the enraged miscreant; "in the name of her you say you loved, I command you—ay, boy as I am, I command you—to shed not human blood. This is no time for vengeance."

"Ah!" cried Harold, "and does the young fawn thus rise against his protector? Boy, behold! the moon turns blood-red at the sight! You know not for whom you plead. But, enough, enough; the time is not yet come. I yield, for there is much more yet to do before I complete my revenge. Blood for blood!"

"Fearful man!" said Sir Laurence, "what is the reason of this outrage? I know you not; and, therefore, what harm could I ever have done you?"

"What harm!" repeated Harold the gipsy, and his eyes seemed to flash fire; "oh! you are most immaculate, Laurence Cleveland; you never could have been guilty of any crime; of course not; ha! ha! ha! you never committed *murder!*"

"Murder!" screamed Amanda; and, overcome by the power of her emotions, she sank insensible on the earth.

"Monstrous!" ejaculated Sir Lawrence, with a look of the utmost disgust and indignation. "Man, have you no sense of shame, that you can recklessly give utterance to such brutal falsehoods?"

"Dare you deny my accusation?" demanded the gipsy, fiercely; "if you dare, hither comes one that may refresh your memory."

Sir Laurence turned his eyes, with an involuntary shudder of dread and horror, in the direction to which Harold pointed, and beheld the man who had hitherto kept back, approaching towards them, accompanied by several females of the wandering

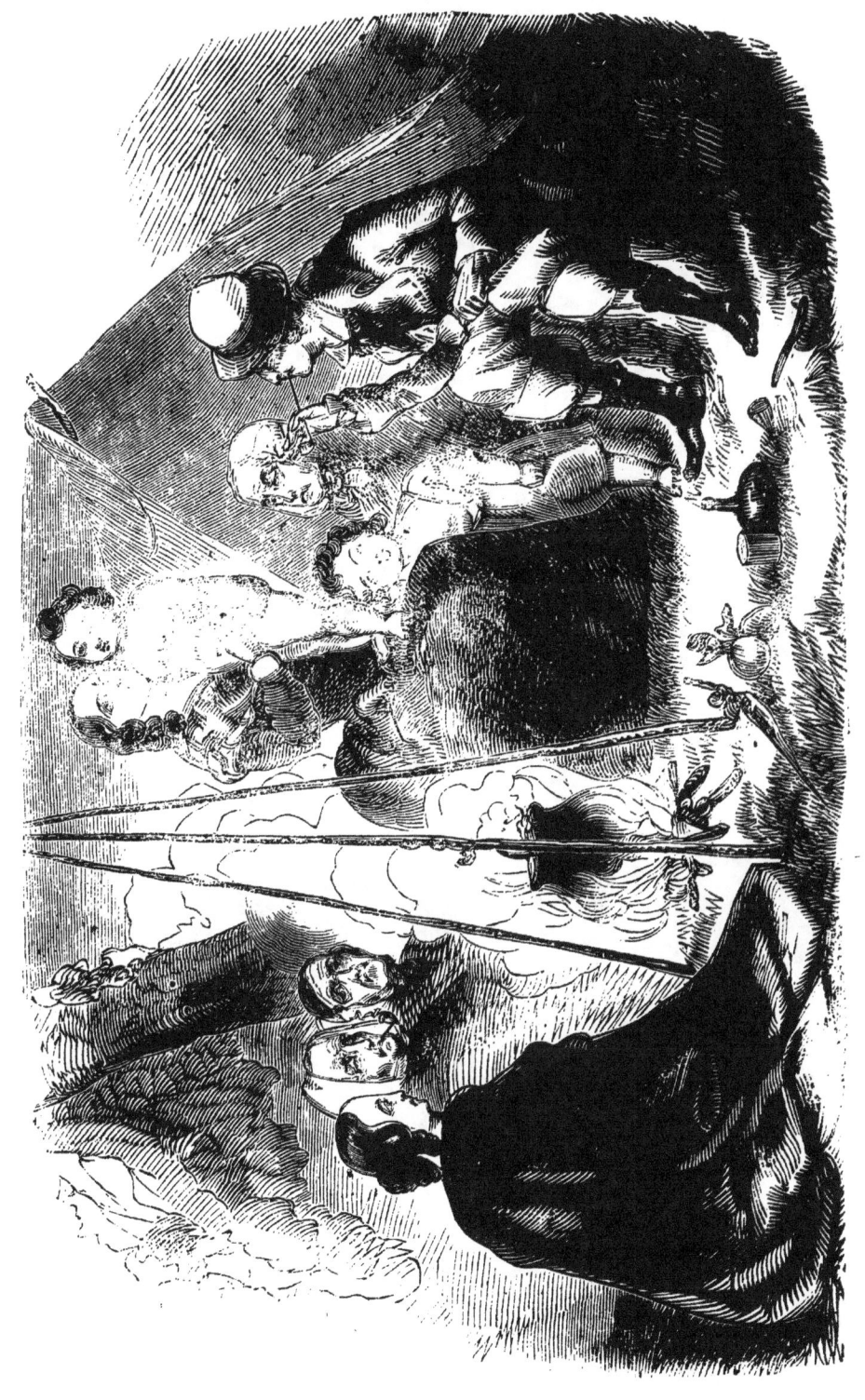

THE ADVENTURE OF AMANDA AND HER FRIEND, BLANCHE LESTER, IN THE ENCAMPME T OF THE GIPSIES.

See p. 15

tribe. He now perceived the full extent of the danger that threatened him; but, notwithstanding, he trembled more for the safety of his sister and the little Angela (who was hanging, weeping bitterly, and with pale looks, over her mother) than his own.

The gipsy boy had all this time been a greatly agitated spectator of the scene; but his handsome countenance expressed a feeling of the deepest astonishment and pity. He now approached the child, with a gentle and respectful demeanour, and smiled sweetly in her face, as if to encourage her not to be alarmed.

"Oh, do not suffer them to harm my poor mamma; do not let them kill my good, kind uncle," supplicated the innocent child, while the tears rolled quickly down her cheeks. The boy ventured to take the delicate hand of the child, and his eyes, at the same time, beamed forth an expression that imparted hope and courage to the fair little being to whom it was directed.

Amanda had now recovered, and, still clinging to her brother, gazed with the most undiminished terror at the motley and uncouth group which now surrounded them. She trembled, and Sir Laurence feared that some dreadful outrage was being discussed and contemplated; for Harold had drawn two or three of the most savage-looking of the gipsies aside, and was conversing with them in under tones, and with significant gestures directed towards him, and he could see by the fierce aspects of these wandering vagrants that danger was threatened. His mind was fearfully racked, but more by the observations of Harold, which recalled all the painful past to his memory, than even the present awkward position in which he stood. There were only he and the other postilion, who was trembling with the most uncontrollable apprehension; and what could they do, unarmed as they were, to defend themselves against such numerous and desperate men?

Involuntarily he looked towards the gipsy boy, as if he would appeal to him to interpose, and Rosario immediately responded to the appeal.

"I know you not, Sir Laurence Cleveland," he said, "for I never before heard your name mentioned; but my heart revolts at the bare idea of shedding human blood, and ——"

Before he could finish the sentence, the gipsies again advanced hastily towards them, led on by the ferocious Harold.

"Yes, there he stands," cried the latter, "the villain Laurence Cleveland!"

"Laurence Cleveland!" shouted several of the ruffians, in a breath, and brandishing their knives; "revenge—revenge! The fourteenth of May, 1798, remember. Down with the murderer!"

"Forbear!" cried the gipsy boy, with an energy and determination quite surprising in one so young, and, at the same time, starting in between Sir Laurence and his fierce assailants; "harm him not; to shed the blood of a defenceless man, however much your enemy, would be cowardly, inhuman murder, not a just retribution for the wrongs he may have done ye. Forbear, I say!"

CHAPTER II.

THE GIPSY QUEEN.—THE FEARFUL TALE.—THE CURSE, AND THE OATH OF VENGEANCE.

APPARENTLY astounded by the resolution of the gipsy boy's manner, the gipsies started back a few paces, but still glared upon Sir Laurence Cleveland with the most threatening looks. Amanda and her child were almost overwhelmed with terror, and clung to Sir Laurence with the most intense emotion, making the air resound again with their piteous shrieks. Rosario still remained fixed in his position before the travellers, and the demeanour of the boy seemed for a minute or two even to awe the gipsies into forbearance.

"Heartless men!" exclaimed Sir Laurence, "I know not in what way I have injured you; why, then, should you seek to murder me in cold blood?"

"The fourteenth of May, 1798, remember!" repeated two or three of the gipsies, and again they rushed towards the spot on which the travellers were standing.

"Hold! 'tis Madela commands. Back—back, I say!" cried a loud and almost unearthly female voice; and the men shrank back, and returned their knives to their belts in submission.

The travellers turned their eager eyes towards the spot whence this mandate proceeded, and beheld advancing towards them a form of the most singular and revolting description, which at length stood before them, and gloated upon them with looks of the most savage ferocity.

The form was that of a female, although it was only the tattered and patch-covered dress she wore that denoted her to be so. She was naturally tall and bony, but nearly bent double with age. Her skin was brown and shrivelled like that of a mummy, her features long and pointed; her hair hung wild and matted over her forehead, and her small grey eyes glared like two balls of fire. A short brown cloak depended from her shoulders, and one of her bony hands was extended in a menacing attitude towards Sir Laurence, while the other rested on a crooked-headed stick. In short, her whole appearance was anything but human, and Amanda and her child shuddered with indescribable horror as they gazed upon her.

"Begone, boy!" commanded the old woman, in a harsh, discordant voice.

"Madela," ejaculated the gipsy boy, in a supplicating tone.

"Away, croaking brat!" shouted the hag; "away, or dread the consequence!"

As she spoke, she seized the boy fiercely by the arm, and forced him from the spot. He retired with slow and reluctant steps, but stood at some distance watching with eager eyes the conduct of Madela.

The old woman now advanced still nearer to Sir Laurence and his trembling companions, and glared upon him with an expression of almost demoniacal malice and exultation, which was sufficient to appal even the stoutest heart, under the peculiar and alarming circumstances.

"Laurence Cleveland," said the hag, "we have met at last. Madela has looked anxiously for this moment for many a long and weary day; but her abode has been in other lands. Welcome, Laurence Cleveland; the gipsy queen greets ye."

"Old woman," returned Sir Laurence, "how you are acquainted with my name I know not. You are a stranger to me; what would you with me?"

"Oh, I have a long account to settle with you, Laurence Cleveland," said the old woman—"a long, a bloody account; but not now. Madela deals not mercy with her vengeance. She has years of misery in store for you—years of torturing anguish, ere she will complete her triumph."

"Woman, why these brutal threats?" demanded Sir Laurence, firmly; "I never wilfully injured mortal being, and ———"

"'Tis false!" interrupted the ancient gipsy, her eyes flashing with tenfold fierceness; "Laurence Cleveland never injured mortal being; oh! the lie should blister his tongue. Shall I repeat the tale of the two fair cousins, and will you then deny that you are a villain? Laurence Cleveland, Madela knows you well. But I will not repeat the tale of the two cousins, one of them your lawful wife, the other ———"

"Oh, forbear! forbear!" ejaculated Sir Laurence, with convulsive emotion.

"Forbear!" repeated the old woman; "oh! then I have touched your guilty conscience, have I, Laurence Cleveland? But I have much,—much more to remind you of yet. On the fourteenth of May, 1798, two poor wretches, father and son, were ordered for death. You remember that,—you must, for you were one of the principal actors in the frightful, the barbarous tragedy."

" They were guilty of murder !"

" 'Tis false! false as thine own black heart. They were accused of the murder of a gamekeeper,—your gamekeeper, Laurence Cleveland, and, on your evidence, were convicted. But they were innocent,—innocent as the child that now stands by your side. They were, as I have before said, father and son; the latter had been your rival in the affections of her you afterwards consigned to misery and death. He was then good and honest, but you destroyed his hopes,—left him to despair, and unable to attend to his work; he became reduced to poverty. He had been the main support of his aged parents, your treachery made him a poacher, for he could not, and would not see his parents starve, whilst wealthy robbers had rich preserves, fattening upon their oppressed tenants, for their mere amusement. What are the facts of the case? One of your gamekeepers, who had made himself generally obnoxious, was found assassinated on your estate; on the same night, you were returning home from a visit you had been paying to one of your friends, when you saw two men retreating from the spot where the body of the murdered man was found, whom you afterwards swore, positively, were the wretched father and his son, and, upon your evidence, Laurence Cleveland, they were condemned. No doubt it was a feeling of revenge that goaded you on; and you knew that you were uttering the most atrocious lies at the time you were giving your evidence."

" By all my hopes," exclaimed the agitated Sir Laurence, " I did not. I really believed them guilty of the dreadful crime that was alleged against them, and I still think so now."

' " Liar!" shrieked Madela, and her frightful countenance became still more hideously distorted with rage; " they were innocent. They were far away from the spot at the time the murder was perpetrated, and there was sufficient evidence brought forward on the trial to prove that; but still their inhuman persecutors were bent on their destruction, and they were convicted."

" Heaven pardon me if they were guiltless!" ejaculated Cleveland.

" If they were guiltless!" repeated the old woman; " dare you doubt it? No; I see from your pale face, and quivering lips, that your conscience will not permit you to do so. Oh! Laurence Cleveland, Laurence Cleveland, you have a severe account to render for this!"

" But they did not both die, they ———"

" No; they did not both perish; it is strange that the murderers should so far relent as to spare the boy! they transported him for life, but they hung the poor, grey-headed, innocent old man like a dog. Laurence Cleveland, the blood of that murdered aged man is upon your head. For that deed you will be pursued to destruction. A curse, a terrible malediction is impending over ye, and, as sure as yon bright moon shall again illumine the heavens, it will be fulfilled."

" Oh! spare him, my good woman; spare my brother!" implored Amanda, with looks of distraction.

" Spare him, lady!" repeated Madela; " oh! it shall be my delight to wring his guilty heart,—to dash the cup of happiness from his lips, and to replace it with one of rankling poison. I have much to do,—much to do; ha! ha! ha! and all is ripe for the execution of my work."

" For Heaven's sake, leave me, woman."

" No, no; not till I have told you all, Laurence Cleveland," returned Madela, with a frightful grin. " Hark ye! the corpse of the murdered old man was stolen from the gibbet, and, while his bereaved widow gazed upon his ghastly face, distorted by the bloody work of the hangman, and the glazed eyes of her dead husband, protruding from their sockets, seemed to gaze upon her in approbation, she breathed a heavy, a dreadful curse on the head of Laurence Cleveland, and swore that she would hunt him through the world to destruction. And that curse shall spread like the night-cloud over you and yours! You may marry,—you may have fair, smiling babes, but the curse shall pursue them as well as you: she who breathed it over the corpse of her murdered husband, will live to see it fulfilled. Yes; she would travel many weary miles to hear the music of the rattling stones upon the coffins of your children!"

"Hold! hold! woman," groaned the distracted Sir Laurence; "I can endure no more."

"Ha! ha! ha!" laughed the frightful old woman; "then my words torture you; you cannot despise them. Oh! this is well,—this is well,—I triumph! What ho!"

Quick at the summons the gipsies approached, led on by Harold, and surrounded the alarmed Sir Laurence and his companions, forming a circle.

"Unsheath you knives, on your knees, and swear revenge to the death against Laurence Cleveland!" fiercely demanded Madela.

Quickly the men and women obeyed this order, but the gipsy boy stood erect amongst them, and gazed with an eye of pity at Sir Laurence and his sister.

"On your knees, boy, and join in the oath of vengeance!" said the old woman.

"Oh! Madela, spare me!" supplicated the boy; "I dare not; my heart revolts at the horrible idea!"

"Your heart revolts, brat, quivering worm! Down, down!"

"I will not swear revenge against one who never injured me!" exclaimed the gipsy boy, firmly.

"Daring recreant!" cried the ruffian Harold, as he struck the poor boy a violent blow, that felled him to the earth. The gipsies then took the oath, crossing their knives, and the women giving utterance to an appalling shriek, that reverberated far around.

They then arose from their knees, and some of them carried the insensible form of the gipsy boy to one of the carts, while the others continued to surround Sir Laurence and his companions.

"Now, Laurence Cleveland," said Madela, "you have heard the oath plighted by the wandering tribe, and, mark me, it will not fail to be fulfilled. You may seek to destroy us—to cast us into prison—but it will be all in vain; and woe to him who dares to attempt to injure one of the gipsy tribe. We will leave you now to your own pleasant reflections; but we shall meet again ere long. In the meantime, remember the fatal day—remember the fourteenth of May, 1798, and tremble!"

Thus saying, the hideous old hag shook her bony fist menacingly at Sir Laurence, and motioning to her companions, they moved away from the spot, and were soon hidden from the sight by a turning in the lane.

What a state of mind was Sir Laurence now in! All the painful occurrences of the past rushed upon his memory with vivid force, and it was in vain that he attempted to treat the threats of the gipsies with indifference, for he well knew their determined and revengeful disposition; and after what had taken place, he felt that he had every reason to dread them. The gipsy boy, too—he could not forget him;

the beauty of his countenance, the manner in which he had interposed between him and the ruffians interested him in his favour; and yet, by a strange anomaly, he could not think upon him without a sensation bordering upon fear.

There were many events in the past life of Sir Laurence Cleveland, which he would have been glad to have had the power to recall, although in some of the most important particulars he could not consider himself altogether to blame.

But his attention was diverted from these meditations to the condition of his sister, who had again become insensible; and poor little Angela was so terrified, that he had the greatest difficulty imaginable to pacify her. At length Amanda recovered, and, looking around her, ejaculated,—

"Where are they? Where are those terrible people, whose frightful threats still ring in mine ears?"

"They are gone, dear Amanda," answered her brother. "Compose yourself; we have nothing more to fear from them."

"Nothing more to fear from them, brother!" said Amanda. "Oh! can I rest assured of that, after the observations of that fearful old woman?"

"They were the observations of a mad woman, Amanda. Heed them not."

"But your face is pale, dear Laurence; their threats have alarmed you, although you seek to persuade me to the contrary. That dreadful tale which the old woman told, say, is it not true?"

"It is," answered Sir Laurence; "but the men were guilty; I can entertain no doubt of it; and surely they merited the punishment, terrible as it was, that they met with."

"Would to Heaven that it had never happened!" said Amanda; "for what fearful enemies has it created against you."

"I fear them not—indeed I do not, Amanda. I have the law on my side to protect me from danger."

"Alas! how can you guard yourself against wretches who have such secret ways of accomplishing their guilty designs?"

Sir Laurence returned no answer, and their thoughts then turned to their immediate situation.

"George cannot be long ere he returns," said Sir Laurence; "but to think of walking the remainder of the journey would be madness."

"It is a most unfortunate accident," said Amanda; "but for that we might have been now at Branscombe House, and the terrors of this encounter would have been avoided."

"True," said Sir Laurence; "but it cannot be helped; and we must endeavour to banish the occurrences of this evening from our memory."

But although Sir Laurence thus advised, he was far from being able to accomplish it himself. The observations and threats of old Madela and the gipsy Harold had sunk deep into his heart, and filled his bosom with conflicting doubts and apprehensions.

"That poor boy, too," observed Amanda; "I can never cease to remember him. How noble was his bearing, how handsome and intelligent his features! Alas! what a pity it is that one so young, and so well calculated to become an ornament to society, should be placed in the power of such wretches."

"It is," sighed Sir Laurence, as he recalled to his memory the melancholy and extraordinary story which the gipsy boy had told them.

The moon, which had all along shone forth so resplendently, now suddenly became obscured by clouds, and the wind began to murmur in fitful gusts among the foliage.

"I fear we shall have a storm presently," said Amanda. "I wish that George would return."

She had scarcely spoken, when the noise of carriage wheels was heard, and presently afterwards she perceived the servant approaching along the lane, with a post-chaise which he had hired at the inn. He had also brought with him two men to repair his master's carriage.

"Did you encounter anything particular on your return?" inquired Sir Laurence.

The man answered in the negative, and Sir Laurence having ordered the other postilion to follow with the carriage as soon as it was repaired, assisted his sister and niece into the post-chaise, and following himself, it was driven off as quickly as possible towards the place of their destination.

It was in vain that Sir Laurence tried to rally his spirits during the remainder of the journey; the extraordinary and alarming events of the evening occupied his whole thoughts, and he became melancholy and abstracted from everything else.

At length they arrived at Branscombe House, the family seat of Sir Laurence Cleveland, and after partaking of a hasty repast, both not being in the humour to converse, they retired to their chambers.

Sir Laurence sat for some time in gloomy meditation upon the adventures of the evening before he sought his couch, and it was then with a mind but ill at ease.

CHAPTER III.

FAMILY PARTICULARS.—THE NUPTIALS.—THE INTERRUPTION.—THE ACCUSATION.

BRANSCOMBE HOUSE was an elegant modern structure, which had been erected by the father of the present Sir Laurence Cleveland. It stood in one of the most lively parts of the county, remarkable for the diversified character of its scenery, and formed a principal object of attraction in that part of the kingdom.

The numberless small cottages that were besprinkled in the vicinity of the mansion bespoke the hospitality of its lord; the happiness and good fellowship of the rustics conferred a degree of lustre on his name that idle ostentation might have blushed to behold, and was pregnant with that tranquillity of mind which is rarely found in the palaces of the most splendid cities.

The parents of Sir Laurence had been dead for many years at the time this narrative commences, leaving him and a daughter, the fair Amanda, we have already introduced to the reader, and who a short time afterwards had married an officer in the navy, who had been slain about twelvemonths before in an engagement with the enemy.

Amanda was for some time inconsolable at this melancholy bereavement, and, therefore, Sir Laurence offered her an asylum in his house, which she gladly accepted, and it was in conveying her and the little Angela to his mansion that they met with the extraordinary and alarming adventure which has been detailed in the previous chapters.

Sir Laurence Cleveland was an extremely handsome man, and his mind was a rich mine of knowledge and elegant acquirements. His character will be more fully developed in the course of our tale; it may be sufficient to state that it was a strange combination of contradictions—of virtues and errors—that clashed with each other, and gave birth to the many misfortunes which attended his life. He was generous and hospitable, almost to a fault; but his passions were powerful, and frequently gained a greater ascendancy over him than he could control.

It was well known that Sir Laurence had been once privately married, to a female of the most surpassing loveliness, but in an inferior station of life; but it would seem that the marriage was an unfortunate one. She suddenly eloped, and it was not known what had become of her, until there was an announcement of her death in the newspapers, and that circumstance appeared to have a melancholy effect for some time upon his mind; but it would mar the interest of our narrative to explain further at present.

After this occurrence, Sir Laurence travelled for two or three years on the continent, where he was introduced to an English gentleman, a widower, and the charms and numerous accomplishments of whose only daughter immediately made a powerful and lasting impression upon his heart, and he paid her the most marked attention, and soon had the gratification to find that his passion was returned.

Blanche Lester was, indeed, a damsel formed for universal love and admiration— fair, accomplished, and amiable; no wonder that she should take such an immediate hold upon the affections of the susceptible and gallant Sir Laurence Cleveland. He loved her with a feeling as pure as it was intense; and Blanche did not hesitate to acknowledge that the sentiments he had inspired her with were as fervent as his own.

Mr. Lester entertained the highest opinion of the character of Sir Laurence, and he, therefore, gave every encouragement to his addresses, confident in his own mind that they were formed to make each other happy. Alas! little could he foresee the many severe misfortunes which were destined to follow their union, or how strenuously would he have endeavoured to nip their passion in the bud.

The happiness of the lovers was now complete, and they looked forward to the future with the most blissful anticipations.

Tired of the continent, they returned to England together, and where, upon their arrival, every arrangement was made, and the day appointed for their nuptials to take place. The fair Blanche and her father looked forward to the happy day with the most sanguine anticipations; for what but happiness, they imagined, could spring from the union of two persons whose dispositions were so much alike? Little did they expect the events which were destined to take place, and which would so cruelly blight the hopes which they had formed; little did they imagine that anything but feelings of the most honourable description, could ever find a place in the bosom of Sir Laurence, or that he could ever have been guilty of a single act which he should feel ashamed to have revealed to the world. But, unfortunately, as we have before intimated, there were many circumstances in the early part of the life of Sir Laurence Cleveland, which he had bitter cause to regret, and which caused him many hours of uneasiness and painful reflection.

That he loved the beauteous Blanche Lester with a sentiment of the greatest purity, cannot be denied, but there were moments when other forms would arise to his imagination, and in such moments he could not but feel himself unworthy of her, and almost trembled in her presence

The note of preparation for the union now resounded throughout the wide domain of Sir Laurence Cleveland, as it was determined to celebrate that auspicious event in a style of the most extraordinary magnificence; but, in the interval, Sir Laurence and

Blanche experienced a temporary separation, as it was his particular wish that his sister should be present on the occasion, and Blanche was anxious to be introduced to that amiable lady to whom she was about to become so closely allied. What took place on that eventful journey has been already related.

Sir Laurence passed a most wretched night, for his mind was tormented with

See p. 19.

racking thoughts, retrospections, and fearful anticipations, and the wild and savage threats of old Madela and the ruffian Harold, in spite of all his efforts to the contrary, inspired him with apprehensions of the most powerful description. The image of the gipsy boy was also constantly present to his imagination, and the more he reflected upon his strange conduct, the farther he became involved in perplexity.

By the morning, however, he became more tranquil, and met his sister with an unruffled brow.   He evinced by his demeanour that he was anxious that no allusion should be made to the gipsies, and she forbore to do so, as she saw that it caused him pain; but she had her own thoughts upon the subject, and she felt extreme anxiety for the safety of her brother, after the threats of vengeance which had been uttered by Madela and the gipsy Harold.   She had heard much of the desperate character of the wandering tribe when their evil passions were excited, and of their secret means of carrying their designs into effect, which it might be difficult to frustrate; and it was evident that they viewed Sir Laurence as an enemy who had done them, or those connected with them, some real or imagined injury, and therefore she saw plainly that there was too much reason to fear them.

Rosario had created the deepest interest in her bosom, and she could not but think of him with astonishment, sympathy, and admiration.   She longed to behold him again, and, if possible, to elicit something more of his history.

We will pass over the introduction of Amanda to Blanche Lester and her father; suffice it to say, that the amiable females were immediately prepossessed in each others favour, and Amanda could not but anticipate every felicity to her brother in a union with one who was so every way worthy of him.

Several days passed away, and nothing more was heard of the gipsies, and Sir Laurence had regained his usual tranquillity; his whole thoughts being occupied with the expected happiness that was in store for him.   And now the auspicious morning arrived, and was ushered in with every demonstration of joy.   Branscombe House had seldom or never before presented so animated an appearance.   The *elite* of elegance and fashion thronged its noble halls, the villagers for miles around had been invited to partake of the hospitalities and festivities of the happy day, and every countenance evinced the pleasure that occupied the breast.   It was, in fact, a complete holiday, and nought but the sounds of exuberant but harmless mirth could be heard on every side.

The spacious gardens of the mansion were crowded with delighted rustics, and a triumphant arch occupied the space from the house to the sacred edifice where the nuptial ceremony was to be solemnized, and around the doors of which anxious crowds were waiting at an early hour, eager to catch a glance of the beauteous bride and her friends, and to give vent to their enthusiasm on the occasion.   In different parts of the neighbourhood bands of music sent forth their joyous strains, and all was hilarity, harmony, and sanguine anticipation.

. The hour approached, and the bridal procession was seen wending its course to the church amid the rapturous shouts of the assembled multitude.   How transcendently lovely appeared Blanche Lester on that auspicious occasion; and yet she looked at times very pale, and a trembling sensation came over her, which might reasonably be attributed to maiden timidity, and the important change which she was about to undergo.

The bridegroom looked contented, but serious, and notwithstanding all his endeavours to banish it, he could not help feeling a sensation of melancholy foreboding, which seemed most unaccountable on an event so important to his future happiness.

Just before the procession reached the church the eye of Sir Laurence suddenly rested upon the forbidding countenance of a man, whom he thought he had seen before, and he involuntarily started; but the man was lost in an instant among the crowd, and the bridal procession entered the sacred edifice.

And now the bride and bridegroom kneel before the altar, the sacred and solemn rites commence, and all is breathless attention. It proceeds; the final benediction is pronounced, the organ sends forth its lofty peal, and its impressive tones are responded to by the simultaneous blessings of the numerous persons assembled; when suddenly between the pauses everyone was startled with loud shouts of rude laughter, which seemed to proceed from several voices, and completely shook the roof of the holy building.

The utmost astonishment, disgust, and horror prevailed at this sacrilegious outrage, this monstrous desecration of so solemn an occasion. The bride turned ghastly pale and clung to her husband, trembling in every limb; a deathly chill fell upon the heart of Sir Laurence Cleveland, and the minister started aghast with pious horror and indignation. But they were not long kept in suspense, for soon, to the indescribable astonishment of all present, a number of men, rudely clad, were seen rushing up the aisle, and the confusion, resentment, and fears of Sir Laurence may be easily conceived, when he recognised in the persons of the daring intruders the gipsies he had recently encountered, who were led on by the ruffian Harold, all being well armed, and having evidently come prepared to perpetrate some desperate outrage.

Nothing could equal the consternation and amazement that prevailed, so singular and so unexpected was this event. The persons assembled in the church involuntarily shrank back, and allowed the gipsies to pass, who advanced boldly up to the altar, Harold confronting Sir Laurence with a stern, malignant, and exulting expression of countenance, and looking with contempt and derision upon the astonished persons assembled.

Blanche uttered a scream of terror, and clung to her father, who was so confounded that he was unable to move, or to utter a syllable.

"What means this brutal intrusion?" Sir Laurence at length found power to exclaim. "Villains, what evil designs bring you here on this sacred and solemn occasion?"

"Villains!" repeated several of the gipsies in a breath, and with threatening looks.

"Hold, lads!" cried Harold; "let the dog have his say; we shall have plenty of time to make him recall his words, and bitterly to repent that he ever gave utterance to them. We come, Laurence Cleveland, and you, fair lady, bride, and no bride, without the just title, we—come, although not invited, to congratulate you on this auspicious event; ha! ha! Oh! it is a bright morning for me, Laurence Cleveland, although black, and heavy clouds hang over your head, and will, ere long, burst, to overwhelm you with destruction. It is the first step to the gipsy Harold's revenge. He holds ye now in his power,—at his mercy! I greet you well, Sir Laurence Cleveland, on your wedding morn."

"Daring men!" exclaimed the minister, "why do you thus profane this holy building by your presence? Are you not afraid that the vengeance of the law, as well as of Heaven will descend upon you? Speak your business and be gone, or tremble at the consequences."

"Old man," returned Harold; "your exhortations have no terrors for us. We are deperate men, and unused to be daunted by the threats of punishment. I come here to do an act of justice, and it will not be you, or any one present, that shall prevent my speaking. Laurence Cleveland, I told ye that we should shortly meet again; once more I greet you well on your nuptials."

Poor Blanche trembled more violently than ever, and glanced with looks of the

most indescribable terror to her husband for an explanation.   But how shall we por·
tray the agony and confusion of Sir Laurence, at the bold effrontery of Harold, and
the fierce looks of malice and exultation which the gipsies fixed upon him?   He felt
a strange apprehension of what would be the result of this alarming event, while he
fancied that every person present looked upon him with doubt and suspicion.   He
almost feared to encounter the eyes of Blanche, for he thought he read in her glances
a sentiment of reproach, and, for a few moments, he was completely deprived of the
power of speech.

   " I command you, as the father of the bride, to explain the meaning of this, and
for what purpose you have come hither ?" said Mr. Lester.

   " You command !" repeated Harold, with a look of scorn.   " But we are no enemies of yours, Squire Lester ; it is only those who do us an injury that incite our
wrath ; nay more, we pity you and your daughter, to think that you have been made
the victims of yon shameless villain."

   " Miscreant !" cried the exasperated Sir Laurence, his eyes flashing with indignation, and every muscle of his countenance convulsed with emotion ; " I will endure
this no longer.   Leave the church, or ———"

   " Leave the church, and at the mandate of Laurence Cleveland !" ejaculated
Harold. " Fool ! see you not that we are armed, and strong enough to crush you and
your trembling myrmidons?   I came here to warn that poor, confiding damsel, to
whom you have just plighted your vows, but which justly belong to another !"

   " Ah !" exclaimed Sir Laurence, and his lips quivered, and all eyes were bent
upon him in suspense and anxiety ; " what diabolical falsehood would you give utterance to now ?   Of what would you dare accuse me ?"

   " I come here to utter no falsehood, Cleveland," returned Harold, firmly ; " I
come here to speak the truth. I accuse Laurence Cleveland of being ———"

   " What ?" demanded Blanche and her father, in a state of agony that was almost
insupportable ; " what do you accuse Sir Laurence Cleveland of being ?"

   " A bigamist !" replied Harold, in a loud voice, and fixing a look of diabolical
exultation upon Sir Laurence.

   The bride uttered a piercing shriek that reverberated through the lofty building,
and immediately sank insensible in the arms of her father, whilst Sir Laurence stood
the perfect effigy of terror and confusion.

CHAPTER IV.

THE FEARFUL CONFLICT IN THE CHURCH.—THE GIPSY BOY WOUNDED.— DISTRACTION OF BLANCHE.

LANGUAGE must fail to do anything like adequate justice to the scene which followed this strange and daring accusation ; but the looks of the wandering tribe fully
evinced the fiendish feelings of triumph which they experienced.   Had the vengeance
of retributive justice at that moment descended upon the head of Sir Laurence Cleveland, he could not have suffered greater terror and dismay than he at that time displayed.   He fixed one hasty look upon Blanche, over whose inanimate form her
father was hanging, in the most unspeakable anguish and consternation.   His chest
heaved convulsively ; and then, in a voice hoarse with the power of his emotions, he
exclaimed,—

" What monstrous falsehood is this? What demon mind could have conceived so diabolical a charge? My fair Blanche, my bride, oh! look up and speak to me."

" Villain!" cried Harold—" liar! Blanche Lester cannot be your bride, whilst she to whom you formerly plighted your vows at the altar, still lives."

" Lives—lives!" ejaculated the distracted father. " Oh! can this—is this, indeed, true?"

" It is," replied the gipsy; " the cruelly traduced wife of Laurence Cleveland, rumoured to be no more, is still in existence, and I can bring unquestionable proof of what I assert, whenever I think proper."

" Lying fiend!" exclaimed Sir Laurence, worked up to a pitch of complete madness, " I will not stand tamely by, and listen to this base assertion. The woman of whom you speak eloped from me years since, and when, abandoned by her paramour, she was stung with remorse, in a moment of despair she committed suicide."

" Oh, but you are much deceived, Laurence Cleveland," returned Harold, with increasing triumph; " your wife—your lawful wife, I repeat—still lives. She was not false to you; and at a fitting time she will herself be able to corroborate the gipsy Harold's statement, and, to your shame and confusion, rebut the foul calumny you have heaped upon her. Oh! I triumph, for I see that your craven heart shrinks beneath my power. But I have tortures yet more exquisite in store for you. Do you remember the treatment of your wretched victim—the fair, the lovely cousin of your wife; shall I recall to your mind ——"

"No more—no more, black-hearted scoundrel," interrupted Sir Laurence, unable any longer to control himself. " Friends, will you stand tamely by, and suffer this ruffian thus to libel my character? On to the villains, I say, and drive them from the neighbourhood."

" Drive us from the neighbourhood, will you? libertine, deceiver, bigamist!" shouted Harold. " Oh! this is a rare bridal morn, Laurence Cleveland. I give you joy of it. To your knives, boys, and death to those who dare to interrupt us!"

" Cowards!" ejaculated Sir Laurence; " is this the gratitude I receive for all the services I have rendered you? Nay, then, since you are so faint of heart, thus will I set you the example."

He rushed upon Harold as he spoke, and struggled with him violently, endeavouring to disarm him. In a moment a scene of riot and confusion ensued that baffles all description; the other gipsies making an attack upon the rustics and other persons in the church, and filling the air with their dreadful maledictions. The minister and the females rushed from the sacred building, in terror and dismay, Mr. Lester following their example, and supporting the still insensible form of his daughter in his arms. The gipsies were, however, more than a match for their opponents, who being only armed with sticks, several of them were wounded.

Sir Laurence displayed uncommon strength and resolution, and having succeeded in wrenching a pistol from the grasp of Harold, he hurled him to some distance from him, and while in the act of discharging the contents of the deadly weapon at him, a piercing exclamation was heard, and Rosario rushed in frantically between them. It was too late for Sir Laurence to avert his hand, and the unfortunate gipsy boy receiving the contents of the pistol in his arm, sank groaning and bleeding to the earth.

Sir Laurence started back, appalled at what he had done, and the gipsies seemed quite panic-stricken at the unexpected calamity.

"Revenge! revenge!" cried the infuriated Harold; "the blood of the Fawn is shed,—the blood of the gipsy boy calls aloud for retribution! Down with his murderer!"

With a terrific shout the gipsies were rushing on Sir Laurence, who was so horror-struck and confounded that he was unable to offer any resistance; but his friends, seeing that his life was placed in imminent peril, determinedly drove them back, and several of them surrounding him, forced him from the church, and hurried him towards the mansion, before he was at all conscious of what was taking place.

The conflict still continued to rage with unabated fury, but at length the whole neighbourhood being by this time alarmed, numbers more rushed to the combat, and the gipsies, seeing their danger, took up the bleeding form of the gipsy boy, and rushed precipitately from the church, in great confusion, pursued by a vast crowd of persons. They, however, managed to keep them at bay, and having gained an adjacent wood, were soon out of sight, and the pursuit was abandoned, until instructions should be issued by the proper authorities.

Surely such a bridal morn as this had never been witnessed, and the excitement it caused in the neighbourhood of the mansion, and for miles around, was most intense. But what were the emotions of all those who were immediately interested in it? It would require, indeed, a powerful pencil to give anything like even a faint idea of them. Poor Blanche had been in a state of insensibility ever since the fearful accusation of Harold in the church, and had been conveyed by her distracted father to his own residence, whither he had been accompanied by the scarcely less agonised Amanda, whose feelings of horror at the bare imputation that was cast upon her brother's character may be easily conceived.

As for Sir Laurence, on his being escorted to Branscombe House, he threw himself into a chair, and for some time gazed wildly and vacantly around him, without being conscious of the full extent of what had happened. His brain seemed to be on fire, and his pulse throbbed with alarming violence. Several of his friends, who had been invited to the marriage festival, were in attendance upon him, and did all they could to soothe him and to arouse him to recollection, but for some time all their efforts were unavailing. At length, however, he suddenly started to his feet, and in a voice of distraction, exclaimed:—

"Where is my wife?—my fair bride—my Blanche? Why is she not here?—she cannot surely believe in this foul calumny?"

"She is at the house of Mr. Lester, Sir Laurence," answered one of his friends.

"At the house of her father!" repeated Sir Laurence; "why is she removed there? This is her future home. Where should she be but at the residence of her husband? Yes, her husband, by all the laws of God and man."

"It would be better for you to endeavour to calm yourself, Sir Laurence, before you attempt to see her again," remarked the gentleman. "This trying event must have proved a terrible shock to her feelings."

"And think you," demanded Sir Laurence, "that I will suffer my beauteous, my innocent Blanche to be torn from me on my nuptial day? I tell you it is a cruel and infamous plot to ruin me. No one can believe the assertions of such miscreants; it would be monstrous to do so. But I will immediately seek my wife; she is mine by every right, human and divine, and no one shall keep her from me."

The friends of the unhappy Sir Laurence saw it would be useless to attempt to remonstrate with him farther, and they, therefore, no longer opposed his departure from the mansion. He hurried, with disordered steps, and a mind bordering on frenzy, from the house towards the residence of Mr. Lester, where he quickly arrived, and demanded an immediate interview with Blanche. He was informed that she was in such a state of mind that such a meeting might be attended with the most dangerous consequences; but this assurance only added to his agony and impatience.

"Who shall dare to prevent my seeing my lawful bride?" he demanded of his sister, who now entered the room, and advanced affectionately, and with looks of the deepest melancholy and sympathy, towards him; "you, surely, will not offer to obstruct me, Amanda?"

"Oh, my dear brother!" ejaculated Amanda; "let me, I implore you, for the present prevail upon you to desist. Poor Blanche is in no condition to bear such an interview."

"Nay, if she does not behold me she will be persuaded that I am guilty of the foul charge with which I am accused. Let me pass, Amanda; I will not, by Heaven I will not, be detained."

He was rushing past his sister and making towards the door, when it was thrown open and Mr. Lester entered. His countenance expressed the greatest grief, and his whole demeanour was extremely agitated.

"Blanche!" exclaimed Sir Laurence; "I must see her. Why have you taken my wife from me?"

"Oh, Sir Laurence," sighed Mr. Lester; "is she, indeed, your lawful wife? I fear that you have blighted the hopes of my poor child for ever."

"Mr. Lester," replied Sir Laurence, with an air of offended pride and reproach, "and is it possible that you can believe me so heartless a villain as thus to deceive you and your daughter? By Heaven I should be a miscreant of the blackest dye, could I, even for a moment, ever have contemplated such a crime."

"I would fain believe you innocent," said Mr. Lester; "but still an unconquerable dread occupies my mind. My daughter must remain beneath her father's roof until you have fully and satisfactorily removed the dreadful stigma that has been cast upon you."

"Would you wish to separate me from her who, in the face of high Heaven, I this morning made my wife? It cannot be. Would you break the heart of your child?"

"Sir Laurence, how am I to act?" said Mr. Lester. "That fearful man not only asserted that the unfortunate woman to whom you acknowledge you gave your hand is alive, but that she will be ready to come forward, whenever she thinks proper, to corroborate the truth of his statements."

"Then let him produce her," returned Sir Laurence; "I defy him to do so. But, oh, it is most cruel and unjust to believe the statements of that abandoned villain; he is only goaded on by a feeling of deadly hatred and revenge against me. But I will pursue him to destruction, and will not rest until I have compelled him to recant the monstrous calumnies he has heaped upon me."

"May Heaven send that you may be able to do so! But let me beg of you to calm your feelings, and not to persist in seeing Blanche in her present state of mind."

"I shall go mad if I do not behold her, and at her feet protest my innocence."

"Alas! I foresee that this fatal day will be productive of misery to us all. Would to God that you had never met! but little did I expect that ever we should be put to so severe a trial as this."

"My patience can endure this no longer," cried Sir Laurence; "I must, I will behold my beloved Blanche. She will not believe me guilty."

He darted past Mr. Lester, as he spoke, followed by him, and immediately made his way towards the apartment in which he heard that Blanche was.

On his entrance, he found her reclining on a sofa, and supported by two domestics. Her lovely countenance was pale as death, and her eyes seemed to glare upon vacancy. He rushed towards her, and seizing her fair hand, covered it with impassioned kisses, while his voice was almost choked with convulsive sobs, which entirely defied all his manly efforts to restrain.

"My wife, my lawful wife," he cried, "oh, speak to me, and relieve me from this maddening suspense! Say that you cannot believe me guilty."

"Ah! Laurence, my lord, my husband!" shrieked Blanche, entwining her lovely arms fondly around his neck, and looking with an expression in his face no language can depict.

"Ah! transporting words!" exclaimed Sir Laurence, as he clasped her more rapturously to his bosom. "She does acquit me of the foul charge. She does believe me innocent."

"My husband," said Blanche, with a fearful shudder, and appearing to recollect herself—"no, no, I must not call you so. Oh, God! that fearful man, he said that you were the husband of another, who is still living; he called me bride and no bride; he——oh, horror! horror!"

"Blanche—Blanche! oh, spare me!" groaned the wretched Sir Laurence, with the most intense agony. "By the Almighty God, I swear that it is all false which that atrocious villain stated. But you will banish the dreadful idea from your mind; you are my wife, my own, my lawful wife; no other woman lives that can claim those holy vows which belong to you alone. Here on my knees I swear it, and may Heaven prosper me as I speak the truth. Blanche, let not the malice of a wretch, unworthy of the name of a man, turn your heart against me. Recall to your memory the many hours of happiness we have passed together; the promises, the asseverations that have passed between us; think of all this, and say, can you, will you discard me from your heart, on the bare assertions of a villain, an outcast from society—a miscreant who would not shrink from the perpetration of any crime?"

Sir Laurence spoke with uncommon energy, for he was worked up to a pitch of madness and despair. Mr. Lester was much affected, and poor Blanche sank sobbing, and unable to speak, upon her husband's bosom, who strained her to his heart with the most frenzied emotion.

"Oh, Blanche," he continued, "and your father would separate us! 'Those whom God joins let no man put asunder,' and yet he would scorn the all-wise decrees of the Supreme, upon the mere accusation of a wandering vagabond, which has no foundation in truth. By all my first hopes of mercy I will not submit to this cruelty; you are my wife, Blanche, the lawful partner of my very soul, and as such I claim you, and will hold you alone under my protection."

"Oh, Laurence, what a cruel destiny is ours!" sighed Blanche, looking piteously in his face, whilst the crystal tears chased each other rapidly down her pale cheeks; "how are the golden hopes of bliss, which my sanguine heart encouraged, blighted. What have I done to merit such a punishment as this?"

"Hear me, dearest Blanche—hear me, Sir Laurence Cleveland—son I dare not, in spite of my yearning will to do so, call you yet," said Mr. Lester, in a voice

See p. 41.

almost choked by the power of his emotions—" I would fain disbelieve the assertion
of the gipsy, especially made under the circumstances they were; but until Sir
Laurence can satisfactorily rebut the charges brought against him, I must, however
painful it may be to me, for your sake, my child, for both your sakes, exercise the
authority of a father, and resist any attempt to force my daughter from beneath my
roof."

" Oh, my father! oh, Laurence, dear Laurence!" ejaculated the agonised
Blanche; " you are my husband, my heart tells me that you are, by every sacred
right; you can, you will substantiate your innocence of this dreadful accusation; say
that you will, or my heart will break, for I can never cease to love you more fondly

than I do at present; and to know that another woman has a just claim to that hand which you joined to mine this morning—oh, horror!"

" It is false! by all the powers of justice it is false!" vehemently exclaimed Sir Laurence, his bosom swelling with the strength of his excited feelings; " it is all a base fabrication of the miscreant Harold, the gipsy, to gratify his brutal and unseemly spirit of revenge. She, to whom I had the misfortune to give my hand, in the full confidence of her love and fidelity, cruelly deceived me, robbed me, abandoned me to fly to the arms of another, and afterwards, stung with remorse, perished by her own hand; even if she were living, her conduct has, by every law and right, rendered her no longer my wife."

" And her name, before her unhappy marriage with you?" eagerly demanded Mr. Lester.

Sir Laurence hesitated, before he returned an answer to this question, and Blanche looked at him with breathless and searching impatience.

" Her name was Clara Roseburn," at last replied Sir Laurence, in a faltering and melancholy voice; " would to Heaven that I had never heard it, or seen her!"

" And you loved her?" gasped forth Blanche.

" I did, or never would I have made her my wife. We were privately married, for I confess that our union was not sanctioned by her legal protector."

" And the gipsy said that this unfortunate woman had a cousin, between whom and you there was some painful connection," remarked Mr. Lester; " tell me, is that the truth?"

Sir Laurence exhibited extraordinary agitation at this question, and beat his breast.

Blanche looked at him with an expression of the most unutterable agony, and awaited his answer in doubt and suspense.

" For the love of God do not press me upon that dismal subject for the present," implored Sir Laurence; " I cannot explain it."

" Were you not guilty?" demanded Mr. Lester, with a stern brow.

" I—I was imprudent, I admit," faltered out Sir Laurence; " the impetuosity of youth led me into indiscretions which, Heaven knows, I have ever since most deeply lamented. Would, oh! would that I could recall the past."

" Enough, Sir Laurence Cleveland," said Mr. Lester, in solemn and impressive tones. " I have heard sufficient to make me firm in my determination that my poor child shall never quit my protection, until you have fully exonerated yourself. Unhappy, misguided young man, what misery has your want of candour and truth brought upon us!"

" Hear me, Mr. Lester; as you hope for mercy hereafter, hear me!" implored Sir Laurence, in accents of burning anguish.

Mr. Lester waved his hand, and shook his head mournfully.

" Laurence—Laurence! oh, God!" shrieked Blanche; and sinking back from his embrace, with a look of agony, which he could never forget, she again became insensible.

" Sir Laurence," ejaculated Mr. Lester, " if you have really any love for my poor child—if you would not at once break her heart, let me implore of you to leave her. I will not deny your seeing her again, and endeavour to enter into an explanation of this dreadful business; but now ——"

" My wife—my Blanche! you shall not, dare not, tear her from me!" cried the frantic Sir Laurence, once more rushing towards her; but, overpowered by the intense anguish of his feelings, he gave utterance to an hysterical laugh, and sank on the floor insensible.

When he recovered, he found himself supported by his sister and one of the servants of Mr. Lester, but that gentleman and his daughter were not in the apartment.

"My dear brother," said Amanda, in the most affectionate accents, "how are you now?"

"How am I!" repeated Sir Laurence, staring at her wildly. "Mad! Where is my wife? Who shall dare to snatch her from me, even on my bridal day?"

"They will not deprive you of her, dear Laurence," said his sister; "but, at present, you are neither of you in a fit state of mind to see each other. Come, come, let us return home, and to-morrow ——"

"To-morrow!" impatiently interrupted Sir Laurence; "no, no; I will not be appeased by any such idle and monstrous evasion. To my home my own sweet bride shall accompany me. What parent's claim can equal the authority of a husband? Let me hasten to her, Amanda; do not detain me."

"But I must, Laurence," said Amanda, firmly; "Blanche is now confined to her bed, and, for her sake, as well as your own, I must intreat of you not to insist upon seeing her until to-morrow. She will be perfectly safe under her father's roof, and, by to-morrow, the feelings of you both will, happily, be more calm. Come, come, remember the fatal consequences that might follow your remaining obstinate, and how bitterly would you repent being the cause of your wife's death."

"Her death! the death of Blanche!" said Sir Laurence, with a look of horror. "Almighty God forbid! I will yield, Amanda, although my heart will surely burst under this awful trial. Oh, heavens! what a bridal day is this!"

Amanda took his hand with the greatest sympathy, and he passively accompanied her from the room, and quitted the house. But he paused upon the threshold of the door, clasped his hands together, and then, with a burst of hysterical agony, he hurried from the spot, followed by his sister, and in a state of mind that must have excited the deepest sympathy in the most insensible breast.

CHAPTER V.

THE SECOND MEETING WITH THE GIPSY QUEEN.—THE THREAT.—THE DISAPPEARANCE OF MR. LESTER AND BLANCHE.—THE LETTER.

In silent agony the wretched Sir Laurence Cleveland proceeded on his way, unconscious of everything but his own misery, and deaf to the attempts at consolation made by his affectionate sister, who foreboded the worst in her own mind, both to her brother and the unfortunate Blanche. But she saw that it was necessary to endeavour to secure Harold, the gipsy, and to bring him to account for his outrageous conduct, and she determined to advise Sir Laurence to do so, as soon as he should have become more calm and reasonable.

They had proceeded only a short distance from the house of Mr. Lester, when a female form suddenly burst from an opening in the lane they were traversing, and crossed their path. They looked up, and Amanda uttered a cry of horror when she recognised the frightful old gipsy, Madela.

"Well met, Laurence Cleveland," cried the old hag, with a malicious grin; "I congratulate thee on the happiness of thy bridal day! Oh! it is a merry season for thee—a very merry season, and thou hast solemnised it by the shedding of more human innocent blood. Thou wilt meet with thy reward, fear not."

"Woman, for mercy's sake forbear, and begone," said Amanda; "are you not satisfied with the misery that your cruel associates have this morning so remorselessly caused?"

"Satisfied! Ha! ha! ha!" laughed the old woman. "No, and I will never rest satisfied until I have wrung every fibre of that trembling villain's heart, and gloated over his destruction."

"Foul hag! I will drag you to justice, and cast your hideous person into a dungeon!" cried Sir Laurence, as he rushed towards her; but, in an instant, the old woman produced a couple of pistols from beneath her cloak, and, levelling them at him, exclaimed, in a fierce and determined voice,—

"Stand back, Laurence Cleveland!—dog—reptile, back with thee, or thou diest before thy time! Thou wilt cast old Madela into a dungeon, wilt thou? Oh, thou art mighty brave—ha! ha! ha! The cur may snarl, but yet he dare not bite. I told thee I would have revenge, and this day I have shown thee that I know how to keep my word. Forsooth thou must be a most happy bridegroom—oh, yes, a most happy bridegroom!"

"Must I endure this?" cried the agitated Sir Laurence.

"Must ye!—ay, and much, much more yet," replied Madela. "I have but commenced with thee, Laurence Cleveland. Remember, I repeat, the fourteenth of May, 1798, and then think of what you may expect. Laurence Cleveland, a bigamist. Oh! 'tis well—'tis glorious!"

"Lying old crone!" exclaimed Sir Laurence—"stand back instantly, and let me pass."

"When I please, dog," replied the old woman, with a look of defiance. "Madela is not used to be commanded, especially by such a thing as thou art."

"Once more I supplicate you to forbear," said Amanda; "this violence can do you no good."

"Oh, but it is rare food to me," answered the gipsy woman. "Hark thee, man, thou hast this day shed the blood of an innocent boy, and the tenfold curses of the gipsy tribe are upon thee for it."

"Woman, you must know that it was only by accident that I did so," returned Sir Laurence.

"Oh, yes, no doubt it was an accident," sneered Madela; "all your atrocities have been committed by accident, have they not, Laurence Cleveland? It was by accident you were the means of condemning two innocent men to the scaffold; it was by accident you deceived and betrayed the two unsuspecting cousins, then left them to misery and shame. It is by accident, too, that you have taken to yourself another wife, whilst your former one still lives. Oh, you have been a most unfortunate man for accidents, truly."

"And who are you that has taken upon yourself to upbraid me?" demanded Sir Laurence.

"Oh, you will know me quite soon enough, Laurence Cleveland," replied the hag. "The time will come—the time will come; look for it, and tremble! The curse— the curse over the corpse of the murdered is still impending o'er your head, and it will be fulfilled—oh, yes, in blood, in blood shall it be realised. Beware! whenever thou seest me, I shall prove the harbinger of evil to thee!"

Thus saying, the old hag once more shook her hand menacingly at Sir Laurence, and quickly retreated from the spot.

"By all my hopes, I will pursue those wretches to destruction!" exclaimed Sir Laurence; "they shall not be allowed to triumph over me with impunity."

"Come, dear brother," said Amanda, "let us hasten home; even now some terrible danger may threaten us from these lawless and revengeful people."

Sir Laurence only sighed, and taking the arm of his sister, walked on, and they soon afterwards arrived at Branscombe House.

But how different was the appearance of that noble mansion to that which it had worn in the morning. The guests had all departed, and the sounds of revelry and gladness were succeeded by a melancholy silence, more in keeping with the character of a funeral than that of a marriage festival.

"Let persons be everywhere despatched in pursuit of those miscreants, the gipsies," Sir Laurence said, addressing himself to one of his principal domestics, whom he met in the hall. "They shall be richly rewarded that secure the villain Harold, and place him in prison."

The servant bowed and departed, and Sir Laurence, accompanied by Amanda, made his way to the library, where he threw himself on a seat, and, covering his face with his hands, gave way to the intense agony of his feelings, in which Amanda did not offer for some time to interrupt him.

"Oh, God!" he at length ejaculated; "and is this the result I expected on my bridal day? Can it indeed be real, or is it only some frightful dream? Blanche—Blanche, where are you? Why do you not fly to welcome your husband to your arms?"

"For Heaven's sake calm your feelings, my dear brother!" ejaculated Amanda persuasively. "This violence of grief cannot avail you. Wait till to-morrow, and all will be well."

"Till to-morrow!" repeated Sir Laurence, impatiently; "and why should I wait till then? By what right does any one hold my lawful wife from me? Oh, I was a fool to leave the house without my fair—my beloved Blanche."

"Mr. Lester has only acted from the best motives, I am convinced; and nothing could afford him greater pleasure than to see you happy."

"Should he have believed the base accusation brought against me by such a villain? And will he not endeavour to prejudice the mind of his daughter against me?"

"Oh, no, think not so meanly—so uncharitably of him, Laurence," said Amanda; "Mr. Lester is incapable of any action that would not redound to his credit. When your feelings have become more tranquillised, you will be able, I have no doubt, to explain everything to his satisfaction, and that of poor Blanche."

"Explain everything!" repeated Sir Laurence, with a shudder; "oh, God!"

"Yes, dear Laurence, will you not?" eagerly inquired Amanda.

"No, no," groaned Sir Laurence, "not all; there is something that my lips dare not reveal."

"Alas! what can that be which causes you so much emotion, and which you dare not reveal even to the ears of your wife?"

"My wife!"

"Yes, your wife, Laurence; is not Blanche so?"

"No," cried Sir Laurence, wildly, and starting from his seat; "I cannot believe it; it is all a mockery; I have been dreaming—dreaming of happiness which can never be my lot. If she were my wife, why is she not here? Why is she absent from her home upon her nuptial day?"

" But she will be here, dear Laurence, and you will yet be happy?"

" Oh, no, you seek to pacify me by false delusions. But still did she not plight her vows with mine at the altar? She did; and who shall interpose to break that solemn contract? Fool! idiot that I am to submit to this. But, by Heaven, my vengeance shall descend upon the heads of those who attempt to do me such an injustice; who seek to commit so monstrous and so unnatural an outrage on my feelings."

" Oh, forbear, my brother, you shock my senses to hear you talk in this manner."

" Shock your senses, Amanda? And how must mine be shocked when all that I hold most dear upon earth is thus unjustly separated from me?"

" But she will not be separated from you for long, Laurence," said his sister; " wait till to-morrow, and then ——"

" Wait till to-morrow," interrupted Sir Laurence, and his countenance glared with the power of his emotions; " you talk erroneously, sister. Why should I wait one hour—one instant—for the possession of her who is mine by every tie, human and divine? The very idea is base, cruel, and unjust. I will return again to the house of Mr. Lester, and demand my bride."

" Nay, dear Laurence, you will not be so rash—so mad?"

" Amanda, this cruel delay will drive me mad. Every moment that I suffer my sweet Blanche to remain away from me, I feel that I am neglecting my duty. What can she think of the husband who could thus so easily abandon her?"

" And were you to venture to see her in your present state of mind, you might be the cause of her death."

" Her death!" repeated Sir Laurence, with a shudder of horror, and sinking again into his chair.

" Yes, brother," said Amanda, " the shock might be too much for her feelings, and think, think then what you would have to reproach yourself with."

" Alas! alas!" sighed Laurence, striking his forehead, " how am I to act?"

" As I advise, dear Laurence," returned his sister. " Wait patiently till to-morrow, and in the meantime endeavour to calm your feelings, and to assume the fortitude of a man."

" Dear Amanda," said her brother, " I know your affectionate solicitude; I know that you speak only for my good. The task is a painful one, but I must try to submit, and may God avert the evils I so greatly apprehend."

" Well spoken, my brother," said Amanda, approvingly; " and now let me tell you to endeavour to snatch a few hours' rest, for you much need it after the excitement of the day."

" Rest! oh, Amanda, there is none for me."

" Say not so, Laurence; just Heaven will look mercifully down upon you, and you will sleep to-night but to awaken in the morning to brighter prospects. Farewell, my brother, and may all good angels guard you!"

" Good night, Amanda, best and most affectionate of sisters, and in your prayers do not forget my poor suffering Blanche."

" My prayers shall ascend to Heaven for her happiness and your own, dearest Laurence," said Amanda.

They embraced affectionately, and the disconsolate Sir Laurence retired to his chamber. Here he threw himself in a chair, and for some time gave free indulgence to the agony of his feelings.

"And this should have been my bridal chamber," he sighed, looking mournfully around him; "oh, God, how dismal do its gaudy trappings now appear to me. Blanche, Blanche, without you, all else can present nothing but an aspect of misery."

He threw himself on his knees, and invoked a thousand blessings on the head of Blanche, and supplicated the mercy of the Most High; then he slowly retired to his couch, but not to rest; oh, no, that came not to him during the whole of the night; his thoughts were constantly on Blanche, and the melancholy events of the day. Then the gloomy retrospection of the past racked his mind, and conscience accused him of many guilty acts. How could he explain to Blanche and her father, without exciting their disgust and condemnation? and should Harold really have spoken the truth, and his former wife be still living, in what a dreadful position would he be placed; what shame, what irremediable misery would he have brought upon her whom he loved almost to adoration! It would break her heart, and he must then accuse himself of being her murderer; but no, it was impossible that it could be so; it would drive him to absolute madness, could he believe it. It must be a base fabrication of Harold's to gratify his vengeance. But who was he, and how had he acquired the knowledge he evidently possessed? He had not the least recollection of his features, and was therefore involved in greater perplexity than ever.

Then the image of the gipsy boy tormented his imagination, and filled him with sensations he had never experienced before, and could not exactly account for. He would have given anything, could he have ascertained to what extent he had wounded him, but he sincerely hoped that it would not prove mortal; for, although it was purely accidental, and he could not blame himself for it, he would not for the world have it upon his conscience.

Thus the unhappy Sir Laurence continued restless and thinking till the morning, when he arose, and although it was yet very early, he could not, without the greatest difficulty, restrain his impatience to depart immediately to the house of Mr. Lester. Every moment of delay appeared to him an age, and he fancied that some fresh danger threatened his beloved Blanche.

On descending into the breakfast room, he found his sister already there, as it was her intention to accompany him. Her looks were sorrowful, and it was evident that she foreboded some fresh impending calamity, although she endeavoured to conceal her feelings from the observation of her brother.

They could neither of them partake of the morning's repast, and Amanda, at last, yielded to the impatience of her brother, and with a melancholy heart accompanied him from the mansion.

As they proceeded, the agitation of Sir Laurence increased, and Amanda feared the consequences which might result from the fearfully excited condition he now was in.

They arrived at the house, and here Sir Laurence was obliged to pause to endeavour to regain some degree of composure, whilst he looked up at the different windows of the mansion with a throbbing heart, for he felt that his future happiness or woe depended upon the result of this interview.

At length he ventured to pull the bell at the gate, and the summons was quickly answered by the porter. The man seemed alarmed and bewildered when he saw

Sir Laurence and his sister; but the former, unable to control the agony of his suspense, was rushing past him, when the porter observed,—

"Pardon me, Sir Laurence Cleveland; but if it is my master and my young lady you seek, they are neither of them here. There are only myself and my wife in the house."

"Neither of them here!" exclaimed Sir Laurence, with a look of astonishment and incredulity. "Man, you surely have not the insolence to attempt to mock me. I must see Lady Cleveland and her father immediately."

"I solemnly declare to you, Sir Laurence," said the porter, "that Squire Lester and his daughter departed from here before daylight this morning, and all the rest of the servants, besides myself and my wife, have left the house."

"Is it possible?" ejaculated Amanda, astonishment depicted on her countenance; "but whither have they departed?"

"I know not, my lady," answered the porter.

"Gone! gone!" gasped forth Sir Laurence. "Can I believe the evidence of my senses? Oh, treachery, most base and monstrous! My Blanche—my youthful bride stolen from me! But no, it is all false! It is a shameful mockery! They dare not, they would not serve me in so cruel a manner. Let me pass, fellow, or you shall dearly repent your insolence and presumption."

"Sir Laurence Cleveland, you are welcome to search the house, if you doubt my word," said the porter; "but my master left a letter with me, with an order to deliver it to you, and that perhaps will satisfy you."

Sir Laurence gasped for breath, the perspiration stood upon his temples in large drops, and he was obliged to support himself against one of the pillars of the hall to save himself from falling. Amanda went towards him, and took his hand, but he repulsed her with almost savage violence, as he exclaimed,—

"And this is what you advised me to wait calmly and patiently for! Oh, may curses ——"

"Laurence, dear Laurence," interrupted the alarmed Amanda; "oh, forbear. You know not what you say. There must be some misunderstanding in this; Mr. Lester could never ——"

"D—n Mr. Lester!" passionately cried Sir Laurence; "he—he—but the letter! the letter! Oh, God! let me at once know the worst."

The porter hastened from the hall, and the unhappy Sir Laurence beat his breast and groaned in agony. In a few moments the porter returned with a letter, which he presented to Sir Laurence, who snatched it eagerly from his hand, and glanced at the superscription.

"Ah!" he exclaimed, "it is in the handwriting of Mr. Lester; Blanche, then, would not condescend me a word, not one single word, in explanation of her cruel conduct. Oh, agony!"

He broke open the seal with delirious haste, and read the following words:—

"Sir Laurence Cleveland,—I would call you son—my heart urges me to do so, but reason tells me that it would be wrong while you refuse to fully explain away the terrible charge brought against you. You may consider the step I have taken as harsh, as cruel; but prudence and justice to both you and my unhappy daughter have prompted it, and Heaven, I trust, will assist me in my efforts to ascertain the facts of this lamentable case. Should it be found that the unfortunate woman to whom you formerly united your destiny is still in existence, Blanche and you must

See p. 46.

never see each other again. God grant that such may not prove to be the fact. This, believe me, is the most sincere and fervent wish of

"Your friend and well-wisher,

"ANDREW LESTER."

"God! God! Spare my brain!" exclaimed the wretched Sir Laurence, when he had come to the conclusion of this epistle; and, casting the letter from him, he sank on a seat, and pressing his clenched fists to his burning temples, he sobbed convulsively in the insupportable agony of his feelings.

"Brother, dearest brother," said the deeply afflicted Amanda, as she picked up the letter, "for Heaven's sake, do not, oh, do not give way to this excessive grief."

He looked up at her, wildly and vacantly, but returned no answer, and burying his face in his hands, he groaned aloud, and swayed his body to and fro, in a manner that was most piteous to behold.

Amanda hastily glanced over the contents of the letter, and then approached her unfortunate brother, and, in the most affectionate and soothing accents, ejaculated,—

" Dear Laurence, look up and revive ; all will yet be well, and ——"

" Well! well !" interrupted Sir Laurence, starting up, and laughing with the wildness of a maniac; " who are you that prate to me thus ? Is it well to rob a husband of his bride even on his nuptial day ? Is it well that harsh parents should thus cruelly rend two fond hearts asunder, and drive them both to madness ? But he shall not triumph ; no, I will pursue him through the world, and never rest until I have snatched my Blanche, my beauteous Blanche, from his cruel power ! Ay, and I will have vengeance, too ; yes, vengeance for this savage outrage ! Let me go ; the voice of duty and justice calls upon me, and I will obey !"

" Laurence, my brother, it is your sister, your own fond sister who appeals to you, and supplicates you to calm the tempest of your agonised feelings, and to listen to the voice of reason !" ejaculated Amanda, clinging to him, and looking with tearful eyes in his face.

" Woman, release your hold ; my brain's on fire ! A hundred men should not detain me ! My wife !—my Blanche ! I come to snatch you once more to my bosom !"

In vain did the distracted Amanda struggle with him, and appeal to him with tears and supplications ; he dashed her furiously from him, and rushed from the house with all the frenzy of the most decided madness.

" Oh, for the love of God, follow him, and alarm the neighbourhood ; my poor brother ! Oh, what a horrible calamity is this !" cried Amanda, wringing her hands, and imploring of the porter.

" Poor gentleman," said the honest domestic ; " I will instantly pursue him. Follow me, please you, good lady ; your persuasions may have the best effect."

They waited for no more, but both hastily rushed from the house, and when they had gained the open air, they beheld the unfortunate Sir Laurence flying with the greatest precipitation towards the wood.

" My God !" exclaimed Amanda, " this rash act of Mr. Lester has driven my poor brother mad. In his delirium, he will lay violent hands upon himself. Oh, save him ! save him !"

At this moment several rustics appeared upon the spot.

" My brother !" shrieked Amanda, pointing towards the wretched Sir Laurence ; " oh, secure him—save him—he is mad !"

The men required no other appeal, but immediately joined in the pursuit, Amanda following as fast as her trembling limbs would permit her. Sir Laurence had, however, got to some distance, and appeared to be entirely deaf to the piteous cries of his sister, who frantically implored him to return. He had now gained the entrance to the wood, when, just at that moment, a wild female form, which Amanda immediately recognised to be that of old Madela, sprang forward, and, pointing to him, laughed aloud in fiendish exultation. Sir Laurence dashed wildly past her, and plunging into the wood, was immediately lost to sight. Madela followed him.

" It is the gipsy—the hag !" exclaimed Amanda; " for the love of Heaven, quick, or she will do him some harm."

The pursuers increased their speed, and soon gained the wood, but nothing was to be seen of the unhappy Sir Laurence, and, overcome with the violence of her emotions, Amanda sank down upon the earth, quite exhausted, and became insensible.

CHAPTER VI.

THE DELIRIUM OF SIR LAURENCE.—THE RETURN OF BLANCHE.—THE DISTRACTED FATHER.—THE APPALLING INTERVIEW.

WHEN the afflicted Amanda was restored to sensibility, she found herself in her own chamber at Branscombe House, with the little Angela standing weeping by her side, and a female domestic attending upon her. In a moment all the horrors of the morning rushed upon her recollection, and, in frantic accents, she inquired after her brother. The servant hesitated to answer her, but at length, on the repeated solicitations and commands of Amanda, she informed her that Sir Laurence was not yet secured, but that the men were still in pursuit of him, and that there could be very little doubt but that they would soon overtake him, and bring him in safety home.

"God of mercy protect him, and shield him from all harm," sighed Amanda; "but alas! I fear that this trial will be much more severe than his reason can withstand. Oh, that Mr. Lester, in his stern sense of justice, had not acted so precipitately!"

She wrung her hands, and wept upon the neck of her lovely child, who, by every innocent means in her power, endeavoured to assure her unhappy parent. Amanda did, by great exertion, become more composed, and arose from the couch, on which she had been reclining; but her mind was still in a state of the greatest excitement and anxiety, until she should hear something of her unfortunate brother.

Another hour elapsed in this state of terrible suspense, when intelligence was brought her that Sir Laurence was secured, and was then being brought to the mansion. She rushed down the stairs, and met the party as they were bringing the unfortunate gentleman into the hall.

His eyes were wild, and his whole demeanor wretched in the extreme. Amanda hastened towards him, and called affectionately upon his name; but he only returned her a vacant look, and did not seem to know her.

"Dear Laurence," she exclaimed, "it is I, Amanda, your sister; oh, do not gaze so awfully upon me, but speak to me, and tell me that you are better."

"Release your hold, fellows," cried Sir Laurence, struggling violently with those who held him. "Do you not know me, that you dare to commit this outrage? I am Sir Laurence Cleveland, he who was married yesterday; but they have robbed me of my bride—off! off! They have torn her from me against her will, and I will go in search of her, and snatch her from their power!"

"Nay, my dear brother," said Amanda, coaxingly, while her heart, at the same time, was ready to burst with anguish, "you are too ill to undertake a journey now; besides, fear not, Blanche will soon return."

"Return!" exclaimed Sir Laurence, fiercely; "it is false! She will never return, unless I force her from the cruel parent who holds her in his power; and what right has he to detain her from her lawful husband? You can all bear witness that she gave her hand to me at the altar, and who shall presume to deprive me of her ?   Let me go, I say, or ye shall pay dearly for attempting to detain me."

He struggled most desperately as he gave utterance to these words, and it required all the strength of several men to hold him.   But at last, completely exhausted by the violence of his exertions, he sank, inanimate, in their arms, and in that state was conveyed to his chamber, and the medical attendant of the family was sent for without delay.

It is needless to say with what emotion and anxiety Amanda watched by the side of his couch, and listened to his melancholy ravings.   But in that state he continued throughout the day, and, at intervals, he became so violent, that it required the united strength of several persons to hold him in the bed.

" He will never recover his reason," sighed Amanda, when she was alone, having left him for a few minutes; " my poor brother will henceforth be a wretched maniac. Oh, if poor Blanche was aware of his present sad condition, how would it wring her gentle and affectionate heart!   No power, I am certain, could prevent her from flying to him. Alas! it was very wrong, it was most cruel to tear her from him so suddenly, and not even to allow her to write one line, to bid him adieu.   Surely the idle statements of the villain Harold should not have been received as truths, without any evidence to corroborate them.   Such a course, I fear, will be the means of breaking the hearts, or destroying the happiness, of Blanche and her husband."

The whole of that weary night Amanda continued unremitting in her attentions upon her brother, but no favourable change took place in him, and she began to fear the most fatal results.

Since the morning Amanda had again seen old Humphry, the porter to Mr. Lester, and had questioned him more narrowly as to the sudden and extraordinary departure of his master and his daughter, but she could elicit no further particulars from him than those he had already imparted, he still positively declaring that he had not the slightest idea in what direction they were gone, or when they were likely to return.   He added, that Blanche was weeping bitterly as her father handed her into the travelling carriage, and that it was therefore evident that she was forced away against her will.

These remarkable and startling events caused the greatest sensation in the neighbourhood of the mansion, and various were the conjectures that were formed upon the subject; but most persons deeply sympathised with the unfortunate Sir Laurence, for he was highly esteemed for the philanthropy of his character, and no one scarcely could believe him capable of the base conduct attributed to him by the ruffian Harold.

A strict search was made after the gipsies, but not the least information could be obtained of them, and this added to the general mystery and perplexity that prevailed.

For several days Sir Laurence remained in the same deplorable condition, and Amanda watched and attended to him until she was almost worn out with constant fatigue.   At length the violence of his delirium abated, and he could weep over his afflictions, and mourn the severity of his fate.   In his sister he ever found a gentle soother of his woes, and he would scarcely allow her to leave him for the shortest interval of time.

" Alas !" he would sigh, " it is but too plain that Blanche loves me not; that her heart is estranged from me, or surely she could not rest without at least addressing one letter to me. Oh, God! and shall I never behold her sweet form again? Shall I never more listen to the heavenly music of her voice, as she used to talk to me in the hours of her love?"

" Despair not, my brother," said Amanda, " for the heart of Blanche, I am certain, can never change towards you, although she is so cruelly separated from you. She must believe you innocent, and will again be restored to you."

" Ah! Amanda," returned Sir Laurence, " I know well your affectionate solicitude for me, and, believe me, I am most grateful for it; but you would inspire me with hopes which, I fear, alas! will never be realized. Blanche, my fair bride, is lost to me for ever. Her father will never relent, and will take good care to keep her from my sight. And if she really loves me, can she long survive the cruel separation, the annihilation of all her brightest hopes? Oh! it drives me to madness, when I think of the sufferings she must at present be enduring."

" I trust, Laurence, that they will not last long. But you must arouse yourself from this abject state of melancholy and despair. Exert all your energies, for by so doing you can alone hope to be able to discover the retreat of Mr. Lester and his daughter."

· " I will, Amanda," replied her brother, vehemently; " your words have aroused me into action, and I will not rest until I have discovered her to whom my soul is rivetted in bonds of indissoluble love."

Amanda was pleased to see this favourable change, and did all she could to encourage him to persevere in his intentions, although, for her own part, she could not flatter herself with any hopes that he would succeed.

Several more days elapsed, and Sir Laurence, having become more calm and collected, exerted himself to the utmost to ascertain what route Mr. Lester and his daughter had taken; but all to no purpose, and he again began to give way to the most intense despair. Nor was his mind less uneasy all this time, upon the uncertainty of the truth or falsehood of the assertions of the gipsy Harold; for should his first wife indeed be still alive, all his hopes would be destroyed, and the misery of himself and Blanche would be complete. But it could not be true. Harold had said that Clara could come forward whenever she thought proper to substantiate his statements. Then why did she not do so without delay? Why had she not presented herself at the time, when she might have prevented the union? This seemed at once to prove the falsehood of all that Harold had said, and Sir Laurence attempted to rest satisfied upon that point; but he found it impossible; dismal forebodings would at times beset his mind, and he could not look back upon his past conduct without regret and self-reprobation. That he had injured, deeply injured Clara and her cousin, his conscience assured him; and how could he ever hope to retain the love and confidence of Blanche (should she ever be restored to him), if she should become acquainted with the melancholy particulars?

And what was the fate of the gipsy boy? Had the wound he had so unfortunately inflicted on him proved mortal? If so, how much more would it add to the anguish of his mind!

It was a beautiful moonlight evening, about six weeks after the occurrence of these painful and melancholy events, that Sir Laurence and his sister were seated in melancholy conversation at the drawing-room window, when their attention was suddenly arrested by the sound of wheels, and immediately afterwards they beheld a carriage approaching rapidly along the principal drive, towards the mansion.

"Ah!" exclaimed Sir Laurence, starting up; "who can that be, at this hour, Amanda?"

The vehicle had by this time turned an angle of the mansion, and they heard it stop at the portal. Another instant, and the hasty tread of footsteps was heard upon the stairs; the room door was thrown open,—one delirious shriek of joy, and Sir Laurence Cleveland clasped the beautiful, but insensible form of his wife—his beloved Blanche, to his heart!

And, oh! what a scene was that which followed this unexpected visit! How rapturously the almost incredulous Sir Laurence strained her to his bosom,—called upon her name,—covered her pale cheeks with his kisses, and wept like a child! And Amanda, too,—but we must pause, for we find our pen far too weak to depicture the affecting scene.

"God! God!" sobbed forth Sir Laurence, raising his eyes towards heaven, "you have, indeed, been most merciful to me in the midst of all my misery. My sweet bride,—my own Blanche, bright, angelic possessor of my soul! and are you indeed restored to me? Do I really clasp you to my heart, or is it only some fair vision sent to entrance my wandering senses? No, no; it is life—reality! I feel her fond heart throbbing against mine! Oh, heaven! I shall go mad with transport!"

"Poor girl! poor girl!" said Amanda, as she gazed with all a sister's most ardent affection in the countenance of the insensible beauty; "how great must have been her sufferings, how powerful her affection, to induce her to brave the anger of her father by this determined step! Oh! my dear brother, Heaven has heard our prayers, and you will be happy. But see, she revives."

Blanche heaved a deep sigh, opened her eyes, and, fixing them upon her husband with an intensity of feeling such as no language can describe, in a paroxysm of frantic joy, she entwined her snowy arms around her husband's neck, and could not utter a syllable.

"Blanche! Blanche! my sweet bride! the empress of my whole affections!" ejaculated Sir Laurence; "has all bounteous Heaven given you to me again? Do you, oh! do you, indeed, still love me?"

"Love you, dearest Laurence?" repeated Blanche, in a voice of thrilling energy; "with all my heart—my soul—my very life! for that life is valueless unless it be a portion of your own,—without it be shared with you! my lord,—my husband!"

"Blessed words!" cried the enraptured Sir Laurence, as he strained her round and beauteous form still closer to his bosom; "and do you, then, acknowledge me for your husband?"

"Oh! yes, my Laurence," replied the young bride; "who shall dare refuse me the claim? Are you not my husband by all the laws of God and man?"

"And you believe me innocent?"

"By all my hopes of mercy, I do. I could not have lived an hour had I thought you guilty, my Laurence, of the foul treachery laid to your charge. I ask for no explanation, I will have none; you have denied it all, my husband, and I should be unworthy of the love I aspire to could I doubt your word."

"Sweet innocence! confiding angel!" ejaculated Sir Laurence, in a voice almost stifled by the strength of his emotions. "Oh! Almighty God! receive my thanks for the inestimable treasure you have given me. And shall we never more part?"

"Never,—never, till we are separated by death, my own Laurence," replied Blanche, with the most solemn and impressive energy. "But, alas! will you not reproach me for having abandoned you? Will you not deem me unworthy of your future protection?"

"Heaven forbid! beloved Blanche," cried Sir Laurence; "for I know that my own fond and faithful bride did not abandon me willingly; and what must have been your torturing anguish during this cruel separation!"

"Words must fail to give even a faint idea of them, my husband. Oh! I marvel that my poor heart did not break!"

"Beauteous sufferer! be mine the care—the constant study to make you a blissful recompense. But your father?"

"Alas!" sighed Blanche, "I fear that he will never forgive me for the step which my devotion and sense of duty to that man on whom I have bestowed my heart and hand, have compelled me to take. But you will pardon him, Laurence, for that which may have appeared to you cruel and unjust. He acted only from the purest motives, and the best of wishes for the happiness of us both. Oh! he has ever been a most kind and indulgent parent to me, and may the Almighty pardon me if I cause his heart a single pang."

"Forgive him, my loved Blanche! indeed I do. But say, has he not come with you?"

"Ah, no! Laurence," answered Blanche; "he is many miles from hence. I fled the place to which he had taken me in secrecy, to return to you."

Again and again did Sir Laurence press the lovely being to his bosom, and weep tears of joy upon her cheeks, and it was some time before their transports had subsided into any degree of composure. And then Blanche related, with touching pathos, all the sufferings she had undergone during the time she had been separated from her husband.

On the evening after their last interview, she had remained for some time in a state of unconsciousness, and, when she recovered, she called frantically upon her husband's name, and it was not until after considerable exertion, and the greatest difficulty, that her father was enabled to pacify her; but at length he succeeded, by promising to take her to him in the morning, and she became more tranquil. She passed several hours in weeping bitterly, and sleep never closed her eyelids during the night.

Before break of day in the morning she was surprised at hearing a carriage draw up to the door, and wondered for what purpose it could be brought there at that early hour. Her heart misgave her, and a fearful foreboding took possession of her breast; but she was not long suffered to remain in suspense. Her waiting-woman entered her chamber, and informed her that her father desired her to get up immediately, as he wanted her instant attendance.

"For Heaven's sake, Mary," said Blanche, with a look of alarm and astonishment, "what can he mean? What is his intention with me?"

"Alas! I know not, madam," answered Mary; "but a travelling carriage is at the door, and I have been ordered to prepare myself to accompany you on a journey."

"A journey! gracious Heaven, my mind forbodes the worst; but, still, my father cannot, surely, be so cruel."

"All the other servants, except old Humphrey and his wife, are about to leave the house," said Mary; "and it would seem as if my master intends to abandon it for some time."

Blanche uttered an exclamation of terror, and it was some time ere she could recover herself sufficiently to obey the injunctions of her father. Then she invoked a blessing on the head of her husband, and supplicated the mercy and protection of Heaven.

A few minutes afterwards, she summoned up all the resolution at her command, and, with trembling steps, she made her way to the apartment in which her father was awaiting her. She found him equipped for travelling, and, sinking on her knees at his feet, she looked up piteously in his face, and for some moments her tears prevented her from giving utterance to a word. Mr. Lester raised her with even more than his accustomed tenderness, and looked affectionately in her pale face.

" Dear Blanche," he said, " you will, I fear, deem me harsh and cruel; but, oh! I need not tell you how it grieves me to take the step which reason and affection for you, my child, have decided me upon. We must go from hence—for a while we must leave our home."

" Oh! my dear father," cried the distracted Blanche, " you cannot mean what you say—indeed you cannot. Am I not a wife? and would you tear me from my husband?"

" Alas! my child," sighed Mr. Lester, " I cannot recognise Sir Laurence Cleveland by that name, until I receive sufficient proof of his innocence of the fearful charges brought against him. You must not yet be united, lest you should violate the most sacred law of God."

" Mercy, mercy, my father! he is innocent—my heart assures me that he is; you cannot surely believe the hideous fabrications of that villain who has accused him."

" Fain would I not, my poor girl," said her father, with the greatest emotion; " but Sir Laurence has not yet been able to rebut them, and I should be unworthy the name of a parent did I consent to sacrifice you to such a dreadful uncertainty. Let him be able to acquit himself, and Heaven forbid that I should for one moment attempt to separate you."

" You, my father, to come to this terrible resolution! Oh! recall your words. Spare me—spare your only child—or you will break my heart!"

" Blanche, Blanche!" exclaimed Mr. Lester, " would you become a thing of shame and reproach? Think of the misery, the disgrace, that would descend upon you, should the accusations of this man be substantiated against Sir Laurence Cleveland."

" Oh! he is innocent, my dear father," energetically exclaimed Blanche; "indeed he is; it were monstrous to believe, for a moment, that my Laurence, my husband—the generous, the noble—could be guilty of such base cruelty—such deliberate, cold-hearted treachery. But you will not tear me from him; you love me too well, I know, to wring my heart thus."

" It is the intense love I bear you, my child," said Mr. Lester, " that urges me to this painful course."

" Then you will consign me to the grave," said Blanche, solemnly; and she covered her face with her hands, and sobbed as though her heart would break.

" Come, my poor child," said her father, in the most gentle and soothing accents, you must not take on so; you will think better of this. But a short time, and all may be proved to our satisfaction; and then it will be your father's pride, his delight, to resign you to the future care and protection of him to whom you have given your hand; but, should it be proved otherwise, and you the partner of a man upon whom you have no lawful claim, your father's heart will be broken, and his grey hairs be brought with sorrow to the grave."

"My God!" exclaimed the unhappy Blanche, "instruct me how to act."

"Reason, discretion, self-respect, virtue, everything should instruct you to act, Blanehe."

Blanche struggled for a few moments with her feelings, and then, in a voice in which acute agony and resignation were blended, she ejaculated,—

"I yield! Bless you, bless you, my dear Laurence, and may Heaven pardon me if I act wrong."

"Heaven will approve your decision, my beloved child," returned Mr. Lester, with the most tender emotion, and affectionately and soothingly taking her hand; "Heaven will approve of your obedience to my wishes, which are prompted only by an anxious wish to save you from shame and misery. Come, my poor Blanche, do not take on so, I entreat. Did you but know the anguish I feel, you would not think so harshly of me as I fear you do at present."

"Oh, no! my father, I do not think so," sobbed Blanche; "for have you not ever been to me one of the kindest, the best of parents? Have you not been to me my only friend, since my poor mother has reposed in the tomb?"

Mr. Lester passed his hand across his eyes at this allusion to his lamented wife, whose death he had never ceased to mourn, and, for a moment or two, he could not speak; but at length he said,—

"And such, my own affectionate Blanche, I trust you will continue to think me; and, great as will be the suspense and misery of mind I know you will experience, I sincerely hope that it will not last long, but that Omnipotence will, in a short time, unravel this painful mystery to the satisfaction of us all, and the exoneration of Sir Laurence."

"Oh, yes! my father, it must be so," said Blanche; "it would be monstrous to believe the assertions of the gipsy Harold or that Laurence Cleveland could ever have acted the villanous part he has accused him of doing."

"Well, my love," returned Mr. Lester, who seemed to be afraid to give expression to his feelings in the present state of his daughter, "we will, for the time being, drop this perplexing and painful subject, with the fervent hope that all will end well. Come, my poor Blanche, the carriage is waiting at the door, and it is necessary that we commence our journey without delay."

Blanche again threw herself sobbing on her father's shoulders, and it was several minutes before she could obtain the least degree of tranquillity.

"Gracious Heaven!" she exclaimed; "and must I, indeed, leave you thus, dear Laurence, upon the mere vague suspicion caused by the accusation of an outcast and a vagabond? Oh, it does seem most cruel, most unnatural."

"But you forget, Blanche," remarked her father, "that Sir Laurence has partly admitted his guilt, and his hesitating to give us a full explanation is calculated to add to the strength of the suspicions we have a right to entertain towards him."

"But you have not given him time to reflect, my father; when he might be induced to give the explanation we require, and which would doubtless remove the foul calumny that has been heaped upon him by the gipsy. I am convinced that his errors have only been youthful indiscretions, and that he never could have been so utterly lost to shame and honour as to act in the manner that Harold has described. The wretches are goaded on by a feeling of revenge against him for some injury they only suppose he has done them, and not the least reliance should be placed upon their assertions."

"Dear Blanche, I cannot blame your generous confidence in the integrity of him to whom you have given your hand; but think you that I can conscientiously resign you to his keeping while this uncertainty of the existence of his first wife remains? I should be failing in my duty if I were to do so, and could never forgive myself, if the assertions of Harold the gipsy should unfortunately prove eventually to be correct."

"But they are false, father; reason ought to convince us that they are," returned Blanche; "had she been living as the gipsy stated, why did she not come forward to make good her claim, and to prevent our nuptials from taking place? The whole story is a base fabrication from beginning to end, and never, never will I believe to the contrary, unless I should behold the unfortunate but evidently guilty Clara myself."

"A short time will probably disclose all, my child," remarked Mr. Lester; "and Heaven knows how sincerely, how fervently I wish that the fond impressions upon your mind may be verified. Come, my dear Blanche, this is a severe trial to your young and bright-formed hopes I admit; but prudence and virtue dictate the course I have adopted, and I am certain that you will acquire fortitude to support it."

"I submit," faintly articulated Blanche; "the will of Heaven be done. Oh, Laurence!" she could say no more, but almost unconscious suffered her father to lead her away, and before she was thoroughly restored to recollection, the carriage which contained her and her father was rolling rapidly on its course far away from the house.

Need we say what were the feelings of Blanche during that melancholy journey, placed as she was under such peculiar, such unexpected, and such trying circumstances? It seemed as if she were being borne away from every hope, from every joy, from all the blessings that could render life endurable, and the pangs that corroded her heart were almost too powerful for human nature to support. Mr. Lester, who keenly felt her distress, endeavoured to console her by every gentle and affectionate means in his power, but with little success. He fully felt the painful task he had to perform, but still he was encouraged by the rectitude of his motives, and trusted that Providence would, in a short time, satisfactorily remove the fearful doubts which, at present, prevailed in his mind, and that he might be able to restore his daughter to that man on whom she had bestowed her hand without the least reluctance or cause for suspicion. But after the evasions and the emotion which Sir Laurence Cleveland had exhibited, he could not entirely divest his mind of the belief that the assertions of Harold were not without foundation; and if that should ultimately turn out to be the case, he saw plainly enough that the happiness of his daughter would be annihilated for ever, and that she would be consigned to the pangs of perpetual misery and disappointment.

In the course of their journey it became necessary that they should pass by Branscombe House, and no sooner did poor Blanche behold that mansion of which she should now be the happy mistress, than her anguish became so great that Mr. Lester found it impossible to restrain the most powerful expression of her feelings.

"Laurence, dear Laurence!" she exclaimed, "and must I leave you thus? Must we not be permitted to exchange one word at parting, perhaps for ever? Oh, God! this surely is most cruel and unnatural. Oh, my father, what a stern, what a severe trial have you put me to; my heart will surely break under it. My husband, what are now your feelings? And what will they be when you find that she, to whom at the altar you have plighted your vows, has abandoned you? It cannot be just; nature, virtue, honour revolt at the idea. Oh, my father, let us return, and suffer not the diabolical aspersions of a miscreant, who is capable of any deed, however base, to mislead us, and plunge us into a fatal error, from which we may never be able to extricate ourselves."

"My child, be calm," expostulated her father. "Heaven will justify our conduct, and, ere long, I trust, restore us to happiness."

"Oh, no, no," sobbed Blanche; "that, alas! will never be; the blow is struck which must annihilate our peace of mind for ever. Laurence can only view my conduct with disgust and abhorrence; and what of comfort will there then be left for me in the world? Would to Heaven that I had died in my infancy, or that I had never been born."

"It may only be a trial of a few days, or a few weeks, at most, my beloved Blanche," said Mr. Lester; "and everything may then be satisfactorily explained, and yourself and Laurence will then be restored to each other. Courage, courage, then, my child. Put your trust in the Most High, and dismal and melancholy though your prospects now appear to be, depend upon it the clouds will be dispersed, and nothing will again occur to interrupt the sunshine of your future days."

Blanche wrung her hands and wept bitterly; and when the noble mansion of her husband faded from her view, she threw herself back in the carriage in despair, and became incapable of uttering another word. Mr. Lester watched her in silence, and his anguish was scarcely less acute than that she was enduring. It was, indeed, most painful to the mind of a father to be compelled, from a strict sense of duty, thus to torture a daughter whom he so fondly loved, and earnestly did he pray to Heaven speedily to remove the fearful doubts and suspicions that at present predominated in his breast.

As the vehicle proceeded on its way, the melancholy which agonized the bosom of Blanche increased, and she reflected upon all the fearful events which had taken place at her union, and since, with the utmost intensity of anguish and despair. That Sir Laurence had been guilty of some serious acts his own admission, and the evasive answers he had given to the questions of herself and her father convinced her; and the discovery of those faults in one to whom her warmest affections were devoted, and whom she had imagined to be the very soul of honour, was sufficient in itself to harass her thoughts almost beyond endurance. But what would be his anguish when he found that she had deserted him, and without so much as leaving him one line at parting! Would it not work a terrible change in his feelings towards her? Might he not believe her false, cruel, and unjust, and as such learn to hate and despise her as one who had deceived him, and become prejudiced against him on the bare assertions of a wandering vagrant, and thus rendered herself unworthy of his love? Oh, yes; it was but too probable that he would do so, and she could not live with the consciousness of possessing his hatred.

The carriage at length having proceeded for some distance on its way, the travellers stopped at the door of a respectable inn to change horses, and to obtain refreshment; but poor Blanche was in too much distress of mind to be able to eat; and it was not without much difficulty that her father was enabled to sustain her at all.

Again they resumed their journey, and the part of the country they travelled through was of the most picturesque and romantic description, and at any other time would have excited the most enthusiastic admiration of Blanche; but now she gazed upon it with indifference, for her mind was completely absorbed by her own painful reflections, and everything appeared to her to wear the grim solitude of death. By that time she imagined that the unhappy Sir Laurence had discovered her flight, and was suffering all the tortures of madness and despair. She could fancy she heard his melancholy lamentations, and beheld his wild and agitated countenance, as he called upon her name, and accused her of having so cruelly deceived him, and plunged him into inextricable misery. She fixed upon her father looks that wrung his very soul, and he knew not what to say to tranquillise her. Then she burst into a violent paroxysm of tears, which lasted some time without interruption, and which Mr. Lester was glad to see, as he hoped it would give her overcharged bosom relief; and in this he was not mistaken, for Blanche, after a short time, became somewhat more calm, but still pondered over the misfortunes that had so unexpectedly befallen her, and could not but anticipate the future with the most gloomy apprehensions.

The uncertain fate of Rosario, the gipsy boy, and to think that he was wounded by Sir Laurence, although it was perfectly accidental, was a source of great uneasiness to her, for she felt certain that it would exasperate the savage feelings of the wandering tribe against him the more, and she was fearful that he would never be safe for a moment. They had fully shown their revengeful nature; and she knew that those people had such crafty and secret means of working their designs, that it was almost impossible for any one who had excited their enmity to guard against them.

And how was it possible for her father to penetrate the mystery of Harold's terrible accusations, was a question which she asked herself, but was unable to answer; and therefore she saw no other prospect but that of endless doubt and misery before her, however much her father might endeavour to persuade her to the contrary.

The remainder of the day passed away without anything particular occurring to the travellers, and just as the long shadows of evening fell around, they arrived at the end of their journey, which was a comfortable and secluded house belonging to Mr. Lester, but which had only been inhabited by two aged servants for several years, and who were completely taken by surprise at this unexpected visit of their amiable master and his daughter, and expressed their regret that they had not been apprised of it, so that they might have made some suitable preparations for their reception.

Blanche entered this abode with a gloomy and despairing heart, for it seemed as if she was abandoning the world and all its joys for ever, and she sank in a chair, and her tears gushed forth unrestrained. In vain did Mr. Lester make use of all the arguments that could possibly suggest themselves to him to reconcile her; she continued for some time quite inconsolable, and talked of Sir Laurence and their blighted es in the most frenzied manner.

Mr. Lester was deeply affected, and regretted the unfortunate circumstances that had compelled him to take such a determined step, but he trusted that a speedy termination would be put to their misery, and that all would end well.

After a deal of persuasion, Blanche was prevailed upon to partake of a slight repast, and then, being quite worn out with the unusual fatigue, both of body and mind, that she had undergone, she requested permission to retire to the chamber that had been prepared for her, and, after a most affectionate parting between her and her father, she quitted the room, attended by Mary, her waiting-maid. Here she sank on her knees, and, in accents of the most powerful emotion, implored the protection of the Supreme, and invoked blessings on the head of her husband, whose sufferings she readily imagined at her sudden and melancholy loss.

In this posture poor Blanche remained for a considerable time, and the anguish of her feelings was far more powerful than language can describe.

"Oh! Laurence," she sobbed forth, in a voice almost inarticulate, " what are now your thoughts? You must hate me—despise me, and I dare not hope to see you again. What can you think of the woman who could plight her vows with you one day at the altar, and abandon you the next, upon the mere accusations of a man who is, I am convinced, capable of uttering a falsehood to gratify his own deadly feelings of vengeance? Oh! my father, you have surely been too precipitate—too severe, and I fear that you will have reason most bitterly to repent when it is too late. God help me, or this heavy weight of care and affliction will drive me to distraction !"

She clasped her hands in extreme agony, and then arose from her knees, and paced the room in a state of absolute despair. It was not until after the lapse of some time that she retired to bed; but wretched, indeed, was the night she passed. When sleep closed her eyelids, the most frightful dreams haunted her imagination, and frequently she started up in bed, unconscious of where she was, and with only a bewildered recollection of what had happened. At length, finding that it was useless to endeavour to obtain any rest, she arose, and sitting down by the window, gave herself up entirely to the dismal thoughts which crowded upon her brain, and caused her to look forward to the future with feelings of the most abject despair.

It was a very beautiful night, and all upon which the eye rested was calm and serene, bathed as it was in the bright moonlight; but all appeared gloomy to the mind of Blanche; nothing whatever could tend to alleviate the misery—the poignant anguish which reigned within her breast.

There were moments, too, when she was tempted, in the frenzy of her thoughts, to brave the wrath of her father, and to depart from the house while the darkness of the night favoured her escape; but a certain feeling of dread, which at that time she could not conquer, prevented her; and, however much she might suffer, she was determined to await the result of her separation from Sir Laurence, her husband, at any rate for a few days.

The morning at length dawned, but the sufferings of Blanche were almost as acute as they had been the night before; and when Mary, who had only slept in the adjoining chamber to her, made her appearance, she found her very pale and weeping bitterly; and she felt the deepest commiseration for the miseries she was enduring, and which there were no means at present of alleviating. A short time afterwards she was summoned to breakfast, and was assisted there by Mary, for her limbs trembled so excessively that she could not walk without support.

Mr. Lester met her with much affection, and was very much grieved to behold her in so deplorable a condition. Again he tried all that argument and remonstrance could do, but with little or no effect. The day was passed in the most melancholy manner, and Mr. Lester resisted all the supplications of Blanche to allow her to write to Sir Laurence, which she considered, under all the circumstances, it was her duty to do; but her father determined to adhere to the plan he had at first fixed upon, and endeavoured to reconcile her to it, and to persuade her that after all his efforts would be attended with the most favourable results.

" The note I left behind for him will be quite sufficient to convince Sir Laurence, if he is not blind to all reason, of the integrity of my motive in having taken so painful but necessary a step," he observed; " and likewise to exonerate you, my dear Blanche, from all blame."

"Alas! alas!" ejaculated Blanche, "think, my dearest father, what his feelings, his anguish must be at this cruel separation from her who is his wife by all laws, human and divine, and pity him."

"I do, Blanche, sincerely, fervently pity him," returned Mr. Lester; " and Heaven knows how happy it would make me to be convinced of his innocence, and to be able to restore you to him without the least doubt or fear upon my mind. But for both your sakes I must persevere in the course I have taken, and unless I am convinced that Sir Laurence Cleveland is innocent of that with which he has been charged, you must never more behold each other."

" Oh, my dear father, retract those terrible words," implored Blanche, with streaming eyes; " you never were cruel to me before, and you cannot—you will not prove yourself to be so now."

"Cruel, Blanche!" repeated Mr. Lester; "indeed you accuse me wrongfully. Never, never could I be cruel to my own beloved Blanche—her whose progress from infancy to womanhood I watched with so much solicitude and anxiety."

" Alas! this is more than I can endure; it will certainly break my heart."

" Say not so, my poor child," observed Mr. Lester, in tones of the deepest emotion; " oh, it will certainly break your father's heart to behold you become the partner of a man upon whom another had a prior and a legal claim."

Blanche attempted to make a reply, but the violence of her grief choked her utterance.

Thus day after day elapsed, without any material change taking place, and Mr. Lester was unable to obtain the least information respecting that which he wanted. Blanche, during that time, was so ill that she could not leave her couch, and her father was obliged to call in medical aid, for he became seriously alarmed as to the consequences. In this dilemma he scarcely knew how to act, but still the accusations which Harold had made against Sir Laurence had made so powerful an impression upon his mind, that he could not banish it, and could not but believe that he only acted according to the dictates of honour and virtue.

But Blanche at length became better, and was able to leave her chamber, and, as she appeared more tranquil and resigned than she had previously been, the fears of her father were considerably abated.

We will not tire the patience of the reader by enumerating all the sufferings of Blanche during the time she was separated from her husband; the reader may well imagine that they were of the most poignant nature, and it was truly wonderful that she was enabled to support them with the fortitude she did. But at length Mr. Lester, having received some intelligence that the gipsies were encamped a few miles off, determined to visit them, with the hope of being able to elicit some further intelligence from old Madela or Harold. Blanche entertained some fears for her father's safety; but, knowing that they had no cause to bear him any animosity, and as they would see, from his being unattended, that he did not go to them with any hostile intentions, he was fully determined, after many injunctions to Blanche, and begging of her not to feel any alarm at the length of his absence, as he intended to put up at the town near which the gipsies had encamped, for the night, he parted from her, and commenced his journey.

For some time after he had departed, Blanche sat wrapped in deep thought. She was now alone; left with the full range of the house, and with no one to control her actions. What was to prevent her from flying to the arms of him whom she firmly believed to be her lawful husband, and from whom she was now so cruelly, and, she could not help thinking, so unreasonably separated? But then she remembered the solemn injunctions of her father, and she again hesitated. She had never yet disobeyed the will of that beloved parent, and could she do so now? He would never forgive her, and the idea of incurring a father's wrath, nay, perhaps his curse, smote her with horror. But love, at length, prevailed over every other feeling, and she determined to put her design into execution. To Mary, in whom she knew she could confide, she communicated her thoughts, and, although she at first attempted to dissuade her from it, consented to become her companion.

It was arranged that they should not depart till the evening; and, when they found that they could leave the house without being observed by the two old servants before mentioned, and as Blanche had a considerable sum of money in her possession, they determined to make their way to the nearest town, where they had no doubt they should be able to procure a vehicle to convey them to the place of their destination.

How varied and how powerful were now the emotions of Blanche at the thought of again so shortly beholding Sir Laurence. Her heart palpitated with impatience, and yet she could not but feel the greatest sorrow and regret at the anguish her disappearance would cause her father. Ardently she supplicated the forgiveness of Heaven for this her first act of disobedience which she was about to commit, and it was some time before she could reduce her mind to any degree of calmness; indeed, at intervals, as the day advanced, she was almost induced to abandon her design, for she could not bear the thought of causing that parent, who had ever been so kind and indulgent to her, one moment's pang; but to remain any longer separated from her beloved Laurence she felt convinced would be more than her reason could support, and her resolution at length became firm and fixed; and she endeavoured, with the aid of Mary, to prepare herself for the task she was so soon about to undertake.

And how would Sir Laurence Cleveland receive her, was a question that forced itself most powerfully upon her. Surely he could not blame or reproach her for the course which she had been compelled to take; he would not spurn her from him, and refuse to receive her as his wife. Oh, no; she knew his heart too well; she had every confidence in the sincerity and ardour of the love he bore her, and felt assured that he could not be guilty of such cruelty towards one whose heart, whatever might transpire, he must always possess.

"Dear Laurence," she ejaculated, "I do believe you innocent, and nothing shall ever estrange my affections from you. And we shall yet be happy together, something convinces me that we shall; that you will be able to exonerate yourself from the foul charges that have been brought against you. And my dear father will forgive me for having disobeyed his injunctions, and we shall all be reconciled to each other. I should go mad, could I entertain a thought to the contrary."

As these ideas occurred to her, hope was restored to her bosom, and she sat down and commenced a most affectionate letter, which she intended to leave behind her for her father on his return, and in which she earnestly implored his forgiveness for that first act of disobedience which she had been urged by unconquerable love for him to whom she had given her hand, to commit, and begged that he would immediately follow her to Branscombe House, as she should be in a state of the most insupportable anxiety until she again beheld him.

This letter she sealed and placed on her dressing-table, and was shortly afterwards rejoined by Mary, who had made every preparation for their journey. Evening advanced, and all was quite still in the house, and as Mary had ascertained that the old servants were both in the kitchen, they considered that this was the most propitious moment for them to depart without fear of being detected. Blanche once more sank on her knees, and supplicated the pardon and protection of Heaven, and then with more confidence she arose, and, having hastily equipped herself, they opened the door cautiously, and with noiseless steps descended the stairs. The heart of Blanche beat heavily against her side, and when they had gained the outer door she paused, and almost repented of what she was about to do. Mary, however, who noticed her hesitation, whispered in her ear the name of Sir Laurence Cleveland, and that at once aroused all her energies into action. The door was opened without the slightest noise, and the next moment they found themselves in the open air. Mary took the

arm of her mistress, and they walked on as fast as their limbs could carry them in the direction of the nearest town, which they knew to be only little more than a mile off. They gained it shortly, and ventured into the most respectable inn, there being no one about to take any notice of them. In the parlour they met the landlady and her husband, who were most respectable people, and to whom Blanche ventured to address herself, stating that they wished to hire a travelling chaise, and offering to pay any sum for the accommodation. It happened, fortunately for them, that they had one disengaged, and the bargain having been quickly made, the chaise was got in readiness, and in a short time they were on the way to the place of their destination. What followed has already been related, and we will now return to that part of our tale from which we have thus long, but necessarily, digressed.

Sir Laurence had listened to this account with the most varied, conflicting, and painful emotions; and while he again clasped the gentle form of Blanche to his heart, and pressed warm kisses upon her willing lips, his feelings of transport were not unmingled with those of anguish and of self-reproach. · He knew that in two or three instances he had already acted, and was still acting, the part of the hypocrite; and when he thought of the generous confidence which Blanche reposed in him—her fervent self-devotion, which had tempted her to brave a father's wrath to return to him, he could not but despise himself for having deceived the confiding girl in any one instance.

But no such thoughts as these occupied the mind of Blanche; she placed every reliance in the truth and integrity, the honour and affection of him to whom she had given her hand, and all other ideas were for a time buried in the transport she felt at her restoration to the arms of her husband.

What volumes of tender feeling did her beauteous countenance express as she gazed with the most intense earnestness in the eyes of Sir Laurence, and felt a sweet belief that they would never be doomed to be parted again, that nothing in future would take place to obstruct their happiness. Poor Blanche! she little imagined at that time how cruelly those fond hopes were fated to be disappointed. She dreamed not of the many bitter sufferings which were even then impending o'er their heads· And it was well for her that she did not, or her feelings would have been far too powerful for human endurance.

"Blanche, my own beloved Blanche," exclaimed Sir Laurence; "if I could ever in my moments of reason and cool reflection, have doubted you, this determined conduct must at once have convinced me of your truth, and of the strength of your affections. Oh, my loved one, how can I express the almost delirious transports that now animate my bosom? For my sake you have braved a father's anger, and scorned the prejudices which might naturally have been excited in your mind by the accusations brought against me by the gipsies, and can I ever be unmindful of the immense weight of gratitude and affection which I owe you?"

"Name it not, my husband," replied Blanche; "what more have I done than that which I feel to be my duty? and, although Heaven knows how much it afflicts me to be the cause of even a moment's pang to my aged and revered parent, I cannot reproach myself for the step I have taken, since Heaven has bound me to you by every fond tie."

"But your father will forgive you, Blanche; so amiable a parent cannot long be angry with a daughter whom he loves so well. He will return to his home, and then be it our task to hasten to him, and throwing ourselves at his feet, implore his forgiveness. He will not refuse us, I am convinced he will not."

"Oh, no, he will not, dear Laurence," replied Blanche; "I know his affectionate heart too well; and we shall all be again united, and be happy."

We must pass over the remainder of the evening, which was passed in conversation similar to this, and in which Amanda most cordially joined, for no one could feel greater pleasure than she did at the return of Blanche, or more admiration at the noble generosity of character which she had evinced.

By the following day all parties were restored to a degree of comparative tranquillity, although, at times, in spite of herself, melancholy misgivings would steal in upon the mind of Blanche, which she almost the next moment, however, chided herself for entertaining.

Sir Laurence, too, was he completely happy? Oh, no; the terrible threats of the gipsy, Harold, and old Madela would at intervals recur most forcibly to his imagination, and, coupled with the gloomy facts of the past, and which he feared must sooner or later be revealed to Blanche, cast a shadow over his hopes, which he found it impossible entirely to disperse. And should the unfortunate being, his former wife, be still living, as Harold had declared she was, what shame and misery would he not have plunged poor Blanche into. He shuddered with horror at the thought, and sought to banish it from his mind altogether

That day passed away, and the next, and still they heard nothing of Mr. Lester, neither did Blanche receive any answer to the letter which she had left behind her on her flight. And now the most agonising apprehensions began to torture her bosom.

"Good God!" she cried; "he surely cannot be so cruel as to discard me from his heart. And will he not even return an answer to my letter? Oh, no; my poor father, I cannot believe that you will ever feel such bitter resentment against your only daughter, because she has been urged to this her only act of disobedience by affection and a sense of the duty she owed to that man to whom she had plighted her solemn vows in the face of Heaven."

"No, my Blanche," replied Sir Laurence, trying to stifle the power of those emotions which he found were gaining such an ascendancy over her, although he feared, indeed, that there was too much reason to entertain the worst surmises; "I cannot think that your father will ever become so stern and inflexible. He will relent. But calm your feelings, my love, and I will myself write to Mr. Lester, and appeal to his goodness of heart for a reconciliation. He is not insensible to the voice of reason, and will surely not continue to place any belief in the base assertion of my enemies.

Blanche threw herself into his arms, and wept upon his bosom; but it was no easy task to conquer the sad forebodings that had taken possession of her mind, and which the continued silence of Mr. Lester served to increase. When she remembered all the observations he had made to her during the time that she had been separated from Sir Laurence, and knew the earnest and ardent solicitude he had at all times felt for her happiness, she could not but fear that her disobedience to his will would have the most painful effect upon him, and she trembled at the consequences which were likely to follow.

Sir Laurence having, after much exertion, somewhat subdued her anguish, left her for a short time, in order that he might compose the important letter to Mr. Lester. This was a task that he scarcely knew how to commence, and he sat for a short time buried in deep and torturing meditation. The whole history of his past life passed in dismal review before his mind's eye, and remorse shook the ardour of his spirit. He felt convinced that the appeal he was about to make to Mr. Lester could make little or no impression upon the mind of that gentleman without he were to enter into a full and satisfactory explanation; and how could he do that, guilty as he would be compelled to admit that he had been? But, at length, he sufficiently conquered his emotions to commence his task, and which he accomplished in a manner much more forcible and eloquent than might have been expected.

He now rejoined Blanche, and having read the epistle to her, over which she shed tears of mingled sorrow, regret, and hope, he sealed it, and immediately despatched it by a messenger to the place where they supposed that Mr. Lester was still remaining.

A quarter of an hour had scarcely elapsed after the departure of the messenger, when a servant entered with a letter, which he placed in the hand of his mistress. Hastily she glanced at the superscription, which merely contained these words,— "To Blanche;" and, uttering an exclamation of emotion, sank in a chair. Sir Laurence hastened towards her, and she placed the letter in his hand, ejaculating, in a faint voice,—

" From my father. Read—read—I cannot."

" Be calm, my dearest Blanche," said her husband. " Where is the person who brought this letter ?" he demanded of the servant. " Send him hither."

" Please you, Sir Laurence, he is gone," replied the servant; " he departed immediately, and without saying a word, after he had delivered the letter."

" This is strange," said Sir Laurence.

" Alas! alas!" sighed Blanche, "it forebodes no good. Oh! read, read, Laurence, and set these horrible doubts at once at rest."

Sir Laurence did, indeed, hastily, but with a trembling hand, break the seal of the letter, and then, in a voice which was partly choked with the power of his emotions, he read the following words :—

" Wretched girl, your deceit and disobedience have severed for ever all ties of affection between us. She who could be thus regardless of her future honour has rendered herself unworthy of a father's love. We meet no more—at least, my fervent wishes are, that we may not do so; for should you ever cross my path, reproaches could be all that you must expect from that aged man whom you have rendered miserable for ever.   (Signed)   " ANDREW LESTER."

Sir Laurence Cleveland had scarcely finshed reading this fatal epistle, when Blanche uttered an exclamation of the most indescribable agony, and sank insensible on the floor. Sir Laurence struck his clenched fist on his burning forehead, with a groan, and then raised his unfortunate wife in his arms ; Amanda standing by, and gazing with the deepest commisseration on her brother and his fair bride.

" Cruel, inexorable man !" at last ejaculated Sir Laurence; " surely he could not have loved his poor child as he professed to do, or he could never have thus discarded her. Oh! my hapless Blanche, it was an unfortunate day for us both when first we met, for misery and perpetual anxiety seem destined to be our portion. Infatuated man! he should have had much more powerful reasons ere he should have been induced to banish his only child from his heart."

He imprinted a fervent kiss upon the pale lips of Blanche, and then proceeded to endeavour to restore her to animation, Amanda having procured the means. It was several minutes before the poor girl, however, recovered, and then she fixed a look of melancholy despair upon the face of her husband, which smote him to the heart.

" That letter.— that dreadful letter!" she gasped forth; " a father discards his only child, upon whom his fondest love has hitherto been lavished, and who, Heaven knows, returned it with all the fervent affection that a daughter could feel towards her parent. Father! father! could you but witness the sufferings of your poor

Blanche, you certainly would recal your harsh and unnatural decree. My God! little did I dream of this! But it cannot be; Laurence, dear Laurence, say that you have been mistaken in reading the letter."

Sir Laurence shook his head, and sighed deeply.

"Alas! it is too true, Blanche," he said; "and I have been the cause of rendering you miserable for ever. But no; I will not believe that your father will persist in this stern and unnatural determination. Disappoinment has only for a time deprived him of reason, and, when he comes coolly to reflect, he will repent him of his stern resolves, and receive you again to his paternal bosom. Dry your tears, my love!—my bride! and still hope for the best. We will seek your excited parent, and, throwing ourselves at his feet, implore his forgiveness. He cannot be insensible to at least your tears and supplications."

"Alas!" ejaculated Blanche; "I did never think that he could have acted as he has already done towards me. I did not believe that he could ever have uttered one harsh word towards that poor child whose constant study it was to render herself worthy of his love. If I have acted wrongly by this one—this only act of disobedience, may Heaven pardon me, and ordain that the fearful doubts he entertains may prove unfounded, as I believe them to be."

Sir Laurence embraced her fervently, but every word she uttered imparted a pang to his heart, and raised a feeling of self-reproach to his breast. Some minutes elapsed ere they could either of them regain any degree of composure, and Amanda stood by, and was at a loss to find words in which she might impart to them consolation. Again the letter was perused, and every word, as they read it, imparted a fresh pang to their bosoms.

"So brief, too," sighed Blanche; "oh! it is not thus he should have discarded me; it is not thus he should have bid me ever more to despair. What has become of the poor old man? Whither has he gone? Surely, he might have granted me at least one farewell meeting, if he even then remained firm in his determination."

"We will find him out, Blanche," said her husband; "nothing shall prevent us from seeking his presence, and supplicating him to relent. He cannot—he will not remain inflexible, for I know his nature too well, and he would despise himself could he close his ears for a moment to the voice of reason and truth."

The eyes of Blanche for an instant sparkled with a ray of hope; but it was only transitory, and her head sunk on the shoulder of her husband, and she sobbed as if her heart would break. Sir Laurence partook himself too much of her anguish to find himself capable of speaking, and a painful silence of some minutes ensued; but which was suddenly interrupted by a knock at the door of the apartment, and on the applicant being desired to walk in, a female domestic entered.

"Now, why this intrusion?" demanded Sir Laurence, hastily.

"Your pardon, Sir Laurence," answered the female, "but Mr. Humphrey, the servant of Squire Lester, is below, and desires to see you immediately."

"Humphrey!" exclaimed Sir Laurence and Blanche in a breath; "oh, show him up directly; he may bring news,—he may be the harbinger of hope."

The servant departed, and presently after old Humphrey made his appearance. Blanche disengaged herself from the embrace of her husband, and, advancing towards the old man, placed her hand upon his arm, and with trembling eagerness demanded,—

"My father, my dear father—tell me, do you bring me news of him?"

"Yes, madam," replied Humphrey, with a look of respectful pity; "my poor, dear master arrived at the mansion not more than an hour since, and so pale and ill he looked, that it was quite melancholy to behold him. He immediately locked himself in his study, and as I thought you, madam, and Sir Laurence, might feel anxious to be made acquainted with his arrival, I slipped out unknown, and hastened here to inform you of it."

"So near to me—my dear father so close at hand, and must I not be permitted to hasten to him, to throw myself at his feet, and implore his forgiveness and his blessing?" cried the violently agitated Blanche.

"Alas! madam," returned the old man, "I fear that it would be useless to attempt to see him to-day, he is in such a state of excitement; but perhaps to-morrow ——"

"Ay, to-morrow," ejaculated Sir Laurence; "by that time he will probably be more calm, and may not refuse to see us, Blanche; till then, let us wait with patience, and try to compose our feelings for the trying occasion."

"Alas! alas!" groaned Blanche, "that we should ever be put to so painful a necessity. Heaven watch over my beloved parent, and move him to reason and to compassion."

Sir Laurence whispered some words of comfort to her, and, after thanking Humphrey, and rewarding him for the trouble he had been at, he dismissed him.

It was some hours after they had received intelligence of the arrival of Mr. Lester at his mansion, before they could gain anything like tranquillity; but Sir Laurence exerted himself to the utmost to compose the feelings of his wife, in order that she might be in some measure prepared for the trying meeting of the following day; but he dreaded its arrival, for he was fearful, from the present conduct of Mr. Lester, that he would remain inexorable, and the shock which the feelings of poor Blanche would thus receive would be more than she could find strength to support. He saw before them no other prospect than that of trouble, and at the same time they would be kept in a continual state of doubt and apprehension from the threats which the gipsies had held out.

Blanche passed a sleepless night, for her thoughts were tortured incessantly by the uncertainty of the results of to-morrow, and the most racking reflections almost drove her mind to entire despair. How fervently did she pray to Heaven that the many apprehensions which she had now so much reason to entertain, might not be realized.

The morning at length dawned, and by that time Blanche had so far struggled with her feelings, as to be more firm and composed than could have been anticipated. Sir Laurence, too, displayed more firmness and confidence than he absolutely felt; and, after they had partaken of a hasty repast, they departed from Branscombe House, to the residence of the unhappy Mr. Lester. How powerful were the feelings of them both as they proceeded on their way; how violently their hearts palpitated, now with hopes, now with despair; and when they had arrived within sight of Mr. Lester's dwelling, the emotions of poor Blanche became so poignant, that it was not without the utmost difficulty she could support herself.

"My father," she ejaculated, "little did I ever expect to approach you with feelings like those which now agitate my bosom. Never did I think that it would be my hard lot to come near you with emotions of doubt and dread."

"Be firm, Blanche," said Sir Laurence, "and something tells me that all will end more happily than you now anticipate.   Your father can never resist the tears and entreaties of his only child, who as always acted with such unbounded affection towards him.   No, no ; he will conquer the present unfortunate prejudices that have taken possession of him, and once more receive you to his paternal bosom."

Blanche returned no answer, for her feelings were of almost too overpowering a nature to find vent in words ; and the carriage, having arrived at the house, drove round to the back entrance, as had been arranged between them and Humphrey, so that they might enter unknown to Mr. Lester, who might otherwise have taken every precaution to prevent their seeing him.

Old Humphrey, hearing the carriage drive up to the door, hastened and admitted them, and they both eagerly inquired after Mr. Lester.

"My master has not yet left his chamber," replied the old man; "but you know it is his usual practice, as soon as he does, to walk into his study; so, if you please, I will show you in there, where you will be sure to obtain the interview you wish."

Blanche sighed deeply ; her heart throbbed more violently than before; and Sir Laurence, taking her arm within his, conducted her trembling footsteps towards the study.   Here she threw herself in a chair, and burst into a copious flood of tears.

"The moment of one of the severest trials of my life is approaching," she sighed. "Oh, God! give me strength to support it.   My dear father, your poor child comes to you a humble suppliant for mercy; surely, you will not refuse it to hear.   You cannot have the heart to discard her for her first, her only act of disobedience to your will."

"Courage, dear Blanche; he will not," said her husband; "I cannot believe him capable of such an act of severity."

In the room were portraits of Mr. Lester, his late wife, and Blanche ; and, before the former Blanche prostrated herself, and with clasped hands, vehemently exclaimed,—

"Dear resemblance of that beloved parent, whose reproachful eye I now dread to meet, how often have I knelt in reverence and admiration before you, and prayed for blessings on the head of the original;   again do I invoke those blessings, and beseech the Almighty to move his heart with pity and forbearance towards me.   And thou, blest shade of my mother, oh! look down with pity from thy heavenly abode, and intercede for mercy for your poor child, who has only been led by the violence of her love for him with whom she has plighted her vows at the altar, to this one act of disobedience to the will of her father."

Sir Laurence was deeply affected, but offered not to interrupt her, and, for several minutes, Blanche remained wrapt in deep meditation and devotion.   At length she arose from her knees, and, beholding her husband hanging affectionately over her, she sank in his arms, and gave unrestrained indulgence to her emotions on his bosom.

"My sweet Blanche," said Sir Laurence, "I feel fresh hope animate my bosom; let the same feeling be imparted to you, and fear not for the result of this painful meeting.   But hark! footsteps are approaching."

"Ah! 'tis he!" exclaimed Blanche; "well do I know his tread. Oh, God! support me."

"Let us retire, my love, behind this screen till after he has entered; it would not be prudent to take him too much by surprise."

Blanche tremblingly complied, and Sir Laurence led her behind the screen, where he did all he could to encourage her, but he had the greatest difficulty to prevent her from fainting. They heard the slow and measured footsteps of Mr. Lester along the gallery which led to the apartment, and the emotion of both Sir Laurence and Blanche increased every instant. At length he entered the room, and so great and painful was the change which only a few short days had wrought in his appearance, that Blanche could with difficulty suppress a scream. His face was very pale, and there was a restless wildness in his eyes which fully showed the distracted state of his mind. His form, too, was bent with care, and, altogether, he presented a perfect picture of grief.

He advanced towards a chair, in which he sank, and, burying his face in his hands, seemed to give himself up entirely to the most agonizing thoughts. All this time Blanche watched him narrowly, and her bosom heaved convulsively. At length he again arose, and advancing towards the portrait of Blanche, he gazed at it with a melancholy earnestness of expression, while the most bitter sobs escaped from his bosom.

"Yes," he said, "it is very like her, at least what she was when she was good and dutiful, and would sooner have sacrificed her life than have disobeyed her fond father's will, or have done aught that could have caused, in his breast, a single pang of regret. But she is no longer Blanche Lester by nature, though, probably, she is still entitled to no other name. Oh! cruel, ungrateful girl, to abandon me at the very moment when I was so very anxious to ensure your happiness, and save you from shame and misery. It is plain she could never have loved me, or she would not thus have opposed my wishes, and after the solemn promise she had made. But she is unworthy of my thoughts, and I will cease to remember her only with shame and loathing."

"Father of mercy, spare me!" shrieked the distracted Blanche, unable any longer to contain herself. Mr. Lester started at the sound, and glared with astonishment and emotion around him.

"Ah!" he cried; "what voice was that? Who was it spoke?"

"Father! father!" shrieked Blanche, starting from the place of her concealment, followed by Sir Laurence, and throwing herself at the old man's feet, and clasping his knees; "it is I, your wretched child, your own Blanche, who here comes to supplicate your pardon for the first, the only act of disobedience she ever committed."

"Ungrateful disobedient," returned Mr. Lester, with a stern brow, and spurning her from him, "begone! You are no child of mine; but probably the degraded paramour of a man upon whose hand another has a legal claim. Begone, I say, nor dare to seek my presence again."

"Gracious Heaven!" exclaimed Blanche; "surely my senses deceive me. Can this be my father, once so kind, so affectionate, so indulgent? Oh, sir, you will not, you cannot, thus cruelly and unjustly discard me; you will recall your dreadful words, and pardon me for that which the violence of my love for my husband alone urged me to do."

"Your husband!" repeated Mr. Lester, with a look of doubt, and still relaxing none of his severity; "has he not been accused of being united to one who still lives, and he has been unable to rebut the charge? Wretched, infatuated girl, you have brought a disgrace upon my name, and have rendered miserable my future days; and a curse, a fearful curse, will ——"

"Horror! horror! forbear!" shrieked Blanche. "Your reason must wander, or you could never give utterance to such dreadful words. Would you invoke a curse upon the head of your only child? Oh, monstrous, monstrous thought!"

"Mr. Lester," said Sir Laurence, "let me implore you to stifle this powerful emotion, and to listen to the voice of reason. Can you blame your daughter that she should be anxious to return to that man to whom she had given her hand in the face of Heaven and of mankind? Would you wish to separate those whom God

hath joined, upon the mere base fabrications of a miscreant, whose actions show him to be capable of falsehood to answer his purposes, and to perpetrate any crime to gratify his revenge?"

"Can you disprove it?" demanded Mr. Lester; "have you not declined to give any explanation?"

"I have already admitted my youthful indiscretions," answered Sir Laurence; "and no one could more sincerely have repented than I have done. Ought I then for ever to be exposed to reproach and calumny? Mr. Lester, I cannot believe that you can be so uncharitable as to view the single offence of poor Blanche with such unmerited, such unnatural severity. For her sake, more than my own, I plead for your forgiveness; and when you discover that I am unworthy of the hand of your daughter, visit me with every reproach; but do not, oh, do not direct your wrath against your own child, who, at any rate, is innocent."

This appeal appeared not to make the least impression upon Mr. Lester, who had suffered his prejudices to gain such an ascendancy of his better sense, that he was blind to all reason, and, for a time, insensible to pity, even for that daughter who had been the very idol of his soul. Blanche still clasped his knees, and gazed up in his countenance with streaming eyes, and the most impressively supplicating looks.

"Away!" he said, again; "I have cast you from me for ever. Quit my sight, lest the feelings with which I now contemplate you tempt me to invoke a malediction upon your head. You have rewarded all my years of foolish fondness and parental indulgence with the most cruel ingratitude, and brought disgrace upon my name; and never, never can I forgive you. Begone! and leave me to that misery which your conduct has created."

"Oh, for the love of Heaven, will nothing move you to relent? I will weep tears of blood, if you will but pity me, and suffer me once more to call you father. By the bright sainted spirit of her who bore me, and the faint resemblance of whom is now before us, I supplicate you to spare me and my husband, and to receive us as we are, by every sacred tie."

"I'll hear no more!" interrupted Mr. Lester, again spurning her from him, and darting towards the door; "get you hence, ungrateful and disobedient; and whenever, in the solitude of your own thoughts, you are brought to a sense of feeling, perhaps you may reflect upon that too fond parent, whose hopes you have annihilated, and whose grey hairs you will bring with sorrow to the grave."

Thus saying, the unfortunate Mr. Lester dashed out of the room with a look that plainly showed he had suffered his feelings to gain such an extraordinary ascendancy over him from the fears he entertained, that partial madness had seized upon his brain.

Blanche uttered one fearful shriek of agony, and sank senseless and inanimate upon the floor. Nor was the anguish of Sir Laurence scarcely less than her own, as he raised her in his arms, and called affectionately upon her name.

"Alas! alas!" he ejaculated, "this will surely break her heart, and thus all the hopes I had so fondly formed will be blighted, and nothing but the most abject misery will in future be my portion. Oh, Blanche, would that fate had never thrown us in the way of each other; then might this have been avoided, and such unmerited sufferings never have been heaped upon your innocence. Curses light upon those wandering wretches—what desolation have they not caused!"

He was interrupted in the midst of these melancholy reflections by the entrance of old Humphrey, who, on beholding the deplorable situation of Blanche and Sir Laurence, evinced much compassion.

"Where is your master, Humphrey?" eagerly inquired Sir Laurence.

"Ah, sir," replied Humphrey, "he has again locked himself in his chamber, and will permit no one to see him. Alas! poor gentleman, I fear that he has gone mad.

Never did I expect to live to see this day. But shall I send my wife to assist to recover your poor lady, sir?"

"No, no," hastily replied Sir Laurence; "procure me some restorative, and I will convey her to the carriage, and to my house with all speed; for, should she recover her recollection here, beneath the same roof with her wretched parent, Heaven only knows what might be the consequences."

Humphrey left the room, and Sir Laurence, raising the form of his lovely bride in his arms, carried her from the house to where the carriage was in waiting. He found Humphrey already there, with a bottle of salts and other restoratives, and having placed his insensible burden in the vehicle, and taken his seat by her side, it was driven off with the greatest rapidity.

CHAPTER VII.

THE DISAPPEARANCE OF MR. LESTER.—THE NOCTURNAL VISITOR TO BLANCHE.

WHAT powerful feelings of agony tortured the mind of Sir Laurence, as he endeavoured to restore Blanche to animation; but all his efforts proved ineffectual, and he, therefore, ordered the coachman to increase his speed, so that they might reach Branscombe House as quickly as possible, and have the advice of the medical attendant of the family.

Sir Laurence saw plainly that it would be useless to attempt to reason with Mr. Lester in his present state of mind, and there was nothing but to leave it to time to convince him of the injustice he was doing his daughter by such harsh behaviour; and, at the same time, he could not help experiencing a feeling of mortified pride at the reproaches and aspersions he had thrown upon him.

But what would be the effect this distressing interview might have upon Blanche? The shock her feelings had sustained she might never recover from, and, certainly, if no ultimate reconciliation could be brought about with her father, her future days would be embittered for ever. And would she not require a full explanation from him of all the circumstances of his past life, to which such fearful allusion had been made by the gipsies? Had she not, as his wife, as one who had sacrificed so much, risked even the hatred and the curses of her father for his sake, a right to demand it? He felt that she had, and yet his very soul must revolt at the task, should she ever require it.

"Poor Blanche!" he sighed, as he hung tenderly over her; "'tis hard, indeed, that all those bright hopes your imagination had formed should be thus sadly blighted. And should the assertions of Madela and the gipsy, Harold, prove correct, and Clara still be living—oh, God! that thought—what horror shall I not have plunged you in! I feel myself unworthy of you, and, although my heart adores, worships you, I regret that ever we met."

They now arrived at Branscombe House, and Blanche was conveyed to her chamber, and Amanda was immediately in attendance upon her, and did all that she could to restore her to animation. Briefly, and as well as his agitation would permit him, Sir Laurence related to his sister what had transpired at their interview with the unhappy Mr. Lester, and she fervently and sincerely expressed her sympathy in the misery which appeared too certainly destined to be the lot of her brother and Blanche.

"Unfortunate gentleman!" she said, "his reason must certainly be affected, or he never could treat with such unnecessary and unmerited severity a daughter whom he so tenderly loved. But Heaven will, I trust, restore his senses; he will relent, and once more receive her to his bosom."

"Alas! Amanda," said Sir Laurence, "I fear that his resentment has gained such power over his better feelings, that nothing will ever be able to subdue it. Oh, had you but heard his fierce observations, as he cast her from him—had you but seen his looks, you would never have forgotten them."

Blanche now heaved a deep sigh, and partially opened her eyes, but immediately closed them again, and relapsed into the same state of insensibility in which she had been before.

"She will never recover," ejaculated Sir Laurence, in the most melancholy accents; "this terrible shock has been too much for her strength to support."

The medical gentleman now arrived at the house, and ordered Blanche to be immediately conveyed to bed, which was accordingly done, and all the necessary remedies were applied for her recovery.

With what anxious care did Sir Laurence watch by the side of her couch, and contemplate the different changes that took place, and which inspired him with alternate hopes and fears; but more than an hour elapsed before she showed any signs of returning animation. She then opened her eyes, but how changed was their expression; it was wild and frenzied, and she glared vacantly around her, apparently unconscious of where she was, and of the persons present.

"My Blanche—my dear Blanche!" ejaculated her husband, in a voice of the deepest emotion.

"*Your* Blanche!" she exclaimed; "no, no—do not mock me. I am no longer your Blanche—no more your child. Did you not tell me so? Did you not discard me—curse me? You have rejected my love, that ardent love and reverence I have ever felt towards you; you have called me hypocrite, deceiver, disobedient, and henceforth poor Blanche must wander through the wide world, despised by her fellow-creatures, and loathed by herself."

"Blanche, do you not know me?" said Sir Laurence, his voice almost choked by the intensity of his emotion. "Oh, look upon me as you were wont to do. I am Laurence, your husband."

"My husband!" cried the poor sufferer. "No, I know you not. I have no husband; he I once called my father told me so, and you must be an impostor."

"Oh, agony!" exclaimed Sir Laurence, striking his forehead; "my worst fears are realised; this dreadful shock has been too much for her, and her reason has fled, perhaps never to return."

"Conquer your emotion, my dear brother," whispered Amanda; "it is only the delirium of the moment, and, in a short time, I trust that her recollection will be restored to her. Hush, she speaks again."

Blanche turned her bewildered gaze towards the doctor, and, in the most touching and pathetic accents, she said,—

"Is it not a dreadful thing to receive a parent's curse, to be banished from his heart for ever, and never more to be permitted to enter his presence, or to kneel at his feet to receive his fond endearments? Oh, 'tis a sad, sad thing to have all one's young hopes blighted. And I have experienced all this; I, poor Blanche, the wretched outcast, the destroyer of a parent's peace."

"Blanche, Blanche," cried the agonized Sir Laurence; "for the love of Heaven, do not suffer this fearful delusion to overpower your senses. It is your husband who appeals to you; oh, speak to me, and assure me that you recognize me."

Blanche stared at him vacantly for a few moments, then uttered a wild and frenzied laugh, and once more sunk into a state of apathy.

"It is all over," groaned Sir Laurence; "oh, Lester, Lester, could you but witness this scene, it would surely wring your heart with remorse, if madness has not completely stifled every feeling."

"You had better retire for a while, Sir Laurence," said the doctor, "and try to subdue your emotion, for I do not despair of being able, before long, to restore your lady to reason; but the greatest care and precaution are necessary."

"Oh, say you so, my dear sir!" said Sir Laurence, grasping his hand; "your words have inspired me with hope, and I will follow your advice entirely."

He then kissed the pale cheek of Blanche with the utmost ardour of affection, and he then left the chamber, accompanied by Amanda, and leaving his wife in the care of the doctor and a female servant.

When Sir Laurence had reached his own apartment, he flung himself into a seat, and for some time was completely absorbed in grief. Amanda approached him, and gently laying her hand on his shoulder, said,—

"Come, my dear brother, you must not take on thus, or you will throw yourself into a dangerous state of illness, at the very time when all your energies may be required to be put into operation. A favourable change will, I trust, shortly take place in poor Blanche, and ——"

"Oh, Amanda," interrupted her brother, "and should she indeed recover her reason, to what a dreadful certainty will she be awakened? Can you wonder at the anguish I endure, when I think of this? Surely Mr. Lester has acted with much cruelty to cast his daughter from him thus, and to allow such terrible prejudices to enter his mind, merely on the assertions of such a miscreant as the gipsy, Harold."

"He has, Laurence," coincided Amanda; "but he certainly will not always remain so harsh and inexorable; he could never have loved his daughter if he does."

"I will see him again," said Sir Laurence, "in spite of everything; and, if he has not banished every sense of feeling from his breast, the present situation of his unhappy and innocent daughter must move him. Yes; in spite of the reproaches he may heap upon my head, I will again appeal to him."

"Be it so, Laurence," remarked Amanda; "I applaud your resolution, for I am in hopes that it will be attended with the most favourable results."

Amanda now returned to the chamber of the invalid, persuading her brother not to venture there until she ascertained how she was. In a few minutes she came back and informed him that Blanche was wrapt in a comfortable and tranquil sleep, which the medical gentleman had no doubt would have the most beneficial effect.

"Thank Heaven!" exclaimed Sir Laurence; "and may she awake to peace and resignation."

He now hastened to the apartment, and approached the bed with noiseless steps for fear of disturbing her. He found her as Amanda had described, in a sound, calm sleep; her face was pale, but, with the exception of a slight expression of melancholy, it was otherwise placid. Sir Laurence ventured to imprint a soft kiss, and breathed a prayer to Heaven for her speedy recovery, and he then turned to the medical gentleman, and inquired his opinion of her.

" Why, certainly her spirits have received a severe shock, Sir Laurence," answered the doctor ; " but she seems to be of a naturally strong constitution, and I have very little doubt that with care she will soon be restored to convalescence."

" Oh, thanks, thanks for that assurance. But her reason ?"

" Oh, there is no doubt that derangement is only temporary ; but above all she must be kept strictly quiet, and must suffer no excitement. But I shall be able to judge better of her when she awakes, which I do not think will be for some considerable time."

Sir Laurence once more kissed the lips of his sleeping bride, and then left the chamber. Thinking that there was now no danger to be apprehended from the situation of Blanche, he determined to hasten to the house of Mr. Lester, and endeavour to gain another interview with him without delay. He surely could not refuse him, and what a consolation would it be to poor Blanche, on her restoration to consciousness, to be assured of her father's forgiveness, and to find him ready once more to enfold her to his paternal bosom. This thought rendered him impatient, and committing Blanche to the care of his sister during his absence, and promising to return as soon as possible, he mounted his horse, and departed on his important mission.

As he proceeded his mind was distracted with various conflicting thoughts, now buoyed up with hope, and then sinking again into despair ; but the favourable change which the doctor anticipated in Blanche urged him on, and he could not bring himself to believe that Mr. Lester could have so closed his breast to every sentiment of paternal affection as to remain obdurate, especially when he was made acquainted with the melancholy state to which his severity had already reduced her.

In a short time he had arrived at the house, and ringing the bell at the gate, it was quickly answered by old Humphrey, whose looks on beholding him augured the most unpleasant intelligence.

" Now, my good Humphrey," said Sir Laurence, hastily, " where is your master ? Can I see him ?"

" Ah, no, sir," answered the old man; " he is gone."

" Gone ! where ?"

" That I know not, sir. Ah ! these are sad doings altogether, very sad."

" I pray you, old man, do not keep me in suspense ; how long has Mr. Lester been from home ?"

" About half an hour, sir, after you and your poor dear lady left here, he quitted his chamber in a state of great agitation, attired for travelling, and commanded me to get his horse ready directly, as he was going a long journey, and it was uncertain when he would return ; but he promised to communicate with me at some future period. In a few minutes, his horse being ready, he mounted it, and, without exchanging another word with me, he galloped from the house with the greatest speed, and, plunging into the wood, was soon lost to my view."

" Rash, misguided man !" exclaimed Sir Laurence ; " what can be his intentions ? Alas ! what will be the anguish of poor Blanche, when she is informed of this addition to her misery—this entire annihilation of her hopes ?"

He beat his breast as these thoughts rushed upon his distracted brain, and after exchanging a few more words with Humphrey, he once more turned his horse's head towards home.

The faint hopes he had recently formed were now crushed, and he dreaded the consequences that would follow, when Blanche should be made acquainted with the disappearance of her father, especially under the state of mind he was labouring.

"Alas!" he cried, "his impetuosity has brought ruin upon us, and I fear will be the death of her to whom my whole soul is devoted. Oh, my poor Blanche, how shall I ever be able to impart this intelligence to you when consciousness is restored to you? How will you receive the information that your father is probably lost to you for ever, and that you can never hope to receive the assurance of forgiveness from his lips? Alas! that Heaven should ever ordain us to meet, since such misery seems destined to alight upon our union."

This anguish increased, and it was in vain he endeavoured to find the least consolation, for whichever way he turned his thoughts, nothing but black despair presented itself. However, he spurred on his horse, anxious as he was to learn the situation of Blanche.

It was a bright, silvery, moonlight night, and every object was as visible as in the open daylight. The soft breeze just gently fanned the surrounding foliage, and the tranquillity of all around presented a melancholy contrast to the tempest of misery that raged within the bosom of Sir Laurence. He had in many respects acted the part of the deceiver, and he felt that he was justly punished; and now, perhaps, the climax of his fate was approaching, for should he be deprived of Blanche, he felt satisfied that life would then become an insupportable burden to him, and he should pray to Heaven to be rid of it as soon as possible. He had got within sight of Branscombe House, when, raising his head, he beheld, standing at a short distance from him in the broad moonlight, what appeared to be a female form, in long flowing robes of white, which, as the moon shone upon them, gave it a ghastly and supernatural appearance. The face was turned towards him, but he was too far off to distinguish the features; but the attitude of the form was fixed, and it seemed as if it was awaiting his approach. He stopped his horse on beholding it, and, notwithstanding he was a man who was not accustomed to fear, he felt a strange tremor stealing over him, which probably the melancholy of his own thoughts, the stillness of the hour, and the suddenness of the appearance of the form, tended to increase. Determined, however, to ascertain its character, if possible, he once more urged on his horse, and, at length, came up to within a few paces of it, but still it offered not to move.

Sir Laurence cast an eager glance towards it. The features were those of a female, lovely, but pale as the moonbeams which shone upon them. But oh, God! those features, as Sir Laurence gazed upon them, what nameless terror and amazement shook his soul; large drops of perspiration stood upon his temples, every limb trembled, but his tongue clove to the palate of his mouth, and he was unable to utter a syllable. The mysterious figure now moved forward with noiseless steps, until it stood close to his horse's head, and he then had an opportunity of observing its features still more narrowly than before. It was no dream; it was no delusion; they were the features of one whom he had never expected to behold again, and which were now fixed upon him with a sad and reproachful look.

" Powers of Heaven !" he at length found strength to utter, in a faint voice, " are the dead permitted to arise again? Oh, God! for what purpose do I receive this awful visitation ?"

The phantom, if such it was, spoke not, but, waving its hand in a menacing manner, slowly retreated backwards, with noiseless steps, until it was lost to view amid the thick, clustering trees which grew at some distance from the spot.

For a few minutes Sir Laurence remained transfixed to the spot, and gazing towards the place where the phantom had disappeared. The most powerful emotions shook his frame, and he was almost ready to sink from his horse to the earth. Could he have been deceived? Oh, no! it was no delusion; he had had plenty of opportunity to mark its features, and they were those of one, the recollection of whom inspired his soul with terror.

" The wrath of Heaven and the dead is upon me," he groaned. " Oh! God! what will become of me?"

He struck his forehead, and almost feared to look around him, lest he should again encounter the ghastly form which had excited such extraordinary emotion in his breast; but at length he forced himself as much into composure as he could, under the circumstances, and dashed on towards the house, where he rang hastily at the gate, and was admitted. He left his horse in the care of the servant, and staggered into the house, his bosom agitated with various feelings, which were too powerful for utterance. When he had gained the sitting-room he sank into a seat, and for a time he was unable to reflect upon anything but the supposed phantom which he had so recently beheld, and which had brought up all the gloomy horrors of the past to his recollection, and made him anticipate the future with still more apprehension. But at length he was aroused to the anxieties of the present, and he was about to hasten to the chamber of Blanche, when Amanda entered the room. She noticed the pale looks and the agitated demeanour of her brother, and she was fearful that he had some more melancholy information to communicate.

" Dear Laurence," she said, " you have then returned; but you look more distressed and wretched than before. Tell me what has been the result of your journey?"

" Anon, Amanda," replied Sir Laurence, impatiently, and with much emotion; " but my poor Blanche—oh! tell me—how is she now?"

" Better, Laurence," said Amanda; " she has awoke once, but it was only for a short interval, and then her mind did not appear to wander as it did, and she is now again wrapped in a calm and refreshing slumber."

" God be thanked for this," ejaculated Sir Laurence; " but, alas! what will be her feelings in addition to her present misery, at what she must too soon learn?"

" Does, then, Mr. Lester still remain inexorable?" eagerly inquired Amanda.

" Alas!" replied Sir Laurence, " it is evident that he does. He has acted throughout the whole of this sad, this unfortunate business with the most unnecessary severity, and now to complete our misery, and to sink us into complete despair, he has left his mansion abruptly, and gone no one knows whither."

" Gone?" repeated Amanda, in astonishment. " Oh, he surely cannot have been so rash and cruel."

" It is true, Amanda," replied her brother. " But let me hasten to my poor Blanche. Oh, Heaven, what insupportable misery have I plunged you into by making you my bride."

Sir Laurence now moved towards the door, and Amanda, laying her hand upon his arm, detained him for a minute.

" One word before you go, my dear brother," she said; " I would advise you not to mention anything to Blanche about the disappearance of her father just now; for in her present weak state it might be productive of the most fatal consequences, and perhaps in the course of a day or two you may receive a communication from the unfortunate gentleman."

"I will follow your advice, Amanda; but I fear that nothing will move the heart of Mr. Lester to relent from its harsh determination. Oh, I never believed that he could have acted in such a manner towards his only child."

"His mind must certainly be wandering, Laurence," said Amanda, "or he could not do so."

Sir Laurence sighed deeply and then quitted the room, followed by his sister. His mind was in a state of the greatest agitation, and anxious though he was, he almost dreaded to enter the presence of poor Blanche. All the guilty proceedings of the past rushed upon and tortured his brain, and those well remembered features which he had never expected to behold again were impressed upon his memory in characters of fire. Such numerous causes for excitement were almost more than he could find strength to support, and he felt and knew that he was in truth acting a part which must not only bring down upon him self-reproach and condemnation, but also that of those with whom he had become so unfortunately connected. It was necessary, however, that he should stifle his feelings as much as possible, and by the time he had reached the chamber door of Blanche, he had by a powerful effort so far succeeded as to have regained somewhat of his usual equanimity.

Amanda entered the room first, and approached the bed of the invalid, who was awake, and having whispered a few words to her, she beckoned her brother to enter. Eagerly he advanced, and taking the fair hand of his lovely bride in his, he pressed it to his lips. Blanche looked in his face for a moment with an expression of the most intense feeling, and then drooped her head upon his shoulder, and her powerful emotions found free vent in a paroxysm of sobs and tears.

"Blanche, my dearest Blanche," said Sir Laurence, "for Heaven's sake endeavour to calm the agony of your feelings, and let us hope that the dark clouds which at present obscure the horizon of our happiness will be dispersed. Oh, my love, think what must be the torture of mind that I am enduring to see you suffer thus."

"I am better now, dear Laurence," sighed Blanche, faintly; "but, oh! my poor father; can I ever forget the terror of his looks—his observations? He who was once so kind, so affectionate, so indulgent; who never gave me a harsh word, but would have been miserable, could he have caused me the slightest pang. And he will never forgive us. The sternness and determination of his manners convince me that he will not."

"Nay, Blanche, do not give way to that thought; when his present delirium has passed away, he will repent him of his severity, and once more receive you to his paternal bosom."

"Oh, no, my husband; I dare not think so. And he cursed us, Laurence; yes, those dreadful words still seem to ring in my ears, and must ever render me wretched."

"No, Blanche," returned Sir Laurence; "he did not curse us; your supplications stayed the fearful malediction his rash lips would have uttered, and Heaven has spared him that which would have embittered all his future days."

"But has he not discarded me for ever?" demanded the agonised Blanche; "has he not said that he will never more acknowledge me for his daughter? Oh, God! surely I have not merited so cruel a fate as this."

"Ah, Blanche," sighed her husband; "and I have been the cause of this. Oh! would to Heaven that we had never met."

"No, my dear Laurence," returned Blanche, throwing her arms affectionately round the neck of her husband; "I will not—I must not reproach you, for I should despise myself could I believe that you are guilty of the base deeds which have been laid to your charge. I feel—I know you are innocent, and no power on earth shall turn my heart against you; no, not even the lasting anger of that parent whom I so fondly love. Come, my Laurence, I am more happy now. Heaven inspires me with confidence, and I will hope that my poor father will relent, and again receive us to his arms."

With mingled feelings of pleasure and grief Sir Laurence heard these observations; he felt that he was unworthy of the generous confidence which Blanche reposed in him, and he feared that something would yet occur to convince her of the same, and then with what horror and abhorrence must she look upon him. Had it been a vision or reality which he had that evening seen? If the latter, his misery and disgrace would be complete, and the hopes of that fair being, to whom he had plighted his vows at the altar, would be blasted for ever.

As these agonising thoughts crowded upon his brain, he scarcely dared to look into the countenance of Blanche, lest he should betray the feelings that were passing in his bosom.

"But will he not see us, dear Laurence?" said his wife; "surely after his first gush of wrath has vanished, he will not—he cannot be so cruel as to banish us from his presence for ever."

This was a question which increased the agitation and confusion of the unhappy Sir Laurence. What answer could he make to it? How would he ever be able to break to her the melancholy intelligence of the disappearance of Mr. Lester? But it must be done, and then he feared that the misery and despair of Blanche would be more than she could find strength to support with any degree of fortitude. He hated evasion, but yet he was compelled to resort to it on this occasion, and he therefore said nothing to Blanche at present about the disappearance of her father, but endeavoured to persuade her that in a few days his reason would return, and that he would then be induced to come to a reconciliation.

Sir Laurence remained with his wife for more than a couple of hours, and he had the satisfaction of beholding her become more composed. When he retired to his own apartment, however, he gave himself up to the most racking thoughts, and it was some time before he could think of retiring to his couch. Long he reflected on the mysterious appearance he had encountered on his return home in the evening, and the more he did so, the stronger became his emotions, and the greater his apprehensions. He did not believe in supernatural appearances, or he must have imagined that he had seen the phantom of her whom he had believed to have been for so many years dead; and if he had not, then was the statement of Harold the gipsy evidently correct, and he had rendered himself amenable to the laws of his country, and had brought shame and misery upon the confiding and affectionate Blanche. What unspeakable agony did these thoughts inflict upon him, and his brain became bewildered, and he scarcely knew how to act.

"My God!" he exclaimed; "should it, indeed, be found that Clara is still living, what will become of me? What atonement can I ever make to Blanche for the ruin I shall then have inflicted upon her? How can I ever again dare to encounter her gaze, or to meet her reproaches? But am I not much to blame to deceive her in the manner which I have done? Oh! yes, I should not have ventured to make her my wife until I had fully explained all the past events of my life, and then left her to decide whether I were worthy of her or not. But I shrink from the task, and never, never can my lips reveal the fatal errors of my youth. My heart shrinks, appalled, at the bare thought."

He was interrupted in this soliloquy by hearing a soft cadence from a female voice of the most melancholy plaintiveness, proceeding apparently from immediately beneath the window of his chamber, and which caused him to start from his seat with astonishment and emotion, so impressive was the effect at that silent hour of the night, and under such singular circumstances. He hastened to the window and looked out, but all was still, and he could not observe any person from whom the sounds could have proceeded. The moon was shining resplendently, and all was tranquil around.

" I must have suffered my imagination to deceive me," he said. " What melancholy minstrel would wander here at this nocturnal hour, and for what purpose ?"

Again he heard the voice—so soft, so beautiful, and every tone of which went to his heart; for to such strains he had often listened in the days of his youth, and every tone presented some familiar recollection to his disturbed imagination. Again he strained his eyes to endeavour to perceive the minstrel, but to no purpose, and his astonishment and agitation increased. He drew in his breath, and, listening attentively, was at length enabled to catch the following words :—

> " Dearest youth, I'll ne'er deceive thee,
>   But faithful prove in weal or woe ;
> By a thought could Clara grieve thee,
>   Or ever cease to love thee ?   No.
>
> Thou art mine, my heart's whole treasure,
>   Our vows are sealed by Heaven on high ;
> And when I cease to yield thee pleasure,
>   What then is left me but to die ?"

" Gracious Heaven !" cried Sir Laurence, as his heart palpitated violently against his side, and every nerve trembled ; " it is the very song that Clara used to sing in those days of transitory bliss, when we first breathed our vows of fidelity together."

His emotion increased to an insupportable degree, and still he listened with breathless attention, but the voice had ceased, and no other sounds met his ear but the rustling of the night breeze, as it wafted among the foliage ; and, as far as his eye could stretch into the gardens beyond, he could not perceive any human form. While he thus stood wrapped in amazement and awe, he heard a slight rustling sound, and the next moment the same female form which had crossed his path in the evening emerged from a bower, and with solemn and noiseless steps approached to beneath the window from which Sir Laurence was gazing. He breathed short and quick, huge drops of perspiration started to his temples, and his limbs trembled violently. He would have spoken and addressed the fair vision, if such it really was, but the power was denied him, and he could only gaze with anxiety and impatience. At length the female raised her head ; and the moon shone clearly and fully upon her features. It was the same pale but lovely countenance which Sir Laurence had seen before, and the sad lineaments of which struck his heart with terror and remorse.

" Spirit of my wife !" he cried, " why comest thou hither ? In the name of Heaven, I implore of you to speak to me !"

The form appeared to sigh deeply, and gazed at Sir Laurence with a melancholy and impressive look of reproach, but returned no answer, and the next moment she turned away, and gliding along the avenue was quickly lost to the sight. Sir Laurence sank upon his knees, and burying his face in his hands, for some moments gave himself up entirely to the agonising and conflicting thoughts which the mystery and singularity of the event excited.

" Good God !" he at last exclaimed, " the vengeance of the dead is pursuing me, for surely this could be no mortal form which I just now gazed upon, and which has left behind, an impression on my heart that nothing can remove."

He groaned with agony, and scarcely dared to raise his eyes, lest they should again encounter some ghastly form. The hour of one now tolled from a neighbouring church-bell, and still Sir Laurence felt not inclined to retire to bed, so much was his mind disturbed by the startling and extraordinary events which had taken place within the last few hours, and which had conjured up the most torturing doubts and apprehensions in his breast. Was it not, indeed, a supernatural being which he had beheld?—Dared he to think otherwise? Oh, no; for, if it was indeed the living form of his former wife that he had seen, his own misery and that of Blanche would be rendered complete.

"All-merciful Father!" he cried, "for the sake of my poor, innocent bride, I pray you to avert so terrible a calamity, and not suffer one so gentle and so blameless to suffer for me."

He clasped his forehead vehemently, and gave himself up to entire despair. He saw at once that fresh troubles were in store for them, and he now almost lamented that his devoted Blanche had fled from the protection of her father, until after all the dreadful doubts which now occupied his mind should have been removed.

Again he looked forth from the window, but no object met his view; and, as all was silent around, he quitted the place, and at length sought his couch; but it was some time before he could go to sleep, and when he did, his imagination was disturbed by the most painful dreams.

The next morning he met Blanche with a heavy and foreboding heart, but he was compelled to stifle his feelings as well as he could, lest he should create any additional fears in her breast.

Blanche was much better, and was enabled to leave her bed. But she noticed the emotion of her husband, and she could not but help thinking that there was something more upon his mind than he had thought proper to make her acquainted with.

"Dear Laurence, I see the emotion that is labouring at your breast, although you attempt to conceal it," she said. "You have not told me all, I am confident you have not; but say, will you not again visit my poor father, and endeavour to move him to compassion and forbearance?"

This was a question that bewildered and confounded Sir Laurence, and he scarcely knew what to answer.

"Dear Blanche," he at length faltered out, "I—I cannot."

"Cannot!" repeated Blanche, with a look of penetration. "What mean you?"

"Blanche," he replied, "will you promise me to bear with composure and fortitude the additional news I have to give you?"

"Oh! yes; Heaven will, I trust, enable me to do so; but keep me not in suspense, my husband, I implore you."

Sir Laurence then related to her the particulars of the disappearance of Mr. Lester, to which she listened with feelings of anguish which may easily be conceived.

"My poor father gone!" she cried; "fled, deserted me, and in wrath! Then there is no hope for me. Oh, surely this is most cruel and unjust! But whither can he have departed? In the present distracted state of his feelings, what may he not be tempted to do? Oh, God! protect the poor old man, and move his heart to relent."

Violent sobs choked her utterance, and she laid her head on her husband's shoulder, and wept bitterly. He exerted himself to console her; but it was some time before he could do so; and he was, in fact, in that state of mind as much to need consolation himself. The midnight adventure still distracted his mind, and he scarcely dared to gaze into her face, lest she should penetrate the thoughts that were passing in his bosom.

"But he must be discovered," said Blanche. "Oh! Laurence, you will not leave any means untried to find him out, and to recall him to reason and justice."

"You may depend upon it, my dear Blanche," answered Sir Laurence, "that I will exert myself to the utmost to do so; but I do hope that his paroxysm will not last long—that he will shortly return, and reinstate you in his affections."

Blanche raised her eyes towards Heaven, and mentally supplicated that the ideas of her husband might be realised; but her mind was tormented by the most painful doubts and apprehensions; and it was some time ere she could attain the least degree of tranquillity.

In the course of the morning, old Humphrey took the liberty of calling at Branscombe House, to inquire after the health of his dear young mistress, as he always called Blanche; and being introduced to her, he answered all the questions she put to him in the most explicit manner, and which convinced her that he was speaking the truth, and rendered her astonishment and anguish at the sudden disappearance of her father greater than before.

"My God!" she ejaculated, "what can be the intentions of the poor old man? Should he in his frenzy be urged to the perpetration of some rash act, I shall ever accuse myself as being the indirect cause."

"Say not so, dear Blanche," said her husband; "in what are you to blame, if you were urged by a sense of the duty and affection you owed to him on whom you had bestowed your hand, to disobey the injunctions of your father, and to fly to his arms? Mr. Lester has acted with unnecessary severity throughout, and I have very little doubt that he will in a short time be brought to a firm conviction of that himself, and will hasten to remove the dreadful anxiety which his sudden and mysterious disappearance has excited in our bosoms."

"Heaven send that he may," observed Blanche; "and that he may be thoroughly convinced of the falsehood of the aspersions that have been cast upon your character."

Sir Laurence shuddered, for his conscience told him that he was deserving of much that had been attributed to him, and he feared that such would ultimately be shown to his shame and confusion.

"And you say that my father did not say whither he was going, or when he was likely to return, Humphrey?" said Blanche.

"No, your ladyship, he did not," replied Humphrey. "But I do hope that it will not be long before he does come back, and that no harm will come to him."

Blanche and her husband heartily responded to this wish, and, after a few more observations, Humphrey took his leave.

The day passed most gloomily away, for Blanche and Sir Laurence were distracted by the most painful thoughts, and in vain sought to impart consolation to each other.

In this manner two or three days elapsed, and they were unable to gain the least tidings of the unhappy Mr. Lester, although Blanche had continued to cherish the hope that if he did not think proper to make them acquainted with the place of his retreat, he would, at least, communicate with them in order to convince them that he was still in existence. But when she found herself thus sadly disappointed, her anxiety became almost insupportable, and the most dreadful apprehensions seized upon her mind, which Sir Laurence found it impossible for them to quiet.

Sir Laurence had taken the earliest opportunity of dispatching a trusty servant to the house where Mr. Lester had conveyed Blanche, in order to ascertain if he was there, but on his return they learned that Mr. Lester had not only not been there since he had left it, but that it was now occupied by another family. This added to the perplexity and apprehensions of them both, and they remained for some time in a state of agitation that admitted of no consolation.

But still Blanche could not, after mature reflection, bring her mind to believe that her father had laid violent hands on himself, and with the hope that time might move him from his stern resolves, and that he would again restore her to his paternal bosom, in which ideas Sir Laurence did all he could to encourage her, she became more tranquil, although her reflections were always of the most painfully poignant nature.

And not less acute the sufferings of Sir Laurence Cleveland, the more so, as he was constrained to stifle his emotions in the presence of his wife, and to try to inspire her with hopes which he did not feel himself. How agonizing were his thoughts when he reflected upon the uncertainty of the existence or the death of his first wife; and it was in vain that he tried all he could to persuade himself that he had been deceived in the form he had seen on two such remarkable occasions. Oh, no; those features were certainly those of that one unfortunate being whom he could never forget, and who, if still living, would be the means of blasting the hopes of himself and Blanche for ever.

In vain he had endeavoured to ascertain whether the gipsies had gone, and, although he affected to heed them not, he lived in daily and hourly dread of their vengeance. His thoughts were often occupied also by the image of the gipsy boy, whom he had accidentally wounded; and he felt a powerful sensation of horror, when he thought of the probability of that wound having proved mortal. The features of that poor boy, so like to one with whom he had been so closely connected, had made a lasting impression upon him, and the brief particulars he had given of his life on their first meeting, had also deeply interested him. He would have been glad to have snatched that boy from the wretches in whose power he was, for, from what he had already seen of him, he was convinced that he possessed a mind which, if properly cultivated, would do honour to any station. In this manner more than a week passed away, and still the place of Mr. Lester's retreat remained a mystery, and not any of the indefatigable endeavours of Sir Laurence to obtain information which might lead to a discovery, were attended with the least success. It was wonderful that Blanche was enabled to support this severe trial with the fortitude she did; but still, amidst all, she could not help believing that Providence would watch over him, and that he would shortly again return to the mansion he had quitted, and, having been convinced of the injustice he had done Sir Laurence, would be anxious to bring about an immediate reconciliation. Daily she and Sir Laurence visited the house of Mr. Lester, with the vain hope of finding him there, or of hearing something from him; but they always had to return disappointed, and every fresh visit increased their fears.

Some particular business calling Sir Laurence from home, Blanche was left alone with Amanda, who did all that she could to divert her thoughts from the melancholy subject that engrossed them. This, however, was no easy task, for Blanche felt more than usually depressed in spirits that day, and the uncertain fate of her father tortured her mind to distraction. She had hitherto endeavoured to control her feelings as much as possible in the presence of her husband, for she knew how much it tortured him to observe it, and that he reproached himself as being the cause of the calamity which had befallen them; but when left alone to her own painful thoughts, her mental agony found full vent, and she indulged in the most gloomy forebodings as to the fate into which her father had precipitated himself.

"I shall never behold him again," she would sigh; "he has abandoned me for ever, and, with that thought upon my mind, what but the greatest possible misery can be my portion? Oh, my dear father, what a terrible infatuation must have taken possession of you to act with such severity towards one who ever behaved to you with the fondest affection, and was always so studious of your happiness. And not to leave one line behind you, merely to inform me of your intentions! Oh! this is most cruel. God of heaven forgive me, if I have acted wrong, but certainly I have not done so wilfully; and would it not have been unjust for me to have abandoned him to whom I had given my hand, merely upon the accusation of a villain who, no doubt, is capable of any crime, however atrocious? Dear Laurence, I should be unworthy of your love, could I deem you the guilty being you have been represented to be."

Unfortunate, confiding Blanche! little did you imagine how fatally you were at some future time to be undeceived. Weak, indeed, was the conjecture you could form of the troubles that were in store for you, or you could never have survived even the bare contemplation.

Sir Laurence had stated that the business he was going upon, would probably detain him till a late hour; therefore, when night approached, Blanche felt no surprise or uneasiness at his not returning, but wishing to be alone, she bade Armanda good night, and retired to her own chamber, where she sat for some time, buried in profound reflection, and forming various conjectures, all alike unsatisfactory, of the fate which had befallen her father. She still, in imagination, beheld his fearful looks, as they appeared on the occasion of their last meeting, and listened to his harsh observations, and her soul shrank appalled, as she recalled them to her memory. But madness, she was certain, must have seized upon his brain, or he could never have given utterance to such fearful expressions; and, believing him to be in that state of mind, had she not reason to apprehend the worst?

Her mind was so tortured by these various thoughts, that she knew it would be useless to attempt to rest, and she therefore did not retire to bed, but continued to watch at one of the windows of her apartment in a state of mind amounting to listless apathy.

The night was very sultry, and the thick, heavy air added to the oppressive languor of her mind. Strange phantasies crowded upon her heated brain, and she could almost imagine she beheld strange and ghastly forms dancing before her eyes in the pale moonbeams. The death-like silence that reigned throughout the house added to the melancholy of her thoughts, and served to increase the gloomy delusions under which she was labouring; but still she felt herself incapable of moving from her seat, and kept her eyes fixed upon the gardens of the mansion, picturing to herself all kinds of frightful images, and fancying that she heard the most fearful and unnatural sounds wafted on the night breeze. It was one of those illusionary moments of horror to which every individual is at some time subject, especially when they have any trouble or anxiety upon their mind, and it was in vain that Blanche endeavoured to shake it off.

She now became most anxious for the return of her husband, as it was fast approaching the hour of midnight; and, as he was only attended by his groom, she began to fear that something might have happened to him, or that he might have been waylaid by some of the numerous and desperate highwaymen that she knew infested that part of the country which he would have to traverse.

In this manner she sat for some time; but she was suddenly aroused from these gloomy reflections by hearing a noise as of some person endeavouring to force themselves through the foliage at the farther end of the garden, and straining her eyes in that direction, she suddenly beheld a female form, apparently very decrepit, and leaning on a stick, emerge into the broad moonlight.

Blanche felt a sensation of fear steal over her, for this time she was certain that she was not deceived, that she had not suffered her distempered imagination to overpower her reason. The woman, if such it was, stealthily approached the house, and when she had arrived to within a few paces of it, she raised her head, and Blanche then recognised that it was the old gipsy woman, Madela.

No. 11.

She could scarcely repress a scream of terror; but the power of her emotions deprived her of the means to quit the spot, and she remained with her eyes fixed upon the actions of the hag, and filled with a mixture of dread and amazement at the visit of that singular being at that nocturnal hour.

Madela drew nearer and nearer, until she arrived immediately beneath the window at which Blanche was seated, when she once more raised her eyes, and seemed immediately to recognise Blanche. The expression of her at any time forbidding features was at that time scarcely human, and Blanche could not meet the stern and stedfast gaze which she fixed upon her without a shudder of horror; but still she could not leave the window, or remove her eyes from the old woman, who seemed to read her feelings, and to exult in them.

A pause of some moments ensued, when the hag raised her long, bony arm in a menacing attitude, and laughed aloud.

"Bride and no bride," she cried, in her usual harsh and grating accents, "I greet thee at the midnight hour—I greet thee, and wish thee joy of the possession of that man whose hand another lives to claim. Forsooth, it was worth sacrificing virtue, honour—it was well worth incurring a father's curse, to gain so rare a prize. Beware! disobedience will bring with it sure punishment. Thou hast already tasted of the poisoned chalice that will embitter thy future days; but thou must drain it to the dregs, and ere long thou wilt have reason to detest the hypocritical villain whom thy weak, fond heart now idolizes. Even now his conscience reproaches him, for he knows that he has deceived thee, as he has done many others, and there is one living who will yet come forward to prove his treachery and thy shame."

Blanche uttered a scream of horror as the hag gave utterance to these words, and looked imploringly towards her; but Madela's eyes flashed with more than their usual vivacity, and she seemed to enjoy the agony she had inflicted on the hapless damsel's heart.

Every word she had spoken seemed to pierce into her very soul; but yet she was unable to move from the place on which she was seated, or to raise any alarm, although she was fearful that some other of the gipsies were close at hand, and contemplated some desperate outrage.

"You are watching for his return, Blanche *Lester*," said the old woman; "and he will come, and you will again receive him to your arms with all the consciousness of rectitude. But mark me, girl! you should cast him forth as you would do the most venomous reptile, although he has worked that ruin which you cannot now recall. Blanche Lester, I tell you again, that Clara Cleveland, the lawful wife of him to whom you have given your hand, still lives."

"Mercy—mercy, great God!" shrieked Blanche, and, unable longer to support her feelings, she sank insensible upon the floor.

How long she had remained in this condition she had no opportunity of knowing, but when she again recovered, her senses were so bewildered, that, for a few moments, she was unable to form only a vague conjecture of what had taken place. At length the awful words of Madela, the hag, rushed with overwhelming force upon her recollection, and, raising herself from the floor, she once more looked from the window, but the old woman was gone.

The moon was now hidden behind a cloud, and all was darkness and gloom. The silence that reigned in the house still remained unbroken; but Sir Laurence had evidently not yet returned home, or he would have sought her presence, and she felt the utmost alarm at his protracted absence; lest he should have encountered any of the gipsies, who were probably lurking somewhere in the neighbourhood, from the appearance of old Madela.

Then the terrible words of the hag rushed upon her brain with renewed vigour, and, for the time, she felt herself the most wretched and degraded of human beings; for, for awhile, she could not but place some confidence in the assertions of the gipsy woman, and, if they were indeed true, her fate was sealed—she was rendered miserable for ever.

"But no, no, it cannot be," she cried, after a pause, during which she had been endeavouring to collect her thoughts; "the dreadful accusation can only have proceeded from malice and revenge. Fate never could have doomed me to such destruction, and it were monstrous to believe my Laurence the villain he is represented to be. Had he really believed his first wife to be living, he would not, he could not, have consented to receive me again to his arms. Alas! alas! what can he have done to these wandering outcasts that they should thus implacably pursue him? Laurence, I will still believe you innocent, and nothing shall convince me to the contrary, until I receive such unquestionable proof that the most sceptical would find it impossible to doubt."

She now endeavoured to move towards the bed, but found herself inadequate to the task, and again sank back exhausted in her seat.

It was now so late that Blanche did not think it was likely that Sir Laurence would return that night; and yet she wondered that he should absent himself so long from home, knowing, as he must, the state of uneasiness and anxiety she would be in.

She cast one more glance from the window, and then closed it, and sinking on her knees, she supplicated the protection of the Almighty, and implored him to watch over, and guard from every harm, her husband and her unfortunate parent, whom she now began to fear that she should never behold again.

She was interrupted in the midst of her devotions by hearing some sounds, like those of cautious footsteps, outside her chamber, but on that side nearest the bed, and where she imagined there was no entrance. She listened with breathless attention, thinking she had suffered her fears, from the state of her mind, to deceive her; but she now heard the sounds more distinctly, and was convinced that they proceeded from human feet; but she was so completely overpowered by terror that she could not give utterance to the least sound, although she felt fully conscious of some approaching danger.

She kept her eyes riveted on that part of the room from whence the sounds issued, and they gradually became louder, until the footsteps seemed to stop immediately behind the wainscot, on that side of the apartment on which the bedstead stood. Blanche trembled, and stared aghast; but still she was quite deprived of the power of creating any alarm, and could only await, with a kind of desperate feeling of resignation, the result of this mysterious adventure. And now she heard a sound like that of some persons trying to force open a lock or spring, and the next moment a panel in the wainscot glided back, and before the astonished and terrified eyes of Blanche appeared the tall and graceful figure of a female, attired in long, flowing robes of white.

The countenance was pale, but the expression of the features was lovely beyond description, and yet so unearthly, that Blanche, believing it to be some supernatural being, uttered a cry of terror, and sank upon the floor insensible.

CHAPTER VIII.

THE ALARM.—THE ANGUISH OF SIR LAURENCE AND BLANCHE.—DEATH OF MR.
LESTER.

WHEN Blanche recovered her senses, she found herself supported in the arms of Sir Laurence, whose countenance evinced the utmost fear and emotion. She could not but shrink from him with an involuntary feeling of horror, when she recollected all that old Madela had said, and she looked around the room almost expecting to see the same ghastly and supernatural-looking form which had so much alarmed her.

" Dear Blanche," said Sir Laurence, " what is the meaning of this? What has occurred to terrify you thus ?"

" Ah!" exclaimed Blanche, staring vacantly around her ; " did you not then behold it ?"

" Behold it !" repeated Sir Laurence, with a look of astonishment; " I do not understand you—explain yourself."

" That spectral form, and yet so lovely," returned Blanche. " But a few minutes since I saw it ; it appeared to me in this apartment, and ——"

" My dear Blanche," interrupted Sir Laurence, " you must have been dreaming, or are labouring under some fearful delusion."

" Oh, no," returned Blanche; " it was no delusion—there, there it appeared;" she added, pointing to the wainscot. " I saw the panel glide back, and the form stalked into the apartment. It was that of a female, so pale, so unearthly, but yet its features were most beauteous and heavenly."

" Most strange," said Sir Laurence, and he felt a powerful sensation of awe steal over his senses, as he recalled to his memory the form he had himself seen, and which exactly corresponded with the description which Blanche now gave of her mysterious visitant. " But who can the individual be, and how could it have gained access to the house ?"

" Oh, Laurence," said Blanche, still clinging to him with terrified looks, " I know not. I am bewildered ; but examine the wainscot."

Sir Laurence did so, and after a minute search, he discovered the sliding panel, which he was not before aware of, and which he now beheld with the most unspeakable amazement.

"Are you not now convinced that I was not mistaken?" demanded Blanche? "Oh, Laurence, never, never shall I forget that mysterious form, and the looks it fixed upon me. A strange destiny pursues us both, and may the Almighty pardon me if I am acting wrongly in his sight. I have seen her, again, too—the hag, the gipsy—and once more she denounced you as a deceiver, and the husband of another, who is still living. Gracious Heaven ! what horrible feelings does that thought create in my bosom! Laurence, may I not still call you husband? Can the dreadful suspicions of my father be true? If they are, wretched, degraded being that I am,— my heart will surely burst."

She threw herself, sobbing, on his bosom, and the emotions of Sir Laurence were so great, that, for a short time, he was incapable of uttering a syllable.

"Oh, my poor Blanche," he said at length, "how can I answer you? My brain is bewildered and distracted. Why is my happiness thus doomed to be continually interrupted? But tell me all the painful particulars."

As well as her agitation would permit her, Blanche complied, and we need not attempt to describe the feelings of anguish with which Sir Laurence listened to her.

"It cannot be," he said, when she had concluded; "it is all a base fabrication of those outcast wretches. Say, Blanche, that you do not believe them, for, were I certain that you could suppose me to be the villain I have been represented, my hopes would, indeed, be all annihilated, and even life would become an insupportable burthen to me, which I must endeavour to rid myself of as speedily as possible."

Sir Laurence could not give utterance to these observations without some confusion and qualms of remorse, for he knew that he had erred—greatly erred; he knew that he had no just claim to the confidence of Blanche, and the recent events—all that had befallen to him, the form which he had seen, and which he had no doubt was the same which had so alarmed her, filled him with apprehensions which he almost feared to encourage, but still could not banish them from his mind. But Blanche could only, for a very transitory period, entertain doubt or suspicion; Laurence could never have acted such a part of duplicity, and she tried to think of the mysterious appearance of the form in the most favourable point of view. Once more her looks beamed with confidence, and, throwing her fair arms around her husband's neck, she ejaculated,—

"No, Sir Laurence, I should be unworthy of you if I could still encourage a doubt upon this painful subject, although, certainly, the events that have taken place are of a very ambiguous and bewildering nature. I am confident that I was as wide awake as I am at the present moment, when the form entered the chamber; and she must have been, if she is not now, concealed in some part of the house, but with what design I can form no conjecture."

Sir Laurence hesitated for a minute or two, and the most painful sensations of fear agitated his bosom. But still he struggled violently with his feelings, and endeavoured to appear as calm as possible, while he observed,—

"The discovery of this secret entrance greatly astonishes me, and I cannot imagine for what purpose it has originally been formed. However, endeavour to calm yourself, my dear Blanche, for a strict search must be made, and the servants undergo a minute examination. It might turn out, after all, to be one of them disguised who appeared to you, prompted by a foolish wish to play a hoax."

Blanche shook her head, and Sir Laurence almost blushed for the suggestion he had thrown out, feeling so certain that Blanche had not been mistaken, but that it was the form of his first wife, whether living or dead, that she had, as well as himself, seen. Those features he could never forget; and the simple ballad he had that evening heard, the favourite song of the unfortunate Clara in happier days, still seemed to vibrate in his ears, and convinced him more forcibly than all that he had every reason not to feel satisfied, while, at the same time, he trembled to think upon the probability of the troubles that were in store for them.

"Ah, no, Laurence," at length said Blanche, in answer to his observations; "I am certain that it was not the person of any of the servants I beheld; nor is it likely that any of them would have the boldness to attempt such a hoax. But let us remove from this apartment; some danger might threaten us, and I do not feel safe while I remain in it."

Sir Laurence whispered some words of consolation and encouragement to her, and he then proceeded to examine the sliding panel, which he opened; but nothing particular met his observation, with the exception of a winding flight of stairs, which appeared to lead to the back part of the house, and which he resolved to examine more particularly in the morning. He secured the secret entrance as well as he could, and then taking his wife's arm, he led her from the place. He afterwards descended the stairs, in order to ascertain whether all the doors were fast, and having satisfied himself that they were, he returned, endeavouring to seem as calm and as re-assured as possible; but his mind continued to be tortured with the same conflicting doubts and fears.

It was some time before he could persuade Blanche to retire to rest, and then it was long ere sleep closed her eyelids. But Sir Laurence in vain courted the drowsy god, and various and agonising were the ideas that crowded upon his brain.

That there was some fatal evil impending over them he felt confident, and yet he was at a loss to form any plan that would be likely to avert it; and the strange events of the last few hours perplexed and agitated him more than all. His conscience reproached him with having been too precipitate in uniting himself to Blanche, at least till he had made a candid acknowledgment of his former errors, and fully and satisfactorily ascertained whether he could make her his bride without bringing shame and misery upon her head. For this want of candour alone he considered himself unworthy of her, and awful was the responsibility he had brought upon himself. Should it, indeed, be found that Clara was still living, his own destruction and that of Blanche would be inevitable, and he must ever accuse himself of being indirectly her murderer. He could not be guilty of the weakness to believe in preternatural appearances, and, therefore, what other character could he give to that he had seen but that of life and reality? The thought was dreadful, but he could not banish it from his breast. He was, however, if the form appeared to him again, fully determined to satisfy those horrible doubts and apprehensions by pursuing it, even though the discovery should bring upon him certain ruin.

As he gazed upon the lovely and innocent countenance of Blanche, calm in sleep, his brain was worked up to a pitch bordering on distraction, and he was almost resolved to fly her presence, and never more to enter it until he was convinced that he could do so with honour; again and again he regretted that she had, in disobedience to the prudence, but stern will of her father, abandoned him, and thrown herself confidingly into his arms; but yet to have been separated from her would have been worse than death, and now, alas! the evil, if any, was past recall.

The disappearance of Mr. Lester, too, and the uncertainty of his fate, added to his anguish; and should he really have been prompted to the perpetration of any rash act, such was the ardent affection which Blanche bore towards him, that she would never be able to look up again, and would reproach herself with having been the cause of his death.

Whichever way Sir Laurence directed his thoughts the most gloomy prospects presented themselves to his imagination, and he looked for the dawn of morn with the most restless anxiety. It came at length, and he arose from his couch, in a state of mind harassed by conflicting terrors. Blanche, on awaking, appeared to be more calm and refreshed; but still the strange adventure of the previous night continued to occupy her mind, and to fill her bosom with wonder and perplexity, which Sir Laurence was in no condition to dissipate. The first thing which the baronet did, was to summon the servants into his presence, and to question them all most narrowly; but he was satisfied, from the unequivocal answers they returned, that they were entirely ignorant of what had taken place, which rendered him more at a loss to unravel the mystery; it also greatly added to the uneasiness of Blanche. Her husband tried to re-assure her, and in some measure he succeeded.

He next proceeded to examine the secret entrance to the apartment in which Blanche had beheld the female form, and the place to which the staircase led, but he met with little or nothing there to repay his curiosity. At the foot of the stairs was a small passage which led to a door, which he found led to a door opening upon the garden, and through which the intruder had doubtless made her entrance and escape; but by what means she had become acquainted with this strange contrivance, of which he had not himself been aware, he was quite at a loss to form even the least conjecture, and he was now more than ever certain that it was no unearthly being that he had seen; and as this conviction flashed upon his brain, he trembled so violently, and such a deathly chill fell upon his heart, that his powerful emotions could not escape the observation of Blanche. She looked at him with an expression that went to his soul; but by a powerful effort he greatly recovered himself, and his wife apparently re-assured, faintly smiled, and gently laying her hand on his arm, said,—

"Dear Laurence, we must leave it to time to fathom this painful and extraordinary mystery; but I tremble lest this should be some design of the gipsies to gratify the feelings of revenge they evidently entertain towards you, and that we may not be able to guard ourselves against them."

"Strict search shall be made after them," said Sir Laurence, "and in the meantime this place shall be secured so as to prevent any person from taking us by surprise by entering this way. I am totally at a loss to imagine for what purpose it has been contrived, and had not the slightest idea that it was in existence. Branscombe House is comparatively a modern building; had it not been so I should not have felt so much surprised."

"And yet," said Blanche, after a moments' reflection, "it does not seem as though the mysterious intruder intended me any injury, or surely if she had done so, she would have taken the opportunity of accomplishing her wishes when I became insensible, and was left entirely at her mercy. Besides, she was in truth most lovely, and from the slight glimpse I had of the expression of her gentle countenance, it seemed as if its soft lineaments could not possibly be the index to a guilty mind."

Sir Laurence shuddered involuntarily at these observations, and scarcely dared to look Blanche in the face, so torturing were the recollections that rushed upon his memory. The features of the unfortunate Clara, and those of another equally lovely and ill-fated, started so vividly to his imagination, that the effect was almost overpowering.

"Come, my love," he said at length, however, "let us retire from this place, and trust to Providence to elucidate this bewildering and ambiguous train of adventures."

Blanche returned no answer, and they walked away. In the course of the day Sir Laurence employed several labourers to block up the secret entrance which had been discovered in so unexpected a manner, and he then endeavoured to tranquillize her feelings, although his own were in no condition to accomplish the task.

He ordered strict inquiries to be made in the neighbourhood, to know whether any of the gipsies had been seen lurking about; but he could not gain the least information concerning them, and that fact added to his uneasiness and astonishment. He was at a loss to fathom exactly the designs of Harold and old Madela, who, if what they had stated respecting the existence of his first wife, were true, had at once the mean in their power of gratifying their feelings of vengeance, and working his complete ruin; and he wondered that they did not avail themselves of it. Why did they not produce her on the day of his union, and thus have corroborated beyond a doubt the charge they had brought against him of being a bigamist? True, their malignant feelings would only have been half satisfied, and Harold had told him that he would not rest until he had wrung his heart to the innermost core, by keeping him in a continual state of suspense and dread; and it seemed but too likely that his inhuman wishes would succeed to the fullest extent.

But amid all these remarkable events, the uncertain fate which had befallen her unhappy father held a predominant station in the mind of Blanche, and she could not, in spite of all her efforts to the contrary, banish the alarming fears that would crowd upon her. It appeared evident to her that madness must have seized upon his brain, or he could never have treated her with what she could not help thinking, notwithstanding her one act of disobedience to his will, the most unnecessary severity; and should he in his frenzy be induced to lay violent hands on himself, she should upbraid herself with being the cause of his untimely end. She remembered (indeed, how could she ever forget them,) all the dreadful observations he had given utterance to on their last meeting, and still imagined she beheld his fierce looks, as he prepared to invoke a curse upon the head of her and Sir Laurence; the manner in which he had discarded her, torn her from his heart for ever,—all was fresh in her memory, as if it had only taken place a few hours since, and drove her at intervals to a pitch of misery and despair, which even Sir Laurence found it a difficult matter to ameliorate; and great was his own suffering at the anguish he witnessed in her.

Amanda deeply sympathised with the distresses of Blanche and her brother; but there were certain circumstances that had come to her knowledge with regard to the latter, and his reserved conduct also, which often excited her suspicions, and rendered her fearful of the consequences that were likely to accrue to them both, particularly Blanche, whom she loved as affectionately as if she had really been her own sister. The circumstance of the mysterious visitant to Branscombe House, also, created her utmost astonishment, and raised a variety of conjectures in her breast, that were rather inclined to prejudice her against Sir Laurence, although she wished not to judge of him too severely, and would fain have believed him innocent.

Two or three days elapsed, and this last adventure was almost entirely superseded in their recollection by the continued absence of Mr. Lester, and their total inability to obtain any clue which might tend to his discovery.

"Unhappy parent!" Blanche would sigh, "whither have you gone, and what has your disordered reason prompted you to commit? I shall never behold you again, and thus will the cup of happiness be dashed for ever from my lips. Alas! I little thought that I should ever be put to such a trial as this."

"Ah, Blanche," returned Sir Laurence, "it is my painful duty to be compelled to admit that you have much to complain of fate, and it has been the greatest misfortune that could occur to you that ever we met. You might now have been happy in the love of a husband every way worthy of you, and about whom no doubts or prejudices existed."

"And are you not worthy of me, dear Laurence?" demanded Blanche, affectionately. "Think you that I would ever have braved a father's wrath, had I not firmly believed you to be so? Oh, no; reason and truth assert the contrary, and I

must ever continue to love you, to confide in you, in spite of all the circumstances that may arise."

Sir Laurence averted his looks for a moment, and sighed. He experienced mingled feelings of confusion and admiration, and scarcely knew what reply to make.

"But the time may come, Blanche," he said at length, "when you may repent this generous confidence, and ——"

"Repent!" warmly interrupted Blanche, in the most emphatic manner; "oh, never; even though I may never behold my poor father again, and though the worst misfortunes may descend upon my head, my love for you must always remain the same, dear Laurence."

No. 12.

Sir Laurence snatched his sweet bride to his bosom, and for some time his emotions were so great as to deny him the power of utterance.

On the evening of that day, Blanche being engaged in conversation with Amanda and the little Angela, Sir Laurence quitted the house and walked forth in the neighbouring fields, in order that he might indulge in those varied thoughts with which his mind was constantly occupied. The generous confidence which Blanche reposed in him, and the unbounded affection she evinced towards him, rendered him, if possible, more wretched, for he could not be without occasional fears that they were destined to meet with a cruel disappointment.

Buried in these profound meditations, he had taken very little heed of the road he was proceeding, when looking up he found himself on the way to the house of Mr. Lester. He had not seen old Humphry for a day or two, and therefore determined to call upon him, although he did not expect that he would have any good news to impart to him, or he would have been sure to have communicated it immediately.

After passing upwards of an hour with the old man, he left the house and returned towards his home, pondering, leisurely in his mind the uncertainty that still remained as to the fate of the unfortunate Mr. Lester; and Sir Laurence now, indeed, from continual disappointment, anticipating the worst.

He had advanced some short distance on his way, when he thought he heard a sound something like that of a human voice, although very low and scarcely articulate, not far from the spot on which he was. He listened attentively, and was soon convinced that he had not been mistaken, and painfully did the tones of that soft silvery voice smite upon his ears; so sweet, so impressive, so plaintive, so unearthly; and that song, the same that he had listened to with such powerful emotions, the other evening. He was rapt, entranced, petrified for a minute or two to the earth, and listened with breathless attention. Then he directed his eyes towards the place from whence the sounds seemed to proceed, but he could not perceive anything, although the bright beams of the moon were streaming full upon every object on which the eye could rest.

"By Heaven, I will solve this mystery!" he cried at length; "spirit, or mortal, reveal yourself, and banish this insupportable suspense."

He darted forward as he thus spoke, but in a moment the voice ceased, and all was as silent as the grave. Still, however, Sir Laurence made towards the spot from whence he had heard the sounds, and forcing his way through a neighbouring thicket, he beheld retreating, at a short distance, the same female and unearthly-looking form which he had seen on two occasions before.

He felt a sudden tremor steal over him, but his curiosity and impatience were worked up to such a pitch, that he was determined, at all hazards, if possible, to gratify them. He therefore increased his speed, but it was to no purpose; the figure appeared to skim over the surface of the earth with the lightness of a zephyr, rather than to run, and Sir Laurence speedily began to despair of overtaking it. Once she turned her head, and then the baronet again recognised those well known features which had impressed themselves so indelibly on his memory. Involuntarily he started back as he encountered them, and when he once more directed his eyes towards the spot, the figure had disappeared.

"Gracious powers!" he cried; "it is the shade of her who once was my wife; why rests she not in the silent grave, to which she has been for so many years consigned?"

He was startled by hearing a loud and malicious laugh of triumph, and, looking up, beheld old Madela standing before him.

"Ha! ha! ha!" she laughed, in her usual manner; "so, Laurence Cleveland, you have again seen her; she has once more crossed your path, and she will continue to do so, until that cup of misery which you must drain to the dregs shall be filled to the brim."

"Old harridan!" replied Sir Laurence, "this is only some contrivance of yours, and the wretches with whom you are connected; some base cheat, got up to mock and torture me."

"Oh! oh! a cheat, is it, Laurence Cleveland? Of course the features are not like that fair damsel to whom you gave your hand but to bring her to destruction? Oh! you have a convenient memory—a most convenient one, but when you are placed within the felon's dock, and confronted, face to face, with your deluded victim; when ——"

"By all my hopes," cried Sir Laurence, fiercely interrupting her, and rushing towards her, "I have you now in my power, and will drag' your old carcase to a prison, there to answer for the numerous offences of which you have no doubt been guilty."

"Stand off, reptile, dog!" shouted the gipsy, in accents that made the place re-echo again, and, raising her staff, she dealt the baronet such a blow that felled him to the earth, where he remained stunned for several minutes, and Madela, again laughing exultingly, retreated from the spot.

There is no necessity for us to attempt to pourtray the feelings of Sir Laurence on this occasion, for the reader can very well guess that they were of the most vexatious and tormenting description; with some little difficulty he gathered himself up, and gazed around him, and his indignation increased when he thought of the insult he had received, and all the perplexing and alarming circumstances that had preceded it.

"Insulted!" he exclaimed, bitterly. "And by that hideous and hateful old hag' who seems to mock at my threats, and to exult, with all the malice of a fiend, at my misery. But, by Heaven, I will have revenge for the indignity that has been offered me! By the frequent manner in which this old beldame crosses my path, she and her miscreant associates must be concealed somewhere in the vicinity; and they must and shall be secured to prevent them doing the mischief with which they have threatened me. This Madela must be the widow of the old villain who murdered my gamekeeper, and who justly suffered the penalty of the law, and whose son, whom I believe to have been equally guilty, was banished for life. She could not have been so well acquainted with all the particulars if she were not; and if such is the fact, there is no need for me to marvel at the deadly feeling of hatred and revenge that she evinces towards me. But can it be possible that the gipsy Harold is her son—that rustic clown who presumed to attempt to rival me in the affections of Clara? I have no recollection of his features; but time, and the life he has led, may have strangely altered them. Oh! if I could discover that he is that individual, I should have him securely in my power—a returned convict, his life would be forfeited to the offended laws of his country, and thus should I rid myself, at once, of my bitterest enemy. The outrage he has already committed, and the threats he has held out against me, render him amenable to the laws; and he and his base associates must be apprehended. But, then, should he have spoken the truth as regards the existence of Clara—and this form I have seen, so like her in features, excites the worst fears in my bosom—what a dreadful retaliation he could make! Shame, ruin, and, perpetual misery would be heaped upon me, and the curses of Blanche—my poor, confiding, lovely Blanche—would descend upon my head, and sink me to the most wretched and degraded of human beings! Oh! torture, torture, most insupportable! How can I act? What course can I pursue?"

Such were the conflicting thoughts that tortured the mind of Sir Laurence Cleveland, as he slowly retraced his steps to Branscombe House; and the further he proceeded, the more his anguish gained strength—the more bewildered did he become to know in what manner to act for the best. He dreaded to meet the penetrating eye of Blanche, for she must observe the unusual agitation of his mind, and how could he enter into an explanation of what had happened? He durst not mention to her his terrible suspicions, and, should they be realised, how awful would be her situation! He would have plunged her into irretrievable ruin and shame, and could never again venture to show his face in society.

"Alas!" he sighed, "why did I ever presume to offer her my hand? Why did I seek to win her affections, when I knew that my past misconduct had rendered me unworthy of her innocence? I feel that I have acted the part of a deceiver, and each hour that I remain with her is adding to my guilt. Why did I submit to receive her under my roof as my wife until all these terrible doubts were removed? The confirmation of the truth of Harold's assertions would doubtless have ruined her prospects, yet still her honour would have been preserved, and the world could never have dared to point at her the finger of scorn or reproach. But can I abandon her? And in a few months, too, she will become a mother. Oh, God! how agonising are all these circumstances! And this little innocent, that should be hailed with the fondest transport, I can but view with pity and regret, since it is more than probable that it may be destined to the greatest misery, and that it may at some future period have occasion to curse the author of its being."

The fearful words of the old woman, Madela, on their first meeting, had impressed themselves most forcibly on his memory, and he now repeated them, as he walked onwards:—

"And that curse shall spread like the night cloud over you and yours. You may marry,—you may have fair, smiling babes, but that curse shall pursue them as well as you. She who breathed it over the corpse of her murdered husband, will live to see it fulfilled. Yes, she would travel many weary miles to hear the music of the rattling stones upon the coffins of your children."

"Oh, this is most horrible," continued Sir Laurence; "and the wretches will not fail to fulfil those threats, should they have the power. But they must be secured—yes; I will not rest until they are so, let whatever may be the consequences to myself."

He now endeavoured to regain some degree of composure, and fearing that his life might be in danger, should any of the gipsy tribe happen to be lurking about, he quickened his pace, and at length came in sight of the mansion, his mind still occupied with the exciting events of the evening.

Blanche had been most anxiously awaiting his return, and she hastened to meet him. Sir Laurence recoiled from her fond endearments with a shuddering sensation of horror, and his confusion increased when she observed:—

"You have tarried long, Laurence, love, and I began to be somewhat uneasy, not knowing whither you were gone, and considering that you are not accustomed thus to play the truant. But you are agitated; tell me, dear Laurence, what has occurred to disturb you ?"

"Nothing, nothing, Blanche," stammered out Sir Laurence; "you are mistaken."

"Your looks are pale, your eyes restless, and you tremble."

"It is nothing, dear Blanche."

"Nothing, Laurence?"

"Only a slight nervousness, nothing more."

"Nay, my husband, to quiet my apprehensions you only seek to evade my questions. Oh! there is blood upon your temple! Gracious Heaven! what is the cause of this ?"

Sir Laurence, in the intensity and anguish of the other thoughts that had so engrossed his mind on his return home, had not noticed that he was slightly wounded from the blow which Madela had dealt him; but he now felt a slight faintness come over him, which he endeavoured to conquer as much as possible, and placing his hand to his head, said, in as indifferent a tone as he could assume,—

"Be not alarmed, my sweet Blanche, it is only a slight scratch, and I feel no ill effects from it."

"But how did you obtain it?" eagerly inquired Blanche, as she examined the wound.

Sir Laurence found that it was to no purpose endeavouring any longer to evade the question, and he therefore briefly related the particulars of his encounter with Madela, but omitted his again meeting with the mysterious object which had so alarmed Blanche on a former occasion. He could not trust himself to disclose that, and he therefore altered those portions of the observations of the old gipsy woman which would have disclosed it.

"Daring woman!" exclaimed Blanche; "her conduct is unaccountable; but oh, Laurence, for Heaven's sake endeavour to avoid those desperate persons, who evidently view you with such feelings of hatred and revenge. They cannot be far from the neighbourhood, and I tremble for the consequences that may ensue from the deadly feelings of malice they bear towards us."

"They are doubtless not far off," coincided Sir Laurence, "from the frequent appearance of Madela; but still I cannot imagine where the villains have been concealed since they quitted the place of their last encampment, for you know that a most indefatigable and minute search has been made in all places that were likely. But I trust that they will not long be able to elude our vigilance, but that they will be detected, and prevented from doing the mischief we have so much reason to apprehend from them."

To this wish Blanche responded, and after some further conversation they retired to their chamber. But Sir Laurence could obtain little or no rest, so sad and fearful were the feelings which agitated his bosom, and banished sleep from his pillow; and most gloomy indeed were the anticipations he formed of the future troubles that were in store for him. He hesitated what to do, whether to persevere in his determination to make a strict search after Madela, Harold, and the rest of the gipsies, or not; but he almost feared to do so, lest the statements of Harold should prove to be correct, and Clara should be brought forward to confront him.

But he could scarcely bring his mind to believe that it was otherwise than a plot of the gipsies to torture him, and that the female he had seen was an impostor; and yet the extraordinary likeness she bore towards his first wife, and the manner in which she had always contrived to escape him, bewildered his brain, and added to the powerful sensations of emotion that reigned within his bosom.

He had not mentioned anything to Blanche about his visit to the house of her father, for he apprehended that it would only have served to increase her uneasiness when she was informed that no intelligence had been obtained of that unfortunate gentleman ; and perhaps it was as well that he did not do so, as it would only have caused her unnecessary pain, and have rendered her incapable of the willing task she was about to be called upon to perform. Sir Laurence felt very little ill-effects from the trifling wound he had received, and by the morning he was quite recovered, and much more tranquil in his mind.

After having partaken of the morning's repast, he set out to his friend, the magistrate, in order to inform him of the outrage which had been committed upon him, and to seek his advice ; but Blanche persuaded him not to venture forth without the attendance of a couple of servants, although there certainly seemed nothing to apprehend in the open day. In order, however, to quiet her fears, Sir Laurence complied with her advice.

He had only just made the magistrate acquainted with the particulars, however, when a servant arrived post haste from Branscombe House with a message from Blanche, begging of him to return immediately, as something particular had happened, since he had been away.

"Ah," ejaculated the baronet, with some alarm, "what is it ? Is your lady taken ill, William ?"

"Yes, Sir Laurence—no, Sir Laurence," stammered the man, who was out of breath with the speed at which he had travelled; "that is, sir, my lady is agitated, but I rather think it is with joy—she has received a letter, sir."

"A letter ?"

"Yes, Sir Laurence," replied William ; "old Mr. Humphry brought it, soon after you left the mansion."

"Ah !" exclaimed Sir Laurence ; "Heaven send that it may contain some joyful intelligence."

He then took leave of the magistrate, and hastily departed towards home, impatient to hear what the intelligence was that old Humphry had brought, though not doubting that it was from Mr. Lester.

On his arrival at the mansion, and hastening to the apartment of Blanche, he found her on her knees, with clasped hands, and dissolved in tears, and Amanda hanging affectionately over her, and in the most gentle and persuasive accents endeavouring to soothe her. Sir Laurence hurried towards her, and clasped her to his bosom.

"Beloved Blanche!" he said, "what is the meaning of this emotion ? Surely nothing else has happened to interrupt our peace ?"

"Alas! alas!" sighed Blanche, her voice almost choked with sobs ; "I shall never more behold him alive in this world. He is dying, Laurence, dying !"

"Dying ! who, my love, tell me, tell me ?" asked Sir Laurence, pale as death with fright.

"My poor father," gasped forth Blanche, placing an open letter in his hand. "Read—read those fatal lines, probably the last that I shall ever receive from the unfortunate and revered author of my being. Oh, God ! in mercy spare him to me but a little time longer !"

She could say no more, but in a paroxysm of grief she drooped her head upon the baronet's shoulder.

Sir Laurence, in a state of agitation almost equal to her own, glanced his eyes over the letter, and read the following few words in the handwriting of Mr. Lester:—

"DEAREST BLANCHE,—If you would ever again behold your poor father in this world, let you and Sir Laurence hasten without delay to Musgrove Abbey, where he is now lying at the point of death, and has something of importance to communicate. I can write no more.   "ANDREW LESTER."

"Cheer you—cheer you, my beloved Blanche," ejaculated Sir Laurence, when he had perused the letter; "your father may not be in so dangerous a condition as he imagines; and this letter should inspire us both with hope. He calls you 'Dearest Blanche,' and that is a convincing proof that his reason has returned; that he repents of the severity with which he has acted towards you, and is anxious to assure you of his forgiveness for the only act of disobedience you ever committed against his will. Conquer your emotion, or you will never be able to undertake the journey to Musgrove Abbey, which it is necessary we should commence immediately."

"Oh, yes," said Blanche, looking up with more composure; "I will try to encourage the hopes you seek to inspire me with, dear Laurence. My poor father would never so have addressed me, had he still entertained the same feelings towards me which he expressed on our last interview. Lord Musgrove is good and amiable, and has, doubtless, interceded with him on our behalf. I feel endowed with fresh strength, and am fully prepared to undergo any fatigue in hastening to the dying couch of my poor father. Come, my dear Laurence, for Heaven's sake, let us not delay an instant!"

Sir Laurence embraced her affectionately, and then hastened from the apartment, while she got in readiness for the unexpected journey, to give instructions for the immediate preparation of the travelling carriage.

When he was gone, Blanche again sank on her knees, in which posture she continued for several minutes, and fervently she supplicated the mercy of the Almighty towards her father, and prayed that his life might yet be prolonged for many years. Then she placed herself in the hands of her waiting-maid, and was quickly in readiness for the journey.

CHAPTER IX.

THE LAST INTERVIEW.—THE PARDON.

MUSGROVE ABBEY was situate about twenty miles from Branscombe House; but, as the roads were very bad, Sir Laurence did not think it was possible to arrive there in less than three or four hours.

Never had any journey appeared half so tedious or so melancholy to Blanche as this did, and Sir Laurence had the greatest difficulty in keeping up her spirits at all.

"Alas!" she sighed, "why did not my unfortunate father apprise me of his precarious situation before the eleventh hour? Something seems to whisper to me that he will have breathed his last ere we can reach his bedside, and I cannot hope to receive from his beloved lips an assurance of his forgiveness, and his dying blessing."

"Do not, I pray you, my darling Blanche, suffer these dismal thoughts to gain ascendancy in your mind," said Sir Laurence; "for something assures me that Mr.

Lester is not so bad as he imagines himself to be, and that he will not only live to see you again, but that he will likewise be restored once more to convalesence."

"Oh, that I could, that I dare encourage such blessed hopes as these, my husband."

"Try to do so, my love, and depend upon it that Heaven will not abandon you entirely to grief and despair."

"The poor old man!" sighed Blanche; "where can he have been all this time? And oh, how truly grateful am I to Heaven, who, in his frenzy, did not permit him to lay violent hands on himself."

"Oh, yes," returned Sir Laurence, "we ought, indeed, to feel most grateful for his preservation from so rash an act, and that he is evidently restored to a sense of reason and of justice."

"It was his fears and his affection for me that caused him to act in the manner he did," observed Blanche; "and most duly can I appreciate the feelings that prompted him."

"Yes, my love," said Sir Laurence, "I am fully sensible that it was out of no ill-will towards me that Mr. Lester acted in the way he did, or he would never have consented to bestow upon me your fair hand; but I trust that something has now occurred to fully convince him of the falsehood of the statements of the villain, Harold."

Sir Laurence almost blushed at the species of duplicity and insincerity of which he was guilty, for he was far from feeling the probability of such a consummation of his wishes having taken place.

"Heaven send that it may be as you predict," ejaculated Blanche; "but never—never can I doubt the perfect innocence of my Laurence."

Sir Laurence pressed an ardent kiss upon her pale lips, and an interval of silence of some minutes ensued.

Having changed horses, the carriage proceeded with increased speed, and at length they drew towards the end of their journey, alternate hopes and fears still agitating the bosoms of them both. Sir Laurence dreaded the result of the interview, and most fervently did he wish that it was over, and that all would terminate more favourably than they both at present anticipated.

Having arrived at the abbey, they alighted in a state of the greatest agitation, and Lord Musgrove received them in the Hall.

"My dear father, my lord," gasped forth poor Blance; "oh, for the love of Heaven, do not keep me in suspense, but tell me how he is."

"Do not alarm yourself, my dear Lady Cleveland," replied Lord Musgrove; "your father is no worse, and probably may yet recover."

"Oh, thank God!" cried Blanche; "oh, pray conduct me to him, my lord."

"Pardon me, Lady Blanche," said his lordship, "but I think it would be more prudent that your arrival should first be announced to Mr. Lester; for there is no saying what such a sudden shock, and under such peculiar circumstances, might have upon him."

"True, my lord," remarked Sir Laurence, "I perfectly agree with your advice. But tell me, how is Mr. Lester prepared to receive us?"

"With open arms."

Blanche uttered a scream of delight on hearing this announcement, and almost fainted in the arms of her husband.

" All-merciful Father !" she exclaimed, " thou hast, then, heard my prayers, and ever must my gratitude be poured forth to thee for this. Oh, my good lord, what a terrible weight have you taken off my mind by this assurance. But pray hasten and inform him that we have arrived, for I am all impatience until I am suffered to throw myself on his bosom, and implore his blessing and forgiveness."

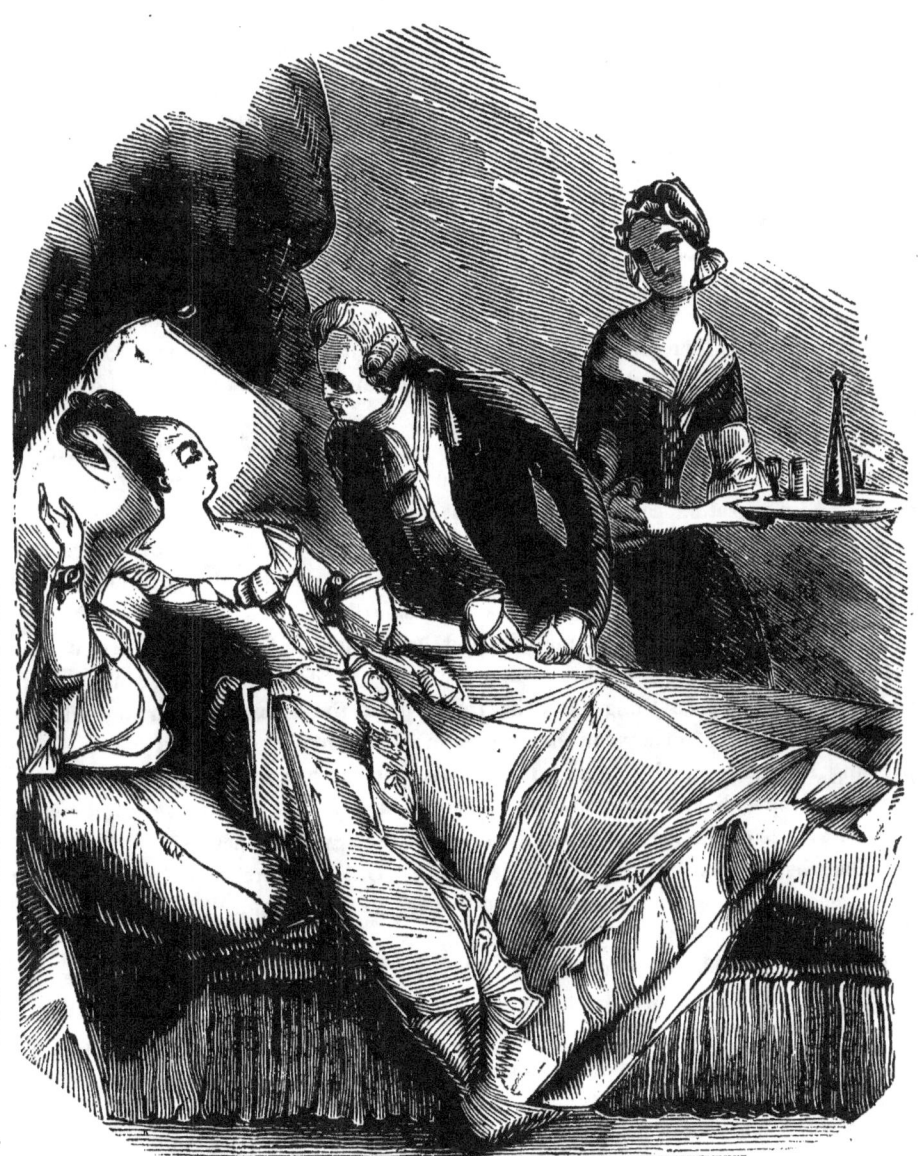

" In a few minutes your wishes shall be gratified; in the meantime, endeavour to tranquillise your spirits, for, in all probability, the meeting will be a trying one, and will need all your fortitude and calmness to support it."

Having thus spoken, Lord Musgrove left them, and the emotions of poor Blanche and her husband, during his absence, it requires no great stretch of the imagination to conceive.

No. 13.

" He has, then, relented," ejaculated Blanche; " reason has once more resumed her seat, and he is convinced of the erroneousness of his former doubts. Oh, my dear Laurence, what unexpected, what joyful intelligence is this."

" It is, indeed, my sweet Blanche," replied Sir Laurence, " and most grateful am I to Heaven for its goodness to us, in the very midst of our despair. Oh, may it restore your poor father to health, and to live for many years to come to be a blessing to us. But struggle with your feelings, and meet this affecting trial with all that fortitude which has ever marked your character in so eminent a degree."

Blanche answered him only by a faint smile of most expressive meaning; and almost immediately afterwards Lord Musgrove returned. Blanche and her husband both eagerly inquired whether Mr. Lester was prepared to see them, and his lordship replied in the affirmative. And now, in spite of all her efforts to the contrary, the agitation of Blanche increased to an almost insupportable degree, and the emotions of Sir Laurence were scarcely less powerful. They, however, made a violent struggle with their feelings, as they followed Lord Musgrove towards the chamber of the unfortunate Mr. Lester, and, by the time that they had arrived at the door, they had, in a great measure, succeeded. Lord Musgrove left them at the door, and they stopped for a moment to listen, for they heard the faint voice of the invalid, who was evidently engaged in prayer.

How the heart of Blanche throbbed, and her bosom heaved, as she listened to those sad, but well remembered accents, and which she had never expected to hear again; and a sensation came over Sir Laurence which he had never before experienced. He could not meet that dying man with an unblemished conscience, and whatever had convinced him to the contrary, he knew not, but he still entertained doubts as to the truth or falsehood of Harold's assertion.

But a few moments, however, elapsed, and the moment of trial arrived. In a tone redolent of all his former fondness, Blanche heard her father repeat her name, and, without waiting for anything else, she threw open the door, and, darting into the chamber, in an instant was on her knees, sobbing convulsively at his bedside, and pressing his damp hand with half frantic emotion to her lips. The poor old man heaved a deep sigh, and then, after struggling violently with his intense emotions, he said, in a voice of the most melancholy and pathetic impressiveness,—

" Blanche, my darling, my own sweet child! Oh, our merciful Father, thou hast been most kind to thy poor dying creature, to grant him this final blessing! Blanche!"

" Father, beloved, ever affectionate, and best of parents!" exclaimed Blanche, and in a moment she was clasped sobbing in the arms of her dying parent, who strained her to his bosom, and wept upon her lovely cheeks like a child, while Sir Laurence still knelt by the side of the couch, and looked up in the countenance of Mr. Lester, unable to utter a syllable.

It was a scene that even the most powerful pen could not do adequate justice to, and therefore we must despair of being able to delineate it.

But what a change had a few short weeks wrought in the countenance of Mr. Lester! Sir Laurence shrank, appalled, as he gazed upon it, for on it were stamped all the ghastly signs of approaching dissolution, and he felt convinced that a very short time would close his eyes for ever in death.

A silence most solemn, and which was only interrupted by the convulsive sobs of Blanche and her father, ensued, and it seemed as if neither of them would ever find strength to speak again; but at length Mr. Lester appeared to recover himself; and parting the beautiful hair from the pale forehead of his lovely daughter, he said, in a voice of the most touching feeling,—

"Oh! my poor child, to what a severe, to what a cruel trial have I put you. But the scene is fast drawing to a close; my moments are numbered, the cold hand of death is upon me; darkness, darkness is rapidly gathering around me, and ——"

"Oh! my beloved father," cried Blanche, again throwing herself upon his bosom, and looking into his pale and careworn face with a bursting heart; "talk not thus, Heaven will not deprive me of you yet; in its infinite mercy it will not. You do but deceive yourself; this illness will vanish before my affectionate, my unremitting attentions, and you will live to bless both me and my husband with your paternal love."

"It may not be, my sweet Blanche," replied her father, in a voice scarcely articulate; "I feel that my earthly career is nearly run, but the will of the Almighty, not mine, be done. I must leave you, Blanche, I must leave you."

"Oh! no, no; I cannot part with you yet; the thought is madness; my brain is wrought to distraction by the bare contemplation of that awful calamity."

"But you must bear it with patience and resignation, my child," said her father; "I am fully prepared for the awful change I am about so soon to undergo, and I am grateful to the Almighty who has permitted me again to behold you ere my soul enters upon eternity. Oh! Blanche, I have acted most cruelly towards you; but it was a sense of duty that urged me on, and I suffered the infatuation to gain such an ascendancy over me, that my reason left me. Thank God, who has preserved me from an act of self-destruction, and has restored me to reason in time to make you the reparation that is due to you, Sir Laurence."

The baronet arose from his knees, and supporting the head of the expiring gentleman, awaited in trembling suspense while he thus continued :—

"Sir Laurence Cleveland, in my last moments I feel satisfied that I have done you an injustice by doubting your honour; but I think that you cannot blame my motives, when I considered that the honour of a beloved daughter was at stake. You have a treasure in Blanche of inestimable value; take her from a dying father's hands, cherish, love, and protect her, and as you do your duty towards her, so may Heaven prosper you."

"And may Heaven desert me if ever I disobey your injunctions, my father, for such I may now call you," said Sir Laurence.

"My child," gasped forth Mr. Lester, clasping her hand more vehemently, and Blanche, eagerly gazing in his countenance, was appalled at the change which had in a few moments taken place.

"Father, father! oh, God!" she cried, "the dew of death is upon your brow; the dread certainty now rushes upon my brain. Mercy, mercy! oh, Heaven! Father, beloved father, speak to me. Where is the physician? Laurence, fly for help!"

Mr. Lester gently waved his hand, as if to signify that it was too late, faintly smiled upon his distracted daughter, and then made a convulsive struggle to speak, but could not.

"Oh, my father," hysterically sobbed forth Blanche; "I have acted in disobedience to your will, and perhaps I have been the cause of hastening your death; for the love of Heaven, endeavour to speak to assure me of your forgiveness."

The dying man for a moment was inspired with fresh strength on this appeal, and at length in a faint, but deeply solemn voice, he said,—

"Blanche, as I forgive you, so may Heaven pardon me. Bless—bless—you both—my children!"

A heavenly smile overspread his features as he uttered these words; he raised his eyes with an expression of Christian resignation, fixed them once more upon Blanche and her husband, then closed them for ever; his hand relaxed its hold, and without a sigh, his soul winged its flight to the realms of eternal bliss.

CHAPTER X.

THE GRIEF OF BLANCHE AND SIR LAURENCE.—THE MOURNFUL CAVALCADE TO THE FAMILY VAULT.—THE DARING INTERRUPTION ON THE ROAD.

THE instant poor Blanche was aware that the vital spark had fled for ever, then she uttered a loud scream, and fell upon the breast of the inanimate corpse in a state of the most indescribable affliction. She clasped the remains of her adored parent in dumb despair; bathing his wan cheek with torrents of tears, and fixing her frantic gaze upon the senseless form of him who had behaved to her with such unbounded affection. At length the horrors of her situation seized upon her shattered brain; the shriek of convulsive agony awoke her from the lethargy of woe, to the eternal and corroding pangs of unavailing anguish. Then nature could support no more, she became insensible, and in that deplorable condition was borne by Sir Laurence from the chamber of death.

For some hours poor Blanche remained in this happy state of unconsciousness, and her husband watched by the side of the couch to which she had been conveyed with the utmost anxiety, and most sad and agonizing were the feelings that occupied his mind. The last moments and observations of Mr. Lester had made an impression upon him he felt that time could not remove, and he felt the full weight of the solemnity of the dying man's injunctions, and the promises he had made; and although he was confident that he could never love Blanche less than he did at present, what sorrow would be his portion should he discover that his first wife was really living, and that he had brought shame, misery, and dishonour upon the head of her whom he had vowed to love, cherish, and protect.

At length Blanche recovered to a full sense of the dreadful calamity which had befallen her, and her violent paroxysm of grief would admit of no consolation.

"My poor father!" she sighed; "fond protector of my childhood—virtuous preceptor to my youthful mind—are you then indeed taken from me for ever? Shall I never more listen to your voice or receive your affectionate caresses?"

"Be calm and resigned, my beloved Blanche," expostulated the baronet. "I own that the suddenness of this melancholy event is enough to cause your affectionate and susceptible bosom the greatest affliction; but still you may find consolation in the blissful assurance that his spirit is in heaven, and in that conviction learn to submit with fortitude to the will of the Almighty."

"Oh, yes, Laurence," replied Blanche; "but to think that we should be so cruelly separated, and that I was not permitted to see him only in his last moments. Had I been by his side at the commencement of his illness, my attention might have prolonged that life so valuable, and which nothing can replace."

"And that you were permitted to see him ere he breathed his last, dear Blanche, to be reconciled to him, and to receive his dying blessing, ought to be a sweet and lasting consolation to your lacerated mind."

"Oh, yes," ejaculated Blanche, while a faint smile of gratitude passed over her melancholy countenance; "that does, indeed, impart consolation to my bosom. Oh, God! what would have been my sufferings had my beloved parent expired before I had seen him, and received an assurance of his forgiveness. I shudder with horror at the bare idea."

Again her tears flowed fast, and her husband did not offer to interrupt her in that indulgence which was likely to afford her so much relief.

Some hours were passed by Blanche in the most frantic grief; but at last, quite exhausted, sleep came to her relief, and she did not awaken till the morning.

Sir Laurence had passed the greater portion of the night in watching by her bedside, and in meditating upon the circumstances of his life, and in picturing to himself what was likely to be the future destiny of himself and Blanche; and after maturely reflecting, he could not but come to the most melancholy conclusions and forebodings. But it afforded him great satisfaction to think that Blanche had seen her father previous to his death, and that she had received his pardon and his blessing; for had she not done so, he felt convinced that the event would have proved fatal to her, and that not all his efforts could have succeeded in reconciling her.

In the morning Blanche was somewhat more calm, but still labouring under the most intense mental anguish, and many were the tears she shed to the memory of that dear parent, whose voice she would never more hear, and whose death had been so sudden and so unexpected.

In spite of all the persuasions of Sir Laurence to the contrary, she would insist upon visiting the chamber of death, that she might weep over her father's cold remains, and pray to Heaven for the repose of his spirit, and as she remained firm in this resolution, the baronet agreed to accompany her.

On their entering the room, the gloom and solemn silence that reigned within it had the most impressive effect upon their minds, and poor Blanche trembled so violently, that had it not been for the support of her husband's arm, she must have sunk on the floor. With faltering steps they approached the bed upon which the corpse of the late Mr. Lester was laid, and throwing back the coverlet, gazed upon his pale face. How calm and placid was it; a sweet smile seemed to play around his cold lips, and his features were as serene as they had ever been in the happiest moments of his lifetime. Again and again Blanche kissed his lips and forehead, passed her lovely taper fingers through his silvery hairs, and wept bitter tears of anguish upon his inanimate bosom; while Sir Laurence stood by, and it was evident, from the working of his countenance, that he was enduring the greatest emotion.

Blanche then knelt down, and in solemn tones poured forth the most fervent prayers to Heaven. It was with difficulty that Sir Laurence could prevail upon her to leave the sad chamber, but at length she did yield, and was conducted to the presence of Lord and Lady Musgrove, who were both most amiable individuals, and sympathised warmly and feelingly in the melancholy bereavement which Blanche had sustained.

From his lordship they learned the manner in which Mr. Lester had come to the abbey, which had only been three days prior to his death.

When the unfortunate Mr. Lester quitted his residence so abruptly, and in such a dreadful state of agitation, as has been related in a previous chapter, he wandered about for some hours, he scarcely knew whither. His reason was certainly disordered; he imagined that his daughter was ruined for ever, and had brought shame and infamy upon his name; he could not divest himself of the terrible and fatal impression, and he cared not what became of him. He had no fixed purpose, other than that he was determined never to behold Blanche again; unless, indeed, that something should occur to prove that she was the lawful wife of Sir Laurence Cleveland, and that the gipsy Harold had spoken falsely. His mind was, as it were, one wild chaos, and it was only surprising, that in some of his moments of frenzy he did not lay violent hands upon himself.

In this manner he continued to travel for several days, stopping only for a short time, or to rest, in one place, and exciting no inconsiderable degree of curiosity by the eccentricity of his conduct. He chose the most gloomy part of the country to wander through, and could he have met with some solitary cell, he would, no doubt, have secluded himself for life. The world, and everything that it contained, was now hateful to him, and, in fact, he became a perfect misanthrope.

It was strange that such a change could come over any one, especially a person of the disposition of Mr. Lester, in so short a time; but so it was, and it could only be accounted for by the shock his senses had received on discovering the flight of his daughter.

At length, however, he was seized with a sudden illness, and fell insensible from his horse, in which state he was found by some peasants ; and as they could perceive by his appearance that he was a gentleman, and there being no inn near the spot, they resolved to take him to Musgrove Abbey, they being the tenants of his lordship, and that being the nearest building where he could be accommodated and properly attended to.

Lord Musgrove was greatly surprised to recognise in him an old and esteemed friend, whom he had not seen for several years, and believed to be still on the continent. He therefore knew not his present address, that he might communicate with his friends, and make them acquainted with his present melancholy and precarious situation.

Advice was immediately called in, and every attention was paid to the unfortunate gentleman, but he continued insensible during the whole of that day and night, and the doctor gave but very little hopes of him, and he said it was a very severe fit of apoplexy.

Towards morning, however, his senses returned, and he was enabled to speak. Lord Musgrove hastened to his chamber, and the surprise of Mr. Lester was great on beholding him, as may very well be imagined.

On his lordship making the necessary inquiries, so that he might make his daughter and his other friends acquainted with his situation, the unhappy gentleman exhibited the greatest emotion, and for some time Lord Musgrove could not elicit any satisfactory answer from him ; but at length he made him acquainted with all those particulars of which the reader has already been informed, and Lord Musgrove could not help expressing his disapprobation of the hasty and severe course which he had taken, and begged that he would immediately allow him to despatch a messenger for his daughter and her husband, as the medical gentleman had pronounced his case to be extremely dangerous. Mr. Lester yielded, and wrote the few lines that have been quoted in the foregoing pages, after which he felt his mind much more at ease. The reason of the letter being forwarded to the mansion of Mr. Lester, instead of direct to

Branscombe House, was owing to a mistake he made in the superscription. With what followed, the reader has just been made acquainted.

With many bitter pangs did Blanche listen to this account given by Lord Musgrove, but he endeavoured to console her, by assuring her that, in his belief, neither she nor her husband were at all to blame; and that the sudden and melancholy death of Mr. Lester was entirely owing to the will of Providence, over which no mortal being could have any control, or should presume to question.

The day passed gloomily away, at times Blanche being so overwhelmed with grief as to be perfectly inconsolable, and Sir Laurence, when he took all the melancholy circumstances into consideration, was in scarcely a better condition.

As soon as the necessary preparations could be made, it was resolved to remove the remains of Mr. Lester to his late residence, in order that they might be deposited in the family vault, and three days after his demise, Blanche and her husband took leave of Lord and Lady Musgrove, whom they invited to visit them at Branscombe House. The mournful cavalcade departed from the abbey.

The anguish of Blanche on the journey was so great, that it needed all the eloquence and persuasion of Sir Laurence to prevent her from sinking completely under it. Little did she expect to have been so soon engaged in so melancholy a duty, and when she considered the whole of the circumstances under which the death of her father had taken place, her heart was fit to break.

For the first few miles they had proceeded from Musgrove Abbey, the weather had been particularly fine; but suddenly the sky became overcast by black and portentous clouds, and added to the gloom and misery which reigned within the bosom of Blanche and Sir Laurence. The distant murmuring of thunder was now heard, which gradually grew nearer, until it broke forth in tremendous and continuous peals, that seemed to shake the very earth as with an earthquake; and the vivid flashes of the lightning were quite terrific, especially as it was some time ere the hot and murky air was relieved by a heavy shower of rain.

Blanche was very much alarmed, and clung to her husband, hiding her face in his bosom, and being completely unable to give utterance to a syllable. What rendered their situation the more gloomy and unpleasant, they were at that time on a desolate heath, and far from any place where they could put up until the tempest had abated. The horses in the hearse and the carriage they were in were frightened, and kept kicking and plunging in the most alarming manner, so that they were in momentary fear that some accident would take place; and this all added to the horror of Blanche, who did not dare to venture to look up, but mentally prayed to Heaven for protection.

The voice of the thunder was still deafening, the lightning, if possible, became more vivid, and such was the terror of the horses, that they became almost unmanageable, so that the progress of the cavalcade was but extremely slow and dangerous.

Sir Laurence tried all that he could to comfort poor Blanche; but this was no easy task, and he scarcely knew what arguments to make use of to do so.

The storm at length gradually abated, until the thunder and lightning entirely subsided, and the rain came not down in such overwhelming torrents as it had done before. Blanche felt greatly relieved, and returned her thanks to Heaven, and the feelings of Sir Laurence entirely corresponded with her own.

They had not proceeded far, however, when the driver suddenly stopped, and informed them that there were a number of suspicious-looking people advancing towards them, who, from their dresses, and the character of the different coarse vehicles they had with them, he suspected to be gipsies.

At the bare mention of the name of gipsies Blanche turned very pale, and Sir Laurence felt a sensation of alarm steal into his breast. He looked from the window of the carriage, and was immediately convinced that the surmises of the coachman were correct, and that a considerable number of the wandering tribe were approaching.

"But still what reason have we to fear them, Blanche?" demanded the baronet; "they may not be our enemies, and even if they are, they will not surely dare to molest us on this solemn occasion."

"Ah! Laurence," replied Blanche; "what have we not a right to fear from those miscreants, especially after the deadly feelings of hatred and revenge which they have evinced towards us. My heart forebodes some approaching danger. Let us turn out of the road they are coming, and endeavour to avoid them."

Sir Laurence gave the drivers instructions to that effect accordingly; but they had no sooner done so, than they heard a loud shout from the gipsies, and they immediately followed their example, and came more rapidly on, men, women, and children, to the number of thirty, at least.

"My God!" gasped Blanche, "what will become of us?. They certainly mean us some harm. And see; know you not that figure who is in advance of them? By Heaven, it is the ruffian Harold!"

Sir Laurence looked eagerly to where his fair bride directed him, and too plainly recognized his bitter and implacable enemy, who was leading on the others, and seemed from his gestures to know who they were, and had been prepared to meet them. Another glance served to show him the repulsive form of old Madela, and several of the villains who had been concerned in the daring outrage in the church on the day of his union.

"Lost—lost!" groaned Blanche; "what means have we of protecting ourselves against their vengeance? Oh, God! and must the cold remains of my poor father be thus insulted on the way to their final resting-place?"

Blanche trembled convulsively as she spoke, and nearly fainted; but Sir Laurence struggled with his feelings as well as he could, and tried to appear firm and composed.

"Courage, courage, my love!" he said; "wretches as they are, they surely cannot be so entirely lost to all sense of shame and pity as to attempt to molest us on our melancholy errand."

"Behold their menacing gestures," remarked Blanche. "They come nearer; oh, my husband."

Sir Laurence gently drew her back in the carriage, and throwing his arm round her waist, he once more sought to inspire her with fortitude; but he did so with a very bad grace, for albeit he was a man who, generally speaking, was a stranger to fear, he could not help feeling seriously alarmed on this occasion, more on account of Blanche than himself.

The shouts of the gipsies now became louder, and the next moment they drew up in a line across the road, and completely impeded the progress of the hearse and the carriage in which Sir Laurence and his trembling and almost fainting bride were seated. Sir Laurence now felt for his pistols, but found that he had left them behind him at Musgrove Abbey, and that he had consequently only his sword to defend himself with; and if he had, what could he and the two or three servants who attended

him do in opposition to such a number, and such desperate villains? It was now quite evident that the gipsies knew who they were, and that they had been apprised by some means or other of the route in which the remains of Mr. Lester were to be conveyed: but they had not much time given them for reflection.

"Stop, fellows!" shouted the voice of Harold to the drivers; "move a step at your peril, till we permit ye; we must have a word or two with your master, Sir Laurence Cleveland, and she who lives with him as his bride!"

Blanche uttered a cry of terror at these words, and looked piteously at Sir Laurence; the next instant Harold and several of the ruffians approached the carriage, and peered in at the window with bold and malicious looks of satisfaction.

Blanche shrank back appalled, but Sir Laurence assumed as intrepid an air as he possibly could, and in an authoritative tone demanded,—

" Hardened villain, what is your purpose ?   Why do you obstruct us ?   Have you no sense of shame or common decency, that you thus sacrilegiously presume to insult the remains of the dead ?   Begone, and let us proceed on our way."

" Not till you have heard all the galling observations I have to make to you, seducer, murderer, bigamist !" cried Harold, in a ferocious voice, and fixing his eyes with a fierce and threatening expression alternately upon Sir Laurence and the terrified Blanche. " Ah, you may frown, Laurence Cleveland, but you feel—you know I speak the truth.   You have seen her, and you, Blanche Lester, for that is still your name, although you have given your hand to the destroyer of your honour."

" Mercy ! mercy !" cried the distracted Blanche ; " I never did you harm, and why should you therefore seek to torture me thus, and even while engaged in the melancholy task of conveying the ashes of my unfortunate parent to their final resting-place ?"

" Curses light upon his memory !" shouted the miscreant ; " even now am I half inclined to desecrate and spit upon his corpse for the hatred I bore him when living. Ah, you may tremble, Blanche Lester, but I pity not your anguish ; I glory in the shame and misery that await you.   Your father was at one period a sapient justice of the peace, and did he ever spare the poor wretches who were brought before him, although he pretended to so much virtue and humanity of heart ?   Did he ever lean to the side of mercy ?   No !   But fortune had not showered upon him the whole of her favours then, and I suppose he could not afford to be merciful or just.   Ha ! ha ! ha !   But I have not told you all yet. 1 was brought before this Dogberry, this father of yours, Blanche Lester, once, twice, thrice, on paltry and false charges of poaching.   Did he ever take the pains to elicit my innocence or guilt ?   No ; ' but to prison, to prison with him ; he is, doubtless, a confirmed rascal, and we must be protected.'   Such was the mercy of your father, such the justice of the benevolent, the all-humane, the great philanthropist, Squire Lester.   But the poacher has lived to exult over his corpse, and to know that he died of a broken heart through the disobedience and the prostitution of his only and darling child !"

It would be utterly impossible for language to describe the horror and agony of poor Blanche while the ruffian was giving utterance to this brutal speech ; but no sooner had he concluded, than she uttered a terrific shriek, and sank insensible in the arms of Sir Laurence.

" Mercy, mercy, Harold, for the poor lady," cried a well-known voice, and immediately the gipsy boy started to the side of Harold, and fixed the most supplicating looks upon his savage countenance.

" Back—back, boy !" shouted the villain, hurling him away. " Intercede for those, and the curse of her who bore thee will light upon thine head.   Thou must learn to hate them as I and all our tribe do, or beware of the vengeance that will pursue thee.   Away !"

The gipsy boy covered his face with his hands, apparently overcome by some powerful emotion, too great for utterance, and immediately retired.

" Monster !" exclaimed Sir Laurence, now for the first time recovering the use of his speech. " Dare you give utterance to such atrocious falsehoods ?   Dare you thus insult the innocence of this unfortunate woman ?   Have you no sense of pity left within you ?"

"Pity for her—for you!" repeated the savage miscreant. "No; your misery, your torture is my triumph. I told you that I would have such a revenge as was never yet before conceived by human mind, and you see that the gipsy knows how to keep his word. But this is only a prelude to the tortures I have in store for you. This moment I could take your life, and that of her whom you hold in your arms; but that is not my purpose; no, I would have more gradual and glorious vengeance. I would goad you on until, overwhelmed with agony and shame, your very heart-strings crack; and the time will come when I shall have that satisfaction. And you would hunt us to destruction, would you, Laurence Cleveland? Oh, most virtuous, most courageous determination! but beware; or you will most assuredly fall in your own net. There is nothing that you do, no place that you can fly to, that can escape our knowledge. Beware—beware!"

Sir Laurence groaned, and looked aghast upon the scarcely human countenance of Harold, but was unable to return any answer.

"You groan, Laurence Cleveland; the steel has already entered your heart; but it will penetrate deeper—deeper," cried the voice of old Madela, and immediately she stood before the window of the carriage, and glared upon Sir Laurence with looks of greater malignance and exultation than ever. "Didst thou never exult in the death of thy fellow-creature?" she continued. "This is the fourteenth of May; hast thou forgotten the fourteenth of May, 1798? Oh, it was a glorious day for thee Laurence Cleveland, that consigned thy hoary-headed victim to the gallows. It must be very refreshing to thy memory. But the curse that was then invoked is now working—working, and will finally sink thee to destruction. The senseless beauty thou now supportest in thine arms will, ere long, become a mother; the offspring of her dishonour and of thy deception will shortly see the light of Heaven but to experience the tortures of hell. Mark me, Laurence Cleveland, my predictions, the predictions of Madela, the gipsy queen, will be fulfilled. Misery, endless misery, to thee and thine!"

"Vengeance—vengeance on all connected with the detested Laurence Cleveland!" cried Harold.

"Vengeance on all connected with the detested Laurence Cleveland!" shouted the gipsies in a breath, and they gathered in front of the carriage, with the most frightful and menacing gestures, brandishing their knives, and otherwise evincing the desperate feelings that animated their breasts. One tremendous shout of triumph and defiance was then given, and the gipsies quitted the carriage, and forming themselves into procession, proceeded quickly across the heath, and were soon lost in the distance from observation.

CHAPTER XI.

THE RETURN TO BRANSCOMBE HOUSE.—THE FUNERAL OF MR. LESTER.

WITH vacant eyes Sir Laurence watched the departure of the wandering tribe, and the anguish and horror of his mind was much more powerful than the imagination can conceive. The words of Harold and Madela had sunk deep into his soul, and the effect they must have upon Blanche, especially in her delicate situation, filled him with the most dreadful apprehensions. He was for some moments so bewildered and horror-struck that he scarcely knew what he did; but at length he gave directions to the drivers to proceed as quick as they could across the heath, hoping to find some inn or other habitation where they might procure assistance.

He kissed the pale cheeks of Blanche, and tried to recall her to sensibility, but in vain ; and he now became more apprehensive than ever, and his emotions were so great that he scarcely knew how to support himself.

"Unhappy Blanche !" he said to himself, "what will be the feelings you must now entertain towards me after this fearful meeting and the opprobrium they lavished upon me ! Will you not, must you not, look upon me with dread and suspicion ? They called me murderer, seducer, bigamist ! Oh, God ! and should the latter prove true, what will become of this poor persecuted angel, deprived as she would be of a lawful protector, and branded by the ungenerous world with shame ? And where could I hide my degraded head ? Should I not become a wretched and degraded being, hateful to myself, and despised and abhorred by every one ? Would not the spirit of Mr. Lester invoke a curse upon my devoted head, which, added to that of his unfortunate daughter, would pursue me to destruction ? Give me courage and fortitude, oh, Heaven, under these accumulated and horrible trials, and avert the evils I apprehend."

He continued to support Blanche in his arms, and to try all the means in his power to recall her to life, but without effect ; and he began to be most seriously alarmed lest the shock she had received should prove too much for her.

At length they gained the extremity of the heath, and beheld a respectable looking inn on the roadside, to which they made their way.

Sir Laurence lifted the insensible form of Blanche from the carriage, and conveyed her to a private apartment, where a female quickly attended them with such necessary remedies for her restoration as they happened to have handy.

Sir Laurence then desired the men to proceed with the hearse towards Branscombe House, not doubting that, if Blanche was sufficiently recovered they should overtake them on the road.

The woman exerted herself to the utmost and was successful, for, after the lapse of about a quarter of an hour, Blanche began to show signs of returning life. The female then quitted the room and left them to themselves.

" Blanche, dearest Blanche !" cried the baronet, as he affectionately embraced her and pressed warm kisses upon her lips, "look up ; the danger is passed ; the villains are gone ; it is your husband that now embraces you."

" My husband !" repeated Blanche, in wild accents, and pressing her fair hands upon her temple ; " am I indeed a wife, or is it only some wicked delusion to work my ruin ? Oh, Laurence, those horrible beings—and have we escaped them ?"

" We have, my love ; cheer up, and try to think no more of it."

" No more of it, Laurence ! Oh, God ! can their dreadful accusations, their maledictions, their threats, ever be effaced from my memory ? But where are we ? We have not reached home ; and my poor father's cold and lifeless remains—oh, where are they ? They have not fallen into the hands of those monsters ? Tell me, Laurence, and do not, as you value my future love, attempt to deceive me."

" They are safe, dear Blanche, indeed they are," answered her husband. " They are now on the way to Branscombe House, whither, as soon as you feel yourself in a fit condition, we will follow."

" Oh, Laurence," sighed Blanche, " what a dreadful adventure has this been ; and the horrible manner in which the miscreant Harold cursed and stigmatized the memory of my poor father; oh, surely that amiable and deeply lamented parent could never have been the harsh and cruel man which the gipsy represented him to be."

"No, my beloved Blanche," replied Sir Laurence, "it were monstrous to believe so base a calumny. You see plainly enough the wretches are capable of saying anything to gratify their malice and revenge. Have they not heaped upon me every opprobrium that their vindictive minds could invent; but you have vowed to confide in me, to believe me innocent, and when I deceive you, when I cease to adore you less than I do at present, may Heaven desert me."

The devoted wife threw herself sobbing on his bosom, and the violence of her emotion for some time choked her utterance. The dreadful observations of Harold had made the most painful impression upon her mind; but could she believe him guilty? No; and her principal fears were entertained for his safety, for what had they not to dread from such desperate villains as the gipsies?

"Alas, Laurence," she ejaculated, "should the wretches succeed in accomplishing their diabolical threats, what will become of us? And in what manner can we escape from them, so secret as they are in their plans, and evidently so reckless of danger?"

"Do not labour under any unnecessary alarm, my dearest Blanche," replied the baronet; "I shall yet be able to devise some means to defeat the villains, and to bring them to justice."

Blanche looked in her husband's face, and it was evident that she read his thoughts, and saw that he only expressed this opinion for the purpose of quieting her fears, and without really entertaining any such ideas himself; but not wishing to create in his bosom any uneasiness beyond that which was caused by the fearful adventure they had already met with, she stifled her emotions, and urged upon him the expediency of their immediate departure.

Having prevailed upon her to partake of some slight refreshment, Sir Laurence complied, and leading Blanche to the carriage, he drew down the blinds, and it was driven off with the greatest speed in the direction which the hearse had taken.

For some time after their departure from the inn, both Sir Laurence and Blanche were too much occupied with their own melancholy thoughts to suffer them to enter into conversation. The baronet pondered over every word which Harold and Madela had uttered, with the most acute anguish, which was fully imparted to the expression of his countenance. He felt a degree of satisfaction that Blanche had become insensible before the conclusion of the scene with the gipsies, for the dreadful observations she would have heard from old Madela and Harold would have increased the agitation of her mind to an insupportable degree; and, in spite of the affection she bore him, some doubts and suspicions might have entered her mind which she would have found it difficult to banish. The re-appearance of the gipsy boy, afforded gratification, for it would have caused him the greatest anguish and remorse, had he been the instrument of taking that poor boy's life, even though by accident. There was something in his features which raised an unusual degree of interest in his breast, and the remarks of Harold, when he appealed for mercy on the behalf of Blanche, increased that feeling tenfold. "Intercede for them," Harold had said, "and the curse of the mother who bore thee will descend upon thine head!" What could be the meaning of this? The gipsy boy had told him and Amanda, when they first saw him, that his mother was no more, and that she had died a death of misery and want.   He felt a burning. curiosity to learn the particulars of Rosario's history, for from what he had elicited from him, there were many facts connected with it that bore a painful coincidence to his own.

Sir Laurence felt a shuddering sensation steal over him, as these ideas recalled to his recollection the events of the past, and made a strong effort to divert his thoughts to some other subject.

Blanche tried also to conquer the emotions which the extraordinary and exciting adventure they had met with, had created in her breast, but that was a task not easy of accomplishment.   To have believed the foul charges of Harold, would have been to have encouraged a gross libel upon her husband, and the memory of her father; and yet what could so have excited the hatred and revenge of the gipsy?   He must have had some cause for it ; either it proceeded from error or truth, and that it was from the latter she could not, she dare not make up her mind to believe.

At length they overtook the hearse, and now the agonising grief of poor Blanche burst forth with renewed energy.

" My dear father," she sobbed, " how rapidly do your revered remains approach their final resting-place.   Alas! it will be long, if ever, before I can recover from the loss I have sustained by your death."

" Say not so, my love," returned the baronet; " time ameliorates the most poignant grief.   Put your trust in the Almighty, and rest satisfied that however gloomy and threatening our prospects may at present appear to be, we shall yet know what it is to enjoy uninterrupted happiness."

" Heaven grant, my husband," said Blanche, " that your predictions may be verified, and that the wretches who now persecute us so terribly, may be induced to abandon their guilty designs.   But have you no recollection of having seen this Harold, before you saw him in the character of a gipsy ?"

" Never, Blanche ; I have not the slightest recollection of the miscreant's features."

" It is most strange; surely he must certainly have made some mistake in your person."

" No ; from many of the circumstances he has related of me, and of which I admit the truth, he must be thoroughly acquainted with me.   But let us for the present drop the subject, my dear Blanche.   The frequent outrages they have committed, and the threats they have held out, must be prevented and punished; and I will not fail in my exertions, until I have brought them to justice."

" I fear, my dear Laurence, you will find them too powerful," said Blanche ; " but still I admit that some plan ought to be adopted, if possible, to put a stop to their guilty proceedings."

Nothing more particular occurred during the remainder of their sad journey, and as the shadows of evening began to fall upon the earth, they came in sight of Branscombe House.

How different were now the feelings of Blanche to what they had been when they departed from Branscombe House.   Then all was dreadful doubt, apprehension, and suspense ; now all was terrible reality.   But with the melancholy death of her revered father, was coupled the soul-felt satisfaction of knowing that she had received his forgiveness and dying blessing, and that with his latest breath he had sanctioned the union of herself and Sir Laurence.

Amanda had been apprised of the death of Mr. Lester immediately after that melancholy event had taken place, and had made every solemn preparation for the reception of his remains. A messenger was sent forward to make them acquainted with their approach, and Amanda and all the servants of Sir Laurence, together with old Humphrey and his wife, dressed in deep mourning, were assembled on the lawn in front of the house to receive the corpse, and their esteemed master and mistress, which they did in solemn silence; and when the coffin which contained the body of her father was removed from the hearse to be conveyed into the house, the grief of poor Blanche burst forth in piteous and hysterical sobs, and it was with difficulty that her husband could support her.

Amanda came forward affectionately to meet her, and to afford her consolation; and she was led into the house by her and Sir Laurence, following the cold remains of her father, which were borne into a state apartment, solemnly prepared for the occasion. No sooner had she entered the drawing-room than Blanche, unable any longer to support the overwhelming weight of anguish that pressed upon her mind, sank insensible in the arms of her husband, and was immediately borne to her chamber, where the family physician was quickly in attendance upon her; and, having applied the usual remedies, her heavily laden breast was somewhat relieved by a violent paroxysm of tears.

Blanche did not attempt to leave her chamber again that night, and obtained some refreshing sleep, during which Sir Laurence and his sister continued to watch by her couch with the utmost anxiety and solicitude.

During the course of the night Sir Laurence related to his sister some of the particulars of their adventures with the gipsies, at which Amanda was much shocked and surprised, and expressed her sentiments accordingly.

"Alas!" she said, "how implacable does the resentment of these men appear to be; and I am afraid, my dear brother, that they will yet find an opportunity of doing you some private and deadly harm."

"I confess, Amanda," replied her brother, "that the thought causes me very great uneasiness, though it would not be prudent to let poor Blanche perceive the whole of my feelings upon the subject. By what means they obtain their information, I am at a loss to conjecture, and one might almost be tempted to believe that they dealt in witchcraft. But could I only secure the villain Harold, and that old hag Madela, my apprehensions would be greatly abated; for their vile associates would be daunted and would never again venture to show themselves in this part of the country."

"Of course they cannot have any means of substantiating the charges they have brought against you, Laurence?" said Amanda, looking at her brother with an expression of melancholy curiosity and anxiety.

Sir Laurence felt somewhat confused at this question, but at length he replied,—

"Most of them, you may be sure, they cannot, Amanda; and one of them, the most important to the happiness of myself and Blanche, I trust they cannot. Should they be able to do so, all my happiness in this world would be annihilated, and I should curse the hour that ever I was born."

Amanda sighed; but she did not wish to enlarge on a subject which was evidently so painful to Sir Laurence, and the conversation upon that topic, therefore, dropped, and a gloomy silence followed, Sir Laurence racking his brain with the numerous and torturing reflections that crowded upon it, and Amanda solely wrapped in the ideas to which her brother's account of their meeting with the gipsies had given rise in her mind.

In the morning Blanche awoke at an early hour, and notwithstanding all the entreaties and remonstrances of her husband, would leave her couch, and visit the chamber in which the body of her father was deposited. They were fearful of the effect this would have upon her feelings, harassed and oppressed as they already were; but, finding it was no use to endeavour to oppose her, they agreed to accompany her.

The scene that ensued in that sad chamber we need not attempt to describe, when Blanche herself drew the lid of the coffin aside, and once more gazed upon the livid countenance of her parent, now locked in the icy arms of death. Her tears gushed forth in torrents, and all the powers of utterance were absorbed in the intensity of her agony. The emotion of Sir Laurence and Amanda was little less than her own, but they did not offer to interrupt her grief, well knowing how the free ebullition serves to disburthen the care-oppressed heart.

The countenance of Mr. Lester had undergone no material change since his death; and Sir Laurence and Blanche, as they gazed upon it, and remembered his last words, could almost imagine that they heard him still addressing them. The idea was too powerful for the baronet, and he averted his looks from the corpse, and sighed heavily as many torturing thoughts occurred to him.

More than an hour they passed in the chamber, when Blanche was at last persuaded to retire; and they returned to the drawing-room.

From that hour, until the melancholy day of the funeral, Blanche became more calm and resigned, and seldom adverted to the meeting with the gipsies. Every morning and evening she visited the chamber of death, and offered up her prayers and lamentations to the memory of her parent, and she looked forward to the moment when his beloved remains must be closed for ever from her sight in the silent tomb with a feeling of the utmost dread.

The sad morning on which the solemn rites were to be performed, at last arrived, and the whole neighbourhood of Branscombe House, and the estate of the deceased gentleman, were wrapped in solemn gloom; for Mr. Lester had been universally respected by rich and poor, and every one deeply sympathised with Lady Cleveland in the sad bereavement she had suffered by the death of so exemplary a parent.

A vast concourse of persons had assembled to witness the funeral procession, and to pay the last tribute of respect to departed worth, and a silence profound as that of death itself prevailed around, as the funeral passed on its way to the church.

There was none of the mockery of pomp or ostentation about it, for that would but have ill accorded with the simple character of the departed, who had ever abominated the tinsel trappings of show and parade. But there was something most powerfully impressive about the whole of the arrangements, which created a feeling of awe in the breasts of all who witnessed the melancholy sight.

The grief of Blanche was almost insupportable; but it was too intense to find vent in tears or lamentations, and she was too much absorbed in her own agonizing thoughts to pay much attention to the attempts of her husband and Amanda to impart consolation to her.

As the sad procession neared the church, the concourse increased, and every one evinced the utmost sorrow at the death of the amiable Mr. Lester, and reverence for his memory.

And now the corpse, followed by the mourners, entered the church, and a funeral dirge sounded in solemn peals from the organ. The church was immediately filled with spectators, who arranged themselves respectfully on either side while the sad procession proceeded up the aisle, and many were the sobs of pity that escaped the sympathising breasts of those who were present, as they noticed the anguish—the deep, the unspeakable anguish of the bereaved young bride, who, had she not been supported by her husband, must have sank to the earth.

See p. 120.

The funeral service commenced, and was conducted with much solemnity and eloquence by the persons officiating; and, at its conclusion, the procession formed itself again, and moved towards the vault in which the remains of Mr. Lester were to receive their final home.

It was a most affecting sight to behold the agony of poor Blanche during this trying part of the funeral rites, and great indeed was the difficulty which Sir Laurence had to sustain her. It seemed as if her heart was going from her, and, at that moment, she could not help entertaining a secret wish that she might be permitted speedily to rejoin her parent, and to be released from the cares and anxieties of the world, in which, of late, she had experienced so much of sorrow and affliction.

The last awful task was performed; his ashes were deposited by the side of those of his wife; a funeral hymn was sung, in which the voices of all the persons joined; the vault closed upon Mr. Lester for ever; and Blanche, unable any longer to support the weight of overwhelming grief against which she had so long been struggling, gave one heavy, heart-drawn sigh, and sank inanimate in the arms of Sir Laurence.

At that moment, when every bosom was absorbed in pity and sorrow, a rude and harsh discordant laugh of malice was heard to ring upon the air. All eyes were instantly directed towards the spot from whence the sacrilegious sound proceeded, and standing at no distance from the crowd, and pointing with her long bony fingers with a gesture of more than fiendish triumph towards the vault and the insensible form of Lady Blanche, stood the hideous figure of the gipsy hag, old Madela, her small but piercing eyes seeming to flash fire, and her shrivelled and repulsive countenance distorted in the most frightful manner by the various diabolical passions that raged within her bosom!

Every one was horror-struck, paralysed by this bold and monstrous interruption at so solemn a moment, and were unable to move from the spot, or to utter a word of execration; and there the ancient gipsy continued to stand for several minutes, gazing with looks of demoniac exultation upon Sir Laurence Cleveland, who trembled so in every limb that it was with difficulty he could prevent himself from relinquishing his hold, and suffering his insensible and lovely burthen to fall to the earth. But suddenly a burst of indignation escaped from the crowd, and they made a rush towards the hag.

For a second or two, Madela did not offer to move, or to alter her position, but seemed to bid defiance to them all; but when they had got to within only a very few yards of her, and it appeared as if her seizure was inevitable, she turned round, and fled with a precipitancy that seemed almost incredible in one of her great age; and notwithstanding her pursuers exerted themselves to the utmost, she fairly outstripped them, and, plunging into the wood, was immediately lost to the view.

CHAPTER XII.

THE BIRTH OF AN HEIRESS TO THE HOUSE OF BRANSCOMBE.—THE FESTIVITIES ON THE OCCASION.—THE WARNING.—THE FETE.— THE ALARM.

Sir Laurence Cleveland gazed wildly and vacantly after the old gipsy, as she retreated from the spot, and the blood ran scalding hot through his veins, while his brain was wrought up to a pitch of frenzy. But when the spectators returned, and informed him of the fruitlessness of their endeavours to overtake her, he beat his breast, and, uttering a deep groan, seemed to give himself up entirely to despair.

Amanda was in scarcely a better condition than himself, but she motioned to two of the attendants, who approached, and, taking their insensible mistress from his arms, conveyed her to the carriage. Amanda then gently laid hold of her distressed brother's arm, and affectionately drew him from the spot, and entering the gloomy vehicle, it was driven off amid the expressions of the deepest sympathy from all who had been spectators of the melancholy and impressive scene.

A sad day was that at Branscombe House, and in the vicinity; Blanche was come pletely overwhelmed with grief, and Sir Laurence, after what had occurred, was in no condition to offer her that consolation he otherwise might have done. Amanda, however, did all that her gentle and affectionate nature could prompt her, and had the satisfaction, at length, of finding that she had succeeded much better than she could have anticipated.

It was a fortunate thing that Blanche was in a state of unconsciousness at the time of Madela's appearance, or how doubly severe would have been her emotions; how overpowering would have been her horror at the insult offered to the memory of her poor father!

Sir Laurence felt some consolation in her ignorance of this circumstance, and cautioned his sister and the servants not to let fall a word in her presence which might make her acquainted with it.

Sir Laurence was now more and more bewildered and alarmed at the mysterious and unaccountable appearance of the old hag, at all times, and in all places. She seemed to be the fiendish mistress of his destiny, to possess supernatural powers, and it was quite evident that unless she was secured, she would pursue both him and all who were connected with him to destruction. These thoughts drove him almost mad, and he dreaded to enter the presence of Blanche any more than he could help, lest he should betray his thoughts, and thus add to the anguish and despair of her mind.

For several days after the funeral of her father, Blanche remained completely overwhelmed with grief, and kept herself almost entirely secluded to her own apartment, seeming scarcely able to endure even the society of her husband or Amanda; and even the fond endearments of the sweet little Angela, to whom she was greatly attached, failed to detach her thoughts from the deep melancholy that absorbed them. There were so many sad and peculiar circumstances attending the death of her father, that she could not eradicate them from her memory, and, in spite of all her efforts to the contrary, she could not help accusing herself of being indirectly the cause of hastening his death.

"Alas!" she would sigh, "my absconding from him took such effect upon his feelings, that his weakened system could not sustain the shock. But yet, did I not act from a pure sense of duty and affection to my husband? Heaven knows that I did, and the poignant anguish it caused me to be obliged to disobey the injunctions of the author of my being, or to occasion in his aged bosom one single pang. But he forgave me that only act of disobedience, he bestowed his blessing upon me and Laurence, and that ought to afford me some consolation, and to banish from my breast these self-reproaches. But then the meeting with the gipsies; their terrible denunciations and threats; the opprobrious epithets the villain Harold applied to me and to Laurence; all these will, notwithstanding my endeavours to the contrary, crowd upon madness."

Thus did poor Blanche continue to indulge in alternate hopes and fears; but at length her husband and Amanda saw the necessity of arousing her by some means, considering her delicate situation, from this abject state of melancholy, and persevered so well in their efforts that they at last succeeded, and Blanche became more tranquil and resigned.

Sir Laurence had ordered a handsome monument to be erected to the memory of Mr. Lester, and to this Blanche and Sir Laurence paid daily visits, and paid their devotions before it to the memory of that amiable being whose loss they so deeply lamented.

At other times they would visit the mansion of the late Mr. Lester, which they would not suffer to be disturbed, and it remained in precisely the same state as when he was alive.

It was the melancholy pleasure of Blanche to ramble over those apartments which had been most used by her father; to peruse the works he had loved to read, or to kneel before the portraits of him and her mother, and pour forth blessings upon their memory.

In these sad occupations, Sir Laurence was gratified to indulge her, for he saw that it afforded her mind relief, and would in time, he hoped, ameliorate, if it did not entirely banish, her sorrow.

Nor had Sir Laurence all this time been indifferent as to the whereabouts of the gipsies, especially old Madela and Harold, but caused the strictest search to be made, and used every precaution he could to guard against any secret outrage they might attempt to commit. But all his efforts to gain any clue to them were unavailing, and he remained in a constant state of dread of their power, after the many proofs of malice and deadly determined revenge which they had displayed towards him.

And now the time rapidly drew nigh at which Blanche expected to become a mother, and, as that interesting and important event approached, the anxiety and fears of Sir Laurence increased, lest he should be deprived of that fair being, that lovely and devoted wife, in whom his sole, his every happiness was centered.

Never had he found the valuable services of his affectionate sister more inestimable than on that auspicious occasion, and, through her efforts, she kept up the spirits of Blanche, and inspired her with hopes of the future happiness that would be conferred on her and her husband by the birth of the little stranger.

But, notwithstanding all, Sir Laurence could not but anticipate the birth of his child with something like a feeling of regret and melancholy foreboding, after the threats and predictions of old Madela; for if it was to be born alone for misfortune, it would be better that it should not be born at all. He could not but feel surprised and ashamed of his weakness, in placing any reliance in the wild prognostication of a wandering old wretch, like the gipsy woman; yet there was something so extraordinary about her conduct and the success with which she managed all her plans, that he could not divest his mind of the impression. And then the uncertainty of the death of Clara, his first wife, tortured him almost beyond endurance; for, alas! what shame would be his, what anguish and misery that of Blanche, should it be discovered that she still lived, and that Blanche had become a mother without having any claim upon the name of wife.

The thought was too horrible for indulgence, and Sir Laurence tried hard to banish it from his bosom; but in that he was unsuccessful.

At length the important day arrived, and, after some hours of severe illness, Blanche was safely delivered of a lovely daughter. With what mingled feelings of transport and melancholy did Sir Laurence gaze upon the little innocent, when it was presented to him to receive his first caress, and fervently did he pray to Heaven to avert from it all those evils and dangers he apprehended, and to shower down every blessing upon its head.

Never does a woman appear half so lovely, as when she presents to her husband the first innocent pledge of their mutual affection; never does her faithful heart more abundantly flow with all the beautiful feelings so peculiar to her angelic sex. With what transport did Sir Laurence gaze upon his beloved Blanche, as her countenance glowed with all the unbounded, the indescribable affection of the young mother upon the father of her offspring.

"Heaven has blessed us, my dear Laurence, with this little innocent cherub," she said, "and we must be happy. Let all the gloomy past be forgotten, and look forward to the future only with the brightest hopes."

"And God grant, my loved Blanche," replied Sir Laurence, fervently, "that in those hopes we may not be disappointed. Sweet child, I hail you with all the fond rapture of a father; may you grow up rich in every virtue and grace, and Heaven guard you from all those sorrows and dangers, those follies and temptations, those arts and seductions, with which this world abounds."

"Amen!" solemnly ejaculated Blanche, and fondly caressed her husband and her babe alternately.

When Sir Laurence was alone, he fervently poured forth his gratitude to Heaven for the safe deliverance of his beloved Blanche, and then endeavoured to banish the doubts and apprehensions which had so long tortured his bosom. But still the accusations of Harold, and the predictions of Madela, together with the curse which she said had been invoked upon his head by the widow of the man whom he had been the means of bringing to an untimely end, haunted his imagination, and banished rest entirely from him.

He had firmly believed that the poacher and his son were guilty of the crime of which they had been convicted, for nothing could be stronger or more conclusive than the evidence which was brought against them; and, consequently, he could not reproach himself for the part he had acted at their trial; but there was one fact of which he could not acquit himself, and that was, his estranging the affections of an innocent girl from one to whom he believed she was devoted, before he lured her with his flattering tongue, and dazzled her with his splendid offers. That youth was the son of the man who suffered death, and, he believed, was honest and industrious, till the disappointment of his hopes rendered him reckless and profligate. That circumstance he could not settle to his conscience quite so well, and, when he reflected upon it, it recalled to his bosom many unpleasant sensations. Should that individual be living, and have escaped his awful doom, namely, that of perpetual banishment, he felt assured that his feelings of hatred and revenge would naturally be excited against him; but why Harold and Madela should thus pursue him, and how they had become so perfectly well acquainted with the particulars, he was at a loss to imagine, unless they were the very individuals he had the most reason to dread; and yet he could not trace the least likeness in the features of Harold to those of the unfortunate young man in question.

Towards the evening, Sir Laurence took a walk around his estates, in order to refresh himself, and that he might indulge, undisturbed, in silent meditation, and, if possible, relieve his bosom of the many cares which, at present, oppressed it.

The evening was very fine, and Sir Laurence, feeling the fresh breeze have an exhilarating effect upon his spirits, was induced to prolong his ramble.

He had ascended a lofty hill, and was occupied in admiring the beautiful effect which the clear and silvery moonlight had upon the extensive scenery around, when he felt his arm vehemently grasped by a bony, but powerful hand, and, startled by the freedom, and apprehending some danger, as he was quite unarmed, he hastily raised his head, and, to his astonishment and confusion, beheld the frightful countenance of Madela peering over his shoulder.

"You have been looking for me, Laurence Cleveland," she said, "and have sent your bloodhounds forth in all directions, in search of me and my people. But we wander where we list; and when we choose to conceal ourselves, to work in secret our plans, the most searching eye cannot discover us. But I am here, Laurence Cleveland, an old woman and alone, and now will you drag me to a gaol, eh? Ha! ha! ha!"

"Mysterious woman," said Sir Laurence, really somewhat appalled by the boldness and defiance of her manner, "why do you ever haunt me thus, and seek to annoy me by your diabolical threats and infamous prognostications?"

"Because I hate thee, Laurence Cleveland, and have sworn to be revenged on thee and thine. The blood of him who died upon the scaffold, and by thy false evidence, calls for retribution; and, mark me, it shall not call in vain."

"Who are you, woman? And why should you take such an interest in that guilty man's well-merited fate?"

"Liar! he merited it not; he was far more innocent than thou art, and thou knowest it. Who am I? Oh! thou shalt know that soon enough, never fear, and to thy sorrow."

"Let go your hold, bold woman, and begone!" commanded Sir Laurence, trying to release himself from her grasp; but she still retained her hold with a strength which seemed almost impossible in one of her sex, of her age, and so decrepid.

"Nay, Laurence Cleveland," she said, "thou hast no puny infant to contend with, as much as thou mayest affect to despise me. Thou goest not until thou hast heard all that I have to say to thee."

"By heaven! this is too much!" exclaimed Sir Laurence, passionately. "Am I to be dared and insulted by such an old wretch as you? Let go your hold, I say! or I will hurl your frightful old carcass into the lake beneath."

"Ha! ha! ha! Fine words, Laurence Cleveland; but, before thou couldst even attempt to put thy threat into execution, behold! I would bury this weapon in your heart!"

She drew forth a long-bladed knife from beneath her cloak as she spoke, and directed it towards his breast; and Sir Laurence, being completely defenceless, really felt alarmed.

"What would you with me, Madela?" he demanded, in somewhat milder accents than before; "why do you thus seek to torture one who knows you not, and who could not, therefore, ever have done you any possible harm?"

"Done me no harm!" repeated the gipsy; "oh! but I could tell thee a tale, if it suited my purpose so to do at present, that should freeze thy very life's blood with horror. But that is not now my design. All is bright and lovely around thee, Laurence Cleveland; and so appear thy prospects, do they not, now that Blanche Lester —the betrayed daughter of he who now rots in the tomb, and over whose funeral I exulted—has borne thee a child? Poor fool! infatuated idiot! Thinkest thou the predictions of old Madela will not be verified? Thinkest thou the murderer, the seducer, the bigamist, will be suffered to go unpunished, while there are those who wander the earth as outcasts, despised, hunted, persecuted, whom his villany hath ruined? No, no! Remember the curse! It will be fulfilled; ay, terribly fulfilled. The clouds are now gathering which shall shortly burst upon thee with the most overwhelming fury. Oh! it is a sweet cherub, is it not? So innocent, so smiling; but it shall grow up a curse to thee; mark my words, it shall. That innocence shall be changed into contamination; those smiles, to the haggard looks of care, and profligacy, and dissipation! After pandering to the vices of such libertines as her father, she shall become the loathed, the horror of all! Mark that, Laurence Cleveland, and rejoice—rejoice in the birth of thy lovely child!"

Sir Laurence staggered back from her hold aghast, appalled, at her awful words, and the vehemence with which they were uttered, and for a moment all his faculties seemed to be suspended; while old Madela laughed aloud and exultingly at the agony which she saw that her observations had inflicted upon him. Had he stood in the presence of a supernatural being, he could not have felt greater horror than he did at that moment, and indeed there was something in the countenance and the whole appearance of Madela, which seemed to denote her anything but human; and now her countenance looked even more than usually hideous; and the reflection of the moon's rays upon her hag-like form, imparted such a ghastly character to it, that it was enough to inspire even the stoutest heart with an unconquerable feeling of dread.

It was evident to Sir Laurence, that in spite of all the vigilance he had used to detect her, she must have been lurking somewhere near his mansion, or she could not have become acquainted with the birth of the infant and its sex; and this the more convinced him, that whatever precautions he might use, still he and his family would never be safe for a moment from the villanous machinations of her and her associates, and therefore there was more occasion for his alarm than ever.

A fearful silence of some minutes ensued, during which Sir Laurence had neither the power to move from the spot, nor to utter a word, and Madela kept her piercing eyes fixed upon him, and her triumph seemed to increase with his anguish.

"Laurence Cleveland," she said, at length, "thou seemest astonished at my prognostications, and well thou mayest, for as sure as thou art a villain of the blackest dye, they will be verified. Yes, and I, old as I am, will live to see it, and to exult in thy misery and disgrace. Thou mayest go home with this consolation, that the sweet babe of her whom thou hast ruined, is born to be a curse to thee."

"Lying, heartless old wretch!" cried Sir Laurence, worked up to a perfect pitch of frenzy; "I will no longer submit to be thus taunted and villified by a miserable old hag like you! Thus do I ——"

"Fool!" interrupted Madela, again brandishing the knife, "wouldst thou rush upon death? Then be it so; come on, and the next instant I will stretch thee a ghastly, disfigured corpse at my feet."

The baronet staggered back in terror, for he saw, from the menacing attitude of Madela, that she was determined to put her threats into execution, and covering his face with his hands, as though he would shut out some ghastly phantom from his sight, he rushed hastily down the hill, and when he had reached the foot, he looked up, but Madela was gone.

He darted on towards his mansion in a state of mind which he had seldom before experienced, and the strange and fearful predictions of the old woman still seemed to ring in his ears as he proceeded. Already he thought that the full weight of the curse had fallen upon him, and that he should never be able to look upon that poor innocent babe again without a feeling of horror.

He had proceeded some distance before he paused to take breath, and then endeavoured to connect his thoughts, and to compose himself, after the unusual excitement which this adventure had caused.

"But a very fool and a coward I am," he said, after reflecting for a few moments,

" to suffer the mad observations of this miserable old woman to agitate and alarm me. Have I become a convert to superstition, that I should place confidence in her predictions? What contempt should I gain were this weakness to be made known! No, no; I will endeavour to shake it off—to place no reliance in them; but to try every means to get her and Harold in my power; then I know I may laugh to scorn their threats of vengeance. They have told me that my first wife, that Clara still lives; that 'tis her I have beheld; but it is all false; it is all an imposition; or why does she not come forward to confront me?"

He was startled at this part of his meditations by hearing a deep sigh, and looking up, to his infinite amazement and awe, he beheld, standing before him at no great distance, the same fair form which had so often of late appeared to him. She was clad in the same robes of pure white, long and beautiful auburn tresses hung flowing luxuriantly over her shoulders, and her eyes, which were fixed intently upon him, had an expression of such intense melancholy and gentle reproach, that it penetrated to the very soul of Sir Laurence, and created a shuddering sensation throughout his veins, which he could not conquer. Her attitude was so still, so marble-like, that she looked not like anything animate, and the manner in which the moonbeams fell upon her added to the illusion.

"Again that form—those features!" cried Sir Laurence; "unfortunate, but guilty Clara, if it is indeed your living self, or only your spirit, oh! speak to me, and banish this terrible suspense; let me at once know the worst, and make me blest or miserable for ever!"

"Be miserable for ever, wretched, guilty Laurence!" replied the mysterious being, in solemn tones; and, waving her hand, she turned round, and immediately glided from the spot.

"God of Heaven!" cried the horror-struck baronet; "this is no delusion—that voice! Fly me not! I will pursue you; and, even though I rush upon immediate death, I will have my doubts removed."

He bounded after the retreating form with the greatest precipitation. He gained upon her—he increased his speed, when his foot came in contact with something that was lying in the road, and he stumbled, and fell heavily to the ground.

It was some moments before he could recover himself from the shock, and gather himself up, and when he did so the form he had been pursuing was gone.

"Still she eludes me," he cried; "how can she thus escape? Surely no mortal being could do so! Oh, torture! torture! These continual excitements will certainly deprive me of my senses. And I heard her speak. My ears could not deceive me; she bade me be miserable for ever! God! God! for what have you reserved me?"

Again he groaned, and struck his burning temples; but suddenly aroused to the recollection of the waning time, and thinking that Blanche would deem it unkind for him to remain so long from home on that particular occasion, he turned away from the spot, and directed his footsteps towards Branscombe House.

It would be a waste of time to attempt to pourtray his feelings as he proceeded on his way home. He had that night received all but confirmation of his worst fears; he felt himself a villain—the betrayer and deceiver of confiding innocence; and how could he dare to enter the presence of her he had so deeply injured, the mother of his child, again? He was bewildered and distracted; and in vain tried to quiet his anguish before he arrived at home.

He trembled when he entered the chamber of Blanche, and gazed upon her affectionate countenance, and that of the little innocent upon her bosom. The predictions of Madela rushed upon his recollection with the most overwhelming force, and already he, in his disordered imagination, beheld those fearful prognostications in the course of being fulfilled.

Blanche noticed the disorder of his manner, although he tried to conceal it, and tenderly inquired the cause. He attributed it to his anxiety about her health, and that of the infant, and with that excuse she was satisfied, for it was so natural, and suspicion never once entered her mind.

No. 16.

Sir Laurence passed a wretched night, and paced his chamber with disordered steps, never seeking his couch, for he knew it would be useless, as it was quite impossible that he could sleep with such a weight of care pressing upon his brain. He endeavoured still to persuade himself that the form he had seen was a phantom, but reason would not permit him to come to that conclusion. And yet, if it was indeed Clara herself, why did she not come boldly forward, and claim him for her lawful husband? Why had she not done so on the day that he gave his hand to Blanche, and thus have prevented that crime with which he was now reproached? And then, again, was it not too probable that she was goaded on by a spirit of revenge, and had refrained from doing so only to render his misery the more complete? There was too much reason and probability in this idea for him easily to reject it, and he gave himself up to entire despair.

"Oh, God!" he groaned, "would to heaven that this poor infant had perished at its birth, rather than to live to know itself the offspring of an unlawful connexion. And you, my poor Blanche, what will be your agony, should you ever discover that there is another living who has a prior claim to that hand which has been given to you? The dreadful discovery must surely break your heart ; and how shall I ever be able to meet your reproaches? They would sink me into the earth with conscious guilt and shame. But it cannot be—I have suffered my fears to carry me too far. Heaven cannot have so much misery in store for those who are, at any rate, innocent. No ; I will try to banish such horrible ideas from my breast, and trust that Providence, for the sake of the innocent Blanche, will avert such horrible calamities."

But, notwithstanding all his efforts, it was in vain that he endeavoured to do so ; and the remaining hours till the morning were passed by him in a state of the greatest possible excitement, and it was only by dint of the greatest perseverance that he was enabled to gain anything like a degree of composure, so that he might enter the chamber of his wife.

He was gratified to find that Blanche and the infant were progressing as well as could be expected ; and he passed some time in the chamber, and conversed with his wife with much greater composure than could have been expected after all that had taken place, and the miserable, restless night he had passed. But the most painful thoughts would steal over him, and when he contemplated the beauteous features of Blanche, and those of her infant, and recollected the predictions of Madela, he could not, without the greatest difficulty, repress a sigh, as he pictured to himself the troubles that were in store for them.

Three weeks elapsed after the accouchement of Lady Cleveland, and she was fast approaching to convalescence. The infant, also, throve amazingly, and gave fair promise of being a lovely child. The event was hailed with much joy by all who had the pleasure of their acquaintance, and when Blanche was sufficiently recovered to leave her chamber, she daily received the congratulations of their friends, and Branscombe House was almost constantly full of visitors.

This served in a great measure to divert the thoughts of Sir Laurence from the painful subjects that had before engrossed them, and he appeared in more than his accustomed spirits. Could he have been certain of one thing, he would, indeed, in spite of the gloomy past, have been supremely happy ; but the uncertainty of that corroded his heart, and haunted him like a grim and ghastly phantom.

The day was appointed for the christening of the little stranger, and Sir Laurence resolved to celebrate that important event with unusual splendour and festivity. For that purpose the most extensive arrangements had been in the course of preparation for several weeks at Branscombe House, and, among the rest of the entertainments, it was determined that there should be a grand masked *fete*. Cards of invitation had been sent to all the nobility and gentry for miles around ; and everything was done to render it most magnificent. Nor were the amusements and festivities to be confined to the higher classes alone, for it was resolved that the peasantry and tenants of Sir Laurence should likewise be partakers of his hospitality, and give full licence to their mirth on that auspicious day.

They were to have a great banquet on the lawn, plenty of hearty old English fare, and partake of all the pleasures of the rustic dance and enlivening song.

The hall was fitted up in the most costly manner, and, when completed, exhibited a scene of the most costly splendour. Nothing could surpass the perfect taste and elegance of its decorations, or the appropriateness of the devices which appeared in different parts of it.

The mansion was also to be illuminated at night, and, in fact, there was nothing left undone to render it such a festive scene as had not been witnessed in that part of the country for many years.

Every person interested looked forward to the auspicious day with the most joyous anticipation, and among the rustics nothing else was talked of, speculated upon, or dreamed about, but " the grand to-do that wur to tak' place on christnun of young mistress."

Lord and Lady Musgrove arrived at Branscombe House a fortnight before the ceremony was appointed to take place, and her ladyship and Amanda had gladly consented to become sponsors for the infant heiress, Lord Musgrove and Sir William Gladhill, the cousin of Sir Laurence, being appointed to officiate in the like capacity.

Lady Blanche looked forward to the day with the most heartfelt pleasure, and bright and sanguine expectations ; but her husband, notwithstanding he tried all he could to conquer it, at times felt a depression of spirits and melancholy foreboding, which made him look forward to the day with something like a feeling of dread. The many troubles he had met with of late had damped the ardour of his hopes, and he was in constant fear of something occurring to crush his happiness, and that of her he valued much more than his own life, at one fell swoop. The wild predictions of Madela, and the words of the form he had seen, in the shape and likeness of Clara, were constantly ringing in his ears ; and he was fearful that the gipsies would not fail to seek some means of annoying him, and interrupting their happiness on so important an occasion. And yet he could hardly believe it probable that they would venture to run the risk of appearing on that day, when the numbers that would be assembled in the mansion and the neighbourhood would be more than sufficient to foil any designs they might have in contemplation, and their own apprehension would be almost certain to follow. However, he used every precaution to guard against them, and employed persons in different parts of the country to give timely notice of any suspicious-looking persons whom they might see lurking about ; and, having made these arrangements, he endeavoured to feel a little more satisfied.

The morning which had been so impatiently looked forward to by so many individuals, was at length ushered in, and at an early hour all was bustle, hilarity, and expectation. The poorest peasants were all attired in their best, and every face bore a joyous smile. The bells of the village church sent forth merry peals, and gay banners fluttered from its lofty spires in the air.

From an early hour the company kept flocking along the road to Branscombe House, and the splendour of the equipages, the costliness of the dresses, and the beauty of the ladies who were going to do honour to the ceremony of baptising the infant heiress of the house of Branscombe, excited universal admiration and delight.

The doors of the mansion were open to all, and the arrangements of the larder, and the beautiful gardens, were not the least attractive portions of the entertainments.

Neither Sir Laurence nor Blanche had slept much during the night; but the feelings that kept them waking were very different. Blanche was all blissful anticipation on the pleasures of the coming morrow; while Sir Laurence felt apprehensive and doubtful, and heartily wished that the ceremony was over, and that the mansion had relapsed into its usual state of tranquillity. Had not the circumstances which had recently taken place have happened, no one could have hailed such an event with greater pleasure than he would have done; but now his feelings were very different; he was labouring under a dreadful uncertainty, upon which the fate of himself and all that was dear to him depended, and he knew not but that at the very moment when [their happiness was at its height, a discovery might be made which would crush it at once, and bring shame, ruin, and misery upon them for ever.

A melancholy feeling of regret would also sometimes steal over the mind of Blanche, when she thought of the delight her poor father would have experienced had he been living to have shared in the festivities of this most joyous occasion; and with what fond transport he would have caressed his little granddaughter, the daughter of his Blanche. But it was useless to give way to these melancholy thoughts, and Blanche therefore exerted herself to the utmost, and at last succeeded in conquering them.

As soon as daylight appeared, a party of excellent vocalists and musicians executed an appropriate serenade under the windows of the chamber of Sir Laurence and his lady, and this, in a great measure, dispelled the sad and bewildering thoughts which had distracted the baronet during the night. They arose cheerful and anxious, and prepared to receive their noble and distinguished guests at an elegant breakfast, at which all the rank and fashion which that part of the country could boast of were assembled, and the scene presented was one of the utmost gaiety and splendour.

The tenantry also had their morning repast on the lawn in the front of the mansion, and at which old Humphrey officiated as master of the ceremonies; and they fully evinced that they had each come there with a firm determination to do ample justice to their master's hospitality.

More merrily rang the bells from every church steeple for miles around; and, as if Heaven smiled upon the proceedings, a more lovely morning had not been known throughout the season.

It was a general holiday for several miles around Branscombe House, and the peasants all hurried to join their friends and companions in the hospitalities that were so plenteously provided for them. There seemed but one disposition to prevail among all classes, and that was to be as happy and as jovial as possible, and to scout anything in the shape of care.

And now came the hour when the ceremony was appointed to take place, and, as the company entered their carriages, the rustics cheered most vehemently; but, when Sir Laurence and Lady Blanche appeared, followed by Amanda and the nurse with the lovely babe, their shouts of gladness rent the air, and were prolonged for several minutes.

The procession to the church was a truly magnificent one, and nothing could equal the animation of the general scene, or the enthusiasm of the crowds of persons that congregated to witness it, and who shouted with joy and admiration as it passed on its way to the church, where the ceremony was to take place. Triumphal arches of flowers and evergreens were formed in different parts of the road, and the effect altogether was extremely beautiful.

The heart of the young and lovely mother bounded with delight, and tears of gratitude and joy started to her eyes, at the demonstrations of esteem and good feeling which were on every side displayed. Even Sir Laurence shook off the cares that had hitherto oppressed him, and gave himself up entirely to the happiness of the scene. In fact, it must have been a sad heart indeed which could not have rejoiced on such an occasion, when all were so smiling and cheerful around.

As the illustrious company passed into the church, loud and enthusiastic cries of "God bless the infant heiress of the house of Cleveland!" burst from every lip, and the sacred edifice was soon filled with anxious spectators.

Never had Blanche looked half so lovely as she did at the moment when the ceremony commenced, and all eyes were fixed on her with admiration and esteem. Sir Laurence felt that he loved her, if possible, more than ever, and a sensation of melancholy came over him when he reflected that probably that fair face was doomed, ere long, to be overclouded with sorrow, and the heart that now bounded so lightly would be loaded with care. But this feeling was only transitory, and he then became completely absorbed by the proceedings.

The infant was baptized in the names of Emeline Amanda Blanche, after the two sponsors and the mother; and the ceremony being completed, the joyful procession departed from the church in the same order in which it had come, the bells ringing their most enlivening peals, and the vast concourse of persons rending the air with their honest shouts of gladness.

No sooner had the company returned to Branscombe House than the festivities commenced, the rustics dancing merrily on the lawn to the gay sound of music, and the noble company deigning, for a short time, to be spectators of the joyous scene, when they retired into the hall to partake of an elegant *dejeuner*, and the peasants continued their sports with unabated hilarity.

It was truly a day of enjoyment and happiness, and not a gloomy countenance was to be seen among all the numerous persons assembled. The company in the hall gave free indulgence to their feelings, and the more humble portion of the guests were allowed to amuse themselves as they pleased; and, certainly, they did not fail to avail themselves of the privilege which was granted them, no one attempting to abuse or disgrace the munificent hospitality of their generous host and benefactor, but fully bent upon doing justice to the ample and excellent fare that was provided for them, and to show the general esteem in which his lady and himself were held by them.

The banquet provided in the hall was sumptuous; and, while the noble guests were at the table, they were entertained with all the charms of vocal and instrumental music, by professors of eminence, engaged for the occasion.

Nor were the rustics without their minstrels, vocal and instrumental; but they were from amongst themselves, and certainly they made up in noise what they were deficient of in ability.

As evening approached, the festivity increased, and the scene became unusually animated. The brilliancy of the illuminations, the variety and splendour of the dresses of the numerous maskers, and the graceful movements of the dance, rendered it altogether one of the most imposing spectacles it is possible for the imagination to conceive; and every one who had the pleasure of beholding it must have felt the greatest admiration and delight.

The peasants' hilarity increased, if possible, with every waning hour, and their noisy mirth made the welkin ring again. Some were engaged in romping and joking with the many rustic beauties who were there assembled; others in drinking, carousing, and singing; while the more young and active kept up the sprightly dance with the most determined spirit.

As the night advanced, and no interruption had taken place to their happiness, Sir Laurence felt contented and unusually cheerful, and Blanche had not felt so free from care for many a day, and could not help thinking the general harmony that had prevailed throughout the day was a fair omen of the future prosperity of her infant offspring.

Sir Laurence had left her for a few minutes engaged in conversation with Lady Musgrove and Amanda, and mingled amongst the numerous gay revellers in the hall. He had noticed that a grey domino had been following him about whichever way he turned for some time, and his curiosity being somewhat excited, he determined to address it; but the individual, who seemed to penetrate his intentions, turned abruptly away, and moved to that part of the hall which was the least crowded.

Sir Laurence, feeling rather surprised at the conduct of the domino, and the peculiar attention he paid to him, determined to follow. He missed him for a few moments; but suddenly turning round, he found him at his elbow, and before he could address it, the domino raised its mask, and gazed full and earnestly upon him. He started back with horror and amazement, for again he beheld those well-known features that bore the powerful resemblance of the unfortunate Clara, his first wife, and he could almost imagine that she stood before him.

Sir Laurence was petrified to the spot, large drops of perspiration stood upon his brow, and his tongue clove to the roof of his mouth; while the female's melancholy and reproachful look remained fixed upon him, and reproach, mingled with pity, sparkled from her eyes.

"God of Heaven!" thought Sir Laurence, "could this be reality, or was it a phantom sent to torture him?" But the moment had now arrived when he had the opportunity of unravelling the mystery, and of ascertaining the full extent of his misery; and, aroused to action by these thoughts, he determined not to lose it.

"Mysterious being!" he exclaimed, "who thus continually haunteth me like a shadow, I will know who you are, whether mortal or the vision of one whose likeness you so strongly bear, even though the knowledge should prove to me decided misery and despair!"

He put forth his hand to seize her as he spoke, but in an instant she again covered her face with her mask, and eluding his grasp, she fled with the velocity of an affrighted deer towards the entrance to the hall. Sir Laurence pursued her, calling upon her to stop, and imploring those persons who were at hand to obstruct her progress; but they did not seem to understand him, and she darted from the hall, fled across the lawn, and was speedily hid from the gaze of the baronet among the numerous persons who were there assembled.

In a state of agitation the baronet flew among the rustics, and hastily inquired of each of them which way she had gone; but they stared at him with amazement, and did not seem to know what he meant. She had again escaped him, and it seemed as if by magic; but still he determined not to give up the pursuit; and he, therefore, darted from the gardens, and took the road before him; but after advancing along it for a considerable distance without perceiving any object, he saw that it was useless, and, therefore, gave up the pursuit in despair.

He paused for a few minutes to recover himself and take breath, and so great was his emotion, that he was compelled to lean against the trunk of a tree to support himself.

"Horror! horror!" he groaned; "I am lost, ruined; the assertions of Harold, the gipsy, were too true, and Clara still lives—I cannot, I dare not longer doubt it. It was no vision that I just now saw; no, there was life and animation in those eyes, those looks, still so fair, yet so reproachful. Oh, God! what a crime I have committed; into what shame and misery have I plunged the most amiable, the most lovely, the most virtuous of human beings; and she is the mother of my child, without having any lawful claim upon my hand! Poor girl! poor ruined girl! I shall go mad. Oh, Clara, why did you not reveal yourself, and thus have prevented this dreadful calamity? Terrible indeed is the revenge you have had."

He beat his breast and gasped for breath as these awful ideas crowded upon his brain, and for some time his mind was so bewildered and confused, that he knew not what to do.

"And must I, shall I continue to contaminate the fair being I have ruined!" he continued. "Can I still continue to deceive her, and to plunge her still deeper into infamy? Alas! there is no alternative, for I dare not reveal the horrible suspicions that now occupy my breast; I dare not arouse her from her sweet dream of confidence and imaginary bliss. It would break her heart were I to do so. Oh, never! never! Fate, since you have thus cast my unhappy lot, I must submit to your decree, even though it bring me destruction. Oh, what misery would have been spared us both had we never have met. Clara, Clara, if you are still alive, you have much to answer for, for this unexampled cruelty."

"Thou hast again seen her, Laurence Cleveland, but still she eludes thy grasp, and will continue to do so, until the fitting time shall arrive to reveal herself, and to confront thee with Blanche Lester to thy shame and confusion. Forsooth, thou must now feel very happy on the celebration of thy infant's christening. Ha! ha! ha!"

"Mocking fiend in human form!"—for it was old Madela who had spoken—"are you here again, to blast me with your odious presence?"

"Oh, then thou dost feel my power, Laurence Cleveland," said the old beldame. "'Tis well—'tis well; but you shall feel it more yet, and quail like a dastard knave beneath it."

"Woman, woman," said Sir Laurence, in accents of agony and supplication; "why do you thus delight to torture me? If I have indeed injured you, I am willing, most willing to make you all the atonement in my power."

"Atonement!" repeated the gipsy, in a fierce voice; "the reptile, Laurence Cleveland, make atonement, and to me! Mark me, the only atonement thou couldst make to me would be upon the gallows, to which it will be my special care to bring thee. But in the meantime it is rare food for me to see thee suffer, and to know that thy peace of mind is ruined for ever. Dost thou now despise the old gipsy woman, Madela? Wilt thou seek to place her and her tribe in prison? Oh, thou art most brave, doubtless. Ha! ha! ha!"

" Must I thus be mocked at—reviled? Woman, if you have no pity for me, at least have some compassion for my wife."

" Thy wife!" repeated Madela, with a look of the most diabolical malice ; " 'tis false! She whom thou hast basely deceived, and whom thou callest thy wife, is no more than thy mistress. Thou hast sunk her to the level of the most degraded being that crawls the earth, and the pretended love thou bearest towards her is nothing more than a base mockery and a cheat. How thinkest thou she will look upon thee when she knows thee in thy real character ? She will loathe thee, curse thee, avoid thee as she would some hideous monster. Yes, and she will teach her child to hate thee too—that child who is destined to be a curse to thee and all connected with thee. Reflect on this, Laurence Cleveland, and be happy if thou canst."

Sir Laurence groaned with the intense agony of his feelings, and covered his face with his hands.

" My God! my God!" he cried, " is there no help for this ? Can this woman speak the truth ?"

" Speak the truth!" repeated Madela ; " darest thou doubt me, libertine ? Oh! but if thou art not yet satisfied, thou shalt have sufficient proof ere long. Madela never fails to keep her word, and so thou wilt find. I shall live to see thee loaded with ignominy, misery, and shame. I shall see thee shunned and loathed by every one. Hunted as a wolf, even as thou wouldst hunt me and my people now. Oh! that will be a rare time for me, Laurence Cleveland ; how will I exult when I see thee branded as a villain, a seducer, a murderer ; how I will laugh when I behold the drops of agony standing upon thy quivering temples. And that time will come ; mark me, I say again, that time will come."

" Cursed prophetess, away!" exclaimed Sir Laurence, worked up to a pitch of frenzy by the galling sarcasm and bitterness of the old woman's words. " I will no longer listen to you, nor place the least reliance in your malicious prognostications."

" Ha! ha! ha! affect to despise them, if thou wilt ; but they *will* be verified—to thy shame and misery they will be verified. But begone, to Blanche Lester, thy foolish, fond, confiding mistress ; she may need thine attendance. Begone, and remember my words!"

As she thus spoke, she once more grinned maliciously and triumphantly upon him, and, waving her hand in a menacing manner, she hurried from the spot, leaving him in a state of mind the reader can most readily imagine.

" Tortured on every side," he exclaimed ; " I shall go distracted. And on this day, too, on which we have all been so happy. A terrible spell is upon me, and it seems but too certain that the doom of myself and poor Blanche is sealed. How can I act?—I know not—my brain is bewildered. Oh, Blanche, Blanche, best of women and most affectionate of wives, I have murdered your peace of mind for ever ! Well do I now admit the wise determination of Mr. Lester ; and, had he been permitted to carry out his plans, though my happiness would have been destroyed for ever, and the hopes of Blanche blighted, at least her honour would have been preserved, and in the course of time she might have learned to have forgotten me, and have become the wife of some man who was deserving of her. An evil destiny has pursued us throughout, and poor Blanche has, alas! been innocently made to suffer for my guilt. Oh, God! why did you not visit your just retribution on my head alone ?"

His agony every moment became more intense, and he feared to return to the mansion ; for how could he meet poor Blanche—how could he meet his guests after what

had taken place? Could he any longer conceal from her all the particulars? And yet, how could his tongue ever reveal the dreadful truth? He could not. The words would choke him.

But the last observations of Madela, which had reference to Blanche, aroused him, and fearing that something might have happened to her during his absence, or that she would certainly feel surprised and alarmed at his disappearance, he exerted all his energies to stifle his feelings, and, with a bewildered and distracted brain, hurried on his way to the mansion.

On his arrival there he was astonished at the silence which prevailed. The sounds of mirth and revelry had ceased, and all seemed buried in profound gloom.

No. 17.

" What can be the meaning of this ?" he said; " can this be the scene of gaiety I left but a short time since ?   Surely my guests, offended at my absence, cannot have retired."

He rushed hastily into the gardens in front of the mansion, and found them entirely deserted; and now his fears increased, and he entered the hall with hurried but trembling footsteps, and found there everything in a state of confusion.   The musicians had quitted the gallery, the lights were partly extinguished ; many of the revellers were gathered together at one end of the hall.

His heart sunk within him; but he rushed up to the end of the hall, and, breaking through the crowd, he beheld Blanche in a state of insensibility, and supported in the arms of Lord Musgrove and Amanda.

" Gracious Heaven!" he exclaimed, " what is the meaning of this ?—what is the matter with my beloved Blanche ?"

Amanda placed an open note in his hand, which he eagerly gazed at, and no sooner had he beheld the characters than he turned ghastly pale ; his lips quivered, and with difficulty he faltered out,—

" Good God ! is it possible ?   Tell me, who brought this ?"

" It was placed in the hand of Lady Blanche by a grey domino, who hastily retreated on delivering it," answered Amanda.

" Ah!" he cried, " the very same.   But how long since ?"

" About ten minutes."

" Oh, horror—horror !" groaned the wretched baronet, as he again cast his eyes upon the note.   Too well did he recognise the characters ; there could be no possibility of mistaking them, and confirmation was made more doubly sure.   For a moment a mist seemed to float before his eyes, his brain swam round, and he could not distinguish a single word ; but at last he partially recovered himself, and then read the following lines :—

" Blanche Lester, beware ! fly the man to whom you have given your hand, but upon whom you have no claim as a wife.   That title belongs alone to her who writes these lines ; she, the injured, the deserted, but who is prevented by a power over which she has no control from coming forward openly to assert her just claims, and who would have saved you from the misery and ruin which have now befallen you, had she not been withheld.   Fly the wretch with whom you have unfortunately connected yourself, if you would avoid further contamination.   The real heir of Branscombe lives !   Beware !   " CLARA CLEVELAND."

" Lost, lost ! oh, horror !" exclaimed the unhappy Sir Laurence, when he had perused these fatal lines, and unable any longer to support the overwhelming force of his feelings, he sank down in the same insensible state as that of poor Blanche.

CHAPTER XIII.

THE EFFECTS OF THE FATAL LETTER.—THE DANGEROUS ILLNESS OF BLANCHE.— THE MEETING BETWEEN HER AND SIR LAURENCE.—THE APPEARANCE OF OLD MADELA AGAIN.

THE confusion and alarm which now prevailed among the numerous persons who yet remained in the Hall, may be imagined, and all of them were wrapt in mystery as to the exact cause, for no one had seen the letter but Amanda; however, that the contents were something very serious and alarming, they were certain.

Sir Laurence and Blanche were both conveyed to their chambers with all possible despatch, and medical assistance was quickly procured. The company looked amazed at each other, and all of them, except Lord and Lady Musgrove, and Sir William Gladhill, having retired, the Hall was quite deserted, the lights extinguished, and silence and gloom succeeded to the splendour and festivity that had lately prevailed. No one could have believed it was the same place, so great was the change that only a few short minutes had wrought.

Sir Laurence was the first that was restored to sensibility; but what maddening thoughts distracted his brain. The letter proved beyond a doubt in his mind that Clara was indeed living, for the handwriting was most unquestionably her's, and how could the poor, ruined, dishonoured Blanche view him but with horror and detestation as a villain of the blackest dye? He could never attempt again to deceive her, and yet, to acknowledge the truth, to make her acquainted with all the horrors of her situation; to leave her, to abandon her, oh, that he felt was impossible. If she indeed believed in the truth of the letter, and should load him with reproaches, with hatred, then indeed would death be a mercy to him, for he should have nothing left to wish to live for.

But he could not believe that she would credit the truth of the statement which the epistle contained, when she came to reflect on it maturely, and fain would he even now have persuaded himself that it was a forgery, but the handwriting so closely corresponded with that of Clara, that he could not; besides, he must, indeed, have been sceptical, after what he had seen and heard if he could have done so.

Then again, was he, after all, so much to blame, after having every reason to suppose that Clara was dead, in having done what he had? No man would sooner have revolted from the perpetration of such an offence than himself, had he been aware that his first wife was alive. He had erred through a fatal error, and, however dreadful the consequences that might ensue, he was certainly, he thought, more to be pitied than blamed.

Such was the manner in which Sir Laurence argued with himself; but it was quite untenable, for, previous to his receiving her hand, he ought in honour to have candidly confessed his former circumstances to Blanche, and then left it to her judgment and discretion, whether she would accept or reject him. Besides, his behaviour to the unfortunate Clara and her cousin had been anything but honourable, as will be explained at a subsequent period; and in regard to the death of Clara, he had only heard of it through the voice of rumour, and had never taken much pains to inquire into the truth or falsehood of it.

However, he determined still to endeavour to persuade Blanche, and tried to believe so himself, that it was all a base fabrication of the gipsies, and that the letter was a forgery.

"I cannot, dare not meet her hatred," he ejaculated; "I can never make up my mind to leave her, so fondly as I love her, and so ardently as I have every reason to believe her affections are fixed upon me. Oh, merciful Heaven, grant, for her sake, that this may all be false, and that the legality of our marriage may not be disputed; but, alas! when I think of that powerful resemblance, my heart sinks within me, and I feel the dreadful certainty but too apparent."

"A RIGHTFUL HEIR TO THE ESTATES OF BRANSCOMBE STILL LIVES."

That line also greatly tortured the mind of Sir Laurence, and filled his bosom with various vague conjectures and apprehensions.

Such were the agonizing thoughts that hurriedly flashed across the brain of the baronet, as he bent his way to the chamber of Blanche. But how he shuddered to meet her, and knew not what answer he should make to her searching inquiries.

He found her in a most pitiable condition, and raving wildly. He approached the bed with a faltering step and took her hand, but she drew it from him quickly, stared vacantly upon him, and did not seem to know him. He sobbed heavily at the fatal change which so short a time had made in her appearance, and turned away to conceal his emotion. But an hour or two since, she was all gaiety, animation, and hope. She had moved the perfect queen among all the beautiful damsels that had thronged the festive scene; now the roses had fled her cheeks, and had given place to a ghastly paleness like that of a corpse. Her eyes, which had shone with such brilliancy and sensibility, were now wild and vacant; and it seemed, indeed, as if a dozen years of care and sorrow had passed over her head in that short space of time.

The affectionate Amanda was in attendance upon her, and she looked at her brother with an expression of searching inquiry and suspicion, which penetrated to his heart, and made him feel abashed, ashamed, and confused. He saw that she entertained the strongest prejudices against him, after the letter which she had no doubt perused, and he knew not in what manner he should be able to remove them; but it was necessary that he should do so, for on her intercession in a great measure depended the reconciliation between himself and Blanche.

"Dearest Blanche," he said at length, in a voice of melancholy affection, and once more taking her hand and pressing it vehemently to his lips; "oh, do you not know me?"

"Who calls me dear Blanche?" she said, with a vacant stare; "who dares to mock me with such words as those? There was one who used to call me so, and to whom I plighted my faith at the altar; but he must no more call me by such endearing titles; he does not belong to me—another claims him; and yet, oh, God! I am the mother of his child!"

"God help her!" sobbed the distracted Sir Laurence; "this dreadful shock has stolen away her reason. But it is all false! That letter is a forgery—I am convinced of it; and the whole proceeds only from the deadly malice and revenge of those heartless miscreants, the gipsies."

"Alas! Laurence," said Amanda, aside to him, "I fear there is but too much truth in that fatal epistle, and I shudder with horror at the consequences. God grant that you may indeed be able to prove the falsehood of this statement, for on that the happiness or misery, the honour or disgrace of yourself and poor Blanche depend."

"Fear not, my dearest Amanda," whispered Sir Laurence; "hopeless and suspicious as all at present appears, I do not despair of being able to prove everything to our satisfaction ere long. I should go mad were circumstances to turn out contrary to my hopes."

Amanda looked at her brother with an expression of pity, and fervently responded to his wishes.

"But my poor Blanche—my unfortunate wife!" sighed Sir Laurence, gazing at the unfortunate sufferer with an expression of the most unspeakable agony.

Blanche started at the word, and looked more wildly around her than before, as she exclaimed,—

"Wife! wife!—no, it is all a mockery; I am not a wife, although I was united at the altar. But I am a mother! Yes, yes; but that will make me the reproach of all. The virtuous will shun me; I dare no more enter the light of day, for the finger of scorn will be pointed at me, and opprobrium will follow me wherever I go. Oh, God! oh, God!"

She now commenced raving in the most frightful manner, and the scene was enough to move the most insensible heart. What must have been the effect it had upon that of the wretched Sir Laurence? He beat his breast, and groaned with insupportable anguish.

The physician who was in attendance upon Blanche, now politely insisted that Sir Laurence should leave the chamber, as the sight of him, and the emotion he was likely to exhibit, were almost certain to increase her malady.

"I trust, Sir Laurence," he added, "that these symptoms will not continue long; but there must be the utmost care used, or your lady's reason may be destroyed; so severe is the shock that her system has received."

"Oh, Heaven, avert so terrible a calamity!" exclaimed the baronet. "Pay every attention to her, I pray you, my dear sir, and my lasting—my deepest gratitude shall be yours."

"You may depend upon it I will do my best, Sir Laurence," answered the physician. "But I beseech you to retire, and to seek your couch, for you yourself need repose, and may become seriously ill if you do not obtain it."

"Think you, doctor, that I can sleep with all this dreadful weight of care upon my mind?"

"But you must try, my dear sir."

"I will—I will; but I fear, alas! that it will be to no purpose. Amanda, will you remain with my poor Blanche?"

"Oh, yes," answered Amanda; "I will not leave her for a moment; and God grant that before long a happy change may take place."

Sir Laurence fixed one agonized look upon the pale countenance of Blanche, and then once more slowly retired from the room, and entered his own chamber, where he threw himself into a chair, and, burying his face in his hands, he for some time gave himself up entirely to the agony of his thoughts. He then arose and traversed the room with the most agitated steps. To retire to bed he could not think of doing, for how could he hope to sleep while his beloved Blanche was in that alarming and melancholy condition?

"It is even more horrible than my worst surmises anticipated," he observed; "impressed with the terrible belief that the contents of the letter are true, it has taken effect upon her reason, which I fear will never more be restored to her, and then indeed will my misery be complete. And, if she recovers her senses, I fear that nothing will persuade her of the falsehood. With what horror will she then look upon me, and what can I say to convince her of my innocence. I rack my brain in vain. She will fly from me with disgust and abhorrence, and I shall be left to misery and despair; for without my beloved Blanche, what is there in life that can impart to me the smallest consolation? And can I with honour remain with her? Should I continue to live with her until I am satisfied that none other has a claim upon my hand? Reason, virtue, tell me I should not; but yet to separate from her would be worse than death."

Thus did the wretched Sir Laurence continue to soliloquize during the night, and never once thought of retiring to rest, although he was worn out with fatigue, both from anxiety of mind, and the exertion he had undergone during the festivities.

Again and again he perused the letter, and, the oftener he did so, the more he was induced to come to the terrible conclusion that it was indeed the handwriting of Clara, and that, consequently, she must still be in existence, and that it was herself that he had so frequently seen, but who had never but upon one occasion addressed him, and then the tones of her voice had struck so forcibly to his heart, that he had never been able to get rid of the impression since.

In fact, everything was so strongly in favour of the assertions of Madela and Harold, that Sir Laurence could scarcely fail to be convinced, and his conscience bitterly smote him for the irretrievable misery and disgrace into which he had plunged her to whom he was sincerely attached.

In the midst of all these torturing reflections, another thought crossed his mind, which he in vain attempted to reject. Should Clara be really living, of which he could now entertain but very little doubt, and he could get her in his power, he might prevent the discovery being made which he so much dreaded. He would have shuddered at the bare idea of doing her any personal harm, otherwise than confining her ; nay, more, he would afford her every indulgence that he could compatible with his own safety, and thus the gipsies would be foiled in their designs, and he might set detection at defiance.

So much did he dread a separation from Blanche, that he never once thought of the absolute villany of such a course, but made up his mind to put it into effect at the first opportunity ; but how that was to be accomplished, he could not at present entertain the least conjecture.

Poor Blanche passed a dreadful night, raving in the most delirious manner incessantly, and the physician entertained the utmost doubts of her ultimate recovery. Amanda was overwhelmed with grief, both on account of her and her brother, of whose conduct she now began to encourage the greatest fears, and she looked forward to the troubles that were in store for them with the most gloomy apprehensions. In spite of all he had said to the contrary, she could not doubt the evidence of her own reason, and she therefore felt all but satisfied, from the extraordinary emotion he had displayed on perusing it, that the letter was no forgery, and, if such was the fact, what a dreadful situation was poor Blanche placed in. She felt for her as keenly as if she had been her own sister, and for ever must she lament the cruel destruction of one whose innumerable virtues entitled her to, and had hitherto gained her, the esteem of every one who knew her. She resolved to question Sir Laurence most narrowly upon the painful subject on the first opportunity which presented itself, and then she should be in a better condition to remonstrate with him, and to advise him how to act. She could not for a moment think him so base as to have married Blanche with the knowledge of the existence of his first wife, but that he erred, through some report of her death, but into which he had not taken sufficient trouble to inquire. But what misery had he caused by that culpable negligence, and which reflected so little credit on his respect for common decency, whatever might have been the faults of the unfortunate Clara.

When Sir Laurence entered the chamber of Blanche, in the morning, his haggard appearance plainly showed that he had not slept, and that the agony he had been enduring was most excruciating, and Amanda felt the deepest sympathy for his sufferings, as well as those of Blanche.

When he ascertained that Blanche was no better, and that the doctor had expressed the greatest apprehensions that she would not recover, Sir Laurence became distracted, and beat his breast, and exhibited altogether such violent grief, that the physician was compelled to remonstrate with him, and to beg of him to endeavour to calm his feelings, lest he should disturb Blanche, who was now lying in a state of complete apathy, and scarcely gave any signs of life.

Sir Laurence endeavoured to do as he desired, but it was an arduous struggle, and he could not stifle the heavy sobs that escaped his bosom, as he hung over the couch of the unhappy, but now unconscious sufferer, and fancied that he saw the cold hand of death already upon her.

"But for me," he sighed, "she might still have been well and happy. Oh, would that Providence had never introduced us to each other. My sweet, my gentle Blanche, oh, little did you merit such a cruel fate as this."

He would have kissed her pale lips, but the doctor prevented him, and would not allow her on any account to be in the least disturbed. But nothing could prevail on him to leave the chamber for several hours, and then it was only on the persuasion of Amanda, who accompanied him to his apartment.

Sir Laurence shrank from her gaze, for he saw that she viewed him with suspicion, and he trembled at the idea of the searching inquiries which he imagined she would put to him.

Amanda remained silent for a few minutes and gazed with mingled feelings of compassion and anxiety upon him, and then said,—

"Alas, my dear brother, what a terrible calamity is this, and what may not be the fatal consequences, should your first unfortunate wife be still alive."

"But you do not believe it, Amanda?"

"I would fain not, Laurence," answered his sister, "both for your sake, poor Blanche's sake, and your little innocent offspring."

"You torture me, sister," said Laurence. "Can you think me such a villain as to deceive my beloved, my adored Blanche, and to marry her with a knowledge of Clara being in existence?"

"Oh, no, dear Laurence; Heaven forbid that I should entertain such an opinion of you. I am convinced that you believed Clara to be no more; although I must say that you were much to blame in not taking more pains to ascertain that fact before you ventured to enter into fresh engagements. But that letter, Laurence?"

"I repeat it is a forgery—a base forgery."

"Why were you then so violently agitated on perusing it?" inquired Amanda, fixing upon him a keen, penetrating look.

Sir Laurence hesitated for a second or two, and he felt somewhat confused; but he soon recovered himself and said,—

"The situation of Blanche, and the boldness of the writer of that letter, I confess, Amanda, shocked, and overcome me; but it was not from any conviction that it was genuine."

"Was you not struck with the handwriting, Laurence?" asked his sister.

The baronet again felt considerable confusion, but he soon regained his composure and replied,—

"The handwriting certainly bears a great resemblance to that of Clara; but I am satisfied that the letter was not, and could not be written by her, and that consequently it is a forgery."

" God grant that you may not deceive yourself, my dear brother; but, alas! taking all the circumstances into consideration, I cannot help still entertaining my doubts."

" Amanda, have you no pity for the anguish of mind you must be aware I am enduring, at the mournful, and apparently hopeless, condition of her I hold most dear upon earth, but that you must still torture me with those painful doubts and questions ?"

" Not for the world would I add to your anguish, my brother," returned Amanda: " but, on the contrary, no one can feel more sincere commiseration for you than I do; but if you entertain any doubts of the legality of your marriage with Blanche, it is a duty you owe to her, as well as to society, to acknowledge them, and although it is too late now to recall the past, it is your bounden duty to avoid the further misery of the future."

" And you would have me separate from Blanche ?"

" You cannot continue to remain with her, unless you have sufficient proof that you can do so with honour."

" Part from my beloved Blanche !" cried Sir Laurence, vehemently. " By Heaven, never! It is a base conspiracy got up to ruin me—it is a diabolical invention of my mortal enemies, the gipsies. But Blanche, should she ever recover her reason, will see through the infamous plot. She will not believe it; I know her gentle, confiding nature too well to encourage such a thought for a moment."

" Well, my brother," observed Amanda, " God grant that the dreadful mystery may shortly be unravelled, and that it may be to the entire satisfaction of all those who are most seriously interested. But Blanche will not, and has no right to be satisfied, without you give her a full and candid explanation of all the circumstances connected with you and your first wife."

" That can never be, Amanda," returned her brother. " I have admitted that I have erred, but the secrets of my past life must be buried in oblivion."

" A man should have no secrets from his wife, Laurence."

" Why should I seek to impart unnecessary anguish to the bosom of Blanche, by revealing mine ?" demanded Sir Laurence. " But, for Heaven's sake, do not torture me any more by such questions. My brain is distracted at the deplorable situation of my poor Blanche; and, should she indeed never again recover, there will be no hope for me but in the grave. I must again visit her, and learn from the doctor whether there is any hope."

" No, Laurence," returned Amanda; " let me beg that you will remain where you are, and I will myself return to the chamber of the poor sufferer. I need not assure you that all that humanity and skill can suggest will be done for her; but, even if her reason is restored, she cannot at present be in a fit state to see you."

Sir Laurence reluctantly yielded to his sister's advice, and Amanda quitted the room, far from satisfied with the interview she had had with her brother. She could see plainly enough that he was not satisfied in what he asserted with so much confidence, and that it was only the dread he had of a separation from the unfortunate Blanche which prevented him from acknowledging it, and she could not contemplate the future without feelings of the most unqualified horror. But Blanche, she feared, would never recover from the shock she had received, and most melancholy was it to contemplate the fate of one so young, so virtuous, and so lovely.

Sir Laurence, too, felt that he had acted the part of the hypocrite in the interview with his sister, and he could not but acknowledge the truth and force of the arguments

she had used on that occasion.   He had asserted many things that he did not sincerely believe, and more especially with respect to the fatal letter, which he was compelled to acknowledge to himself was too much like the handwriting of Clara to be
an imitation, and was satisfactory proof of her being in existence.   Besides, had he
not himself seen her—and even within a few minutes of when she placed the letter in
the hand of Blanche?   Oh, yes; it was all too evident for him any longer to doubt,
and he acknowledged, at once, the triumph of the gipsies, and his own fatal error.

But there was another fact which now tormented his mind.   By his marriage with
Blanche he had rendered himself amenable to the laws; and thus he was entirely at
the mercy of the gipsies, and was not a moment safe.   This rendered him the more
anxious to get Clara in his power, and he determined to do so, though at present his

mind was too much agitated to allow him to devise the means of accomplishing it. Clara secured, most of his fears would be at an end, for the gipsies would have no proof of the truth of their assertions, and would, consequently, be defeated.

Blanche continued in much the same condition during the whole of that day; no favourable change took place, and the fears of the physician were still unabated. She had her senses at intervals, but it was only for a very brief period, and then she would weep and sob bitterly, and neither Amanda nor the doctor could obtain any observation from her. She would speedily, however, relapse into her wild fits of delirium, and then it was quite awful to hear her.

Amanda, although she was much fatigued from the number of hours that had elapsed since she had been in bed, continued unremitting in her attentions upon her, and watched her with the utmost anxiety and pity. Her sad wanderings were indeed most melancholy to listen to, and touched the compassionate and sensitive Amanda to the heart. She feared that she would never recover; and, if she did, would not her happiness be destroyed entirely, believing, as she undoubtedly would, in the truth of the statement of the fatal letter? Sir Laurence she well knew would insist, as he had done with her, in the falsehood of the same; but would he be able to convince Blanche? Must not the circumstance have destroyed all the confidence she had reposed in him, and she would look upon him with horror and abhorrence as the destroyer of her hopes.

And how fallen, how degraded would poor Blanche be in her own estimation, Amanda reflected. Surely the dreadful trial would be more than she could sustain with any degree of fortitude, the more especially as Sir Laurence, refusing to enter into an explanation, which was undoubtedly her due, would naturally cause her to believe that the contents of the letter were too true, and that he felt confident of the same, although he might endeavour to persuade her to the contrary. Amanda herself entertained the worst apprehensions and surmises on the subject, in consequence of the extraordinary emotion her brother had betrayed on beholding the letter, and the evasive answers he had given to the interrogatories she had recently put to him. She saw no other prospect than that of misery before them, and deeply did she lament that they had ever met.

Blanche underwent very little change during the day, but towards night her wild and delirious wanderings abated, and she became more calm; but still her mind remained in a disordered state, and the physician, although he now expressed strong hopes of her ultimate recovery, strictly desired that she should be kept perfectly quiet, and that every precaution should be used to prevent her from suffering the least excitement, and for that reason he enjoined Sir Laurence not to enter her presence until she was in a better condition to support the interview, which, under the circumstances, was sure to be a painful one.

The baronet could scarcely endure this restriction with any degree of patience, notwithstanding he could not help experiencing a sensation of dread in meeting the eye of Blanche, and knew not how he should be able to reply to the searching interrogatories she would be sure to put to him. It was utterly in vain that he endeavoured to persuade himself that the letter was a forgery, the handwriting too closely resembled that of Clara to be mistaken; and then the likeness which the female whom he had so frequently seen, bore to that unfortunate woman, carried with it conviction to his agonized heart. What a dreadful offence had he been led to commit, an offence that nothing could remedy, and which was rendered doubly torturing from the certainty that he could never find courage sufficient to acknowledge to Blanche the real extent of his fears, and the inevitable misery into which he had plunged her, and that he must live in constant dread of the gipsies fulfilling their threats, and, by producing Clara, bring both him and Blanche to complete destruction.

"And am I, indeed, a bigamist!" he soliloquized; "and as such amenable to the laws of my country, while I have plunged one of the most lovely and amiable of nature's works into the lowest depths of degradation! My God! the thought is enough to drive me to madness. Oh, Clara, if you are indeed still living, what a terrible, what a monstrous revenge you have had. Had you revealed yourself before my nuptials could have taken place, great as the trial would have been to me and Blanche to have had our hopes thus unexpectedly blighted, and to be compelled to separate, I could have forgiven you; but now, alas! what prospect is there for us both but that of utter ruin and misery?"

He beat his breast, and paced the room with disordered steps, in the extreme and almost insupportable anguish of these thoughts, and it was some time before he could acquire even the least semblance of tranquillity.

His mind was so bewildered that he was totally incapable of forming any satisfactory idea, which he did not almost immediately reject as soon as it had suggested itself to him. But still he entertained the hope of being able to get Clara in his power, and thus prevent that discovery from taking place which he had so much reason to apprehend. Could he but accomplish that, the designs of the gipsies would be frustrated, and he might set their threats at defiance; but that was a task more easily conceived than executed, and, as yet, Sir Laurence could not form even the most remote conjecture as to in what manner to set about it. That Clara, if she was living, was in the power of the gipsies, he could entertain no doubt; and to remove her from them in secrecy, and to get her into some place of security, was what he was at present at a loss to know how to accomplish, and before he could have an opportunity of putting his designs into effect, all the evils he apprehended might take place, and his misery and shame be rendered complete.

Thus was Sir Laurence harassed with conflicting thoughts, and, whichever way he directed his ideas, he could not find the least cause for consolation. The interview he had had with Amanda had greatly disturbed his mind; for the searching questions she put to him, and the observations she had made use of, convinced him that she placed too much reliance in the truth of the statement contained in the letter, and that she looked upon him with suspicion, notwithstanding the solemn asseverations he had made, and with which his conscience now severely smote him, for he could not have believed that he could ever have acted such a part of hypocrisy. He well knew the sincere affection which his sister felt towards him, and he therefore reproached himself for having deceived her in the manner he had done. But how could he venture to confide even to her the terrible thoughts and apprehensions which occupied his mind? To do so, he must reveal all his past errors, and he shrank with repugnance from such a task. How great was the anxiety he experienced during the night, for the doctor would not permit him on any account to visit the chamber of Blanche for the present, fearful of her experiencing the least excitement, and which would, in all probability, be attended with the most serious consequences; but it afforded him considerable relief to understand from him that a favourable change had taken place, and that, if she did not suffer any relapse, her speedy recovery might be anticipated. But, alas! could anything banish from her mind the painful impression which the latter had made! Would she not look upon him with dread and suspicion? And how could he reply to the penetrating questions she would be sure to put to him so as to satisfy her, or without betraying his own thoughts upon the subject? Could he deceive her who had ever placed such affectionate confidence in him; and yet to suffer her to remain in ignorance of her real situation would be a mercy to her. Should she indeed become convinced of the fatal truth, she could never survive so terrible a blow; such a perfect annihilation of all her hopes. Shame and horror would overwhelm her, and madness must then indeed seize for ever upon her brain. And he must separate from her; he must leave that lovely being who was more valuable to him than his own existence, but who would then look upon him with horror and abhorrence. This thought alone was sufficient to drive him to distraction, and it was some considerable time before he could at all tranquillize his feelings.

In the meantime, Amanda continued to watch in the chamber of Blanche, and she forgot her own fatigue in the anxiety she felt for the recovery of the sufferer. Blanche had, fortunately, obtained two or three hours' most refreshing sleep, and when she awoke again, the change was most visible. Her mind no longer wandered, and recognising Amanda, she extended her hand towards her, while her eyes filled with tears.

Amanda fervently grasped her hand, and pressed it to her bosom.

"Dear Blanche," she ejaculated, "you are better now; I see you are, and Heaven be thanked for it."

"Better!" repeated Blanche, passing her hand over her still aching temples, as if to collect her thoughts. "Oh! yes, I am better now. But tell me what is the meaning of all this? Have I experienced only some frightful dream? or is it, indeed, true that I am ruined—degraded—the partner of a man upon whose hand I have no legal claim? Oh, God! that dreadful letter! I remember it all now, and I shall go mad at the thought."

"Pray, my dear Blanche," expostulated Amanda, "do not give way to these dreadful ideas, but endeavour to be calm, and to look forward to the future with hope."

"Hope!" cried Blanche. "Oh! no, it cannot be; that fatal letter has annihilated all the hopes I had formed, and plunged me into terror and despair. Sir Laurence, to whom I plighted my vows at the altar—he, the father of my child, to be the husband of another! Oh, Heaven! what will become of me, degraded—lost as I am? I must no longer remain under his roof; henceforth, I must become a wretched outcast, hunted, calumniated, despised by all. Oh! my poor father, had I attended to your advice, this dreadful fate would have been spared me. Terribly, indeed, am I punished for my disobedience to your solemn injunctions."

"Nay, Blanche, banish such thoughts from your mind. My brother declares the letter to be a forgery, and, believe me, it is all a scheme of the gipsies to gratify their feelings of revenge."

"Say you so, dear Amanda?" said Blanche, eagerly, and her countenance, for a moment, brightening up. "Oh! would to Heaven that you could prove your words; what a terrible weight would it remove from my breast. But that female form which I have more than once beheld—oh! who can it be? My heart misgives me. Those features, so lovely and so sad; they have made an impression upon my heart that nothing can ever eradicate. It was the same mysterious being that delivered to me the letter, and, when I think of her, and the strange expression of her countenance, a shuddering sensation of terror runs through my veins, which I find it impossible to conquer. Alas! alas! should it, indeed, be proved that the first wife of Laurence is still in existence, what will become of me? How am I again to venture to show my face? Will not the finger of scorn and opprobrium be pointed at me, whichever way I turn? And my poor innocent babe, too—oh! would to Heaven she had never been born."

Poor Blanche sobbed bitterly, as she gave utterance to these melancholy observations, and Amanda, who feared that there was too much reason for the terrible apprehensions she entertained, knew not what argument to advance to console her, and she anticipated the future with the utmost dread, which the remarks of her brother at their recent interview were not at all calculated to dissipate.

"My dear Blanche," she said, at length, "I own that this adventure is calculated to raise the worst fears and surmises in your breast; but put your trust in the Most High, and do not doubt but that everything will, ere long, be explained to your satisfaction. There cannot be any truth in the statement of the letter, or why do not the gipsies immediately put their threats into execution; and why does not Clara, at once, come forward and advance her claims? Indeed, it seems evident that it is all a wicked design of those wandering wretches to annoy and distract you both, and to gratify those malignant feelings they have, what reason I know not, engendered towards my brother. Clara must be no more; or she would, long ere this, have revealed herself, and not have suffered Sir Laurence to give his hand to another."

"Fain would I think so, Amanda," said Blanche; "but, in spite of all my efforts to the contrary, the most dreadful apprehensions will continually haunt my imagination; and shall I continue to remain with Sir Laurence in this awful state of uncertainty?"

"Could you leave him? could you abandon him, Blanche?"

"It would break my heart to do so; but better that I should meet death—anything, rather than continue to sin. Oh, Laurence, Laurence, it would have been better for us both had we never known each other."

She wrung her hands in the agony of her despair, and again wept and sobbed bitterly. The anguish of mind which Amanda was enduring was almost equal to her own, for she saw too well the utter uselessness of endeavouring to inspire Blanche with hopes which might never be realised, and which she was herself far from encouraging. It was indeed a most delicate subject to have to deal with, and Amanda was completely bewildered, and was at a loss for words to impart comfort to her unfortunate friend.

A silence of some minutes ensued, which neither of them seemed inclined to interrupt, and during which the most racking thoughts crowded upon the brain of Blanche, and kept her in a state of the most insupportable anguish. Fain would she have believed that the letter was a forgery, and had only been written for the purpose of creating her alarm and destroying the peace of her and Sir Laurence; but she could not, and the more she reflected, the more bewildered and distracted she became. She now saw how necessary it had been for her to have demanded every explanation of the baronet concerning his first marriage, previous to her consenting to become his wife, and by which all the misery she now endured, and that which seemed likely to be in store for her, might have been avoided; and deeply she lamented that she had not persevered in such a course, and upon which the future happiness of herself and

Sir Laurence, and all who were connected with them, depended.   But it was too late to repent now, and she had therefore nothing to do but to endeavour to resign herself to her fate, whatever it might be.

The little Emmeline had been brought to her by her desire, and as she pressed the innocent infant to her bosom with maternal fondness, she wept tears of sorrow and affection upon its beauteous face.

" My sweet babe," she ejaculated, " surely Heaven can never have destined you for a life of sorrow and misfortune, or it would be a mercy if it were to take you at once to itself.   I could better resign you at once, than to see you afterwards buffetted about at the mercy of the cruel world ; to behold the finger of scorn and calumny pointed at you, which would certainly be the case, should this dreadful statement prove to be correct.   Oh, God ! hear my prayers, and avert so awful—so terrible a calamity."

" And He will, Blanche," remarked Amanda, with renewed energy and confidence ; " He will never permit the innocent to suffer so cruel a fate as that you apprehend for yourself and your child.   Place your whole reliance on the goodness of the Supreme, and depend upon it He will not forsake you.   But come, my dear sister, stifle these agonising thoughts, and the designs of your enemies will be defeated, and all will yet be well."

" I know the affectionate regard you bear towards me, dear Amanda," said Blanche, " and will endeavour to follow your advice ; but, alas ! it is a task not easy of accomplishment."

" True, it is a most difficult one, Blanche ; but persevere, notwithstanding, and depend upon it you will succeed.   Try and calm your feelings, which this adventure has so much excited, and to seek that rest which is so necessary to you after what you have suffered."

" Alas ! Amanda," replied Blanche, " my mind is too much agitated to suffer me to find rest.   But where is Laurence ?   Why is he not here ?   Surely he cannot treat this painful event and my illness with indifference ?"

" Oh, no, Blanche ; you would do my poor brother the greatest injustice by encouraging such an idea.   His anguish has been, and is now, most intense ; and most anxious has he been to be with you, and to offer you all the consolation in his power ; but he has been prohibited by the doctor from doing so, for fear that the excitement it would cause you in your present delicate state of health might be attended with the most dangerous consequences.   But exert yourself to the utmost to regain your fortitude, and in the morning you shall behold him again, and Heaven grant that the interview may prove favourable to your speedy recovery."

" Oh, Laurence," sighed Blanche, " and may I indeed still call you husband, and with the blissful certainty that there is no other being who has a prior claim ?   May I still look with honour and affection upon the father of my child, and with the assurance that she will never find the blush of shame mounting in her cheek when she recalls his name to her memory ?   God grant that this may be the case, and, in spite of all the troubles I have hitherto endured, my happiness will be then complete."

" Oh, yes, Blanche," returned Amanda, who felt her own hopes now revive ; " you may indeed do so.   Something convinces me that all will shortly be explained to our mutual satisfaction, and that the diabolical designs of the wandering tribe will be frustrated, and the falsehood of their assertions proved beyond dispute."

"I will try to think so, Amanda, and may the Almighty grant that I may not be disappointed."

After some further conversation, Blanche gradually became more tranquil than could very well have been expected, and at length fell off into a calm sleep, which Amanda was very glad to see, as she was certain that it would tend in a great measure to advance her recovery.

Amanda then left her in the care of a female servant, and hastened to the apartment in which her brother was seated, and who hastily arose on her entrance, and eagerly inquired after Blanche. Amanda informed him, and we need not say what a relief it was to his mind to hear that all danger was past, and that her senses were restored to her.

"Dear Blanche," he exclaimed, "let me immediately hasten to you, and at your feet pour forth my gratitude to Heaven."

"Hold, Laurence," said his sister; "you must not be too hasty, or the meeting may be attended with the most painful results. Blanche, as I have before told you, now sleeps, and by the morning will probably be greatly refreshed, and in a condition to meet you. Till then you must, therefore, wait with patience."

Sir Laurence nodded assent, and after a short time passed in conversation, Amanda left him, and retired to her chamber to snatch a few hours' repose, of which, after the fatigue she had undergone, she stood so much in need.

The baronet, however, notwithstanding the pleasure it afforded him to hear the favourable change which had taken place in his beloved Blanche, passed a restless night, and looked forward to the following morning with the greatest anxiety. How would poor Blanche receive him? Would she believe in the statement of the letter, and in consequence recoil from him with shame and horror; or would his arguments and asseverations succeed in convincing her that it was all a base invention of the gipsies, and that the letter itself was a forgery?

We have before mentioned the anguish of mind, and the numerous conflicting thoughts and apprehensions which Sir Laurence had been enduring ever since the alarming event, and the deplorable condition of his wife; and it would, therefore only be a waste of time to describe very minutely the meeting that took place between them. Suffice it to say that it was one of the most affecting and interesting nature, and that it was some time ere either of them could gain sufficient composure to talk calmly.

It was a painful task for the baronet, and his conscience could not help accusing him with duplicity; and his mind entertained the greatest dread of what the future consequences might be to them both. Unsupported by truth, reason, or sincerity, his arguments were necessarily weak; but the powerful affection which Blanche bore towards him, and the still unlimited confidence she placed in his truth and honour, prevailed over everything else, and she threw herself sobbing upon his bosom, and fervently implored the Almighty to protect them from the evidently deadly malice of their enemies, and to frustrate any base designs they might have in contemplation to destroy their happiness.

Poor Blanche, so great was the love she bore the father of her child, that she would not cause him a single pang by demanding from him that candid explanation of his past life which was so justly her due; and Sir Laurence was thus saved that trial he so much dreaded, and from which he must have shrunk with the greatest repugnance and shame.

But although he had succeeded in effecting a reconciliation with his wife, and in quieting her doubts and suspicions, could Sir Laurence be really happy? Oh! no; he bitterly reproached himself with the part he was acting, and, notwithstanding all his efforts to the contrary, lived in constant dread of exposure, and of the shame and misery that would be brought upon himself and Blanche in consequence.

The gipsies, it was evident, were determined to have a terrible revenge, and he had too much reason to fear that they had the power to carry their threats into execution. In vain he tried to persuade himself that the female he had so frequently seen was an impostor; the likeness she bore to Clara was too great to be mistaken, and therefore had he every reason to apprehend the worst, unless he could by some means get her into his power, and thus prevent her from coming forward. But would that at all alter his position? No; his conscience would still reproach him for his cruel deceit towards one of the most virtuous, affectionate, and confiding of women, and of the greatest injustice towards the unfortunate Clara, although, if she was, indeed, really living, she had taken the most terrible means of gratifying her revenge against him and one who had never injured her. If he had really been guilty of the great offence, he had committed it in ignorance, and Clara might have prevented it all by revealing herself in time, and thus have saved an innocent woman from irremediable misery and shame.

Such were the agonising thoughts which for some time tortured the bosom of Sir Laurence Cleveland, and confused and bewildered him in such a manner that he was unable to form any idea what to do for the best. He trembled to meet the eye of Blanche, and yet he was utterly miserable when out of her presence, and left entirely to the anguish of his own thoughts. Her fond endearments, and the generous confidence she placed in him, seldom or never alluding to the late event, strengthened his self-reproaches and remorse, for he felt that he was unworthy of them, and that he was acting the part of a hypocrite and villain towards her. And yet how sincere and ardent was the love he bore towards her; how willingly would he have laid down his own life could he be certain that by doing so he would secure the future happiness of herself and their lovely and innocent offspring!

But there was another portion of the letter which greatly perplexed and tortured him; it was that part in which the writer declared that the real heir to the house of Cleveland lived. When Clara disappeared from him she was far advanced in pregnancy; but what if that child had been born alive, and was still in existence? He could not believe that he was its parent, after what he suspected had taken place, and of which he supposed himself to have had the most unquestionable proof; and, therefore, no law could establish its right to the title that was sought to be claimed for it.

"It is all in keeping with the dark designs of my enemies," he said, "and only intended to add to my torture, and to increase my apprehensions. But I will learn to treat it with contempt. And, after all, should she to whom I formerly, unfortunately, gave my hand, still live, from the number of years that have elapsed without my hearing anything of her, but, from the reports which were current, I having a right to suppose her no more, she can have no possible claim on me. Under these circumstances the law must exonerate me from all blame, if even she had not previously forfeited all right to the title of my wife by her infidelity. I will banish from my mind all fears and doubts, and learn to think of her only with pity and contempt."

But it was in vain that he tried to do so; he could not stifle the recollection of his own guilty conduct, nor forget that he had been the originator of all the misfortunes and faults of Clara, and the destroyer not only of her prospects and happiness, but likewise the seducer of her beauteous and once virtuous cousin. It is a sad story of youthful indiscretion and crime, which will be fully disclosed at some future portion

See p. 126.

of this narrative, and it is to be hoped will serve as an useful warning to the young and inexperienced, who, blinded by vanity, ambition, or flattery, are too apt to suffer their worst passions to obtain a fatal ascendancy over them, and to plunge themselves into endless misery and shame, only to awaken to a sense of their folly and madness when it is too late.

By dint of great perseverance, however, Sir Laurence so far conquered his fears and emotions as to appear calm and happy, when in the presence of Blanche, if he did not sincerely feel so; and, encouraged by his conduct, and his affectionate attentions to herself and the infant Emeline, she became tranquil, and struggled to banish the remembrance of what had so recently taken place from her mind. She succeeded much better than could have been thought, and when more than a month passed away without anything more occurring to disturb them, she resumed nearly all her wonted confidence, although she was still apprehensive that the deadly malice which the gipsies had evinced towards her husband, would induce them to attempt to do him some further injury.

The baronet was unremitting in his endeavours to trace them out, but he met with no success, nor did it seem to be at all likely that he would ever be able to gain the least clue to them, although he could not believe that, desperate and determined as they were, they would readily abandon the designs they had formed against them.

Amanda, knowing the anguish it would cause to both her brother and Blanche, never alluded to the circumstance that had occurred at the christening; but she still had her doubts and misgivings as to the fatal truth of the contents of the letter, which suspicions were not at all diminished by the evasive answers Sir Laurence had returned to the questions she had put to him on the subject; and greatly did that amiable woman fear that the tranquillity they then experienced was not destined to remain without being interrupted; and she feared that the troubles which were in store for them were greater than those they had hitherto endured. These apprehensions were doomed too fearfully to be realised, as the sequel will show.

Two months had elapsed since the christening of the infant Emeline; and the event, which had caused considerable sensation and discussion at the time, ceased to be talked of in the neighbourhood. The hopes even of the baronet began to revive, and he again endeavoured to persuade himself that the female he had seen was only an impostor, and an instrument in the hands of the gipsies; and the letter nothing more than a forgery, notwithstanding, whoever the author might happen to be, they must have been thoroughly acquainted with the handwriting of Clara, to have given so close an imitation. He would have been much more satisfied, however, had he been able to have got her in his power, when he should at once have every opportunity of satisfying his doubts, and likewise to have placed her beyond the power of injuring him.

About this period circumstances compelled him to leave Branscombe House upon matters of a private nature, which he expected would detain him from home about a week; and after a most affectionate parting with Blanche, and seeing that everything was done to secure her from any outrage that might be attempted during the time he was away, he took his departure, attended by his favourite groom only, and mounted on horseback.

At the end of the first day's journey, they put up at an inn for the night, and Sir Laurence, after partaking of some refreshment, retired to the chamber allotted to him. But he did not at first feel inclined for rest, and as the night was particularly fine, he seated himself by the open windows, and gave himself up to the various thoughts that crowded upon his imagination. He mentally supplicated Heaven to protect his beloved Blanche and her infant from all danger during the brief period that he expected to be separated from them; but notwithstanding all the precautions he had taken, he could not help entertaining some apprehensions, and felt most anxious for the time to arrive when he should return home.   Then he recalled to his memory all the painful events that had lately taken place, and all his uneasiness was in a great measure revived.   Under all the peculiar and trying circumstances it was impossible that he could be entirely happy, or that he could feel satisfied with his own conduct, but yet he tried to justify it, and to trust that the Almighty, for the sake of Blanche and their tender offspring, would avert the many serious evils he had too much reason to apprehend.

The window at which he was seated commanded an uninterrupted view of an extensive range of fields and meadows, the inn being situated at the top of a long lane, and far away from any other house.   The night was tranquil, and the moon shone clearly upon all around.   Sir Laurence felt the refreshing cool night air gradually revive his spirits, and he endeavoured to divert his thoughts into another channel to that which they had previously wandered in, and to look forward to his return home without any apprehension of danger, in which effort he was far more successful than he had at first anticipated.

While he was thus occupied, he was aroused by hearing the trampling of several feet, apparently in the lane, but as there was nothing very extraordinary in this, he took but little notice of it, but continued with his eyes fixed upon the landscape before him.   In two or three minutes he beheld several persons, male and female, together with a number of children of both sexes, emerge from the lane round an angle of the inn into the open fields, attended by two or three horses and carts.   He had a distinct view of them from the clearness of the night, and almost a single glance convinced him that they were gipsies, but whether the same he was so anxious to find out, he had no means of ascertaining, no more than by the resemblance which the persons of two or three of them bore to some of the tribe to which old Madela and Harold belonged.

Sir Laurence watched them with much anxiety as they proceeded on their way, and he was almost certain that they were the same tribe who had already caused so much mischief to him and those with whom he was connected, but he could not recognise amongst them any individuals who were at all like Madela, Harold, or the gipsy boy; but they might not be with them, and he still retained the impression that they were those whose place of retreat he had been so long anxious to discover.

They moved slowly on their way across the fields, but at length they were hidden from the sight of Sir Laurence in the distance, and all remained the same as before they had made their appearance.

This circumstance caused the baronet considerable reflection, and he was not without apprehension that he should encounter them on his journey, and if they should happen to be the same individuals he so strongly suspected they were, they might be tempted to commit some outrage upon him, from which he would have no means of protecting himself.   It would be advisable in him, he considered, to avoid the route they had taken, although he was most eager to know the place of their destination, which, however, he might be able to learn on the road, and if he did so he would then take the readiest means of securing those who had already shown the deadly malice and spirit of revenge they entertained towards him.

Having come to this determination, Sir Laurence closed the window and retired to rest.   If they were indeed those whom he suspected, it would have afforded his mind a considerable relief, as he should know then that Blanche, at present, at any rate, was in no danger from them, which she might have been had they been aware of his absence from home.

After reflecting upon this circumstance for a short time longer, the baronet fell asleep, and did not awake till the morning. Previous to his departure from the inn he called the landlord to him, and after making him acquainted with what he had seen, inquired whether he was aware that the gipsies ever located themselves in or near that neighbourhood?

" Oh, no, sir," answered the landlord, " they would not be so bold as to do that now, I should think, though they did so two or three years since, when they committed so many depredations that they became the terror of the whole place. But the magistrates interfered, and had not the rascals quickly departed, they would very soon have found themselves the inmates of the gaol. There was one frightful old woman among them, whom they called the queen, who was certainly a most determined creature, and I do not believe that she would have hesitated to commit any crime if she had had the opportunity."

" And did you ever see this old woman ?" eagerly asked Sir Laurence.

" See her, sir," replied the landlord; " oh, yes, frequently, and many a time have I been compelled to give her and her tribe both victuals and drink, to prevent them from pulling my house about my ears."

" Can you describe this woman to me?"

The landlord answered in the affirmative, and then did so, and Sir Laurence was perfectly satisfied that it was old Madela, and he had no doubt but that it was the same tribe to which her and Harold belonged, whom he had seen the night before. The landlord not being able to give him any further information, he departed from the inn, and made the best of his way on his journey.

Nothing more particular occurred to him on the way, and he saw nothing more of the gipsies, nor was enabled to gain any intelligence of the route they had taken.

Sir Laurence transacted the business he had gone upon with as much expedition as possible, but it was protracted beyond the time he had anticipated, and it was more than a week before he was enabled to return home.

Anxious to arrive at Branscombe House, the baronet travelled early and late, and on the second night, him and his servant were overtaken by the darkness in the midst of a most dreary part of the country, some distance from any town, and with every prospect of an approaching storm. He now regretted that he had departed from the inn where he had put up for refreshment, but pushed on his way, hoping to reach the nearest town before the storm came on. They kept to the road as much as they could, but the prospect before them was anything but inviting, a wood being on one side of them, and a dreary moor upon the other, and seemed a very fit haunt for the worst of characters. The wind also swept across the moor in howling gusts, and added to the extreme cheerlessness of the hour.

They had proceeded in this manner for some distance, when a harsh, grating, rattling noise met their ears, and casting their eyes in the direction from whence it came, they beheld a dark object swinging in the air by the road side, which they immediately knew to be a gibbet, and the sight at that dismal hour of the night, and in such a place, was calculated to inspire them with a powerful feeling of awe; but the baronet's attention was quickly drawn to the three objects which seemed to be human forms that were moving near the gibbet.

Wondering what their purpose could be at that time, and on such a spot, and apprehensive that danger might be at hand, Sir Laurence placed his hand upon the spot where he expected to find his pistols, and then found, for the first time, that he had forgotten to bring them with him, and his servant was no better provided. This was a most provoking discovery, but there was no help for it now, and all that they could do was to remain firm, and to make the best of it they could.

They still perceived the three objects moving about the empty gibbet, and which they must pass, but they clapped spurs to their horses, and determined to do so as quick as they could ; but the persons, whoever they were, looked up on hearing their approach, and immediately crossed from the gibbet to the centre of the road, so that they were obliged to slacken their speed or to run over them.

" What, ho ! why come ye on with the swiftness of the w2irlwind ? Would you trample us to death as if we were no more than dogs ?" shouted a loud, coarse voice, which the astonished and somewhat alarmed Sir Laurence recognised in a moment ; and having now got to within a few paces of them, he discovered, to his amazement, that it was Madela, Harold, and another gipsy, who stood before them. They recognised the baronet at the same moment, and approached with looks of diabolical malice and triumph, but the baronet and his attendant assumed as much firmness as they could, and awaited the result of this nocturnal meeting with the greatest impatience.

" Laurence Cleveland," cried Harold, " once more—once more we meet. Oh, it is a fair spot, and a most appropriate hour."

" Ha ! ha ! ha !" laughed Madela ; " a fair spot, truly ; look, murderer, perjured miscreant, at yon empty gibbet now grating in the air ; knowest thou whose mouldering bones it was meant to contain, had not the relations of the slaughtered victim borne his disfigured corse away and committed it to the earth ? Ask thine own conscience, heartless wretch, and it will tell thee that was the gibbet erected for the body of that aged man whom thy lying tongue condemned to an ignominious death ! Oh, villain, villain, would it not be a fair retribution to immolate thee on the spot, and leave thy carcase for the crows to peck at ? But, no ; we have a more sanguinary revenge to gratify, and therefore do we suffer thee yet to live, that our triumph may be the more complete in thy protracted tortures."

Sir Laurence started at the frightful old hag aghast, and for a short time he was unable to speak, while Harold and the other gipsy reiterated her fierce denunciations and pointed with demoniacal looks towards the gibbet.

" Inhuman, hardened wretch," at length said Sir Laurence ; " why do you thus continually cross my path, and loading me with your base and false charges ? Are ye not satisfied with the mischief you have already done, in seeking to break the heart of an innocent woman ?"

" What, reptile," demanded Harold, " dare you attempt to deny the truth of our charges ? Are you not a murderer—seducer—hypocrite—bigamist ? Is not she, Clara, your only lawful wife still living ? Have we not promised you that we will at some future time produce her to your shame and confusion ? Nay, more, have you not seen her, spoken to her ; and will you deny the truth of those features that ought to be so indelibly impressed upon your memory in characters of fire ?"

" 'Tis false !" ejaculated Sir Laurence ; " although he could not help quailing as he spoke, and his conscience belied the contradiction he was giving. " The being I have seen is an impostor, and ——"

" An impostor !" repeated Madela, at the same time fixing upon the baronet a look of contempt and triumph which penetrated to his veins with horror; "an impostor, say you, Laurence Cleveland?" she reiterated, with increased bitterness; "oh, but I can penetrate thine inmost thoughts, villain, and read the conviction they bring to thy dastard heart of the lie thou utterest. An impostor! Oh, forsooth, the time will come when, to thy shame and confusion, thou wilt be compelled to retract that foul calumny in the face of abhorring multitudes. But not yet, not yet; no, our vengeance would be only half complete did we at once bring about the consummation of thy destruction. But the time will come, ay, as surely as the dark clouds which now are pending o'er our heads must disperse before the bright beams of the morrow's sun. And she whom thou hast vowed to love, to whom thou hast given thine hand, the wretched deluded fool, Blanche Lester, will, with a broken heart, see thee in thine own hideous deformity, and heap damning curses upon thine head!"

Sir Laurence Cleveland trembled in every limb as the hideous old woman gave vent to these fearful observations, and a terrible conviction flashed upon his mind that her predictions would be realized. He saw plainly that he had no common enemies to deal with, and, in spite of all his efforts to appear firm, and to treat them with contempt, his heart shrank appalled from them. Fain would he have passed on his way, and at once have ridden himself of their dreaded presence, but they still remained fixed in the position they had taken, and by their savage looks evidently exulted in the mental agony which their words had inflicted on him. And then to be alone, defenceless, in that dismal spot with them, was more than sufficient, notwithstanding that he was naturally courageous, to excite his utmost apprehensions, and gave to them additional advantage. He would have tried the powers of persuasion and remonstrance with them, to induce them to depart, and to suffer him to proceed unmolested on his way, but he knew that with such determined wretches any such attempt would be only worse than an useless waste of words, and he was therefore at a loss in what way to act. The hour, too, was getting late, and the storm which had been so long threatening now commenced, which all added to the terror of his situation.

"Ah!" cried Madela, "I see thy blanched cheeks and quivering lips, Laurence Cleveland; thou tremblest before those whom thou wouldst fain affect to despise. 'Tis well; but thou wilt yet have more cause to quail. And hark, the loud voice of the thunder reiterates the curses I have uttered against thee, and yon creaking gibbet rattles in the blast in concert with it; fit music for such an hour, such a spot, and such company. It only needs the mouldering bones of thy murdered victim to complete the scene."

"I implore you, woman, to desist, and suffer me to proceed," said the baronet in a faultering voice. Madela and Harold laughed aloud in their fiendish delight, as they witnessed his anguish.

"Ho! ho!" croaked forth the former; "so the proud Sir Laurence Cleveland, he whose words, whose threats were lately so large and commanding, now condescends to implore; of me, the gipsy outcast, whom he would hunt to death, he deigns to supplicate forbearance. Ha! ha! ha!"

"By all my hopes," cried Sir Laurence, worked up to a pitch of madness, "I will endure no more. Get out of my path, I say, or I will trample ye beneath my horse's feet."

"Dog!" shouted Madela and Harold, in a breath, and levelling their pistols at his head; "stir but an inch until we permit thee, and thy life's blood shall be shed upon the spot!"

Sir Laurence drew back his horse in terror, and his attendant was so alarmed, that he could scarcely retain his seat in his saddle. The tempest now raged with the greatest violence, and, as the lightning flashed upon the savage countenances of Madela and the other gipsies, they appeared like the evil spirits that ruled the storm.

"So, reptile!" exclaimed Madela; "thou wouldst again venture to threaten us; thou, who art entirely at our mercy, and whom we could immediately sacrifice to our terrible vengeance. Fool! were it not that it would be a mercy to thee to spare thee the punishment we have in store for thee, thou shouldst never more be permitted to quit this spot alive, but thy carcase should be left to decorate yon swinging gibbet! But, go thy ways; seek thy proud home, and much joy may it give thee the reception thou wilt there meet with. Oh! it is gathering; it is gathering; the torch is placed to the pile, and the flames will shortly ascend in blood-red flakes of vengeance! Ha! ha! ha!"

There was a mystery about the latter words of the hag which struck a deadly horror to the heart of Sir Laurence, and palsied every limb.

"Woman," he gasped forth; "what meaning do your portentous words convey?"

"Go—go, reptile, dog!" answered Madela; "and gain the information thou seekest. Misery, perpetual misery is the lot of the murderer, the hypocrite, and the betrayer of confiding innocence. Go thy ways, and mark me, thou wilt have good reason to remember this meeting at the intended gibbet of thine aged, slaughtered victim."

As the old woman uttered these words, she and her fierce companions set up a wild shout of triumph and defiance, and, pointing significantly at the gibbet, slowly retreated from the spot, and left Sir Laurence for some moments in a state of indescribable consternation.

But, at length, the impetuous fury of the raging elements aroused him, and, after once turning his eyes to catch a glance of the retreating forms of his terrible enemies, he spurred on his horse, and pursued his dreary journey.

CHAPTER XIV.

THE RETURN HOME. — THE FEARFUL CATASTROPHE.—THE GIPSY BOY CHARGED WITH INCENDIARISM.

DISTRACTED with conflicting thoughts and dismal forebodings, Sir Laurence pursued his way, almost regardless of the pelting rain, so much was his mind occupied by the impressive events that had just occurred to him. Every word that Madela and Harold had uttered was stamped upon his memory in the most vivid characters, and which he felt that neither time nor circumstances could efface. It was in vain for him to attempt to treat their observations with indifference, for their conduct throughout was characterised by so much mystery, and they spoke to so many painful subjects which his conscience could not deny, that he was perfectly confident he had everything to dread from them, and that they had the power to carry their terrible threats into execution: and he, therefore, felt assured that he was never safe from them, even for an hour.

Their strange appearance to him, also, at all times, in all places, and at the very moment when he had the least right to expect them, filled him with the most unbounded amazement, alarm, and confusion; but, more than all, this last nocturnal meeting created his excitement. Madela might have spared herself the trouble of warning him to remember it, for he was satisfied that nothing whatever could cause him to forget it; and there were several of the reproaches she had heaped upon him which he could not help inwardly acknowledging he richly deserved, and that rendered the poignancy of his anguish the more severe.

But the last words the hag had uttered had made a more indelible impression upon his mind than all, and he was lost in perplexity to understand what they could mean, although he doubted not that some fresh evil was intended him.

Most agonising and unsatisfactory were the various conjectures he formed, and greatly anxious was he to arrive at home, to have his doubts removed, or at any rate to banish the insupportable suspense from his bosom. But he was yet a long way from Branscombe House, and it would be impossible for him to reach there that night in such a pelting storm, and as his horse and that of his attendant were already considerably fagged.

This was torture almost insupportable, but Sir Laurence endeavoured to conquer it, and goaded on his horse to the top of its speed, almost regardless of the tempest, although he was already drenched to the skin, and his servant was filled with the greatest apprehensions, which he in vain endeavoured to subdue.

They at length, however, emerged from the dreary road they had so long been traversing, and, to their infinite satisfaction, came in sight of a town, and observed lights glimmering from the windows of the principal inn, which convinced them that notwithstanding the lateness of the hour, the inmates had not yet retired to rest.

" We shall find every accommodation for the night here, sir, no doubt," said the servant of the baronet, cheering himself at the idea.

" No, not for the night, George," returned his master; " we must not delay the completion of our journey any longer than possible."

" Bless me, sir," said the disappointed groom, " you can never think of proceeding in such a storm as this, wet and weary as we already are; besides, our poor horses are completely knocked up, and it is impossible that they can proceed much farther."

" We shall no doubt be able to procure fresh ones, or a post-chaise from the inn," replied Sir Laurence. " At any rate, in spite of the consequences, I am determined to proceed."

They now stopped at the inn, and the landlord meeting them at the door, they alighted from their horses and entered, Sir Laurence hastily ordering refreshments for himself and his servant, and desiring the landlord of the inn to come to him again as quickly as possible. In a few minutes he returned.

" Can you accommodate me with a post-chaise directly?" inquired the baronet.

" What, at this time of the night, sir, and in such a tempest?" inquired the landlord, with a look of amazement. " Why, your honour is already very wet, and seem to have travelled far, and ——"

" No matter," interrupted Sir Laurence, impatiently; " can you accommodate me in the way I desire?"

" Why, sir, I certainly can, but if you would take my advice ——"

" Never mind your advice, but get the chaise ready with all the expedition you can, and I will reward you accordingly."

The landlord vanished immediately, and Sir Laurence having partaken slightly of the refreshments which had been brought to him, gave himself up to the most gloomy thoughts while the chaise was being got ready. The last warning of old Madela continued to harass and torture his mind, and it was in vain that he tried to fathom the meaning of it, although he foreboded some fresh trouble, which had never failed to follow the predictions of that strange and fearful woman.

Such was the manner in which the gipsies defied him, and the evident power they had of carrying their evil designs into effect, that he entertained a stronger dread of them than ever, and he feared to take any future steps to detect them, lest they should indeed have it in their power to denounce him as a bigamist, and to bring forward the proof they threatened.

During the short interval that was employed by the landlord in getting the chaise ready, the storm fortunately greatly abated, and with it a considerable poition of the fears of George, the baronet's groom, and presently afterwards the worthy host entered the room in which Sir Laurence was sitting, and informed hi··· that the chaise awaited his pleasure. The baronet thanked him for his promptitude, and having liberally rewarded him, he stepped into the vehicle, telling the postillions to drive as quickly as possible, and with an anxious heart was soon again rapidly pursuing his journey.

The men took a different and far better route than that which the baronet had come, and consequently they could proceed with much greater speed, so that in a little more than an hour they had accomplished nearly half the journey.

The storm had now entirely subsided, and to it succeeded a darkness that was almost impenetrable. But presently the heavens became illumined with an ensanguined reflection, which evidently proceeded from fearful fire at a distance, and as Sir Lawrence beheld it, a terrific foreboding flashed upon his mind. He remembered the words of Madela,—" The torch is placed to the pile, and the flames will shortly ascend in blood-red flakes of vengeance!" and, as he did so, his heart sunk within him. Moreover, the conflagration seemed to be raging in that part of the country where Branscombe House was situated, and that served to increase his dreadful apprehensions.

" Quick—quick as lightning!" he said, addressing himself to the postillions; " any money shall be yours, if you will but use all the expedition in your power."

The men obeyed this command, and increased the speed of their horses till the vehicle was carried along almost with the velocity of the wind. Sir Laurence watched the spreading reflection with the greatest anxiety, and the further they proceeded the more convinced he became that his surmises as to the direction in which the fire was raging, were correct, and his agony was almost more than his strength could endure.

" Good God!" he cried, beating his breast; " should the fire proceed from my mansion, what will become of my beloved Blanche and my poor child? Oh, Almighty Father, avert, I beseech you, so horrible a calamity!"

The fire now seemed to abate in fury, and gradually nothing was visible in the sky but a faint streak of red, just like the last hue left by the departing sun, and a large body of smoke, which still continued to ascend from the spot where the flames had lately so fiercely raged. Sir Laurence was now convinced that it was his own mansion which had so fatally suffered, and his brain was distracted.

" The wretches have fulfilled their threats," he exclaimed, " and I am ruined. Gracious Heaven! my wife, my child, what have become of you?"

He was interrupted in these agonizing exclamations by the loud shouts of men, and eagerly turning his eyes in the direction from whence they proceeded, he perceived a number of persons approaching, apparently forcing some other individual along with violent execrations. They came nearer, and Sir Laurence beheld—could he believe his eyes?—yes, it was Rosario, the gipsy boy, they held, and so roughly handled, and who was making vain appeals to them for forbearance.

" My wife—the Lady Blanche!—my sister—my child!" hastily demanded the baronet, as he alighted from the chaise, and forced his way into the middle of the group.

" They are all saved, Sir Laurence!" replied two or three of the men, in a breath. " Oh! what a fortunate thing it is you have arrived. They are all safe, Sir Laurence."

" Gracious Heaven be thanked!" cried Sir Laurence, clasping his hands. " But," he added, fixing his earnest looks upon the pale countenance of the gipsy boy, " what is the meaning of this?—what are you about to do with that youth?"

" He is the young villain who has done this," answered one of the men; " he is the base incendiary."

" Good God! is it possible?" exclaimed the baronet.

" Sir Laurence Cleveland," said the gipsy boy, in a firm voice, " I am commanded by my tribe to hate you and yours. I know not for what reason it is they thus enjoin me, but my feelings have ever revolted from doing so; and on more than one occasion, as you know, I have interposed between them and you, when they, probably, would have shed your blood. I am innocent of this charge—by my mother's spirit, I swear that I am!"

" Believe him not, Sir Laurence," said two or three of the men; " he is a hardened young villain. We caught him almost in the fact, leaving the house, and with a lighted torch in his hand, with which he had, no doubt, kindled the fatal flames."

" Wretched boy!" ejaculated Sir Laurence; " can this be true? Harm him not, but convey him to a place of security."

" Sir Laurence Cleveland," cried the boy, in tones of anguish and reproach, " you may repent this. I repeat that I am not guilty of the monstrous crime of which these men accuse me."

" Heaven send that you may not be so, for your own sake," returned the baronet. " But at present suspicion is strong against you. I will see you to-morrow."

The gipsy boy clasped his hands in apparent agony, and Sir Laurence then turned away from him, and made his way, with rapid steps, to his mansion.

The fire, which had been confined to one wing of the building, was now quite subdued, and Sir Laurence, rushing into the hall, quickly clasped his beloved Blanche and child to his bosom, while Amanda stood by, and gazed with feelings of the most powerful emotion on the affectionate scene.

CHAPTER XV.

THE GIPSIES' RETREAT IN THE OLD ABBEY RUINS.—THE GIPSY BOY AND HIS FRIEND OF MYSTERY.

WE must now return to that eventful day on which Sir Laurence and Blanche were united, and when Rosario, the gipsy boy, was accidentally wounded by the baronet. Situated in a beautiful valley, and surrounded by lofty hills, that reared their verdant summits almost to the clouds, were to be seen the mouldering ruins of a venerable edifice, known by the name of Oakshall Abbey; or, the Haunted Ruins. It stood in a most beautiful and retired part of the country, and about fifteen miles from Branscombe House; and, though oft the traveller paused to admire it, and the sylvan scenery by which it was surrounded, the persons in the immediate vicinity most carefully avoided it, especially after nightfall, in consequence of the absurd superstition to which allusion has just been made.

Many ages had passed since the erection of that ancient fabric; many, many changes had taken place since that remote day; numerous proud buildings, that were contiguous to it, had crumbled in the dust; but time had failed to sweep that gothic pile entirely away, and there still stood its ivy-mantled remains, as if, even in their gradual decay, mocking the universal and unrelenting devastator.

How different were the inhabitants the old abbey now contained from those who in former days had occupied it; for there the gipsy wanderers now found a safe retreat, and claimed the beautiful scenery around as their dominions, for no persons offered to interrupt them, and there were few, in fact, who knew that they had there taken up their residence, although, at the time we are at present alluding to, they had been there many months, having been going there on the memorable evening when they were first encountered by Sir Laurence Cleveland and his sister, and at which period our tale commenced.

No place could possibly be better suited to those outcast wanderers than the old abbey ruins, situated as it was, so secluded, so romantic, and protected from the prying eye of curiosity by the superstitious rumours which the inhabitants of the neighbourhood so industriously circulated among all who travelled that way. It was certainly a very different mode of living to their usual encampment, and not quite so characteristic of their peculiar life; but under all their present circumstances, and with the deep-laid designs they had in contemplation, no place could possibly be better adapted for their purpose. To the inhabitants of the adjacent villages they were civil, and, therefore, engaged their friendship, and that therefore operated as another means of protection to them in case they should be attacked; but they were so numerous, and possessed such hardy and resolute spirits among them, that they entertained but little apprehensions of such an event, and were fully prepared for it, if it should take place.

One wing of the abbey was in pretty good preservation, and there the principal portion of the gipsies resided, while the remainder pitched their tents in the more ruinous part of the ancient edifice.

It must have been seen, that the gipsies had spies constantly secreted in the neighbourhood of Branscombe House, to ascertain all that transpired there, and they were thus enabled to carry their plans better into effect, and without the parties against whom they were directed having the least suspicion as to the way in which they gained their information, so that their transactions had the appearance of being conducted by some supernatural agency, and were likely to have the powerful effect which they desired. It was by these means that Madela and Harold were enabled to make their appearance to Sir Laurence at all times, and in all places, being so thoroughly acquainted with all his movements, that even almost his very thoughts reached their knowledge.

The reader must remember the eventful day on which Sir Laurence led the lovely Blanche Lester to the altar; and that which should have been a day of joy, was converted into one of horror, by the interruption of the gipsies, and the dreadful accusation which Harold brought against the baronet. Whether or no there was any truth in that charge, remains to be shown hereafter.

We have stated the excitement of the gipsy Harold and his companions, on seeing Rosario fall, as they imagined, dead or mortally wounded. It was a wonder that they did not immediately sacrifice Sir Laurence to their wrath; and they doubtless would have done so, had they not been prevented by Harold, who, as well as Madela, had determined on a far more deliberate and horrible revenge; seeing, therefore, the danger which threatened them from the numbers which fast crowded to the assistance of the baronet and his friends, he thought it most prudent to make a retreat, while the confusion which prevailed might enable them to make their escape, and accordingly did so, as has been previously described.

Their enemies having given up the pursuit, the gipsies were enabled to pursue their way to their retreat in the old abbey ruins in safety; and speedily the wound of the gipsy boy was examined, the blood stanched as well as they could, and everything done to restore him to sensibility, but in vain.

Harold exhibited more emotion than could have been expected from a man of his hardened and insensible character; and, for a few moments, hung over the form of the gipsy boy with looks that sufficiently spoke the intense mental anguish he was enduring.

"Now, by all the evil stars, I swear to have a tenfold vengeance for this deed of blood," he cried, clenching his fist, and raising it in the air. "The blood of the innocent has been shed by the being I hate, and I will contrive such schemes to wring his guilty soul, as never yet the mind of fiend in human shape conceived. But should he die! but no—I cannot entertain that thought, for how much depends upon this child's life. On, on my lads, as quick as ye can, we shall shortly meet Madela and her companions; our queen has always remedies about her for such accidents as this. Ah, see; they come."

Bending her footsteps up the side of a steep hill, from the romantic valley beneath, the aged woman was now seen, followed by several more of the gipsies, and, on beholding her, Harold and his companions set up their usual shout of vengeance, to signify that they had received some injury or insult, and the old hag hastened towards them.

"What mean those shouts?" she cried. "Who has dared to insult my people?—speak, Harold!"

"Behold!" replied Harold, taking the arm of Madela, and leading her to the cart in which the insensible form of the gipsy boy was laid.

"Ah!" exclaimed Madela, her eyes flashing fire, and every muscle of her frightful countenance agitated by the power of her excitement; "blood! blood! the blood of the fawn shed. A dreadful curse, the heaviest that the gipsy can invoke light, upon the wretch who has done this. His name, his name?"

"Laurence Cleveland!" answered Harold.

"Ah, the bloodhound!" cried Madela, with looks that were enough to appal the stoutest soul to gaze upon; "has he dared thus to provoke the wrath of those whom he has already so much injured? Revenge! revenge against him and all connected with him—revenge even more terrible than that which we before contemplated. Oh, did he but know the extent of his crime. But he is not dead. Let me see to him; the young fawn must not perish thus."

Carefully the old woman examined the wound of the gipsy boy, which she found not to be mortal, and that he had merely become insensible from loss of blood. Then she applied such remedies to it as she constantly carried about with her, and having bound it up, they proceeded on their way with as much rapidity as they could. Harold making her acquainted with all that had happened in the church.

When the gipsy boy recovered his senses, he found himself supported in the arms of one of their tribe whom he had often beheld, but had seldom had an opportunity of speaking to; in fact, he was not permitted to mingle much with the other gipsies, and when he did so, he was watched most narrowly and mysteriously by Harold and Madela, and he seemed afraid to speak but as they dictated.

Azrah, as he was called, was indeed a man who, once seen, must make a lasting impression. He was tall, graceful, but most delicately formed, and seemed ill calculated for the hardy life of the gipsy tribe. His complexion was remarkably fair for a gipsy, and his features were regularly formed, and possessing almost feminine delicacy and loveliness. His eyes were brilliant as the stars of Heaven, yet they beamed forth a constant expression of intense melancholy, and a smile was never seen upon his countenance. When he spoke, there was a gentle softness and delicate timidity in his tones that was anything but masculine; and those who heard them could not fail to be fascinated by their melancholy sweetness, and to wish to listen to them again.

Frequently had Rosario discovered this interesting and mysterious being watching him with the most intense looks, and thought he observed tears in his eyes; but when he sought to address him, Madela or Harold were almost sure to interpose, and to force Azrah roughly away. On more than one occasion, too, on awaking from sleep, Rosario saw the same strange being on his knees by the side of his rude couch, and apparently invoking blessings on his head; but no sooner did he behold that he was awake than he would start to his feet, and flee from the spot with the greatest precipitation, and before the gipsy boy had an opportunity of speaking to him.

These circumstances made the most powerful impression upon the mind of Rosario, and caused him the utmost perplexity, and many hours of deep reflection. Most anxious was he to know more of him, but regretted that there seemed to be no probability of his ever obtaining such an opportunity. That he had been the victim of misfortune, there could be very little doubt, and Rosario felt a yearning of respect towards him of the most powerful description.

There were times when Azrah would be absent from the tribe for days together, and it seemed to be known only to Madela and Harold what had become of him; but he would return as suddenly as he had departed, and always, on such occasions, he appeared more melancholy than he had been before, and would remain in secret conference with Harold and Madela for hours together.

Rosario had frequently felt an inclination to question Harold upon the subject, but the fear of incurring his anger prevented him, and none of the other gipsies would, if they could, give him any information.

Such was the mysterious being who now supported the wounded boy in his arms, and gazed in his pale countenance, with the most tender solicitude and emotion. Tears were trembling on his cheeks, but he hastily dashed them away, and, on beholding the gipsy boy open his eyes, uttered an exclamation of delight, and raised his eyes, as if in thanksgiving, to Heaven.

"Where am I?" ejaculated Rosario, in a faint voice; "have I been dreaming? Ah! Azrah, mysterious man, you here?"

"Hush! hush!" said Azrah, in his usual gentle tones. "We must not be heard. I have but stolen to you for a few moments, and Harold or Madela may quickly interrupt the happiness of this moment. Tell me, how do you feel, Rosario?"

"Better—better now, kind Azrah," replied the gipsy boy. "I shall soon be quite well, and the happiness of seeing you alone is a pleasure that I would undergo greater pain, at any time, to experience."

Azrah seemed deeply affected by the artless fervour of the poor boy's manner, but he endeavoured to conquer it, and he said,

"Do you, then, esteem me, Rosario?"

"Esteem you, Azrah?" answered the gipsy boy. "Oh! if you could only read my heart, you would find that I could love you better than if you were even my brother."

"Your brother!" repeated Azrah, with peculiar emphasis, and his countenance evinced the most powerful emotion. "Oh! thank Heaven for this!"

"That voice so sweet, those words so tender, go to my very heart! Oh! tell me, I pray you, who are you?"

"Your friend."

"My friend! blessed assurance!"

"Your *best* friend, Rosario," sighed Azrah.

"Let me, then, pay my homage to you in your true character," ejaculated the gipsy boy, energetically; "you are not what you seem to be."

"*You* are not what you seem to be, Rosario," returned Azrah, fixing a penetrating look upon the poor lad's countenance, and his chest heaving with emotion.

Rosario started and trembled.

"Gracious Heavens!" he cried; "what do you mean?"

"*I know your secret!*" replied Azrah, in a low but impressive voice. "No disguise can keep it from me."

It would be impossible to describe the agitation of Rosario on hearing these words, and the deepest blushes suffused his cheeks. Tears then gushed to his eyes, and, sinking on his knees at the feet of Azrah, he sobbed forth,—

"Mysterious man, how have you acquired this knowledge? In what manner can I possibly have betrayed that secret which I am warned, at the peril of my life, not to reveal?"

"Do not alarm yourself, poor Rosario—for such I will still call you," said Azrah, with the greatest tenderness, and sighing deeply as he spoke; "you have not betrayed yourself; it has never, it never could be, a secret *to me*. Oh, that my lips were permitted to reveal more. But as you regard me, as you value, perhaps, my very life, do not let a word escape your lips as to what I have said to you at this interview."

"By all my soul's hopes I will not! But will you not disclose to me your real name, and who you are? I ——"

"It must not be, child," interrupted Azrah, in faltering tones. "My lips are sealed upon that painful subject for the present; but the time may come, and then ——"

He paused, and seemed afraid to finish the sentence.

"Oh! Rosario," he said, at last, "the last few hours only have witnessed the completion of that which is enough to break my heart, already so deeply lacerated."

"You know me, Azrah," said Rosario; "and, oh! may I not hope for a greater share of your confidence? Tell me, I beseech you,—know you the name of my wretched parents?"

Azrah exhibited more powerful emotion than he had done before on this question being put to him, and he turned away his face, clasped his forehead, and sobbed heavily.

"Why are you so violently agitated?" said Rosario, approaching him as well as his strength would permit him. "Azrah, if you are indeed my friend, answer the question I have put to you."

"Do I know who were your parents, Rosario?" said Azrah; "oh, yes! well—too well."

" Their name ?"

" I must not—dare not—reveal it to you. But, hark! some one approaches; I must begone. Remember my words, and ere long we may meet again. Farewell, farewell! and rest assured that you have no kinder earthly friend than Azrah !"

Thus saying, he waved his hand with the greatest affection, and departed by one door just as Harold entered at another.

" Ah! then," exclaimed Harold, " you have recovered your senses, Rosario; tell me, how do you feel now ?"

Rosario seemed to shudder in the gipsy's presence, and crimson blushes mounted in his before pale face, as he faltered out, in a faint voice,—

" I am better, Harold, much better, but faint and weak with loss of blood."

" You are more than usually agitated. There are tears upon your cheeks ; you have been weeping."

" And is it surprising that I should weep, Harold, after what has happened ?" demanded Rosario.

" Yes; hatred, deadly hatred and revenge should take the place of this feeling," replied Harold, in fierce accents; " your lips should breathe curses on the head of that villain who inflicted the blow which aimed at your life."

" I forgive him, Harold," returned the gipsy boy, mildly; " I freely forgive him, for it was an accident; I cannot, will not, curse him."

" Ah!" cried Harold, grasping his arm, and looking in his face with an expression of even more than his usual ferocity; " dare you say so? Beware—beware! I say again that you must hate Sir Laurence Cleveland as you would the most loathsome reptile that crawls the earth."

" Never !" exclaimed Rosario, vehemently. " In spite of all you have said, and the accidental injury I have received from him, my heart revolts from such a feeling."

A heavy execration passed the lips of Harold, and he paced the room for a second or two in the greatest disorder.

" And does the young fawn thus revolt against his protectors ?" he said, turning again to Rosario; " would he lick the hand of the wolf who has just shed his blood and whom he should detest with a loathing I cannot express ? Rosario, recall your words, or you will have bitter cause to repent this opposition to our will."

" Harold," said Rosario, with firmness, " is it because you hate Sir Laurence Cleveland that I should also do so? He has never injured me, and I can never hate those who have not been the cause of any pain to me. Why did you commit the daring outrage you did against him, and thus obtrude yourself upon the day of his nuptials ?"

" Presumptuous !" exclaimed Harold, furiously; " and dare you question my conduct ? But I waste words with you; away to rest, and learn obedience, as you value your life. To rest, I say !"

" To rest !" repeated Rosario, with a sigh. " Alas! miserable, mysterious, and revolting as is my fate—young as I am, what rest is there for me ?"

Harold stamped passionately and impatiently, and taking the arm of Rosario, weak and ill as he was, forcibly led him from the room.

CHAPTER XVI.

THE GIPSY BOY'S REFLECTIONS. — HIS RECOVERY. — THE DISAPPEARANCE OF AZRAH. — THE PLOT, AND ROSARIO'S RESOLUTION.

WHEN Rosario stretched himself on his rude pallet, and was left alone, he suffered much more from the agitation and anguish of his mind than he did from the pain of his wound, which, as has been before observed, was but slight. The interview he had had with Azrah he could never forget; but it left him, if possible, in a greater state of mystery and excitement than before. He was at a loss to form a conjecture as to who he really was; but it was evident from his manners that he was far above the present vagrant life he was leading, and the deep interest he expressed in his fate made Rosario imagine that he was in some way connected with him.

But Azrah knew his *secret*, that important secret which his lips were forbidden to reveal, although so revolting to his nature, and with which he had thought that no one but himself, and Madela, and Harold were acquainted. The cheeks of the gipsy boy glowed, as this thought occurred to him, and his bosom heaved with the most violent emotion; but what that secret was must remain so at present to the reader.

Azrah was also acquainted with the names of his parents, but he refused to reveal them; and the extraordinary emotion he had displayed on his putting the question to him, had not escaped the particular observation of Rosario. Why should he feel so deep an interest in them? He was at a perfect loss to conceive.

How deeply did the gipsy boy regret the interruption to their interview which had been caused by the entrance of Harold, for he might have been able to elicit much more than he had done, and most anxious was he to have the opportunity of meeting with him again.

There was something in the countenance of Azrah, too, that particularly struck him, and he had every lineament of it as fresh before his mind's eye, as if he was now gazing at it. The peculiar delicacy of its expression, so unusual in one of the male sex; its uncommon beauty, and the gentle expression of his lovely eyes, were such as the imagination of Rosario had never before conceived. And then the almost silvery sweetness of his voice, which touched the tenderest chords of his heart, still seemed to vibrate in his ears, and made him long to hear them again. And although he had told him that he dared not reveal more at present, he had also given him some reason to hope that he would at some future period make a disclosure, till which time Rosario must endeavour to wait with patience.

These thoughts and the observations of Harold kept poor Rosario waking nearly the whole of the night. We have stated that he was struck with the appearance of Sir Laurence Cleveland from the very first moment he beheld him, and that favourable impression gained greater ascendancy over his mind the more that the gipsies persecuted him. Could he hate him—could he curse him, as he was commanded to do? No; his gentle nature recoiled from the bare idea, and quite opposite feelings daily, hourly gained strength in his mind. He pitied Sir Laurence, and he deeply commiserated with his unfortunate lady, who Rosario felt satisfied could never have done anything to justify the deadly vengeance of the gipsies. Yet, at the same time that these thoughts crossed his mind, a strange feeling came over him for which he was entirely at a loss to account.

The state of mind Rosario was in retarded the progress of his restoration to entire convalescence, and he was for several days unable to leave his couch, and when he did he was but a shadow of his former self. He beheld the gipsies with feelings of dread, and they looked upon him with eyes of suspicion—at least, Harold and Madela, after the observations he had made respecting Sir Laurence; but, at the same time, they were convinced that he entertained such a dread of their power, that he would not dare to attempt any direct act of disobedience towards them, much less than to venture to betray those designs with which he was acquainted.

How anxious was the gipsy boy to again behold Azrah, but he looked in vain for him. He had again left the abbey, and had gone on one of those secret expeditions which Rosario in vain attempted to fathom.

In this manner several weeks passed away, without any change taking place in the scenes of the old abbey ruins. Rosario was now entirely recovered, but his spirits had lost their usual elasticity, and he kept himself as much as possible apart from the gipsies, wandering forth alone at every opportunity, and pondering over the strange events of his life, few as were the years he had numbered. But there was one thought which caused him more anguish than all, and, as it occurred to him, the blush of shame would mantle in his cheek, and a feeling would come over him which at present cannot be explained.

The cause of this was the strange, the painful facts to which Azrah had alluded when he assured him that he was acquainted with his secret. In that one word was summed up the most important point of the gipsy boy's peculiar destiny; on that secret, and the mystery with which his origin was enshrouded, hinged his future happiness or misery.

And Azrah had told him that he was acquainted with the names of his parents, and no doubt knew the whole of their history; and, surely, after the deep interest he had expressed in his welfare, he would not hesitate at some future period to disclose all that he knew to him. Indeed, he had told him that he would not, and in that assurance he endeavoured to make himself contented.

He was well convinced that his mother had endured the greatest misfortunes, and he had been told that they had been caused by the cruelty of her husband, whom he had been from earliest childhood commanded to abhor, to curse; but, deeply as he sympathised in the sorrows of his mother, and her supposed untimely fate, his heart revolted at the idea of hating the author of his being, however unjust he might have been. He was told that he was still living; but should he ever be permitted to know him—would he ever acknowledge him as his offspring, and endeavour to make atonement to him for the injuries he had inflicted on his mother? He would fain try to hope that he would, and that hope imparted a ray of comfort to him in his darkest gloom.

Thus passed away weeks, months, and still Rosario saw nothing of Azrah, and he began to fear that he had quitted the tribe altogether, and, in that apprehension, his uneasiness increased to an almost insupportable degree. Notwithstanding the pains which Harold had always taken to prevent Azrah from holding any communication with the rest of the gipsies, particularly with him, Rosario's impatience at last increased to such a degree that he could not help venturing one day to inquire of Harold what had become of him, and whether he would never again return to the abbey. The gipsy frowned at the question, and fixing a penetrating look upon Rosario, demanded,—

"And why do you feel such an interest in Azrah, Rosario?"

"Because he is good and kind," replied our hero; "and I should much regret if he were to leave us."

"He dare not leave us, boy," said Harold, with a significant look; "those who are once accepted in our tribe are bound to it for life, and Azrah, more especially than others, would not attempt to leave us."

"And why so particularly, Harold? And what is the meaning of the mystery which envelopes his actions? Why is he not permitted to associate with us the same as the rest of our companions?"

"Ask no questions, boy," sternly commanded Harold; "and beware that you seek not to hold communication with Azrah, though you may regard him with feelings of friendship and esteem. Above all, remember the oath which binds you to secrecy upon a subject to which I need not more particularly allude."

Rosario sighed deeply, and tears trembled in his eyes, while his bosom heaved with the most extraordinary emotion, and in other respects he evinced that something more powerful than can at present be explained was passing in his mind.

"Alas, Harold!" he ejaculated; "you know too well that you need not remind me of that. But shall I never be released from that terrible restriction so revolting to my feelings?"

"Hold, Rosario," exclaimed Harold; "you know how useless it is to remonstrate with me upon that subject. Reasons the most powerful have compelled us to adopt the course we have towards you, and you must not murmur. The time may come when you may be permitted to appear in your real character; but till that period shall arrive, you must learn to wait with patience."

The gipsy boy sighed, and cast his eyes to the earth; and Harold gazed at him for a few moments with looks of a peculiar expression.

"Oh, Harold," at length said Rosario, "why do you hesitate to reveal to me the names of my parents?"

"It's enough for you to know that I have my reasons," answered Harold; "therefore interrogate me no farther."

"But my father still lives?"

"I have told you so, and you must learn to hate him as you would the greatest miscreant who draws the breath of life."

"Oh, Harold," returned the gipsy boy, "notwithstanding all the faults of which he may have been guilty, he is still my parent, and I cannot hate him—nature revolts from the thought."

"Boy!" fiercely demanded Harold, "would you esteem the murderer of your mother?"

Rosario shuddered, and could not make any reply. He remembered the oath he had taken at his mother's grave, and his anguish of mind was the most intense. He saw, however, that it was useless to put any further questions to Harold, and therefore quitted his presence, and wandered forth from the abbey into the neighbouring woodlands, in order that he might give free indulgence to his thoughts.

Young as he was, Rosario possessed a mind far more capacious than his years gave authority to, and his nature was susceptible to the most tender feelings. He seemed born to adorn the most elevated station of society, and no one who beheld him could help regretting that he should be placed in the degraded situation in which he was. And Rosario was fully sensible that he was qualified for a far better position in society, and that those with whom he was unfortunately associated, were unworthy of him; but still there was something in the wild, romantic, and wandering life he led, which was consonant with his feelings, and he would have felt loth to have quitted it, even had the opportunity been offered him. Besides, in spite of all the severity with which Harold and Madela had treated him, and the ferocity of their dispositions, he could not help feeling some degree of respect and gratitude towards them for the protection they had afforded him from infancy, when he was left without a friend or protector in the world.

"Would they only permit me to appear in my real character," he exclaimed, "in spite of all the mystery which is attached to me, and which they refuse to solve, I might endeavour to be happy. And why should they hold me under such restraint!

Alas! how can I know peace or contentment while I am forced to assume a character so repugnant to my feelings?"

Rosario sighed deeply as he uttered these words, and tears flowed fast from his eyes. How agonizing were the thoughts that crowded upon his brain, and banished all hope of serenity from his breast.

He continued to wander in the woodlands the whole of the afternoon; and, even when evening set in, he felt no inclination to return to the abbey.

The moon arose in chaste splendour, and Rosario, seating himself on a green hillock, for some time diverted his thoughts by the contemplation of the tranquil beauties of the scene.

He was suddenly aroused by hearing a light footstep behind him, and, looking round, he beheld the form of a man approaching towards the spot on which he was seated. The figure was familiar to him, and, looking more narrowly, he was enabled by the light of the moon to distinguish the man's features. It was Azrah.

The amazement and delight of Rosario at this unexpected meeting with that being who had so constantly occupied his thoughts, may be very well conceived; and Azrah, who recognized him at the same moment evidently with some confusion, paused, and the gipsy boy hastened towards him; but, as the moonbeams fell upon his countenance, he was surprised at the change which had taken place. The features were the same, but they were marked by such a curious expression, that Rosario could not help gazing at him with the greatest astonishment. His face was very pale, and his eyes were more than usually melancholy.

"Oh, Azrah," said Rosario, extending his hand towards him, " and do I then, indeed, once more behold you? I began to fear that you had left us for ever. But how pale and ill you look! Oh, tell me, and deem me not impertinent that I ask the question, whither have you been, and what has happened to you to detain you so long from us?"

Azrah looked at him with the deepest emotion, and then passed his hands across his eyes.

"Go—go; leave me, Rosario," he said; " I—I am glad to see you, but we must not commune together."

"Oh, why not?"

" I have told you, Rosario, and that must suffice for the present. If you value my friendship, my happiness, you will not urge me. Where I have been, and what errand I have been upon, must remain a secret. Alas! Heaven knows what I have suffered, what I am still suffering. Bless you, bless you, Rosario; bless you, fair child of sorrow, and farewell."

"Nay, dear Azrah, friend, for such you have permitted me to call you," said the gipsy boy, imploringly, " do not leave me thus. We are here alone, where no one can observe us, and surely you need not hesitate to grant me the indulgence I seek so anxiously."

"Already have I told you more than my lips were permitted to reveal," said Azrah; "and with that you must rest satisfied until Providence will suffer me to disclose the whole truth. Should Harold or Madeline suspect what has taken place between us, I dare not say what the consequences might be that would ensue to both you and me."

"Azrah," returned Rosario, "you know me for what I am; you know my parents, you are acquainted with all the melancholy circumstances of their history. Oh! think of what my anguish and suspense must be, and do not refuse to impart to me at least their names.''

"I must not,'' replied Azrah, in a voice choked with emotion; "and the knowledge of it would only render you more miserable than you are at present."

"Oh, how could it do so?''

"Time, my poor child, will probably reveal it. But tell me, Rosario, do you remember the fatal night when you were brought among our people? Oh, no; it is impossible, for you were so very young at the time."

"I was, but still so strong was the impression that dismal event made upon my mind, that nothing can eradicate it. Oh! well do I recollect how my poor mother carried me through the wet and the cold, till her exhausted limbs could support her no longer, and she sank on the spot from which she was taken by the gipsies but to die. Methinks I still feel her poor cold arms as they encircled my neck, and hear the blessing she invoked upon my head. I remember no more than that she was conveyed into the gipsy tent, where I was afterwards informed that she breathed her last.''

Sobs choked the gipsy boy's voice, and Azrah exhibited the most powerful emotion, so much so, that he was unable for a few moments to speak.

"Rosario," he said at length, "and have you no recollection of the features of your unfortunate mother?''

"All that I recollect is, that they were very beautiful, but careworn. They frequently arise indistinctly to my imagination like a dream.''

Azrah paused for a minute or two, and seemed to be communing with himself; at length he turned once more to Rosario, and said,—

"Rosario, if I deliver to your care a treasure you no doubt will think inestimable, will you have the prudence to keep it concealed from every eye save your own?''

"Oh, yes, yes!'' eagerly replied the gipsy boy. "I will guard it as carefully as my own life.''

"Take this, then, my poor child," said Azrah, taking a miniature from his bosom, and placing it in the hand of Rosario; "and, while you gaze upon the countenance it represents, know that it is the resemblance of that unfortunate woman who bore you. Bless you, bless you; farewell."

And, before Rosario could recover from his astonishment and confusion, Azrah had fled from the spot. Indescribable were the feelings that rushed to the bosom of the gipsy boy, as he pressed the miniature to his lips; his heart palpitated with an emotion it had never experienced before; but, when he ventured to look at it, and to inspect it minutely, which he was enabled to do by the bright moonbeams, how greatly was that increased.

The likeness he gazed upon was that of a beautiful young woman, apparently not more than twenty-two years of age. The features were of the Grecian order, and soft and gentle as those of an angel. The eyes were brilliant as diamonds, and redolent of every intellectual expression. The hair was parted gracefully across the forehead, and flowed in rich and luxuriant tresses over the shoulders. A sweet smile played around the lips, which were parted, as if in the act of speaking. The complexion was beautifully fair.

"But, gracious Heaven! what is the meaning of this?'' exclaimed Rosario, after he had gazed at the portrait for a minute; "I gaze upon the exact likeness of Azrah; the features are the same, only more delicate, and the complexion more fair. Such, too, is the expression of his eyes, only more melancholy. No brother could be more alike than is Azrah to this, the resemblance of my poor mother. Almighty Father, unravel this mystery! Do I, indeed, in Azrah behold a relation ?"

He sunk on his knees with the greatest emotion, and continued to gaze upon the miniature, and the longer he did so, the more forcibly was he struck with the extraordinary likeness it bore to Azrah, and nameless feelings shot through his frame. Then, again and again, did he press it vehemently to his lips, and weep tears of melancholy joy and reverence upon it.

"Spirit of my mother," he exclaimed, "look down upon thy poor child, and unravel this painful mystery. And am I, at length, permitted to gaze upon the features of her who bore me ? This is, indeed, a sad gratification, which I never expected to experience."

Once more he kissed the miniature, and, rising from his knees, placed it carefully in his bosom, next his heart, and slowly bent his way towards the abbey ruins.

It would be impossible to do justice to the feelings of Rosario, as he proceeded on his way; but the likeness which existed between the features of Azrah and the miniature astonished and bewildered him more than all, and most anxious he was to behold that mysterious man; and yet, after the solemn injunctions he had given him, how could he persist in tormenting him with questions, after he had, again and again, assured him that he could not, at present, satisfy his curiosity ? The esteem he had before felt for him was now greatly increased, from the impression that he was, in some way, related to him. How could he have known so much of the family history of his parents, which it was evident he did, if he had not been immediately connected with them ? And by what means did the miniature of his mother fall into his possession ? These questions were so much involved in ambiguity, that he found it impossible to fathom them.

On arriving at the abbey ruins, he was questioned narrowly by Harold and Madela as to the reason of this long absence; but he managed to answer them to their satisfaction, and, not beholding Azrah among them, he quickly retired to the room in which he slept, where he again gave free indulgence to his thoughts, and passed several hours in contemplating and weeping over the portrait of his mother. The longer he gazed at it, the more he was convinced of the striking and extraordinary resemblance it bore to Azrah, and he was lost and bewildered in a chaos of fruitless conjecture.

When sleep, at length, descended upon his eyelids, the most remarkable visions flitted before his busy imagination, and he awoke, in the morning, very little refreshed.

The whole of that day he looked in vain for Azrah, nor could he hear anything from the gipsies in allusion to him. He wandered from the ruins, at the first opportunity, and passed his time in the woodlands, in weeping over the dear resemblance of her who had borne him, and whom he believed had met with so untimely and sad a fate.

Thus several days elapsed, without anything worthy of notice occurring, and still Rosario saw nothing of Azrah, and he could scarcely believe that he was an inmate of the abbey; but he was determined not to rest until he had, by some means or the other, ascertained the fact. He could perceive by the manners of Harold and Madela that they had something of evil in contemplation, and, from the hints which he accidentally overheard them drop, he was satisfied that their designs were directed against Sir Laurence Cleveland. He was soon satisfied that his suspicions were correct.

He happened, one evening, to enter the ruins unperceived by any of the tribe, and was passing on to his chamber, when he overheard the voices of Madela and Harold in deep and serious conversation, in an adjoining part of the ruins; and, as he could do so without being observed, curiosity prompted him to stop and listen, thinking that he might elicit something that would be of service to him, and might serve to unravel the mystery in which his fate was enshrouded. Not expecting the proximity of any person, they did not conduct their conversation in guarded tones, so that Rosario was enabled to catch distinctly every word they uttered.

"Zephania and Malachial are those most fitting for the task," observed Harold; "and they will be able to accomplish it without any danger of detection."

"Aye," returned Madela; "and I am all impatience until the deed is done. Oh! it will be glorious revenge. How will the heart of Laurence Cleveland be wrung, on his return, to find his noble mansion a heap of smouldering ruins, and his fair Blanche torn from him for ever. We must despatch the order immediately."

"Yes," replied Harold; "and, by to-morrow night, if our plan fail not, Branscombe House will be in flames, and Laurence Cleveland will return to his home but to meet with desolation and despair. Oh! he little imagines the power and determination of those whom he affects to despise. He must be made to shed tears, tears of blood, and, by my murdered father's spirit, I swear never to rest until I have accomplished that."

"Well said, Harold," remarked Madela; "our revenge must be slow, deliberate, but certain. We must keep the mind of Sir Laurence in a constant state of dread and suspense, until we have worked him up to the utmost pitch of human endurance, and then ——"

"Ah! then," added Harold, "we will resign him to that fate, that shame and punishment, from which he cannot escape. Oh! how little does he believe the power we hold in our hands to work his destruction. Little does he conceive that we can produce those who will sink him into infamy. But come, we are wasting time while we are conversing here. Let us immediately despatch our instructions to Zephania and Malachial; by to-morrow night, Branscombe House must be destroyed."

"It must—it shall!" ejaculated Madela, and they both directly quitted the spot, and left Rosario in a state of amazement and horror at what he had overheard.

"Monstrous!" exclaimed Rosario, when they were gone; "what can urge those with whom I have been from childhood connected, to such an act of outrage? And shall I remain quiet while such a dreadful act of incendiarism is contemplated, against those to whom my heart, by some strange, some unaccountable influence yearns? They have commanded me to hate Sir Laurence Cleveland, but I cannot; no, no, my heart revolts at the very idea; and as to his amiable lady, can I dare even to think of the awful calamity with which she is threatened? No, I cannot. I will thwart the plans of Madela and Harold, and save Lady Cleveland, if possible; but how? Would that I could behold Azrah now, that I might consult with him upon this subject, and take his advice. But there is no time to be lost. Already have they, perhaps, despatched their infamous instructions to Zephania and Malachial, who are in the neighbourhood of Branscombe House, and, if promptitude is not used, it will be too late to prevent the evil contemplated. In spite of all the danger that might accrue to myself, I will away to Branscombe House, and warn Lady Cleveland of the plot. I am well acquainted with the nearest route, and, if I use expedition, I may not be too late to prevent the threatened destruction. If I can only leave the ruins unseen, my absence will not cause any suspicion, especially as no one is aware that I have become acquainted with the plans of Madela and Harold. It shall be so, in spite of the consequences to myself. Providence will, I trust, approve of my intentions, and protect me through them."

He felt inspired with the greatest confidence, and made his way to that part of the ruins in which the gipsies were assembled, with the hope of being enabled to elicit something more to forward him in the accomplishment of his wishes.

The most perplexing thoughts agitated the mind of Rosario, and he could not but

No. 22.

look upon Madela and Harold with a feeling of greater horror than he had ever experienced towards them before.   But he subdued his feelings as much as possible, to
prevent their eliciting any suspicion in their breasts, and listened to the conversation
which passed between them with the greatest attention, hoping to hear something
more of their plans; but he was enabled to gather no more than that it was the intention of Harold, Madela, and two or three more of the tribe, to leave the ruins that
evening, on some secret expedition, and that they probably would be absent two or
three days.   Rosario was delighted to hear this, as it would afford him a better opportunity of putting his designs into effect; and he was determined, as soon as they
had departed, also to quit the abbey, and to rest not until he had arrived at Branscombe House.   A short time afterwards Madela and Harold, whom Rosario now believed to be the son of the old woman, left the ruins, and he immediately retired to
his own chamber to prepare himself for his journey.   Here he took forth from his
bosom the portrait of his mother, and pressing it fervently to his lips, invoked of her
spirit a blessing on his head, and protection in the virtuous cause he was about to undertake, and he then felt inspired with more than usual confidence, and all being still
in the old abbey ruins, and darkness having fallen upon the earth, he ventured forth
from his chamber, and was soon after traversing the road which he had designed to
take.   He would have been doubly satisfied had he been able to have seen Azrah,
communicated to him what he had overheard, and had his advice, for he felt assured,
from the manners of that mysterious man, that he could never for an instant lend
himself to such atrocious designs; but that, on the contrary, he would do all that he
could to frustrate them.

The idea of the dreadful danger to which the Lady Blanche was exposed by the
contemplated vengeance of the gipsies, added speed to his footsteps, and he travelled
on without fear, and, in the course of a very brief space of time, had got a considerable
way on his journey.

"But why should I feel such an extraordinary interest in the fate of Sir Laurence
Cleveland, and all connected with him?" he asked himself.   "He is almost a stranger to me, and I have never beheld him but under the most disadvantageous circumstances.   I am commanded to hate him as my deadliest enemy; yet I cannot do so;
my heart revolts at the bare idea, and, on the contrary, I am prepared to look upon
him with the warmest esteem.   What inscrutable power is it that has engendered
these thoughts in my breast?   And must I ever remain in the character I now assume?   Shall I never be permitted to shake off that disguise which is so revolting to
my feelings?   Oh! Azrah, you are acquainted with my secret, and from all you have
said, and from your behaviour towards me whenever we have met, I feel convinced
how deeply you sympathise with me; yet why not unravel the mystery, the impenetrable mystery connected with me?   Would you but disclose to me the names of
those to whom I owe my being, even though the intelligence might bring me pain,
I would endeavour to be satisfied; but to be kept in this state of suspense and doubt
is intolerable.   And then the likeness which Azrah bears to the portrait of my mother,
that is unaccountable, unless, indeed, he be a near relation.   And by what means did
he acquire that knowledge of my parents which he evidently has?   By what means
did he become possessed of the miniature?   All these facts are beyond my comprehension, and the longer I reflect on them, the more do I become involved in perplexity.   Providence assist me, and release me from my present painful situation."

These words he uttered with the greatest fervour, and any one who could have beheld his impassioned looks at that moment, might have read the tumultuous and agonizing thoughts that were passing in his mind. He, however, endeavoured to recover himself, and proceeded on his journey with increased speed, only stopping to rest himself occasionally, and partaking of the refreshments he had taken care to provide himself with previous to his leaving the ruins. He met with but few persons on the road, and those whom he did, did not seem to take any notice of him, notwithstanding the lateness of the hour for one so young to be out. But at length he could not struggle against fatigue, in spite of his anxiety to lose no time in arriving at the end of his journey, so momentous as was the errand upon which he was going, and having arrived at an old barn on the roadside, he entered it, and having committed himself to the care of the Almighty, he was soon asleep.

He did not awake again until daylight, and then arising from the rude couch which he had formed himself, he resumed his journey, with renewed hope and determination. In consequence of his having become foot-sore, however, he was unable to proceed as fast as he had before done, and evening approached, and he had yet several miles to travel, before he would arrive at Branscombe House. The most torturing apprehensions took possession of his mind, and he exerted himself to the utmost.

" I shall never reach there in time to thwart the diabolical plans of old Madela and Harold," he soliloquised ; " and should I not do so, the destruction of Lady Blanche is inevitable. Heaven assist me in my wishes, and suffer not the guilty to triumph in their schemes."

Still he proceeded on his way with all the rapidity he could, and felt convinced that Providence would not frustrate him in his praiseworthy intentions. But now the storm commenced with great violence, and everything served to retard his progress. He was soon wet through to the skin, and was compelled to seek shelter for awhile in the first place he came to, until it should in some measure have abated. This unavoidable delay was most torturing to him, and he began to despair of being able to put his humane wishes into execution, and that his journey would all be to no purpose. Zephania and Malachial had probably by this time received their instructions, and would be sure to put them into execution without delay, and he shuddered at the idea of the destruction which he would be too late to prevent.

At length the storm greatly abated, and Rosario resumed his journey with increased speed and energy, and at length arrived within two miles of Branscombe House. His heart palpitated with mingled doubts, hopes, and fears, but suddenly a lurid glare shot up into the sky, and which proceeded from the very direction of the doomed house.

" Alas ! alas !" ejaculated Rosario, as he watched the progress of the conflagration; " it is too late—the villains have done their diabolical work, and nothing can now prevent the destruction. Heaven spare the unfortunate Lady Blanche. Oh ! what a monstrous deed is this."

Notwithstanding the violent agitation of his feelings, and knowing that he was now too late to furnish the information he had wished, Rosario proceeded on his way towards the mansion, and flew rather than ran, and as he approached nearer, the full extent of the scene of destruction was made more apparent to him, and he paused in despair, and was at a loss to know in what manner to act. While he thus stood, he was all at once aroused by hearing approaching footsteps, and looking in the direction from whence they proceeded, he beheld two men coming at a quick pace towards him, and, by the red reflection occasioned by the fire, he immediately recognised the two gipsies, Zephania and Malachial, the miscreants who had committed this fiendish act. Knowing what the consequences would be if they beheld him, he turned aside, and concealed himself behind a tree until they had passed him, which they did without observing him, and then he once more hurried on his way, and anxious to know the extent of the damage, and whether Lady Cleveland had been preserved from the flames.

"The monsters!" he ejaculated; "well have they performed their diabolical task, and all my good intentions have been thwarted. And they will escape the punishment, while I dare not betray them, knowing that my own destruction would be sure to follow. And shall I continue to associate with such wretches? Alas! how can I help myself? The strange secret connected with me, and the power they hold over me, places my fate in their hands, and entirely at their disposal, and I must not, dare not separate myself from them."

He sighed deeply with anguish of these thoughts, and then once more hastened on his way, and soon perceived that only one wing of the mansion was on fire, and that a number of persons were exerting themselves to extinguish the flames, which were fast yielding to their united efforts.

In the confusion of the moment, scarcely knowing what he did, he rushed into the gardens of the mansion, and on the way picked up a torch which was burning on the ground, and which had probably been dropped by accident, or very likely by one of the incendiaries themselves, and he was about to move towards the house, when he was surrounded by several men, and accused of being the author of the nefarious outrage, in the manner which has been described.

CHAPTER XVII.

THE GIPSY BOY IN PRISON.—THE INTERVIEW.—THE MINIATURE.

"You are preserved, my dearest Blanche, from a hideous fate. Heaven in its infinite mercy has yet spared to me my soul's treasure, and our cherub babe," ejaculated Sir Laurence Cleveland, as he strained them both to his bosom; "and my soul rises in unbounded, in unspeakable gratitude to the Almighty Ruler of events. Oh, God, had you perished in this awful conflagration, kindled by the base hands of the incendiary, what could have redeemed the dreadful loss? My soul shrinks appalled with horror at the thought."

"Oh, Laurence, dear Laurence," sighed Blanche, as she wept tears of mingled joy and anguish upon his bosom; "and do I indeed behold you again? Alas! alas! this must be the work of our bitterest enemies, for I feel convinced that it was not occasioned by accident."

"Too much reason have I to fear that it did not," returned the baronet; "it is those miscreants, the gipsies, who have been the authors of this inhuman deed."

"Ah! my husband, for what reason do you suspect them?"

"Whom else have we a right to suspect; have they not by their actions, and the avowals they have made, shewn the deadly hatred they bear towards us? Have they not several times threatened us with their vengeance? and their daring conduct hitherto, ought to satisfy us that they would not hesitate to put those villanous and desperate threats into execution at the first opportunity."

"'Tis too true," coincided Blanche; "but still, Heaven forbid that we should judge them too hastily of this frightful crime. From the vigilant inquiries that we have for some months made, it is quite evident that they are nowhere in this neighbourhood."

" And it is equally clear, my beloved Blanche, from what has in that interval transpired, that they have their agents lurking about, and I have good reason to believe that it was by them that this diabolical attempt at destruction was made."

" Ah! my husband, what have you then seen or heard?"

" I will make you acquainted with everything anon," answered Sir Laurence ; " but tell me, my love, how did you first discover the flames, and in what manner were your own precious self and our infant so happily saved from so horrible and so untimely a death?"

" Amanda will tell you everything," returned Blanche; " my thoughts are too disordered to enable me to do so."

Sir Laurence turned to his sister with an inquiring look, and she gratified his wishes in the following words:—

" The little Emeline had long been placed in her cot, and slumbered in peaceful innocence, but Blanche and myself did not feel inclined to go to rest, for the storm raged with frightful fury, and we were deeply engaged in anxious conversation on your quick return, after the letter we had received from you; in fact, as you are aware, dear Laurence, we expected you yesterday, and knowing your usual punctuality it is no wonder that we should feel some alarm at your delay. However, we endeavoured to persuade ourselves that you could not get the business you had gone upon completed so soon as you anticipated, and were satisfied that you would not procrastinate your return any longer than you could possibly help. While we were thus seated, we were suddenly aroused by hearing a confused noise below, which was almost immediately followed by loud cries of ' fire!' We were both, as you may suppose, terribly alarmed, and, in the confusion of the moment, scarcely knew how to act. But now the reflection of the flames met our gaze, and fully convinced us of the extent of our danger. I snatched the infant from the bed, and taking the arm of the trembling Lady Blanche, advanced with her towards the room-door, which I opened, but had no sooner done so, when we were met by a dense and suffocating body of smoke, which drove us back into the room, and for a few seconds deprived us of all power of action. Our situation was now extremely perilous ; we heard the crackling timbers, and were convinced that the fire had got strong hold, and was gaining rapid progress. ' My child! my child!' frantically exclaimed Blanche ; and we once more rushed to the door, and endeavoured to make our escape, but were again forced back by the overpowering volumes of smoke that rushed up the staircase. Our senses nearly left us, and we gave ourselves up for lost. But, at that moment, amidst the confusion from the numerous persons which the conflagration had gathered together, we heard the shouts of two or three men who were apparently, at the risk of their lives, endeavouring to force their way up the stairs Blanche was so overcome by terror and the effects of the smoke, that she fainted, and I scarcely remember anything more than being seized and conveyed by several persons through the flames and smoke, to that part of the mansion which the fire had not reached. Thank Heaven, we were in safety; with the rest you are, I believe, acquainted."

" How miraculous was this preservation!" remarked Sir Laurence, when his sister had concluded; "this was no accident, and a just and terrible punishment overtake the wretches who have been guilty of this atrocious, this fiendish deed. And were your preservers your own servants?"

"They were," answered Amanda; "to their courage and fidelity we are indebted for our lives."

"Brave, honest fellows!" ejaculated Sir Laurence; "they shall not go unrewarded. But it is the villains—the gipsies, who have done this; and, by all my hopes, I will not rest until I have pursued them to destruction."

"And what makes you so strongly suspect those wandering, outcast people, dear Laurence?" eagerly inquired Blanche.

"Oh, I have almost convincing proof of their guilt," answered the baronet. "But you are not aware, my love, that one of them is in custody on suspicion of being the incendiary?"

"No, no; is it possible?"

"It is true, Blanche; and that person is no other than the gipsy youth who has so deeply interested us."

"Rosario?"

"The same."

"Oh, it cannot be," said Blanche; "I will not credit it. One so young, apparently so innocent, and noble in manners, and who has on more than one occasion interposed to save us from the outrages of the tribe with whom he has been from childhood, it seems, connected, could never have been guilty of so hideous—so frightful a crime."

"Oh, no, it is impossible," exclaimed Amanda.

"Believe me," observed Sir Laurence, "that I would fain think the same; for that boy has, from the first moment I beheld him, made a powerful impression upon me; but suspicion appears to be very strong against him, and I fear that he has been made the instrument of the villains with whom he associated. He was detected coming from the mansion with a lighted torch in his hand soon after the flames were kindled."

"Unfortunate boy!" said Blanche; "but still I cannot bring my mind to believe him guilty on such evidence alone. It seems impossible that one so gentle in manners, could ever be persuaded to act so inhuman a part."

"I cannot but be of your opinion, dear Blanche," remarked Amanda; "and you, my brother, must scout the fearful idea from your mind, when you remember the manner in which Rosario interposed to save you from the vengeance of the gipsies, on the occasion of our first meeting with them, and the horror he expressed at the shedding of human blood."

"I repeat, Amanda," answered the baronet, "that all these circumstances have prepossessed me in favour of the gipsy boy; but although he be not the actual incendiary, he may be acquainted with the authors of the brutal outrage, and it is necessary that he should undergo the most searching examination; the real guilty parties must not be suffered to escape punishment, or we shall never be safe for a moment from their acts of violence."

"And did you, then, behold the unfortunate lad, Laurence?" demanded his wife.

"I did, on my arrival at home, and gave instructions for his being conveyed to a place of security. It is true that he strongly protested his innocence, and said that he had come here to warn me of my danger, and ——"

"And that is not at all improbable," said Blanche, eagerly interrupting Sir Laurence. "Oh, I am confident that he will be able to prove his innocence, or never can I believe the human countenance again."

"I sincerely hope that he may, Blanche," said the baronet; "but he must give every satisfactory explanation."

"Which, doubtless, he will do," observed Amanda. "His own words prove that if he is not himself the incendiary, he knows the guilty parties, and he must not endeavour to shield them from punishment, if he would not implicate himself in their crime. However, I have very little doubt but that the gipsies are the scoundrels who have perpetrated this outrage."

"And what makes you so strongly suspect them, Laurence?" asked Blanche.

"Because they have openly avowed themselves our bitterest enemies," replied Sir Laurence; "but I have other reasons."

"Name them."

The baronet then briefly related to Blanche and his sister such of the particulars of his encounter with Madela, Harold, and the other gipsy, on his return home, as he thought prudent, and also the vague threats they had given utterance to; and the astonished females both expressed their horror, but at the same time could not believe that it was at all likely that the gipsies would employ him in, or that Rosario would undertake, such a monstrous and dangerous task.

"They might do so thinking that he was the least likely to be suspected," returned Sir Laurence. "Certainly, if the statement of the men who seized him be correct, the case looks remarkably black against him. They saw him coming out of the outhouse attached to the wing of the mansion to which the fire was confined, and in which a number of faggots are kept. But I will suspend my judgment until after his examination has taken place, and to which I am now going."

Blanche and Amanda made use of a few more observations, and shortly afterwards Sir Laurence left them, and proceeded on his way to the house of the magistrate where the examination of Rosario on the serious charge that was made against him was appointed to take place.

On his way thither, the mind of the baronet was tortured by various ideas, and he could not but hope that circumstances would turn out that would entirely establish the innocence of the gipsy boy; for the feelings he excited in his breast, whenever he thought of him, were of the most unaccountable description; nor could he bring his mind to believe that one so young, and apparently so gentle in manners, could be guilty of such an atrocious deed.

On his arrival at the magistrate's house, he found a number of the gentlemen of the neighbourhood, who were attracted by curiosity, and the indignation they felt at the outrage which had been committed, to witness the proceeding; and shortly afterwards Rosario was brought in by the officers from the place where he had been confined during the night. His appearance excited the deepest interest, and a murmur of admiration and astonishment ran through the justice-room.

Rosario's countenance was very pale, and he had evidently been weeping; but that added, if possible, to the simple beauty of its expression, an expression that gave the lie to guilt, and was the index of a pure and innocent mind. He seemed by far too delicate for a boy, and no one could gaze upon him without admiration, in spite of the heinous charge which was about to be preferred against him.

Sir Laurence Cleveland felt a strange sensation stealing through his veins as he gazed upon him; and, when Rosario's eye timidly met his, crimson blushes suffused his cheeks, and he hung down his head, as if in shame; but he quickly seemed to re-cover himself, dashed the tears away that had gathered in his eyes, and then stood calm and erect, awaiting the commencement of the proceedings.

The usual preliminaries having been gone through, the examination began.

"Prisoner," said the magistrate, "do you not belong to those gipsies who, at dif-ferent times, create so much alarm in this and other neighbourhoods?"

"I am connected with the wandering tribe, sir," answered Rosario. "They have been my only protectors from early childhood."

"You have parents?"

"My mother rests at peace beyond the stars," replied the boy, solemnly; and tears again trembled in his eyes.

"And your father?"

"He lives, I believe, but I know him not."

"Were you not born among the gipsy tribe?" demanded the magistrate.

"No, your worship."

"Beware; you will only prejudice your case, if you do not speak the truth."

"My lips never yet gave utterance to a wilful falsehood," answered the gipsy boy, firmly, and with a dignity of demeanour that astonished every one.

"Your name, boy?"

"Rosario."

"Have you no other name?"

"They call me the Fawn."

"But your surname?"

"I know it not. It has ever been kept a secret from me."

"Again I caution you not to equivocate."

"I have spoken nothing but the truth, sir, and intend to do so, let whatever may be the consequences."

"You know this gentleman, Sir Laurence Cleveland?"

"I have seen him several times before," answered Rosario, with a sigh.

"Are you aware of the nature of the offence with which you are charged?"

"I am; and solemnly assert that I am as innocent of that foul charge as your wor-ship yourself."

The different witnesses were now examined at great length; and, when they had concluded their evidence, the magistrate observed,—

"Prisoner, you have heard what the several witnesses have said; what have you to reply to the charge?"

"No more than to repeat my solemn assurance of my entire innocence," replied Rosario.

"And what was you doing at Branscombe House, at the time of the fire, and under such suspicious circumstances?" interrogated the magistrate.

"Having accidentally overheard the plot against Sir Laurence Cleveland, I came to warn his family of their danger. The lighted torch that was found in my possession, I picked up in my path."

"Then, although you assert your own innocence, you acknowledge you know the persons who have been guilty of this heinous offence?"

"I do, sir."

"And what are their names?"

The gipsy boy hesitated for a moment or two, and then said,—

"I will not reveal their names."

"This, to say the least of it, looks suspicious," said the magistrate; "you had better retract your words."

"Let whatever may be the consequences, I cannot."

"Where are your tribe at present remaining?"

"That question I also decline to answer."

"Are any of them now concealed in this neighbourhood?"

"I cannot say."

"Prisoner," said the magistrate, "the evasive answers you have given to the questions that have been put to you, and your obstinacy in refusing to furnish us with the knowledge you admit that you possess, all serve to add to the suspicion against you. I shall remand you for a few days, when you will be again brought before me, to complete the evidence against you; and I sincerely hope that, in the interval that will be thus allowed you, you will well consider the awful position in which you stand."

" Sir Laurence Cleveland," said the gipsy boy, in a voice of the deepest emotion, and fixing upon him a look that left the most powerful impression upon his mind, "if I suffer on this charge, before high Heaven I declare that it will be innocently, and in my earnest endeavour to serve you, and save your amiable lady from destruction. But I forgive you, and ardently pray that you may be protected from the vengeance of your enemies."

" Unhappy boy," said Sir Laurence, " if you are indeed guiltless of this atrocious charge, of which I would fain believe you to be, why do you hesitate to denounce the real offenders, and thus save yourself from farther annoyance, and perhaps punishment ? You will have nothing to fear, for every protection would be afforded you."

" It must be sufficient to say that *I dare not*," answered Rosario.

Sir Laurence looked upon him with an eye of the deepest pity, and the gipsy boy was then removed from the justice-room.

Sir Laurence continued in conversation with the magistrate for some time after the examination had taken place, and could not help expressing to that gentleman the deep interest he took in Rosario's fate, and the strong belief that he entertained of his innocence; but still, under all the circumstances, he felt bound to admit that the magistrate had no alternative but to act in the manner he had done.

" I would willingly believe that one so young, and so prepossessing in his manners and appearance, could not be guilty of this abominable crime," remarked the magistrate; " but the obstinacy with which he refuses to answer the important questions I have put to him, looks very suspicious indeed; and I am afraid that he has been made the instrument of the rascals with whom he is connected to put their designs into execution. He is certainly a very handsome lad, and his manners are far superior to what you might expect from one who has been brought up to the vagrant life he has."

" True," coincided Sir Laurence; " and there is an air of mystery about him that greatly interests me."

" That may only be assumed to effect some sinister purpose," returned the magistrate.

" And yet I cannot think that so young a lad could act with such duplicity," said the baronet.

" Consider the tutors he has been among. But, in the course of a few days, we may be able to elicit much more than we know at present; and I only hope that it may prove to be in the prisoner's favour."

In this wish Sir Laurence perfectly coincided, and he shortly afterwards took his leave of the magistrate, and returned towards Branscombe House; his mind filled with various conjectures by the unsatisfactory result of the examination.

The looks and observations of Rosario were vividly impressed upon his memory, and he could not but believe him innocent, and strongly hoped that he would yet be prevailed upon to reveal all he knew, and not to permit himself to suffer for the guilty. He regretted that Rosario had ever been taken into custody at all, and would gladly have unbarred the doors of his prison if he could; but he was determined that every means should be used to detect the gipsies, for that the outrage had been committed by the orders of Madela and Harold, he could not entertain the least doubt; although he had mentioned nothing of the circumstance of his meeting with Madela and Harold at the old gibbet to the magistrate, as he did not think it would serve in any way to exculpate Rosario.

The solemn asseverations which the gipsy boy had made of his innocence, the baronet could not help placing the most implicit confidence in; and the longer he reflected on them, the stronger that belief became impressed upon his mind. But the features of Rosario gave rise to thoughts which he could not account for or understand, and he determined to visit him in his prison, with the hope that he should be enabled to persuade him to furnish him with some important information, especially when he should be satisfied that it was his earnest wish to exonerate him from the odious offence with which he was charged, and to restore him to liberty. Connected as he was with the gipsies, it was not likely that he was not acquainted with most of their secrets, and he might therefore have the power of at once removing his terrible doubts and suspense, as to whether or not Clara was really in existence, and if she was not, who the individual was whom the gipsies represented to be her, and who bore so extraordinary a resemblance to her.

Filled with these thoughts and resolutions, Sir Laurence arrived at home, where Lady Blanche and Amanda had been awaiting most anxiously his return. On hearing the result of the examination of Rosario, they both expressed their deep regret, for, notwithstanding his evasive answers, and all the circumstances under which he was taken, they both entertained a strong idea of his innocence, and were greatly interested with the peculiar circumstances of his tale, and the mystery that was connected with him.

"Poor lad!" said Blanche; "it is quite evident that he was formed by nature to fill a far better station in society than that he now occupies. It is a pity that some kind and benevolent person does not step forward and snatch him from the power of the abandoned wretches with whom he is now so unfortunately associated."

"That would I myself most willingly do, were it in my power," said Sir Laurence; "but he seems entirely wedded to his present wild and wandering life, and that nothing can prevail on him to leave it."

"But they will not convict him of this terrible crime, surely?" said Amanda.

"What alternative is there," returned the baronet, "so powerful as are the circumstantial facts adduced against him, and while he refuses to denounce those whom he asserts to be the real guilty parties? However, it is my intention to-morrow to have an interview with him, and nothing shall be wanting on my part, you may depend, to endeavour to prevail on him to be more communicative, and not to plunge himself into inevitable ruin by remaining obstinate."

"Do so, dear Laurence," said Lady Blanche, "and Heaven grant that you may succeed. Would that the men had not been so hasty in seizing him."

"They only acted as the circumstances of the case authorised them, and ought to be commended for their honest zeal in our welfare."

"Very true," said Blanche; "but after what fell from the lips of Madela and Harold on your meeting with them, there can be but little or no doubt that they were the instigators of the outrage, and they would never have employed a boy like Rosario to commit such an atrocious act of incendiarism."

"No, my love," coincided Sir Laurence; "I cannot believe that they would; but Rosario says that he knows them, and I am fearful that he entertains too great a dread of the tribe to betray them. He has also refused to disclose where the gipsies are at present concealed. But, with the assistance of the magistrates, I am not without strong hopes that I shall yet be able to detect them, and to bring them to justice."

" Alas!" sighed Blanche, " how unfortunate it is that we should have incurred the hatred and revenge of that determined and terrible race of people. They form their plans with such secrecy, and so cleverly, that no person whom they intend to injure can be on their guard against them, and we are therefore not safe from them an hour."

" Do not give way to any unnecessary fears, I pray you, Blanche," said her husband. " Providence has hitherto frustrated their evil designs against us, and I do not doubt but that, with proper precaution and vigilance, we shall still be enabled to defeat them."

" God grant that we may!" ejaculated Lady Cleveland; " but the seizure and imprisonment of Rosario, especially if he is convicted, is sure to exasperate them still more against us."

" All that we must be prepared for, my dear Blanche; but I rather think they will find the law too powerful for them."

" I know not that," remarked Blanche; " nor do I think they will be intimidated by it. They are most desperate and reckless people, as we have already had sufficient proof of."

" I do not attempt to deny that, Blanche," said Sir Laurence; " but still we must not be frightened by them, and, shortly, they may be caught in their own trap."

Blanche and Amanda appeared to be satisfied by the observations of the baronet; but in truth they were not, and he himself laboured under secret apprehensions, which he found it quite impossible to conquer, notwithstanding all his efforts.

In the meantime, Rosario, in his dungeon, was a prey to a variety of the most torturing emotions, and, after his examination before the magistrate, his agitation increased. He paced his dismal cell to and fro, and heavy sighs escaped his bosom.

" Oh, Providence!" he exclaimed, " why did you not permit me to be in time to warn them of their danger? What misery would then have been prevented, and I should have been now at liberty! And it is in my power to prove my innocence of this hateful crime, but I cannot, will not betray those with whom I am associated, though I would fain have frustrated their designs. But will they convict me? Oh, surely Sir Laurence Cleveland will intercede for me, after the deep interest he has evinced in my fate. He cannot believe me guilty. If I were permitted to reveal the painful secret connected with me, how sincerely, how fervently would every humane person sympathise with me, and marvel at the extraordinary character of my destiny. But, should I even be permitted to escape, shall I not incur the vengeance of the gipsies for the part I have played? On every side I am surrounded by danger, and am completely bewildered by the thoughts that are engendered in my breast."

He took forth the miniature of his mother from his bosom, pressed it vehemently to his lips, and shed scalding tears of anguish upon it.

" Spirit of my mother!" he ejaculated, raising his eyes towards Heaven, " I supplicate your protection in this my trouble; I implore you to guide my conduct, and teach me how to act. Heaven knows that I would act for the best, and would foil the guilty machinations of the gipsies; but I cannot, I dare not break the solemn oath I have taken, let my own sufferings be whatever they may. Oh! Azrah, what will be your sufferings when you come to know of my situation? You have stated yourself to be my best friend, and your own conduct proves the truth of your words; what anguish, then, will your generous bosom endure at the danger of my situation. Would to Heaven that I could have seen him before my departure from the abbey, that I might have had the benefit of his advice; then might all this evil have been avoided. But it is useless to regret now; there is nothing left for me to do but to trust in the goodness of Providence, who knows the purity of my intentions, and surely will not suffer me to fall a victim to my humanity."

Thus did Rosario continue to soliloquize at intervals during the night, and he gained but little repose; and the morning brought with it no hope, no consolation. He remained firm in the resolution he had formed not to betray the gipsies, or to reveal where they were concealed, notwithstanding the consequences that might accrue to himself for his determination. What a relief would it have afforded him, could he have had an interview with Azrah in his prison; for surely he would then, under all the circumstances, be induced to become more explicit than he had hitherto been, and would no longer refuse to make him acquainted with all those particulars of his birth which he was so anxious to know.

The features of Azrah haunted his imagination there, and the longer he gazed upon the likeness of his mother, the more forcibly was he struck with the extraordinary resemblance between that and Azrah, and the deeper he became involved in mystery and perplexity. Certainly Azrah must be some relation to his deceased mother, for in no other way could the remarkable likeness be accounted for. Perhaps he might even be her own brother. The idea was not an improbable one, and gave rise to the most powerful sensations in his breast. It seemed quite clear to him that he must have been in some way closely connected with his mother, or how could he have acquired the knowledge of her history that he had, and by what means had he got possession of the miniature?

He was deeply immersed in these thoughts, when he heard the key of his cell door turn in the lock, and the gaoler entered, followed by Sir Laurence Cleveland. The former immediately retired, and the baronet, having walked to the centre of the cell, paused and gazed upon the youthful prisoner with looks of the deepest interest and commiseration. The bosom of Rosario heaved with some extraordinary emotion as his eyes met those of Sir Laurence, and while his cheeks became pale and red alternately, he averted his looks, and seemed to be awaiting impatiently for the baronet to address him.

"Unfortunate youth," said Sir Laurence, at last, "think not that I come to exult over you in your painful situation, or to reproach you for the injury you are suspected of having done me; no, I would endeavour to persuade you not to remain obdurate, but to reveal all that you know of this guilty transaction, so that you may avoid the consequences that probably will otherwise befall you, and from which, in consequence of the deep interest which you have excited in my breast, I am most anxious to save you."

"Sir Laurence Cleveland," said Rosario, fixing upon the baronet a look of the deepest expression, "do you believe me capable of committing this diabolical outrage?"

"No, Rosario," returned Sir Laurence; "I cannot think that one so young could possess a mind so base; besides, I must confess that your appearance and manners, and the way in which you have upon more than one occasion interposed between me and the brutal violence of those with whom you are associated, have prepossessed me in your favour, and most happy should I be to snatch you from the degrading course of life which you are at present pursuing."

The countenance of the gipsy boy beamed with a peculiar expression as the baronet made use of these observations, and he sighed deeply.

"Sir Laurence Cleveland," he said, at length, "I know not how it is, but I have, from the first moment I beheld you, felt the same interest towards you as that you have been pleased to express you take in me, and fully do I appreciate your kindness; but I am wedded to the wild and wandering life I have, from my earliest childhood, led, and I must not leave it. But as respects this foul charge, I again, in the face of Heaven, solemnly declare my entire innocence. At the greatest risk I left my companions, with the hope of being able to warn you of your danger, but unfortunately I was too late."

"But you know the villains who perpetrated the deed, Rosario?"

"I do."

"Then why refuse to disclose their names, and where they are likely to be found, and, by so doing, exonerate your own character, and regain your liberty?"

"For reasons which I have before given, Sir Laurence," answered Rosario. "And, in spite of what the consequences to me may be, nothing whatever shall induce me to alter my determination."

"So young, and yet so obdurate? Bethink yourself, Rosario, ere it is too late."

The gipsy boy shook his head, and it was plain to be seen that his breast was undergoing the deepest emotion.

"I am fully satisfied that the outrage was committed through the instructions of the gipsies," continued Sir Laurence; "and I am determined not to rest until I have detected them. You, of course, know where they are concealed, and your refusal to divulge it looks, at least, suspicious."

"And would you have me betray those who, however rude their manners, have, at any rate, protected me from earliest infancy?"

"Rosario," said Sir Laurence, gazing with the utmost intensity at the handsome countenance of the lad, "there is something about you altogether, and the strange mystery with which you are enshrouded, that greatly creates my curiosity and anxiety. Tell me, and rest assured you will lose nothing by the confidence you repose in me, what is your name, and who are your parents?"

"I have before told you, Sir Laurence, that I know not," answered Rosario— "that assurance must suffice."

"I am afraid, boy," said the baronet, "that you are persuaded by the people with whom you are connected to maintain this unaccountable secrecy."

"I have ever scorned to speak an untruth," said Rosario, with a look of indignation. "Sir Laurence Cleveland, it is useless to question me farther, for I have nothing more to answer."

"Strange, unfortunate boy! you seem determined to rush on your own destruction. But one question I beg of you to answer."

"Name it, and if it is possible, and I am permitted to answer it, I will."

"You are aware of what Harold and Madela have stated at different times respecting the existence of my first wife?"

"I am, Sir Laurence."

"Are you aware whether it is a fact?"

"I know not."

" Pray answer me candidly, sincerely."

" I do."

" Have you never seen among your tribe a fair woman, about five-and-thirty years of age, and who will correspond with the form that has several times crossed my path in so mysterious a manner ?" eagerly demanded Sir Laurence.

" We have plenty of fair damsels amongst our people, but I have not seen one that answers the description you have given," replied Rosario.

" Strange," remarked the baronet ; " and yet it is certain that she is the instrument of the gipsies."

" She may be, Sir Laurence ; but I know her not. Have you any more questions to put to me ?"

" I have not, and have only once more to urge you to change your determination, and, by disclosing all you know, restore yourself to liberty."

" My determination is fixed, Sir Laurence," said Rosario ; " but here on my knees I once more solemnly protest my innocence, and that, so far from bearing any feelings of resentment against you and your amiable lady, I entertain towards you the most sincere esteem."

He was interrupted by an exclamation of astonishment and emotion from Sir Laurence, and found his eyes earnestly fixed upon something that was hung suspended from his neck. It was the miniature, which had accidentally escaped his bosom, and which was fully revealed to the baronet's anxious gaze. Rosario was astonished, and in the confusion of the moment he could not replace it.

" Gracious Heaven !" exclaimed Sir Laurence, in a tremulous voice, " those features so like !—boy, tell me, how came that miniature into your possession ?"

" Why are you so anxious to know, Sir Laurence ?" demanded Rosario.

" For the love of God, answer me ; do not keep me in suspense."

" This miniature but a few days since was given to me by a valued friend," replied our hero.

" One of your people ?"

" He is."

" And his name ?"

" It could serve you little to know."

" Torturing mystery ! Rosario, know you whose features that miniature represents ?"

" I am told," answered Rosario, in a voice of deep emotion, and tears gushed to his eyes as he spoke, " that they represent the beloved features of my unfortunate and ill-fated mother."

" Your mother !" cried Sir Laurence, trembling in every limb ; " good God ! is it possible ?"

" What means this fearful emotion, Sir Laurence ?" eagerly asked the astonished and agitated Rosario ; " know you the features that are here delineated ?"

" Do I know them ! Oh, Heaven !—Boy, let me look more narrowly into your countenance !"

He grasped the arm of the gipsy boy, as he spoke, and fixed his penetrating eyes full upon his countenance. Rosario trembled, and his cheeks became pale and red alternately.

" Ah ! those looks, those eyes !" ejaculated Sir Laurence ;—" boy, I must and will know more of you."

"Do not grasp my arm so tightly, Sir Laurence," said the lad; "you pain me, and your looks alarm me. I have told you all I know or am permitted to reveal."

"Gold, liberty, all that you can wish, shall be yours, Rosario, if you will but part with that portrait."

"Part with the likeness of that beloved mother whose soul is now in Heaven; sooner would I suffer death in its most horrible shape. Why should you wish to get the miniature in your possession?"

"Why should I wish to do so!—But away with this weakness; why should I suffer such a trifle to affect me thus?—and after all there may be no foundation for the ideas it has engendered. Rosario, once more I demand of you whether you know the name of your mother?"

"Have I not again and again protested that I do not?" returned Rosario. "She died in want and misery. My father I am told is still living, but I know him not, and I have been taught to curse him, hate him, for that he was the murderer of her who gave me being."

"Her murderer, boy!"

"Ay, for ill-treatment caused her death."

"And could you hate him if you were to know him, Rosario?"

"Methinks I could, when I recalled to mind the fate of my mother."

Sir Laurence paused a few moments, and seemed to be endeavouring to recover himself, while he gazed with ardent looks upon the gipsy boy.

"Rosario," he said at last, in calmer accents, "for the present I will leave you; but when we meet again, I trust to find that you have changed your mind, and that you have resolved to become more communicative."

"My mind is fully made up, Sir Laurence, and I cannot reveal more than I have already done," answered Rosario. "Heaven knows my innocence of the crime of which I have been accused, and I do not fear that it will protect me through my troubles."

"Strange as is the mystery of your actions, Rosario," said Sir Laurence, "you shall find in me a sincere friend, if I do not find that you are undeserving of it; but the wretches with whom you are connected I will pursue to destruction; I will not rest until they are detected, and brought to that punishment which their crimes so richly merit."

"Beware, Sir Laurence Cleveland," said Rosario; "you know not the enemies you have to contend with. Their designs are worked so secretly, that they may set detection at defiance, and they seldom fail in accomplishing anything upon which they have fixed their minds."

"And yet you would screen such villains, boy, and would still continue to associate with them."

"It is my fate; I cannot help myself," replied the gipsy boy.

"Wretched youth!" exclaimed Sir Laurence; and once more fixing a look upon Rosario, in which pity, surprise, and mental anguish were blended, he quitted the prison.

CHAPTER XIX.

THE OLD ABBEY RUINS AGAIN.—THE RAGE OF THE GIPSIES.—THE ATTACK
ON THE PRISON, AND THE RESCUE OF ROSARIO.

FOR some minutes after Sir Laurence Cleveland had departed, Rosario stood
lost in bewilderment and amazement. He recalled to mind every word that the
baronet had uttered; but the extraordinary emotion he had displayed on beholding
the miniature, created his wonder more than all. It was evident that the portrait
recalled some agonizing thoughts to his memory, and the eagerness he evinced to
obtain possession of it, served to increase that idea. The interest he seemed to take
in his welfare strengthened the esteem he had imbibed for him from the first moment
he had seen him, and he could not but believe that he would exert himself to the

utmost to rescue him from the dangerous situation in which he was at present placed; however, whether or no, Rosario was resolved that nothing should induce him to betray the gipsies, let whatever might be the consequences.

Rosario's anguish increased every hour, and it was in vain that he endeavoured to form some reasonable conjectures as to the real cause of the powerful emotion which the baronet evinced on beholding the miniature.

The whole of that day, these thoughts occupied his mind, and he still remained in as great a state of perplexity as ever. And, by this time, he thought to himself, the gipsies had, probably, become acquainted with his situation, and the rage they would experience at the discovery tortured his imagination. He had not the least doubt but that they would make an attempt to rescue him; but, if they should even succeed, he dreaded their vengeance, should they have become acquainted with his real intentions, which no doubt they would from the examination he had already undergone before the magistrate. Would that he could escape from them altogether, he thought; but he had no power to do so. What was to become of him? where could he find a place of shelter? or how could he subsist, without any means or a friend in the world? And could he make up his mind to leave Azrah? Oh, no! besides, the peculiar nature of the secret connected with him rendered such a step totally impracticable, and placed the power of the gipsies over him beyond dispute. No; should he ever regain his liberty, he must continue with them, and submit entirely to the will of fate, who had cast his destiny in so extraordinary a mould.

But the feelings of Sir Laurence, on leaving the prison, were, if possible, more acute even than Rosario's. The features pourtrayed in the miniature haunted his imagination, like some grim and ghastly phantom. He could not be mistaken; they bore an exact resemblance to those of the unfortunate woman to whom he had first given his hand, and upon the uncertainty of whose death or existence rested his future happiness or misery. And Rosario had said that the likeness represented that of his mother. A strange sensation shot through the frame of Sir Laurence, as this recollection flashed upon his brain, and he clasped his burning temples, with a feeling of the most exquisite agony.

And then the features of that poor boy, so beautiful, yet so painfully familiar to him. What a variety of curious conjectures did they create in his mind, and yet he scarcely dared to venture to trust himself with an attempt at their solution. The singular and melancholy history of the gipsy boy, also, or such portions as he had been enabled to elicit from him, had made a lasting impression upon his mind.

But there was one circumstance that afforded some relief to him (and he was fully inclined to think that he spoke the truth), and that was, the assurance that there was no female among the tribe who answered the description of the form which had so often appeared to him, and which had so powerfully created his alarm; yet he was far from being entirely satisfied, nor was the mystery at all elucidated. It was quite evident that the woman, whoever she was, was the instrument of the gipsies, and was entirely in their power; and the likeness she bore to the unfortunate Clara, the letter she had delivered to Blanche, and various other circumstances, were all calculated to excite the worst fears in his breast, and to keep him in a constant state of suspense, doubt, and apprehension.

"But this boy, this Rosario," he said; "he must, he shall be saved; I cannot believe him guilty; my heart instinctively yearns towards him, notwithstanding the deep and impenetrable mystery by which he is surrounded, and I should never forgive myself if anything were to happen to him on my account. Would to Heaven that I could persuade him to throw himself under my protection, and to quit the abandoned wretches with whom he is now unfortunately connected; but I fear there is no chance of doing that. He is bound to them by some mysterious tie which I am at a loss to fathom, and which he either cannot or will not explain Poor youth, your destiny does, indeed, seem to be a singular and a melancholy one; and it is to be regretted that one so young, so intelligent, and so fair, should be thus made the sport of fate. There is a nobility in his manners and general demeanour, which shows him fitted to adorn the most elevated state, and shall he be permitted to suffer the doom of a felon? Oh, never! I must believe his solemn protestations of innocence, especially after the manner in which he has at different times interposed to save me from the brutal vengeance of the gipsies, and the esteem which he has possessed for me, after having been commanded by his fierce companions to hate me, and to curse me. Would that the men had not been so hasty in seizing him; but they acted for the best, and certainly the suspicious circumstances under which the gipsy boy was taken, fully authorized them in what they did. The obstinate refusal of Rosario, too, to give a more explicit explanation of the circumstances under which he overheard the infamous plot, and to reveal the place where the gipsies are concealed, all serves to strengthen the cause of suspicion against him, and renders my wish to serve him the more difficult. But still I must exert myself to the utmost, and save him if possible."

With these intentions, and filled with a variety of conflicting ideas, Sir Laurence bent his way towards the house of the magistrate, whom he found at home, and immediately informed him of the visit he had paid to Rosario in prison, and communicating to him most of the particulars of what had taken place at the interview, omittting, however, the circumstance of the miniature, in which he considered he could not possess any interest.

"There is something, certainly, very mysterious in the circumstances connected with this lad," remarked the magistrate. "It is a great pity that he should have fallen into such vicious hands, and which seems likely to lead him to destruction."

"I would that he be dealt leniently with in this case, sir," returned Sir Laurence, "for I really believe that he is innocent. I do not think it possible for one so young, and who possesses so intelligent a mind, to have been guilty of such an act of atrocity; nor do I consider that there are any very strong causes of suspicion against him."

"Excuse me, Sir Laurence," replied the magistrate; "although I am inclined to take the most merciful view of the case, still I must beg leave to differ from you in that opinion. The obstinacy of the boy in refusing to disclose all he knows, so that the actual guilty persons may be brought to justice, is a fact, at any rate, to say the least of it, of very great suspicion; and, unless he becomes more communicative, he must take the consequences. We have it already in the evidence adduced before us by the several witnesses, that he was detected in the act of coming from the mansion with a lighted torch in his hand, and the account he gives of having picked it up in his path, does not to me appear very reasonable. The outrage is a most abominable one, and the perpetrators of it must not be permitted to escape punishment.. Besides, unless they are detected, the lives of yourself and your family will not be safe one hour from another."

"I am much obliged to you, sir," observed the baronet, "for the interest you express in my security; but I trust that knowing the precautions that are being used, will be sufficient to deter my enemies from making any further attempt, and that by using vigilance they will, ere long, be detected. I have no doubt that some of the gipsies are the vile incendiaries."

"Rosario has admitted that he knows the actual perpetrators of the crime, but yet he has refused to divulge their names, or the place where they may be found; and therefore, if not the incendiary himself, has become an accessory to the fact. I should not be doing my duty if I permitted him to escape, unless I have the most undoubted proofs of his innocence. Perhaps he may repent of his obstinacy, and be induced to give a satisfactory explanation of that which we demand to know, at his next examination; and I can assure you, Sir Laurence, that it will afford me the greatest pleasure to find that our suspicions against the prisoner are unfounded."

"I am afraid, sir, that Rosario will remain determined."

"Then there will be but one alternative left for me, however much I shall regret it."

"But do you really think, sir, that there is sufficient evidence against the lad to justify his being committed to take his trial?"

"I certainly do, Sir Laurence," answered the magistrate.

"I am sorry to hear it; but still I do hope that something will transpire to render such a step unnecessary, and to exculpate the character of this unfortunate boy, in whose fate I feel the greatest interest."

"I am equally anxious for such a result, as yourself, Sir Laurence. There is something very superior in the appearance and the manners of the prisoner, and the mystery which seems to be connected with him is of the most extraordinary kind."

"It is," coincided the baronet; "and I am disposed to believe all that he has stated. I consider him to be the child of misfortune cast among the gipsies by some remarkable circumstances, and that he is really, as he says, unacquainted with the names of his parents. You noticed his powerful emotion when they were alluded to?"

"I did," answered the magistrate; "and it is that circumstance which has the more excited my sympathy in his favour. Had he been placed in other hands, I do not doubt but that he might have become a bright member of society."

"And even now I feel satisfied that his mind is untainted," said Sir Laurence. "Never did I behold a fairer youth, approaching, as he does, to almost feminine loveliness and gentleness."

"There is certainly something peculiarly delicate in his personal appearance and manners."

"Of course, sir, I need not request of you to allow no more restraint to be put upon the unfortunate boy in prison, than is compatible with the rules and regulations of the place?"

"Certainly not, Sir Laurence; I will take especial care that he shall receive every indulgence that the prison will afford."

Sir Laurence thanked him, and then took his leave, agitated by emotions of the most perplexing description. He could not but acknowledge the justice of the magistrate's observations, and he feared that if Rosario remained resolute, that he would be placed in a situation of the most imminent peril, when his future liberty, if not his very life, would be at stake. He shuddered at the thought, especially after the interview he had just had with the unfortunate object of his anxiety. But surely, he reflected, Rosario would repent of an obduracy which would involve him in such danger, and be induced to render what could only be considered as an act of justice.

He would again visit him, and once more try what the force of argument and persuasion would do.

Lady Blanche and Amanda had been most anxiously looking for the return of the baronet, to ascertain what had been the result of his interview with Rosario; and on his entering the apartment in which they were sitting, they could immediately perceive, by the expression of his countenance, that his errand had not been crowned with any success. Sir Laurence quickly related to them what had taken place, with the exception of the fact of the miniature, and his thoughts upon that subject, and they could not help giving expression to their feelings upon the occasion.

" Unfortunate boy," said Blanche, " if he remains determined not to divulge what he knows, it will appear like a confirmation of his guilt, in the eyes of the prejudiced, and nothing can save him from punishment."

" 'Tis too true," returned Sir Laurence, " and I cannot look upon it without dread, for I feel thoroughly convinced of his innocence."

" Oh, yes," remarked Amanda; " it would be a libel upon humanity to suppose that one so young and so gentle could be the perpetrator of such a frightful deed. The statement he has made is very probable; the guilty parties, no doubt, are some of the gipsies, and it is only the dread he entertains of them, or some false notion of honour, that prevents him from disclosing the whole truth. But I trust that he will yet think better of this, and not suffer himself to fall a victim to the guilt of others."

" Most heartily do I respond to that wish, my dear sister," said Sir Laurence; " and it shall be no fault of mine if the real villains are not discovered and brought to punishment. It would be a fortunate thing for Rosario if he could be snatched from the degrading and vagrant life he has so long been leading; for I am certain, from what little I have seen of him, that he possesses a mind that would render him fitting for any grade of society; and there appeared to be that melancholy interest attached to his history, which must excite the compassion of every humane individual."

" Very true," replied Amanda; " and never shall I forget his simple but impressive observations, on the occasion when we first met him, Laurence."

" Oh," ejaculated the baronet, with a sigh which he could not suppress, " they have haunted my recollection ever since."

The baronet then related what had passed between him and the magistrate, but offered no observation upon it.

" Mr. Clavering is a most excellent and humane man," remarked Blanche, " and I feel satisfied that no one would be more happy than himself if the innocence of Rosario should be established. What he says is very just, and he can certainly, if he does his duty, only administer the law as he finds it; therefore, if Rosario remains obstinate, strong as circumstantial evidence is against him, the magistrate, as he observes, has no alternative, but to commit him for trial. Poor lad! may Heaven avert this; and deeply do I regret that he was ever taken into custody at all."

" And so do I, beloved Blanche," said her husband; " but still we ought not to reproach ourselves, for it certainly was no fault of ours. If he is not guilty, however, Heaven will, I am confident, watch over his safety, and something will occur to bring the real criminals to light. But I will see Rosario again in his prison, and, in the meantime, every search shall be made after the gipsies, and should we be able only to secure Madela and Harold, we shall be perfectly safe from any future outrages, and the innocence and safety of the gipsy boy fully established."

" I am fearful, my dear Laurence," said Blanche, " that you will find that a much more difficult task than you seem to imagine. The gipsies are so secret in their actions that they seem to defy detection; and even now I fear that they will take some means for which we cannot possibly prepare ourselves, to seek revenge for the imprisonment of Rosario."

" They will not surely be so bad," returned Sir Laurence, " knowing the excite.. ment that at present prevails in the country against them."

" Alas !" said Blanche, " have we not already had sufficient proof of what they will dare attempt to do?"

" Very true, my love; but we must not suffer any unnecessary fears to take possession of us. I have ordered a sharp watch to be set over the neighbourhood, and we should receive immediate notice were anything to occur to excite suspicion."

Lady Blanche and Amanda seemed satisfied with these assurances, and, after some further conversation, they separated.

  * * * * * * *

We must now return to the old abbey ruins, to which Madela, Harold, and the other gipsy returned, after their meeting with Sir Laurence Cleveland at the gibbet on the moor, exulting in the misery which would greet him on his return home; for they had despatched a messenger in the evening of the day before to Zephania and Malachial, and they had no doubt but that those ruffians would not fail to carry their diabolical intentions into effect.

It was late when they arrived at the abbey, but several of the tribe were up, and indulging in their usual carousal.

" Are all the tribe within?" demanded Madela.

" All, I believe, except Rosario," replied the gipsy.

" Ah!" exclaimed Harold; " Rosario absent, and at this hour! this is very unusual. How long has he been away from the ruins?"

" Ever since yesterday evening."

" Ah, by Astaroth!" cried Madela and Harold in a breath; " there is something wrong in this. Fools! what have ye been about not to keep a stricter watch over him, after the strict commands which were given to you to do so? Have you made no search after him?"

" Yes," answered the gipsy; " we have made all the search we could after him in the neighbourhood. It is no fault of ours, Harold."

" Curses light upon thee," exclaimed Harold, stamping furiously; " has he dared to desert us? By every power of mischief, if he has, the vengeance of our tribe shall pursue him to destruction. Where is Azrah?"

" He returned not long since, and is now in the room in which he always sleeps when he is among us."

" Was Azrah in the ruins when the disappearance of Rosario was first discovered?" demanded Madela

" He was not," replied the gipsy.

" And did you make him acquainted with the fact?"

" We did, for he quitted abruptly, and as he usually does, and retired to his own room."

" Attend me, Harold," said Madela, and they immediately ascended a broken flight of stone steps, which led to two or three rooms that were not quite in such a ruinous state as some other parts of the ancient building. A faint light was seen glimmering through the crevices of a carved oak door, and a low melancholy voice might be heard, as if in prayer, proceeding from the room. Madela and Harold looked at each other significantly, and then frowned, and, dashing open the door, Azrah might be seen on his knees, and with clasped hands, apparently totally absorbed in devotion. The attitude was strange, for one of that wandering tribe, but it did not seem to create any surprise in the bosoms of Madela and her companion; and, walking hastily up to Azrah, Harold roughly laid his hand upon his shoulder, and repeated his name. Azrah started, and, beholding the gipsies, exhibited the greatest confusion and emotion.

"How now," said Harold, in harsh and savage tones; "this is not the time for foolery. Important business demands our attention. Where is Rosario?"

"Rosario!" repeated Azrah, in a peculiar voice, and with a look of astonishment; "Harold, where should he be, at this hour, but in the abbey, and, I hope, at rest?"

"But he is not."

"What mean you?"

"Know you not that he has been away from the ruins ever since yesterday evening?" demanded Harold.

"Rosario gone!" exclaimed Azrah, turning ghastly pale, and fixing his eyes upon Harold and Madela attentively, with an expression of doubt and astonishment. "Oh, surely there must be some mistake in this?"

"There is no mistake in it," returned Harold; "but why do you exhibit such extraordinary emotion?"

"And is it wonderful that I should evince emotion on receiving such intelligence?" demanded Azrah, with singular emphasis.

"Rosario has fled those who have protected him from childhood," said Madela; "the secret will be betrayed, and, by all the evil planets, I swear that we will have a terrible revenge. You—you, too, must join us in hunting the treacherous fawn to destruction."

"Oh! hold, forbear!" cried Azrah; "know you what you say—to whom you talk? Some accident has befallen Rosario, dear Rosario, more precious to me than the life-blood which circulates throughout my veins, for confident I am that he would never of his own free will abandon us. Alas! fair, beauteous, beloved unfortunate, thou for whom alone I cling to life, and shall I never again behold thee? Harold, Madela, for years past you have found me subservient to your will, and I have submitted to the dreadful, the cruel fate you have subjected me to, almost without a murmur; but, by the great God of Heaven, I swear that if you carry your threats against that unhappy being into effect, I will at once shake off the yoke, reveal myself to the world, and ——"

"Ah!" interrupted Harold, fiercely, "dare you threaten?"

"Ay," returned Azrah, with remarkable energy, and a look which only Madela and Harold could understand; "I not only threaten, but will perform too; for degraded being as you have made me, Harold, my spirit is not yet broken entirely, and I will, to the best of my power, protect that unfortunate being who is more precious to me than my very life's blood."

"Your language betrays you," said Madela; "it is you who have connived at the escape of Rosario."

"'Tis false," replied Azrah; "I solemnly declare that I knew not of the disappearance of Rosario till you told me. Think you that I could willingly part from one so closely, so fondly allied to my heart?"

"Yes," said Harold; "to conceal him where you could at any time behold him, and communicate to him your thoughts, your mind. For some time past I have noticed the peculiar looks that have been exchanged between you whenever you met; the anxiety you seemed to feel to speak with him."

"And can you wonder at that? Think you that every feeling of humanity or affection is stifled within my breast?"

"And you would reveal to him the secret?" demanded Harold.

"No," answered Azrah; "anxious as I am to clasp the poor unfortunate victim of a cruel destiny to my heart, I would not do so, until the fitting time shall arrive. Harold, hitherto, I have yielded entirely to your plans, and never uttered one word of complaint; why then should you now reproach me, and accuse me of that of which you must feel convinced I am not guilty? Oh, Rosario, my heart forebodes that something fearful has happened to you, or you would never have quitted your wood-land home—that wandering life, which, from your association with it from earliest childhood, has become so dear to you."

The countenance of Azrah exhibited the most intense emotion as he uttered these words; tears flowed down his cheeks, and he spoke in tones of singular plaintiveness and sweetness, which must have made a powerful impression upon any sensitive heart.

"Enough of this weakness," said Harold, sternly; "and see that you do not ex-hibit it among any of our people. Do you mark me?"

"I do; and too well do I understand you," said Azrah. "But let me begone; I cannot longer remain here; I must go in search of Rosario, and will not return until I have ascertained what has become of him."

"Nay," returned Harold, determinedly, "you go not from hence; we do not choose to trust you; we will, ourselves, institute a strict search after Rosario."

"Would you then make me a prisoner?"

"For the present, until we have ascertained whether or not you have spoken the truth."

"Heaven help me, then," said Azrah, solemnly, "and watch over and guard from danger that unfortunate being on whose safety my very life depends. Harold, Madela, you will not attempt to confine me? I promise you that I will not attempt to leave the abbey without your permission, unless any urgent necessity, upon which the safety of us all may depend, should require me."

Harold and Madela consulted together aside for a few minutes, and then the for-mer, turning to Azrah, said,—

"Upon those conditions, we will trust you. Besides, we shall keep a strict watch on your actions, and it will therefore be useless for you to attempt to deceive us. We need not tell you what the consequences would be if you were to venture to do so."

Azrah sighed, and Madela and Harold hastily quitted the room. When they were gone, Azrah sunk on his knees, and, with clasped hands and streaming eyes, seemed for some time wrapt in mental prayer. What the nature of his thoughts were at that moment, we will not in this place attempt to describe; but it was evident from his heaving bosom, and his otherwise agitated manner, that they were of the most tortur-ing description.

Madela and Harold lost no time in despatching several of the gipsies in different directions, in search of Rosario, while, in spite of the remonstrances which had been uttered by Azrah, they vowed to punish the boy severely, if they should get him again in their power, and discovered that he had abandoned them willfully.

"Perhaps, ere now, the secret which we have so long and so carefully kept, may be

See p. 183.

divulged," said Harold; "and if so, all our future plans will be rendered abortive. By all the infernal host I swear, that should this be the case, I will have such a revenge, that shall make even those who in future shall read it, tremble with horror."

"Aye, Harold," returned Madela; "we are sworn to revenge, and nothing shall prevent our having it. But I am inclined to be of Azrah's opinion, that some accident has befallen Rosario, for I do not think that he would, of his own accord, desert us; besides, whither could he go? what would become of him, friendless as he is? Our vengeance is working by degrees; doubtless, ere this, Branscombe House is a heap of blackened ruins, and Laurence Cleveland, and all connected with him, reduced to misery."

"Yes; Zephaniah and Malachial would be certain not to fail. But I trust that Blanche has not perished in the flames, for that would interrupt our plot, and render our vengeance but half complete."

"True; the time must yet come when we shall have her in our power."

"It must," said Harold; "and to that time I look forward with impatience. But why should Rosario have dared to wander to any distance from the ruins, without our permission? He may have fallen into the power of those who are anxious to discover us, and, should he have done so, we shall not be safe an hour in our present place of concealment."

"I do not believe that Rosario would ever betray us," observed Madela.

"We know not what intimidation may do," returned Harold; "besides, they may discover him, and then ——"

"Enough; it is no use anticipating danger."

"It is always as well to be prepared for it."

Tired, most of the gipsies now retired to rest, and all was silent in the old abbey ruins till the morning.

But no repose did Azrah obtain, but continued pacing his room wrapt in the most agonizing thoughts, of which the reader would be unable to form any adequate idea, unless they were acquainted with all the melancholy particulars of that mysterious being's history. Ever and anon, he muttered strange and incoherent sentences to himself, and then his emotion would become more powerful, and he would beat his breast in a manner that showed the state of his mind was bordering on distraction. Notwithstanding the threats of Madela and Harold, and the promises he had made to them, he was several times worked up to such a pitch of suspense and torturing anxiety, that he was half resolved to leave the ruins, and proceed in search of Rosario, to whom he believed that some fearful accident had happened, for he could not suppose, for a moment, that he would willingly desert the tribe, knowing that he would be certain to be pursued by the vengeance of the gipsies, and especially after what had taken place between them; but, after awhile, he succeeded in restraining his wishes, and determined to endeavour to wait with patience the result of the searching inquiries which Madela and Harold would be sure to make.

In the morning, the gipsies were all up and moving at an early hour, and Azrah made his way to that part of the ruins in which they were assembled, anxious to know their proceedings, and whether anything had yet been ascertained of Rosario; but none of the men who had been despatched in search of him had yet returned, and the rage and impatience of Harold and Madela increased.

"There is some daring treachery in this," said the former, "and we must be on our guard, to resist any sudden attack that may be made on us. Rosario has broken his oath, and, probably, by this time, betrayed us to the myrmidons of the law."

"'Tis false!" exclaimed Azrah, vehemently; "and you must feel it to be so, Harold. Rosario would never act the traitor's part; he possesses a soul too noble, too generous for that."

"He should know us too well to dare to make the attempt," returned Harold.

"Oh, he will have to answer dearly for this, should he ever again fall into our power."

"You will not dare to harm him?" said Azrah.

"Not dare!"

"No; beware! for terrible would the consequence be if you offered to injure him."

"Again do you venture to threaten us?"

"Yes; while you threaten that ill fated being," answered Azrah, boldly. "Harold, I need not remind you of the secret link which binds us together; one act of injustice on your part, and in spite of all that might follow, that link would be broken asunder for ever, and destruction spread around."

Harold and Madela gazed at Azrah for a few moments with fierce looks, then, muttering a bitter curse between their teeth, retired to another part of the ruins. In a short time afterwards, Zephaniah and Malachial, who had departed immediately from the neighbourhood of Branscombe House, after having accomplished their villanous act of incendarism, arrived at the abbey.

"How now?" said Harold, greeting them hastily; "you have returned; say, have you fulfilled the instructions we sent you?"

"We have," answered Zephaniah. "We left Branscombe House in flames, and I should think nothing would save the entire building from total destruction."

"Oh, monstrous!" exclaimed Azrah, who had advanced towards the group on seeing the two ruffians enter the ruins. "What fiendish work is this?—Cowards!"

"Hold, croaking fool!" exclaimed Madela; "dare you murmur? Would you, forsooth, extend mercy to Laurence Cleveland? Nay, then it is time to beware of you, and to keep a more vigilant eye than ever upon your actions."

"I care not," answered Azrah, coolly. "Heaven knows that I have little cause to sympathise with Sir Laurence Cleveland; but my heart shrinks appalled from such hideous crimes as this."

"Heed him not," said Harold, "we shall know what conduct to pursue towards him in future. Know you not whether the house was entirely destroyed, Zephaniah, or whether Blanche or her child were rescued from the flames?"

"We cannot say," replied the gipsy; "for as the alarm was given, and a number of people were fast congregating at the scene of the conflagration, we quitted the spot as speedily as possible, and thought it was best to leave the neighbourhood, lest we should be suspected."

"You acted prudently," remarked Harold; "but we have fresh work for you. Rosario has disappeared from the abbey."

"Rosario gone?"

"Yes, absconded; and even now several of our comrades have gone in search of him."

"The boy has appeared very dissatisfied of late," said Malachial; "can he have dared to betray us?"

"No; bloodthirsty dog!" cried Azrah, in tones of the greatest wrath and indignation. "Rosario possesses not the black heart that beats within your guilty bosom. Dare not to calumniate him!"

"Better words, Azrah," said the ruffian, "or we may perchance quarrel. You may not find me very ready to submit to your abuse, because I merely suggested that which is most reasonable. Bloodthirsty dog, indeed!"

"Aye, dog I call you again," returned Azrah, with equal boldness and vehemence. "Your readiness to perform any act of villany, proves you to be a miscreant of the blackest dye."

"Miscreant in your teeth, reptile," fiercely cried Malachial, and he aimed a violent blow at Azrah's head; but Harold interposed between them, and arrested his arm.

"Hold!" he exclaimed, "he is no match for you, Malachial. And you, Azrah, again I warn you to restrain the violence of your language, and to retire."

Azrah fixed upon them both a look of contempt, and folding his arms, offered not to move from the spot. At that moment two of the gipsies who had been sent in search of our hero, hastily entered the ruins, and the expression of their countenances showed that they had something of importance to communicate. Azrah drew closer to them, and anxiously awaited the intelligence they had to impart.

"How now; what have you heard? Quick!" eagerly demanded Harold and Madela, in a breath.

"All that is bad; Rosario is in prison, accused of having set fire to Branscombe House!"

"God of Heaven!" groaned Azrah, and his countenance became as ghastly pale as that of a corpse; "can this be possible? Fiends! shall that innocent and unfortunate being suffer for your crime? No, I will fly to save him, though I perish in the attempt."

"You stir not hence," cried Harold, seizing the arm of Azrah. "Rosario in prison, and suspected of being guilty of this offence?—tell me, how is this, and what brought him near that spot?"

"He was seen coming from the mansion, soon after the fire broke out, with a lighted torch in his hand," answered the gipsy; "he has acknowledged in his examination before the magistrate, that he overheard the plot to destroy the house, and that he had, at the hazard of his life, hastened to warn the inmates of their danger, but arrived too late."

"Revenge! revenge! the Fawn has betrayed us!" shouted Harold and Madela, and their eyes were bloodshot with rage.

"Oh, horror! horror!" groaned Azrah; "but 'tis false; false as your own black hearts! Let me go; let me hasten to the deliverance of all that is dear to me on this earth!"

"Away with him to his own room," said Harold, "and there let him for the present be strictly confined."

Several of the gipsies seized Azrah immediately, and in spite of all his violent struggles, and pitiful exclamations, overpowered him, and forced him away.

"Now, Mark," said Harold, addressing the gipsy, who had given him the intelligence; "are you certain that what you have been stating is correct?"

"I am positive," answered Mark; "we gained our information from a source upon which we can depend."

"Curses light upon the treacherous brat!" exclaimed Harold; "who would have believed this? and how could he have become acquainted with our designs, so secret as we kept them?"

"We have not a moment to lose," said old Madela; "Rosario has, doubtless, revealed everything to the authorities, and it will be no longer safe for us to remain where we are."

"No, on that score we need not entertain any apprehensions," said Mark; "Rosario has refused to name who the real guilty parties are, or the place in which we are concealed."

"Ah!" ejaculated Harold; "is it so? Then, in that, at any rate, he has done well. But has the fire done much damage?"

"It was confined entirely to one wing of the mansion."

"Would that it had levelled it with the ground. And were all the family preserved?"

"Yes."

"Then they yet remain to meet with our vengeance," said Harold. "But we must not be daunted; we must make a bold effort. Rosario must be saved, and it will be for us to punish him for his contemplated treachery afterwards. As soon as the shades of evening have set in, we will depart, so disguised that nobody will know us, or suspect us, and taking different routes, meet at an appointed spot in the neighbourhood of the gaol, be prepared to act with caution and determination. I know the old prison well, and am certain that an attack can be made upon it without much danger."

The gipsies all approved of these proposals, and they immediately separated to make the necessary preparations for the expedition.

To describe the anguish of Azrah upon being removed to his own room, and finding himself a prisoner, would be an arduous task; he dashed himself on the floor, and clasping his aching temples, for some time gave vent to the most wild and piteous exclamations of agony. Then he arose upon his knees, and with clasped hands continued in silent prayer for several minutes. Large drops of perspiration stood upon his brow, with the intense, the almost insupportable anguish of his feeling, and his heart palpitated so violently against his side, that it seemed as if it would burst from its tenement.

"All is lost! all will be discovered!" he ejaculated; "in prison, and accused of this dreadful crime, alas! what can save the unfortunate Rosario from the vengeance of the law unless he reveals the whole truth? Oh, God! why did you not avert this dreadful calamity?—Headstrong, but humane, and innocent being, why did you thus recklessly venture? and the secret will be discovered; that awful secret on which so much depends. Laurence Cleveland, methinks even your hard heart would be stung with remorse did you but know the facts. But am I not to blame for all?—Oh, yes, it was in my power to have prevented all this, had I not yielded to those in whose power I am, and kept my lips sealed. But I will no longer do so; no, I will form a bold resistance, and even at the risk of a life not worth preserving, at length shake off the fetters with which I am bound, and unmask the truth to the world. But am I not also a prisoner, and deprived of the power to put my wishes into execution? All-merciful Father, hear my prayers, and assist me in this fearful hour of my bitterest affliction. Rosario, had I but seen you previous to your departure from the ruins, I might have prevented all this evil, and yet have safely warned Sir Laurence Cleveland of the dangers which threatened him. But I am so linked with those wretches that I cannot rescue myself."

Again did Azrah strike his forehead with his clenched hands, in the agony of his excited feelings, and gave himself up to all the frenzy of despair. He paced the chamber to and fro, with disordered steps, and looked around to see whether there were the least possible means to escape, but none presented themselves; all was secure. Many, many bitter sufferings had the unfortunate Azrah experienced, but none that excelled the anguish he endured, and which was increased to an insupportable degree by thoughts of the most remarkable, the most torturing description, and which cannot at present be explained. His fate was of that dark and mysterious character that few had ever known, and which it would seem impossible that any human being could endure.

An hour passed away in this manner, and no one came near Azrah, although he could hear the gipsies busily moving about below;—but, at length, the bolts of the room door were withdrawn and Azrah entered.

The expression upon the countenance of both when they met was remarkable; Azrah seemed to view Harold with a feeling of shuddering horror, and the latter appeared to shrink within himself at meeting with Azrah. But, at the same time, there was that subdued tone, if we may so express ourselves, in the demeanour of Azrah, which showed at once that he was labouring under a sense of injustice, to which he was so fettered by circumstances, that he could not at the moment release himself; that of Harold was the character of the reckless ruffian who knows himself to be placed in a position that his intended victim cannot resist.

But there was something more in the characteristics of the individuals we mention at that period, the one was that of savage triumph, and partial dread, the other that of meek but regretful subservience under unmerited wrong. The look that was bestowed upon Azrah by Harold was one of brutality; the one returned was that of silent reproach, pity, and contempt; while at the same time the look that countenance bore at the moment, was one that might have left the observer involved in doubt and mystery as to the meaning it was meant and did convey.

" And you mean to keep me a prisoner Harold?" said Azrah, after a pause of some minutes; " you would prevent me from hastening to the place which holds that one loved being, and endeavouring to extricate *him* ?"

Azrah placed peculiar emphasis on the last word, at which Harold frowned, and seemed, for the time being, at a loss to return a fitting answer; but at length he said,—

" I would prevent, and I will prevent, your holding immediate communication with Rosario, even should the life of that individual be sacrificed in consequence. I have even now my suspicions that you have done so, and were I certain, not only should you not have the opportunity of holding communication with each other, but you should never see each other again. You understand me, Azrah ?"

" Azrah, ah ——"

" Beware !" interrupted the ruffian, half drawing a knife from his belt, with a threatening aspect; " mention another word in allusion to what I see your will would lead you to, and it will be the last that you shall ever have the opportunity to offer."

" And I would court the blow," said Azrah; " only that, by the preservation of my own, I save that which is far more precious to me. Oh, Harold, can you, knowing all the circumstances of my hard, my cruel fate, thus take delight to triumph in the misery you have principally wrought?"

" I have principally wrought?"

" Yes, you."

" Is there not one who first taught you misery ?"

" True, true; alas, that he did."

" And you do not hate him ?"

" I can abhor his deceit, but can never hate him personally."

" And what think you of the individual he first injured ?" demanded Harold, eagerly.

" I can pity him."

" Pity him ?"

" Yes; because both he and the one being who bears the most prominent part in this painful drama, were, by fate, placed in a wrong position. Harold, why keep these fetters on me? There was a time, I acknowledge, when different sentiments inhabited my breast towards you; but you have descended from the man to the savage, and wherefore need you wonder that you should now hold a different position in my esteem, my opinion? You force me, by powers that I have no means of resisting, to assume a character that belongs not to me, and consequently ———"

" Hold !" once more interrupted Harold, ferociously, and his eyes flashed forth a meaning, which himself and Azrah could only understand at the time ; " even to me you must not murmur one syllable in allusion to the compact which so indissolubly binds us together. And what would you with Rosario?"

" I would seek an interview with him," answered Azrah.

" To tell him *all;* to divulge to him the important secret ?"

" No; to endeavour to effect that unfortunate being's escape."

" The plan is projected already."

" You cannot save him."

" And how would you ?"

" I would sacrifice my life but he should be at liberty."

" I will not trust you."

" I have trusted *you;* and in doing so have sacrificed myself, and all that is much dearer to me than my very self. But hear me, Harold; you have pledged yourself to rescue Rosario from his present imprisonment; do so, and return him unscathed to *me*; and you shall hear me murmur no more; but, fail in your promise, attempt to pursue him with your vengeance, for having acted as humanity dictated to him, and you will kindle a fire that even your power cannot extinguish. Yes, you may mock me; but humble, subservient, as you imagine me to be, I will prove to you that I have the determination and the means of revenge. I will cast aside the fetters with which you have hitherto bound me, and even to the risk of my own life, expose you and myself to the world in our real characters. Think of this, Harold, and know that what I promise, borne down by trouble and oppression even as I am, I have the power, and likewise the resolution, to carry into operation."

The countenance of Azrah expressed far more, as he uttered these words, than it is possible for us to explain at the present time, and Harold, apparently astounded by the boldness of his manner, stood by for a few moments in amazement, unable to utter a syllable, and gazing upon him with looks that showed the extraordinary feelings that were passing in his mind. After some considerable pause, he advanced nearer to Azrah, and grasping his arm with vehemence, gazed stedfastly in his face, while he ejaculated,—

" Is it come to this ? Am I to be bearded, threatened, and by *you?* Are you dreaming, or mad ?"

" Neither," answered Azrah, calmly; " though I have too long been doing so for the maintenance of my own self-respect, and the welfare and safety of that one individual far dearer to me than mine own existence. Harold, I command you to keep me no longer confined here like a dog in the kennel, lest that spirit which you have so long curbed, should arouse itself into that of the wild savage, hunting you to destruction."

"By h—l I will not brook this!" cried Harold, fiercely.'

"But you must," returned Azrah, with a smile of superlative contempt.

"Fool! what if I now plunge my knife to your heart?"

"You dare not."

"Dare not?"

"No."

"And why?"

"Because my death would be the warrant for your own."

"Ah!"

"Aye, Harold," said Azrah, with a look of triumph, "think not that because you have for so many years held me in subjection, and confined me to a mystery abhorrent to my feelings, that I have neglected to provide myself against any emergency that might arise. Let me not make my appearance in the world, and after a certain period, there are those *sealed* documents left with certain parties, to be then opened and perused, *that will reveal everything*, and will not fail to bring the guilty parties to justice and punishment."

The eyes of the gipsy became bloodshot with rage, and he glared upon Azrah, with looks of the most ferocious meaning. As his rage appeared to increase, so did the calmness and defiance of Azrah, and when Harold could first give vent to his feelings, he did so in the most brutal execrations.

"Aye, Harold," observed Azrah, with a smile; "you may curse, but I heed it no more than the idle wind. What I state is the truth, and I dare you to test it."

"Have you forgotten your oath?" demanded Harold.

"No," returned Azrah; "my conduct throughout has shewn my too nice observance of it; I now demand that you should adhere to yours."

"And have I not done so?"

"No."

"What would you have, insolent?"

"Insolent!—ha! ha! ha! that sounds well, coming from *you!* However, I would have, and am determined to have, justice, that justice which you have so long denied me."

"Beware! beware!"

"Oh, I am too used to your threats, to be now intimidated by them," said Azrah.

"By all the infernal host, I swear, I will not brook this."

"Get not out of temper; it is but a simple thing I demand of you."

"And what is that?"

"I have told you before," answered Azrah; "simply, justice."

"And what are your notions of the way it should be administered?" asked Harold, with a malignant scowl.

"I can expect little of it in its most liberal sense from *you*," said Azrah, in reply, with a look of bitter irony. "But I demand that you no longer keep me a prisoner."

"And for what purpose do you seek your liberty?"

"That I may endeavour to give liberty to Rosario."

"That I have determined on."

" And to follow it with revenge ?"

" It was Rosario's design to thwart our plans, and thereby to break the solemn oath which binds him to secrecy and fidelity."

" He would have foiled your atrocious attempt, but still not have denounced you."

" And you would sanction Rosario in such a proceeding ?"

" I would."

" And thus become an obstacle in the way of the gratification of our just revenge against one whom you have so much reason to hate ?"

" Yes."

" You have deceived me."

" You have deceived yourself."

" What mean you ?"

" Put the question seriously to your own conscience, and explanation is unnecessary."

" For the present, at any rate, you must remain a prisoner."

" Must ?"

" Yes."

" And for why ?"

" Because your over ardour to save that being, whom, of course, I admit you have a right to feel so great an interest in, may be the very means of frustrating my wishes."

" And would you release Rosario from prison ?"

" I would."

" Are you sincere ?"

" If you do not take my word, I am satisfied that I can say nothing to convince you."

" And you will not visit him with your vengeance ?"

" I will make no promise."

" You will not dare to injure that being upon whom your own fate—the fate of all the tribe hinges ?"

" Not dare ?"

" No."

" And what is to daunt me in the carrying out of any determination to which I may have come ?"

" That which I have before told you," answered Azrah; " the fear of exposure, and consequent destruction."

" D——n !" exclaimed Harold; " am I to be thus braved and threatened ?"

" Harold," observed Azrah, with the greatest calmness, and fixing upon the ruffian a look which it was impossible for him to mistake, " I seek not to brave or threaten you, that you must be aware of; but I want justice—I demand justice, and, by the living God, whom you acknowledge not, that justice will I have !"

" What do you seek ?"

" Do I not tell you, justice? But you have so long abused its laws, that you have become an entire stranger to its impulses."

" Azrah," said Harold, with a frown, " try not my patience too far, or you know not what I may be tempted to do."

" You cannot do worse than you have done already," answered Azrah; " unless you take my life, which is no longer valuable to me, only for the preservation of Rosario."

" Bah ! I waste words by parleying with you thus. It is useless for you to murmur against my will. You know that, I believe ?"

" Alas ! too well," returned Azrah, with a sad and impressive look. " Harold, do you intend to persist in keeping me here confined a prisoner ?"

" You have advanced no reasons that I should alter my determination. You would madly rush to the prison of Rosario, and seek an interview with him; and thus throw yourself at once into the arms of danger. Besides, what reason have I to believe that you would not, in the present excited state of your feelings, reveal all, and thus frustrate those plans which have been so long and so deeply laid ?"

" I promise you faithfully that I would not."

"But I will not trust you. I tell you again that I have determined to release Rosario, and for that purpose myself and some of the most trustworthy of our people intend to depart from the ruins immediately. That must suffice you."

"Harold," ejaculated Azrah, "I dread your purpose after the observations you have made use of."

"Why should you?"

"You will not harm that unfortunate being—promise me that you will not."

"Think you not that Rosario merits punishment after the mischief he has done, and the act of treachery he has committed?"

"He has not betrayed you."

"But he has said enough to convince our enemies that we are the authors of the outrage committed at Branscombe House; and he would have thwarted our plans by warning the inmates of the danger which threatened them. Has he not himself admitted this? and he must have turned spy upon our actions, or how could he have become acquainted with our intentions?"

"It was humanity that urged him on."

"Humanity towards Laurence Cleveland and those connected with him!" repeated Harold, with a malicious look.

"Ay," returned Azrah; "and the same feeling would have prompted me to do as he has done."

Harold stamped with rage, and he fixed his eyes upon the countenance of Azrah with an expression that told the feelings which were passing in his mind.

"Has it come to this?" he exclaimed. "Do you forget your oath—the degrading wrongs that we have all experienced from Sir Laurence?"

"Forget them! No, Harold; oh, would I could bury them for ever in oblivion. But once more I solemnly adjure you not to harm that one dear individual upon whom my fate depends."

"It is not by conduct such as this that you will restrain me. But enough; you had better reflect maturely upon what I have said, and be prepared to submit to my decrees, whatever they may be, or I will not answer for the consequences. I go to rescue Rosario."

Azrah clasped his hands, and looked imploringly in the face of the ruffian, who, however, frowned more fiercely than before, and, without making use of any further observations, hurried from the room, securing the door after him. When he was gone, Azrah threw himself on his knees, and, raising his eyes towards Heaven, offered up a silent but fervent prayer to the Supreme. There was a singular expression in his countenance, and in his whole demeanour, which would have excited the greatest surprise and mystery in the breasts of all who might have beheld him at that moment, and must have caused the utmost curiosity to become acquainted with the secret thoughts that were passing in his bosom; and when they beheld the tears that started from his eyes, that wonder and curiosity must have been increased. It would have been a difficult matter to have penetrated into the real character of that strange being; and the longer they gazed at him, the more would they become involved in the mazes of fruitless conjecture.

"Almighty God!" he said at length, "oh, watch over and protect from harm that one unfortunate being, who is far more precious to me than even the purple current of life that flows within my veins; teach me how to act, I beseech thee, under my many trials. Alas, alas! what can I do under my present circumstances? Am I not a prisoner, and entirely at the mercy of Harold and the rest of the tribe? Weak, foolish man that I have been, to resign myself to those galling and degrading fetters which I cannot now remove. Oh, Rosario, did you but know me in my real character; were you acquainted with the peculiar and bitter troubles of my past life, what would be your feelings! And must I never be permitted to reveal the melancholy secret? Oh. Laurence, wretched, guilty man, this is all your doing; but yet I cannot entertain those deadly feelings of hatred and revenge towards you which those who hold me in their power would fain inspire me with."

Again he became silent; but the intense agony he was enduring, was plainly evinced by the convulsive heaving of his bosom, and the quivering of his lips. He traversed the apartment with the most disordered footsteps, and heavy groans frequently escaped his bosom.

"But they will not dare to attempt to harm Rosario," he said, at length, "should they get him once more in their power. Harold may threaten, but he will not, must not venture to put them into operation against that individual, on whose safety so much depends. Let him do so, and, braving everything, I will at once shake off the restraint under which I now labour, and reveal the whole important truth. Alas! that I did not see Rosario, and become acquainted with his designs, before he could have attempted to put them into execution; then might I have prevented all this mischief, and, at the same time, have found the means of warning the inmates of Branscombe House, without involving any one in danger. And should they not succeed in effecting Rosario's escape, what may not be his fate, if committed on this serious charge? I shudder with horror at the thought."

Such were the reflections of Azrah,—at least, such of them as we are permitted, at this moment, to reveal; and the poignant anguish of his mind increased almost to distraction.

In the meantime, Harold, and the other gipsies he had selected to join him in the hazardous expedition, having got everything in readiness, prepared to depart from the ruins. They were all so disguised, that it would have been next to an impossibility for any person to have entertained any suspicion of their real character; and they, therefore, expected to travel in complete safety.

"Let there be a strict watch kept in the ruins during our absence, so that you may be prepared for any surprise," commanded Harold; "above all, be careful that Azrah is not permitted to leave the room in which I have thought proper to confine him."

"Ay, we will see to that," replied the gipsy to whom these orders were addressed.

"We will divide ourselves into small parties of only twos and threes," said Harold, to his companions; "and, travelling by different routes, all meet together in the Black Hollow, in the wood near the town, where we will further arrange our plans. The prison is situated in a good spot for our purpose. We are well armed, and I do not entertain much doubt of the success of our designs."

"The prison is an old building," remarked another of the gipsies, "and we shall not find much difficulty in forcing an entrance. But we must use all the promptitude we can, before the neighbourhood is alarmed; and how to find out the cell in which Rosario is confined will be the principal trouble."

"Oh, that difficulty we shall be easily able to surmount, I believe," said Harold; "the gaoler must conduct us to it, or he will have to pay for his refusal with his life. It will not do to stand parleying on such an occasion as this."

"True, Harold," coincided Zephaniah; "in desperate cases desperate means must be resorted to. The headstrong boy, a pretty hobble he has got himself into, through his mistaken humanity."

" He has," said Harold ; "but he must be prevented from attempting any such conduct in future. How he became acquainted with our designs, I am at a loss to imagine."

" Why, he states in his examination before the magistrate, that he overheard the plot."

" I cannot conceive how he could have done so, after all the precaution that was used. However, he must give a thorough explanation, which will enable us to be on our guard for the future. Come, it is time to depart. You remember the place of appointment—the Black Hollow in the wood? We must use all the expedition we can, and by that means I expect we shall arrive there before daylight to-morrow morning."

After a few more observations, they quitted the ruins, and separating, they departed by different routes, as had been agreed upon, to the place of their destination.

We must now once more return to Rosario, who, in his solitary cell, was still suffering under a variety of the most afflicting thoughts and apprehensions, but still he determined, let the consequences be whatever they might to him, never to reveal the names of the real perpetrators of the outrage, and he could scarcely make up his mind to believe that he would ever be convicted upon such evidence as was at present adduced against him, and he could not but think, after the deep interest he had expressed in his fate, that Sir Laurence Cleveland would exert himself to the utmost to save him.

Most happy did Rosario feel to think that no further damage had been done to Branscombe House, and that all the inmates had been preserved uninjured ; but more than all was he astonished at the extraordinary emotion which the baronet had displayed on beholding the miniature, and the searching questions he had put to him in consequence. In spite of all that had been urged upon him against the character of Sir Laurence, he could not help entertaining towards him a feeling bordering upon esteem, and he could have made a confident of him, but after the oath he had taken, and the peculiar circumstances he was placed under, he feared to do so.

" But, alas," he sighed, " if I do not escape from my present situation, can my secret long remain undiscovered? It is impossible. And why should I dread it? Will it not release me from the dreadful restraint, so revolting to my feelings, under which I now labour? And surely every feeling breast would commiserate with me in my unfortunate and extraordinary fate? And why am I compelled to assume a character so abhorrent to my feelings? What object can those who hold me in their power have in view? Oh, Azrah, you have said that you know all, and if you are indeed the sincere friend you have professed yourself, and which I believe you to be, why do you not relieve me from this insupportable weight of suspense, and let me know who I really am? And what will be your anguish when you become acquainted with my situation? Surely you will devise some means to release me from the fate with which I am threatened, and to avert the vengeance of Harold and the other gipsies! Had I but seen you before I quitted the Abbey ruins, this might not have happened, and still the designs of Harold and his associates against Branscombe House have been averted. And shall I never behold you again? Oh, yes; Providence will not deny me, at least, that gratification; I cannot endure the thought."

Thus tediously passed away the hours, and Rosario suffered no change in his situation, nor did anything occur to revive his hopes. Another miserable day and night elapsed, and the prisoner obtained but little or no rest, and when he did, his imagination was haunted by the most frightful visions, which rendered sleep even more torturing to him than his waking moments. The day after Sir Laurence Cleveland had had an interview with him, the magistrate visited him in prison. Rosario received him with the utmost respect, and the magistrate seemed to be greatly prepossessed in his favour.

"I have been induced to visit you," he said, "in the hope of being able to persuade you to alter your determination, and, by at once revealing all you know, and being the means of bringing those whom you say are the real guilty parties to justice, save yourself from the consequences which must otherwise result from your obstinacy. From your appearance and manners I am inclined to entertain a favourable opinion of you, notwithstanding the suspicious nature of the circumstances against you. I feel no inconsiderable interest towards you, but unless you are candid, and explain everything, as far as lies in your power, I shall have no other alternative, upon the evidence adduced against you."

"I am much obliged to you, sir," answered Rosario, "for the good opinion you are pleased to express towards me; but I cannot avail myself of your proposal. I can only still solemnly protest my innocence, but nothing can ever induce me to reveal the names of those who are the actual perpetrators of this outrage."

"Foolish boy," said the magistrate, "have you well considered the situation in which you stand, and what the consequences will undoubtedly be, if you are convicted of this heinous charge?"

"I have, sir, and put my trust in providence to release me."

"I can entertain but very little doubt that the gipsies, with whom you are connected, are the authors of this guilty plot, if not the absolute perpetrators of it!"

The gipsy boy returned no answer.

"There is a mystery about you, boy," continued the magistrate, "which I cannot unravel, and which, after the interview Sir Laurence Cleveland has had with you, is greatly increased. Do you still persist in declaring that you are ignorant of your real name, or who are your parents?"

"I have spoken nothing but the truth, sir," replied Rosario.

"I am fearful, prisoner," said the magistrate, looking at him seriously, "that you have suffered yourself to be made the instrument of those bad people with whom you are associated, for the purpose of furthering their evil designs; which is much to be regretted in one so young, and, in other respects, so prepossessing."

"I am sorry, sir, that you should feel disposed so soon to abandon the favourable opinion you were just now pleased to express towards me," said Rosario; "but, however unfortunate my destiny has been, I can conscientiously declare that you do me wrong by encouraging such an idea."

"You have now an opportunity of extricating yourself from an abandoned and degrading course of life, which cannot fail, sooner or later, to bring you to destruction. Sir Laurence Cleveland, as well as myself, feels the most lively interest in your welfare, and, by being candid, you may secure a most valuable friend and protector."

"Believe me, sir," said Rosario, fervently, "I have a full sense of the kindness of yourself and Sir Laurence; but pray urge me no farther, since I cannot swerve from that which I have already stated. Nay, more; even were I at liberty this moment, I could not accept of the honour the baronet might intend me. Many as are the troubles I have experienced, I would not consent to abandon my wandering, woodland life."

"Unfortunate youth," remarked the magistrate; "I fear, indeed, that you are lost. I sincerely pity you, but I shall be compelled to do my duty."

"Sir," returned Rosario, "I would wish you to act only as justice shall dictate to you; for my own part, in the consciousness of my entire innocence of this foul charge, I am content to resign myself to the will of the Almighty, in the hope that He will not forsake me in the hour of need."

The magistrate looked at him with mingled feelings of pity, astonishment, and admiration; and, after a short time, finding that all arguments or persuasions were useless, he took his departure from the prison.

He called upon Sir Laurence on his way home, and informed him of what had taken place at the meeting between him and Rosario, which the baronet listened to with much regret, for he saw at once that the resolution of the gipsy boy was not to be broken; and he could not but feel the utmost grief at the probable fate that awaited one, who had excited feelings of so extraordinary a description in his bosom.

"There is certainly something very remarkable in the conduct of this unfortunate lad altogether," he said. "I cannot believe that he is speaking an untruth, and am firmly of opinion that he is innocent."

"I am inclined to think the same as you do, Sir Laurence," said the magistrate; "but that a jury must be left to decide upon; for, after the evidence that has been already brought forward against him, and his refusal to disclose all he knows, I cannot do less than commit him for trial. I will have him brought before me again, the day after to-morrow, for further examination, and I then hope that something will transpire in his favour."

"I hope there may," said Sir Laurence; "for I should be sorry to see him suffer for a crime, of which there is so much reasonable doubt as to whether he is the actual perpetrator. Could we but find out the place where Harold and the other gipsies are concealed, I have no doubt that the real guilty persons would be brought to light, and everything be properly explained."

"All the exertions we have made, have hitherto not been attended with any success," remarked Mr. Clavering; "and it would almost induce me to believe that they are not in any part of the country."

"But I have had sufficient proof that they are," returned the baronet; "besides, the appearance of the gipsy boy is quite enough to convince us. It is really most remarkable where those people, numerous as they are, contrive to conceal themselves. But it is quite evident that they have agents in the neighbourhood, to supply them with all the information they may require."

"Why, it does appear like it, Sir Laurence, and Rosario even hinted as much. But it is impossible to come to any satisfactory conclusion upon the subject in its present state. However, I do sincerely hope that if this unfortunate and mysterious lad is really innocent, that Providence will make it apparent; and that it will be my pleasant duty to discharge him on his next examination."

"Most heartily do I coincide in that wish, Mr. Clavering," said Sir Laurence; "and I sincerely regret that Rosario was ever apprehended at all."

"The circumstances under which he was found were most suspicious," said Mr. Clavering; "and your tenants were fully justified in what they did. You cannot possibly blame yourself for the manner in which you have acted."

"Oh, no," said Sir Laurence; "and yet I am sorry I did not order him to be set at liberty."

"That would have been highly imprudent, to say the least of it," observed Mr. Clavering.

"It would have saved me a great deal of trouble and anxiety. I cannot fully explain to you, Mr. Clavering, the extraordinary feelings this lad has excited in my breast; but I can only say that I would not, for nearly all the wealth which I possess, see him convicted of this crime. It is natural that I should feel the greatest interest in his destiny, from the manner in which he has, upon more than one occasion, interposed to save me from the wrath of the gipsies, and the warmth of the esteem which he has evinced towards me."

"Well, I fervently trust, Sir Laurence, that a short time will explain all to our satisfaction, and that you may not be deceived in the impressions you have formed of the innocence of Rosario; no one can possibly feel more gratified than I shall be on the occasion."

Mr. Clavering then took his leave, and left Sir Laurence to reflect upon all that he had said, and in most of his observations he entirely agreed with him. Still the obstinate determination of Rosario annoyed him greatly, and excited many painful doubts and apprehensions in his mind; and he trembled to think what the consequences must unavoidably be should he remain obdurate.

"Unhappy youth!" he ejaculated; "I could never forgive myself, even should I be the indirect cause of bringing you to such a wretched fate as that which is always awarded to persons convicted of the crime with which you stand charged. But you surely will repent of your obstinacy, and, seeing the absolute danger of your situation, yield the real criminals to the justice of the law. The strange and inexplicable mystery connected with Rosario has raised the most unaccountable feelings in my bosom; and that miniature—ah! the well-known resemblance it bears to the features of one who has proved the evil star of my destiny, opens afresh the wounds which I hoped would long ere since have closed. I have erred, greatly erred, but was I not in turn deceived, and has not the bitter remorse I have for years endured, sufficiently atoned for the unfortunate indiscretions of my youth? She could not have been innocent of that with which she was accused; if indeed she were, oh, then have I been most guilty. And I am told that she lives!—and that mysterious form I have so frequently seen—the letter, so like her handwriting, serve to strengthen my worst apprehensions. I can scarcely believe that any one could so closely personate Clara, or forge her writing. My God! and should she be really living, what a dreadful position shall I find myself placed in, and what irremediable shame and misery shall I have plunged my beloved and confiding Blanche into! The thought is madness. Oh! Heaven, for her sake, and that of my child, in your infinite mercy, avert, I beseech you, so awful a calamity!—I can endure any punishment myself, but the curses, the reproaches of her, that fair, that innocent being who is the idol of my very soul. And the boy said that the miniature pourtrayed the features of her who gave him being! Terrible, impenetrable mystery, when will you be satisfactorily elucidated? Alas! how fearful is the punishment that always attends one single act of crime!"

He beat his breast, and paced the room, in a state of mind most torturing in the extreme. Again and again he regretted that Rosario had been detained, and sincerely hoped that something would occur to restore him to liberty. In spite of all his efforts to the contrary, he feared the vengeance of the gipsies, and, notwithstanding the exertions he was himself making to apprehend them, he could not help secretly hoping that they would not succeed; for, although it might be proved that their assertion of the existence of his first wife was false, still he was convinced that

See page 198.

they were acquainted with all the transactions of his former life, and that they would not fail, in revenge, to divulge them; and his very soul shrank appalled from the disclosure, and the shame and obloquy it would bring upon him. How must Blanche despise, abhor him, should she ever become acquainted with the degrading particulars. That love which she now bore him must be converted into disgust and hatred, and his misery would then, indeed, be complete.

He was interrupted, in the midst of these reflections, by hearing the door of his apartment gently opened, and Blanche entered. She could not have come at a more painful moment, and it was in vain that Sir Laurence tried to subdue his emotion.

Approaching him, she affectionately threw her fair arms around his neck, and, gazing with fond solicitude in his face, she said,—

" You look pale, love; you are agitated. Tell me, are you unwell ?"

" No, no, my sweet Blanche," he replied; " I am well—quite well; but I confess that I am distressed in my mind."

" And what has occurred to disturb you, Laurence?"

" The painful situation of the gipsy boy, Blanche, in whose fate I cannot help feeling the deepest interest."

" The feeling does honour to your heart, my husband; you do not then think him guilty ?"

" I cannot. After the warm esteem he has expressed towards me and you, and the gentleness of his manners, and the innocence of his looks, it seems to me impossible that he could have been guilty of such a heinous crime; but then the mystery of his behaviour, and many other circumstances connected with him, bewilder me, and fill my mind with various conjectures. Should he be convicted, and subjected to punishment, it will cause me the greatest anguish."

" But he will not, dear Laurence," said Blanche; " something, I feel convinced, will yet transpire to exonerate him from this guilty charge. I lament that he should ever have been apprehended."

" You cannot do so more deeply than I do, Blanche," returned the baronet; " but it was unavoidable; and, if he speaks the truth, he has even now the power of restoring himself to immediate liberty."

" Mr. Clavering, the magistrate, has been here, has he not ?"

" He has."

" And what says he in relation to this unfortunate youth ?"

" He is as much interested in him as we are, Blanche, and no one, I am convinced, would be more rejoiced to have his innocence proved; but of that, I fear, there is no prospect, while Rosario still remains obstinate."

" Has Mr. Clavering visited him in prison ?" inquired Blanche.

" He has, this very morning," answered Sir Laurence.

" And he still refuses to reveal the names of those whom he asserts to be the real guilty individuals ?"

" He does."

" It is strange; and renders every effort to save him fruitless. But I think that there can be very little doubt that our enemies, the gipsies, are the real authors of the outrage, although it is remarkable that none of them were seen in the neighbourhood."

" In the confusion," observed the baronet, " which naturally prevailed at the time of the conflagration, they had every opportunity to effect their escape unseen."

" And will no persuasion prevail with this unhappy boy ?"

" From that which has already transpired at my interview with him, and that of Mr. Clavering, I fear not, Blanche."

" Then do I indeed tremble for the fate which is impending o'er his head, and which I pray Heaven to avert. He must have some strong and mysterious reasons for thus remaining obdurate in the midst of so much danger."

" He must," coincided the baronet; " and I have in vain racked my brain to try to penetrate them. It cannot surely be the fear of the vengeance of the wretches with whom he has so unfortunately been associated, for that could not surpass the punishment of the law, if he is found guilty of this crime; besides, if he revealed the truth, he would receive every protection. I myself would feel most happy in affording it to him, and snatching him from the degrading life in which he has been placed."

"Oh, yes!" ejaculated Blanche, eagerly; " and most gladly would I assist you in the performance of so praiseworthy a task. Poor lad, young even as he is, his must have been a strange and chequered life."

" It must," said Sir Laurence; " and yet, is it not extraordinary that he should express such attachment to that wild and wandering career?"

" It is; but he has known no other from earliest infancy. And yet one would think that the coarse habits and frequent outrages would shock his gentle nature, and render him anxious to have an opportunity of escaping from them. Heaven send that something may occur to induce him to change his present determination; for it would be dreadful to see one so young sentenced to an ignominious punishment for an offence of which he appears to be entirely innocent. But surely the evidence adduced against him is not sufficiently strong to convict him?"

" I am afraid it is, my dear Blanche," replied Sir Laurence; " but still I cannot believe that Rosario will, on his last examination, which Mr. Clavering has fixed to take place the day after to-morrow, any longer refuse to reveal all he knows, that the active perpetrators of the outrage may be brought to that punishment which they so justly merit; and thus to exculpate himself from a charge of so heinous a description."

" It does not seem probable that a youth of the prepossessing manners of Rosario, can be so devoted to the cause of such miscreants, as to suffer rather than betray them to the hands of justice."

" He must surely be mad to do so," said the baronet. " But come, my love, let us for the present drop the subject, which is so painful to us both, and hope for the best. It shall not be through any want of exertion on my part if the unfortunate boy's character is not vindicated."

Blanche expressed her warmest satisfaction in what he said, and they then changed the conversation; but nothing could remove the painful thoughts and apprehensions which had taken such firm hold of the baronet's mind, although he endeavoured to stifle his emotion in the presence of Blanche; and as soon as he had an opportunity he retired to his study, where he gave free indulgence to his reflections, and tried in vain to reconcile the conflicting thoughts that occupied his breast.

Rosario was more than usually agitated after the visit of Mr. Clavering; but he still remained fixed in his determination to suffer anything rather than he would break the oath he had taken, and betray Harold and his associates.

" They must already have heard of my imprisonment," he reflected; "and although their rage must be excited at my absconding from the ruins, and with the intention of frustrating their plans, they must still applaud my firmness, in resolving to suffer myself rather than betray them. And they will not surely allow me to suffer without making some attempt to rescue me. Should they not, the secret so important to them and to me must be revealed, and Heaven only knows what may be the consequences. Oh, Azrah, would that I could behold you; for now, in my present dilemma, you might be induced to disclose all that I am so anxious to know, and which would guide me better how to act. And should you know my present situation, which no doubt you do, after the interest you have expressed in my fate, how agonising will be your thoughts. Why has not the strange mystery in which my destiny has been enveloped been allowed to be unravelled before this? What misery it might have saved to me and others!"

Once more he took the likeness of her whom Azrah had told him was his mother from his bosom, and, as he gazed upon it, tears streamed from his eyes, and his bosom heaved with a nameless and powerful feeling. He pressed it to his lips, and as he examinèd every lineament of the beauteous countenance it there represented, his agitation increased.

"Yes," he said; "here are the exact features of Azrah, and I could almost imagine, were it not for the revered female it portrays, that he was gazing upon me, and speaking to me, as he did when we last met, and he delivered to me this treasure, so inestimable. Strange mystery—what can it mean? And should I be convicted, will it not be taken from me? No; surely there cannot be beings who would be so cruel as to do that. They shall not! I will lose my life first in attempting to preserve it. And Sir Laurence Cleveland, how powerful were his emotions on beholding it; and how anxious was he to become possessed of it. What could be his motives for that, and the unconnected and ambiguous observations he made use of? Mystery upon mystery! The more I become bewildered the longer I reflect."

Rosario clasped his forehead, and continued in the same state of mind throughout the day; nor could he find anything to alleviate his agony in the least degree. Night came on, and, worn out with thinking, and in the hope of being able to snatch a few hours' respite from his cares and anxieties in sleep, he stretched himself on the rough couch allotted to him, and courted the drowsy god. For some time, however, these efforts were to no purpose; but at length nature was exhausted, and sleep came to his relief.

He must have slept several hours, for when he was suddenly aroused by hearing a loud noise in the prison, he heard the old church clock strike the hour of three. He rubbed his eyes, scarcely conscious as to whether he was asleep or awake; but the sounds that had before reached his ears were repeated louder than ever.

Rosario started hastily from his pallet, and, hurrying towards the door of his cell, listened with breathless attention. The confusion above increased, and a violent struggle of some description seemed to be going on between several individuals. He could also distinguish the voices of men, as if in noisy altercation, and immediately afterwards a hollow groan met his ear, followed by the falling of some heavy weight above his head.

"Good God!" he exclaimed, "what has happened? What is the meaning of this uproar? Surely the prison is attacked; but can it be I who am the cause of it?"

He had scarcely a moment given him for reflection; the sound of the hasty closing of numerous and heavy doors met his ears, succeeded by the hurried treading of several feet. They approached nearer; they were evidently making their way to the cell in which he was confined. The heart of Rosario palpitated, evidently with mingled hope and fear.

"This way, this way!" he heard a voice exclaim, which he immediately recognised as that of Harold, and he sunk on his knees, and clasped his hands with a feeling which it is needless to attempt to describe.

"It is the gipsies!" he exclaimed. The next moment he heard them at the door;

the bolts were withdrawn, the door burst open, and Harold and several other of the gipsies entered,

"Ah! he is here," cried Harold; "and our plans have succeeded."

Rosario could not repress a scream.

"Hold, boy," commanded Harold, with a fierce look; "this is not the time for the display of any childish emotion. Come, you must with us, or the neighbourhood may be alarmed before we can effect our escape."

He laid hold of the arm of Rosario as he spoke, and forced him from the cell, and the gipsy boy was so overcome with emotion, that he had not the power, if he had even had the will, to offer any resistance.

So sudden and unexpected was the event, that Rosario was completely bewildered, and scarcely knew what was going forward. They hurried him through the different passages of the prison, and ascending the steps, entered the small court-yard which led to the house occupied by the master of the gaol. Here Rosario, to his horror, beheld two of the officers of the prison stretched apparently lifeless on the pavement, and weltering in their blood; and, on entering the house, he also saw the mangled body of the principal gaoler, who it seems had offered all the resistance in his power, when the ruffians forced the doors, and had paid for his daring with his life. The sight completely overpowered the poor boy, and, after fixing a look of horror upon Harold, he became insensible. The ruffian raised him in his arms, and then said,—

"Follow me, lads; quick, quick! The least delay may prove fatal to us."

They rushed from the prison as he spoke, and looking around them with eager eyes, beheld the coast was perfectly clear, for daylight was only just beginning to dawn.

"It is all right; fortune favours us," cried Harold.

"She does," said Malachial; "we have managed this business with promptitude and ability. To the wood, to the wood; and, before any one is aware of what has happened, we shall be far away."

They hurried away from the prison as fast as they could, and entering a field which led to the wood, they beheld a couple of horses grazing.

"This is fortunate," said Harold, as he hastened towards them; "we must take the liberty of hiring these for a short time. I will mount one, with the boy; you, Malachial, can take the other; and, before an hour has elapsed, we shall be far out of the reach of danger. Our companions can follow us by different routes, but let them be careful to take the roads that are the least frequented, for no doubt there will be a rare hubbub as soon as the escape of Rosario is discovered."

Quickly Harold threw the insensible Rosario over one of the horses, Harold leaping up behind himself; Malachial mounted the other, and they galloped off with all the speed they could make; the other gipsies separating into small parties, and taking different roads, as they had been commanded.

CHAPTER XX.

THE EXCITEMENT IN CONSEQUENCE OF THE ESCAPE OF ROSARIO.—THE BIRTH OF ANOTHER CHILD.—THE INFANTICIDE.

IT was not until more than two hours had elapsed after the flight of Harold and the other ruffians, that the escape of Rosario was discovered, and the consternation which the scene at the prison excited, quickly spread itself all over the neighbourhood, and every one was on the alert to discover the villains who had committed so atrocious and bloody an outrage. Communication was immediately made to the magistrate, and shortly reached the ears of Sir Laurence Cleveland, and they both hastened to the scene of the fearful event.

The head gaoler was quite dead, his skull having been frightfully beaten in; and so was one of the officers; but on examining the other, it was found that life was not quite extinct, and, being placed under proper surgical care, every means were promptly resorted to for his recovery, and with every hope of success, as none of the vital parts had received any injury.

We need not attempt to describe the horror of Mr. Clavering and Sir Laurence, at this dreadful and unexpected event, and the latter, while he secretly exulted in the escape of Rosario, could not but feel the most unbounded disgust at the means by which it had been effected, and immediately concluded that it was the gipsies who had accomplished his liberation, and, therefore, felt satisfied that the poor lad had only for a short time escaped one fate, to meet with another more dreadful; for, attached to such heartless and bloodthirsty miscreants as those, what else could ultimately attend him, but misery and shame? He was also not without his doubts as to whether or not Rosario was, after all, absolutely guilty of that act of incendiarism with which he was charged, in obedience to the command of the gipsies, and the assertions of his innocence, and affected gentleness of disposition, were not merely a subterfuge to evade the punishment that was due to his crime. But still there was something so repugnant to his feelings in that idea, that he quickly banished it from his mind.

Mr. Clavering's suspicions also fell upon the gipsies, and he lost no time in sending persons in every direction in search of them; at the same time placards were printed with the utmost despatch, offering a large reward to any one who could give such information as would lead to the apprehension of the atrocious miscreants who had committed the murderous outrage. But much depended upon the recovery of the wounded man, and, in the meantime, the villains would have every opportunity of effecting their escape.

"It appears to me," observed Mr. Clavering to Sir Laurence, "that, after all the favourable impressions which this boy has made upon us, he has been so well tutored by the miscreants with whom he has, from his own admission, from childhood been associated, that he has become an accomplished and consummate hypocrite; and I begin to fear that he is really the individual who was guilty of the act of incendiarism at your mansion, Sir Laurence."

"I would fain believe otherwise, Mr. Clavering," answered the baronet; "but, certainly, I must admit that circumstances look very suspicious against him. Yet it is not likely that he could carry on a correspondence with the tribe, and neither could he by any means have prevented their committing the present outrage, and rescuing him from prison, however anxious he might have been to do so."

"True," returned the magistrate; "but still, if his wish was to render justice, he would at once have divulged who were the perpetrators of the heinous crime at Branscombe House, given every information where they were to be found, and thus have prevented this monstrous crime. As I said before, I am afraid that Rosario, as he calls himself, has been thoroughly debased by his connexions; and, should he be again apprehended, however plausible he may make his conduct appear, unless he at once candidly discloses the whole of the transactions of these ruffians, renders the means of bringing them to justice, and exonerates himself from the odium which circumstances at present cast upon his character, he will have to suffer the full penalty of the law."

" And you would regret that, Mr. Clavering ?"

" Certainly I would. But would he not have himself to blame ?"

" In one respect, I think he would. But, after all, I cannot believe that so amiable an exterior, and in one so young, can cover a depraved heart. He must be the dupe, the inexperienced dupe of those who, from earliest childhood, have held him in their power."

" I would charitably think so also," said Mr. Clavering. " But, after all, I have my doubts; I am inclined to think, after maturely weighing all the circumstances in my mind, that he is old in art, if not in years; that he is the offspring, and knows it, of one of the tribe, and that he has been instructed to assume this air of mystery for the purpose of exciting sympathy, and the better forwarding the diabolical plans of the gipsies."

" Oh, no," exclaimed Sir Laurence, and his mind warmed with different recollections; " I cannot, I will not thus judge of the character of the boy, Rosario ; I will never believe that he is the child of one of those lawless miscreants, after what I have seen and heard."

" Seen and heard ?"

" Yes."

" You surprise me, Sir Laurence ; what may you have seen and heard ?" inquired Mr. Clavering.

" Excuse me, sir," answered the baronet, " I decline answering that question."

" It is strange."

" It may appear so ; but his features ——"

" Do they remind you of any particular individual, Sir Laurence ?"

" Do they remind me of any particular individual !" repeated Sir Laurence, with a deep sigh. " Oh, yes; of one, whom I would fain, but can never, forget. The resemblance is most extraordinary, and I cannot in any way account for it."

" And who might that individual be, Sir Laurence ?"

" Pardon me, Mr. Clavering, but I dare not mention the name. Let us change the subject."

" Well, Sir Laurence, I do not wish to be so bold as to press you upon a subject which appears so painful to you ; but, of course, you will exert yourself to discover these wretches?"

" Certainly," answered the baronet ; " nothing would gratify me more than to see the real villains brought to condign punishment."

They now returned to the prison, in one of the chambers of which the wounded man was lying ; but they found that, although he had been restored to sensibility, and the medical men expressed it as their opinion that he would ultimately recover, he was in yet too weak a condition to speak, or to give any explanation of the dreadful transaction that had taken place. This was very unfortunate, as it all afforded time for the ruffians to escape detection ; and so solemnly and closely were they bound to each other, that it was generally feared, even the offer of any reward, however large, would not induce any of their associates to betray them.

The two horses, which belonged to Mr. Clavering, having been missed, it was immediately supposed that the same parties who had committed the outrage had stolen them, and, if so, they must have had plenty of time in making their escape, especially with the gipsy boy; and thus everything seemed to bear against their detection.

Mr. Clavering and Sir Laurence now separated for a time, and the latter made his way to Branscombe House, to make Blanche and his sister acquainted with the extraordinary particulars; but he found that the intelligence had already reached them, and that they both were in a state of great excitement, awaiting his return, in order to hear further news.

" And they have found no clue to the course which the desperate ruffians have taken ?" eagerly inquired Blanche.

Sir Laurence replied that they had not.

" And the gipsy boy has escaped?" said Blanche.

" For the present, he has," answered the baronet.

" Thank Heaven !" ejaculated Blanche.

" Ay, my love," returned her husband; " had it been by less sanguinary means, I should have rejoiced that he had done so. But the obstinacy that he has hitherto maintained has prejudiced most persons against him, and they now believe him to have been the individual who committed the act of incendiarism upon our mansion."

" But you do not—you cannot believe him guilty, Laurence ?"

" I know not what to think."

" Oh, no," remarked Amanda; " depend upon it that it was the gipsies who committed both acts. It was only natural, for their own sakes, that they should run any risks to effect the poor boy's liberation."

" Certainly," said the generous hearted Blanche; " I am firmly of that opinion. Would that he could have been prevailed upon to reveal everything, and thrown himself upon the protection of those who were disposed to become his friends; all this might then have been prevented."

" The gipsy boy at liberty," added Sir Laurence, " and our bitterest enemies secured, and the lives of those two unfortunate men saved, I perfectly agree with you, my dear Blanche; but, anxious as I am to know more about him, I dread Rosario's now being discovered, for nothing can save him from punishment."

" Poor boy !" said Amanda; " his has been a hard and mysterious lot, to be thus placed among wretches who could only bring him to destruction."

" Yes," coincided Blanche; " and when he is so well calculated, both from appearance and manners, to fill the most exalted station. I feel satisfied that he cannot be the child of obscure parents."

" That is my belief," said Sir Laurence; " and yet Mr. Clavering has expressed an opinion to me that he is the offspring of one of the tribe."

" Oh, no, that can never be," replied Blanche; " something speaks convincingly to my mind that he is not. The tale he has told is a remarkable, but still a most plausible one."

" It is," said the baronet; " and has made the strongest and most lasting impression upon my heart."

" How much, if it is true, is he to be pitied !" remarked Amanda. " Had he fallen into other hands, what a bright and valued ornament might he not have formed to society !"

" Alas! he might," sighed Sir Laurence; " but now ———"

" He seems doomed, by the most terrible destiny, to some deplorable fate," added Lady Cleveland; " and if it is true that he has a father living, who deserted him and

his mother, and left them to misery, shame, and degradation, how much has that man to answer for!"

Sir Laurence felt a pang of remorse steal through his bosom at these remarks, and he averted his face to conceal his emotion from the observation of his lady and Amanda, and was unable to return any answer.

"One of the unfortunate officers of the prison, you say, is not dead?" said Amanda.

"He is not," replied the baronet.

"And is he likely to recover?" eagerly inquired Blanche.

Sir Laurence replied in the affirmative.

" Then, if he does, he will doubtless be able to give such an account of the affair as will elucidate it, and lead to the detection of the ruffians."

" Probably he will; but still I think there can be little doubt that it is the gipsies. Who else would feel such an interest in, or run such a risk to release, Rosario?"

" Very true," coincided Amanda; " but they have had time sufficient to effect their escape, and we have had quite proof enough of the difficulty there is to discover them."

" Yes," said Sir Laurence; " one might almost be inclined to think that they had some supernatural means of accomplishing their designs."

" Could I be convinced that the gipsy boy was in safety, I should be satisfied," said Lady Blanche.

" Yes," returned Sir Laurence; " but we may never behold him again, or ascertain anything of his fate; and, indeed, should he ever again appear in these parts, the doom that awaits him, I dread to think upon."

" But he might then be prevailed upon to reveal all he knows, and to exculpate himself from all blame."

" I fear he would not; Rosario seems to be very determined, and would rather sacrifice his own liberty, or even his life, than betray those with whom he is connected. Surely, it must be something very powerful and extraordinary that can thus hold such a control over him."

" It must, indeed," coincided Blanche; " my mind is bewildered in trying to form a conjecture as to the cause."

" The more we reflect upon it, the more likely are we, it seems, to become perplexed," remarked the baronet.

" It is evident, from what we have seen, that he is savagely treated by the gipsies, and therefore is it the more remarkable that he should be so much attached to them."

" That they hold him entirely under subjection, and in their power, there can be no doubt," said Amanda; " but I hope the time will arrive when he will be able to shake off their trammels, and to convince the world that he is entirely innocent of that with which he is charged. For my own part, I must ever believe him innocent."

" That opinion does honour to your generous mind, my amiable sister, and I firmly trust that it will be found to be correct."

After having partaken of a hasty repast, Sir Laurence again left home, and made his way once more to the prison. On the road he deeply ruminated upon all that had taken place, and his bosom became the receptacle of various conjectures, doubts, and apprehensions.

" Would that I could discover what has become of this mysterious boy," he soliloquized; " and be able to place him in a position of security. Something convinces me that he is innocent of that of which he is suspected, and that he has truly represented himself; and my heart throbs towards him with a feeling for which I cannot account. Never can his features be effaced from my memory, and the more I recall them to it, the stronger hold does he take upon my interest and affections. And then the miniature which he holds in his possession, that tortures my recollection with nameless thoughts. His *mother* too! But why should that interest me so much, and thus agitate my mind? Are there not many faces in the world alike? and yet, when I gazed upon that portrait, I could have thought that the living countenance of Clara was before me. Just so did she look when I first became acquainted with her, and when I believed her to be all purity, love, and innocence. Oh, memory! how dost thou delight to torture me! and why should I then thus feel the bitter pang of remorse? Alas! alas!" he added, with a groan; "and did I not also act the part of the deceiver? did I remain constant to the vows I had plighted with her at the altar? did I not act the part of the sensualist, the hypocrite? did not my affections wander from her to her too fair cousin? and what, after satisfying my passions, became of that unfortunate being? Oh, I have been a villain; conscience will continue to reproach me as such, and I ought never to have dared to unite myself to such purity and virtue as that which Blanche possesses. I can never hope to be happy with all this weight of guilt upon my conscience, and I deserve not to be so. Oh, would that I could recall the past!"

He smote his breast as he thus spoke, and hurried on his way, his anguish increasing at every step. On arriving at the prison he found that Mr. Clavering was already there, and he eagerly inquired after the state of the wounded man.

"He is much better than he was," replied Mr. Clavering; "but he is still in too weak a state to enter into the explanation that we require."

"And have you yet received any information that may lead to the detection of the villains?" asked Sir Laurence.

"None whatever; neither have any of the men whom I despatched in pursuit of them yet returned. Every suspicious place in the neighbourhood has been strictly searched, although I do not think it likely that they would remain in the vicinity of the scene of their atrocity."

"Certainly not," coincided the baronet; "I am afraid they are far out of the reach of detection by this time. It is a great pity, I think, that the prison was not better protected."

"Why, I must admit," said Mr. Clavering, "that it was a great and unfortunate oversight; but who would have thought that any one would have been bold enough to venture an attack upon it?"

"It certainly was a daring act," remarked Sir Laurence; "and such an one as I think none would have ventured to attempt but such daring and reckless characters as the gipsies."

"I am perfectly of your opinion; and they must be discovered and brought to justice, for, the sooner the country is rid of such villains, the better. They must not be permitted thus to outrage society with impunity, or no individual will be safe."

"No; and the miscreants will become more bold from continual success. It is most extraordinary where they can have contrived to conceal themselves so long."

"It is; and the refusal of Rosario to betray the place of their retreat, renders his conduct the more suspicious. Had his wishes been as praiseworthy as he professed them to be, he would have shown no hesitation in the matter, especially when he was assured of being protected from their vengeance."

"What the motives of that unfortunate boy were," said Sir Laurence, "I cannot undertake to give an opinion; but, so prejudiced am I still in his favour, that I should be sorry to judge too hastily of him."

"I trust that you, Sir Laurence," replied Mr. Clavering, "will do me the justice to suppose that such are decidedly my wishes as regards the unfortunate lad; but, at the same time, I think you must admit that all the facts that have hitherto transpired in evidence, and the subsequent events, are very prejudicial against him."

"Very true, sir; but still we must make allowances for the intimidation, or, rather, the effect that intimidation is likely to have upon the mind of a youth—a complete boy. And then there are other excuses, I think, to be c ': for instance, the having been associated with those individuals from the e? ,oments of recollec-tion; the mystery attached to his birth; and ———''

"Pardon me, Sir Laurence," interrupted the magist 'but it strikes me that the very argument you now make use of, tends to confir suspicions that the boy has been made an instrument of, and so well tutored b; \ese wretches, that, taking his prepossessing appearance and manners into consideration, his misrepresentation of facts was more likely to receive credence, and to screen his coadjutors from justice. Throwing a veil of mystery over any individual is the most likely way of exciting sympathy, and, consequently, giving those who have the wish, the readiest means of transacting their nefarious business."

"Then you do not believe in the truth of the boy Rosario's statement as to his ignorance of the authors of his being?" observed Sir Laurence.

"I certainly have very strong doubts upon the subject; it is so like the tricks of these wandering vagrants to excite, as I before observed, a false sympathy. Had not Rosario every offer given him of protection, if he would divulge the truth? Yet he preferred to screen those miscreants, and run any risk himself, rather than do an act of justice. Had he really been the honest and virtuous youth we would fain be-lieve him to be, he would not have hesitated a moment. I am, indeed, afraid, after maturely deliberating upon all the circumstances, and with every sincere wish, the same as yourself, Sir Laurence, to see the gipsy boy fully and satisfactorily excul-pated from all blame in respect to the outrage of which he was accused, that he has been so well tutored as to be able to prepossess us in his favour, and that he is un-worthy of the sympathy he has excited."

"I cannot, Mr. Clavering," replied the baronet, "indeed I cannot subscribe to your opinion."

"And perhaps, Sir Laurence—and, indeed, I imagine, from the observations of which you have made use—you have reasons for thinking to the contrary, into which I, of course, shall not make so bold as to inquire."

"It is true, sir, that I have other reasons for being prejudiced in Rosario's favour than those I have mentioned, but which I, at present, cannot explain. I would that the poor boy could be extricated from the power of his present associates, and the mystery with which he is enveloped could be explained, and I feel satisfied, in my own mind, that he would be found to be fully worthy of the deep interest and sym-pathy which he has excited in my mind and that of others. I will not deny, that I should have rejoiced in his escape, had it been effected by less sanguinary means, and were I convinced that he was in the hands of those who would not abuse their power, but do justice to the excellent qualities which I cannot but believe Rosario possesses."

"Those sentiments do honour to you, Sir Laurence," said Mr. Clavering; "and I sincerely hope that future events will prove that the good opinions you have formed of the gipsy boy are not erroneous. But, as I have before remarked, those gipsies must be detected, if possible, and then it will rest with Rosario himself to prove that he is not a willing instrument in their hands, which his refusal to divulge the place of their concealment at present gives every possible reason to suppose that he is."

Sir Laurence made no answer to this, and, after some further conversation, they repaired to the chamber in which the wounded man was lying, and found him in a condition to be able to give some explanation of the facts they were solicitous to know.

It appeared from his statement that himself and his brother officer, the murdered man, were aroused in the room where they slept, about three o'clock, by hearing a loud noise, like the smashing in of doors, from above, and hastily throwing on their clothes, and seizing such weapons of defence as they had at hand, they hurried to the scene of uproar. There they found the room filled with men, in many of whom, notwithstanding the disguise which they had assumed, they recognised the gipsies, and Mr. Hutchins, the head gaoler, doing all he could to resist them. The next moment, and before they could fly to his assistance, he received a stab in the side from one of the ruffians, and fell dead, without a groan, at their feet. Notwithstanding the disparity of their numbers, they rushed upon them, but were immediately felled to the earth, and he remembered no more.

" And you firmly believe that those whom you recognised were the gipsies who were formerly located in this neighbourhood ?" inquired Mr. Clavering.

" I do," answered the wounded officer; "nay, more, I am convinced of it, for one of them I had formerly in my custody on a charge of poaching; but he was rescued from me by his companions on our way to your worship's house."

" And do you know his name ?"

" They called him Malachial."

" That, at any rate, so far, is satisfactory," remarked Sir Laurence.

" It is," coincided Mr. Clavering; "but," he added, addressing the wounded officer, "do you know one of the same tribe who is called Harold ?"

" I have heard of his name," answered the man; "but I do not know him personally."

" Then, of course, you cannot say whether or not he was present at the outrage ?"

" I cannot."

This was all the information it was possible for them to elicit for the present; but it was quite sufficient to satisfy Sir Laurence and the magistrate that the gipsies were the perpetrators of the outrage, and fresh steps were immediately adopted to detect and apprehend them. Bills were posted, offering a much larger reward than at first, and giving a full description of the persons of Harold, Malachial, and Madela; at the same time a free pardon was promised to any of their associates who had not actually committed the murder, if they would come forward and reveal all they knew, and thus be the means of bringing the villains to justice.

The whole affair caused the greatest possible excitement, and the utmost exertions were made to discover the miscreants; but week after week elapsed, and still nothing transpired to throw the least light upon the subject, and it became the opinion of every one that the gipsies had taken good care to retire to some distant and obscure part of the country, and that, in all probability, they would never venture to approach that neighbourhood again.

Sir Laurence, however, could not make up his mind to this, and he firmly believed that the gipsies would never abandon their thirst for vengeance against himself, especially after the threats they had uttered, but would only wait and watch their opportunity, till the excitement which at present prevailed had subsided, and they could do so with greater chance of success, and without the fear of discovery.

These ideas kept the baronet in a constant state of apprehension; and he was, likewise, most anxious to learn what had become the fate of Rosario, whom he could not help still believing to be the innocent being his manners and appearance denoted him to be, and which he himself professed. He avoided communicating his thoughts to Blanche, for fear of betraying any extraordinary emotion; but she fully participated in the same, and anxiously longed to gain some information of the gipsy boy, and to see him placed in a position which she believed he was born to adorn.

While they were thus occupied in fruitless conjecture, a letter was, one morning, delivered to Sir Laurence, at breakfast, written in an unknown hand.

"Where is the person who brought this?" the baronet demanded.

"He went away immediately on delivering it, Sir Laurence," replied the servant.

"It was a man, then?"

"Yes, Sir Laurence."

"And do you ever remember to have seen him before?"

"I do not, sir."

"What sort of a person did he seem to be?"

"He had all the appearance of a simple rustic, and seemed to be very impatient to get away."

Sir Laurence opened the letter, and read the following words aloud, to the astonishment of himself, Blanche, and Amanda:—

"The gipsy boy is safe. The writer wonders not that Sir Laurence Cleveland should feel so deep an interest and anxiety concerning him. At some future period he may probably appear in a new character; let Sir Laurence prepare himself for that event. The truth must be revealed—atonement for past wrongs be made—and justice done, ere Sir Laurence can hope to be contented, much less happy."

The voice of Sir Laurence faltered, his countenance became pale, and his lips quivered, as he read the last lines, and he scarcely dared to raise his eyes to Blanche or his sister.

"What can be the meaning conveyed in those lines?" asked Blanche. "Can you explain them, Sir Laurence?"

"I—I cannot," stammered out Sir Laurence; but his conscience gave an explanation which he dared not utter.

Blanche fixed her penetrating eyes upon him, as she repeated,—

"At some future period he may probably appear in a new character; let Sir Laurence prepare himself for that event. The truth must be revealed—atonement for past wrongs be made—and justice done, ere Sir Laurence can hope to be contented, much less happy! These words are mysterious, and imply a threat, sufficient to excite dread. Sir Laurence, are you acquainted with this handwriting?"

"I can safely assert that I never saw anything resembling it before," answered the baronet. "But probably it is written by Rosario himself."

"And why should he hold out such threats, after the professions of esteem he formerly declared to entertain towards you?"

"I know not; but probably the letter was dictated by the gipsies, and is all a scheme of theirs to keep us in a constant state of apprehension and excitement.

Blanche appeared to be satisfied, but those particular passages in the letter had made an impression upon her mind that she could not easily eradicate. Sir Laurence also, when he was alone, reflected with great pain upon the contents of the epistle, and the longer he did so, the more did his anguish increase. But with respect to the gipsy boy, he could form no conjecture as to what they implied, and why he should so particularly prepare himself to meet him in a new character. Surely he could have nothing to dread from that boy; and yet there was that impenetrable mystery attached to him, which he would fain have explained. That he had committed past wrongs, he was, to his sorrow and regret, compelled to admit; but in what manner could he make atonement? If bitter remorse could be received as any reparation, surely he had already made abundant amends, which he was ready to strengthen by his future conduct, if the means could be pointed out to him. But after maturely deliberating upon the contents of this strange epistle, he could come to no other conclusion than that it was another dark scheme of the gipsies to harass and torment him, and to disparage him in the estimation of Blanche; and his worst apprehensions, therefore, were all but confirmed, that they were secretly at work to do him some serious injury, and he knew not in what manner to guard against them. He communicated to Mr. Clavering some of the contents of the letter, and that gentleman was firmly of opinion that it came from the gipsies, and that they had, therefore, certainly not abandoned their designs of vengeance, but still was as much at a loss as ever to devise any plan for their detection.

Several months elapsed without anything more particular occurring, when Blanche was safely delivered of a beautiful boy, which was welcomed with feelings of transport, not unmingled with melancholy and fear, by Sir Laurence Cleveland.

The mother and infant progressed well, and Blanche was soon restored to convalescence. Maternal affection induced her to suckle the babe herself, and she was not happy if it was for a moment absent from her presence.

She had retired one evening, with the infant, rather sooner than usual to her chamber, and Sir Laurence was preparing to follow her, when he was suddenly startled by hearing a piercing shriek from her apartment, and he rushed towards it with the greatest precipitation; a feeling of the most uncontrollable dread coming over him at the same time. All was still when he arrived at the chamber; but, on entering it, what a spectacle of horror presented itself to his eyes! It was a wonder that madness did not at once seize upon his brain. Blanche was perfectly insensible, and her infant was lying by her side, a blackened, disfigured corpse!

CHAPTER XXI.

MORE SUFFERING FOR SIR LAURENCE AND BLANCHE.—THE VAIN ENDEAVOUR TO FIND OUT THE MURDERER OF THE INFANT.—ANOTHER CALAMITY.

No language can properly pourtray the agony of Sir Laurence as he gazed upon this dreadful scene. He uttered a loud exclamation of horror, which brought two of the female servants into the room, and it is needless to say that they were as much appalled as himself at the sight which presented itself. Sir Laurence threw himself, with the most unspeakable agony, upon the form of his wife, at first believing her dead; but he just felt the slight throbbing of her heart, and, almost delirious, and scarcely knowing what he said, he ordered them immediately to summon the family physician.

He then turned his distracted gaze once more upon the infant, and was too quickly convinced that the little innocent was dead. From the discoloured aspect of its countenance, the first idea that suggested itself to him, was, that it had died in a convulsive fit; but, on examining its throat, the impression of fingers was plainly to be distinguished, and convinced him that its death had been caused by violence.

At this moment the family physician arrived, and, having examined the unfortunate infant, immediately pronounced it as his opinion that it had died of strangulation. Sir Laurence looked aghast, and the greatest sensation was caused in the mansion. Who could have perpetrated this hellish deed? Surely it must be some one in the establishment, for who else could have gained access to the chamber without being discovered?

"Where—who is the fiend that has done this?" groaned Sir Laurence. "Oh! God!—oh, God! what have I done to deserve to be visited with this dreadful calamity? My wife, my poor Blanche, this will certainly prove your death-blow."

He threw himself in a chair, and groaned as if his heart would burst. The doctor tried to soothe him, and then turned his whole attention towards the recovery of Lady Cleveland, after having had the disfigured corpse of her infant removed to another room.

It would be a fruitless task to endeavour to describe the dreadful agony of Sir Laurence; but no persuasion could induce him to leave the bedside of his insensible wife, and he beat his breast and tore his hair, in a state of mind bordering upon absolute frenzy.

"The curse of Heaven is upon me!" he exclaimed. "Oh, Blanche! Blanche! into what continual scenes of horror have you been plunged by your union with me. And my poor, innocent babe; monsters! why should they seek its life? My wife, my soul's idol, you will never again recover."

"Pray, Sir Laurence," said the doctor, "do endeavour to tranquillise your feelings, and retire, for a time, to another apartment. I have every hope that, in time, I shall be able to restore Lady Cleveland to her senses. It is necessary, likewise, that an immediate and minute inquiry should be made into this dreadful affair."

"Leave the chamber!" cried Sir Laurence, with a frenzied look; "leave the chamber, and my Blanche in this state? Oh, no! nothing shall draw me from her side. Heaven retain my senses, or these accumulated calamities, these monstrous acts of vengeance against the good and innocent, will assuredly lead me to commit some act of violence. My poor babe! and could not even your smiling innocence, your cherub looks, avert the murderer's hand? What have I ever done to deserve this terrible retribution?"

He covered his face with his hands, and again sobbed with the most convulsive agony, and it would have been completely useless for any one to have endeavoured to expostulate with him in such an hour of dreadful trial. The worthy doctor saw that, and, therefore, did not offer any farther to interrupt the violence of his grief.

Amanda now entered the chamber, having been made acquainted with the full extent of the horrible event, and her emotion, as may be expected, was nearly equal to that of her brother. She went to him, offered some few words of consolation, which he did not either appear to hear or to comprehend the meaning of, and then lent her whole assistance, as far as her agitation would permit her, to that of the physician, towards the recovery of the unfortunate Blanche, to whom she feared that this dreadful and unparalleled calamity would prove a death-blow.

In the meantime, the greatest possible consternation prevailed amongst the establishment at Branscombe House; and Mr. Clavering, to whom all the particulars of the melancholy catastrophe had been immediately forwarded, arrived at the mansion, and entered into a searching investigation of the various domestics. But nothing whatever could be elicited from them calculated to throw any suspicion upon the wretch or wretches who had perpetrated this atrocious crime. The statements of the domestics, given in the most simple, unaffected, and candid manner, went at once to remove all suspicion of the guilt of the hideous charge from them, and the circumstance, the more it was investigated, became more and more involved in the most inscrutable mystery. A strict examination of every part of the mansion was made, but no clue whatever was obtained. According to the statements of the servants, no

See p. 239.

person unconnected with the house had entered or repassed from the house during the day, up to the time that the murder must have been committed, and there was nothing whatever to show how they could have done so, without their knowledge. It now rested entirely upon the restoration of Lady Cleveland, to give any explanation that might throw a light upon the subject, and that was greatly retarded, for no sooner was she restored to a state of consciousness, than, looking round, and not beholding her hapless infant, all the fearful horrors of the calamity appeared to rush upon her recollection, and convulsive fits succeeded one another with such violence, that the medical gentleman fully expected she must sink under them.

Mr. Clavering exerted himself to the utmost of his power, in order to elucidate this most mysterious and melancholy affair, and lost no time in forwarding full particulars of the same to the proper authorities in all parts of the country, and great was the sensation that was created; but, at present, all chance of the detection of the miscreant or miscreants, who had committed the barbarous murders seemed to be futile.

The anguish of Sir Laurence Cleveland bordered upon madness, and no argument or persuasion would prevail upon him to leave the chamber of his lady, even for an instant. Throughout that night she continued in much the same state, but, towards the morning, the violence of the fits abated, and she was restored to something like consciousness.

Looking around her, and seeing her husband by her side, she ejaculated,—

"Ah! Lawrence, my husband, you, then, are not taken from me; but our child, our little innocent, where is that? Oh, God! oh, God! what have we done, that we should thus be visited?"

"My poor, my beloved Blanche!" said Sir Laurence, in a voice nearly choked with the violence of his emotions. "Endeavour to bear up against this dreadful calamity, and to give us such information as may lead to the fiend or fiends in human shape, who have perpetrated this monstrous crime."

"Ah!" cried Blanche, with a ghastly smile; "then it is too true; it was no frightful dream, but stern reality; and the ghastly, blackened corpse I beheld on awaking, was that of my own sweet babe! Laurence, whatever is the cause I know not, but a curse, a dreadful curse is upon us, and it were better that neither of us had ever been born."

She uttered the latter words with a peculiar solemnity of tone and gesture, and Sir Laurence, struck with a nameless feeling of remorse, buried his face in his hands and groaned aloud.

Amanda advanced to the side of the couch, and taking the hand of Blanche in the most soothing and affectionate accents, said,—

" Dear Blanche, I implore you to endeavour to compose yourself, and to give some explanation of this horrible affair, so that there may be a clue furnished to the perpetrators of the hideous crime. Did you observe any one in your chamber at the time you awoke?"

" Yes, yes," hastily gasped forth Blanche, passing her hand across her damp forehead, to recall her scattered senses; " I—I remember that I was awoke from a frightful dream, by hearing a loud laugh as from a fiend exulting over his deluded victim. I looked up, and by the light of the lamp burning in my chamber, I caught the hasty glimpse of a retreating form, enveloped in a large black mantle. Which way it went I know not. Instinctively I turned my eyes to my poor babe, and beheld it, oh, horror, black, disfigured, and struggling in the last convulsive gasp of death. I remember no more; my—my senses left me."

" God of Heaven!" groaned the wretched baronet, striking his forehead deliriously, " I invoke thy most terrible vengeance on the head of the demon who has done this! Reveal him, I beseech thee, to our knowledge, that he may meet the just punishment due to his inhuman, his unparalleled crime. Oh, Blanche, my soul's adored, look upon me, speak to me one word of ———"

But, before he could finish the sentence, Blanche, overpowered by the indescribable emotions that distracted her bosom, once more became insensible.

The scene that ensued was one of the most distressing which can be imagined. Sir Laurence threw himself upon the bosom of his wife, and it was not without the greatest difficulty that he could be removed, and, when he was, he tore his hair, and beat his breast, and exhibited every other symptom of the uncontrollable anguish that afflicted his mind. In vain did the doctor, Mr. Clavering, and Amanda, try to prevail upon him to retire, for a while, from the chamber, while they endeavoured to restore his unfortunate lady once more to consciousness; he was deaf to expostulation, and they dreaded the most serious consequences.

From the brief statement that Lady Cleveland had been enabled to make, they could gather nothing whatever which might lead them to a detection of the murderer, and by what means he could have obtained admission to the mansion, and afterwards effected his escape, they were all at a perfect loss to conjecture.

While the doctor and Amanda were using every effort to recover Blanche, Sir Laurence threw himself in a chair, and swaying his body to and fro, and uttering the deepest, heart-drawn groans, his agony was quite pitiable to witness. Suddenly, however, he was aroused from the immediate absorption of his grief, by a loud exclamation which proceeded from Amanda, and looking up, he beheld her with an open note in her hand, which it seems she had found near the spot where the murdered child had been lying.

From her alarmed aspect, it was evident that she had hastily perused the contents of the epistle, and Sir Laurence, darting towards the bed, hastily snatched it from her hand, and with a breathless agony, which cannot be adequately described, he perused the following words, in a handwriting of which he had not the slightest knowledge,—

" The same spirit of vengeance that has hitherto pursued the detested villain, Sir Laurence Cleveland, has destroyed his illegitimate offspring, and that of the wretched, betrayed woman with whom he cohabits. It will continue to pursue him till his brain is wrung to madness, and he is sunk to the lowest depths of shame, misery, and degradation! Send forth your bloodhounds; the game ye may seek defies the skill of the huntsman!"

The paper fell from the hands of the distracted baronet, and, with a loud groan, he sank insensible upon the floor.

He was immediately conveyed to his apartment, and one of the medical gentlemen who were in attendance was left in charge of him, while every one became more and more involved in mystery and horror.

"This note at once confirms my suspicions," remarked Mr. Clavering; "the gipsies are the perpetrators of this frightful murder, as well as the other atrocities that have recently taken place. What is to be done to detect them, and to bring them to justice, I am at present at a loss to imagine, for they seem to set the law at entire defiance."

Amanda was in such a state of agitation, that she could not return any answer, and it was with the greatest difficulty that she could support herself at all; but she was firmly of the same opinion as the worthy magistrate, and foreboded at once the most dreadful consequences. The aspersions also cast upon the character of her brother, and for which she was fearful there was too much foundation, filled her 'bosom with the most unutterable anguish, the more so, as she could not give any expression to her feelings.

"But, I pray you," she said, addressing herself to Mr. Clavering, the physician, and the other persons present, "do not make Lady Cleveland acquainted with any particulars of the receipt of this epistle; it can do no good, and might be productive of the most serious consequences."

"I agree with you, madam," said Mr. Clavering; "and care must be taken to caution Sir Laurence to make no allusion to it. It is evidently only a scheme of these abominable and hardened miscreants, to give greater effect to the deadly spirit of revenge which they have unaccountably imbibed against him."

"Oh! sir," ejaculated Amanda, "what will become of us, possessing such terrible and desperate enemies as these? How are we possibly to defend ourselves against them?"

"I will take care, madam," replied the magistrate, "you may depend upon it, to use every means to detect them, and to protect you from any farther outrages from them. Notwithstanding the secresy with which they have hitherto conducted their plans, I do not think it is possible that they can much longer escape apprehension. Such blood-thirsty miscreants must not be allowed to outrage society; and I am certain that every one who entertains a proper abhorrence of such atrocities, will do the utmost to aid in the detection of the ruffians."

Poor Blanche was only conscious at intervals during night, and then the agony she endured was far greater than the most eloquent pen could describe, and which must be left to the imagination of the reader. The medical gentlemen continued unremitting in their attentions upon her, and but for their skill, and the gentle soothings of the affectionate and amiable Amanda, she must have sunk under her sufferings. She could furnish no other account of the horrible transaction than that she had already given, and it was thought advisable not to refer to it any more than possible, for fear of the consequences.

Sir Laurence Cleveland had been placed in bed, and after some time he was restored to sensibility, and would immediately again have hastened to the chamber of Blanche, had he not been prevented, and assured that such a step would be sure to endanger the life of his unfortunate lady.

"And it is I—I who have murdered her!" he said, striking his forehead—"but for me, she might now have been happy. Why did Providence ever suffer us to meet? Oh, God! that letter and its contents rack my soul! And what power have I of protecting myself from such terrible, such implacable enemies? They have a secret way of working their inhuman designs, which I cannot fathom, and consequently have no means of averting. My poor murdered babe! Alas! my beloved Blanche, this must certainly prove your death; and my conscience must ever reproach me with having been the indirect cause. I must have been a villain, or never could I have united myself to one of whom I was so unworthy."

Again he beat his breast, and the persons who were in attendance upon him stood by, wrapt in astonishment, but the deepest commiseration, for they charitably believed that he reproached himself undeservedly, and that the shock of the late dreadful calamity had taken an effect upon his intellect. At that moment Mr. Clavering entered the chamber, to inquire how he was, and endeavoured to assuage his anguish as much as possible.

"You tell me to be calm," said the wretched baronet; "but how think you I can be so, after the horrors of this night; the bloody murder of my innocent child; the dreadful situation of my unfortunate Blanche, and the receipt of that fearful letter ?"

" I will not attempt to deny, Sir Laurence," said the magistrate, " that the horrible and mysterious events of this night, are more than sufficient to excite your utmost anguish; but still, for the sake of your amiable lady, for your own sake, I beg of you to try to subdue your feelings, and be prepared to offer Lady Cleveland that consolation she will so much need under all the trying circumstances. One thing, above all, I would advise you to do, and that is to keep that letter, which Lady Blanche has probably not seen, a secret from her. Your amiable sister and myself have consulted upon the subject, and that is the conclusion we have come to, as the most advisable course to pursue."

" But the threats contained in that note," said the baronet; " how are we to guard against them ? In what manner can we protect ourselves against those bloodthirsty miscreants, who have proved how fully capable they are of carrying their inhuman designs into execution ?"

" I do hope, my dear Sir Laurence," replied Mr. Clavering, " that before many days, perhaps hours, have elapsed, something will transpire to lead to their apprehension. I need not assure you that I will exert myself to the utmost, and will leave no means untried to bring the monsters to justice. That the gipsy tribe to which Harold, Madela, and Rosario belong, are the perpetrators of all those dreadful crimes which have so shocked the neighbourhood of late, there cannot be the least doubt, and it is impossible that they can remain concealed much longer."

Sir Laurence shook his head, and heaved a deep sigh, and after some time Mr. Clavering left him, and quitted the mansion.

We need not attempt to describe the sufferings of the baronet during the night; the more so, as he learned that Blanche still continued in the most melancholy and distressing state; and it was with difficulty that he could be prevented from hastening to her chamber. By the morning, however, he was a little more tranquil, and at an early hour he arose, and hurried to the chamber of Blanche.

He found that his sister had never for a moment quitted her bedside, but had watched her with the tenderest solicitude, and the utmost anxiety.

It was not till the day had advanced, that poor Blanche was restored to anything like a degree of sensibility, and then the meeting which took place between her and her husband was agonizing in the extreme. It is needless to dwell upon it, for the reader we are certain can form an adequate conception of it. They mingled their tears together at the dreadful fate of their innocent offspring, and invoked the just vengeance of Heaven upon the head of its cowardly and monstrous assassin.

Many days elapsed before Lady Blanche was able to leave her chamber, and when she was, she had the melancholy, the heartrending duty to perform of following the remains of her murdered infant to the tomb. How she was enabled to support so severe a trial at all, was wonderful; but when the tomb closed upon its ashes for ever, she uttered one piercing shriek, that appalled the hearts of all those who heard it, and sunk inanimate and insensible in the arms of her distracted husband. She was conveyed without the least delay to the mansion, and removed to her chamber, where the unfortunate lady remained for several hours afterwards in a state of utter unconsciousness, and Sir Laurence Cleveland was scarcely in any better condition than herself.

Nothing could surpass the poignant anguish of mind which the baronet endured;

for, in addition to the tortures inflicted by the dreadful calamity which had befallen them, his bosom was stung with remorse, and he was in a constant state of dread, not only of the vengeance of the gipsies, but also of exposure; and, at the same time, he could not but consider that he was acting the part of the deceiver and the hypocrite, by refraining from making Blanche acquainted with all the particulars of his past life, yet his very soul shrank appalled from the odious task, although he might have been convinced that Blanche loved him too fondly not to view his former errors with a lenient eye.

It was many weeks after the horrible murder of their infant ere Blanche or her husband were restored to anything like tranquillity, and how much more acute would the sufferings of the unhappy lady have been had she been acquainted with the cir-cumstance of the letter which the monstrous assassin had left behind him; but that, in compliance with the advice of Mr. Clavering and Amanda, was kept a profound secret from her; but most torturing were the reflections which the contents of that epistle caused Sir Laurence. He was in a constant state of the greatest dread, for he could have no doubt that the wretches from whom it emanated would not fail at every opportunity to put the threats it contained into execution, and he shuddered with horror to think what further horrible calamities were yet in store for them: and yet he in vain racked his brain to hit upon some means of averting them.

Rewards had been offered—the utmost vigilance used to detect the wretches from whom they had already experienced so many troubles; but all to no purpose. Every-thing remained involved in the same state of mystery as before, although they could entertain little or no doubt that the gipsies were the authors of all the atrocities that had been perpetrated against them, and the success with which they kept themselves secure from detection astonished every one. It seemed impossible that the tribe could be located in any part of the country, or they must be discovered; they could not keep themselves concealed from every eye, and the large rewards that were offered for their apprehension would surely induce some one to betray them. But yet there could be very little doubt they had their agents in the neighbourhood of Branscombe House, who made them acquainted with everything which took place there, and watched incessantly to carry their diabolical plans into effect.

Several persons had been taken up on suspicion, but, after having undergone the strictest examination, nothing could be elicited against them, and they were conse-quently discharged.

Thus month after month passed away, and matters remained in the same state of mystery. Time, in some degree, ameliorated the grief of Blanche and Sir Laurence for the untimely loss of their infant, and they devoted the whole of their affectionate attention to the little Emeline, in whose innocent gambols they endeavoured to find their greatest consolation; but often as he contemplated the lovely child, the dreadful threats and predictions of old Madela and Harold would rush on the memory of the baronet, and fill his bosom with the most painful and uncontrollable apprehensions.

"Even this fair child," he would sometimes soliloquise, "the wretches have prog-nosticated, will prove a curse to me, instead of a blessing—that she will learn to hate me; and so fearfully have their predictions been hitherto fulfilled, that, although I am not prone to be superstitious, I cannot help entertaining a dread that they will be realised. Oh, how horrible is that thought! But surely the Almighty will avert anything so unnatural. That beauteous child can never become so depraved, so de-graded. Could I be convinced that she would so, fondly as I love her, with all the fervour that parent can feel for his offspring, most ardently should I pray that Heaven would take her to itself ere one vicious thought has entered her breast. But away with such gloomy ideas; they are revolting to human nature, to reason, to affection, everything. Providence will, I trust, shield my innocent offspring from every harm, from every temptation, and make her a blessing to her fond parents, instead of a curse."

Such were the thoughts that continued to haunt and harass the mind of the baronet, and threw a constant gloom over his hopes and prospects.

A twelvemonth had now elapsed since the dreadful occurrence which has just been recorded, and nothing had been seen or heard of the gipsies; and it was, therefore, concluded that they had quitted the country; but Sir Laurence in vain tried to flatter himself with the idea that they had abandoned their designs.

" They have only deferred the execution of their plans," he said, " until the excitement caused by their last dreadful outrage has subsided, and an opportunity presents itself for them to accomplish what they wish with more safety to themselves. I know not in what way to guard myself against them; for it seems that they can gain access to my house whenever they please. The manner in which they are enabled to carry their plans into effect, and without being detected, is entirely beyond my comprehension. Surely none of my servants can be conniving with them? Oh, no; they are all well tried and honest; and I am convinced that I should be doing them an injustice, by entertaining any suspicion against them."

Frequently did the image of the gipsy boy present itself to his imagination, and most anxiously did he long to know what had become of him, commiserating, as he did, in the peculiar circumstances of his fate: believing him to be innocent, and after the interest which his features and the miniature he had seen in his possession, had excited in his breast. How glad would he have been to behold him again, with the hope that he might prevail upon him to give him some further explanation, and also to furnish him with such information as would lead to the discovery of the gipsies, and, by bringing them to justice, thus frustrate any further designs they might have in contemplation. But he feared that the gipsies would keep such a watchful eye on the actions of Rosario, that he would not have the opportunity, if even he had the will, to put him on his guard against them.

It was about this period, that Sir Laurence and his lady received a pressing invitation from Lord and Lady Musgrove, to pass a few weeks with them at their noble seat; and the baronet gladly accepted it, hoping that the change of scene and society would be conducive to the health and spirits of his beloved Blanche.

Before they departed, however, they left strict injunctions with the servants to keep a strict look out against any suspicious persons who might be seen lurking near the mansion, and to give immediate information to Mr. Clavering, who would be ready promptly to assist them, should occasion require.

CHAPTER XXII..

THE ABDUCTION AND RESTORATION OF THE CHILD.—THE REVELATION.—THE FLIGHT OF THE GIPSIES.

NOTHING particular, or worthy of being recorded in these pages, occurred to them on the journey, and, in due time, they arrived at Musgrove Abbey, and were heartily welcomed by the noble lord and his amiable lady. No persons could more deeply commiserate with the misfortunes that had befallen Sir Laurence and Lady Blanche than they did, and they exerted themselves to the utmost to alleviate their distress, and to lead them to hope for happier days.

Nothing could be more beautifully romantic than the situation of Musgrove Abbey, and the picturesque scenery by which it was surrounded often tempted them to take long rambles; and in these excursions, and in the society of their noble host and hostess, Blanche felt her spirits greatly exhilarated, and she learned to submit with more patience and fortitude to the will of fate, however severe its decrees might at present appear to be.

Sir Laurence beheld, with the most infinite satisfaction and gratitude to Heaven, the change that had come over her, and began to hope that, if no further troubles befell them, she would, in time, be able to banish the bitter past from her memory, and to look forward to the future with the most sanguine anticipations.

Several weeks passed away, at the abbey, in the greatest tranquillity and enjoyment, and Sir Laurence and his lady needed no very pressing invitation to persuade them to prolong their visit. Lord and Lady Musgrove contrived everything they could to amuse them, and to divert their thoughts from other subjects; and they were gratified to find that they succeeded beyond their most sanguine expectations.

Lord and Lady Musgrove enjoyed a select circle of amiable friends, and they paid frequent visits to the abbey; thus serving to add to the pleasures of Blanche and her husband, and, by their enlivening conversation, to banish those reflections which might otherwise have disturbed their minds. They indulged in no riotous pleasures, but everything was in strict keeping with the taste of Sir Laurence and his lady.

Time flew away on gossamer wings, and still Sir Laurence and Blanche thought not of returning home, so admirably was everything contrived for their amusement at the abbey. But another event was about to take place, to interrupt their happiness, and to fill their minds with the most indescribable grief and consternation.

The little Emeline was frequently taken out for a walk, accompanied by her nurse, alone, who was an honest, simple young woman, and one in whom they could place the strictest dependence; but she was always cautioned never to go any great distance from the abbey, and always to return at a certain hour. One day, however, she had greatly exceeded her time, and as the clouds had become louring, they began to be alarmed, and sent a domestic in search of her.

Some time elapsed, and still Susan did not return with the child, and as the rain began to descend pretty heavily, both Sir Laurence and his lady became more seriously alarmed than before, and Blanche, with a throbbing bosom, could not but express her apprehension that something had happened to them.

" The foolish woman," said Sir Laurence, " she has been induced to stroll too far with her tender charge, and, being overtaken by the storm, they have probably stood up somewhere for shelter until it has subsided. Do not alarm yourself, my love; I will myself immediately go in search of them."

Sir Laurence instantly seized his hat and cloak, and, accompanied by Lord Musgrove, left the abbey, consigning Blanche to the care of Amanda and Lady Musgrove.

They proceeded in the direction which they thought it was likely Susan had taken, but they could perceive no signs of her, nor learn anything of her, although they made the strictest inquiries of every person whom they chanced to meet. Sir Laurence

See p. 227.

became dreadfully alarmed, the more so when they beheld the servant who had been despatched in search of them coming towards them alone. From him they learned that, although he had searched every place where they were likely to be, and had made inquiries at several cottages where he thought they might have sought shelter from the storm, he had not been able to obtain the least intelligence of them.

"Good God!" exclaimed Sir Laurence, "what fresh trouble is in store for us? My heart forebodes the worst; something terrible has happened to my poor child and her imprudent attendant. Thoughtless that we were to entrust her with so precious a charge."

He was interrupted by hearing the loud cries of lamentation, and immediately afterwards they beheld Susan emerge from an adjacent lane, wringing her hands, uttering piteous exclamations, and giving other signs of deep distress. When she beheld her master and his companions, she seemed overwhelmed with horror and anguish, and sank upon the earth. Sir Laurence and Lord Musgrove hastened towards her, and raised her up, and so violent was her agitation, that it was several minutes before they could elicit anything from her.

"Oh, my poor, dear, young lady," she at length sobbed forth, wringing her hands; "oh, what will become of me, miserable woman that I am? Mercy, Sir Laurence; mercy—mercy!"

"Answer me, woman!" said the baronet, impatiently, and his agitation, at the same time, was almost insupportable; "where is the child?"

"Oh, dear! oh, dear!" stammered out Susan.

"Keep me not in suspense!" cried Sir Laurence, sternly; "where is my child?"

"Oh, Sir Laurence, oh, my dear, good master, how shall I tell it? And my poor lady too, it will certainly break her heart to hear it; my sweet young lady, Miss Emeline, is gone—stolen from me! Oh, that I should ever live a moment to tell the dreadful truth."

"Gone! gone! My sweet child stolen from me!" cried the distracted baronet, striking his forehead in all the frenzy of despair. "Great God! why am I thus continually persecuted? And it is you, wretch, who have been the cause of all this, through daring to disobey the injunctions I gave you. What atonement can you make for the misery you have occasioned?"

"Oh, spare me, spare me, my dear, kind master," said the unhappy woman; "I know I have done wrong, very wrong, in straying so far from the abbey, after you had commanded me not to do so; and never, never shall I forgive myself; but who would have thought——"

"Tell us everything, and without equivocation," interrupted Lord Musgrove; "how did this dreadful affair happen?"

"Oh, yes, my lord—yes, Sir Laurence, I—I will," stammered the poor woman; "oh, that I should ever live to see this day. It was so very fine when I took Miss Emeline out, and I was so amused with her gambols and her innocent prattle, sweet little angel! that I did not notice the time or the distance, but all at once, a gipsy woman, with a little boy in her hand, made her appearance before me, and said that if I would let her cross my hand with a silver sixpence, she would tell me my fortune; how I was to become a great lady, and keep my full set of servants, and ride in a carriage, and——"

"No more of this nonsense, woman," interrupted Sir Laurence, fiercely, and bursting with impatience; "tell us at once all that has happened, and what became of your young lady. The delay of a moment may be worse than death."

"Oh, yes, Sir Laurence," answered Susan; "I will tell everything. Heaven help me; I am a miserable woman; but oh, pray forgive me. Well, the gipsy woman used so many persuasions, and told such fine tales, and held out to me such promises, that I could not resist her; so I gave her the sixpence, and then she commenced telling me my fortune."

"And where was Miss Emeline at the time of this your foolery?" eagerly demanded Sir Laurence.

"By my side, dear, sweet, young soul," replied Susan; "but suddenly, while I was deeply engaged with the woman, I received a violent blow on the head, from some one behind, which felled me to the earth, and when I recovered my senses, the gipsy woman, and her little boy, and my poor young lady were gone. Oh, how I ——"

"Gracious Heaven!" exclaimed the distracted Sir Laurence; "then the truth is apparent; those miscreants, the gipsies, have again been at their inhuman work; they have stolen my child, my only hope! Horror! horror! what a tale is this to tell my poor Blanche."

"Compose yourself, Sir Laurence," said Lord Musgrove, "and let us return to the abbey with all possible speed, and despatch persons in search of the villains. It may not yet be too late to overtake them."

Sir Laurence could only utter a groan in reply, and was hurried away from the spot by his lordship, scarce conscious of what he was doing, and the distracted and terrified Susan was left to be escorted to the abbey by her fellow servant, deeply deploring her imprudence, and anticipating the most dreadful punishment for the calamity of which she had been the cause.

On the way to the abbey, Sir Laurence and Lord Musgrove were met by several of his tenants and domestics, headed by Grab, the parish beadle, who had been informed of Susan and her precious charge being missed, and had issued forth, anxious to distinguish himself, in search of them. To him Lord Musgrove detailed all the particulars, as they had been related by Susan, and ordered him and his companions to hasten immediately in search of the villains, offering them a handsome reward if they succeeded in apprehending the daring wretches, and safely restoring the little Emeline to her distracted parents. Grab was very glad of the job, and promised that he would discover the villains, and bring them to justice, or never hold office again; and he and his companions then commenced the pursuit with all possible speed.

Sir Laurence and Lord Musgrove made their way to the abbey with heavy hearts, and, when the unfortunate Blanche was made acquainted with the whole of the dreadful particulars, the scene which followed baffles all description. Poor Blanche sunk in an hysterical fit upon the floor, and was immediately conveyed to her chamber, followed by her husband.

The scene of consternation which prevailed in the abbey, when the abduction of the little Emeline became known, was of the most intense description, and the excitement soon spread around the neighbourhood. Persons were despatched on horseback, in every direction, and every person was willing to exert themselves to the utmost in this painful emergency.

With what agony did Sir Laurence hang over the insensible form of his wife, and beat his breast, and bewail the sad, the terrible destiny that pursued them! He was completely deaf to all the efforts of Lord Musgrove and Amanda to console him, and the consequences that seemed likely to follow this unexpected event were of the most fearful description. It was more than an hour before Blanche could be restored to consciousness, and then, beholding her husband hanging over her, she threw herself sobbing on his bosom, and ejaculated,—

"My child! my sweet Emeline, where are you? Oh, God! are you, indeed, stolen from me? Where are the monsters who have torn my innocent from me? Was it not enough that they should brutally murder my last born? Oh! it needed but this to complete their hellish work, and my misery. My heart will break; it can never sustain these accumulated horrors."

Sir Laurence pressed her still closer to his bosom; but his emotion was so great that it was some moments before he could find power to utter a syllable.

And what could he indeed say? What could he advance in argument on this melancholy and unexpected calamity, that was likely to impart consolation to Blanche—that consolation which he really so much needed himself? He felt conscience-stricken, spirit-broken, and despairing; for this blow, he felt convinced, must prove fatal to that amiable and beloved being, whom his former guilt had plunged into so much misery. That the gipsies were the inhuman authors of the outrage, after the statement of Susan, there could not be the least doubt, and therefore had he a right to apprehend the worst.

What means had they of tracing those wretches now, who had hitherto kept themselves so well concealed? and probably the poor child had already fallen a victim to their bloody revenge. She had, it was too much to be feared, shared the same fate as the infant, and, if so, the vengeance of the gipsies would be complete; for they would not only have murdered their two innocent offspring, but also the unoffending mother. And could he himself long survive such an unexampled accumulation of calamities? Oh, no; he felt that he was indirectly the author of all; that his punishment, however terrible, was just; but it was dreadful that the innocent should have to suffer with the guilty.

Most fearfully did he feel the force of what Blanche had observed, namely, that the curse of God seemed to have descended upon them, and that curse he had provoked by his own misconduct in early days; a misconduct that rendered him, he must acknowledge, unworthy to associate himself with such virtue and purity as that of Blanche, however well he might be disposed to act towards her. Had he not grossly deceived her, by exhibiting himself to her only as a very paragon of honour? Yes; he felt, and keenly he now felt it, that he had acted an hypocritical and despicable part, in not having at once acknowledged and divulged to her his past errors, and thus have afforded her the opportunity of receiving him or rejecting him, as her own prudence or affections might have prompted. And yet he had not now the moral courage to make that revelation, and the generous confidence she placed in him was a more bitter reproach than all upon his conscience.

As he looked in the countenance of that suffering woman, he could have wept tears of blood, and yet he had not a word to utter in consolation—no syllable of hope to breathe, for his own mind was all dark and abject despair.

"Oh, God, oh, God!" cried the distracted mother; "what have I done that thou shouldst thus severely visit me? Was it not enough that my last born, my little innocent, should fall a victim to the hands of the assassin, but that my only child, my dear, sweet girl, should be thus monstrously snatched from me? Alas, alas! better would it have been had I never been born, than that I should be doomed to meet with these continual and insupportable visitations. My husband, my Laurence, have you not a word to say to me? Can you not form any idea why we should thus be selected for the wrath of Heaven?"

This appeal was too much for the feelings of the unhappy baronet, and he groaned aloud.

"Alas, alas!" he sighed, "I feel, I admit, that I have formerly erred, greatly erred; but why should you, my innocent bride, be thus visited? Oh! Blanche, you must look upon me with hatred, with horror!"

"Hatred, horror!" repeated Blanche; "and this from you, Laurence! Oh! what has there ever been evinced in my conduct to excite such horrible, such revolting suspicions in your breast?"

"Blanche," exclaimed Sir Laurence, with a burst of agony, which he could not control, "I feel that I have been a curse to you instead of a blessing—that I have plunged you into misery, which nothing on earth can ever recompense. It would have been fortunate for us both had we never met; and even now, were I to act as justice would dictate, I should flee your presence, and no longer——"

"Flee my presence, Laurence!" interrupted Blanche, with a look of the most indescribable agony. And is, indeed, then, your love for me so weak, so evanescent, that you could for a moment contemplate deserting me, and that in the midst of all my severest afflictions? Oh, Heaven! what have I done to merit this?"

"I feel myself unworthy of you, Blanche," ejaculated the baronet, in a voice almost choked with emotion.

"Unworthy of me, Laurence! Have I ever by word or act shown that such is the opinion I entertain towards you? Fate has frowned upon us; but still you, my husband, cannot be, are not to blame; and I would stifle my own emotions, even till my heart burst, sooner than by my sorrow I should lead you to imagine that I meant one sentiment of reproach against you. I know not what your former errors may have been; I ask not what they were; but I am convinced that they could never have been such as to merit the terrible retribution with which both you and I have been visited."

"Sweet, confiding, generous, noble-hearted woman," cried Sir Laurence, again pressing her more ardently than ever to his bosom; "surely the Father of all Mercy will reward such virtue as this; and will not suffer you to continue the victim of such unexampled sorrows. Our child, our beauteous little Emeline, will be restored to us. Something tells me that she will. Cheer you, then, my beloved Blanche, my only comfort, and, before many hours have elapsed, indulge the sweet hope that we shall again clasp our little innocent offspring to our bosom."

"Oh, yes, yes," remarked Amanda, who had stood by and witnessed all that had passed between her brother and his wife with the deepest interest, and the most anxious solicitude; "I am sure she will. The outrage was discovered so soon after it had taken place, that the wretches who were guilty of it cannot have proceeded far, and will doubtless be overtaken by those who have gone in pursuit of them."

"Alas!" cried the distracted mother; "fain would I encourage the hope with which you are anxious to inspire me; but I cannot divest myself of the horrible forebodings that have taken possession of my heart. The gipsies had probably made every preparation to bear the child away to a place of security, or perhaps, more horrible still, they have already sacrificed her, as they did our other poor infant, to their sanguinary and fiendish vengeance. My God! my God! preserve my brain under these accumulated and insupportable horrors."

In vain Sir Laurence and Amanda still endeavoured to offer her consolation; they needed it too much themselves to render anything they could say effective, and there appeared too much reason in the apprehensions of Blanche for them to controvert them.

Language must fail to do justice to the dreadful state of suspense in which they remained, as hour after hour elapsed, and still nothing was heard of the poor child, or of those who had been sent in pursuit of her. It seemed but too evident that the villains had succeeded in effecting their escape, and it was wonderful that Sir Laurence' or his unfortunate lady, could succeed in retaining their senses at all.

And the excitement which prevailed in the neighbourhood was nearly equal to that of Musgrove Abbey, for Sir Laurence and Lady Cleveland were universally respected, and every one deeply sympathised in their misfortunes, which had followed each other in such rapid succession. They needed nothing to urge them to use their best efforts to detect the miscreants who had perpetrated the cruel outrage ; but, as it seemed to be, with little chance of success. Having been furnished with a full description, as well as the fears of poor Susan would allow her to give, of the persons of the gipsy woman and the ruffian who struck her to the earth, persons started off, on horseback, different ways, to scour the country, and to give notice of the outrage that had been committed, in the various towns and villages they might pass through; and, in the interim, Sir Laurence, Blanche, and Amanda, remained in a state of mind of the most melancholy description.

Lord and Lady Musgrove remained with their unfortunate friends, and did all that they could to tranquillise their feelings, and inspire them with hope ; but this was a task most difficult to accomplish, and it required all the force of argument and persuasion they were possessed of, to keep them like anything within the bounds of reason. In fact, after the dreadful murder of the infant, no doubt by the same heartless and revengeful wretches, they could not but apprehend the worst.

But, if possible, the anguish of Sir Laurence was greater than that of Blanche, for, in spite of all his efforts to the contrary, his conscience would continue to smite him, and to accuse him of being the indirect, if not the absolute, cause of all these horrors.

" And Blanche," he reflected, " although she does not do so now, must afterwards deem me so, and look upon me with horror and aversion. Oh, God ! I can never bear to witness her anguish. Death itself would be preferable to such a life of incessant torture. Father of Mercy, if it is not thy will to restore our child uninjured to us, suffer me no longer to live."

Blanche turned a look of agony upon him, as these reflections passed in his mind, and seemed to read his thoughts ; however, her emotions would not suffer her to make use of any observations, and she threw herself sobbing hysterically upon his bosom.

Another hour passed in this manner, and still nothing transpired to relieve the terrible doubts and fears which distracted their minds. Blanche had given herself up entirely to despair, and her husband was so wretched himself, that he could not make the slightest effort to tranquillise her feelings ; had it not been for the exertions of Amanda, and Lord and Lady Musgrove, they must have sunk under it ; but nothing could induce poor Blanche to retire to bed, and Sir Laurence could not be prevailed to quit her presence even for a moment.

Suddenly, however, they were aroused from the deep agony of their thoughts by hearing a confused noise below, and Lord Musgrove was about to go to ascertain the cause, when a servant abruptly entered the room, and, without any ceremony, exclaimed,—

" She is found, she is found ! my dear young lady is restored uninjured ; the beadle and all of them are in the hall, and they have got the wretches who stole her, and ——"

A simultaneous exclamation of joy and gratitude from Blanche and Sir Laurence interrupted the man, and they rushed down into the hall, and the next moment the distracted parents clasped their little darling once more to their hearts.

What a scene was that which followed this joyful and unexpected occurrence! No pen could portray it in language sufficiently powerful or eloquent, and we must therefore pass hastily over it.

Grab, the beadle, and his companions, had fortunately taken the right way, and having received some valuable intelligence from persons they met with, were enabled to trace the wretches, and to overtake them. They secured the child, and also the prisoners, without any difficulty, and brought them with them to the abbey, in order that Sir Laurence might put any questions to them he might think proper, before they were conveyed to prison.

The woman, who led a little boy by the hand, and also the man who accompanied them, seemed to feel keenly the danger of the position in which they were placed, and ready to communicate all they knew.

"Wretch," demanded Sir Laurence, addresing himself to the woman, "what could induce you to commit this cruel and daring outrage?"

"I am willing to reveal all, Sir Laurence," said the woman, " and I beg for mercy, for the sake of my poor child."

"That will depend entirely upon the truth of what you utter," said the baronet, " and your readiness to make all the atonement in your power."

"I will do so, your honour," replied the woman.

"You are a gipsy?"

"I am."

"To what tribe do you belong?"

"To that of which Harold and Madela are the chiefs?"

"Ah! and was it those miscreants who employed you to steal this innocent child?"

"It was, your honour."

"And what was their intention, had they got her in their power?"

"I know not."

"And know you anything of the dreadful murder of my other poor infant?"

"It was by Harold's orders that deed was perpetrated?"

"Oh, monster!" groaned forth Blanche, straining the little Emeline to her bosom; "and, but for the interposition of Providence, this poor child would probably have shared the same fate. Surely the most terrible vengeance of Heaven will pursue these fiends in human shape, for such odious crimes."

"It must,—it will," said Sir Laurence; "but were not the gipsies also the authors of the conflagration at my mansion?"

"They were," answered the woman; "it was Zephaniah and Malachiel who set fire to the mansion."

"Ah, then the boy Rosario was innocent of that crime?" eagerly demanded the baronet.

"He was," answered the gipsy woman; "what he stated on his examination before the magistrate was the truth."

"And where is he now?"

"In the power of Harold and his associates."

"Was it they who rescued him from prison?"

"It was; and he has thus been cruelly treated, and kept a close prisoner ever since."

"And know you who that mysterious boy really is?"

"I know him only as Rosario and the Fawn."

"Do you believe that his parents are amongst your tribe?"

"I do not."

"And where have your base associates kept themselves so long concealed?"

"In the old abbey ruins at ————, about thirty miles from this place."

"Ah," ejaculated the baronet, "then we have at last discovered the miscreants, and we may at length get them in our power, and bring them to that punishment which their numerous and atrocious crimes merit. But beware, woman, that you do not attempt to deceive and mislead us; for, as I have said before, on the candour and truth of what you utter depends your own safety."

"If your honour finds me speak falsely," said the woman, "I am ready to abide by the consequences. I left Harold and the rest of the tribe secreted in the old abbey ruins on leaving them."

"You appear to be speaking the truth," said Sir Laurence.

"We can have no interest in doing otherwise now," interposed the man, speaking for the first time; "since Norna has thought proper to divulge so much. Our tribe are, as she observes, for aught we know to the contrary, at present located in the old abbey ruins."

"It is only by speaking the truth that you can expect mercy to be extended to you," said Lord Musgrove.

"We can have no possible object in not doing so," observed the man; "since we are already in your power, and you have the means of proving our truth or falsehood."

"Answer me, I pray you," said Sir Laurence, with peculiar emphasis; "answer me, and that with candour, are you and the woman, your companion, thoroughly acquainted with the secrets of Harold and Madela?"

"No more than we have divulged to you," answered the gipsy.

"You are aware of the statements he has made respecting me?"

"I am."

"Are they true?"

"I know not."

Blanche looked on while these interrogations were taking place, with the greatest anxiety and interest, at the same time she still hugged her beautiful and innocent child to her heart, and wept tears of maternal transport upon its healthful roseate cheeks.

"Know you a female among your tribe, called Clara?" demanded the baronet.

The bosom of Blanche heaved with increased emotion, and Amanda waited with impatience the answer of the gipsy.

"I know no female among our tribe of that name," answered the man.

"She may not be recognized among your people by that name," said Sir Laurence.

"Possibly not."

"Ah! there appears to be a doubt conveyed in those words. Answer me, I again beseech you, and not only shall liberty but fortune be the reward of a satisfactory reply; know you the female who has several times appeared in so mysterious a manner to me and Lady Cleveland?"

"I solemnly declare that I do not, Sir Laurence," replied the gipsy.

"Nor you, woman?"

"I do not."

"And yet you must be admitted deeply into the secrets and schemes of the gipsies," added Sir Laurence; "or they would never have entrusted you with the execution of this outrage."

See p. 251.

"This woman is my wife," replied the man; "it is not more than two years since we have joined the tribe, of which Harold and Madela are the heads. We were bound to obey what they commissioned us to do; what their motives were for employing us, we have nothing to do with; we have spoken the truth; we have imparted to you all we know; believe them, or believe them not, we will stand by our assertions let the consequences be what they may."

There was a degree of honest candour about the man's observations and general demeanour, which greatly impressed the baronet; his mind felt a certain relief from a portion of his statement; and he, therefore, for the present, forebore to urge him or the woman further, more especially as his joy was so great at the restoration of the little Emeline.

"It will be necessary to detain you for the present," he remarked; "but no other restrictions shall be placed upon you than circumstances demand; according as the truth of your statements is proved, so will the amount of the punishment for the offence you have committed be awarded."

"Very well, your honour," said the man; "we care little how it is; no more than that we have a wish to render some atonement for the offence we have committed. If we are not punished by you, and Harold and the rest of the tribe still remain at liberty, we shall be pursued with their vengeance."

"If we discover that you have not deceived us," said Sir Laurence, "depend upon it, you will meet with every protection."

"We thank your honour for your forbearance," said the man, civilly; "and again solemnly declare that we have not attempted to deceive you in a single particular. We are very sorry that we committed the offence, and for the suffering and suspense we must have caused you."

The gipsies were now conveyed to a place of security, and the fond parents gave free vent to the feelings of transport, which the restoration of their child naturally created in their breasts. Again and again they pressed the little Emeline to their hearts, and poured forth their gratitude to Heaven in the most fervent and eloquent language.

"Oh, Laurence!" ejaculated Blanche, "how thankful ought we to be to Providence for having thus frustrated the diabolical intentions of our mortal enemies, the gipsies. I shudder with horror to think upon the fate which threatened our poor child. Never, never could I have survived her additional loss. It wanted but that, to make our wretched condition complete."

"Thank Heaven that we have not been put to such an additional and dreadful trial, my beloved Blanche," said her husband. "The retreat of the wretches also being now discovered, steps must be taken for their immediate apprehension; and we shall thus be rescued from their future vengeance."

"And yet, Laurence, I fear that the attempt to apprehend them will be fraught with great danger."

"I do not think so, my love," answered Sir Laurence; "they will be taken by surprise, and will, consequently, not be prepared to resist us. However, any risk must be run, rather than permit such dangerous miscreants to be at large. There is one thing that affords me great satisfaction, and that is the discovery of the innocence of Rosario."

"Yes," said Blanche; "and most deeply do I commiserate his situation, and the sufferings he must be enduring from the gipsies. Would that he could be rescued from their power."

"I will endeavour to do so," said the baronet; "for it is a pity that a youth of his superior manners and disposition should be lost. The great interest he has inspired in my mind continues undiminished, and the mystery connected with him is most inexplicable."

"It is," coincided Blanche; "and I cannot but believe that he has spoken the truth, and that he is as entirely ignorant of his origin as he has represented himself to be."

Composure now being restored to the inmates of the abbey, they retired to rest; and, on entering their chamber, Sir Laurence and his lady again fervently poured forth their gratitude to Heaven for the preservation of their child.

But the parent slept but little during the night; for his mind was harassed with various thoughts, and he still could not help entertaining some apprehensions as to the future. He remembered all the answers of the gipsy; and, notwithstanding they were generally satisfactory, they left him in doubt and suspense upon many points. He had said that he knew of no female among the tribe who answered to the description of Clara, or the woman who had so frequently crossed his path, and who bore such an extraordinary resemblance to her; but yet, might he not have deceived him on that point, thinking he ran no risk of being detected? In spite of all he had said to Blanche, Sir Laurence almost apprehended the detection of Harold and the other gipsies, lest they should have it in their power to put their threats into execution, and thus render at once his shame and misery complete.

"But it cannot be," he reflected; "all they have asserted is false; or would they not, if Clara were really living, have produced her before this? They would; and I will therefore endeavour to banish all fears from my mind. The woman who has so often appeared to me, and in such a mysterious manner, is some vile impostor employed by them. And, yet, Harold and Madela are evidently well acquainted with my past history, and, should they be apprehended, will doubtless, to gratify their vengeance, reveal all they know. My very soul recoils at the thoughts of the fearful exposure, which must inflict such anguish on my beloved Blanche, and perhaps change the warm sentiments she now entertains towards me into those of abhorrence and scorn. But, oh! no; I cannot believe that that will ever be. Surely no one, especially my own Blanche, will believe the statements of such wretches as Harold and Madela. And, yet, can I deny their truth? My conscience will not permit me to do so. It would have been much better that I should candidly have divulged all to her, than that the painful revelation should come from the lips of such a villain as Harold, who will be sure to distort facts, and render them in appearance more revolting than they absolutely are. But never, never can I find courage to disclose the truth. How could I ever offend the ears of my poor Blanche by repeating the degraded tale? Alas! I am most wretched, and know not how to act."

Such were the thoughts that continued to torture Sir Laurence throughout the night and rendered him anxious and most wavering. But towards the morning he became more composed, and sought an early opportunity of having another interview with the gipsies. However, he could not elicit any more information from them than what they had already told him; and they closely adhered to their former statements, so that he was disposed to place the greatest reliance on their sincerity.

It was determined to send a number of men to the old abbey ruins without delay; and Sir Laurence would have accompanied them, had it not been for the earnest solicitations of his wife and Amanda to the contrary; for they were fearful that, in the contest which would probably take place, something fatal might befal him, and those who were sent to apprehend the gipsies could very well dispense with his services. The baronet, therefore, yielded, and the men departed on their expedition.

Sir Laurence had promised the gipsy and his wife that, if what they had stated was found to be correct, they should be pardoned the offence they had committed, and set at liberty; and they fully expressed their acknowledgments for this act of forbearance, which they had so little right to expect.

All persons interested, now waited with much anxiety, the return of the men, entertaining but very little doubt that the gipsies being taken by surprise, they would succeed in taking them prisoners. Yet, at times, when Sir Laurence took everything into consideration, he could not help wishing that they might escape, lest they should out of revenge, and which they would be almost certain to do, expose all the fatal facts they knew respecting him, a circumstance from which he shrunk with the greatest dread.

It was not, however, till the following day that the men returned; and it was then found that their journey had been fruitless; the gipsies, doubtless, entertaining some suspicion that Uriah and his wife had been detected, and that they would in consequence, run the risk of being discovered, had abandoned the abbey ruins, and they could not gain the least clue as to the way they had taken, or whither they had gone.

"But," observed Lord Musgrove, "the villains must not be suffered thus to escape if possible. You and your family will never be safe a single day, Sir Laurence, while they are at liberty, and entertaining the deadly feelings of revenge that they do towards you."

"Their feelings of revenge certainly appear to be most implacable," said the baronet; "and they are much to be dreaded; but still I do not see what course to adopt, and what chance there is, at present, at any rate, to approach them. All that we can do is to guard ourselves as well as we can against any sudden attack they might make upon us, and any future outrage they may in their vengeance attempt to commit."

"And, alas!" said Blanche, "I fear they will not hesitate to make such an attempt at the first opportunity; and they manage their plans so secretly and artfully, that it is next to an utter impossibility to guard ourselves against them. Would to Heaven they had been detected and brought to punishment, then our fears would have been at an end. Perhaps, however, Uriah can form some idea of the route they have taken."

The gipsies were narrowly questioned accordingly, but they could afford no farther information than that they had furnished already; but they had no doubt they would seek some distant part of the country, where they might remain undiscovered, until the excitement had in some measure been worn away, and suspicion be lulled as to the evil designs they had in contemplation.

"But I would have you, Sir Laurence," said Uriah, "not to make too sure that they will abandon their designs altogether. Their vengeance is at all times most deadly, and what they threaten they seldom fail to perform."

"I believe the truth of what you assert," said Sir Laurence; "but I wish to ask you, whether if we set you all at liberty, you will be ready to furnish us with any information which may at any future time come to your knowledge."

"Your honour may depend upon me," answered Uriah.

"And what course do you yourself intend to pursue?"

"Why, that of honest labour, if I can. But we must disguise ourselves, and try to keep ourselves concealed from Harold and his associates, or they will be sure to have our lives."

"Keep that determination," said the baronet, "and you shall find a freind in me."

Again Uriah and his wife thanked the baronet, and having presented to them a small sum of money, they were restored to liberty.

The search after the gipsies was continued with unabated energy, but with no better success, for not the least clue could be gained to them; and Sir Laurence became more surprised than ever at the manner in which they were enabled to avoid detection; but began to hope that they would no more be annoyed by them, and that they would abandon the designs they had so long contemplated against them.

They passed another month at Musgrove Abbey, and then returned to Branscombe House, where Blanche and her husband exerted themselves to the utmost to regain their tranquillity. But the recollection of the calamities that had befallen them, and the constant dread they were in of the gipsies, cast a deep shadow over their feelings, which only time could remove.

CHAPTER XXIII.

A FRESH SOURCE OF ALARM AND SORROW.—THE COMMUNICATION.—FRESH SUSPICIONS.—THE DEMAND OF BLANCHE, AND THE AGONY OF SIR LAURENCE.

TIME flew away on rapid wings; a twelvemonth had elapsed since the occurrence related in the preceding chapter; and the tranquillity at Branscombe House remained uninterrupted, and nothing was heard or seen of the gipsies. It did, indeed, seem as if they had abandoned their diabolical designs, and quitted the country altogether.

Blanche, by degrees, shook off her former melancholy, and the sorrows that had constantly haunted her, and she appeared at times even cheerful.

The baronet was delighted at this unexpected change, and began himself to hope that their future days would be allowed to pass in peace. Yet could he not altogether banish from his mind the apprehension that the gipsies only slumbered, and that they would, at the first opportunity, put into execution those threats they had given utterance to. These fears he did not reveal to Lady Cleveland, for he well knew how uneasy it would make her; but they caused him many a miserable hour, and he was in constant fear of exposure, which he could not but think would entirely estrange the affections of Blanche from him.

The little Emeline grew apace, and was really a most beautiful and interesting child, and was made the complete idol of her parents, and her youthful playmate, Angela, who loved her with the same affection as if she had been her own sister. Yet, when Sir Laurence reflected on the prognostications of Madela and Harold, he could not help feeling the deepest anguish, which he was the more surprised at, considering it must proceed from weakness and superstition, which he had hitherto flattered himself he was not prone to.

Thus stood affairs at Branscombe House, when one day Sir Laurence, having been absent from home, on his return, on inquiring for his lady, learnt from Amanda that she had retired to her chamber in a state of agitation, and had locked herself in, refusing to admit any one.

"Gracious Heaven!" exclaimed the astonished and alarmed baronet, "what can be the cause of this extraordinary conduct? Can you not in any way account for it, Amanda?"

"Alas! I fear, my brother," answered Amanda, "that some fresh trouble is in store for you. A short time since, a stranger brought a letter to the house, addressed to Lady Blanche, and no sooner had she glanced her eyes hastily over the contents, than she uttered an exclamation of emotion, her countenance became very pale, and, regardless of my anxious inquiries as to the cause, she abruptly quitted the apartment, and retired to her own chamber with the letter in her hand."

"Alas! what can this mean?" said Sir Laurence, his heart sinking within him. "Did you not see the person who brought this mysterious letter, Amanda?"

"I did not," answered the latter.

"Was it a man?"

"No; I understand it was a woman, and that no sooner had she delivered the letter than she started off at full speed, and was soon out of sight."

"It is some guilty scheme of the gipsies again," cried Sir Laurence; "will their vengeance never be appeased? Oh! Blanche, Blanche, I had fondly hoped that our troubles were all at an end; but it seems that the wretches are determined to ruin our peace of mind for ever."

He beat his forehead with emotion as he spoke, and hastily quitted the room to go to the chamber of Blanche. For a moment he listened at the door; but all was still as death, and he knocked loudly, and called upon her name. But no answer was returned, and the astonishment and alarm of both Sir Laurence and Amanda were greatly strengthened.

Once more the baronet called in distracted tones on the name of Blanche; but all remained as profoundly quiet as before. He then placed his eye to the key-hole, and then, to his horror, beheld his beloved wife stretched, pale, ghastly, and apparently lifeless, on the floor.

"Good God!" cried Sir Laurence, "she is dead! What horror is this that is in store for me? Blanche, Blanche! oh! agony unspeakable!"

"Do not give way too suddenly to those dreadful apprehensions, my dear brother," said Amanda. "It is more than probable that Blanche has only swooned. Force the door, and let us ascertain the worst at once."

The baronet immediately placed his shoulder to the room-door, and it flew open, and he and Amanda entered the chamber, and flew towards the spot where Blanche was lying. With almost delirious haste, Sir Laurence raised the unfortunate lady in his arms, and although her face was ghastly pale as that of a corpse, he felt the throbbing of her heart against his own.

"God of Heaven!" he cried, as he kissed her pale, cold lips, "I thank Thee! She still lives. My poor Blanche, what can have reduced you to this melancholy state?"

He placed her inanimate form upon the couch, and Amanda flew to her assistance, having rang the bell to summon the attendance of a servant, who quickly appeared, and was ordered to call in the attendance of the medical adviser of the family immediately.

The attention of Sir Laurence was now called to the spot where his wife had been lying, and he beheld on the floor a letter, which he had no doubt was the one which had been brought to her, and had caused all the mischief. Eagerly he seized it, and glanced at the handwriting. He knew it not, but it was written in a masculine hand. One word elicited from him a groan of agony, and hastily, by motion, imploring his sister to see to the recovery of Blanche, he rushed from the chamber to his study, where he sunk in the chair with the letter still clasped in his hand, and for some time he drew his breath short and quick, while he was unable to read a syllable, although his eye could take in the horrors of a whole sentence at a single glance.

Large drops of perspiration started coldly to his forehead, as he hastily glanced at the contents of the communication, the truth of which his conscience would not allow him to deny. His limbs trembled, and he felt as if he was already standing at the bar of public justice, as a criminal of the blackest dye.

"Oh, God!" he at last exclaimed, "my ruin effected. The enemies whom I have so long had cause to dread, have taken the readiest means to effect that object. They have stated facts in this epistle so pointedly, that Blanche must demand an explanation, and I cannot any longer evade it. It would be the basest of hypocrisy, viler than any of which I have hitherto been guilty, to attempt it. And what must Blanche think of me after having perused this? Will she not despise me—shudder at the very sight of me, and what arguments can I make use of to console her? Oh, God! I have broken her heart, and no misery whatever that can attend me, can be too severe a punishment for me."

For a few minutes he again rolled himself backwards and forwards in his seat, before he could peruse the contents of the fatal communication throughout.

They ran as follows :—

"To Blanche Lester, *alias* Lady Cleveland.

"Unfortunate woman, under certain circumstances the writer of the present communication pities you, because he believes you to be innocent (although, from the author of your being, he has suffered the greatest injustice), because you are the victim, the confiding victim of a man whose mind was formed only to betray, and to sport with the feelings of those over whom his seductive arts have unfortunately prevailed. Sir Laurence Cleveland is a villain, and facts shall be briefly stated in this letter to prove him so, which the writer defies him to bring proof to contradict.

"You have, Blanche Lester, been told that you have no legal claim upon the name you now bear—and rest assured it is the truth—and that every day you remain with the libertine, the seducer, the murderer, you are adding to your own misery and culpability. The time will come, when everything shall be fully explained, but circumstances will not at present permit it. In the meantime, you are forewarned, and, if you do not avail yourself of the opportunity of escaping from further degradation, you must take the consequences.

"You have been told that 'you are a wife, and no wife!' This, doubtless, does appear to you a paradox, and it is; but it is to be simply solved. You have, at the altar, given your hand to Sir Laurence Cleveland, but you must still remain legally, Blanche Lester, and only the concubine of him, whom you believe to be your husband, while Lady Clara Cleveland (formerly Clara Roseburn) still lives! That she does live, can, and will be proved, to the shame and misery of the villain with whom you are cohabiting, under the impression of being his wife; therefore, if you would not become the mother of any more illegitimate offspring, brought into the world to be ultimately discarded by their father, and left to the scorn and opprobrium of that world, abandon him, and every protection shall be afforded you.

"He may ask you for facts to corroborate those accusations; let him deny the accuracy of these if he can, if he dare.

"Seventeen years since, there resided in the town of Summerford, an aged man named Redmond Roseburn. He had formerly been a farmer, and, being prosperous, had for several years retired. Children, wife, he had none, nor any relations, except two orphan girls, his nieces; one, the daughter of his only brother, the other, the daughter of his only sister.

"Oh, how lovely were those two cousins; how virtuous, how amiable, till the deceiver came. They were the pride of their aged relative, the prop of his declining years, and no other protector had they to look to.

"Clara Roseburn was the eldest of the cousins, rather seriously inclined; beautifully sensitive and confiding. Mirah Alston, her cousin, was equally lovely, but light and giddy, and more disposed for the frivolities of the world. But I will not enter into minute particulars of their different merits and demerits; these you will doubtless become acquainted with at some future period.

"Not far from the residence of Mr. Roseburn, lived an honest couple, who had dwelt there from their earliest childhood, named Martin and Dorothy Glebeland. They had but one child, a son, Walter Glebeland, who was their main support by his own honest labour. No individual had ever attempted, or could cast the slightest imputation upon his character, and, indeed, he and his parents were universally respected for miles around the neighbourhood.

"Between this Walter Glebeland and Clara Roseburn, an intimacy of the most tender nature sprang up, which was encouraged by her uncle, and matters had even gone so far as the time for their nuptials to be appointed, and all was blisful anticipation; when the demon stept in to destroy all, and to render future and immeasurable misery.

"Accident brought Laurence Cleveland, then a very young man, to the neighbourhood of Summersford, and the same accident introduced him to the lovely cousins. Curses light upon that hour. His rank, his personal attractions, and his practised arts of seduction, made a fatal impression upon Clara, and unfortunately secured him the triumph over her virtue; I must do him the credit to say, that he promised to make her his lawful wife, and fulfilled that promise, but as it will be seen only to gratify his passions, and to seek the earliest opportunity of discarding her, and leaving her to despair and shame.

"Old Redmond Roseburn suspected his character, and forbade his future visits to his house, notwithstanding his promise to marry her; his asseverations that his intentions were honourable. How could he give his assent to that alliance when he had previously promised her hand to Walter Glebeland, and, as the writer has before stated, the time was appointed for their nuptials? The consequence was, that Clara eloped with her betrayer, and *they were privately married*, at St. Mildred's church, and a short time after this, Mirah, who had conceived an affection for him, also eloped, sought them out at their residence, was received with *sisterly* affection, and fell a victim to the villanous arts of her cousin's husband!

"A black tale of villany this; but it is not half complete. In a short time the passion which Laurence Cleveland had pretended for Clara ceased; the more lively disposition of her cousin suited him best, and they both became anxious to get rid of her. A story was trumped up of her infidelity; it was supposed that she eloped with her paramour, and afterwards, stung with remorse for her misconduct, committed suicide. But *she was innocent—she still lives, and likewise the lawful heir to the house of Cleveland*, as the villain, Sir Laurence, shall ere long know to his cost.

A few months only, and Sir Laurence Cleveland also banished his other victim, Mirah, from his *protection;* yes, he discarded her, left her friendless, for poor old Redmond Roseburn, deserted by his only relatives, had sunk into the grave broken-

hearted, leaving his property to charitable institutions. And what became of Mirah? Why, she became the victim of every sensual ruffian, and after enduring some months of infamy in the metropolis, sunk into a pauper's grave!

"And this all the work of the *virtuous*, the *honourable* Sir Laurence Cleveland, the man to whom Blanche Lester has given her hand, but upon which she has no claim! Certainly, she must feel most happy in having such a companion in future.

"But the writer is not yet done. Walter Glebeland, having all his hopes blighted, became a reckless youth. He neglected his labour, and became wild and dissipated, until, as no one would employ him, he became dishonest, at least, as far as poaching may be termed dishonest, and for which he was several times innocently punished by your own father, Blanche Lester.

"Now comes one of the principal portions of the drama; it has been told to you before, Blanche Lester; but I will now repeat it to you, in order that it should properly impress itself on your memory.

"One of the gamekeepers of Sir Laurence Cleveland, who had rendered himself particularly obnoxious, was found assassinated on his master's estate. On the same night he was returning home from a visit he had been paying to one of his friends, when he saw two men retreating from the spot where the body of the murdered man was found, whom he afterwards swore positively were Walter Glebeland and his father. No doubt what his motives were. They were objects of terror to him, not only for the revenge they should naturally seek, but the exposure which it was in their power to make; and he was anxious to rid himself of them as soon as possible. He did so. Upon his evidence both father and son were condemned to death; the aged man perished like a dog; but the son's sentence was commuted to transportation for life. That son escaped; he is in England; he has his eyes constantly fixed upon the miscreant whom he alike loathes and despises, and will not rest until he has wrung his heart to the utmost, and brought down upon him the full weight of overwhelming misery.

"Such, Blanche Lester, is the true history of the amiable career of Sir Laurence Cleveland. Let him deny it if he can. Again the writer warns you that, if you would escape further misery and degradation, you should cease to cohabit with the husband of that woman who has the only legal claim upon his hand. Beware!"

It was not without the greatest difficulty that Sir Laurence could go through the whole of the contents of this dreadful epistle; but when he had done so, it fell from his hand, and he clasped his burning temples, with both hands, competely appalled.

"Ruined! ruined! lost!" he cried; "I cannot deny most of the facts here recapitulated by the writer, and the exposure I have so long dreaded, is now made. Oh God! this will prove the death blow of the unfortunate Blanche, and with what horror and abhorrence must she look upon me. How can I ever dare again to meet her glances, after this terrible revelation, the truth of which I cannot, I dare not deny? Who can be the writer of this? How did he become possessed of the principal facts of the painful history? He must have been one of the principal actors in it. Perhaps Walter Glebeland himself, and he whom I know and fear as Harold, the gipsy, may be him, only time and various circumstances have so altered his features, that I do not now recognise them. Alas! then, if such is the fact, have I not plenty of reason to fear him? Oh! how my conscience goads me with many of the statements which the writer makes. 'Tis true that I was the seducer of the unfortunate Mirah, and that I afterwards abandoned her, and knew not, and took no trouble to inquire what became of her. Alas, alas! I have been most guilty. But surely Clara deceived me, and I had sufficient proof of her infidelity; for if she knew herself to be innocent, why did she take to flight? But what can poor Blanche think of me after all these exposures? Will she not look upon me with horror and disgust? She must—she must; and I can have nothing to offer in extenuation of my conduct. And should Clara indeed be still in existence! Oh, no, the thought is far too dreadful; I dare not, I will not encourage it. But how is it possible for me to disprove it, and to convince Blanche that such is not the case? I am distracted and bewildered on every side."

Again he beat his breast, and paced the room in a state of almost insupportable agony. [He was suddenly aroused from these distracting thoughts by hearing a knock at the room door, and opening it, Amanda entered. Eagerly he inquired after the condition of Blanche.

"She still remains in a state of insensibility, Laurence," answered his sister, "notwithstanding all the efforts of the medical gentleman to restore her. Oh, my brother, what can have been the contents of that fatal letter, that they should have such a terrible effect both upon her and you?"

"Oh! Amanda," groaned the baronet; "how can I answer you? I fear that there is nothing but misery and ruin for me and Blanche. Alas! I have been most guilty, and should never have united my fate with that of her who is supposed to be my wife."

"*Supposed* to be your wife, Laurence," repeated Amanda, with a look of astonishment and emotion. "My brother, there is a fearful mystery about your words. Did you not legally give your hand to Blanche at the altar?"

"I would fain think differently," replied the baronet, half choked with the violent anguish of his feelings; "but, alas! I have too much reason to fear that I did not *legally*."

"My God, Laurence!" ejaculated the alarmed Amanda; "you surely cannot mean what you say. Your mind wanders."

"My brain is distracted, Amanda. These continual horrors—the recollection of the past—this insupportable state of doubt and suspense, will surely drive me mad. Oh, that I had never been born."

"My dear brother," said the anxious Amanda, "what can that letter contain that it should affect you in this violent manner?"

"Read, read, Amanda," answered her brother, thrusting the letter in her hand; "read that fearful epistle, and then marvel not at mine or my beloved Blanche's emotions."

Amanda took the letter from him, and, as she perused it, her countenance underwent a painful change, and she trembled, while Sir Laurence covered his face with his hands, and sobbed convulsively.

With much difficulty did Amanda go through the contents of this fearful letter, and when she had done, she looked at her brother with an expression of the greatest dread, and eagerly awaited an explanation. The baronet, however, for a short time averted his gaze, and his anguish and shame increased every instant.

"Dear Laurence," at length said his sister, "what can you say to the fearful contents of this letter? Pray ease my doubts; be candid with me, and tell me, can you deny the truth of them?"

"Alas, alas!" groaned the baronet.

"The agitation of your manner alarms me; do you then acknowledge them to be correct?"

"Part of them, wretched man that I am, are too true, Amanda."

"Gracious Heaven!" ejaculated Amanda; "can you then, my brother, ever have so degraded yourself as is here represented?"

"I have been most guilty, but not of all that is therein stated, and which originates in the malice only of my bitter and implacable enemies. I feel that I have done an irreparable wrong by ever uniting myself with Blanche, of whom I was so unworthy. What can that poor innocent, suffering woman now think of me? Must she not hate me—despise me? And yet Heaven knows how deeply I have for years past repented of my former errors, and the deep, the unalterable love I bear towards her to whom I have given my hand."

" This is a terrible discovery, Laurence," said his sister, looking upon him with an expression of the deepest commiseration, not unmingled with gentle reproach.

" Oh! plead for me, Amanda, I implore you," said the baronet, " plead for me with Blanche ; your gentle persuasiveness can do .much, everything for me, and the dreadful results of this fatal communication which I now anticipate, may be averted."

" That I pity you, Laurence, I need not assure you," replied Amanda, " and regret that your want of courage or candour did not prevent many of the difficulties that I have now too much reason to apprehend. Alas! the contents of this letter may have the most terrible effect upon the delicate constitution of Blanche, and I wonder not at the shock her feelings have sustained."

" Oh! no, no ; wretch that I have been to deceive her, the discovery of my vices will certainly break her heart."

He struck his forehead violently in the despair and agony which these thoughts created, and gave himself up to the most absorbing grief.

" Should it be proved that the statement of the writer of this letter be true, and that your first unfortunate wife is still in existence, I shudder to think of the ruin and misery into which yourself will be plunged."

" Name it not, Amanda," ejaculated Sir Laurence; " it cannot be. Clara has long since rested in the grave ; she died by her own hands, otherwise she would have come forward to have prevented my nuptials. It is all a base fabrication of my enemies to keep me in a constant state of suspense, and to break the heart of that unfortunate woman, who could never, by any possible means, have injured them. Clara, for her infidelity to me, deserved the punishment she met with, and could never again have dared to claim me for her husband."

" And were you convinced that your suspicions against her were correct ?" eagerly asked Amanda.

"Oh, yes," answered the baronet; " I could have no doubt of it. She was most guilty."

" It is a most melancholy, a most painful affair throughout, Laurence ; and it seems that nothing short of the destruction of yourself and Blanche will satisfy the gipsies, if it is indeed from them that this letter emanates."

" There can be no doubt of it, Amanda. Who else but them could send such a communication ?"

" I know not."

" Have you no advice, no consolation to offer me, my dear sister ?"

" Alas! what can I do more than pity you under the circumstances ?"

" You then condemn me ?"

" For many of the fatal errors you acknowledge to have committed, I do. It was unjust, ungenerous, dishonourable in you to estrange the affections of Clara from the youth on whom they were previously placed, and to whom it appears she was already affianced."

" True—true; but the blindness of love, and the impetuosity of youth, goaded me on ; but had not my sentiments towards her been sincere, and my intentions strictly honourable, think you that I should ever have made her my wife ?"

" Alas! I fear, Laurence," returned Amanda, " that however ardent your affection for the unfortunate and misguided Clara might have been at first, they too soon evaporated; but what have you to say respecting her equally unfortunate cousin, Mirah, as she is called in this letter?"

"For mercy's sake, do not press me upon that revolting subject," implored the baronet.

"I have no wish to do so, my brother; but your words convince me that she, at any rate, became your victim."

"In a moment of blind infatuation, I acknowledge that I became guilty, Amanda," returned Sir Laurence, in a voice of the greatest emotion; "but she was the tempter; and, had it not been for her acts of levity and seductive arts, I should at least have been spared that crime."

Amanda shook her head, and Sir Laurence could not but feel the reproach it conveyed at his weakness in offering such an excuse.

"As the cousin of her to whom you had given your hand, you should have resisted your passion, Laurence," she said.

The baronet returned no answer, for he felt the full force and justice of his sister's observations, and all that he could say would not tend in the least to exonerate him.

"And did you not, as this letter states, banish the misguided Mirah from your protection?" she interrogated.

"No, no," stammered forth the baronet; "I—I did not; she fled from me of her own accord. Alas! I feel that I have much to answer for, but already have I been most severely punished. Do not torture me farther, Amanda, by these painful, these revolting allusions. If the bitterness of remorse may be received as any atonement for my faults, no unhappy individual could ever feel it more keenly than I do at present. And, oh, how dreadful will be the reproaches that I may expect from Blanche, unless you intercede for me."

"I will do all that I can, you may depend," said his amiable sister. "But equivocation or disguise is now no longer possible. Blanche will demand, and has a right to have, from your own lips, a full explanation."

"Oh, God!" groaned Sir Laurence; "and how can I give that dreadful explanation? My soul shrinks with horror from the revolting task. But Blanche can never believe the dreadful story."

"It would be worse than folly to suppose that she will not, after these repeated accusations, and the present one in particular. It would be cruel and unjust any longer to deceive her."

"Then I am lost—lost entirely. The acknowledgment of my guilt must destroy all her affection towards me, and life then will prove to me an insupportable curse instead of a blessing. Alas, Blanche! poor, suffering, innocent woman, why did we ever meet? But she is the mother of my child, and however she must and will regret my errors, confident of my repentance, and my sincere devotion to her, she can never hate me."

"Be calm, Laurence," said Amanda, "for this violent agitation will only serve to increase your misery, and that of Blanche, instead of ameliorating it."

"Can I be otherwise than wretched, Amanda, with all this weight of dreadful thoughts upon my mind? The wretches! they have, indeed, sought a terrible way of gratifying their vengeance."

"And why should your past errors, my brother, have excited these deadly feelings of revenge in the bosoms of the gipsies?"

"I know not; and have often racked my brain, to no purpose, to form a conjecture upon that point, and to imagine who Harold or Madela can really be, and why they should be so inveterate against me."

"Have you no recollection of their features?"

"None."

"May not Harold be the very man who, through your evidence, as here stated, was with his father convicted of murder, and whose sentence was afterwards commuted to transportation? Madela may also be his mother."

"That idea has often suggested itself to me, and yet I cannot trace the least resemblance in their features to those of the persons you mention. But, oh, Amanda, you must commiserate my feelings, and the anxiety I feel to know the condition of my beloved Blanche. Return, I beseech you, to her chamber, and see to her recovery, and in pity endeavour to prepare her for the trying interview that must take place between us. Much, very much depends upon you, my dear sister, and I am certain that your own amiable feelings will prompt you to undertake the task, painful as it is, with promptitude."

"You do me but justice by that supposition, Laurence," said Amanda; "and Heaven send that my efforts may be crowned with success. In the meantime, you remain here, and try to tranquillize your feelings, and to prepare yourself for the scene which must shortly take place between you."

"I will, I will, dear Amanda; I will exert myself to the utmost. But, alas; I fear that the shock she has sustained is such as she cannot easily recover from, and should she be taken from me, what can ever recompense me for her loss?"

"Do not anticipate so fearful a calamity, my brother," said Amanda; "for painful as the shock must be to the feelings of Blanche on such a discovery, I trust that the Almighty will support her through it. But should the unfortunate Clara really be still living, then, indeed, might we have reason to apprehend that the consequences would be most fatal."

"Oh, no—no—no," said Sir Laurence; "that cannot be; my heart shudders at the bare idea of such a possibility."

Amanda now quitted the apartment, and returned to the chamber of the unfortunate Blanche.

The baronet felt somewhat relieved in having disclosed his mind to his sister, but still he was in a state of almost insupportable agony and suspense; and he looked forward to the meeting with Blanche with the most unbounded dread. He saw plainly enough that he could no longer avoid giving a full explanation to her of all his past conduct, and what excuse could he offer in extenuation of the faults of which he had been guilty? Would it not appear at once to Blanche how cruelly he had deceived her? and could it be expected that she could ever again view him with the same ardent and devoted affection that she had previously done? Oh, no; it was out of all reason to imagine that she could; and he, at the same time, must ever feel his degradation in her eyes.

"And this might all have been averted," he said to himself, "had I had the courage or the honour to have freely opened my mind to her previous to our marriage. It would have convinced her that I was truly penitent, and would not, I firmly believe, have changed her sentiments towards me. But now, she will look upon the subterfuge I have practised as mean, contemptible, and dishonourable, and will probably, if she is again reconciled to me, ever view my future conduct with doubt and suspicion. Harold, if you are the author of this fatal epistle, which there can be little doubt that you are, you have, indeed, had an ample revenge. Oh, God! spare my poor Blanche; but for myself I feel that I am justly punished."

He continued to traverse the apartment in the most disordered manner, and was half disposed to hasten to the chamber in which Blanche was lying, as Amanda did not return; but fearful that should his wife have recovered her senses, his sudden appearance might cause a relapse, he restrained his feelings, and soon afterwards his sister entered the apartment.

"Tell me, Amanda," he eagerly demanded; "tell me how is my poor suffering Blanche now?"

"Much the same," answered Amanda.

"Ah! is she then still insensible?"

"She has recovered the use of speech, but her mind wanders, and it would not be prudent for you to visit her just yet."

"Oh, torture most unbearable!" groaned the baronet; "and all this then is my doing. I must be blamed for all the consequences that may follow. But tell me, Amanda, what says the doctor? does he apprehend any danger?"

"He does not," answered Amanda; "but, as he says, she requires to be managed with a great deal of care and prudence. Leave that duty to me, Laurence; I will continue by her side during the night, and nothing shall be wanting on my part, you may depend, that can tend towards her recovery."

"Oh, my kind, my amiable sister," said Sir Laurence; "well do I know with what anxious solicitude you will attend to your painful task; but how can I support this intolerable suspense?" In what agony will pass the tedious moments of this terrible night. May I not be at least permitted to see her?"

"Not for the world," answered Amanda. "When you consider, Sir Laurence, what the fatal consequences might be, you cannot continue to urge it. By the morning, perhaps, Blanche may become more composed, and you can then be permitted to see her probably without danger; as I will use my utmost exertions to prepare her for the interview."

"I submit," said the baronet, with a sigh; "and may the just God of Heaven watch over my poor afflicted Blanche, and assist you in your amiable task. But give me immediate notice should any unfavourable change take place."

"You may depend upon me, Laurence," replied Amanda. "I will do all that is in my power."

"Oh, God! how terrible is the agony my mind is enduring," said Sir Laurence, striking his forehead, as Amanda once more left the apartment. "What would I not give could I recall the past! But nothing can ever make atonement for the misery I have caused. I long, yet dread, to behold the poor sufferer; for how can she receive me? Must it not be with feelings of horror, and to ring her reproaches in my ears? And I deserve it all. Oh, yes; my conduct towards her has only rendered me worthy of her hatred, and we can never be happy together again. The exposure I have so long dreaded is made, and I tremble beneath its power."

Thus painfully did the unhappy baronet continue to soliloquise, and to reproach himself for hours, and nothing could induce him to seek his couch. He sent several times to inquire after Lady Blanche, but the answers he received were not at all calculated to remove his suspense. She continued in much the same state, talking wildly and incoherently, and not seeming to recognise any one near her; and it was quite evident that the fatal letter had made an impression on her that she was not likely soon to be able to get rid of, and which the doctor was fearful might be productive of the most dangerous results to her reason.

Blanche underwent no material change during the night, and Amanda continued to watch with the most anxious solicitude by her bedside, totally regardless of fatigue. Towards the evening of that day, however, she so far regained her senses as to recognize Amanda, and, dropping her head on her bosom, she burst into a copious flood of tears.

"Dear Blanche," said Amanda, after having suffered her for a few minutes to weep uninterrupted, "you are better now, are you not?"

"Better, Amanda!" she replied; "oh, no—no—no! The blow is struck which has destroyed my hopes of happiness for ever, and death would be to me the greatest release. But why am I still beneath this roof? I have no business here where another should rule as mistress! I have been deceived, cruelly deceived, and by one whom my fond heart believed to be incapable of a single dishonourable action. Oh, how could he thus tamper with my feelings? And the monstrous charges that are brought against him. His discarded wife—her ruined cousin! Oh, God! who could ever have believed that Sir Laurence Cleveland, he whose lawful wife, whose beloved wife I flattered myself that I was, could have been so abandoned, so depraved?"

"For Heaven's sake, Blanche," said Amanda, "do not judge my unfortunate brother too harshly or severely. That he has erred he does not attempt to deny, but still how sincerely penitent is he; nor is he so guilty as that fatal letter represents."

"Ah! that fatal letter!" ejaculated Blanche, with a look of horror; "its dreadful contents are impressed upon my memory in characters of fire. The unfortunate Clara lives, and I have become another confiding victim of the seducer. Let me arise, and quit this house for ever; let me fly somewhere where I may hide my shame and misery from the light of day."

"Dear Blanche, do not—oh, pray do not give way to this excessive grief. It is false; depend upon it that Clara lives not; sufficient proof can, no doubt, be procured that she is no more; or, if she still lived, would she not long ere this have come forward? Bear with this event with fortitude, and judge not too hastily, until you have seen my unhappy brother, whose agony is equal to that you are yourself now enduring."

"See him!" ejaculated Blanche; "oh, could I see him with the same confidence that I did, what a consolation would it afford me under these painful circumstances. But reflection drives me to madness. Has he not dishonoured me by making me his wife when even the doubt existed of his former wife being living? Oh, God! would that I had never seen the light of Heaven, or that we had never met. Laurence, never—never could I have suspected you of so much duplicity! Clara lives, and her offspring, so says the writer of this letter; and in what position, then, stand I and my child? Horror—horror! this is shame and misery that I never anticipated."

"Dear Blanche," said Amanda, "once more I implore you to endeavour to view this unfortunate business more calmly, and not to condemn your husband until you have heard him in explanation."

"My husband!" repeated Blanche, with a look which expressed far more than language could have done. "Oh, God! were I convinced that he were legally so, independent of his past errors, I could be comparatively happy. But there is too much the appearance of truth about this epistle, and the other circumstances con-

nected with the charges brought against your brother, Amanda, that I cannot divest
my mind of the dreadful impression that they are correct."

"Oh, Blanche!" remarked Amanda, "this is an uncharitableness that I never
thought you capable of.   Specious as the charges brought against my unfortunate
brother may at present appear to be, they, in my opinion, carry a falsehood on the
very face of them."

See p. 259.

"How? in what manner?" demanded Blanche, eagerly.   "Sir Laurence does not
deny that he is guilty of many of the delinquencies of which he is accused.   Explain
yourself, Amanda."

"My brother pleads guilty to the whole of the charges, with the exception of having banished his wife from her home. This, he maintains, was her own voluntary act, after the discovery of her infidelity. He also declares, and he still believes, that Clara was not living for some years before he paid his addresses to you; and, therefore, if it should be even now discovered that she is still in existence, he surely is not to blame no more than for his misguided want of candour in not disclosing these circumstances to you. But I will go farther, and state it was my firm belief, that the statement of her existence and that of her child is false; or why have they not before, or why do they not now appear to place the matter beyond a doubt? It is all an invention, originating in the implacable hatred of those heartless wretches, the gipsies. Dismiss the dreadful impression that you have suffered to take possession of you from your mind, Blanche, and receive Sir Laurence as your husband, and the sincere penitent of his past errors."

"That I have loved him, that I still love him, as well as mortal can love its fellow-being, Heaven knows," said Blanche, with a deep sigh. "But how can I receive him as my husband with all these horrible thoughts upon my mind? How can I remain with him under the uncertainty whether or not another lives to claim him as her lawful husband?"

"And what means has Sir Laurence of ascertaining that fact?" inquired Amanda. "Surely the doubts are in his favour. Were the statements of the gipsies correct, they would lose no time in bringing forward their corroboration, if it were only for the purpose of completing your misery. Come, Blanche, assume your natural reason, and learn to look with more suspicion upon what I firmly believe to be these base fabrications."

"Oh, Heaven, teach me how to act!" exclaimed Blanche.

"The love which you bear to your husband, and which you say has not diminished, will be one of your best guides. Oh! Blanche, could you but see the bitter anguish that my poor brother is suffering, you would, I am certain, be disposed to judge more mercifully of him. Will you grant him an interview, calmly and dispassionately?"

Blanche hesitated before she offered any reply, and it was evident, from the powerful working of her countenance, that she was undergoing a severe struggle with her feelings.

"Alas—alas!" she at length sighed, "that I should ever discover that he whom I believed to be formed in honour's mould, to be all perfection, has been the heartless betrayer of innocence."

"He was not the betrayer," said Amanda, "if we are to believe his solemn assertions, and I cannot, will not doubt my brother. Consider that he was young, very young at the time, and inexperienced, and that Mirah ——"

"Oh! Amanda," interrupted Blanche, "I know that your strict sense of honour and virtue will not suffer you to offer any apology for he who certainly acted the libertine's part. Mirah was also young, with all the weakness of her sex; she had formed an unlucky passion for Sir Laurence; but he ought to have had the moral courage to resist it, when he knew that the passion could not be encouraged in an honourable way. But no; he received the attentions of the poor infatuated girl; he lured her on to ruin; he made her a thing of shame and reproach, and then abandoned her; left her to the wide and merciless world, with all the weight and degradation upon her, and never troubled himself to inquire what became of her. Oh, this was most heartless—it was monstrous! Can he deny that? No; I feel convinced that he cannot. And I am associated with him; I have given up my very soul to him; for him I sacrificed my poor father's life, by breaking through all those injunctions which virtue and affection prompted. And he may abandon me, he may consign me to the same state of misery and degradation."

"Oh, Blanche, Blanche!" said Amanda, "your reason surely wanders, or you could never thus form such an opinion of my brother, whose very soul is fixed in adoration upon you. Reflect, reflect, and I am certain that your generous nature will never allow you to condemn your husband unheard."

"He cannot exonerate himself," said Blanche; "I feel convinced, from what you have observed, that he cannot. A feeling of horror has come over me which I cannot conquer. Oh! Amanda, never did I expect to live to see this day. Would that I had died before Laurence and I met. But I cannot see him; the sight of him would cause those blushes of shame to mantle in my cheeks, that I never expected would have cause to gather there. I have no business here. Give me my poor illegitimate child, and let me wander forth to hide my misery, shame, and disappointment in some remote corner of the earth."

She sobbed hysterically as she gave utterance to these words, and Amanda gazed at her with feelings of agony and commiseration which may be imagined, but cannot be adequately described. Again she tried to expostulate with her; but it was all to no purpose; so powerful was the impression which the contents of the fatal letter had made upon her mind, that neither argument nor remonstrance could remove it; and after the most convulsive weeping, and incoherent expressions, she again sank into a state of utter insensibility, and the physician now expressed the most alarming apprehensions as to the result, and desired Amanda to communicate the same opinion to her brother.

Need we attempt to describe the distraction of Sir Laurence, when he became acquainted with these melancholy facts, and likewise the result of the interview, which was communicated to him in the tenderest and most cautious terms by Amanda? We are certain that we need not.—He beat his breast, tore his hair, and it was not without the greatest difficulty that Amanda could prevent him from rushing to the apartment of his wife.

"All is lost!" he wildly exclaimed; "she believes me guilty of all the charges that have been brought against me, and the triumph of my bitter enemies is complete. They told me that she would learn to hate me, and to teach our offspring to curse me, and are not their fearful predictions about to be realised? Oh, God! oh, God! I can never support this terrible visitation. Blanche believes me to be a guilty, contemptible wretch, and life is therefore now hateful to me. Let me at once end it, and with it my misery!"

As he thus spoke, the wretched man started towards the other side of the room, and snatched a pistol that was hanging over the mantel-piece. With a shriek of horror, Amanda darted after him, and arrested his hand, as he was, in his despair, about to place the muzzle of it to his head.

"Hold, hold! Laurence," she cried, "what would you do? Oh, forbear; this conduct unmans you!"

"Hold me not, Amanda,'" said the baronet; "Blanche hates me—she refuses to hear me in extenuation of my former offences—crimes if you so think proper to call them; and therefore the sooner I am rid of this wretched existence the better; I I cannot live, with the knowledge that I am no longer beloved by Blanche. And she will die, too; she cannot survive this terrible blow; and shall I then be anything less than her indirect murderer? Let go my arm, Amanda; I cannot, I will not survive these accumulated misfortunes. Hope of happiness is at an end, and with it let my existence terminate. Oh, God! that it should come to this!"

"Laurence, my dear brother," said Amanda; "this is madness. Blanche will recover from her present state of distraction, and all will yet be well. She will listen to your explanation, and affection will prompt her to judge you with clemency."

"Oh, no," returned the deeply agitated baronet, striking his forehead vehemently; "you would inspire me with hopes, Amanda, that I cannot encourage. I dare not meet Blanche; my heart would sink beneath the weight of her reproaches, and how could I ever repeat the melancholy, the guilty tale which she would demand of me? I am surrounded by despair, and see no means of extricating myself from this insupportable misery."

Again he beat his breast, and traversed the room in a state of the most indescribable agitation. Amanda knew not what to say to tranquillise him, and while he was in that terrible state of excitement, she was afraid to leave him, (although she knew well that her attendance must be required upon Blanche), for she was fearful that, in his despair, he might be urged to lay violent hands upon himself.

"My dear brother," she said at length, "giving way to this violent excess of anguish will only add to the evils that at present beset you, while it deprives you of the reason and fortitude to act as prudence should dictate under the circumstances. Try to be calm, and, in the course of a few hours, Blanche may recover, and consent to see you, with a hope of reconciliation. You may depend upon it, that my exertions will be used to the utmost to bring about that desirable object."

"Oh, Amanda!" returned Sir Laurence; "can you talk to me of being calm, with all this weight of anguish upon my mind? I feel my senses reeling, and would to Heaven that they were gone for ever, rather than that I should continue in this state of conscious agony. I have been a villain; my conscience reproaches me most bitterly with having been so, and the curse of God is upon me, and all with whom I have unfortunately become connected."

"Say not so, dear Laurence," said his sister; "dismal and cheerless as your prospects are at present, depend upon it that bright sunshine is yet in store for you and Blanche."

"Oh! never, never! in vain may you endeavour to inspire me with such a hope! I cannot, I dare not encourage it. Blanche will still continue to retain the impression that Clara is living, and, unable as I am to contradict the assertion, how can I hope to retain her confidence and love? She will fly me, she will abandon me, as something odious; and what hope is there then for me but the grave?"

"The anguish that Blanche has displayed was to be expected, after the receipt of that fatal letter; but a short time, perhaps only a few hours, will ameliorate her sufferings, and she may be prepared to meet you with calmness. Exert, then, all your fortitude; for much, perhaps everything, depends upon that. Remember, that displaying this weakness, may be misconstrued by many into a confirmation of your guilt of all with which your anonymous enemy has charged you."

"And can I ever repeat that sad tale?" said the baronet.

"Oh, yes," returned Amanda; "it will relieve your mind, and the love, the generosity of Blanche will not suffer her to condemn you altogether; although she must regret those errors for which you are now so severely suffering."

"Love, Amanda! and think you that Blanche can still love me? Oh, no, it is impossible. I have deceived her; I have plunged her into irremediable misery, and she must in future look upon me with shame and abhorrence. It was my duty to have made her acquainted with all the particulars of my past life previous to my making her my wife, and then, though I might have compromised her happiness, and should have destroyed my own hopes, I could never have endangered her honour."

"That you were not more candid, Laurence," answered his sister, "I admit was unfortunate; but what is past cannot be recalled, and it is only by your future conduct that you can hope to make atonement, and to banish the sufferings of Blanche. She will, after the paroxyms of her grief have subsided, and the revelation once made, she will learn to bury the past in oblivion."

"Oh, would that I could think as you profess to do, Amanda," replied the baronet; "but that I feel is impossible."

"Say not so, my brother; it is only by a due exercise of your reason and your fortitude, and all may, and rest assured will, be accomplished. The heart of Blanche is too fondly devoted to you ever to suffer her to view you with hatred and scorn. I will cheerfully undertake the task of mediator between you, and fear not but I shall succeed."

"My kind, my amiable sister; how much I am indebted to you for this generous solicitude! I—I will endeavour to become calm, and to hope that Blanche will not banish me entirely from her breast."

"That assurance strengthens my confidence," said Amanda; "and in a few hours I trust that I shall be able to prevail on Lady Blanche to meet you with composure. But, in the meantime, you must try to conquer the violence of your agitation, and prepare yourself to enter into such an explanation as Blanche will be certain to require; for, as I have before said, much, very much will depend upon your own conduct."

"I will endeavour to follow your advice, Amanda," returned Sir Laurence, with more calmness, "and may Heaven aid me in the task. Go, my dear sister, to the chamber of Blanche without delay, and let me know her condition; my very existence itself depends upon you."

Amanda retired from the room, happy to see her brother reduced from his state of frenzy to this temperament, and made her way to the chamber of Blanche.

But, although Sir Laurence had become more composed, and had listened with the strictest attention to his sister's advice, he was far from feeling satisfied that her opinions would be realized in all respects. He felt the full weight of his own offences, and gentle and generous as he knew his beloved Blanche to be, he doubted much whether the explanation he had to give her, could do otherwise than prejudice her against him; and, in another respect, he had his own doubts as to the truth or falsehood of the statement that Clara was still in existence; and if it should transpire that she really was, what would be the position of himself and Blanche? For his own part he would be amenable to the laws of his country, and Blanche would be left to shame and sorrow, which must ultimately bring her to a premature grave.

He continued to traverse the apartment for some time, sending at intervals to inquire as to the state of Blanche; but the answer she received were not at all calculated to alleviate the misery of his mind.

Night came on and it was one of the greatest misery to the baronet, and wraught but little change for the better in Blanche. Worn out with the fatigue of thinking he at length threw himself upon his bed, and endeavoured to court sleep, but he did so in vain. His mind was far too much agitated to allow him to receive the genial blessings of the soothing god, and he arose at an early hour of the morning, feverish and bewildered.

Shortly afterwards a servant appeared from Amanda, to inform him, that, although Blanche had passed a wretched night, she was now considerably more composed and rational, and that she (Amanda) hoped, before many hours had elapsed, an interview might take place between them with safety, and that the best result might be anticipated.

" Thank Heaven !" exclaimed the baronet, " for that ; and may it give me strength to meet the poor sufferer in the spirit that I ought to do ; and to give that explanation, the very recollection of which freezes my soul with horror, and so lowers me in my own estimation. But surely the sufferings, the acute sufferings I have for so many years been enduring, have rendered some atonement ; and why should my sins be visited on my innocent, my unoffending wife ?—Oh, God ! look down upon her with an eye of mercy, if you do not upon me."

The morning was particularly fine, and the baronet thought that a walk would not only tend to refresh him, but to prepare his mind the better for the interview with his wife. He continued to wander among the delightful and romantic scenery by which Branscombe House was surrounded, for some time, but nothing could divert his thoughts from the painful subject that engrossed them ; and, at length, tired of walking, he threw himself on the green sward, and gave himself up entirely to his various and complicated feelings.

The spot on which he had cast himself was at the entrance of the woods, and commanded a very extensive and picturesque view, which, under any other circumstances, would have called forth his most unbounded admiration ; but now it attracted but very little, if any, of his attention.

In spite of all the arguments that his sistet had made use of, and the hopes she had held out to him of the reconciliation of himself and Blanche being so easily effected, he was not without the most painful misgivings, which were strengthened, after the account which Amanda had given him of the observations of Lady Cleveland, and the horror she had evinced at the mere mention of his name. And how could he find courage to recapitulate to her the revolting particulars of his former life ?—Gloss it over as he might, still the account must create the greatest disgust in the breast of Blanche ; and must excite a feeling of sympathy for both Clara and Mirah ; while she could not, in spite of the affection with which he had inspired her, look upon him in any other character than that of a reckless libertine and deceiver. She might pardon him ; but still her future confidence in him would be shaken, and she would ever view him with doubt and suspicion.

Such were the agonising thoughts that continued to occupy the mind of Sir Laurence Cleveland, and rendered him indifferent to the lovely scenery around, and fearful of the arrival of the time, when it might be considered safe for him to seek the presence of the deeply afflicted Blanche.

He was suddenly interrupted, however, in the midst of these reflections, by hearing a soft and plaintive voice, evidently that of a female, singing near him. A nameless feeling of emotion came over him, and he started from his seat, and gazed around him, listening attentively, for the tones struck upon the tenderest chords of his heart, they were so familiar to him, as was likewise the melody of the song the unseen minstrel was singing.

"God of Heaven!" he exclaimed; "those tones. Surely it must be the spirit of Clara that breathes upon my ear, awakening in my soul all the painful reminiscences of the past. Or is it only my disordered imagination that thus deceives me?"

He drew in his breath, and listened with more attention, and deeper interest than before, and was at length enabled to distinguish the following stanza of a ballad he had himself composed, and had often sang to Clara, when he was paying his addresses to her:—

> " I can ne'er forget those sparkling eyes
>   That taught me first to love ;
> Those beauteous looks, expressing thoughts
>   As pure as Heaven above ;
> That sylph-like form, so airy, light,
>   All redolent of bliss ;
> Those ruby lips, with smiles begirt,
>   Inviting virtue's kiss.
> I can ne'er forget those sparkling eyes,
>   That taught me first to love ;
> Those beauteous looks expressing thoughts
>   As pure as Heaven above."

"Agony! agony!" ejaculated Sir Laurence, again looking eagerly around him; "this can be no delusion. The voice, the very words are the same. Mysterious minstrel, who art thou? Let me behold thee, that I may at least banish the terrible suspense that now holds possession of my mind."

He darted towards the spot from whence the sounds seemed to proceed, as he spoke, but before he had advanced many paces, he beheld, from an opening in the wood, the retreating form of a man of light and graceful make, but whose apparel was mean, and seemed to denote him for a person who occupied one of the lowest grades in society.

"This cannot be the unknown minstrel," said the baronet; "for it was a female voice, and one of the most impressive sweetness."

Loudly he called upon the man to stop, but although he heard him, he heeded him not, but rather increased his speed. Once he turned his head, and although Sir Laurence was at some distance from him, he had a distinct view of his features. He started back in amazement, and a feeling of horror came over him; for he could, had it not been for the male apparel, have sworn that he once more beheld the countenance of the woman who so strongly resembled Clara, and who had so frequently crossed his path.

"Gracious Heaven! what fearful mystery is this? Stop, stranger, for the love of Heaven, and answer my questions."

The man, however, if such it was, continued to hasten on, and indeed increased his speed, so that the agitated baronet, unable to keep up with him, soon lost sight of him entirely among the thickly clustering trees of the wood.

Sir Laurence paused to take breath, and to endeavour to recover himself, and most tumultuous and conflicting were the thoughts which passed in rapid succession through his brain. It must have been the stranger who had so hastily retreated from him that had sang the words of the song which so deeply riveted his attention, and conjured up so many bitter recollections in his breast; but yet the voice, so plaintive, so sweet, was a direct contradiction of his sex. Again Sir Laurence threw himself upon the grass, and gave himself up entirely to the strange and bewildering reflections which this adventure naturally gave rise to.

The features of the stranger still seemed to be vividly present to his imagination, and they bore so strong a likeness to those of the female whom he was so anxious to discover, and to ascertain who she really was, that, the more he reflected, the more did he become lost, perplexed, and agitated.

"They were the words of the song I have so often sung to Clara," he said; "and the voice was hers. Its dulcet tones can never be obliterated from my memory. Will nothing ever unravel this insupportable mystery? And what can have brought this singular being to this neighbourhood, and to the very spot which I had sought to indulge my gloomy thought? It would seem as if he must have been aware of my intentions, and had watched me from the mansion. And yet, what could have been his purpose? This must be another scheme of the gipsies, and I know not what fresh danger may threaten me and Blanche, from their deadly and insatiable feelings of revenge. Surely this continued state of suspense and dread, is more than any human being can support."

He beat his breast, and remained for some moments in a state of the most powerful emotion, and at a loss in what manner to act; but at length, anxious to learn how Blanche was, and fearing that his protracted absence from home might cause some surprise and alarm, when the state of his mind was so well known, he arose, and slowly, and with a melancholy heart, retraced his steps towards the mansion.

Soon after his return home, and before he could send a messenger to the chamber of Blanche, Amanda entered his apartment.

"You have been walking, Laurence," she said; "and I hope the fresh morning air has revived you. But still you look pale and agitated."

"No—no, Amanda," hastily replied Sir Laurence; "I am better—much better, and fully prepared to know the crisis of my fate. But, my beloved, my suffering Blanche, oh, tell me how she is."

"Better, Laurence," returned Amanda; "she is fully restored to her senses, and, by the dint of argument and expostulation, has become much more tranquil than could have been anticipated."

"Oh, thank Heaven for this," said the baronet, fervently, and vehemently clasping his hands. "But what says she now of me? Does she still reproach me with having deceived her, as one who is unworthy of her, and who has brought her to shame and misery?"

"Oh, no, Laurence; you anticipate the worst. Blanche, having now recovered from those violent paroxysms of grief which the receipt of the letter naturally excited, is disposed to view all the circumstances more calmly and rationally. She is most anxious to see you; but I must warn you that everything depends upon your own conduct on the occasion; or she may suffer a relapse, and then there is no saying what the consequences might be."

"Alas! alas! I shudder at the thoughts of the interview, for what can I say in excuse of myself; and will she not demand that explanation which I had vainly hoped there would never have been any necessity to pass my lips?"

"Undoubtedly Blanche will require you to explain everything," said Amanda; "it is the only way by which you can restore her to confidence. But exert yourself; it will doubtless be a painful trial of your feelings, but it will soon be over, and by it

See p. 263.

terrible doubts, which at present occupy the mind of Lady Cleveland, will be removed."

"Oh, Amanda!" ejaculated the baronet, "it is, indeed a most arduous task, and Heaven only knows how I shall accomplish it. But it must be done, and let me then muster all the fortitude that is in my power."

With a drooping heart he now left the room, and made his way towards the chamber of Blanche.

When he arrived at the door, he paused, and again hesitated to open it. He listened, but no sound met his ears, and again mustering all the resolution he could, he threw open the door, and rushed into the room. His entrance startled Blanche, and beholding him, she gave utterance to a faint scream, and hid her face with her hands.

Sir Laurence in a moment sank on his knees by her bed-side, and, in a voice almost choked with the violence of his emotion, exclaimed,—

"Oh, Blanche, my beloved, much injured Blanche; it is your husband who kneels by your side, and supplicates your mercy and forbearance."

"My husband!" repeated Blanche, in a faint and hollow voice; "oh, Laurence, dare I still call you by that name? Is there not another being who has a prior claim on your hand? Alas! alas! what dreadful thoughts crowd upon my brain. Little did I ever think that he on whom my every hope was fixed, in whom I had placed such implicit confidence, could so have deceived me."

"Reproach me not so severely, Blanche," implored Sir Laurence; "I have erred, greatly erred; but still I am not so guilty as I have been represented to be."

"Oh, Laurence," sighed Blanche; "what think you must be the tortures, the trible doubts on my mind after the receipt of that fatal letter?"

"But you do not, you cannot believe the statements made in that anonymous epistle, Blanche?"

' Can you deny them?" eagerly demanded Lady Cleveland, and she fixed her penetrating eye full upon the countenance of her husband.

"Part of them, to my sorrow and shame I own, I cannot," answered the baronet. "But Clara was more guilty than I was. She deceived me; became the paramour of another; brought dishonour upon my name, and then eloped with her seducer."

"And is that, indeed, true, Laurence?"

"By all my hopes it is."

"And that you believed her dead when you paid your addresses to me?"

"I did—I did; oh, I must have been a villain, indeed, could I thus willingly have betrayed you, Blanche. She perished by her own hands, as I have often before asserted, and therefore that part of the gipsies' statement is proved to be entirely false."

"But Mirah," said Blanche, fixing upon him her full and beautiful eyes; "Mirah, her cousin, her fair cousin, can you deny the allegations laid in this letter against you, respecting that individual?"

Sir Laurence trembled, and felt at the same time much discomposed in other respects, at this question. It was the very one upon which the principal business that affected himself and Blanche hinged, and, with all his reflections, he was unprepared to answer it.

"Blanche," he said at last, "why cannot you waive that point for the present, until we are both in a more composed state of mind to enter into a mutual explanation?"

"A *mutual explanation!*" repeated Blanche; "what mean you, Laurence? I have nothing to explain; I gave up my heart, my soul, my whole being to you, without wilful thought or feeling prejudicial to your character; have you in one instance found me act differently to what a wife, loving her husband, and acting the duty of a wife towards him should do?"

"No; no!" answered the baronet.

"What explanation then have I to give?"

"I am bewildered, distracted!" returned Sir Laurence. "Oh, Heaven! how can I enter into an explanation of that unfortunate event without shame? Why should I call the blushes upon your face, my dearest Blanche?"

"You admit, then, that that part of the communication in the letter, is, in certain respects correct?" asked Blanche.

"I do—I do," replied the baronet, partially covering his face with his hands, at the same time his bosom was heaving with the intense agony of his feelings.

"Oh, Laurence!" ejaculated Blanche, "and you could exert your powers of fascination but to lure this poor girl from the paths of virtue, and then desert her?"

"Spare me, spare me, Blanche; I did not so. I will admit, to my shame, that I made a conquest of her."

"A conquest of her!—The language of the confirmed libertine. Oh, shame, shame, Laurence Cleveland—husband I dare not, must not call you."

The baronet beat his breast in despair; he knew not what to say in reply; he felt the keenness, the justice of the reproaches his wife was pressing upon him, and therefore his own weakness and incapacity of evading the explanation she in justice demanded. Yet would he have given worlds to have been excused that dreadful ordeal.

"Blanche, dear Blanche," he at last said, "you try me to the utmost; but to prove the sincerity of the love I have ever professed and felt for you, I will enter into the full explanation which you demand. Then judge of me as you may; judge of me by my past conduct and my present; consider that those offences, for which I now feel the keenest and the deepest remorse, were committed in my youth and with every temptation around me; and I am certain that your gentle nature will induce you to place the most favourable construction upon the circumstances."

"Alas, Laurence!" said Blanche, "and why had you not the candour to explain these circumstances prior to our marriage?"

"Because I was anxious not to offend your sensitive and delicate mind by a recapitulation of my past errors, confident as I was that my future conduct would defy reproach, and that you would never have cause to complain. And I now ask you, Blanche, whether, in every respect, since you have become my wife, you have had any reason to suspect that my professions of love were not sincere?—whether I have in any one instance deceived you, as regards those professions?"

"No, no," answered Blanche; "but after these repeated charges, which must leave a weight of doubt upon my mind, can you feel surprised that I should require—nay, demand, a full explanation of the facts that have given rise to the accusations?"

"True, Blanche, true," answered the baronet; "and yet would I willingly have spared your feelings, as well as my own, by avoiding the painful recital. I admit I have been most wrong, most guilty; but I have paid, and am now paying, a deep penalty from the bitter remorse I feel."

"And you banished Mirah," said Blanche; "you discarded her, after vowing affection for her, and taking advantage of her weakness?"

Sir Laurence averted his face, and could return no answer. A pause ensued, and then the baronet, turning to his lady, said,—

"Dear Blanche, have I not admitted my guilt in every respect where I am guilty? Why, then, add to the almost insupportable agony of my mind by repeating these facts? Blanche, have they so prejudiced your mind against me, that you are prepared to look upon me as an individual only worthy of your scorn and hatred? Tell me, Blanche, and let me know the extent of my misery."

"Hatred!" repeated Blanche, looking up in her husband's face with an expression that no language could do ample justice to; "oh, no, Laurence; guilty however you may prove to be, I must still love you, even though regret should break my heart. It is only that you may, by the explanation, remove some portion of the stigma that is placed upon your character by these terrible people, that I thus urge you to enter into particulars."

" And you will listen patiently and with forbearance to me ?" interrogated Sir Laurence.

" I will—I will," answered Blanche, and she drooped her head upon his shoulder. The baronet threw his arms around her neck, and kissed her rapturously.

" My own Blanche, my sweet, my confiding wife," he ejaculated; " there you speak like yourself. But I could expect nothing less from you. Your words have inspired me with confidence, and renewed my energies. Listen, then, to my narrative, and, dismissing all prejudices from your mind that the anonymous letter may have inspired you with, judge me only by the facts which I will truly relate."

" I will, Laurence," answered Blanche, yielding herself to his fond embrace. " But Clara, your first wife, do you really believe that she is no more ?"

" How can I think otherwise, Blanche, under all the circumstances of her reported death ?"

" But you took no particular pains to inquire into the correctness of those reports."

" In that I admit my guilt or error."

" And that female form that has so often appeared to both you and me ?"

" I admit," replied Sir Laurence, " that her resemblance to my first wife is most striking; but still I cannot but think she is only an impostor, colleagued with the gipsies to carry out their diabolical scheme of vengeance against me."

" Heaven send that it may prove so !" said Blanche ; " for should it really be Clara, alas ! what misery and shame will it not plunge us both into ?"

" Entertain not such terrible ideas, my beloved Blanche," said her husband ; " for Providence surely can never ordain that innocence like yours should be so severely visited. And do you then pardon me, my love, for the errors of my youth ? Do you still place the same reliance upon the fidelity of the professions of my affection that you formerly did ?"

" It has been a severe trial to me, Laurence," answered Blanche ; " but, indeed, I do ; and had you been prudent enough to have evinced the candour that you now do, previous to our marriage, what misery, what suspense, would it have spared us both."

" And could you still have loved me, Blanche ? Would you still have been willing to become my bride ?" asked the baronet, eagerly.

" Oh, yes, yes !" replied Lady Cleveland. " Much as I might have regretted, and do now, regret your errors, nothing whatever could have changed my sentiments towards you."

" Sweet confidence ! Most amiable of women ! Oh, how unworthy do I feel myself of you. How bitterly do I reproach myself that I could ever have been guilty of a single act that I should feel ashamed to acknowledge to you, or which should cause one pang within your gentle bosom. But, if remorse, if my future conduct can make any atonement to you, I do not despair that we may yet experience every happiness."

" And we may still continue together, without the fear of reproach or shame ?"

" Oh, yes, yes, my love. Divest your mind of these horrible doubts ; had there been any truth in the statements of the gipsies, that Clara was living, would they not have produced her to confront me ere this, and to have proved her identity beyond all doubt ?"

" True—true," returned the confiding Blanche ;. " that argument does appear most feasible. I will place every confidence in your assurances, Laurence, for life would be a curse to me could I not do so. But can you wonder at the dreadful shock my feelings received on the receipt of that epistle? Can you wonder that constant repetition of the same charge, and with such apparent reason, should create these doubts and suspicions in my mind? But you will explain everything, will you not? and then I shall be the better prepared for anything that in future may take place."

"I will, my love, my fondest, my most forbearing Blanche," replied the baronet; "but had it not better be deferred to a future day, when you will be in a better condition to listen to the painful details I shall have to relate?"

"No, no," returned Blanche; "I am fully prepared for everything now, and even the assurance of the worst that I might anticipate could not be equal to this dreadful suspense which I am now enduring. You shall find me not interrupt you by a single remark, no word of reproach shall escape my lips, and I trust, therefore, that you will deal with me in the true spirit of candour you profess."

Sir Laurence embraced her with the truest affection, and his breast was relieved from a heavy and almost insupportable weight of anxiety which had before oppressed it.

"That assurance, my dearest wife," he said, "is enough, and inspires me with fortitude for the arduous and disagreeable task that devolves upon me. I will explain everything; I will not endeavour to extenuate any of my former errors, which have been productive of so much misery; and whatever may be the impression the disclosure should make upon you, I will strive to submit with patience to your decision. But, Amanda, my sister, that amiable mediator in all that so immediately affects us, and to whom we are so much indebted, I would wish her to be present while I enter into the particulars, that she may become acquainted with all her brother's faults, and know the better how to advise us."

"Oh, yes," replied Blanche, "the presence of Amanda will be a relief to me; and, more than all, assures me of the sincerity of your intentions, Laurence."

"Could you for a moment suspect that I now intend to endeavour to deceive you, Blanche?" he said, with a look of gentle reproach.

"No, no, Laurence," returned Blanche; "I will, I do, place every confidence in you. But let Amanda be summoned, and at once reveal those facts which must be a great relief to your own mind, at the same time that it removes my anxiety."

Sir Laurence moved to the bell, and summoned the attendance of a servant, whom he desired to request that Amanda would immediately join them. In a very few minutes she entered the chamber, and could not help expressing, most warmly, the gratification she felt at the composure which both her brother and Blanche evinced.

"Yes, Amanda," said the baronet, "the painful ordeal is passed; my beloved Blanche is disposed to view my youthful errors with a lenient eye, and I request your patience and attention while I disclose those offences for which my conscience now so bitterly reproaches me. I admit that I have been wrong, sadly wrong; but still not so guilty as I am represented by those wretches, who can have no other feelings to gratify than their own vindictive passions, originating from what cause I know not."

"This resolution reflects the highest credit on your reason and justice, my brother," remarked Amanda, "and must afford the greatest satisfaction and confidence to Blanche of the strict honour and sincerity of your intentions. Never could I be_ lieve that Laurence Cleveland could be guilty of all that is imputed to him. It would be a libel on the memory of my revered parents to entertain such a thought."

" My good, kind sister," said the baronet, vehemently pressing her hand, and looking gratefully in her countenance, "you do me but justice by those observations. It is true that I have been guilty of many errors, for which for years past I have felt the deepest remorse. Alas! no one but myself and Heaven know what I have suffered, when left to my own thoughts, and how anxious I have ever been to make all the atonement in my power. But, still, all my faults have originated in youthful impetuosity and misguided, or, I might say, too sanguine passions; and, certainly, I cannot help still thinking that I have been more sinned against than I have sinned. I feel the sincerest love for Clara Roseburn, and believed her all virtue and innocence; and that my intentions were strictly honourable, is proved by my having made her my wife, when I might have exercised the influence I possessed over her by seducing her from the paths of virtue. That I estranged her affections from the man to whom she was affianced, I admit; but when ardent love is the stimulant, and the object is a young and lovely being, whom you have every reason to believe reciprocates your passions, where is the mentor who can restrain you in the gratification of your wishes? That I did not reveal my sentiments to her guardian, and that I eloped with her from that place in which she had ever found the tenderest home; that I married her in secret, and without consulting the will of my father, I admit was wrong; but dearly have I paid for my imprudence, and bitterly have I suffered for the disappointment of my hopes. My conduct to Clara was ever all that a woman could expect from a fond and faithful husband; but her ambition once gratified, she basely, cruelly deceived me, as I shall be prepared to prove in the narrative I am about to submit to you. She deceived me—dishonoured me, I repeat; and, even were she really living, no laws, human or divine, could give her any just claim to the title of my wife. But allow me a few moments to collect my thoughts, and then I will commence my melancholy, and, it may be, degrading story."

Blanche and Amanda made no reply, but the expression of their countenances was quite sufficient to shew their assent; and they offered to make no observation while the baronet was wrapped in reflection.

It was evidently a long and a severe struggle with his feelings; many disheartening and black clouds passed over the horizon of his memory; but they were, at length, dispelled by the sunshine of reason, and he commenced his narrative as follows :—

CHAPTER XXIV.

THE NARRATIVE OF SIR LAURENCE CLEVELAND.

It is now nearly nineteen years since—when our beloved father was alive, Amanda —that I was invited by a fellow collegiate to pass a short time with him and his relations, at their family seat, near Summerford. I need not tell you how gladly I availed myself of his invitation, so delightfully situated as Roslinwold Manor is, and the enthusiast which you know me to be in the picturesque architecture of nature.

Roslinwold Manor is of the Elizabethan epoch, possessing all the graceful and commodious style of architecture—a style divested of the heavy, cumbrous, and prison, or hospital-like appearance of the dwellings that our present gentry and aristocracy seem to think it proper to confine themselves in; and, therefore, it possessed advantages which, in every respect, were in unison with my taste.

The manor stood near the entrance of a wood, backed by rich pasture land, in a luxuriant state of cultivation, and comprised within its demesnes several prosperous villages, the inmates of which were most of them tenants of Sir William Clerivalle, the father of my friend.

Summerford was situate about a mile and a half from this delightful spot, and also possessed many attractions, which drew me and my companion frequently to visit it. Above all, was one ancient, but comfortable dwelling, that stood in the immediate suburbs of the town, on the brow of a hill, commanding an extensive range of scenery of the most beautiful description. But it was the inmates of that dwelling which induced me and Herbert Clerivalle to visit that neighbourhood so frequently more than anything else.

At that period, as you must be aware, Amanda, I was young (little more than eighteen years of age), volatile, and thoughtless. I had wealth at my command, from an indulgent parent; so had my friend; and therefore, without any really vicious intentions, we were likely to be fascinated into certain extravagances which we might afterwards sincerely regret.

It is from too great a susceptibility to the all-powerful fascinations of your sex, that I date all my misfortunes, and from an imprudence, a self-over-estimated opinion of my own judgment, I think that is natural to youth. Be it as it may, it is from the dwelling on the brow of the hill, which I have been so particular in describing, that I firmly believe I may trace all those calamities which it is now my painful task to recount, and your's to listen to.

And who were the inmates of this dwelling? I will tell you; and while I do so, I implore you, my dearest Blanche, and my amiable sister, to bear with me patiently, and to excuse me, if I, in the effervescence of my feelings, excited by the recollection of the past (would that I could, and were permitted, to bury it for ever in oblivion), give too glowing a description.

The situation, as I have before said, was romantic and retired, and myself and Herbert had frequently stopped to admire the neatness of the dwelling, which showed the exquisite taste of those who inhabited it, and the most refined judgment was displayed in the manner that the garden attached to it was laid out.

" Ah," said Herbert to me one day, when I was giving expression to those ideas, " I guess well the lovely minds from which all these beauties you so much admire, have sprang; and I doubt not but you would be most captivated could you but obtain a sight of them. I am afraid that I should be deemed bold and obtrusive, or I certainly would introduce you to the fair inmates of this happy dwelling. They were most lovely, when I last saw them, and three years must, if possible, greatly have added to their charms."

" To whom do you allude, Herbert?" I asked, my interest and curiosity being greatly excited by his observations.

" To two lovely orphan cousins who live here under the protection of their uncle, an aged man," answered my friend ; " Clara Roseburn and Mirah."

" Are are they very handsome?" said I.

" Two fairer beings you never beheld, Clara especially, who I believe is two years the senior of her cousin Mirah. But I hope that we shall have an opportunity of seeing them before we leave this neighbourhood. However, I caution you, Laurence, to look well after your heart, or I imagine that it will be taken captive by one of those beauteous rustics."

" In which case, I fear that I should meet with a rival in you, my friend," I returned, with a smile. " For it seems to me to be impossible that your heart can have remained proof against these fair cousins."

" I own," remarked Herbert, " that they made a great impression upon me from the first moment that I beheld them, Clara Roseburn especially ; and had she moved in a superior station of life, I should not have hesitated in paying my addresses to her ; but as it is, I can only admire, without the hope of any further gratification."

" But surely it is not possible that two such beauteous damsels as you describe Clara and Mirah to be, have remained without lovers," said I.

" I dare say not," answered Herbert ; " in fact, I am aware Clara had a suitor when I was last here, and I understand that he is still paying his addresses to her, and no doubt he will make her his wife."

" And who is this fortunate swain, Herbert?" I inquired.

" An honest rustic who resides in the adjacent village ; Walter Alston, by name," answered my friend.

" If Clara is such as you have described her to be," I remarked, " she is too fair a prize for a simple clown to possess.   I must see these incomparable cousins."

" You shall, if possible, Laurence," returned Herbert ; " but, after all, it would be better if you did not, for I apprehend it will only raise passions in your breast which can never be gratified."

" And why is it impossible that they should be gratified ?" I demanded.

" Your station would not permit you to make either of them your wife, if even they were to accept you as a lover."

" But would they not either of them make a charming mistress—a delightful enjoyment to retire to in some snug country box, from the severities of study?" I said.

Ah, Blanche ! well may the blushes of shame and virtuous indignation mantle in your cheeks at this avowal of my depraved thoughts ; and severely am I now punished in the bitterness of my remorse.   But I pray you to bear with me patiently, while I candidly reveal all my past errors, but which I would fain have spared your gentle nature the pain of listening to.

" Flatter not yourself, Laurence, with any such ideas," replied my companion ; " for you may depend upon it that Clara and Mirah are too strictly virtuous ever to fall the victims to the seducer's arts ; and I do not believe that you could ever find it in your heart to become the betrayer of such beauteous innocence, although you now talk with so much levity."

" I am afraid, Herbert, you give me more credit than is due to me," said I ; " you know that I am not made of the most invulnerable materials.   The glowing description you have given me of the cousins has aroused my most unbounded curiosity, and I must see them, or I shall surely die of disappointment.   Cannot you form some excuse to call at the house ?"

" Oh, no !" replied Herbert ; " I cannot think of taking such a liberty ; besides, the suspicions of old Redmond Roseburn, who watches over his fair charge with a most jealous eye, would be sure to be excited.   No, Laurence ; you must content yourself to leave it to chance to gain you the introduction you so anxiously seek."

" Well, this is confoundedly tedious.   But what sort of an old gentleman is this Redmond Roseburn, as you call him?   Is he some crabbed old churl, who looks upon everything and everybody with a jaundiced eye?"

"Oh, no!" answered Herbert; "I believe him to be a very excellent man, of a superior mind; and his conduct shows that he loves his two orphan nieces, who, from childhood, have been left without any other protector, with the same fondness as if they were his own children. Clara is the daughter of the only brother he ever had, and who was killed in battle, his wife dying shortly afterwards of a broken heart.

See p. 376.

Mirah is the daughter of his sister, and she was left parentless when she was not more than three years old. The old man has taken the greatest pains with their education, and they are more accomplished than most young girls of their station in society."

"And shall such beauty and accomplishments be sacrificed to some rustic hind?" I demanded. "But you say that the old gentleman is independent?"

" He has, I believe, sufficient to keep him in comfort, and something to leave his fair nieces to advance them in the world when he shall cease to live. The house he inhabits is his own freehold property."

The account which Herbert gave, more and more increased my curiosity, and rendered me the more anxious to behold the fair cousins. Every day we visited the neighbourhood of their dwelling, and sometimes I went alone; but still the opportunity I wished for was not granted me, although I frequently saw Walter Alston pass and repass from the house. I felt vexed and disappointed, and could not help thinking that Mr. Roseburn watched them with too jealous an eye, to keep them such close prisoners. I was already a lover of those hidden beauties whom I had not yet seen. I could not but form the most ardent and extravagant ideas of their charms from the pains that were taken to keep them concealed from the dangerous gaze of man; and I determined never to rest until I had, by some means or other, gained an interview with them. But for a considerable time I was doomed to be disappointed.

I had been a month at Roslinwold Manor, when I received a hasty summons to return home immediately, as our revered father, Amanda, was taken suddenly ill, and his malady had assumed so serious a character, that he was not expected to live.

You may be sure that this melancholy intelligence diverted my thoughts from every other subject, and I lost no time in departing from Roslinwold; and, on my reaching home, I found my father at the point of death, and in less than two hours afterwards, he breathed his last, strictly enjoining me, as you are aware, Amanda, not to marry for three years after his demise. Alas! how bitterly do I now, and must ever, reproach myself for having disobeyed the dying injunctions of that excellent parent. I have been severely punished, for a curse has seemed to pursue me ever since.

I was now left with a large fortune, to follow the bent of my own inclinations without control; and young, wild, and thoughtless as I was, it was one of the greatest misfortunes that could have befallen me. You, although younger than myself, Amanda, was already betrothed to Captain Gordon, and, only a few months after the demise our father, became his wife; and I thought it hard and unjust that I should be tied down by such injunctions as my father had, in his last few moments, given me. I, however, paid every respect to his memory, and for some time felt his loss most keenly. But time, aided by a sanguine and volatile disposition, served to ameliorate my grief, and I began to think of seeking those pleasures and enjoyments which my ample fortune would allow me to indulge in.

My thoughts now returned to the fair cousins at Summerford, and my anxious curiosity to behold them revived. The opportunity was soon afforded me, for I again received an invitation from my friend Herbert, to pass a short time with him at Roslinwold; and I need not say that I accepted this second invitation with even greater pleasure than I had done the first, and lost no time in proceeding to that place on which my thoughts had been so long fixed.

" Well, Herbert," I said to him, after we had been in conversation for a short time; " what about those beauteous cousins?" I inquired.

" I have only seen them once, and then I had not an opportunity of speaking to them. Oh, they are, indeed, more lovely than ever, and must captivate the most insensible heart. I do not feel mine exactly in my own keeping since I have seen them. Mirah is a light, smiling, graceful thing; but Clara, in my opinion, far surpasses her in dazzling beauty."

"And she has not yet married that clown, has she?" I eagerly demanded.

"She has not," replied Herbert; "but is it possible, Sir Laurence, that these damsels, whom you have never seen, should have continued to occupy your thoughts."

"Indeed, they have!" I returned; "the description you have given me of them has never for any length of time left my memory, and you must, indeed you must contrive some means of getting me a sight of them."

"How can I do so, my dear fellow? I am not on intimate terms with Mr. Roseburn, and consequently I could not, with any appearance of decency, obtrude myself upon his dwelling. I regret that I mentioned anything to you about the lovely girls, since it seems that it has and is likely to cause you so much anxiety and uneasiness."

"Well," said I, "perhaps it would have been better if you had not; but now my curiosity is excited in the most unbounded degree, and I shall not rest until it is gratified."

In vain Herbert tried to banish these thoughts from my mind; a strange infatuation seemed to urge me on, and I determined not to abandon my wishes until they were crowned with success; and with that design I spent whole hours every day in wandering about the dwelling, but only once caught a glimpse of the cousins at one of the windows up stairs, but they were so quickly gone that I had not the opportunity of distinguishing their features, but even the slight glance that I had induced me to fancy they were still more lovely than my friend had described.

You cannot, I am sure, but condemn the egregious folly of my conduct, and I cannot acknowledge it without shame. It was the behaviour of an infatuated idiot, for no person in their senses could be supposed to have acted in such a way.

From that moment my impatient curiosity increased, and Herbert in vain attempted to rally me out of it. I continued my visits every day, but with no better success; still, my patience was not exhausted, nor would I alter my determination, although there seemed to be no more prospect of its being gratified than at first. However, a circumstance was about to occur which afforded me my desire.

Herbert and me had been rambling a few miles from home, and we did not turn our steps towards the Manor until the evening was approaching. As we were crossing the wood near which the dwelling of Mr. Roseburn stood, we were suddenly alarmed by hearing loud cries, apparently those of a female, proceeding not far from the spot we were traversing, and, fearing that some outrage was being committed, we hastened towards the place, with the determination of rendering all the assistance in our power. The cries were repeated, and we were then convinced that they proceeded from more females than one, and we redoubled our speed, and after forcing our way between the thickly clustering trees, we came to a more open part of the wood, where we beheld two females struggling violently in the grasp of a couple of desperate-looking ruffians.

"Oh, by Heaven, it is the cousins!" exclaimed Herbert.

My blood glowed at the intelligence, and my heart palpitated with uncontrollable emotion against my side. Here, then, was the opportunity I had so long and so anxiously sought, afforded me, and that of introducing myself to the lovely damsels under the most favourable circumstances.

"Hold! villains! miscreants!" I shouted at the top of my voice; and, clutching the stout walking-sticks we had with us, both me and Herbert rushed to the rescue of Clara and her cousin, who had now fainted, and were held in the arms of the ruffians. On beholding us, however, they instantly resigned their senseless and beauteous burthens, and precipitately took to flight.

We hastened to the spot, and raised the insensible girls in our arms, and I gazed with feelings of admiration and rapture upon them. To my sanguine imagination then, they appeared to me the most lovely beings I had ever before seen, and far surpassed the eloquent description Herbert had given of them. But Clara, whose graceful form I supported, appeared to me perfection's self. Pardon me, Blanche, for this description; but it is only right that I should openly reveal to you what were my impressions at the time, since they were the origin of all the misfortunes and miseries that have since occurred to me. Would that we had never met; I might now have been sincerely happy.

I cannot do justice to my feelings at that moment; my heart throbbed at double its natural height, and I could have pressed warm kisses upon those lovely lips, but a feeling of shame restrained me, and I trembled with the power of my agitation.

"Herbert," said I, "how faint, how weak was the description you gave me of these beauteous creatures, but especially of her whom I hold in my arms. And shall such perfection be sacrificed to some rude clown, who cannot appreciate the value of such a treasure? Never! By Heaven! it must not, shall not be!"

"Restrain your feelings, Sir Laurence," said Herbert; "this is neither the time nor the place to give expression to them. We must see to the recovery of the fair cousins, and then we can protect them to their home."

It happened that, close by the spot where we were standing, there was a small brook, and we therefore bathed the temples of the insensible girls, and in a few minutes we were delighted to find our efforts crowned with success. They sighed, and opening their eyes, gazed upon us with astonishment, not unmixed with terror; and then the deepest crimson blushes suffused their cheeks, and rendered their modest charms truly irresistible.

Clara gently disengaged herself from me, and then stood apparently bewildered, and uncertain how to act.

"Be not alarmed, fair damsel," I said, in a tremulous voice; "the ruffians who insulted you are gone, and you are now with friends."

"Oh, kind gentlemen," said Clara, in a voice of most impressive sweetness, "how can we thank you for the service you have rendered us?"

"We need no thanks, Miss Roseburn," replied Herbert; "we have done no more than our duty, and we are only too happy to think that we arrived on this spot in time to save you from the power of such desperate villains. But do you not know me, Miss Clara?"

"Oh, yes," answered the blushing damsel. "You are Mr. Herbert Clerivalle, if I am not mistaken. I cannot but again assure you of our gratitude for the kindness of yourself and your friend. But it is getting late, and our dear uncle will begin to feel alarmed at our absence; we must return home as quick as we can."

"You must allow us to accompany you, fair Clara," I said, "for the villains may still be lurking near the spot, and you might be again subjected to their insults, if you had no one to protect you."

Clara fixed upon me a look, which went immediately to my heart, as she modestly replied,—

" I thank you, sir, for your generous offer ; but Mr. Clerivalle knows that we are not many minutes' walk from our residence, and it is therefore unnecessary to trouble you farther."

" Pardon me, Miss Roseburn," said Herbert; " but you must allow us to escort you home, for, short as the distance is even, there may yet be danger."

Clara, seeming fully to appreciate our intentions, raised no further objection, and taking her arm, while Herbert did that of Mirah, we walked on towards the dwelling of their uncle. Sincerely did I regret that the distance was so short, since we must so soon be parted from the lovely cousins, and the looks of Herbert convinced me that his thoughts were the same as mine.

We had but little conversation on the way, but the answers of Clara and Mirah, though simple, were most expressive and eloquent, and at once displayed the superior qualifications of their mind. My senses were completely captivated, and never had I before experienced a few minutes of such pure bliss as those I then enjoyed.

When we came in sight of the house, we saw old Mr. Roseburn standing at the door, and, no doubt greatly surprised at seeing his fair nieces so accompanied, he hastened to meet us.

" My dear children," he said, " you have at last then returned. How anxious and uneasy have I been about you; I really must chide you for absenting yourselves so long from home. But, Mr. Clerivalle, and you, sir, whom I have not the pleasure of knowing, to what accident may I be indebted for the honour of this visit?"

" It has been our good fortune, Mr. Roseburn," answered Herbert, " to rescue your two fair nieces from the power of ruffians in the wood, and we therefore took the liberty of escorting them home, lest they should be exposed to farther danger."

" Ah !" exclaimed the old man, " is it indeed so? Oh, gentlemen, how can I properly acknowledge my gratitude ? Had anything happened to my darling girls, it would certainly have broken my heart. Pray walk in, gentlemen, and rest yourselves awhile, and then you can, if you please, give me a further explanation of this adventure."

This was just what I wanted, and I could hardly help giving expression to the pleasure I felt ; and I know not whether it was only fancy, but I could not help thinking that both Clara and her cousin were far from being dissatisfied. The manners of Mr. Roseburn, too, were most gentlemanly and prepossessing, and the invitation was, therefore, doubly acceptable.

We entered the house, and found it furnished with that taste and elegance which so well corresponded with the exterior. Having taken our seats, we related the particulars of the adventure in the wood, and when we had concluded, Mr. Roseburn once more repeated his thanks to us, and the looks of Clara and Mirah plainly shewed the sincere and ardent gratitude they felt.

" But who could the villains have been that thus dared to insult you!" said the old gentleman, when we had concluded.

" I cannot say, my dear uncle," replied Clara ; " they were complete strangers to us, and I never remember to have seen them before."

" My God !" ejaculated Mr. Roseburn, " had it not been for the fortunate arrival of these gentlemen, what might have happened to you ? You must never again venture, my dear girls, to be so late from home, for there is no knowing what villains may be lurking about; and should you fall into their hands, all my hopes of happiness in this world will be destroyed."

After about half-an-hour passed in conversation, we could see, by the manner of Mr. Roseburn, that he began to think our stay had been protracted quite long enough, and we therefore, though very reluctantly, arose to take our departure.

"This is a charming residence of your's, Mr. Roseburn," said Herbert, "and me and my friend here, Sir Laurence Cleveland, have often, in the course of our rambles, stopped to admire it. Will you permit us to visit you occasionally while we remain in this neighbourhood, that we may enjoy the pleasure of your company?"

In my heart, how warmly I thanked Herbert for this; and I looked eagerly in the countenance of Mr. Roseburn to see what effect it might have upon him. He seemed unprepared for such a question, and hesitated, while I could not but observe that Clara and her cousin awaited his answer with some impatience.

"I should feel honoured by the friendship of yourself, Mr. Clerivalle," he said at last, "and that of Sir Laurence Cleveland; but I am afraid that you would not find the conversation of an old and lonely man like me very agreeable. However, any time when you feel disposed to honour me with a visit, I shall be most happy to see you."

This answer filled me with delight; it was more than I could have hoped on so short an acquaintance, and I augured the greatest success to my wishes from it. But what were my wishes? Could I bear to contemplate the destruction of Clara, and thereby break the heart of her fond guardian, and blight the hopes of that man to whom she had promised her hand? I cannot venture to describe the tumultuous thoughts which rushed through my mind at that moment; I was bewildered and unsettled, and undecided how to act; but that I could conquer the passion with which Clara had inspired me on this our first meeting, I found to be impossible.

We now took our leave, and made our way towards Roslinwold manor.

CHAPTER XXV.

THE NARRATIVE OF SIR LAURENCE CLEVELAND CONTINUED.

I NEED not attempt to describe my feelings as we proceeded on our way home, and could not help giving free vent to the emotions of my throbbing heart.

"What a heavenly creature!" I exclaimed; "what features, what grace, what intelligence! Oh, Herbert, I have at last seen that beauteous being whom my imagination has so long painted, and who is the only woman that I can ever love. Thanks to this accident which has introduced me to her. Mirah is most lovely, but the gentle Clara far surpasses her; she is perfection's self; and I shall be permitted to behold her again—to enjoy the felicity of her conversation. Oh, this is bliss most unspeakable. Herbert, my friend, I am eternally indebted to you for your conduct this night; and for the invitation you have elicited from Mr. Roseburn."

"And yet I am afraid, Sir Laurence, that I have done wrong; and that we ought not to avail ourselves of the kindness of Mr. Roseburn," observed Herbert.

"Why so?" I eagerly demanded.

"Because it will be the means of feeding a passion that you ought to persevere to stifle in the bud," answered my friend; "and I am fearful that my heart will be in danger from the superlative charms of the little Mirah, towards whom my family connexions will never allow me to encourage sentiments of honour. No, Laurence; after all, this is a very unfortunate business, and it would have been much better had we never seen the beauteous cousins; but we must avoid their too dangerous society, and endeavour to forget them."

" Forget Clara!" I exclaimed; " oh, never! that is impossible!"

" And could you for a moment entertain a wish to estrange her affections from that youth to whom she is affianced ?"

" He is humble, rude, uncultivated; such a man must never possess a treasure so precious."

" But surely, Sir Laurence, you can never wish to betray Clara Roseburn to ruin, and to bring sorrow and shame upon her now happy relatives ?"

" Oh, no, no," I returned; " I could never do so; my heart revolts at the very idea."

" Then this at once shows the absolute necessity of your abandoning all thoughts of her altogether," remarked Herbert. " Your wife she can never be, if even you should win her heart; and you must be base, indeed, if you could for one moment contemplate the destruction of her virtue."

" Herbert," I returned, " I am bewildered; I know not what to say, or what to do; but to banish all my hopes of possessing Clara is utterly impossible, even though I make her my wife."

" Your wife, Sir Laurence ?"

" Ay, my wife !" I repeated.

" You cannot be serious," said Herbert.

" Indeed, I am."

" You do not reflect upon the insurmountable obstacles which are thrown in your way."

" Am I not my own master, Herbert ? Who is to control my actions ?"

" This is talking absurdly; for what likelihood is there of your ever being able to supplant Walter Alston in the affections of Clara, now that she is betrothed to him ? And think you that Mr. Roseburn would ever give his consent, or descend to such injustice and cruelty towards a worthy young man to whom he has granted the hand of his fair niece. You must entertain a very erroneous opinion of the character of Mr. Roseburn if you think so. Besides leaving alone the disparity of your stations."

" The disparity of our stations!" I interrupted impatiently; " oh, what are rank and riches compared to the treasures of Clara's mind?   Is she not worthy to become the bride of an emperor ?"

" You are far too romantic in your notions, Sir Laurence," said Herbert.

" You may deem me so; but I feel convinced that nothing whatever can alter the sentiments with which Clara Roseburn has inspired me."

" Time and absence may, if you will but persevere."

" Never! my feelings spurn the very idea."

" But you certainly would not disobey the dying injunctions of your father, which restrain you from marrying for three years from the period of his death ?"

This question, I confess, tortured and bewildered me, and it was some moments ere I could return an answer.

" The injunctions of my father were cruel, unreasonable, and unjust," I said at length; " and it would not be remarkable if I should neglect to obey them, solemn even as the circumstances were under which the promise was exacted."

" I am sorry to hear you make use of such observations, Sir Laurence," returned Herbert; " and I more than ever regret that I should have ever mentioned the names of the cousins to you. But, after all, I do trust that you will think differently upon this subject, and see the necessity of subduing the sentiments which you have unfortunately suffered to take possession of your mind."

I shook my head, and the conversation ended, and we soon afterwards separated for the night. I retired to my chamber, but could I think of seeking rest? Oh, no; that, in my present state of mind, was impossible.

I can scarcely dare to shock your ears, my dearest Blanche, by describing all the varied thoughts that now occupied my breast, and kept me in one continued state of anguish till the morning. The beauteous form of Clara (for, indeed, she was most beautiful, and innocent as she was beautiful, she was then) never for an instant quitted my imagination; and still I seemed to listen to the music of her voice, and to remark the looks of gratitude which she bestowed upon me when she was made acquainted that I had rescued her from the power of the villains. But could I ever dare hope to inspire her with the same sentiments as those I felt for her? Could I expect to supplant Walter Alston in her affections? and should I not be acting the villain's part in doing so? I shuddered at the thought, but still I could not subdue my feelings. The more I reflected, the more my anguish, my doubts, my perplexity increased, and I continued to traverse the room for hours together, without one idea calculated to inspire hope or impart consolation to my mind, suggesting itself to me. I could not deny the force of the arguments which Herbert had made use of, yet I thought it would be impossible for me to avail myself of them, without at once sacrificing all my hopes.

My heart, as I have before said, revolted from the idea of betraying Clara; to obey the dying injunctions of my father, I could not, at present, make her my wife; and yet, could I see her sacrificed (as my vanity—for by no other name could I designate it—at that time led me to consider it) to a simple rustic? Allow him to carry off the triumph that I might strive for in vain? Oh, never! I thought to myself I would run every risk, of character—everything, rather than that should take place.

I have often since reflected to myself upon the madness of the infatuation which had at that time got such strong hold of me, and I cannot but now despise myself for the vain and selfish motives that must have guided my conduct, although I prided myself so highly upon my honour. Oh, Blanche! how degraded do I now feel myself, and even, though I firmly believe the deceit with which Clara afterwards acted towards me, how keenly do I reproach myself for having suffered my passions to throw temptations in her way that probably might never otherwise have presented themselves to her.

I must do her the justice to say that I believe she was the very soul of innocence and purity when I was first introduced to her, and that she might have been happy with the man who had engaged her affections; but I spurned the advice of my friend Herbert; I courted her favours, instead of avoiding the too powerful attraction of her charms, and by that means was the indirect course of leading to the ultimate destruction of her virtuous principles. It was natural to suppose that a young and educated man should possess more attractions for the mind of the highly cultivated woman, independent of his rank, than the simple rustic, and thus it was that the advice of Herbert was the more valuable, and should have been the more duly appreciated by me.

"I should have shunned the dwelling of Mr. Roseburn, and have avoided the too

dazzling charms of one who was the affianced of another; then would' Clara, in all probability, have been sacred from vice, and I should never have experienced the misery, shame, and remorse which I am at present enduring. But, alas! the impetuosity of my disposition would not suffer me to think of such a thing with any degree of patience.

Such thoughts as these continued to engross my mind till the morning, when I quitted my chamber with the full determination of seeing the lovely object of my reflections at the earliest opportunity. At the same time, I was equally resolved, if I could gain her affections, notwithstanding the dying injunctions of my father, to make her my wife.

It was an early hour when I quitted my apartment, and I did not expect to find any portion of the family risen; I, therefore, made my way to the beautiful park attached to Roslinwold Manor, with the hope of there being allowed to give uninterrupted indulgence to the thoughts which were passing in my mind; but in that idea I was doomed to disappointment, for I found that, early riser as I was, my friend Herbert was there prior to me.

" Ah!" he exclaimed, when he saw me, " I observe, Laurence, from your careworn, I might say, countenance, that Somnus and you have not been upon the most agreeable terms during the night."

" Somnus!" I answered. " I have never once attempted to court his influence; how could I, with the beauteous form that has been floating in my imagination?"

" And yet you must forget her, my dear fellow," said Herbert.

" Forget her!" I repeated—" never! I must first forget myself."

" Romantic nonsense!"

" Herbert," I returned, " I must say that you treat with too much levity the impression which that lovely damsel, Clara Roseburn, has made upon me."

" Indeed I do not," he answered; " on the contrary, I perhaps view with more seriousness than you imagine the sensations it has excited in your breast, from the evil consequences that may result from them; and I take the greatest blame to myself for having been the indirect cause of introducing you to the fair being whose superior charms may be the means of leading you into those errors you would otherwise not have thought of, and which you will afterwards bitterly repent."

" Repent! Can I ever repent loving so amiable, so lovely a creature as Clara Roseburn!"

" Yes; because you may be inspiring her with false hopes—with hopes that can never, by any possibility, be realized."

" And why impossible!"

" Would you make her your wife?"

" Yes."

" And destroy the hopes of the youth to whom her hand is already promised?"

" I would win her heart and hand upon any terms," I replied.

" And disobey the last solemn injunctions of your father?" said Herbert.

I confess that this question staggered me, and that I remained silent for a few seconds, not knowing what reply to make.

" Come, Laurence," remarked my friend, placing his hand upon my shoulder, " you must exercise more manly fortitude in this business, and not allow this too fascinating damsel to lure your better reason from the paths of honour and rectitude. You must forget her in any other character than as some beautiful painting you have seen, but the original of which you can never hope to possess."

" Forget her!" I ejaculated. " By Heaven, never! I could as soon forget mine own existence. Spite of everything, of all the consequences, I would woo her and wed her in an honourable way."

" You cannot do so, when she is the affianced of another, even if you could win her affections. You must not behold her again, Sir Laurence."

" And who shall prevent my doing so?"

" I would *persuade* you not to do so," returned Herbert.

" I must die of sheer despair, were I not."

" Nonsense!" said Herbert ; " you are by far too enthusiastic, my dear friend."

"You underrate the character of my sentiments, Herbert," I replied.

"Indeed I do not, Sir Laurence. I am satisfied that they are sincere, and strictly honourable; but knowing the utter impossibility of their being gratified without the sacrifice of the best interests of your family connexions, and without destroying the hopes and arrangements of Mr. Roseburn, I would have you subdue them, as I have resolved to do the passion with which the beauteous Mirah has inspired me. There are many other females in the world, of equal charms, no doubt, your equals in rank, and disengaged, with whom you may seek an alliance."

"There is not one, be she ever so lovely, or let her station in society be ever so elevated, who can engage my heart's most ardent affections after Clara Roseburn. No, Herbert; no change of place, no distance, no circumstance whatever can banish her from my thoughts."

"But is not her heart already engaged?"

"And who shall dare to rival me in my pretensions?"

"Psha! Laurence; I did not think you capable of such egregious folly."

"You may call it folly if you will, Herbert; but time, I trust, will convince you to the contrary."

"And time, I trust, my dear friend, will also teach you more reason. Here is a damsel with whom you have never spoken but once, whose heart you know to be previously engaged, and more than whose respect you can never hope to gain, whom you confess yourself to be stark-staring mad in love with; at the same time that you know, even were you to win her affections, you are prohibited by your station in society from making her your wife. Reflect—reflect, Sir Laurence, and 1 am convinced that you will see the value of the advice I offer you—namely, to abandon all hopes of possessing the damsel, and to avoid seeing her again, as an innocent enemy to your peace."

"I tell you, Herbert, that to follow your advice, given, I know, in the true spirit of friendship, is utterly impossible," I replied. "To my warm imagination, Clara seems marked out by destiny for me; and not only see her again I will, but that this very day. You can accompany me or not, as you think proper."

"Nay, if such be your determination, my headstrong friend," returned Herbert, with a smile, " I *will* be your companion. I have been the primary cause of leading you into this dilemma, and I should consider myself highly culpable were I not to attend you to its result. But, still, let me advise you to postpone your visit for, at least, a day or two."

In fact, I should become tedious, were I to detail all the particulars of the endeavours of my friend Herbert Clerivalle to stifle the imprudent passion which I had suffered so suddenly to enter my breast; indeed, when I recall to my mind my conduct at that important epoch of my life, I cannot but feel ashamed of it, and to look upon it as very little better than that of an absolute madman; and mad I certainly must have been, or such extravagant ideas could never have entered my breast. I imagined that Clara, even on our first interview, had noticed me with favour; and that impression urged me on to perseverance in those resolutions which proved the ultimate ruin and misery of us both. The knowledge of her being affianced to Walter Alston, accepted by her own choice, ought to have restrained my passions, and caused me to avoid her too dangerous presence. You will thus see, my dearest Blanche, that I do not seek in the least to extenuate my own blind misconduct and infatuation; on the contrary, it has ever since been to me a source of the deepest regret and compunction. Would that I could recall it! From what a weight of care and self-reproach would it relieve me.   *   *   *   *   *   *

Sir Laurence was obliged to pause in his narrative; for his feelings overpowered him. A look from the gentle Blanche (who, much as she regretted the errors of which he had been guilty, deeply sympathised with him in the compunction and consciousness of self-debasement which he now experienced) reassured him, and he continued in the following words:—

I yielded to the persuasions of Herbert, and deferred my second visit to the residence of Mr. Roseburn until the following day; but I must confess that it was with extreme reluctance that I did so, and Clara never, for an instant, quitted my thoughts during the whole interval.

It was not until the evening of the following day that we could find the opportunity I was so anxious for, as visitors to Roslinwold Manor detained us. Mr. Roseburn received us with much cordiality; but I felt uneasy and disappointed on finding that Clara and her cousin were from home. After some trifling conversation with Mr. Roseburn, I took the liberty of inquiring after the health of the two cousins, and expressed my anxiety to know whether or not they had suffered anything particular from the fright which the outrage committed upon them by the ruffians must have occasioned them.

"No, Sir Laurence," answered the old gentleman; "I am happy to say that they have suffered no ill effects from that alarming adventure. They have gone on a visit to the neighbouring village, and will doubtless soon return; but they are perfectly safe, as they are under the protection of honest Walter Alston."

The name went to my heart, and a death-like chill shot through my veins. How I envied the rustic his office; I bit my lips, and could scarcely repress a frown.

"Walter Alston is a worthy young man, I believe?" said Herbert.

"Yes, sir," replied Mr. Roseburn, "he is steady and industrious; I have known him from childhood, and I entertain the highest opinion of his merits, which I need scarcely say, when I inform you, that I have consented to bestow upon him the hand of my darling Clara, and in three months from the present time they are to be united."

Had a dagger been planted in my breast, it could not have imparted greater agony to me than did these observations, and Mr. Roseburn must surely have noticed my emotion.

"Happy man!" I could not help ejaculating, "to have won the heart of so inestimable a treasure."

Mr. Roseburn looked at me with some surprise, and I felt somewhat confused, considering that I had said too much.

"My Clara is a good girl," said the old man, after a pause; "and will make an excellent wife. Walter Alston and her have been companions from the earliest days of childhood, and I know that their love is mutual and ardent, as it is pure and virtuous."

My agitation increased, and I knew not how to keep it concealed from Mr. Roseburn. I could not but curse Walter for his good fortune in my heart, and secretly vowed from that moment that, let whatever might be the consequences, he should not possess her who had so enslaved my affections, that I was prepared to make any sacrifice to secure her. Herbert watched my countenance, and guessed the feelings which were passing in my mind, and he endeavoured by a significant look to restrain me; but I had suffered the charms of Clara to gain such an ascendancy over me, that I had little or no command of myself.

"Walter Alston," I observed, "must be a very fortunate man to gain the affections of such a damsel as your fair niece, sir; for, from what I have seen of her, she is a prize worthy of the highest noble of the land."

"Clara looks only for honour and integrity, sir," returned Mr. Roseburn; "which I am certain that Walter possesses in an eminent degree. She has not the ambition to aspire to wealth and station, which, in themselves, she is well aware, cannot be productive of any real happiness. Humble happiness, in preference to splendid misery, is her choice, and I admire her for it."

I knew not what to say in answer to these just and pointed observations, and Herbert, seeing that the conversation was likely to become too painfully interesting, and fearing that I might commit myself, seized the opportunity to change the subject.

I sat in misery and suspense, and must have appeared very dull and stupid to Mr. Roseburn, for I took but little part in the conversation which followed, and know that I made some very vague replies to the questions that were put to me, for my mind was occupied with other subjects, and I felt vexed, dispirited, and disappointed.

What would I not have given to have been in the situation of Walter Alston! how much I envied him the place he evidently held in the heart of Clara! And only three short months were to elapse before they were to be united. The thought was madness, and I then resolved, in spite of everything, that the union should not take place, but that Clara should either become my mistress or my wife. Yes, possess her I was determined to do, upon any terms; I disregarded the dying injunctions of my father, and even flattered myself that I should be enabled to estrange the affections of Clara from the man to whom they were devoted, and to whom she was betrothed, notwithstanding what Mr. Roseburn had said. I had the vanity to imagine that I had made a most favourable impression upon her, at our first meeting, and, unfortunately for us both, it too soon appeared that I was not wrong in my conjectures. Secluded as the life of Clara had hitherto been, and humble as were the notions that had been instilled into her breast by her uncle, she was still not proof against the temptations of rank, or the delusive pleasures of the world, and thus it was that my triumph became far more sudden and complete than I could have anticipated.

An hour elapsed before Clara and her cousin returned home, and then they were accompanied by Walter Alston.

I scarcely remember in what manner I greeted the fair cousins, but I know that my principal attentions were devoted to Clara, and I did not fail to notice the flushes that suffused her cheeks, and the pleasure which evidently throbbed in her bosom at beholding me again. It flattered my hopes, and encouraged me to persevere, in spite of all the difficulties that presented themselves in my way.

To my imagination, Clara appeared ten times more lovely than when I had first beheld her, and this second interview confirmed the sentiments with which she had inspired me.

Walter Alston was at that time a good looking young man, and more intelligent and better conducted than most persons in his humble station of society usually are; but still I could not endure the idea of such a rustic becoming the husband of so beauteous and accomplished a damsel as Clara, and I determined, at all hazards, and in spite of all consequences, that he should not. I could not but look upon him with a feeling of hatred, and I thought that he observed me with an expression thatnearly approached to jealousy; but it might have been that he felt himself uneasy in the presence of his superiors. However, I have no doubt that he looked for the departure of myself and Herbert with impatience.

I could not but notice the pleasure which Mirah seemed to experience at this visit, and the peculiar glances which she ever and anon cast towards me, although Herbert tried to engage her in conversation. She was less reserved, and of a far more vivacious turn of mind than her cousin; but yet, great as was her beauty and accomplishments, how inferior did they appear in my eye, when compared with those of Clara. Unfortunate girl! she had suffered the insidious poison to steal into her breast, and I afterwards understood, she loved me from the first moment she saw me. I may appear here very egotistical in thus speaking of the impression I made upon both the cousins, but I assure you that I am guided by no such feeling, but from an earnest desire to speak the truth, and to give the candid explanation of my conduct which I promised you on the commencement of my narrative.

As it was getting late, we could not prolong our visit long after the return of Clara and her companions, and I observed the pleasure which Walter evinced on seeing us arise to depart. He had joined but little in the conversation, which no doubt proceeded more from jealousy than timidity or bashfulness; and every now and then I had caught him eyeing me with no very pleasurable expression of countenance.

On taking our leave, Mr. Roseburn did not receive our promise to do ourselves the pleasure of visiting him again with that degree of warmth which I could have wished; but there was a certain expression in the countenance of Clara when I bade her adieu, which added fire to my hope, and encouraged me to proceed in the accomplishment of my wishes, at the same time that I could perceive that Walter Alston knitted his brows, and evinced other signs of dissatisfaction. But I heeded him not; I treated him with contempt, as one who was beneath my notice, and whose influence over the affections of Clara I had already impaired, and was determined ultimately to destroy entirely.

Oh, Blanche, what shame do I now experience, that I should ever have suffered such despicable, such degrading feelings to enter my breast; but such was the ardour, the impetuosity of my passion, that it seemed to have worked a complete revolution in my nature, and to have blinded me to those sentiments of honour and reason, which had hitherto guided my conduct. I cannot attempt to deny that I acted a base part towards Walter, and, by blighting his hopes, plunged him into that career of vice which afterwards brought him to shame and ruin. I have ever since bitterly upbraided myself for having thus acted, and must continue to do so, and surely I have been most severely punished for having thus committed myself. Had I taken the advice of my friend Herbert Clerivalle, all these misfortunes would never have happened."

" But do you believe that Walter Alston and his father were really guilty of the crime of which they were afterwards convicted?" inquired Blanche.

"Oh, yes," answered the baronet, " or I would never have given the evidence I did on their trial. I was not influenced by any vindictive feelings towards them, for at that time Clara was my wife, and therefore I had no further occasion to view Walter with an eye of jealousy. But to continue my narrative.

As we returned home, I became more enthusiastic in my praises of Clara than ever, and the language I made use of on the occasion was most extravagant, and which I never bring to my recollection without shame and regret.

"Sir Laurence," observed Herbert, "I am really astonished at your observations. That you should have allowed Clara to take such a powerful hold upon your feelings in so short a space of time, and considering the difference of your stations, and, moreover, that her affections were devoted to another, to whom her hand is also promised, is most remarkable. I cannot believe that you can wish to blight the hopes of Walter Alston, who seems to be in every respect worthy of the love of Clara."

"I say again, Herbert," I impatiently replied, "that I cannot, I will not endure the thought of Clara being sacrificed to such a rustic as Walter Alston."

"Is it not with her own free will, and by the consent of her guardian?"

"I care not."

"And what use is it for you to entertain such thoughts? You cannot, if you have the will, prevent their marriage."

"But I will do so."

"This is madness."

"Call it what you please, Herbert," I returned; "such is nevertheless my determination."

"Psha! if you could ever hope to supplant Walter in her affections," said my friend, "which it does not appear at all probable to me that you are likely to do, you may depend upon it that Mr. Roseburn is too honourable a man to break his word to the young man, and you hear that in three months time he is to lead Clara to the hymeneal altar."

"By all my hopes, that shall never be!" I exclaimed, vehemently; "even though I cannot obtain the love of Clara, she shall never become the wife of Walter Alston."

"Why, any one, to hear you talk, Sir Lawrence, would certainly think that you had taken leave of your senses. But you will think better of this; and, as the charms of Clara Roseburn possess too powerful an attraction for you, you would only act with reason and prudence were you to take my advice, and refrain from visiting the residence of the amiable cousins again."

"How easy it is for you to advise, Herbert," I replied; "but I feel that it is utterly impossible for me to follow it. I must and will visit the house again, and I will never rest until I have achieved my wishes, extravagant as they may now appear to be. I do not despair, believe me; I watched the looks of Clara narrowly, and I am much mistaken if I have not already made a favourable impression upon her."

"Mere imagination, my dear fellow; I can scarcely resist laughing at such absurdity."

"Indeed it is not mere imagination, Herbert, although you may think it so," I returned; "and is there anything improbable in such a circumstance?"

"Very, I think," replied Herbert. "Besides, even if you should succeed in luring the affections of Clara from Walter Alston, what would be the future course you would adopt?"

"Make her my wife," I replied. "It is to that alone my ambition soars."

"Make her your wife! Impossible!"

"And why so?"

"Mr. Roseburn would never give his consent."

"And that should not prevent me, if Clara herself was willing."

"But can you entertain such an opinion of Clara," demanded Herbert, "as to believe that she could be induced to act contrary to the wishes of that kind guardian who has ever acted towards her with the affection of a parent? Oh, it would be most cruel and ungrateful in her were she to act so. Besides, you must certainly have more respect for the memory of your father than to disobey his solemn injunctions."

"I have every respect for my late father's memory," I replied; "but still I cannot hold such an extravagant demand as binding."

"But then consider the difference of your stations."

"Nonsense!" ejaculated I, impatiently; "what care I for rank or station? Has not Clara charms intrinsic and external far beyond all wealth? By Heaven! if she were even a beggar, I would sooner become her husband than that of a princess."

"I see that it is useless to argue with you," remarked Herbert, "while you are in this state of mind; but I hope you will reflect more seriously upon the subject, and see in time, before it effects further mischief, the folly of such conduct, and the dishonour of entertaining such ideas."

"Dishonour!" I repeated.

"Yes; the word may sound harsh, but it is nevertheless a proper one. Would it not be most dishonourable to lure the affections of this amiable damsel from the man upon whom they are fixed, and to whom her hand is engaged, and to destroy the harmony which at present exists between her and her guardian? But you will banish these thoughts from your mind, I am certain you will; and, by avoiding the presence of Clara in future, prevent the occurrence of those evils which I apprehend."

"Avoid her presence! oh, no, I cannot;—I am wretched while she is out of my sight."

"But you must have observed that Mr. Roseburn received our promise to visit him again very coldly," said Herbert.

"No matter; nothing can restrain me in the prosecution of my wishes."

"I am sorry to hear it, and deeply do I reproach myself for having ever mentioned the names of the two lovely cousins to you."

"You have nothing to reproach yourself with, Herbert," I observed; "I am master of my own conduct, and even if you had not described Clara to me, accident might have revealed her to me, and the effect would have been the same."

"But like myself, Laurence," replied Herbert, "you are young, and have seen but little of the world; and may there not be another damsel whom you may behold, whom you can love as ardently as you profess to do Clara, and to whom you can pay your addresses without compromising your honour, or sacrificing your interests?"

"Oh, never!" I answered fervently; "there is not, I am certain, that being in existence, whom I can ever love as I do Clara. To possess her, I would sacrifice fortune, friends, everything; and were I certain that I could never win her affections in return, life would no longer possess any charms for me; in fact, it would become insupportable to me!"

"What a strange infatuation is this, Sir Laurence; and how deeply do I lament it."

"I am obliged to you for your good wishes, Herbert," I answered; "and well know and duly appreciate the sincerity and value of your friendship. But I cannot avail myself of your advice, and must persevere in my endeavours to win the affections and the hand of Clara, in spite of whatever consequences may ensue."

"Well, my friend, then it is useless for me to argue further, although I sincerely wish that you and Clara had never met. Even should you win the affections of the maiden from Walter Alston, of what else can it be productive than the greatest misery to you both, since you must feel convinced that you have for ever ruined the hopes and prospects of a worthy young man, and probably incurred the resentment of that aged, and generous man who has been her protector from childhood."

See p. 291.

"Surely, Mr. Roseburn cannot be so blind to the future interest of his niece," I remarked, "as to refuse his consent to her alliance with me, in preference to the lowly peasant, Walter; especially if her heart accompany her hand? As for Walter, I would establish him in a farm of his own, and no doubt he would soon be content to bind his lot with some other damsel."

No. 37.

"Place yourself in his situation," said Herbert, "and ask yourself whether you could be content to relinquish all your fondest hopes and expectations so coolly."

This query, I admit, confused me, and I knew not how to answer.

"I see, Herbert," I at length said, "that you and I shall never agree upon this point, and therefore it is only a waste of time to argue the matter further. To resign all hopes of Clara I find to be utterly impossible; but, depend upon it, my intentions towards her are strictly honourable and virtuous."

"Pardon me, Laurence," he replied, "but they cannot be so, when the heart of Clara Roseburn is previously engaged, and the time is even appointed for her nuptials."

"They shall never take place with Walter Alston," I said, determinedly.

"What folly it is to talk thus, Sir Laurence; I am really surprised at you."

"I care not by what name you call it, Herbert, but I am fully determined, and I firmly believe that I shall succeed in the accomplishment of my wishes."

"Certainly, my dear fellow, this displays a vanity that I thought you were incapable of."

I made no answer to this, for we had now arrived at Roslinwold Manor, and not being in the humour for further conversation, I excused myself to Herbert and his relations, and retired to my chamber, in order to indulge in my own thoughts alone. What these thoughts were it is needless for me to describe minutely, as you may form a pretty shrewd guess of their nature. But Herbert had truly charged me with vanity, which must have principally guided my conduct, and I have, ever since, never recalled it to my memory without shame and disgust.

The more I thought of Clara (and her image was constantly present to my mind's eye), the more powerful became the impression she had made upon my heart, and the stronger became my determination to persist in my designs. I repeated every observation she had made use of during our interview, and remembered the peculiar glances she had at different times fixed upon me, and more strongly convinced than ever was I that I had made a favourable impression upon her.

"Oh, yes," I ejaculated, "those crimson blushes, that tremulous voice, that throbbing bosom, revealed the tender secret, and adds fire to my hopes. Dear Clara, to gain your love, what sacrifices would I not make! Honour would prompt me, as my friend Herbert has suggested, to avoid her, but can I thus easily discard my hopes? Must I wait patiently, and see her become the bride of another? By Heaven, never! To witness such a sacrifice would be worse than a thousand deaths to me; and it will not even bear the slightest contemplation. Clara shall be mine, or never shall she become the wife of another man."

I slept but little during that night, and when I did, my imagination was haunted by the most troublesome dreams. I arose at an early hour of the morning, and met the family at breakfast with a haggard and careworn countenance. I requested Herbert to accompany me in a walk, but he pleaded a prior engagement as an excuse, and disappeared; I therefore left the house alone. I saw clearly enough that Herbert had only excused himself from my society, lest I should wish him to accompany me on another visit to the residence of Mr. Roseburn, and anxious although I was, I could not think of obtruding myself alone, and I was fearful, too, that Mr. Roseburn would think me bold, and begin to suspect me, and thus my plans would be frustrated at the outset. I, however, bent my steps in the direction of the house, and my mind continued to dwell upon the numerous charms and accomplishments of Clara, and to endeavour to devise some means of ingratiating myself in her favour, and of supplanting Walter, towards whom I could not help entertaining a feeling approaching to hatred.

"Were it not for him," I muttered to myself, "I should probably find but little, if any, obstacle in the way of the accomplishment of my wishes, and I could make my advances towards her without any hesitation; but still I must not suffer him to triumph; I must and will destroy the influence he at present possesses over Clara. Honest and worthy although he may be, he must not be permitted to carry off so bright, so invaluable a treasure, to bury it for ever in obscurity and indigence."

I walked on, wrapt in these reflections, and at length arrived to within a few yards of the house. I gazed towards it with eager eyes, and longed but in vain to obtain a glimpse of the beauteous object of my thoughts, although her form was presented as distinctly to my imagination as if she stood before me. With feelings of rapture I viewed the flowers which I believed to have been planted by her hand, and eagerly I plucked a rose from a tree which grew near the palings that inclosed the garden, and I placed it carefully in my bosom, after having pressed its odorous leaves again and again, with the most extravagant transport, to my lips. Indeed, any one who had seen me at that time, must have thought that I had taken leave of my senses; and, indeed, my conduct was more that of a madman than anything else.

I walked round the house, and looked up at all the windows, but I could see nothing of Clara and her cousin, and I felt vexed and disappointed, although, if I had been seen, my behaviour must have been thought singular and suspicious.

Two or three times I was partly tempted to venture to the house; but a fear of offending, restrained me, although I found it impossible to move from the spot. Everything about the place possessed an indescribable charm to me, and I could have occupied my mind for hours in their contemplation; but an adventure was about to occur to me, which I deem it necessary to relate.

While I thus stood, I was astonished on hearing my name repeated by some person from behind me, and, turning round, I beheld a woman, about the middle age, and from whose complexion and features I knew to be a gipsy, gazing intently upon me.

"Who are you, woman, and how have you become acquainted with my name?" I demanded.

"How do I know you, Sir Laurence Cleveland?" replied the woman; "what is there with which I am unacquainted? I can tell of things past, present, and to come. Would you have me open to you the book of fate?"

"Psha!" I ejaculated impatiently, and throwing her a piece of money; "reserve your wondrous prognostications for those whose heads are weak enough to believe in them, and begone; I have something else to occupy my thoughts."

"I know you have, Sir Laurence Cleveland," said the gipsy; "shall I prove that power you affect to despise, by telling you what they are?"

"Do not trouble me with your idle nonsense, woman," I ejaculated; "and go your ways."

"Indeed! but even the thoughts of the fair Clara Roseburn, which at present engage your mind, need not prevent you from bestowing some little attention for a few minutes on the gipsy sybil."

I started in amazement at these words, and stared at the woman with searching eyes, and without being able to utter a syllable.

"Does not the gipsy sybil speak the truth, Sir Laurence?" she continued. "You love the damsel, and would fain supplant Walter Alston in her affections."

" Strange being," I cried, " by what means have you acquired this knowledge ?"

" Have I not spoken the truth ? Nay, more, I will tell you that the damsel will love you in return ; and that for your sake she will banish Walter Alston from her heart, and, in disobedience to the will of her uncle, become your wife."

" Mysterious woman," I exclaimed ; " can I place confidence in your strange predictions ? But no ; I am ashamed of myself for allowing this weakness even for a moment to take possession of my reason. Begone, and trouble me no further."

" Believe them or believe them not," returned the woman, " they will be fulfilled. But a sorrowful day it will be for you and Clara when you become united, and will be the cause of misery, shame, and endless care to you both. Such do I prophesy, Sir Laurence Cleveland, and as surely will those prophecies be realised, as that you now draw the breath of life. Mark my words, and farewell !"

" Stay, mysterious woman ; do not leave me thus," I exclaimed ; but, regardless of my supplications, she darted hastily from me, and plunging into the wood, was out of sight in an instant.

For some moments after she was gone, I stood petrified to the spot with amazement, and I could not form the least conjecture as to how she had thus become acquainted with my thoughts and wishes. In spite of all my efforts to the contrary, this adventure made the most powerful impression upon me, and I have frequently thought of her prognostications since, so painfully as they have been verified."

" It was certainly most singular," remarked Amanda ; " but might not the woman have been employed by your friend, Herbert, in order to banish your wishes as regarded Clara ?"

" Oh, no," replied the baronet ; " that idea occurred to me ; but still, after mature reflection, I could not bring myself to believe that Herbert would descend to any such an artifice."

" I cannot comprehend it at all," said Blanche ; " but did you ever behold the gipsy woman again ?"

" Never," answered her husband ; " although I have frequently endeavoured to discover her."

" And did you mention the circumstance to your friend ?" asked Amanda.

" I did," replied Sir Laurence, " as soon as I returned to the manor, and expressed the utmost surprise, and could scarce believe it.

" However, Sir Lawrence," he remarked, " whether there be any truth or not he in the predictions of this woman, which it would be absurd to believe there is, the warning she has given to you is not, in my opinion, to be despised, and I think the advice conveyed in it is very excellent. Most undoubtedly, if you should succeed in making Clara Roseburn your wife, it cannot but be productive of misery to you both."

" Misery with Clara !" I repeated ; " oh, impossible ! Let me but possess her heart and hand, and my happiness will be complete ; but without her, life will be no longer endurable."

" Strange infatuation !" said Herbert. " Will nothing drive it from thy brain ?"

" I cannot—dare not resign my hopes of possessing her."

" Try what change of scene and society will effect."

" It is useless, Herbert ; for absence from the neighbourhood of that too captivating girl would only add to my misery. Think you that I could endure the thought that while I was away, she would bestow her hand upon Walter Alston ?"

" And yet, what madness is it in you to think you can prevent it. Come—come,

Sir Laurence, be a little more reasonable, and I am certain that your good sense and honourable feelings will induce you to banish such wild ideas from your mind."

"No, Herbert, my resolution is fixed."

"Then I must candidly tell you, that I cannot think of lending you any assistance in the furtherance of designs of which I so highly disapprove."

"Be it so,' I returned; "but nevertheless, in spite of all the difficulties in my way, nothing shall daunt me. Clara is a prize worth any trouble to obtain possession of."

Herbert returned no answer to this, and we soon afterwards separated.

I continued in the most agitated state of mind for two or three days after this, and I could not prevail upon Herbert to accompany me in another visit to the house of Mr. Roseburn, nor, in all my rambles near the dwelling, could I catch a glance of either of the lovely cousins, neither could I muster courage to call myself. I reflected deeply on the adventure with the gipsy woman, and it filled me with a variety of conjectures and painful thoughts; but I saw no more of her, and was unable to come to any satisfactory conclusion upon the subject.

At length my impatience became beyond endurance, and I resolved, at all hazards, to visit Mr. Roseburn by myself.

I walked two or three times round the house, however, before I ventured to knock, and my heart palpitated violently, to know what kind of a reception I should meet with.

In a few minutes my eyes were again captivated with the sight of Clara, who opened the door to me, and I could see by the agitation of her manner, and the soft blushes that suffused her cheeks, that my visit was far from being an unwelcome one to her; and this idea imparted a sensation of transport to my breast, which I need not attempt to describe. Mirah, also, seemed to behold me with equal pleasure, and there was a peculiar expression in her countenance which I could not help remarking.

Mr. Roseburn received me with formal politeness, but I could plainly perceive that it was not with the same warmth of feeling that he had done on the first occasion. He inquired after my friend, and said that the intimacy of myself and Herbert was an honour which he had never expected.

"And the pleasure of your society, my dear sir," I returned, "is a gratification which I trust I shall be able to prove I am worthy of."

"But do you intend to remain much longer in this neighbourhood, Sir Laurence?" inquired Mr. Roseburn.

I caught the eye of Clara eagerly fixed upon me when this question was put to me, and I could not help thinking that she seemed anxious to hear my answer.

"Why, sir," I replied, "I have not fixed any time for my return to Branscombe House at present; but I am so delighted with the scenery around, and the hospitality of my friends, that I shall, probably, remain here for some weeks to come. By-the-bye, there is to be a fete next Monday, at Roslinwold Manor, to celebrate the birth-day of Herbert Clerivalle, and I am certain that my friends would feel great pleasure in seeing you and your fair nieces among the guests."

The eyes of Clara became more than usually animated, and it was clear that she awaited the answer of her guardian with anxiety.

"Excuse me, Sir Laurence," said the old gentleman, at length; "but I must decline the honour you offer me."

"Oh, pray, my dear sir, do not say so," I ejaculated; "for I am certain that my friend Herbert will be greatly disappointed if you do not accept the invitation. Try what your sweet powers of persuasion can do, Miss Clara, and Miss Mirah."

Clara blushed more deeply, but returned no answer; but, to judge from Mr. Roseburn's expression of countenance, he was far from being pleased with my familiarity.

"And my nieces are unused to society, Sir Laurence," said Mr. Roseburn, " and should cut but sorry figures in a scene of festivity; I must again beg leave to decline the invitation."

" But, indeed, sir, I must continue to press you," I returned.

Clara and Mirah now looked more anxiously in their uncle's face, and he seemed to understand their thoughts, for he said,—

" Well, well, since you are so pressing, and I am half inclined to believe that my dear girls would like the recreation, I will consent to step out of my regular course for once in a way, and do consent."

" Thanks, my dear sir," I exclaimed, with a feeling of pleasure which I could not conceal; " I am certain that you and your amiable relations will be delighted at their reception, and the amusements that will be got up on the occasion."

" It may amuse them, Sir Laurence; but the time has gone by for me to feel any relish for such entertainments; however, you will do me the favour to return my acknowledgments to Squire Clerivalle for the honour he has done me.

" Most certainly, sir," I replied; " and most happy shall I be to do so. As I before said, you will find everything conducted there on the most innocent and rational principle. It is the wish of Mr. Clerivalle to entertain all his neighbours and tenants on that auspicious occasion, whatever their station in society; and I am certain it will afford you and your amiable nieces much more recreation than you probably now anticipate."

The fact is, that Mr. Clerivalle, senior, always having heard the characters of Mr. Roseburn and his nieces spoken of in the most praiseworthy manner, had expressed a wish that they should be invited to become participators in the entertainments got up on the occasion, and Herbert had indirectly promised to forward the invitation; but I saw plain enough that he would rather decline doing so, fearful, no doubt, that it would afford too great an encouragement to the fatal passion which Clara had excited in my breast.

I need not attempt to describe the pleasure and satisfaction with which the success of my plans so far inspired me. I should see Clara again in the midst of pleasure and excitement; I should be permitted to feast my eyes on her charms, and that was an enjoyment I had never hoped so soon to be allowed to indulge in. And then, as I have before stated, I had observed the pleasure with which she received the invitation, the joy which sparkled in her eyes, the soft and delicate, yet expressive confusion of her manner while in my presence, and I augured from it every success to my wishes. Honour should have restrained my passion, when I thought of the connexion which existed between her and Walter Alston; but, alas! I was completely blinded by the infatuation of my own sentiments, and was determined, in spite of the prudent watchfulness and reserve of Mr. Roseburn, that nothing should prove an obstacle to me in the way of my accomplishing them.

After some other conversation, of no particular importance, I took my leave, and caught the eyes of Clara at parting, and could not help thinking that they beamed with an expression of encouragement and pleasure; but it might have been that it was only vanity, and the warmth of the sentiments I had suffered to take possession of my breast that deceived me; however, I indulged in the flattering idea all the way as I proceeded home.

"She is mine! I am determined she shall be so," I soliloquised; "I will suffer no obstacle to stand in the way of my possession of her whom I do so much prize. She become the bride of a clown like Walter Alston! Never! Such a sacrifice I cannot bear even to contemplate with any degree of patience. But yet the time appointed for their nuptials is very brief, and I must be prompt, or I shall yet be foiled. Before many days have elapsed I must contrive to gain an interview with Clara, and make her acquainted with the sentiments she has engendered in my breast, for it will be utterly impossible for me to wait any longer in this state of suspense. Would to Heaven that I were rid of Walter; for old Roseburn is so prejudiced in his favour, that nothing whatever can induce him to break his promise with him, and I can see that he already begins to view me with some degree of suspicion, and would fain decline my too frequent visits. But I must not allow this to dishearten me. Oh, no; Clara is a prize too rare and precious for me not to persist in contending for her to the last; and something flatters me, and that strongly, too, that my efforts will be crowned with success."

Thus did I give way to the indulgence of the feelings and the hopes with which Clara had inspired me, as I proceeded on my way to Roslinwold Manor; and indeed, my dearest Blanche, I trust that you will believe me when I assure you that it is with heartfelt pangs of shame and remorse that I acknowledge to them now, when the confession must so shock your ears; but I have promised that I will keep nothing concealed from you, and I will keep my word, however hurtful it will be to my feelings, and however much it may change your sentiments towards me. * *

Blanche sighed deeply, and tears came to her eyes, but they were called forth by feelings more of regret than reproach; and she extended her hand to her husband, which he pressed fervently to his lips, and for some moments the power of his feelings choked his utterance.

"Thanks—thanks, my beloved Blanche, for this," he said at length. "Oh, unworthy do I feel myself of it, and how doubly do I repent ever having been the cause of one single pang to your gentle bosom. But, alas! the actions of the past cannot be recalled, and I can only by the sincerity of my future conduct make atonement."

"You are penitent, Laurence," returned Blanche, looking affectionately in his face; "I believe you are, and, therefore, do I forgive you; for it was shame, I must consider, that alone prevented you from before revealing to me your secrets. There is but one fearful doubt that tortures me, and fills me with the most dreadful apprehensions."

"And what is that, my dearest Blanche?" eagerly inquired Sir Laurence Cleveland.

"The doubt whether or not Clara is still in existence," replied Blanche.

"Oh! no; it is impossible," said Sir Laurence. "Do not suffer such an idea to torture your mind for a moment; reason and facts are opposed to it. It is all a diabolical invention, springing out of the deadly feelings of revenge which the gipsies entertain towards you and me. Again I state, the wretched and misguided women perished by her own hands. Had she been really still living, she would have come forward ere this, to prove the truth of the first charge which Harold brought against me; but, certainly, I take the greatest blame to myself for having, in the first in-stance, lured her affections from the man on whom they were placed, and for having led her to act in disobedience to the will of that man who had ever acted towards her with all the affection of a father. But youth, and an impetuous disposition, added to the numerous attractions which she possessed, led me on, and would not suffer me to reflect seriously, when, by doing so, I might have avoided all the misery and dis-grace which afterwards followed."

" But her offspring; should that survive, Laurence ?"

" It is no offspring of mine, but a proof of her infidelity," answered the baronet, passionately.

" Alas! poor little innocent," said Blanche, feelingly; " why should it have to suf-fer for the faults of its unhappy mother? Better for it that it should rest in the silent grave; but, should it really be discovered to be living, I could never have the heart to treat it with scorn or indignity; and I am certain that you could not, Lau-rence, however much you might be prejudiced against it for the uncertainty of its origin."

" True, my love," answered Sir Laurence. " You only do me justice, by enter-taining such an opinion. But let us hope that the child, if Clara indeed bore an off-spring, perished in its infancy; for, left as it was, it could only be exposed to misery crime, and shame. But to continue my narrative.

I returned to Roslinwold Manor, and met Herbert soon after my arrival. He could see by my countenance that I had met with something to please me.

" Well, Sir Laurence," he remarked, "it seems that my society is not so agree-able to you as it once was; since you have taken it into your head to wander forth alone."

" Indeed, my dear friend," I answered, "you mistake me; your society is just as pleasant and as welcome to me as ever; only latterly you have become so much the sage and the moralist, that I can scarcely persuade myself it is the same Herbert Clerivalle I once knew."

" If I have become the sage, Cleveland," returned Herbert, "it is merely to offer you what I presume to be good advice, in endeavouring to persuade you to stifle a passion you can never hope to gratify, and which can only be productive of misery to you and the fair object of it."

" You are very kind, Herbert, and I know well the strict feeling of friendship that prompts your observations; but indeed I cannot conquer the passion with which the lovely Clara has inspired me; and the more I reflect on her, the more powerful becomes that sentiment in my bosom. But I have seen her again."

" Ah !"

" Yes; I have once more had the felicity of gazing upon her."

" Is it possible that you have had the resolution to visit her residence?" inquired Herbert.

" It is no less possible than true, my friend; both her and Mirah received me with smiles."

" You flatter yourself too warmly, Laurence; but, again I say that you would act with more prudence were you to resist such dangerous temptations. It cannot but be destructive of your peace, and that of Clara and her friends."

" I trust not," returned I; " for it is my fervent hope to contribute only to their happiness and prosperity."

"And you are not destroying the hopes of a worthy young man like Walter Alston?"

"He is not a fair match for Clara Roseburn; besides, I can make him ample compensation for his loss, and no doubt he will soon find a suitable wife among the rustic damsels of the village. If he really love the damsel, he will not stand in the way of her future fortune."

"Psha!" returned Herbert, impatiently; "this is talking preposterously. What can be a sufficient compensation to Walter Alston for the loss of such a damsel as Clara Roseburn? There can be nothing on earth to justify such conduct, especially now that Walter and Clara are already betrothed. Besides, as I have before often observed, if you should even succeed in captivating the maiden's heart, which I do not believe is at all likely, do you think that Mr. Roseburn would ever dishonourably break his word with Walter Alston, and give his consent to your paying your addresses to his niece."

" Well, if you please, Herbert, we will argue that subject no further at present."

" And how did Mr. Roseburn receive you?" inquired Herbert.

" Why, I certainly have no cause to complain, and he has even consented to be present, with his fair nieces, at the festivities which are to take place on the anniversary of your birthday on Monday next."

" Indeed!"

" Yes, I took the liberty of inviting them, as I knew it was the wish of your honoured father."

" And did Mr. Roseburn readily accept the invitation?" demanded Herbert.

" Why, no," I answered; " I must admit that he did not. He pleaded his age, and the secluded life he had hitherto led, as an excuse for his not joining in such festivities; but he could see plain enough, by the looks of Clara and Mirah, that they wished to be present, and he, therefore, yielded."

" Well," observed Herbert, " much as I should wish the cousins to honour the festivities by their presence, I would rather, under all the circumstances, that they had not come. It will only be adding to the temptation that has already been thrown out to you, and may be the cause of many evils to you."

" What a strange being you are, Herbert," I remarked.

" I may appear so, Sir Laurence; but I only speak for your good, and that of Clara and her friends. Nothing good can come of this misplaced attachment, and you would show both firmness and prudence by at once subduing it."

" I am sorry that you and I should disagree upon this point, which is so important to me," I remarked; " but I trust that you will see the matter in a different light to that which you do at present."

" That I can never do," returned Herbert; " for reason is opposed to your encouraging so hopeless, so dangerous, and, I must add, dishonourable a passion."

" Dishonourable, Herbert?"

" Yes; it cannot be otherwise when Clara is already, of her own free will, betrothed to Walter Alston. But, come, come, you must, after all, think better upon this subject."

" I am afraid that I shall never think otherwise than I do now."

Herbert shook his head, and, for the present, the conversation ended. My thoughts were now all elate at the prospect of so soon again beholding Clara, and under such favourable circumstances, and I looked forward to the arrival of the following Monday with the greatest impatience, for I hoped then to enjoy the conversation of her who had so enslaved my senses, and who would appear doubly charming, enlivened as she would naturally be by the festivities of the occasion.

The preparations that were making for that joyous occasion were on the most extensive and magnificent scale; and a general invitation was sent to all around, both rich and poor.

" I have before observed that Mr. Clerivalle was a gentleman of the most hospitable disposition, and he was determined that nothing should be wanting on his part to afford gratification to the numerous guests, which he anticipated would be present.

Every room in the spacious mansion was called into requisition, and splendidly decorated with rich hangings, and all the other paraphernalia of grandeur. The gardens too, were laid out in magnificent style, and, in short, everything that taste could suggest, or wealth and munificence could supply, were called into requisition for the festival.

My thoughts were fully occupied with the most joyous anticipations, till the time arrived, and they even haunted my imagination in my dreams at night.

I was anxious again to visit the residence of Mr. Roseburn previous to the day of the festivities, but I could not find resolution to do so, lest Mr. Roseburn should think me too obtrusive, and alter his mind; and I therefore endeavoured to satisfy myself by imagining all sorts of sweet things, which I would say to the lively occupier of my thoughts, and flattered myself that I should on that auspicious occasion succeed in making some impression on her. Vain fool that I must have been to have entertained such an idea for a moment, especially when honour forbade it, as she was already the affianced bride of another. But I must have been goaded on by a species of madness, for which I cannot now even account. The bare thought of Walter Alston possessing the affections of Clara, filled my bosom with the most ungovernable rage, and I feel ashamed to own it, that I cursed him in my heart, although I really believe that Walter was, at that time, a worthy young man.

When we suffer an imprudent passion to take possession of our minds, into what strange and unaccountable acts may we not be tempted; acts which we should never before thought ourselves capable of performing. And thus it was with me; I was so completely infatuated, that I never gave myself time to reflect, or I must have seen through the folly and injustice of my conduct, and been thoroughly ashamed of myself. But, it seems, it was to be my fate, to plunge into the disgrace and misery which, had I taken the advice of Herbert, I might have avoided, and better cause have I since had to repent of it.

At length the important day arrived, and it was ushered in with all those sounds of mirth and enjoyment, which the most sanguine and vivacious mind could have anticipated. No sooner had the sun darted his first golden rays in at my chamber window, than I arose, having slept but little during the night, and immediately repaired, with the assistance of my *valet de chambre*, to the duties of my toilette. Never before had I taken such pains in the decoration of my person; and, when I recall that circumstance to my memory, I despise myself for my consummate folly and vanity.

The moments seemed like seconds to me, until the guests began to assemble; but how much more impatiently did I await the arrival of Mr. Roseburn and his two charming nieces. But at length that long-expected moment came, and I again beheld Clara, but a feeling of sad disappointment and vexation passed through my mind, when I saw that she was accompanied by Walter Alston, as well as her uncle and Mirah.

I could scarcely help giving expression to my feelings, but I stifled them as well as I could, lest they should meet their observation; but I must acknowledge, and I do it with shame and remorse, that I could at that time have committed any outrage upon the innocent cause of my wrath. And he viewed, or I fancied he viewed me with an eye of jealousy. Whenever I attempted to make any advances upon the conversation of her who enclosed my heart, a dark frown sat upon his brows, and he took every possible means, I am certain, to thwart me in my object.

Mr. Roseburn, too, was grave and sedate; and, while he allowed his two nieces to enter into the festivities of the occasion, he took especial care to lose not sight of them, or to permit them to share my conversation alone.

In consequence of this, the day which I had marked out to myself as one of supreme bliss, passed off remarkably dull, with the exception of the occasional glances exchanged between me and Clara; for I could see that I had made a favourable impression upon her, and determined to follow up the advantage I had thus gained. Whenever her eye met mine, a crimson blush suffused her cheek, and I could perceive that she rested not easily upon the arm of her rustic swain.

Herbert, too, pursued me, like my annoying sprite, and whenever I had an opportunity of addressing my conversation to Clara, he was ready with himself and friends to attract me another way, and it was so cleverly managed, that I could not even appear to feel displeased, or to object to the interruption.

The banquet was over; the ball commenced; fortune smiled on me. Mr. Roseburn and Walter were by some means drawn away from their companions; the two lovely cousins were alone. I requested the hand of Clara in the dance; Herbert, who was by my side, that of Mirah; with blushing timidity they were accepted, and through the graceful movements of the dance we passed.

Need I say what transport filled my breast at that moment? Never had I experienced such felicity before. Clara, I thought, moved through the moves of the dance with the grace of ten thousand nymphs, and I had the opportunity, the blissful opportunity I had so much sought for, for which I would have, at that time, laid down my very life, of whispering soft words in her ear. What replies she made I recollect not, but there was sufficient in them, and the expression of her eyes, to convince me that my advances were not disagreeable to her.

Before the dance was concluded; Mr. Roseburn and Walter Alston entered the room. Clara became confused, suddenly relinquished the hand I held, and before I could offer an observation retired from the dance and joined her uncle and lover; the former beckoned to Mirah, and they abruptly left the saloon.

I must confess that I was completely astonished, and stood like a fool, until Herbert placed his hand on my shoulder, and observed,—

"Now, Sir Laurence, what think you of your fair inamorato? Do you not agree with me in beliving that you have made a most consummate fool of yourself? The bumpkin will prove more than a match for you, after all; mark my words he will."

"Herbert," I replied, with a look of anger, "this is no joking subject. By all my hopes, I will not thus be foiled. They have not left the mansion, surely."

"It strikes me rather forcibly that they have," said Herbert. "And if they have not, you certainly would not further thrust your society upon the damsel, when you have thus received from her guardian the cut direct?"

"I will see her if she is near the mansion," I returned passionately; "and not only see her, but speak to her, in spite of the Argus eyes of her prudish old uncle and the clown who has the presumption to aspire to her hand."

"Nonsense!" ejaculated Herbert. "Are there not other maidens equally fair and worthy in this beauteous galaxy to attract the attention of my amorous friend? See! Lady Clarissa Melrose."

"Confound Lady Clarissa Melrose," I interrupted, with a burst of passion, scarcely knowing what I said or did, and I rushed from the room.

I flew all over the ante-apartments with the air of a madman; I searched among the throng of smiling, beauteous guests that filled the mansion on that joyous occasion, but in vain did I seek her who had so infatuated my senses. She was gone, and with her the only charm that the festivities presented to my imagination.

I walked into the gardens. All was hilarity and splendour; but I moved like a spectre amid the happy throng. Their very mirth was full of misery to me. I could in my heart have cursed them for being so happy when I was wretched.

I walked from the house, and only seemed to breathe when I got away from the festive sounds. But why should Mr. Roseburn thus abruptly withdraw his nieces from the scene? was a question that I put to myself. Was there anything so offensive in my conduct? Had I committed myself in any shape? I knew not that I had done so; and to me, therefore, his behaviour seemed to be altogether uncouth, unreasonable, and inexplicable. It was grossly insulting to Mr. Clerivalle, I considered, as well as pointedly offensive to me. I was determined to have an explanation, let it cost me what it might.

These were my thoughts, when I felt a hand upon my arm, and, turning round, beheld Herbert by my side.

"Where are you going in such a hurry, my dear fellow?" he said. "You surely are not going to leave all our worthy friends without the benefit of your society?"

"I go to seek an explanation from Mr. Roseburn, for his unmannerly conduct in so abruptly retiring from our festivities," I answered.

"Are you mad, Laurence?" said Herbert.

"You may deem me so."

"The explanation you require is here;" said Herbert, placing a note in my hand. "Read, and satisfy yourself."

"From whom is this note?" I asked

"Mr. Roseburn."

I hastily glanced over the contents; they were as follows:—

"Sir,—You will probably excuse the apparent uncourteousness of my departure with my nieces, in so abrupt a manner; but sudden illness is the only cause. I find that retirement is best suited to me, as I hope that domestic and simple enjoyment is more in unison with the tastes of my nieces. Yours very truly,

"REDMOND ROSEBURN."

"A mere subterfuge," I exclaimed, "to force his relatives from a scene which his insensible mind cannot appreciate. I will see them in spite of everything."

"Psha!" exclaimed Herbert; "you are absolutely deranged, Sir Laurence. Return with me, and let the festivities banish these absurd notions from your mind. It is evident that Mr. Roseburn, and wisely too, approves not of your familiarity, and you, in your more serious moments, cannot but applaud his prudence. She is the the betrothed of another; one worthy of her, and——"

"She loves him not."

"Confirmed madness!" ejaculated Herbert. "By Jupiter, I did not think tha you, my friend, possessed half the vanity I perceive you do."

"By all my hopes," I cried, "I will not rest until I have once more seen her; made her acquainted with the impression she has made upon my heart, and received from her own lips either my death warrant, or the consummation of my earthly bliss."

"Very romantic," returned Herbert, with a smile; "upon my word, Sir Laurence, you would make an excellent hero in a novel or a romance."

"I am serious, Herbert," I said.

"And so am I," he answered; "and it is because I am so, and would banish those ridiculous ideas from your brain, that I offer you the advice of a sincere friend Sacrifice your ill-placed passion to prudence and honour."

"And think you, Herbert, that I cherish one dishonourable thought towards Clara Roseburn?"

"No; but you would seduce her from him to whom she is affianced; and should you do so, and thereby disturb the peace of her amiable guardian, you must act a part which honour cannot sanction."

"I would make her my wife."

"And blight the hopes of a man who is every way worthy of her."

"By Heaven he is not."

"And why not?"

"Her intrinsic merit is too great for one in his situation. Some humbler mind will do for him to mate with."

"Very generous!" ejaculated my friend. And in truth, I could not but feel the force of his sarcastic reproof, and blush for the vanity I evinced throughout the whole of the unfortunate affair. I must have been mad, as I have often since reflected, or never could I have plunged myself into such extravagance.

"Come, come, Sir Laurence," said Herbert, "return with me; you must, you shall; and in the festivities of the scene, and the gay and beauteous beings that throng the saloon, banish these absurdities from your brain. Come, come."

"The magnet of attraction to me is departed," I returned; "there is nothing there which can now afford me any gratification."

"Upon my word you are very complimentary," said Herbert, with a smile. However, I am determined not to be offended. I know my friend too well to imagine for a moment that he will refuse to do honour to the anniversary of my birth."

"Pardon me, dear Herbert," I said, fervently grasping his hand; "pardon me for my apparent rudeness; but, indeed, this disappointment, so unlooked for, has unmanned me. I scarcely know what I say or do; I am distracted."

"A fiddle-stick!" returned Herbert; and forcing my arm within his, he led me from the spot towards the manor, I scarcely knowing what I did.

We returned to the mansion; all there was hilarity and gladness; music sent forth its gayest notes; bright eyes sparkled, and graceful forms trod the giddy mazes of the dance; but nothing could remove the ennui from my mind; all was dull and uninteresting to my jaundiced eye. I moved about a poor spiritless being, and must have appeared most strange and uncourteous to the many lovely damsels that courted my gallantry. I recollected the look of displeasure which Walter Alston had fixed upon me, and in my heart I wished my innocent rival dead. The more did my hatred of him increase, when I remembered the glances which Clara had fixed upon me, and which all but convinced me that her heart throbbed responsive with mine own."

And shall an ignorant rustic like this, I muttered to myself, dare to aspire to the affections I court? He become the husband of Clara Roseburn! By Heaven! never! A few hours shall decide; I will see her; reveal to her my thoughts, and learn from her own lips, whether or no I have made a favourable impression upon her heart. The frigid coldness of her prudential guardian shall not daunt me, and interpose an obstacle to the consummation of my happiness. Death, if Clara love me not, will be welcome, for life, without her, would be a most insupportable burden."

The festivities did not close till a late hour, but how heartily did I wish them at an end. I was in no humour to converse with any one; I was out of temper with myself, with everything, and a great relief was it to me, when the guests separated and I was allowed to retire to my chamber. But not to rest did I go. Oh, no; distracting thoughts banished sleep from my eyelids, and I tossed about on my pillow feverish and half mad.

Daylight found me still waking, and I arose, not having undressed myself, and immediately left the house, undecided how to act, or what step I was about to pursue. Involuntarily I wandered on towards the residence of her upon whom my whole thoughts were fixed; and arriving there, I walked around the building, and it not been for the earliness of the hour, I should have ventured to call, notwithstanding the reception it was likely I should meet from Mr. Roseburn.

I looked up at each window with the vain hope of beholding Clara, and many were the wild observations I made use of, and the singular antics to which I committed myself. Any person who could then have seen me, must have concluded, and with reason, too, that I was a madman.

The sun now burst forth in all its golden splendour; it was a delightful morning, and to my imagination that was the loveliest of nature's spots, for there resided her who at that time had enraptured all my senses. There was my whole world of delight, and all beyond it was dark, drear, and uninteresting.

Again and again I walked round the house. I was unable to move from the spot; I was, as it were, spell-bound, held prisoner within a magic circle, and Clara was the fair enchantress who held me within her power. Oh, but for one glance of that angelic countenance, I thought to myself; heaven itself could afford me no greater bliss.

How long I had remained in this state I know not, but I was suddenly aroused from my lethargy of thought by hearing the bolt of the door which opened into the garden withdrawn, and she on whom my thoughts were fixed, came forth. Oh, how beautiful, how enchanting did she then appear to my infatuated imagination. She was alone; I endeavoured to open the gate which led into the garden, but could not It was so well secured that it resisted all my efforts.

Clara advanced along one of the walks towards the spot at which I was standing, and my soul rose in transport, as I feasted on her charms. At first she did not observe me, but in a few moments she did, and the crimson blushes that suffused her cheeks, shewed the confusion and surprise into which my unexpected appearance had thrown her. For a moment she stood confounded, and I was so much taken by surprise that I could not at first address her.

"Beauteous Clara," I said, at length; "one word with you—only one word; it will save me from misery the most insupportable."

She looked at me for an instant with an expression of countenance which made a lasting impression upon my mind, and assured me that I was not without taking some position in her esteem; yet, immediately she seemed to recollect herself, and without deigning me a reply, she started back into the house, and left me alone to my own reflections.

Yet, although I was disappointed, in the opportunity thus afforded, of exchanging a few words with her, I flattered myself that I had made a favourable impression upon her, and I was determined to proceed, at all hazards, in the prosecution of the unfortunate passion I had formed.

I continued to wander round the dwelling of her who had so enraptured my senses, for some time, with the hope of seeing her again, but she appeared not, and I then walked disconsolately towards the manor, brooding in my mind various schemes to explain my feelings to Clara, and to obtain a private interview with her; one of which was to address a letter to her, but how to get it conveyed to her hands I was at a loss to imagine.

While I was thus reflecting, I was startled from my reverie, by hearing the sound of horse's hoofs, and looking up, I perceived Herbert proceeding towards me at a most rapid rate. His horse had evidently taken fright, and it seemed to me as if he had, either from alarm or exhaustion, lost all control over him. I made an effort to stop the progress of the excited animal, but it was ineffectual, and he passed me the same as a flash of lightning. Herbert, I could perceive, was fainting, and I followed as quick as I could, expecting every moment to see him precipitated to the earth. My fears were, unfortunately, soon realised; the horse, with its unfortunate rider, reached a declivity, and there both horse and rider were prostrated to the earth.

I rushed up, and beheld my unfortunate friend bleeding from a frightful wound upon the temple. He was quite insensible, and the horse seemed to have inflicted such severe injuries upon itself, in its wild career, that it was evidently dying. I raised Herbert in my arms; he moaned heavily, but could not speak, and I feared that life was passing from him fast.

I was now placed in a most awkward and awful predicament; for I was far away from any habitation, and assistance was immediately required. The earliness of the hour, too, seemed to preclude the possibility of any person passing, who might render me help; notwithstanding, I shouted at the top of my lungs, and, after the lapse of a few seconds, I was relieved from my terrible anxiety by hearing a voice or two in reply. I redoubled my shouts, and immediately afterwards two stout labouring men made their appearance, and hurried towards the spot. They happened to be persons living upon the estate of Herbert's father, and immediately rendered their assistance in carrying them home.

I need not attempt to describe the sensation that was caused in the breast of poor Herbert's father, and all in the establishment, on becoming acquainted with the melancholy catastrophe. The poor old gentleman was nearly distracted, and it was a difficult and almost hopeless task to endeavour to console him.

Medical aid was quickly in attendance, but so severe were the injuries that poor Herbert had received, that not the least hope was expressed of being able to restore him. He never rallied, or for an instant was restored to his senses, and, only two hours after the fatal accident, he was a corpse.

The shock upon my feelings at this awful calamity was very great, and, for a time, banished all thoughts of Clara from my mind. Mr. Clerivalle was perfectly distracted, and was deaf to all attempts to console him, although I exerted myself to the utmost to do so. Indeed, the loss was so great to the afflicted gentleman that nothing could replace it, and I felt that I was deprived of a friend whose equal I should be at a loss to discover.

CHAPTER XXVI.

THE NARRATIVE OF SIR LAURENCE CLEVELAND CONCLUDED.

At this portion of the baronet's narrative, as the time was getting late, he paused, and solicited the suspension of the curiosity of his wife and sister till the following day.

Blanche fixed upon him a melancholy glance, yet it was one of affection and confidence, as she said,—

"Dear Laurence, of what a terrible weight of doubt and anxiety does this recital relieve me, painful though it is. You admit your errors openly and candidly, and al.chough I regret that my husband should ever have been led into those indiscretions, it is a consolation to find that he has no wish to deceive me."

"Deceive you, Blanche," returned Sir Laurence; "Heaven forbid that I should. But it was a feeling of unconquerable shame and remorse only that prevented me from making these disclosures before; and can you marvel at it?"

"I do not, Laurence," answered Lady Cleveland.

"And can you forgive me? Will you not in future look upon me with shame and disgust, to think that I could ever have been so guilty?"

"Oh, no, my husband," said Blanche; "as I before observed, I must regret it, and pity the misfortunes of her to whom you previously gave your hand; but I will not, cannot reproach you."

"Sweetest, best of women," exclaimed Sir Laurence, embracing her; "and Heaven favour me, as I endeavour to repay this affectionate condescension and forbearance. Oh, how bitterly do I lament that I should ever have acted unworthily to you, or have been the cause of a single pang within your bosom."

The looks of Lady Blanche spoke much more than words could have done, and Sir Laurence felt far happier than he had done for some time before. Still his mind, during the night, was a prey to the deepest anxiety; for, in spite of all his efforts, he could not persuade himself that the statement of the gipsies was false, and that Clara and her offspring were not still in existence: and, if such was the case, the destruction of all his hopes, and those of Blanche, was certain. The form and features of the gipsy boy also haunted his imagination, and filled him with strange ideas. The mystery attached to his origin was altogether inexplicable to him, and the miniature which he had seen suspended from his neck, was one that he could never forget. And that, he had said, represented the features of his mother. Those features, so closely resembling Clara, that when he had beheld the portrait, he could almost have imagined that the unfortunate being was gazing at him. Yes, such had she appeared when he first beheld her, in all her innocence and beauty; and such might she have remained, had it not been for his seductive arts. However much he believed she had afterwards erred when she became his wife, he fairly thought that, had she never have seen him, she would have remained pure, and have become the happy wife of, at that time, an honest and industrious man. He could not deny that he had much, very much to lay to his charge, and that he had a right to view the after errors of Clara more with pity and regret, than revenge.

He slept but little for these torturing thoughts during the night, and at an early hour in the morning he arose, and walked forth from the mansion, in order that he might collect himself for the completion of his painful task.

He had wandered to some considerable distance, and was deeply immersed in rumination, when he was suddenly aroused from his lethargy, by hearing his name repeated in a harsh and disagreeable voice, and looking up, to his amazement and confusion, beheld Madela glaring malignantly upon him, and standing at only a few paces from him. He was startled at a meeting so totally unexpected, and he drew back, gazing at the old hag with a mingled feeling of astonishment, disgust, and apprehension.

"Good morning, Laurence Cleveland," she croaked forth, with a sardonic grin; "I wish you much joy on the prosperity of your prospects. The confiding fool to whom you have given your hand, still, no doubt, labours under the delusion that no other still exists to claim it. Ha! ha! ha! It is rare food to witness the constant state of doubt and dread in which you are placed; but the time will come when the terrible conviction will come home to you both. Oh, yes, the time is coming, Laurence Cleveland; the time is coming."

"Hideous old wretch!" exclaimed Sir Laurence; "again do you cross my path, the harbinger of evil. Is there no power to stop you in your career of vengeance? Are you not content with the misery you have already caused?"

"Content!" shouted Madela; "no, no; what limit can there be to my deadly vengeance? Never will I rest till the fate of the murdered, grey-haired old man is fully avenged. Never will I cease to pursue you till I see you swing at the gallows like a dog—aye, and much as you may now despise my predictions, that wish will be accomplished; mark me, villain, murderer, libertine, bigamist!"

"By the great God above us," cried Sir Laurence, excited beyond endurance, "I will not submit to this. I will drag your frightful old carcase to justice, and ——"

"Ha, ha, ha!" laughed the old woman, contemptuously, and at the same time raising the staff which she carried in a menacing manner; "you talk largely to an old woman, brave Sir Laurence Cleveland; but dare to move an inch towards me, and I will fell you to the earth, as I have before done. It is not such reptiles as you that can alarm the gipsy queen."

In spite of everything, the baronet was awed by the manner and words of this mysterious woman, and withdrew himself further back, and gazed with speechless wonder and horror upon her. He could scarcely believe that she was a human being; and, indeed, there was nothing earthly in her demeanour and the expression of her countenance. She seemed to exult in his emotion, and muttered some unintelligible words to herself. It was several moments before Sir Laurence could speak at all, and he knew not what course to adopt. He looked around him, with the hope of seeing some one whom he might call to his assistance, and to help him in securing the woman; but the coast was quite clear, and therefore he felt himself entirely at her mercy and in her power.

"Brave Laurence Cleveland!" said the old woman, in still more sarcastic and contemptuous tones than before; "I read your thoughts—ay, well do I read them, and despise them. Oh, it would be a sad day's work for you if you dared to attempt to drag me to prison. It would but hasten your own fate, and bring immediate destruction upon the heads of those connected with you. You may affect to despise my threats, but you do not; for never did I yet utter one that I did not accomplish. You would discover where I and my tribe are at present concealed; know that we are where we can constantly watch your actions, and yet defy detection. There is scarcely a thought which passes in your mind, with which we do not immediately become acquainted, and in a moment could we sacrifice you to our vengeance, and you could not offer the least resistance. Mark that, Laurence Cleveland, and rest assured that I make no empty boast."

"Strange and fearful woman!" said the baronet, in a tone of surprise; "who and what are you?"

"Madela, the gipsy queen, and your most implacable enemy. You will know me better by-and-bye, to your sorrow."

"In what have I ever injured you, that you should pursue me with such deadly hatred and vengeance?"

"Oh, the tale of the wrongs you have done me is too long, and it answers not my purpose to tell it at present," answered Madela; "but you will know it soon enough, and when the time comes, if you are not more than man, it will freeze your blood with horror. Ask your own conscience."

"I know you not."

"At present you do not; and a terrible day will it be for you, when we become better acquainted."

"Why do you perpetually cross my path?"

"To ring my curses in your ears, and to exult in your misery. Oh, I will make both you and her whom you call your wife shed tears of blood yet."

"Alas! alas! have not you and your fiendish associates already brought upon us the most insupportable misery? It is you who murdered my infant child."

"Ha! ha! ha!" laughed Madela, with the most diabolical exultation.

"Monster in female form, can I endure this?" exclaimed Sir Laurence, clenching his fists, and again advancing a step or two towards Madela; but without moving from the spot on which she was standing, she drew a pistol from beneath her cloak, and presenting it at his head, she exclaimed,—

"Fool! if you would precipitate your fate, come on, and I will scatter your brains upon the ground."

The baronet started back aghast, and gazed with horror upon his strange and terrible enemy.

"Ha! ha! ha!" laughed the old hag; "you have not courage to brave the old woman, Sir Laurence Cleveland; and yet you dare to talk of bringing to justice me and my tribe. Once more I tell you that we defy both you and the laws; those who have attempted to molest us, never yet escaped our vengeance. But get you home, reptile, and finish the recital of your guilt to the fond, confiding fool, Blanche; no doubt, it will greatly elevate you in her affections."

It would be impossible to pourtray the astonishment of Sir Laurence at these observations. He stared at Madela aghast, and again he could not help believing that she was some supernatural being.

"Woman," he cried—"if such, indeed, you are, which your observations lead me to doubt—again I demand who you really are, and by what means you thus become acquainted with all my actions?"

"*You* demand!" said Madela, ironically. "But will you now any longer deny my power, or affect to despise my predictions? No; your blanched cheek and quivering lips convince me that you cannot, and I triumph. What is there that Madela, the gipsy sybil, knows not? Be prepared, for there is more misery in store for you. And when we meet again it will be my task to exult in your additional misery. Begone to your mistress, and console her with the conclusion of your honourable narrative."

"Stay, woman!" exclaimed the baronet; "I am determined to know more of you, and by what means you have acquired your knowledge, before you leave me."

The only reply he received was a derisive laugh from Madela; and shaking her long, thin, bony hand menacingly at him, she quickly vanished out of sight.

Sir Laurence stood for several minutes after she had gone, and his mind underwent the greatest agony. He knew not how he could sufficiently collect himself to meet Blanche, and to resume his narrative, and yet it would not do to make her acquainted with this adventure, which would so alarm her, and destroy the tranquillity she had at present gained. And who could this fearful old woman be who seemed to be thoroughly aware of all his actions, and even his thoughts, as soon as they occurred to himself? It was altogether a mystery which he could not penetrate, and the longer he reflected upon it, the more he became bewildered. He was not prone to superstition, or certainly he would have been disposed to imagine that Madela was no human being. Let it be whichever way it might, after the evil that had already been effected through her means and that of her infamous and daring colleagues, he felt that he had every reason to dread her, and he looked upon her re-appearance to him as the certain foreboding of some fresh calamity.

"And in what way can I protect myself?" he said; "how thwart the diabolical designs they have against me? I cannot even fathom their secret machinations, and they hold both law and every power apparently at defiance. She said truly that those who dared to attempt to obstruct them never failed to meet with their deadliest vengeance; and therefore am I, and all those against whom they entertain any malice, completely the slaves of their caprice, and dare not attempt to resent their dreadful persecutions and outrages. My God! and should it indeed be true that Clara and her offspring still live! The very thought freezes the blood within my veins with horror. She says she will never rest until she sees me die the death of a dog upon the gallows; and yet of what crime can I ever, or have ever been guilty to merit such a fate? I am distracted; I know not how to act. And where can they be? How is it possible that they can thus escape detection, and yet appear to me whenever they think proper? Conjecture can supply no answer."

He beat his breast, and the anguish of his mind increased every moment. Every word that Madela had uttered was as fresh in his memory as if she had spoken it but that very moment; and he remained for some time transfixed to the spot, lost, confounded, and appalled. He feared to return home and to meet Blanche, lest, by the violence of his emotion, he should betray himself, and be compelled to give her an explanation of the morning's adventure; and yet, if he delayed, she would become alarmed at his absence. And another apprehension seized him, namely, that the gipsies were in the neighbourhood, and might seize that opportunity to commit some fresh outrage; and that idea prompted him not to procrastinate his return.

But how could Madela obtain the information she had gained, unless she had some secret spy upon his actions, was a question he asked himself. Notwithstanding all their protestations to the contrary, it seemed evident to him that there must be a traitor among his own domestics; but how to discover that individual was the difficulty.

"It seems," he soliloquised, "that they have so secretly and ingeniously entangled me in their meshes, that I cannot escape from them, and, therefore, it is absurd for me to attempt to defy their power. Alas! alas! to what horrors have my youthful indiscretions exposed me, and all connected with me. Would to Heaven that I could recall the past! I have, indeed, been most guilty; for had I followed the advice of my friend Herbert, I should have stifled a passion that I could not encourage with honour; I should have been spared this terrible self-reproach and constant dread; and Clara might have been the happy and virtuous wife of an honest man."

He was suddenly startled from these reflections by hearing the same plaintive and familiar voice which had on a former occasion saluted his ears, singing that song he used to sing to the unfortunate Clara when he was paying his clandestine addresses to her. Thunderstruck, he looked around him, but could not perceive anything of the minstrel, although she (if woman it was) seemed to be at no great distance from him. The sounds appeared to proceed from a woody glade, near which he was standing, but he was so electrified and entranced, that he could not move from the spot; and again he listened to the following well-known words :—

> "Can I e'er forget those sparkling eyes,
> Which taught me first to love;
> Those beauteous looks, expressing thoughts
> All pure from heaven above?"

"Gracious powers!" he exclaimed, unable to listen any longer; "this can be no delusion of the senses. The voice—the words are the same! Clara, if it is indeed you, I command you to come forward and confront me! I defy the consequences, and am ready at once to meet the consummation of my fate. Certain misery cannot be half so fearful as this dreadful state of suspense and anxiety. Clara, I say, if it be you, appear!"

No answer was returned to him, and he darted towards the spot from whence the sounds had issued, and the moment he broke from between the trees, he beheld the graceful form of a man retreating. It was the same figure he had before seen, and he called upon it to stop. It turned round, and revealed to him a countenance which so closely resembled that of Clara, that, had its dress been that of a female, he would have felt convinced that it was either her or her spirit. And sad, melancholy, and reproachful was the hasty glance which met his, and struck a chill of horror to his heart; but it was only for a moment, and then, plunging into the deepest thicket, he disappeared from the view.

"Mystery upon mystery!" cried Sir Laurence; "you shall not escape me till I know who and what you are. Stop, stranger, I command you, nay, I supplicate you!"

Wildly the distracted baronet rushed into the thicket where the singular being had disappeared, but he had no sooner done so than Madela once more crossed his path, with a malicious grin of triumph upon her hideous countenance that was perfectly unearthly, and he started back completely appalled.

"Cursed fiend, in human shape!" he exclaimed; "again do you appear before me, as if in mockery of my anguish! What would you now?"

The mysterious woman returned no other answer than a wild laugh, and waving her staff, as if in defiance and mockery at him, she retreated from the place, and left him in a state of mind which the reader can very well conceive.

"By Heaven!" he ejaculated, "this torture is unsupportable. Have the fates conspired against me altogether, to mock me? Oh, who is this mysterious being that has appeared before me, and with that voice, those features, which I can never forget? Is it some spirit conjured up to drive me to madness? And Madela, too; she is aware of its appearance, and exults in my misery. By all my hopes! this horrible state of suspense is more than human nature can support.

He struck his forehead in the intense anguish of his feelings, and remained transfixed to the spot, undecided what to do. Then he once more looked around him, but perceived no object to attract his attention, and yet to his imagination the countenance of the stranger was presented as vividly as if he had gazed upon it, and the tones of the voice rang in his ears, recalling all the actions of the past to his memory in the most painful colours.

"The form was that of a man," he said, "and yet the voice and the countenance were those of a woman, and of one whose image must ever remain stamped upon my memory. What can explain this inexplicable mystery? Had it not been for the dress, I could have sworn that Clara again stood before me. This must be unravelled before I can hope to gain a moment's peace; but how? And should it indeed prove to be correct that Clara is living, and only waits to come forward, to my shame and confusion, till the gipsies permit her! Oh, God! for the sake of my beloved Blanche, if not for me, forbid this."

Slowly he turned away, and walked towards his mansion. His mind was completely bewildered, and he could find no consolation; for the longer he reflected, the more threatening did his prospects appear to be.

He dreaded to meet Blanche and his sister; for he was fearful that the agitation of his manner would betray him, and that they would put such questions to him that he could not avoid answering; and should he make Blanche acquainted with the startling events of the morning, he was apprehensive that they would have the most dangerous effects upon her, and might shake the confidence she had now reposed in him. And how could he ever find nerve enough to resume his narrative, while his mind was in this terrible state of agitation? He deeply regretted that he had left the mansion at all, then would the anguish of this adventure have been spared him. But it was no use to encourage these thoughts, and all that he had to do was to put as bold a front upon the matter as he could. Alas! he reflected, he was, perhaps, after all, only holding out false hopes to Blanche; and if so, when the truth was made apparent, how great would be her shame and horror. She would never support it. She must sink under the dreadful blow, and could he do otherwise than accuse himself of being indirectly her murderer? Would he not be degraded in the eyes of the whole world; and if the existence of his first wife was proved, his destruction would be inevitable. These thoughts were of themselves sufficient to drive him to frenzy, and it was several minutes after his arrival at home, before he ventured to enter the house.

When he did, he found that the morning repast awaited him, and that Blanche and Amanda had expressed some surprise at his absence. He conquered his emotion as well as he could, and excused himself for having so long absented himself from home, by stating that the fineness of the morning had induced him to ramble farther than he had at first intended. With this answer Blanche appeared to be satisfied, and the breakfast passed off without anything worth noticing occurring. But still Sir Laurence could not banish from his mind the events of the morning, and the agitation of his manner did not escape the observation of Lady Cleveland, who questioned him concerning it. He pleaded indisposition as an excuse, and requested that Blanche would favour him by allowing him to postpone the conclusion of his narrative until the next day. Of course, anxious though she was to hear the sequel, she could offer no objection to this, and the baronet was thus allowed a short respite from his painful task.

After some trifling conversation, he pleaded increasing illness as an excuse to retire to his chamber, and being thus left alone, he was permitted to indulge in the harassing thoughts which rushed tumultuously to his mind. Again and again he reflected upon all the words of old Madela; and the more he did so, the greater became his perplexity. That she had the power and the determination to fulfil her threats, after what he had seen of her, he could entertain but little, if any, doubt; and what means had he of protecting himself against her diabolical machinations, and those with whom she was associated? None; for she seemed to set both law and everything else at defiance; and the plans she adopted were so artfully devised, that it appeared next to an utter impossibility to frustrate them; and even should he attempt to apprehend them, it was not at all unlikely that it would only be precipitating his own ruin. But the form he had seen, the voice he had heard, had made a far deeper impression upon him than anything else; and in vain he tried to form a single idea which might afford him any consolation. The features were an exact counterpart to those of Clara, and the plaintive tones of the voice were exactly the same. To him the mystery was totally impenetrable, and he only tortured his brain the more he sought to fathom it. He determined, however, to keep a stricter watch over his domestics than he had previously done; for, after what Madela had said to him, he could not help thinking that one amongst them was connected with her and the other gipsies, and communicated all that transpired in the mansion to them; or else, how was it possible that she could have obtained the knowledge she possessed, and that she should have become acquainted with almost his very thoughts? And yet they had all been in his service for a number of years, and he had never had the slightest reason to doubt their honesty or fidelity.

This was a day of agonising thought and perplexity to Sir Laurence Cleveland; but towards the evening he became more tranquil, and fearing that he might alarm Blanche if he any longer pleaded illness, he ventured to enter her presence, and to her solicitous inquiries he replied that he felt himself much better, and trusted that a night's rest would perfectly restore him to health. Blanche, by her looks, expressed the pleasure she felt at this intelligence; and an hour or two having elapsed, in conversation upon different topics, they retired for the night.

In the morning, the baronet had so far conquered his emotion, that he met Blanche with even more than his accustomed composure; and the morning repast being over, he resumed his narrative in the following words:—

I am afraid that I have hitherto been far too tedious, but I will endeavour to come to the conclusion of my painful recital in as few words as possible.

I need not tell you how shocked I was at the untimely death of Herbert Clerivalle, between whom and myself so warm a friendship had existed; but his father was for some time in a state of mind bordering upon distraction. He requested me to prolong my visit at the manor; and of course, under the melancholy circumstances, I could not decline, even if it had been my inclination so to do; which it was not; for I could not even bear the thought of leaving the neighbourhood in which Clara resided; and I was determined, with as little delay as possible, to obtain an interview with her, and, in spite of the consequences, at once to reveal to her the impression she had made on my heart. It was a bold resolve, considering that her faith was already plighted to another, and that the time for their nuptials was appointed; but reason was entirely banished from my mind, and thus I was hurried on to ruin.

The remains of Herbert were consigned to the tomb, and I followed them to their final resting-place, deeply lamenting the melancholy fate which had put a period to his existence.

A week passed away, when the opportunity I had so long prayed for was afforded me. In the course of one of my rambles—for I had not yet ventured to visit the residence of Mr. Roseburn again—I beheld Clara tripping across the fields towards her home, and to my unspeakable pleasure she was alone. On seeing me, she blushed deeply, and dropped a low curtsey with modest grace, and hesitated, seemingly confused, but not at all displeased at the meeting. I approached her; my heart palpitated violently, and I scarcely knew how to address her; and yet a volume of words was on my tongue; and I was fully resolved not to let such an opportunity pass, without revealing my thoughts, and ascertaining whether or not I had made a favourable impression upon her. I will not tire you by detailing all that passed at that interview; but, suffice it to say, that I put my bold resolution into effect, and revealed

See p. 320.

to the astonished and blushing damsel the place she held in my affections, and implored her, with all the eloquence I could make use of, not to leave me to despair.

It was some moments ere she could reply, and her bosom heaved with emotion: but I was vain enough to flatter myself that it was not with displeasure, and I pressed my suit with still greater fervour.

I had taken her hand, and endeavoured to press it to my lips; but she quickly withdrew it, apparently surprised and abashed at my boldness; at the same time, she said,—

" Sir Laurence Cleveland, leave me; this is language to which I must not listen, and which I was little prepared to hear from you.   Suffer me to return home, and do not, by your conduct, alter the good opinion I had formed of you."

" And will you not bless me with one word of kindness and hope, lovely Clara?" I ejaculated.   " Oh! did you but know the hours of anguish I have passed, when deprived of your sweet presence, you ——"

" Forbear, sir !" interrupted Clara; " and do not offer to detain me.   This convinces me of the necessity of our never meeting again."

" Meet no more, Clara!" I cried; " by Heaven, if I thought that such was to be my d,om, I should be driven to madness.   Oh, I could endure anything but your scorn."

" Think of the difference of our station, Sir Lawrence," said Clara; " remember that I am the affianced bride of another, and do not venture to further urge those vows which honour cannot sanction.   I may hold Sir Laurence Cleveland in my esteem, but he can never hope to possess my heart."

Thus saying, she fixed upon me a look which I could never forget, and before I could recover from my confusion, she darted from me, and made her way with all the speed that her agitation would permit, towards her dwelling.   I did not dare to follow her, but I gazed after her with the most intense feelings of admiration, until she entered the house.

I need not attempt to describe to you minutely my feelings after this meeting. Clara had bid me despair ; but I could not, and I determined to persevere in my suit even at all hazards.

Fortunate would it have been for me could I, at that critical moment, have seen through the folly of my misplaced attachment, and have taken the advice of my late unfortunate and excellent friend, Herbert, and that tendered to me now by the object of my passion.   But there was that expression in her eyes and general demeanour, which seemed to convince me that however sincere she might be in her counsels and asseverations, it would not be disagreeable to her for me to prosecute my suit.

But the time was so brief that must elapse before her proposed nuptials to Walter Alston, that I almost despaired of my efforts being crowned with success.

" And must she," I said, " must she become the bride of such a man as Walter Alston?   She, whose charms have rivetted my very soul, and to obtain possession of whom I would willingly make any sacrifice, however great ?   No, no; I will sacrifice riches, life, everything, rather than such a consummation should ensue; for I feel that it would be utterly impossible to live, and to behold Clara the bride of another."

In this mood, I walked to the old manor, but, on the road, was compelled to endeavour to conquer my powerful emotions, in order that they might not meet the keen observation of Clerivalle; and yet, in spite of all my efforts, I could not rid myself of the excitement which had been created by my interview with Clara.   There was much to inspire me with hope, and plenty to sink me to despair; but, nevertheless, nothing whatever could daunt me in my resolution to follow up my addresses to the maiden who had taken such a strong hold on my affections.

" She would hold me in her esteem, she said," was a portion of my soliloquy, as I proceeded towards the manor ; " her esteem! much as I value that, it is not half the satisfaction that my hopes aspire to.   No ; by all my hopes, let whatever may be the consequences to myself and others, she shall become my wife. That clown shall never have the felicity of carrying her away as his bride."

I arrived at the manor, but I was too much agitated in my mind to meet the company that was then assembled there, and I therefore excused myself, and was allowed to retire to my own apartment. There I reflected, with mingled feelings of satisfaction and disappointment, upon the interview I had had with Clara; but, still, in spite of all she had said, I was resolved not to be daunted in the prosecution of my designs; and with that determination I retired to bed.

Throughout the night Clara was never for a moment absent from my thoughts, and as soon as the sun peeped in at my casement the following morning, I arose, and once more wandered to the neighbourhood of her residence. All was still around; no one was stirring, and I climbed the gate which opened upon the garden, and there indulged in the thoughts which every flower created in my mind, and which I fondly imagined had been fostered by the fair being who had so transported my senses, and had, in fact, made a madman of me. What strange freaks I performed there, I will not annoy your ears, or shock your good sense by reciting; but, as I was leaving the place, I met Walter Alston, as he was passing by the house on the way to his daily occupation. I know not that he saw me leave the garden, but he paused as soon as he recognised me, and a frown of displeasure passed over his countenance, while, at the same moment, he seemed to endeavour to subdue the feelings that were probably passing in his mind, and slightly touched his hat to me, and was passing on, when I called out to him,—

" Hoigh, friend Walter; you are not about to pass me in that way, surely, are you?"

"You do me honour, Sir Laurence Cleveland," he replied, " by thus condescending to address me ; but I be going to my employment; you have none of the anxieties of that to trouble your mind. You be a lucky man, squire; a very lucky man."

There was a quiet, sarcastic tone in his observations, and the manner in which he delivered them, which abashed me, and I scarcely knew how to answer. I was convinced that he felt me to be an enemy to him, and I could not but reproach myself with the intention of doing him the most serious injury ; and, consequently, I sank into insignificance before his honest indignation. Yet I stifled these feelings as well as I could ; and, after a pause, said,—

"You should be doing better than you are, Walter ; can I forward your views in any way? Rest assured, I should feel most happy to do so."

"I am obliged to you for your kindness, Sir Laurence," returned Walter, with a half sarcastic look, and I could perceive, at the same time, that he bit his lips ; "but I am perfectly contented in my present station of society, as my forefathers have been before me. I have a strong arm and a willing heart to work, and a spirit independent enough not to be beholden to any one. Good morning, sir."

As he said this, he moved from the spot, and was hurrying on his way, when, vexed that I should have allowed myself to be thus defeated, I called after him, and he returned.

"Now, Sir Lawrence," he said, with an air of contemptuous pride, which stung me to the quick, "what may be your pleasure with me?"

"You appear to misunderstand me," I said, after a pause. " I would congratulate you on the happiness which you flatter yourself is in store for you, in your union with the fair Clara Roseburn."

" Which I *flatter* myself is in store for me, Sir Laurence Cleveland !" he repeated, with a frown ; " I certainly *do* understand you when you address me in that way; and, mark me, those who dare to cast an insinuation against the truth of Clara Roseburn, or to endeavour to interpose between me and my honourable suit, be they squire or prince, they shall have to answer it, and that dearly, to a *man*."

He fixed upon me a look of meaning which I could not mistake, as he spoke; my bosom swelled with offended pride and resentment, but before I could offer a word in reply, he was out of sight.

"So," I said to myself, as I retraced my steps to the mansion, " this clown reads my thoughts, and thinks to supersede me in my wishes. But he shall find himself mistaken. I am convinced, in spite of what Clara said to me on our last interview, that she views me not with indifference, and I will pursue the course I have adopted until I have triumphed."

With these thoughts and determinations, I returned to the mansion, but my mind was too much disturbed by this meeting with my rival to suffer me to enter with any spirit into conversation.

On retiring for the night, I racked my mind in vain to hit upon any plan to forward my designs. It now wanted but two months to the time appointed for the union of Clara and Walter Alston to take place, and, therefore, there was not a moment to be lost. And yet I knew not what course to adopt. In the loss of Herbert, I was deprived of a friend, who, however obstinate I might be at first, would, no doubt, ultimately have saved me from the misery which afterwards, and has subsequently befallen me. But without that, I went on my own headlong course, and worked the evils which afterwards ensued.

I passed a sleepless night, but at last I resolved, at all hazards, to pay another visit to Mr. Roseburn, and before I did so, as it was probable that I should not be able to snatch a word privately with Clara, to write a letter to her, expressive of my thoughts, which I might find an opportunity of slipping into her hand.

Filled with these hopes, I left my bed on the following morning, and employed all my eloquence in addressing this epistle to Clara; assuring her of the honour of my intentions, my readiness to make her my wife, although it would be prudent that such a ceremony should be conducted privately, in consequence of the dying injunctions of my father; and I concluded by requesting that she would grant me a secret interview on the following evening, in the elm grove, not far from their residence.

My heart fluctuated between hope and fear, as I quitted the manor, and once or twice I was half inclined to return and abandon my hopes, half astonished and ashamed of the boldness of my designs. But still the too fascinating image of Clara prevailed over all my scruples, and I proceeded on my way.

Mr. Roseburn received me with cold reserve, and I could perceive that he would rather have declined the visit. Neither Clara nor Mirah appeared for some time after I had been there, and I began to despair of seeing the object of my anxiety, and knew not how I could with any decency prolong my visit. But at last she came, and to my enraptured imagination she appeared far more lovely than I had ever before seen her. She was evidently confounded and confused at my presence, but still, as I had before imagined, there was a feeling of pleasure mingled with it. I ventured to address her, and she replied with a modest sweetness of demeanour which I felt was an encouragement to my hopes, and Mirah, too, blushed deeply, and seemed to be far from dissatisfied at again beholding me.

An hour more was passed at this interview, and although Mr. Roseburn behaved with his accustomed friendship and politeness, I could see that he was anxious for my departure. More than once I caught the glance of Clara, and there was everything in its expression, but yet so modestly displayed, to encourage my hopes, and embolden me to proceed with my plans.

In going to perform some domestic part of her duties, she had occasion to pass me, and I seized that opportunity to slide the billet-doux into her hand. She took it, and I felt her hand tremble as she did, and her cheeks were crimsoned with blushes; but she seemed to recover herself immediately, and returning a suitable answer to my farewell, retired from the room, followed by her cousin.

After a few more observations of no moment with Mr. Roseburn, I departed from the house.

My heart felt elated, for the looks of Clara had inspired me with confidence, and I entertained every hope that my letter would make a favourable impression upon her. I returned to the manor, and met Mr. Clerivalle in far better spirits than I had done for the last day or two.

"She does not despise me," I soliloquised, "I am convinced she does not, and I shall yet triumph. She will yield to my persuasions; her uncle will give his consent, and I shall become possessed of the brightest treasure that could ever fall to the lot of man!"

Weak, unprincipled fool, which I must acknowledge myself at that time to have been, I did not for a moment reflect upon the misery, the ruin, that I was likely to produce. Oh, keenly, severely, do I take shame to myself, for the conduct I then pursued.

It would be a waste of time to attempt to describe to you my anxiety and impatience until the evening arrived; and the various doubts and fears which occupied my mind during that tedious interval; but still I flattered myself, from the glance I snatched of Clara, that she would, if possible, comply with my request. And yet it was a libel upon her modesty and prudence to encourage such an idea. But a man, blind and infatuated with unlicensed love, as I was at that time, has no reason. Alas! unfortunately for her, she had suffered herself to be conquered by my protestations, and could not resist the temptation that was held out to her.

As soon as the shades of evening had fallen, I made my way to the elm grove, which was little more than a quarter of a mile from Clara's dwelling. I had to pass it in going there, and my heart throbbed with mingled doubts and fears to know whether she would have the opportunity of meeting me there, and if even her will prompted her to do so. And yet, when I came to reflect seriously upon the assignation, I could not but consider that it was a preposterous one, for was it likely that her uncle would allow her to leave the house at such a time, and would she, if even she had the opportunity, do so without his knowledge? However, I was agreeably mistaken.

It was a beautiful evening; never had the moon shone more brilliantly; the sky was one vast expanse of liquid silver, and the tranquillity of all around was enough to soothe the most agitated feelings. The air was mild and refreshing, and while I paced the spot where I hoped to meet her who had so captivated my every sense, I felt inspired with new hopes and ideas. Presently I heard a light footstep, not proceeding from the direction of Mr. Roseburn's house, and, looking round, I beheld Clara approaching. She had been to the neighbouring hamlet, as I afterwards understood, to visit some person who was sick; but there is no doubt that she seized upon the opportunity with avidity, in order to comply with a request which her own heart could not refuse. How eagerly I hastened towards her, and with what affectionate words did I greet her, which she received with blushes, but still in such a manner as did not discourage me from proceeding in my advances. But I must pass hastily over that important meeting. It lasted but a short time, but suffice it to say, that my eloquence, my protestations, prevailed, and that Clara acknowledged that I had made a favourable impression on her heart, and entirely changed her sentiments as regarded Walter Alston.

With what different thoughts did I return to Roslinwold Manor that evening, after my separation from Clara. My heart leaped again with joy, and the exultation of my mind was so great that I could scarcely control it.

My dreams that night were those of bliss, but never for a moment did I think of the dishonour with which I was acting towards Walter Alston, and the misery—the inevitable misery I must inflict, if not upon Clara, upon her uncle and cousin.

Several interviews we had after this, and my triumph over her affections was complete. She was ready at once to become my bride, if I could gain the consent of her uncle; but there was the difficulty; was it at all likely that he, as a man of honour, could break the solemn promise he had made to Walter Alston? and how could I have the boldness to make such a proposal to him, or expect that Clara could at once cruelly reject the companion of her youth, to whom she was solemnly plighted? It was a terrible difficulty, and one which I knew not well how to surmount; but there was not a moment to be lost, and, let the consequences be what they might, I was determined (encouraged by the knowledge that I possessed the heart of Clara) to make the confession. The following day I called upon Mr. Roseburn, and, finding him alone, I disclosed my thoughts, and pleaded my suit with all the energy I was capable of using.

It would be impossible to describe the emotion he evinced while I was addressing him; and when I had concluded,—

"Sir Laurence Cleveland," he said, "is it possible that you, a gentleman, and professing yourself to be a man of honour, can make such a proposal to me? Know you not that the hand of my niece is already plighted to the companion of her childhood, to Walter Alston; and that I have solemnly pledged my word they shall be united?"

"True, Mr. Roseburn," I answered, with more coolness than I had thought it was possible I could assume; "but bear with me while I confess to you that the beauteous Clara has possessed my heart ever since the first moment I beheld her. She is a gem too precious to become a peasant's bride; and I now make proposals to you, as her affectionate guardian, for that hand which even an emperor might covet!"

"Impossible!" ejaculated Mr. Roseburn; "she is affianced to a noble-minded and worthy youth, and, by Heaven, I will not blast his hopes, and degrade myself in my own estimation as a man of honour."

"Then you would sacrifice the happiness of your niece, Mr. Roseburn," I remarked.

"Nay," he returned, "by giving my consent to their nuptials, I am positive that I best consult her happiness. They have been companions from earliest youth, and have ever loved each other."

"She loves him no longer," I observed.

"Impossible!" replied Mr. Roseburn; "they were the companions of the earliest childhood; their tastes, their sentiments, were the same; they had not a thought which they did not each anticipate and reciprocate; their virtues rendered them worthy of each other; and I felt an honest gratification in being able to form so fortunate, and, as I considered, so happy an alliance. Clara's consent was given freely, joyfully, and what has Walter Alston done that such a change should be wrought in her sentiments? Oh, it is as I said before, impossible; I know my niece too well to believe that she could thus act; or, if it indeed be true that you have thus estranged her affections, allow me to say, Sir Laurence Cleveland, that you must have exercised some extraordinary arts over the inexperience of the poor girl, alike unworthy of yourself, and redolent with future misery to us all."

"Sir," I returned, with a feeling of mortified pride which I could not suppress, "honour alone, and a sincere affection towards your beauteous niece, have alone guided my conduct; and I am certain that she will acknowledge to you that I have used no unfair means to win her love. Allow me to say that the seclusion in which you have kept her, has left her no opportunity of choice, and ——"

"Sir," interrupted Mr. Roseburn, warmly, "her choice fell upon one worthy of her; she has consented, she has pledged herself to become his wife, and you, knowing this, should in honour have stifled your own sentiments, and have withdrawn every temptation from the poor girl which could never be encouraged without the sacrifice of her own truth, and the future hopes and prospects of a worthy young man. I have solemnly affianced her to him, and, by all my hopes, I will not break my word."

"Then, would you, sir, destroy the happiness of your niece?" I demanded.

"Heaven forbid that I should do so," he answered.

"And you will do so, if you do not give your consent to my addresses," I said emphatically. "Clara will never, I am convinced, and I speak it not out of vanity, now, of her own free will, consent to become the wife of Walter Alston. But allow me to say, that I regret the situation in which this circumstance has placed him; but surely he would not possess the hand of any individual, when he knew that her heart was that of another? I respect Walter, and if I could compensate him for the loss of Clara ——"

"Compensate him for the loss of Clara!" interrupted Mr. Roseburn, with indignation; "I am astonished to hear you, Sir Laurence Cleveland, who pride yourself upon being a gentleman and a man of honour, talk after that fashion; why, the *roue* and libertine could do no more. What compensation could you make to Walter Alston for the loss of her whom you affect to prize beyond all earthly things? Could you renew the hopes and prospects he has formed, and which by that you would cruelly blight? No, Sir Laurence; I most positively and emphatically decline the honour that you intended me and my niece; and pardon me for adding, that I consider it would be most prudent for all parties if your future visits here, until you you have conquered the unfortunate passion which you have allowed to take possession of your breast, are abandoned."

You may imagine my feelings at this moment; my pride was sorely mortified, and it was not without the greatest difficulty that I could suppress my resentment. But I knew how much was depending upon my forbearance, and I therefore controlled my passion much better than could have been expected.

"Mr. Roseburn," I exclaimed, after a pause, "my intentions towards Clara are of the most strictly honourable description, or I should not have ventured to acknow. ledge to her my love, or to have pleaded my suit with you. I would make her my wife; she has confessed to me that her heart's warmest feelings respond to mine, and that she can never in future bestow upon Walter Alston more than her esteem and friendship; would you thwart the hopes, and inflict everlasting misery upon her to. wards whom you have ever behaved with even more than the affection of a parent?"

"By Heaven! I cannot believe it!" ejaculated the old man. "Clara could never have become so weak; she could never have thus permitted her affections to be estranged from the object on which they were placed, and whose conduct has ever rendered him so worthy of her."

"Question her yourself, Mr. Roseburn," I said, "if you doubt my word, and you will find that I have stated nothing but the truth."

"I will, I will," replied Mr. Roseburn, "and that in your presence, Sir Laurence Cleveland. But, understand me; my word is pledged to Walter Alston, and let whatever may be the consequences, I will not break it. If Clara Roseburn, my niece, fail in her duty, I will not in my honour; and either she becomes the bride of Walter Alston, or an alien to me and my affections."

"Forbear, Mr. Roseburn," I said; "make not so rash, and I may add, so cruel a vow."

"Sir," he returned, with a determined look, as he rang the bell, "my mind is fixed."

The female servant who attended upon them, made her appearance, and she was ordered to request the attendance of her young mistress. This was an interval of the greatest excitement to me and Mr. Roseburn, and we neither of us ventured to look at each other. Deeply did I feel for the emotion and confusion which Clara would be certain to experience, and much did I dread the result of the interview from the agitated manner of Mr. Roseburn. Fain would I have been absent when that important and peculiar question was put to the fair object of my affections, and when I heard her light footsteps approaching, my agitation increased. She entered blushing and trembling, and when she caught a hasty glance of me she dropped her head, and I could perceive she was most violently agitated in every limb, no doubt fully aware for what her presence was required, and, from her uncle's looks, apprehensive of what the results of the interview would be.

I cannot describe to you the scene which followed. Mr. Roseburn at once put the question to Clara as to the state of her affections, and she as candidly acknowledged them. She confessed that she could no longer love Walter Alston, and that if she was compelled to accept him for her husband, her heart must still be mine. We both on our knees pleaded our passion, and implored Mr. Roseburn to relent; but he was inexorable, and the more we supplicated, the greater his excitement became. He loaded us with reproaches, and to all my remonstrances turned a deaf ear. Clara fainted, and was conveyed to her chamber, and Mr. Roseburn retiring abruptly from the apartment, I was compelled to quit the house. However, as I did so, I met Jane the female attendant, who was most devotedly attached to her young mistress, and was the confidant of all her secrets, and I felt convinced that I could win her favour, slipped a guinea into her hand, and whispering in her ear, "Let me know all that take place, and you shall be handsomely rewarded," I departed.

My mind was now completely distracted by conflicting doubts and fears, bu from the determined manner, and the observations of Mr. Roseburn, I felt thoroughly convinced that I had nothing at all to hope from his relenting; but still I was resolved, at every hazard, that Clara should be mine, and I set all my ingenuity in immediate operation to bring about the accomplishment of my designs.

In the furtherance of these I had no doubt that I should find great assistance from

See p. 333.

Jane, and I did not entirely give myself up to despair. To know that I really possessed the love of Clara, was a bright consolation to me under all the obstacles which presented themselves to me, and encouraged me to persevere. And yet, in spite of his inflexibility and opposition to my suit, I could not but admire the honour and integrity of Mr. Roseburn, and blame myself for thus supplanting Walter Alston in the affections of her to whom he was betrothed, and thus destroying his hopes and prospects altogether.

That day was one of infinite misery to me, and I avoided society as much as possible, retiring at an early hour to my chamber, but not to sleep. No; the image of Clara continued to haunt my imagination, and I felt that I could never rest until I had beheld her again? Her uncle would be sure to use every precaution to keep us apart: and after what had taken place, it was not likely that I could venture to intrude myself again upon him. I pictured to myself all the anguish that she must now be enduring, and formed a thousand projects in my mind, which I rejected as soon as formed, to accomplish my wishes, and to frustrate the designs of her amiable guardian; and I blush now to think of the various projects which at that time suggested themselves to my imagination. But that she should not become the bride of Walter Alston, I was fully resolved, and secretly swore. Alas! fate allowed me too well to accomplish my oath.

The next morning, immediately after the breakfast, I excused myself to Mr. Clerivalle, and, departing from the manor, bent my way towards the residence of Mr. Roseburn, and his fair nieces, with the hope of seeing Jane. I walked about there, my mind in a state of feverish agitation, which I need not attempt to pourtray, during the whole of the day, and I had only walked a few paces on my way home, when I was aroused from my lethargy of vexation and disappointment, by hearing my name repeated in no very ceremonious voice from some person behind me. I turned round and beheld Walter Alston, who had evidently just left the house of Mr. Roseburn, coming towards me. I paused, and I could not but feel confused and abashed at his appearance, especially as I saw, from the expression of his countenance, that he had become acquainted with all that had happened, and was, naturally enough, filled with indignation; but still I collected myself, and conquered my feelings as much as possible, and felt my pride greatly mortified at the familiarity with which he had used my name.

"So, Sir Laurence Cleveland," he said, when he had got up to me, "I see the blush of shame is mounting in your cheek, and well it may, when you meet the man you have so deeply injured."

"Injured!" I repeated, scarcely knowing what reply to make.

"Ay!" he answered, and his broad chest swelled with the excitement of his feelings; "deeply, most basely injured. Can you, will you attempt to deny it, and thus add falsehood to the other wrongs you have done me. Nay, Sir Laurence Cleveland, you may frown, but different though our stations in society are, your conduct has reduced us to a level. I am a plain man in speech, but I have truth and honesty on my side, and I will speak my mind. Before cursed fate sent you to this neighbourhood, I was happy, and my hopes were brighter than the most sunshiny day, knowing that I possessed the love of her who was dearer to me than my own existence. I had formed the most sanguine expectations of future felicity in the possession of that envied treasure; but those hopes you have crushed, and laid desolate my mind by alienating from me the affections of Clara. What then should be my feelings towards you? What have I ever done towards you that you should injure me in so vital a part? Oh, Sir Laurence, your conduct has been truly honourable, and well befitting one who holds the station of a gentleman."

"Walter Alston," I replied, unable to control my resentment at the pointed irony with which he addressed himself to me; the more so as I keenly felt the truth and force of his observations: "this language, allow me to say, ill becomes you; and, therefore, if you are determined to be insolent, our interview must end."

"Indeed!" he said, with a bitter sneer; "but I marvel not that you should shrink from the meeting. Your own conscience must convince you how richly you merit my reproaches. Insolent, indeed! and so it is insolent for a man who has received a mortal injury, to speak his mind to him who has done him wrong, because he happens to be placed in a more elevated station of society. I tell you, Sir Laurence Cleveland, that you have degraded yourself, when, on the contrary, from your position it was your bounden duty to set an example of honour and integrity to your inferiors in rank."

"Is it my fault that I have won the heart of Clara Roseburn, or that I should have been captivated by the charms of one whom you yourself describe, and truly so, as all perfection?" I demanded.

"Yes," replied he quickly: "when you knew that the damsel was betrothed to me —that the day was even fixed for our nuptials—you should have stifled your passion, and not have thrown temptation in the way of her who was happy in the choice she had made, until she beheld you. But mark my words, Sir Laurence Cleveland—your hopes will be disappointed, and, in spite of your efforts, Clara Roseburn shall become my wife."

"And would you unite yourself to one whose heart you must be now aware you can never possess?" I asked.

"Yes," he fiercely replied; "even though it should break that heart which is no longer mine. Your conduct, Sir Laurence, has driven me to desperation, and there is nothing that I will hesitate to do to prevent Clara Roseburn from becoming your's."

"Hear me, Walter Alston," I remarked, "and let reason have some influence over your excited feelings."

"Reason," he repeated, with a look of the most supreme contempt; "you wound a man in the most vital part; you blast all his hopes and prospects; you create misery and despair where all was before happiness and blissful anticipation, and then you coolly talk to the man you have so injured, of reason. Bah!"

"This indignation can do you no good, Walter. I admit that, to a certain extent, I have injured you; but I would be your friend, and make you some atonement."

"Atonement for the loss of Clara's affections," he cried; "oh, this is, indeed, monstrous. Do not add mockery to irreparable wrong. But I only waste my time by talking thus to one who is evidently insensible to every proper feeling. The time may come, Sir Laurence Cleveland, when you will have reason to repent this."

"Ah! dare you threaten me?" I exclaimed, with uncontrollable indignation.

He returned no answer to me, but fixing upon me a look of mingled contempt, reproach, and defiance, he quitted the spot, and was quickly out of sight.

I stood for a few moments after he was gone, and bit my lips, while my bosom swelled with the mingled feelings of offended pride and shame. I could not deny the truth and justice of Walter's observations; but to receive such biting reproaches from one whom I considered to be so far beneath me, was more than I could, with any patience, endure.

"Insolent menial!" I ejaculated; "you may, and shall have reason to repent of this boldness. And so you dare to threaten me that you will thwart me in my plans, and make Clara your wife, in spite of me? Well, we shall see; but that assertion makes me more determined than before. She shall be mine, even at any sacrifice."

With these thoughts, after lingering for some time longer in the neighbourhood, I returned to the manor. But, notwithstanding my efforts, I could not but feel at times the greatest apprehensions that my wishes would be frustrated, and the anguish of mind which I felt convinced Clara must now be enduring, tortured me more than all.

And what chance was there of seeing her now, or of communicating with her, so strict an eye as Mr. Roseburn would be sure to keep upon her actions? My only dependence was upon Jane, and, however great her inclination might be to serve me, she might not be afforded the opportunity. Thus was I racked between doubt, hope, and fear.

That day and the next I passed in the same state of mind, and although I wandered in the immediate vicinity of Mr. Roseburn's residence for several hours, I could not see anything of Jane.

At one time the house looked so lonely and deserted, that I imagined they had left it; and indeed it was not at all unlikely that Mr. Roseburn would remove Clara secretly, in order that he might with certainty defeat my plans, and enforce her union with Walter Alston, without any fear of interruption; and this idea so tortured my mind the more I encouraged it, that I was almost mad.

"But surely;" I reflected, "when he finds that Clara's heart is firmly devoted to me, he will never compel her to become the wife of Walter Alston? He is too much attached to her to sacrifice her to one on whom her affections are no longer placed, especially when he is convinced that my proposals are dictated by honour and sincerity. And Clara, after the solemn declaration she has made to me, will not, let the consequences be what they may, ever consent to become the bride of Walter Alston. No, no—I will not despair—Clara loves me; she has acknowledged that she does so, and she must, she shall be mine. And yet the time is so short ere the day will arrive that is appointed for their nuptials to take place, that I must be prompt in my plans, or, in spite of all my resolutions, they will be frustrated. Let me decide quickly, and use measures accordingly."

Such were the guilty, the dishonourable reflections which occupied my mind; but it was some time before I could come to any decision, so surrounded by difficulties did my peculiar and embarrassing case appear to be. However, at length, as I had not an opportunity of seeing Jane, and I felt confident that Clara must be in a most painful state of suspense; also, that I was prohibited from again visiting her residence, I determined to write to Mr. Roseburn, again urging my suit with the utmost energy, and imploring him to consider the misery he would inflict upon his niece if he persevered in compelling her to bestow her hand upon a man whom she could no longer love; at the same time pointing out to him, in the most forcible language I could make use of, the honour of my intentions, and my readiness to make Clara at once my wife, although family matters would render it necessary that the ceremony should be performed in secrecy. As regarded Walter Alston, I again disavowed any feeling of ill-will towards him, and offered to make him all the compensation for his loss and disappointment that it was in my power to do, confident that he would not persist in forcing Clara to complete a compact which was no longer in unison with her feelings, but which, on the contrary, must render her wretched for the remainder of her life.

Compensation! oh, how heartless and vain must I have been at that time, to think that I could ever render sufficient compensation to that man whose hopes I sought to blight for ever. But nothing could remove the infatuation that had taken such firm possession of my mind.

This letter I despatched by a trusty messenger to Mr. Roseburn, and awaited his reply with the greatest anxiety. It came, and was of that description which I might fully have anticipated had I allowed reason at that time to hold the least sway over me.

He rejected my offers with stern decision; expressed his determination to compel his niece to become the wife of Walter Alston, or to discard her for ever; and bitterly reproached me for my obstinate perseverance in encouraging a passion which could never be gratified, and for thinking him capable of forfeiting his solemn word to a worthy young man. He concluded by requesting me not to address any future letters to him, as, after he had so explicitly expressed his resolution, he should not again condescend to answer them.

This epistle greatly mortified my pride, and I could not help cursing Mr. Roseburn in my heart, for an obstinate old fool; but still was determined not to be daunted in my resolutions, flattering myself that the sentiments which Clara had confessed towards me remained unchanged, and that even the fear of incurring the wrath of her aged relative and guardian, would not restrain her from consenting to become my wife, should an opportunity offer itself. But still the time was so short, that I could not but entertain some apprehensions for the success of my wishes. What means I could adopt to behold Clara again, that I might hear from her own lips an assurance of the continuance of her love, and her willingness to enter into any plan which I might suggest, I knew not, for Mr. Roseburn would be sure to keep such a watchful eye over her actions, and would not lose sight of her for a moment.

That I could not see Jane, annoyed and perplexed me much, and I looked most anxiously for her coming to the manor every day, and had already written a letter for her to convey to Clara, in which I again most eloquently repeated my vows of unalterable affection, expatiated upon the anguish I was enduring, and implored her to brave every risk, and appoint some place, and a certain hour, where we might have a private interview, and to decide immediately upon the course it would be necessary for us to adopt under the peculiar circumstances of our situation.

Three days elapsed in this state of almost insupportable anxiety, and I had almost made up my mind once more boldly to visit Mr. Roseburn, and to urge my suit, when I accidentally met Jane one morning as I was wandering in the vicinity of her master's residence.

She seemed no less pleased at seeing me, than I was gratified in meeting her, and evinced the utmost readiness to answer the numerous questions I so eagerly put to her, almost in a breath. She informed me that Clara had never once quitted the house since I had last seen her; that she was very melancholy, and was almost constantly in tears, keeping herself secluded in her own apartment. Mr. Roseburn had endeavoured again and again to convince her of the folly and injustice she was guilty of in encouraging a passion for me, which could never with honour be gratified, and thus destroying the hopes of that youth to whom she was so solemnly affianced. But Clara repeated her former asseverations, namely, that Walter Alston no longer possessed her heart, and that if she were not permitted to bestow her hand upon the real object of her affections, she would remain single for ever.

Jane added that never before had she beheld her master so sternly determined; he had reproached Clara for her obstinacy and ingratitude, and had expressed his firm resolution to compel her to become the wife of Walter Alston, or to banish her for ever from his affections, and no longer to own her for his relation.

"By Heaven!" I exclaimed, passionately, when Jane had concluded, "his hopes shall never be gratified; I will possess her, though I risk my very life in trying to do so. Obdurate, inflexible man! is this a proof of the affection he bears his niece? Would he not sacrifice her to a man whom she has declared she can no longer love, and thus break her heart? It shall not be! No, dear Clara; I find that you are faithful and sincere in the vows you have made to me, and, in spite of all the difficulties which now present themselves, you and no other shall become my bride. Jane, convey to your young mistress this letter, and beg of her to return me an answer as speedily as possible. I shall be all impatience until I behold you again."

As I said this, I placed the letter and a guinea in Jane's hand, and she having faithfully promised to meet me on the following evening, returned home to the cottage.

The account which Jane had given me increased my hopes, for I was certain that Clara's sentiments towards me were still the same, and that, notwithstanding the determination of her uncle, she would hazard everything rather than bestow her hand where her heart could not accompany it. But I saw no other means by which our wishes could be accomplished, than by an elopement, and, after all, Clara might feel an unconquerable repugnance to such a step as that.

Most anxiously and impatiently did I await the arrival of the following evening, and long before the time which Jane had promised to meet me I was at the place of appointment; and I formed various conjectures as to the message she would bring me, although I could not but flatter myself with the best hopes.

She came at last, and I eagerly advanced towards her, and, before I could put any questions to her, she placed a letter in my hand.

The fine and delicate characters I knew immediately were in the handwriting of Clara, and with feelings of the most unbounded transport I pressed the epistle to my lips, and loaded it with my kisses. I then broke the seal, and with eager eyes, in the broad rays of the moonlight, I perused the contents. They were all that I could wish, most warmly yet modestly responding to those sentiments of affection I had expressed for her, deploring the obstacles which presented themselves to the encouragement of our vows; but, at the same, protesting her determination to suffer anything rather than consent to become the wife of Walter Alston. She placed the utmost reliance on the honour and sincerity of my intentions, and concluded by promising to meet me at nine o'clock the following night, in the dell near her uncle's residence, she having no doubt that she should be enabled to leave the house secretly at that time, as Mr. Roseburn would imagine she had retired to her chamber, as was her custom almost always at that hour.

With what delight did I read this letter, which was so confirmatory of all my hopes and expectations; and I entrusted Jane with a most affectionate message, which I desired her to deliver to her young mistress, assuring her that I would be true to the appointment, and should endure the most torturing suspense until the time had arrived which would once more transport my eyes with her presence.

Jane promised to obey me to the very letter, and I could place the strictest confidence in her integrity. Certainly, under all the circumstances, I considered her an almost inestimable friend; whereas, if I had not been blinded by my misplaced passion, I should have looked upon her rather as the contrary, since she was making herself an instrument to my future misery, and that of Clara and her amiable guardian.

On returning to the manor, and retiring to my chamber, which I did as soon as I could excuse myself, I perused the letter which I had received from Clara again and again, and every time I did so, it afforded me the greater gratification.

"Beloved damsel!" I cried, "I can no longer doubt the sincerity and ardour of your attachment to me; this precious epistle proves it, and how can I ever sufficiently return the passion of one so enviable? And shall I suffer anything to frustrate our wishes? By Heaven, never! Great as the obstacles now appear to be, I may surmount them, and I will persevere at any hazard. Oh! Clara, how great, how unspeakable will be the transport I must experience on again beholding you, and being allowed to press your angelic form to my heart. What heavenly music will it be to my ears to listen to your tender vows, and to receive the assurance from your own lips of the ardour of your affection!"

Thus did I continue to soliloquise for some time, and I could not think of retiring to rest, and when I did, my mind was so busily occupied that I could not sleep. I was glad when the morning dawned, so that I could walk forth from the manor, and endeavour to compose my feelings in a ramble; for I did not wish Mr. Clerivalle to behold me in my present agitated state, lest it should excite his suspicion, and he should put such questions to me as it would not be pleasant or convenient for me to answer at present.

After walking about for more than a couple of hours, I did become composed, and, buoyed up with the most sanguine hope, I endeavoured to await with patience the arrival of the appointed hour in the evening, when I was to meet the object of my most ardent affections, and I trusted that nothing would occur to prevent her from keeping her promise. I considered to myself all that I should say to her, and was resolved to urge her to consent to become my wife clandestinely, since it appeared that nothing could persuade her uncle to give his consent to our nuptials. This, I had very little doubt that I could prevail on her to do, and I had already partly formed a plan in my mind by which our wishes might, I thought, with certainty be carried into execution.

In order that I might not excite the surprise or suspicion of Mr. Clerivalle, by leaving the manor at so late an hour in the evening, I departed soon after dinner, merely stating that I was going for a walk; and I wandered to the wood, where I threw myself on the green turf, under the shadow of a lofty tree, and gave myself up to reflection on my approaching interview.

The time passed tediously away, but at length the evening set in; I heard a church clock strike the hour of eight, and I arose from my recumbent posture, and made my way towards the place of assignation.

The night was very fine, and the moon shone forth with silvery splendour, seeming to smile upon my hopes. With a throbbing heart I proceeded on my way, and every step I took, my sanguine expectations gained strength. It was not long ere I arrived at the dell, and there I awaited the arrival of the time when Clara had promised to meet me, with the greatest impatience. Never had the minutes appeared half so long or so tedious to me; and a thousand fears entered my breast that something would occur to prevent her coming to me, although I was convinced that her anxiety for the meeting would be as great as mine.

At length, however, nine o'clock struck, and scarcely had the last tone died away upon the tranquil air, when I heard a light rustling sound upon the grass, and hurrying forward in the direction from which it proceeded, I beheld the beloved object of my anxiety approaching. I flew towards her with an exclamation of delight, and the next instant I enfolded her lovely form in my arms, and felt her heart violently palpitating with the most uncontrollable emotion.

I need not relate all the particulars of that meeting; suffice it to say that we repeated our vows of unalterable affection, and Clara expressed the dread she felt as the time approached which was appointed for her union with Walter Alston, and declared that death would now be less awful to her than a fate which was so thoroughly repugnant to her feelings. Now did the opportunity present itself for which I had been so anxious, and I immediately urged her to elope with me, when we might be privately united, and thus put an end at once to all the cares and apprehensions which at present tormented us, and afterwards, no doubt, effect a reconciliation with Mr. Roseburn.

Clara at first seemed to recoil from the idea of taking such a step, for she hesitated thus to disobey the will of that guardian who had ever behaved with so much affection towards her ; and she feared, after what she had said, that he would never forgive her; but, at length, my persuasions, and the affection which I firmly believe she at that time felt towards me, prevailed, and, with many blushes, she yielded, and promised to be in readiness to fly to my arms when I had made the necessary preparations, which would occupy two or three days.

My extacy was now complete, and again I clasped her to my bosom, and breathed a solemn vow to Heaven that I would never deceive her; and as there might be danger in any further delay, we were constrained to part. I attended her till we came in sight of her dwelling, and, promising to forward a letter through the means of Jane, as soon as possible, we bade each other adieu, and I perceived that she entered the house by a back entrance, unobserved ; I then made my way back to the manor in a state of mind I shall not tire your patience by attempting to describe. The consummation of my hopes I now considered was certain, and I indulged in ideal scenes of future happiness.

It was necessary, however, that I should depart immediately from the manor, in order to make the necessary preparations for my clandestine union, which I was resolved should take place at my house at Broxley, where, for the present, it would be prudent for us to reside.

Lord Elworth resided in the same neighbourhood; he had been one of my earliest friends, and I knew I could confide in him. I had not the least doubt that he would readily enter into my plans, and assist me in my union, and there would be very little difficulty, I flattered myself, in getting a minister to perform the ceremony, and thus I considered that all would go as well as I could wish it.

The next day after this interview with Clara, I informed Mr. Clerivalle that I regretted I should be compelled to leave him directly, as I had some important business to transact, which demanded my immediate attention; but that I hoped, ere long, to be honoured by a visit from him to Branscombe House.

Mr. Clerivalle expressed some surprise at the suddenness of this intention, but promised to avail himself of my invitation. The next evening I saw Jane in the neighbourhood of the cottage, who informed me that her mistress was quite as anxious as myself, and that she had retired to her chamber at a very early hour, under the pretext of being indisposed. She also informed me of the tender

See p. 338.

expressions her mistress had made use of, regarding me, in confidence to her, and delivered to me that which was more precious than all, a small locket, inclosing a miniature likeness of herself, accompanied by a few lines, modestly requesting me to accept the gift, as an assurance of her sincerity in entering into the solemn compact between us.

I pressed the precious gift to my lips, and invoked a thousand blessings upon the head of the generous-hearted, the confiding, the lovely donor, and taking a valuable ring from my finger, desired Jane to deliver it to her mistress with all secrecy, and then, having arranged with her in which way she was to receive my letters, and instructed her to call every day at the post-office, to ascertain whether they were waiting for her, we separated.

I returned to the manor, and I now felt that my triumph was all but complete. My plans, I considered, were so admirably arranged, that it would be next to an impossibility to frustrate them; and, what was more, the assurance of the sincerity and ardour of Clara's affections towards me inspired me with confidence.

"She is mine!" I ejaculated in tones of transport; "she is mine, by her own consent, and other fortuitous circumstances, and no earthly power can prevent our union. True, Mr. Roseburn, her too precise guardian, may, for a time, feel indignant at this disobedience to his will, and Walter Alston may be wrathful at the disappointment to his hopes; but I have no doubt, that time and circumstances will reconcile them both to a marriage, which, however clandestine, originates in affection, and that they will be ready to come to some amicable arrangement. Nevertheless, at any risk, I cannot resist a blessing which is thus laid within my grasp. Dearest Clara, to sacrifice you, would be to abandon my every hope of happiness in this world."

Such were my selfish reflections; I thought not of the misery that I was sure to inflict upon others—I thought not of the injustice to the humble Walter Alston; of the ingratitude to Mr. Roseburn; every feeling of honour and rectitude was absorbed in the one idea, the one paramount determination to make Clara my wife at any cost. Thus was I hurried down the stream of madness and folly, and awoke not from my dream, until it was too late to redeem the errors of which I had been guilty.

How many times, during that night, did I take the miniature of Clara from my bosom, and gaze enraptured upon those fair features which had so infatuated my senses. I thought that every charm was concentrated in that beloved resemblance; that it was indeed the likeness of perfection itself; and that every blessing must attend my union with such an inestimable being. To imagine that one thought could ever harbour in that fair bosom, which an angel should blush to acknowledge, would have constituted me at that time, as I believed, little better than a monster; and the manner in which she had yielded herself to my will, was a flattery to my vanity, which rendered me still more ardent and firm in my determination.

Little did I anticipate that that beauteous damsel, who had so completely, as I might say, taken my reason prisoner, who was then, as I firmly believe, the very soul of innocence, could ever have descended to deception towards him for whom she had sacrificed so much; but time cruelly proved to me how fatal was the mistake which I had made, and brought upon me a just punishment for my obstinate perseverance in my advances towards one who was honourably affianced to another. I certainly must admit myself all to blame in this unfortunate affair, and, had I taken the advice of my excellent friend, it would never have happened.

The following day I took my leave of Mr. Clerivalle, and departed for Branscombe House, merely intending to stop there until I had arranged some private matters, and then to hasten to Broxley; for there was now no time to be lost, as it wanted only a fortnight to the time which was fixed for the nuptials of Clara and Walter Alston to take place; and I was certain that Mr. Roseburn would not delay them one day; no, not one single hour.

As soon as I arrived at Branscombe House, I despatched a letter to my beloved, teeming with affection, and urging her to hold herself in readiness for the day of trial, as it was uncertain how soon it might occur, and that I would make such arrangements as would leave not the least doubt upon her mind of the honour of my intentions.

By the return of post I received a letter from Clara, the contents of which were all that my most sanguine hopes could have anticipated. She assured me of her confidence, and her willingness to abide by anything I suggested ; but at the same time informed me that her uncle remained inflexible, and that Walter Alston continued his visits, the same as before, and seemed to flatter himself that, after all, she would become his wife from affection, and not from compulsion alone, although she now took the greatest pains to convince him of the contrary.

It appeared, from the statement of Clara, that my departure from the Manor had somewhat eased the anxiety of Mr. Roseburn, and dispelled his apprehensions, and he seemed to hope that his firm rejection of my suit had abashed me, and caused me to abandon my hopes ; the consequence of which was that he placed not so much restraint upon the actions of his niece ; raised no objections to her taking her customary walks, and thus offered every facility to the favourable operation of our schemes.

This intelligence gratified me much, and I resolved to take, as you may be sure, every advantage of it. The success of my wishes now appeared certain, and I could not but exult in what I then considered a triumph.

Having settled all my business at Branscombe House, I departed for Broxley, and immediately sought the presence of my friend, Lord Elworth. He was, as I have before observed, very much attached to me, and I knew that I could place every confidence in him.

His lordship had not been married more than a twelvemonth to a very handsome and accomplished lady, who was of a most vivacious disposition, but accustomed to pay the utmost deference to her lord's will and judgment ; and, therefore, in securing the aid of one, I was certain of obtaining that of the other.

I made Lord Elworth acquainted with all the particulars of my amour, and the peculiar circumstances in which the object of my affections was placed ; and he entered most readily into my plans, and volunteered to render me all the assistance in his power towards the consummation of my wishes, and introduced me to a minister, who was a particular friend of his, and who undertook to perform the marriage ceremony at any time, in private, while his lordship promised that he and his lady would become attesting witnesses to the validity of the proceedings. This was all I required ; my plans seemed to prosper as well as I could hope, and I immediately despatched another letter to Clara, apprising her of all that had taken place, and telling her to be in readiness to meet me on the twenty-fourth, in the wood not far from the residence of Mr. Roseburn, where I would be in waiting at seven o'clock in the evening, with a post-chaise, and accompanied by my friend, Lord Elworth, to carry her to Broxley. I repeated my vows of constancy, and implored her to place every confidence in my honour.

Two days after this, I received a letter from Clara, breathing the same sentiments of love and confidence which she had before so ardently expressed towards me, and promising to be in readiness to meet me at the time and place of appointment.

My happiness was now all but complete ; everything went on as well as my most sanguine wishes could have anticipated, and I could foresee nothing that could possibly prevent their being satisfactorily carried into effect. Lord Elworth also warmly congratulated me on the prospect of their success, and all the preparations being completed, on the morning of the twenty-third, myself and his lordship departed from Broxley, for a town situated about two miles from the dwelling of Mr. Roseburn. We arrived there at a late hour in the evening of the same day, and put up at the principal inn, but, of course, most prudently concealing our real names and titles.

Notwithstanding Lord Elworth tried to persuade me to the contrary, I could not resist the temptation to ramble in the vicinity of the residence of the object of my affections, with the hope of seeing her, although it was not likely that she would venture forth at such a time, and when her more serious attentions must be fully engaged in making preparations for her elopement on the following evening.

I muffled myself up in my cloak, so that I might not be recognised by any one whom I should encounter, and who might have a knowledge of my person, and walked on, filled with the most anxious thought.

It was a fine moonlight night, and I had not proceeded far when I perceived a female form, which I thought I knew, advancing towards me. I looked more narrowly, and was then convinced I was not deceived; it was Jane. I hastened to meet her, and repeated her name; she looked up, and recognising me, she uttered an exclamation of astonishment. Eagerly I inquired after her mistress, and learned from her, to my satisfaction, that she was as well as could be expected, and that she had made all the arrangements for the hour of trial, although it caused her the most painful regret at being thus compelled to act in disobedience to the will of her uncle, and probably to forfeit his affection for ever. She stated, also, that Walter Alston was confined to his bed through indisposition, and had not been able to visit them for two or three days past; and, as for Mirah, although she had been very melancholy ever since I had quitted the neighbourhood, she seemed not to entertain the least suspicion of what was going on, but rather to imagine that they would never behold me again, and that her cousin would in time learn to forget me, and to stifle the unfortunate passion I had created in her bosom. But what afforded me more satisfaction than all was, that Mr. Roseburn had stated he would be compelled to leave home on the following day, on business, which might probably detain him till a late hour in the evening; and thus every opportunity would be afforded for the escape of Clara, and we should be far away from the neighbourhood, before he would be aware of her flight. Fortune seemed to smile upon us, and I hailed it as a harbinger of future success.

I loaded Jane with presents, and sent by her the most affectionate message to her mistress, and then I returned to the inn, full of glee, and the most delightful anticipations. Lord Elworth congratulated me on the favourable aspect of my affairs, and expressed the most anxious wish to behold the lovely being who had so completely captivated my senses, and whom, he considered, must certainly be perfection's self.

I slept but little that night, so busily was my mind occupied with the anticipations of the following evening; and when I did, the most strange and perplexing visions flitted before my imagination. I arose in the morning, sanguine with hope, and tedious seemed the hours until the evening advanced. The long—long looked for time came at last, and everything being in readiness, myself and Lord Elworth stepped into the carriage, and were driven off to the wood, where, at the spot appointed, and in one of the most secluded parts, we alighted, and awaited the arrival of the moment when we might expect to behold Clara with feelings of impatience and anxiety you may readily form an idea of.

We had not to wait long, for exactly as the appointed hour struck from the neighbouring church, Clara and Jane (who it had been agreed was to be her companion) were perceived coming along the avenue. On beholding the vehicle, and myself and

Lord Elworth standing near it, the emotions of Clara seemed to overpower her, and she paused, and leaned on the arm of Jane for support. I fled towards her, and caught her almost fainting in my arms. I called her by every endearing title, and pressed her lovely form with the greatest transport to my bosom; but it was some minutes ere she could recover anything like a degree of tranquillity, and then she looked up timidly, with tearful eyes and blushing cheeks, in my countenance, but could not speak.

"Courage, courage, my love, my affianced bride!" I exclaimed, fervently pressing her hand; "the painful ordeal is passed; Heaven smiles upon our love, and you are now mine for ever!—No earthly power shall prevent our union; and, in a few days, fear not but we shall effect a happy reconciliation with your guardian. Come, then, my beloved Clara, the carriage waits, which in a few hours will convey us to the place of our destination."

"Oh, Sir Laurence," sighed Clara; "even at this critical moment, though I doubt not the honour of your intentions, or the strength and sincerity of your affection, a dismal foreboding comes across my mind, and I regret —— Oh, surely it is most cruel to leave that venerable and beloved relative, who has ever behaved to me with such unlimited kindness and attention, thus."

"Nay, Clara," I remonstrated; "it is no time to hesitate now; it is stern necessity that alone compels the step; but fear not, your uncle will forgive us, and nothing will be wanting to render our happiness complete. Come, dear Ciara, for should we any longer delay, we may be observed by some one who knows us, and our plans frustrated, and all our hopes annihilated. You do not leave your uncle for long; in the course of a few days you will probably behold him again, and it will then be, I am convinced, to receive his forgiveness and his blessing."

Clara threw herself in my arms, and after giving vent to her emotions for a minute or two, she suffered me to lead her towards the carriage.

I introduced her to my friend, Lord Elworth, who seemed much struck with her appearance, and having handed her into the carriage, we followed, and closing the blinds, were quickly driven from the spot.

It required all the arguments I could make use of, however, to tranquillise the feelings of Clara, as we proceeded on our journey, and the further we withdrew from the neighbourhood where all her days from childhood had been passed, the greater her anguish became, and her tears flowed unrestrained. But at length she became more composed, and listened to my vows and asseverations with patience and confidence. Lord Elworth was much prepossessed in favour of her, and it seems he had made the same favourable impression upon her.

Clara informed me, when she had sufficiently tranquillised her feelings to do so that she had left letters behind her for her uncle and cousin, in which she explained everything, and earnestly implored their forgiveness, at the same time that she had been compelled to disappoint the hopes of Walter Alston, for whom, she stated, she felt the greatest esteem, and trusted that he would be able to place his affections upon some damsel who could return his passion, and who was worthy of his merits.

I could not but highly approve of the tenour of these epistles, and predicted that they would have their due effect; but it was some time before I could persuade Clara to think so too, or to dissipate the dismal forebodings which she had suffered to take possession of her mind.

Nothing worthy of recording occurred on the journey, and at an early hour the following morning we arrived at Broxley, and immediately proceeded to the mansion of Lord Elworth, where it was arranged that Clara should remain under the care of Elworth until the hour fixed upon for our nuptials. Lady Elworth received her with every kindness, and Clara, inspired with fresh confidence, became more calm, and, soon after her arrival at the mansion, retired to the chamber allotted to her, with the hope of being able to snatch a few hours' repose, which she stood so much in need of after the fatigue of her journey.

My happiness was now all but complete, and I could scarcely control the excess of my joy. Lord and Lady Elworth passed the most flattering eulogiums upon the personal attractions and manners of Clara, and wondered not that she should have so captivated me, and they ardently wished that every prosperity might attend us, and that we might soon be able to effect a reconciliation with Mr. Roseburn; which they had no doubt would be the case, when that gentleman should be satisfied that we were honourably united; but, for my own part, I must confess, although I had endeavoured to persuade Clara to the contrary, that my anticipations were not sanguine; for Mr. Roseburn had evinced, from scruples of honour, from the first moment that my sentiments towards his niece had become known to him, such a thorough repugnance to the union; and I could perceive that he was a man who, when he had once formed a resolution or a prejudice, could not be easily moved to abandon it. This opinion, however, I must endeavour to conceal from Clara; for it would be sure to make her miserable, and greatly diminish those joys I had so long and so fondly contemplated.

It was not till the afternoon that I was again permitted to behold my intended bride, and I had then the satisfaction of observing that she was much refreshed, and evidently more calm, and in better spirits than when we had recently parted.

The kind attentions of Lord and Lady Elworth inspired her with confidence, and divested her of much of that timidity, which was natural under the circumstances. But let me at once come to the more important facts.

The day following our arrival at Broxley, the marriage rites were performed in the chapel attached to the mansion of Lord Elworth, and I considered I had now attained the very pinnacle of earthly felicity. Short-sighted fool that I was, I never reflected how hopeless it was that permanent happiness could ever be the result of an union contracted under such circumstances; little did I then imagine that that beauteous being to whom I had resigned all my affections; to obtain possession of whom, I had broken the solemn pledge given to my late lamented father on his death bed, could ever deceive me. But a few months only, and I was awakened from my delusive dream. But I have other circumstances to relate, ere I come to this melancholy part of my story.

No sooner were our nuptials over, than Clara requested that I would write to her uncle, informing him of the fact, and craving his forgiveness for the step we had been compelled, from the strength of our love, to take. Much depended upon his answer, and we both awaited it with the utmost anxiety and impatience. It came at last; the letter I had dispatched inclosed in another, containing these brief lines :—

" Abandoned pair, henceforth you are strangers to Redmond Roseburn."

I need not attempt to describe the distraction of Clara, on the receipt of this brief epistle; she fell into a fit, and it was several hours before she could be restored to anything like a degree of consciousness; and then, so abject was her despair, that it was a considerable time before I could reduce her to a state of tranquillity.

In the meantime, I had forwarded another letter to Mr. Roseburn, to which no answer was returned, and this all added to the agony of Clara. But I endeavoured to persuade her that it was all the passion of the moment, which would speedily evaporate, and that her uncle, knowing us to be honourably married, would once more receive us to his bosom.

Fain would Clara have hastened to her late home, and, throwing herself at her guardian's feet, supplicate his forgiveness, and I had the greatest difficulty in persuading her not to do so; but at length she became tranquil, and everything was absorbed in the affection which, I have every reason to believe, she at that time bore towards me. From Mirah we received a letter, in which she informed us, that her uncle was in a state of mind bordering upon madness; that he looked upon her with suspicion, if not absolute hatred; and that Walter Alston had sworn revenge against me, and all connected with me. The latter threat I treated with superlative contempt; for I considered that he would never have the courage, if he should have the opportunity, of putting it into execution. However, I could not conceal from myself, that his feelings were justly provoked, and that I had acted towards him in a manner which was highly discreditable to myself; and Clara, I could perceive, could not help reproaching herself for the manner in which she had annihilated his hopes and prospects; worthy as she firmly believed him to be, of every happiness that could befal him.

And now I must readily admit, that I consider, had I not thus have ruined the hopes of Walter Alston, and rendered him reckless of himself and what became of him, he would always have remained a respectable member of society; but I firmly believe that he and his father were guilty of the atrocious crime of which they were convicted, and certainly it was only in honesty and justice that I gave the evidence I did against them. Bitterly have I lamented their fate ever since; and, although I know not why Harold, the gipsy, and Madela, should entertain such implacable feelings of hatred and revenge against me, and how they can have become so well acquainted with all these circumstances, I cannot imagine that they are in any way connected with Walter Alston or his family; for Harold resembles him not in features, and certainly not in disposition; as for the old woman, I never saw her, that I am aware of, and, consequently, cannot say whether Madela and her are the same individuals.

A month passed away, and myself and Clara, during that time, had sent several letters to Mr. Roseburn, which he never condescended to answer; but many were the epistles that were received from Mirah, in which she stated the change that had come over her uncle; from being one of the kindest and most indulgent of men, he had become one of the most austere and suspicious; seldom gave her a kind word, and continually averred it as his firm belief that she would treat him with the same ingratitude as Clara had done.

It was in those letters that I first became convinced that I had excited the same tender sentiments in the bosom of Mirah, as I had done in that of her cousin, and the truth could not long remain a secret from the keen penetration of Clara. This conviction, coupled with the wrath of her uncle, rendered her miserable, and notwithstanding my fond attentions, and the kindness shown to her by Lady Elworth, I had the greatest difficulty in arousing her to anything like a degree of composure. She was anxious for us to seek the presence of Mr. Roseburn, that we might personally solicit his forgiveness; but I always strenuously combatted this desire, fearing that the excitement might be too much for both parties, and trusting that in a short time his anger would subside, and that he might be willing to come to a reconcilia- tion. I could not imagine that it was in the nature of that excellent man, to bear animosity for any length of period, especially towards one whom he had ever loved as fondly as if she had been his own child; but I did not at the time properly appreciate his feelings, and how deeply, by thwarting his hopes and wishes, I had struck at the root of his happiness; and another was shortly afterwards about to take place, which was destined to break his heart altogether. Mirah informed us that he frequently absented himself from home for hours together, and when he was at home he was peevish, morose, and abstracted, and although she did her utmost to please him, he always appeared to view her exertions with suspicion, and treated her with reserve, if not with absolute unkindness. It was quite evident, from the tenour of Mirah's letters, that that home which had once been so happy, was now rendered miserable, and that conviction naturally rendered Clara wretched, and I felt myself at a loss for arguments to console her.

Mirah also informed us that Walter Alston had become quite another individual. He neglected his usual employment, was often inebriated, and seldom visited Mr. Roseburn's house. Nay, more, she had often heard him utter vows of vengeance against me, and she apprehended that his feelings of resentment would lead him into some act of violence. This idea I, however, treated with indifference, and endeavoured to persuade Clara that time and reason would reconcile him to his disappointment. But it was no easy matter to bring her to that conclusion; and she could not but deeply regret that she had been the means of bringing a naturally worthy young man to ruin and despair.

Another month passed away, and Clara had become a little more tranquil, when a circumstance took place which completely destroyed all the good that I had laboured so hard to accomplish.

I was seated alone one day in my study, when a servant suddenly made his ap- pearance, and informed me that there was a man waiting in the hall, who demanded an immediate audience of me. I demanded his name, but he refused to furnish me with it, or to name the business he had called upon; and I therefore declined to see him. This message was no sooner delivered by the servant, than I heard a loud disturbance in the hall, and the angry voice of a man, which I thought I had heard before. I was about to go to inquire the cause of this uproar, when a hasty and heavy foot was heard upon the stairs, and the next instant the room door was burst open, and Wal- ter Alston, with a countenance and demeanour rendered furious by the malevolence of his feelings, stood before us.

Clara was so alarmed, that she uttered a loud scream and immediately fainted in my arms; and I was so confounded and astonished by this unexpected meeting, that I was unable for a few moments to speak; while Walter Alston all the time, with clenched fists, stood gazing upon me and Clara alternately, with looks of the most deadly malice.

At length, I recovered sufficiently to demand in a peremptory tone what he meant by such an abrupt intrusion, and what his business was with me.

"To tell thee, Laurence Cleveland," replied Walter, in fierce accents, "that you be a villain, and that the poor deluded victim you hold in your arms——'

"Hold, man!" I interrupted, passionately, and my bosom swelled with insulted pride at the boldness of the man whom I had, in truth, so deeply injured; "dare you use such language to me? Begone, or you may have reason to repent having made this visit."

"Indeed I shall not go, Sir Laurence Cleveland," returned Walter Alston, "until I have told you my mind. Nay, you may frown, and you may threaten, but you have a desperate man to deal with, on whom you have inflicted the most cruel wrongs;

and who, viewing you with the contempt you merit, cares not a straw for you. I repeat that you are a treacherous scoundrel, who, under the guise of friendship, have seduced that wretched girl from the man to whom she was honourably, solemnly betrothed; you have made her act a cruel part of duplicity, and prompted her to break through that love and duty which she owed to her generous benefactor; and for that a heavy curse will light upon your head. Yes, I, the despised Walter Alston, whose prospects you have ruined, and rendered him an outcast, come to tell you so; and mark me, my predictions will be fulfilled as surely as that I now stand before you."

I will not become tedious by relating to you the particulars of this painful interview. Indeed, I think it would be better for us all that I should pass over it as briefly as possible. Suffice it then, to say, that the taunts of Walter Alston so enraged me that I could not at last keep my passion with the bounds of reason, and that Clara regained her senses to behold us engaged in a fierce struggle together, and but for her interposition, some fatal injury would probably have been inflicted upon one or both of us. Walter Alston at length quitted the house, vowing a deadly revenge.

This event had the most painful effect upon the feelings of Clara, and I found the greatest difficulty in at all tranquillising her. She could not but admit the truth and justice of Walter's observations, and I, also feeling the force of them, was at a loss to find any arguments to persuade her to the contrary.

Several weeks passed away in this manner, and at last nothing would satisfy Clara, but that we should both seek the presence of Mr. Roseburn, and solicit his forgiveness. I tried all I could to dissuade her from this step, for I shrunk with dread from the bare idea of meeting the reproaches of the incensed Mr. Roseburn, and felt convinced that all our efforts to reconcile him would be unavailing; but Clara was determined, and I was at last reluctantly compelled to yield. Two days afterwards we departed for the neighbourhood of Mr. Roseburn's residence, and put up at an hotel in the vicinity. My fears were fully realised: Mr. Roseburn refused to admit us to his presence, and, after many fruitless attempts to prevail upon him, we were forced to abandon our efforts in despair, and we returned to Broxley without so much as being able even to see Mirah.

Clara was almost heartbroken at the stern inflexibility of Mr. Roseburn, and I had the greatest difficulty imaginable, in being able to bring her to anything like a degree of composure.

Clara had scarcely recovered from this shock, when another event occurred to cause us much uneasiness. One day we were seated in the parlour of the mansion, when we were aroused by hearing a vehicle driven up to the door; hasty footsteps on the stairs followed, the room door was abruptly and unceremoniously thrown open, and the next instant Mirah sunk fainting in her cousin's arms.

Yes; unable any longer to endure the unkindness of Mr. Roseburn, and prompted by far more powerful feelings, which I afterwards discovered, she had abandoned him, and the poor old man was thus left alone to his misery and anguish.

I could not but blame Mirah for the step she had taken; but Clara, I found, was greatly comforted by the presence of her cousin, and I therefore endeavoured to reconcile myself to it, although I confess that I felt the greatest uneasiness; for, as I have before stated, I had discovered, by the tenor of her letters, that she had imbibed an unfortunate passion for me; but I determined not to give any encouragement to her hopes, and I had no doubt, that justice to Clara would induce her to subdue her passion.

At the earnest request of Mirah and Clara, I now addressed another letter to Mr. Roseburn, informing him where Mirah was, and beseeching him to forgive her, and to become reconciled to us all; but the letter was returned unopened, and it was but too evident that all chance of a reconciliation with Mr. Roseburn was at an end.

Another month elapsed, and then we heard that Walter Alston was in prison for poaching, and that he had become one of the most abandoned characters in that part of the country; and I could not but bitterly reproach myself as having been the cause of his ruin, and I could perceive that Clara viewed his fate with pity and regret.

But shortly afterwards we received a shock more severe than any we had yet experienced. Mr. Roseburn was found dead in his bed, and, upon opening his will, it was found that he had carried his animosity to the grave, for he had bequeathed all the property he possessed to a perfect stranger, and never once alluded to the names of Clara or her cousin.

This melancholy event greatly agitated Clara and Mirah, and they were for some time inconsolable; but time wore away their grief, and I began to hope that happier days were in store for us; but, alas, we were yet fated to endure much greater misery.

It was a short time after this, that as I was returning home one night, when I was in the immediate neighbourhood of my own residence, I was alarmed by hearing the report of a gun, and soon afterwards two men rushed past me, in whom I immediately recognised Walter Alston and his father, the latter of whom carried a gun. They retreated as fast as they could, and were quickly out of sight; but I had had so distinct a view of their features, that I was certain that I had not been mistaken, and I felt the greatest apprehension lest they should have committed some dreadful outrage.

These fears I found were not groundless, for, on advancing nearer to the house, I was horror-struck on beholding my principal gamekeeper stretched lifeless, and weltering in his blood.

There could be little doubt that Walter Alston and his father were the perpetrators of this atrocious deed, for there were several other persons who saw them retreating from the spot, as well as me. They were accordingly apprehended, and brought to trial, and although they both positively protested their innocence, the evidence against them was too conclusive to be doubted, and they were accordingly convicted, and sentenced to be hanged. The result of this unfortunate tragedy you are already acquainted with. Walter's father was executed, but the sentence of the former was commuted to perpetual banishment. I can solemnly declare that in all the share I had in the conviction of these wretched men, I was not instigated by any feeling of animosity, but that I was stimulated by a strict sense of justice, and I still feel satisfied that they were guilty of the horrible crime for which they suffered.

Soon after this, I thought that I perceived a great change in the conduct of Clara; she did not seem to take that pleasure in my society that she was wont to do, and was melancholy and reserved. This alteration very much surprised and disturbed me, and I sought from her an explanation, but she evaded my questions, and I could get no satisfactory reply. As her melancholy and abstractedness of manner increased, so also did the attentions of Mirah towards me, and I at length began to fear that she was excited to feelings of jealousy, and deeply regretted Mirah had ever become an inmate of my mansion, and avoided her all that I could.

A young man, named Cyril Percy, being on a visit to Lord and Lady Elworth, he was introduced to us, and possessing much fascination of manners, I took a great fancy towards him, and the consequence was, that he was frequently a guest at Broxley. Alas! it was a fatal intercourse for me, as you will soon learn; and now comes the time when the guilt of her to whom I had sacrificed my hand will be made apparent, and when you will find that, however much I may in other respects have erred, that at least I am not altogether so guilty as my implacable enemies would make me appear to be.

Soon after the appearance of Cyril Percy, the melancholy of Clara increased, unless when she was in his society, and then her countenance always brightened up, and she seemed to feel the greatest pleasure, and to listen to his lively conversation with the greatest admiration. But when he was gone she would relapse into her usual gloom, and it was in vain that I endeavoured to arouse her from it.

This singular behaviour caused me much uneasiness, especially as I could not imagine the cause, nor could I elicit any explanation from her. But never for a moment did I suspect her fidelity, or entertain the least idea of the thoughts that were then passing in her mind. Could I suspect that woman whom I believed to be all perfection, and to be devoted heart and soul to me? It was impossible; and yet, alas! I was fated too soon to be awakened from this delusive dream, and to be plunged into that abyss of shame and misery which I never thought to experience.

As this change in the behaviour of Clara became the more manifest, that of Mirah was not the less remarkable, and she took every opportunity of being in my company, and making up, by her volatile conversation, for what I had now lost in that of my wife; and I must confess that I began to feel a greater pleasure in her society than I had hitherto done.

Weeks flew on much in the same manner, and without anything occurring worthy of particular notice; but the storm was gathering that was shortly to burst over my head with overwhelming fury. The whole fearful truth was about to be revealed to me when, and in a manner I had little expected.

Cyril now became much more frequent in his visits, but still I never suspected his base designs, so well did he know how to act the part of the wily hypocrite, and to assume those virtues which he did not possess. At length, however, his visit to Lord Elworth terminated, and he expressed his regret at being compelled to leave such agreeable society, and to return home.

For some days after Cyril's departure, Clara was even more gloomy and thoughtful than before, and excused herself, to keep herself almost entirely secluded in her own chamber; still I had not the least suspicion of the truth, and attributed her melancholy to the reflections which constantly occupied her mind upon the death of her uncle, and his having gone to the tomb without having awarded to her his forgiveness. I tried all I could to arouse her from this gloomy state of mind, and at last I flattered myself that I had succeeded, for she appeared more cheerful, and I began to hope that nothing would again occur to interrupt our happiness.

One day I had been from home since an early hour in the morning upon business, and did not return until the afternoon had far advanced. The porter having opened the gate to me, I entered the garden, and proceeded towards the house. On my way I had to pass a summer-house, and I was about to do so, when the voices of two persons, speaking in under, but earnest tones, attracted my attention, and, stimulated by something more powerful than mere curiosity, I was induced to pause at the door and listen. For a moment or two all was silent, but at length I heard the voice of a man, and breathing the most ardent vows of affection.

"He loves you not," I heard him say; "his conduct of late shows that the love he once pretended to entertain for you exists no longer, and that ———."

I could not catch the conclusion of the sentence, but what I had heard caused my heart to palpitate with the most violent emotion, and I drew in my breath and listened more attentively than before. What reply was made by the person to whom this speech had been addressed I could not distinguish; but, gracious heaven, how my bosom swelled with astonishment and indignation when I recognised the tones of my wife.

The whole dreadful truth flashed at once upon my brain, and worked me instantly into a pitch of frenzy. I burst open the door without any more hesitation, and judge of my horror when I beheld the villain, Cyril Percy, on his knee before my wife, and pressing her hand to his lips.

"Vile miscreant!" I exclaimed, rushing upon him, and immediately felling him to the earth. I then, with all the fury of a madman, rushed into the house, and, snatching up a pistol, returned to the spot where I had left the supposed guilty pair, with the determination of having immediate revenge; and I certainly should have had the life of Cyril, but although I had been absent only two or three minutes, Percy had made his escape.

I gazed with horror and disgust upon the insensible form of my wife, and had it not been for the sudden appearance of Mirah, I know not what fatal act, in the fury of my wrath, I might have been tempted to commit. I briefly explained, as well as my agitation would allow me, what had happened to Mirah, and she seemed scarcely less astonished and disgusted than myself. However, she endeavoured to calm my rage, and had Clara conveyed into the house.

It would be useless for me to attempt to describe to you the state of my feelings now that the guilt of Clara appeared manifest to me. I raved like a madman, invoked curses upon her head, and it was a wonder that, in my despair, I did not lay violent hands on myself. At last, I rushed from the house, with the determination of seeking out Cyril, and wreaking upon him my vengeance. I hastened to the mansion of Lord Elworth and made him acquainted with what had happened. He was thunderstruck, and could scarcely believe the evidence of his ears, especially as he had seen nothing of Cyril, and had not the least idea that he was in the neighbourhood. He tried to tranquillise me, but all his efforts were for some time completely unavailing. I abruptly left him, and ran all over the neighbourhood in search of Percy with the air of a maniac; and, in fact, madness had partially seized upon my brain; but I could neither hear nor see anything of the villain, and I returned home.

Clara was still in a state of insensibility, and continued so all the night; but I never once entered her chamber, nor could I be induced to retire to rest, but paced my apartment during the whole of that night—the most dreadful that I had ever experienced—giving vent to my feelings in the most bitter exclamations, and forming different plans of revenge.

In the morning, Clara had regained her senses, and I entered her chamber. The scene that followed you may easily imagine. How bitterly did I reproach her for her infidelity; but she solemnly protested her innocence, and implored me to treat her with forbearance, out of pity to the delicate situation she was then in, she being at that time *enceinte*; but nothing could control the fury of my wrath, and, overcome by the terror of my reproaches, she again became insensible, and I left her.

I now determined to seek out Cyril at all hazards, and having left Clara to the care of Mirah, I immediately departed for the place where Percy resided, Lord Elworth accompanying me, for he was fearful of the consequences if I should be left to the indulgence of my own unguarded rage. He did his best, as far as advice and argument could go, to persuade me that Clara was not really so guilty as she appeared to be; but I could not listen to him with any degree of patience, so incontesti-ble to me did the evidence of her guilt appear to be.

On arriving at the mansion of Cyril Percy, we found that he had been absent from there for some weeks, nor could we obtain the least clue from any of the servants as to the place where he had gone. It was very evident that the cowardly villain, fearful of the consequences, had concealed himself in some place of security; but I was fully resolved that I would never rest until I had discovered him, and brought him to a severe account for the injury he had done me.

Lord Elworth now endeavoured to persuade me to return home, and to listen with patience and forbearance to the explanation of Clara, who he firmly believed would be able to exonerate herself. But this I would not listen to, so perfectly satisfied was I of her guilt. Instead of returning to Broxley, I made my way to Branscombe House, where I determined to take up my residence for the present, and I was undecided as to the course I would adopt for the future. To take Clara, who I believed had so cruelly deceived me, again to my bosom, I could not think of doing; and yet I could not make up my mind to abandon her entirely, for, in spite of all that had happened, I could not banish the love with which she had at first inspired me, when I had fondly imagined that she was all innocence and purity.

I had not been many days at Branscombe House, when I received a letter from Mirah, earnestly requesting me to return to Broxley, and become reconciled to her unfortunate cousin, who still protested her innocence of encouraging the unlawful passion of Cyril Percy, which he had dared to acknowledge to her. But I could not make up my mind to believe this statement, and I still continued at Branscombe House, one of the most wretched beings in existence, since all my hopes and pros-pects were now entirely blighted. Sometimes I was half resolved to quit the country altogether, and never more to behold Clara; but I found it impossible to make up my mind to this desperate course, and I remained in a state of doubt and indecision, and every day and every hour my misery increased. Nor could I gain the least in-formation which might lead to the discovery of the villain Percy, whose mysterious disappearance was a source of wonder to all who knew him.

At last I received a letter from Clara, couched in the most forcible language, and in which she again solemnly protested her innocence, and declaring that she had never wronged me by word or deed. But when I recalled to my memory the coldness and reserve of her behaviour towards me for some time previous to the discovery I had made, and remembered also the pleasure she had always evinced in the society of Cyril Percy, I threw the letter by with indignation and disbelief, and felt convinced that she was only adding hypocrisy and insult to her other faults; and such was the tenour of the answer I returned to her."

"Unhappy woman!" said Blanche; "the unfortunate circumstances of the case did certainly appear very suspicious; but still I think that you should not have disregarded her protestations altogether, Laurence."

"My conduct may appear to have been harsh, dear Blanche," returned Sir Lau-rence; "but you will hear how soon my suspicions were fatally verified, and the cruel duplicity with which this wretched, fallen woman had been the whole time acting towards me.

Not more than a week after I had received this letter had elapsed, when I had another in great haste from Mirah, in which she informed me that the guilt of Clara was too fully confirmed. She had herself surprised her and Cyril together, and the same night Clara had fled from Broxley, no doubt with her guilty paramour, as they had been seen together when they took the coach at the inn.

This intelligence drove me to madness, and I invoked the heaviest curses on the head of her who had so shamefully deceived me, and vowed never more to think of her but with the deadliest hatred.

I was for some days in such a state of distraction, that I was unable to leave my chamber, and the physicians even feared that my life was in danger; but at length I somewhat recovered, and immediately made my way to Broxley, where I found Mirah most anxiously awaiting my arrival, and who entered more fully into the painful particulars of the elopement of my guilty wife, and deeply sympathised with me in my misfortunes. But, alas! nothing could tend to console me under this insupportable calamity, and again I invoked the bitterest curses on the head of Clara and her seducer.

From Lord Elworth I learnt that Cyril Percy had sold off his estates, and was gone no one knew whither; but that it was most likely he and Clara had quitted the country together.

For some months I gave myself up to despair; but at the end of that period my grief began to abate, and I tried to banish Clara from my memory altogether; but this was a much more difficult task than I had expected.

And now I come to another of the most painful events of my history, and which I would fain pass over in silence, for I know that I must incur your heaviest censure.

I have told you that I had long perceived from the behaviour of Mirah that she had imbibed a fatal passion for me, and, after the elopement of Clara, it displayed itself in a yet more unmistakeable manner; nor did I indeed make any effort to discourage it. Let me be as brief over this guilty part of my narrative as possible. Day after day the behaviour of Mirah became more glaring, and she possessed a power of fascination which I found it impossible to resist. In a moment of weakness Mirah confessed to me the love she entertained towards me, and, alas! she fell!"

Sir Laurence paused, and his looks sufficiently showed the shame and remorse he was feeling. Lady Blanche and Amanda sighed deeply, and it was some time ere the baronet could resume his narrative, which, however, he did at length, in the following words:—

"I feel that I can offer nothing in extenuation of my conduct in this event, and I will not, therefore, insult your ears by attempting it. I would have made her my wife had Clara been no more; but that was an obstacle which I could not surmount, and yet we could not make up our minds to separate, but continued our guilty intercourse.

In this manner eighteen months passed away, when there appeared in all the newspapers a paragraph stating that the beautiful Lady Clara Cleveland, who had some time since eloped from her husband, after having been deserted by her seducer, and driven to the greatest distress, and the extremity of destitution, had committed suicide.

This announcement caused me considerable emotion; but, after all, I considered that it was no more than a just punishment for her guilt, and my grief soon abated. I took but very little trouble to inquire into the truth of this report; but hearing that the body of the unfortunate woman had been stolen in a most mysterious manner from the place where it had been lying to await a coroner's inquest, I took no further steps in the matter.

"Most extraordinary!" said Blanche. "Who could have stolen the corpse of the unfortunate woman, and what could have been their motives for so doing?"

"I have often reflected upon that extraordinary circumstance, but without being able to form the least conjecture upon the subject," answered Sir Laurence; "but there can, I think, be no doubt of the truth of the statements in the newspapers, and, therefore, the falsehood of the assertions of old Madela and Harold as to Clara being still in existence, you must admit is satisfactorily proved."

"Oh, yes," said Blanche, "I feel convinced of the truth of this; and although I cannot but deplore the melancholy fate of the misguided Clara, this explanation has removed from my mind an insupportable weight of care. But did you never hear what became of the guilty Cyril Percy?"

"I did not," replied Sir Laurence; "but I have no doubt that retribution overtook him, and that, ruined in circumstances, he perished in obscurity.

"I have now but little more to add to bring my melancholy narrative to a termination, and would that I could bury that for ever in oblivion. Mirah, now finding me at liberty, urged me to make her my wife; but the sentiments with which she had inspired me were greatly abated, and I could never think of uniting myself to one with whom I had been so long carrying on an illicit intercourse. I therefore firmly rejected her pressing importunities, and she loaded me with reproaches for the manner in which I had deceived her, having before held out to her the most sanguine hopes of making her my wife in the event of her cousin's death. This led to frequent quarrels between us; and in a moment of excitement and wrath I cast her from me, and she quitted the house. What became of her I never properly ascertained, but I am inclined to think that her fate was a melancholy one; and Heaven knows the bitter pangs of remorse I have endured ever since. I blush with shame to have to make this confession to you, my Blanche; but I have yielded to your wishes, by candidly revealing to you all the particulars of my history, and I trust that your gentle nature will prompt you to award me that forgiveness, without which I must be for ever miserable."

Blanche threw herself into her husband's arms, and, in a voice which told the sincerity of her feelings, she ejaculated,—

"Dear Laurence, I do indeed forgive you—and may kind Heaven, in its infinite mercy, do the same. But did you never learn whether the offspring of the unfortunate Clara survived?"

"I did not," answered Sir Laurence; "but as there was no mention made of any child in the papers which contained the account of Clara's death, I am inclined to think that there was no child in existence."

Thus Sir Laurence Cleveland concluded his narrative; and when he had thus disburthened his mind, he felt far happier than he had done for many years before; and Blanche once more bestowed upon him all her love and confidence. But still she could not entirely banish from her mind the horror she had imbibed of their secret enemies; and to apprehend that they would yet contrive some means to put their threats of vengeance into execution, and she was at a loss to imagine in what manner they could guard themselves against their evil machinations.

CHAPTER XXVII.

THE LAPSE OF YEARS.—THE YOUNG BARONET.—ROSARIO RE-APPEARS IN A NEW CHARACTER.

A PERIOD of five years has now elapsed, without anything worthy of particular notice in this narrative occurring. They had been five years of comparative tranquillity to Sir Laurence Cleveland and his family, for they had received no further annoyance from the gipsies, neither could they hear what had become of them, so that they began to hope that they had abandoned their evil designs, and that they consequently had nothing more to fear from them.

One thing, however, appeared certain, and that was, that the statement of Madela and Harold as to the existence of Clara was false, although both the baronet and his lady frequently reflected upon the mysterious being that had so often appeared before them, and Sir Laurence, in particular, recalled to his memory the extraordinary likeness she bore to his misguided wife, with feelings of astonishment and mingled emotions.

And there was another individual who held almost a constant place in their thoughts, so deeply interested as they were in his fate, and so worthy as he appeared to be of their pity and solicitude. Need we say that being was the gipsy boy, Rosario? His handsome appearance, and the peculiar gentleness and delicacy of his manners, coupled with the mystery of his origin, had made a deep and lasting impression upon their minds, and they were most anxious to behold him again, or to know what had become of him. But they apprehended the worst had befallen the poor boy, placed as he was in the power of those who were evidently capable of any atrocity.

The little Emeline grew apace in beauty and innocence, and was the complete darling of her parents, and the admired of all who saw her.

The amiable Amanda, who was still a very beautiful woman, had received many desirous and flattering offers of marriage, but her heart was buried in the tomb of her late husband, and she resolved never again to alter her condition, but continued to reside with her brother, Sir Laurence, to whose happiness, and that of Lady Blanche, she was indispensable.

Angela Clearmont, the daughter of Amanda, was now eighteen years of age, and the beauty of her person could only be surpassed by the elegancies of her mind. She was indeed a being, whom but to know, was to love, admire, and esteem. It would be a libel upon the taste and sensibility of the opposite sex, to say that she had not had amongst them the most ardent admirers, who would have felt themselves the most fortunate and blest of human beings, could they but have made an impression upon her heart; but Angela had not yet seen the man whom she could love as her husband, although there was one youth, and that was Evelyn Manners, the son of the baronet of that name, who held the most prominent place in her regard, and whom her uncle and her mother would have been happy to have seen united to her, when time should have matured their affection, and tried their constancy.

Evelyn Manners was three years older than Angela, and was possessed of every personal and intrinsic attraction; independent of which, he was the heir to a large fortune, which would be considered no trifling desideratum in the estimation of most persons. But, although Angela regarded him as a friend, and admired his virtues, she could not look upon him with feelings of a more ardent description. Evelyn Manners had now been about two years on the continent, when he received a summons to return home without delay, in consequence of the declining health of his father.

"So Evelyn Manners is expected to arrive at the Grange to-morrow," said Sir Laurence Cleveland, as the family were seated in the parlour of Branscombe House one afternoon. "Time, no doubt, has worked a great improvement in him, and I expect that my sweet niece will scarcely know her young and gallant friend. The addition of his society to our little circle will be productive of the greatest pleasure to us all, I am certain."

Angela blushed deeply, and averted her looks, while she felt a fluttering at her heart, which she scarcely knew how to understand. Strange, too, at that moment the image of Rosario arose to her thoughts, and she felt confused and embarrassed.

From the very first occasion of her meeting with the gipsy boy, when a child, he had made an impression on her mind which nothing could ever remove, and frequently he arose to her recollection in a manner so striking that she blushed to think he should be so forcibly stamped upon her memory. Tears would often start involuntarily to her eyes, when she thought of his amiable and gentle manners, and recalled to her memory the melancholy circumstances of his fate, nor could she banish the anxiety she felt to know what had become of him.

"But what says my fair Angela," continued Sir Laurence, "to the return of her amiable companion? Will she not be prepared to give him a hearty welcome, and feel the same gratification that I imagine she always did in his society?"

Angela blushed more deeply than before, and her confusion increased, nor was it unnoticed by her mother and the baronet, but they were not at all surprised at it.

"I shall ever feel honoured by the friendship of Mr. Manners, my dear uncle," said Angela, at length; "but the precarious state of his father's health will, I imagine, prevent his devoting much of his time to us, at present, at any rate."

"A circumstance which, if I judge aright, you will greatly regret, Angela," added Sir Laurence, archly. But a look from Amanda, who noticed the confusion and agitation of her daughter, restrained him, and, after a pause, he observed,—

"I confess I feel some curiosity to behold this extraordinary youth, of whom Evelyn has so frequently written to us about."

"Horace Milton, as he calls himself," said Amanda; "the object of his benevolence."

"Ay," returned the baronet, "and who has shown such an amiability of manners, and such an ardent devotedness to him, that Evelyn looks upon him more as a friend and companion, than a servant. You remember the way in which he met him?"

"Yes," answered Amanda; "Evelyn was returning one evening from a visit which he had been paying to a friend, when, in crossing a forest, he was alarmed by the dismal moans of some person evidently in great distress, and, on hastening to the spot from whence the sounds seemed to proceed, he found a youth, wretchedly clad, and apparently dying, extended upon the earth; he immediately had him placed in the carriage and conveyed to his hotel, where he was placed in a bed, and medical assistance called in. By dint of great exertion and attention he recovered, and when he was able to leave his chamber, he was admitted to the presence of Evelyn, to return him his acknowledgments for the kindness and humanity he had experienced."

"Yes," said Sir Laurence; "and Evelyn, it seems, was much struck with his appearance, for his form was graceful and elegant, and his features peculiarly handsome and delicate; he, therefore, put several questions to him, from which he elicited that his name was Horace Milton, that he had never known his parents, who had died in his infancy, and left him in the power of lawless wretches, who had endeavoured, but in vain, to lure him into crime; but, after experiencing many years of misery from them, he had made his escape, and had since been wandering about the country, in a state of the greatest distress, until, worn out with want and fatigue, he laid himself down to die on the spot where Evelyn found him. This melancholy tale naturally interested Evelyn; and, being in want of a servant, he offered him the situation, which Horace gladly accepted, and soon, by his gentle and willing manners, and the strict probity of his conduct, so ingratiated himself in the favour of his master, that he treated him more as an equal than a menial.   Evelyn describes him as one of the most faithful and devoted beings that can be imagined, and says that he never seems happy but when he is in his presence.   But still he says there is a mystery at times in his behaviour which he is at a loss to understand.   He has frequently caught him gazing with looks of the most intense earnestness and melancholy upon him ; and when he has found himself observed, he would blush deeply, and averting his looks, sigh as if he was oppressed with some agonizing thought.

"Poor youth!" ejaculated Lady Blanche ; "really, I feel quite anxious to behold him.   The humanity of Evelyn Manners reflects the highest honour on him."

"It does, indeed," said Sir Laurence ; "and I sincerely hope that this young man will never abuse his kindness."

"His name bespeaks him to be a native of England," remarked Amanda.

"It does," coincided the baronet.

"His narrative has deeply interested me," said Lady Cleveland : "but do you not think that it greatly resembles that of Rosario ?"

"It has often struck me that it does," returned her husband.   "I wonder what fate has befallen that unfortunate youth, and whether we shall ever behold him again."

Angela could scarcely repress a sigh at the mention of Rosario's name, and a pang shot through her bosom, which she was unable properly to understand.

"I fear the worst has happened to him," said Lady Blanche, "if he be still in the power of those lawless people."

"But he has now arrived at years of maturity," remarked Amanda, "and surely would resist their guilty will."

"Alas," observed Sir Laurence ; "it seems, according to his own assertions, in spite of the cruel treatment he received at the hands of the gipsies, that he was so attached to the wandering life, that nothing would ever induce him to leave it.   Did he not firmly reject all my offers of protection ?"

"True," replied Blanche ; "but time may have altered his opinions, and he might now feel most happy to abandon those guilty people, if he had but the chance.   I am certain that he is possessed of principles which would do honour to any society."

"In that opinion I agree with you, Blanche, and should feel most happy could I be the means of snatching him from a life of shame.   But it is not unlikely that he is now no more."

Angela trembled and turned pale, but, surprised at herself, she concealed her emotion as well as she could.

The conversation was now changed, and they soon afterwards separated.

When Angela was left alone, she reflected deeply upon all these circumstances, and they gave rise to a variety of feelings in her breast.   She could not help anticipating the return of Evelyn Manners with something like a sensation of dread, for she saw plainly enough that both her mother and Sir Laurence entertained a strong hope that she would receive his addresses with favour, and her heart told her that she could never bestow upon him more than her esteem.   She honoured his virtues, but whenever she thought upon him in the character of a husband, a sensation of re-pugnance followed.   At such times, too, the form of Rosario would arise before her mind's eye, and she felt both surprised and ashamed that the poor wandering gipsy boy should have made so extraordinary an impression upon her.   But so it was, and notwithstanding all her efforts, she could not banish him from her memory.

The allusions which had been made to Rosario in the conversation just quoted, had re-kindled all these feelings in Angela's bosom, and when she thought of the probable sufferings he was enduring, and the danger to which he might be exposed in his association with the gipsies, she could scarcely restrain her tears; but mentally she offered up her prayers to Heaven for his preservation.

That night Angela's dreams were of Rosario, and he was presented to her imagination in the most remarkable characters. She awoke melancholy and oppressed.

At the time expected, Evelyn Manners returned to the Grange, but he was too occupied with his father (whom he found much worse than he expected) that day, to visit Branscombe House, although he was most anxious to behold the beauteous Angela again.

The following day, however, Sir Laurence and his lady visited the Grange, in order that they might welcome Evelyn on his return to his native country, and after some time being passed in conversation, the baronet observed,—

"Really, the interesting accounts you have forwarded us from the remarkable object of your humanity, this Horace Milton, as he calls himself, have greatly excited my curiosity, Evelyn; you must do me the favour of introducing him to me."

"He is, indeed, a most extraordinary young man, Sir Laurence," answered Evelyn; "and I have no doubt that you will be immediately prepossessed in his favour. But since he has been aware of my intended return to England, he has evinced the most unaccountable melancholy and uneasiness, and although at one time he was never happy unless he was in my presence, he now keeps himself as much as possible secluded from my sight, and he appears to feel fearful of being seen by any one."

"That is strange," said Sir Laurence; "but it only adds to my curiosity. Will you desire him to favour me with an interview?"

"I will," answered Evelyn, and he immediately rang the bell, and told the servant to request Horace to attend, as he and Sir Laurence Cleveland wished to have a short conversation with him.

After a few moments the servant returned and said, that Horace, immediately on hearing the message and the name of Sir Laurence Cleveland, had exhibited the most remarkable agitation, and had desired him to request Mr. Manners to excuse him, as he felt indisposed, and not at all in a fit state to receive the honour intended him.

"What can all this mean?" said Evelyn. "Horace must have some stronger reasons for this excuse than those he has named. I must have an explanation. Go and tell Mr. Milton," he continued, addressing himself to the servant, "that it is my particular wish that he should attend to the summons, and that I shall feel offended if he any longer refuses."

The servant left the room accordingly, and in a few minutes afterwards the door was opened with a tremulous hand, the graceful figure of a young man entered, and threw himself at the feet of Evelyn and Sir Laurence Cleveland, the latter of whom started back with the most inexpressible astonishment as soon as he beheld his features, for in them he recognized those of Rosario!

CHAPTER CXXVIII.

THE EXPLANATION.—THE MEETING AT BRANSCOMBE-HOUSE.—ANGELA AND
ROSARIO.

IT was indeed the gipsy boy, but so altered in personal appearance, that had it not
been for the same expression of features, as when he was first introduced on the stage
of this narrative, it would have been impossible to have recognized him.   Nothing
could surpass the almost feminine graces of his form; while, as the baronet gazed upon
his handsome but melancholy countenance, he felt a sensation steal through his frame
of the most powerful and unaccountable description.

" Good God, is it possible !" he exclaimed.   " Rosario !"

" Rosario !" repeated the astonished Evelyn ; " the gipsy boy of whom I have so
often heard Sir Laurence Cleveland speak ?"

" The same, my honoured master and benefactor," sighed Rosario ; " oh, pardon
me for the deceptive part I have acted towards you in concealing from you my real
name; but I was only tempted to do so to prevent my being discovered by the
gipsies, and—but I must reveal no more at present ; the time may come when I shall
be permitted to shake off the horrible mystery in which I am now enveloped, and to
appear in a character which you little anticipate.   Oh, pity me, for I am indeed a
wretched, deeply persecuted being."

The voice of Rosario was choked by sobs, and tears chased each other rapidly down
his cheeks.

" Mysterious youth !" exclaimed Evelyn ; " why should you be thus bound to
secrecy, and selected for persecution ?   But rise, and fear not; while you continue to
deserve it, you shall ever possess my friendship."

The countenance of Rosario beamed upon Evelyn an expression more powerful
than gratitude; and he pressed his hand respectfully to his lips, and while he did so
Evelyn could feel him tremble violently.

It was several minutes before either of the three could sufficiently recover from
their emotion and astonishment to speak, but at length Sir Laurence observed,—

" Rosario, it is with the most unfeigned pleasure that I behold you again, for it
was ever my wish to snatch you from the power of the wretches with whom you were,
unfortunately, for so many years associated.   Believe me, you have frequently occupied my thoughts, but never did I expect to meet you again.   Tell me, are my
enemies still living ?"

" They are, Sir Laurence," answered Rosario ; " and I would have you still be on
your guard against their evil designs."

" Where are they at present ?" demanded the baronet.

" I know not," returned Rosario ; " but when I escaped from them they were in
France, whither they fled about four years since.   Oh, Sir Laurence, did you but
know all that I have suffered since I last saw you, you would pity me ; and should
they now discover me, they would not rest until they had sacrificed my life to their
vengeance."

" Fear not, Rosario," said Sir Laurence ; " under the protection of Mr. Manners
and myself, you will be perfectly safe."

" Would that I could think so," said the youth ; " but their cruelty was so great
that I could endure it no longer ; and one night, when most of the gipsies were absent

from the place of our retreat, I seized the opportunity, and absconded without knowing whither to direct my steps, or what was in future to become of me. Many days and nights I wandered, ekeing out a miserable existence only by the charity of strangers. The rest, Mr. Manners, I believe, has made you acquainted with."

" He has," said the baronet; " but oh, Rosario, who would ever have thought of meeting with you again under such extraordinary circumstances? I need not assure you that I feel the deepest solicitude and interest in your mysterious destiny, and that my power and influence shall be joined to that of Mr. Manners, in protecting you from your enemies."

Rosario endeavoured to return his thanks, but his voice was choked with sobs, and he cast his eyes to the ground, while the deepest blushes suffused his cheeks, and his bosom appeared to heave with the most remarkable emotion. In fact, there was something so peculiarly delicate, timid, and retiring in the whole of Rosario's behaviour and appearance, that both Sir Laurence and Evelyn could not help gazing at him with increased astonishment and anxiety. Time had added to the graces of his person, and the melancholy beauty of his countenance, but still there was the same feminine expression of features and modesty of demeanour, while his voice retained all that soft and melodious expression of tone which had distinguished him when a boy.

Whenever Evelyn Manners addressed him, he seemed to tremble with emotion, and tears glistened in his eyes; but although Evelyn and the baronet could, of course, only attribute it to gratitude, the power of its expression filled them with amazement, and involved them still farther in perplexity.

" Strange youth!" said Sir Laurence; " would that I could penetrate the mystery with which your fate is enshrouded; for I feel convinced that you are not really what you have hitherto appeared to me to be."

Rosario's agitation increased; he covered his face with his hands, and sinking into a chair, gave free vent to the secret and almost insupportable feelings that oppressed him.

Sir Laurence and Evelyn looked on with the greatest sympathy.

" Rosario," said Evelyn, " for such I suppose I must in future call you, why keep this painful secret confined to your own breast, when you can with safety confide it to me and Sir Laurence, who feel so deep an interest in your welfare, and would protect you from all danger?"

" Oh, my kind, my generous benefactor, and you, Sir Laurence," returned the youth in a faltering voice, " for the love of Heaven, I again implore you not to urge me on this fearful subject; for I cannot, I dare not comply with your wishes."

" You dare not, Rosario?" repeated the baronet.

" I dare not, indeed I dare not; for I am bound by a dreadful oath of secrecy."

" An oath extorted from you by such wretches as those who held you in the r power, cannot be binding in the sight of Heaven, Rosario," remarked Evelyn; " and why, then, should you hesitate?"

" Oh, no, no," ejaculated Rosario; " my soul shrinks with horror at the thought. Accident alone must reveal that which my lips cannot give utterance to."

" You have nothing more to fear from the gipsies, Rosario, while you are under our protection," said Sir Laurence; " they will not venture again to this neighbourhood; be candid, then, and fear not."

" Mr. Manners—Sir Laurence Cleveland," said Rosario, solemnly, " I have told you that I dare not for the present divulge more than I have; and if then you are not satisfied, but entertain doubts of my honesty and sincerity of purpose, much as it would grieve me to lose your friendship and esteem, I would rather be suffered again to return to the wide world, and battle with my fate in the best manner I can. Oh, deem me not ungrateful; but—but ——''

Sobs choked his utterance; and once more he buried his face in his hands, completely overwhelmed by the agony of his emotion.

"This must not be, Rosario," said Evelyn; "I should for ever reproach myself were I to suffer you to leave my protection, and to become again exposed to those dangers from which you have now escaped. Compose yourself, my poor youth, and rest assured it is only from a wish to serve you, and to see justice rendered you, that I and Sir Laurence Cleveland have been thus urgent. None can more deeply sympathise with you in your extraordinary misfortunes than we do."

"Oh, my esteemed benefactor," replied the youth, looking up in the countenance of Evelyn with tearful eyes, and a throbbing bosom; "well do I know that; and never will I cease to pour forth blessings on your head; and though we may be separated "— his voice faltered, and he averted his looks while he added, "my prayers shall be constantly offered up to Heaven for yours—for Sir Laurence Cleveland's welfare and happiness. Believe me, it is not for the preservation of my own life that I feel so much anxiety; but that of one who, by his kindness and manners, has so greatly endeared himself to me, and who would fall a sacrifice to the vengeance of the gipsies, were I to divulge all I know."

"And he knows your secret?" said Sir Laurence.

"He does; but it was not imparted to him by my lips."

"And who is he?" eagerly demanded the baronet.

"The same kind but mysterious being who—but no, that must I also not disclose."

"His name?"

"I know him by no other than that of Azrah," replied Rosario.

"And he is one of the tribe?"

"He is; but oh! how unlike any of the others. So kind, so gentle! While I speak of him, a feeling of reverence animates my bosom, and my brain is distracted. Alas! I left him a prisoner with the gipsies, and Heaven knows what he may now be suffering, if he be still alive! Oh, Azrah, shall I never behold you again?"

Once more Rosario was almost suffocated with the intensity of the grief that these thoughts gave rise to, and Sir Laurence and Evelyn suffered him to indulge in it for a few minutes, without offering to interrupt him.

"Rosario," said the baronet at length, "since it seems to afflict you so much, we will not at present urge you further to reveal the remarkable secret connected with you, hoping that time will render concealment no longer necessary; but there are two or three questions I wish to put to you, which I trust you will have no objection to answer. In the first place, are Madela and Harold the right names of the two gipsies from whom I have experienced so much annoyance?"

"I know them by no other, Sir Laurence," answered the youth.

"And they are mother and son?"

"I have always been taught to believe them so."

Sir Laurence remained silent for a few moments, and reflected deeply. The features of Madela and Harold bore no resemblance to those of Walter and his mother, at least, as far as his recollection could trace; but still there were many circumstances connected with them that coincided with them, particularly the knowledge which they possessed of all his past history, and the deadly feelings of revenge which they had always evinced towards him.

"And you have before said," continued the baronet, "that you know of no female among the tribe who answers the description of that misguided woman who was once

See p. 352.

my wife, and whom Harold and Madela have declared to be still in existence, and that it is in their power to produce her whenever they think proper?"

"I solemnly declare that I do not," replied Rosario.

"Then," said the baronet, apparently relieved from the weight of anxiety that oppressed him, "it is clear that it is all a base fabrication. And yet that mysterious being that so often appeared before me—who could she be? Rosario, are you positive that no female, mild and beautiful in aspect, formed one of the members of your tribe ?"

"I again assure you, Sir Laurence, that there was not," said Rosario. "And yet, such a being have I oft beheld."

"Ah !" eagerly exclaimed the baronet ; "where—where, boy ?"

"In my dreams," answered Rosario, with a sigh. "Such a fair and gentle being has often arose to my imagination in my visions, smiling serenely upon me, and my heart has whispered to me the tender name of 'mother!'"

Rosario dashed the tears from his eyes, as he uttered these words in a faint voice, and he then clasped his hands together in the agony of thought.

"And yet you never knew a mother," observed Sir Laurence, with the deepest sympathy.

"Alas, no," sighed the youth; "only when I was too young to appreciate her worth."

"And that portrait," muttered Sir Laurence to himself, "so like, that while I gazed at it I could almost have imagined that Clara was again presented to my sight."

"I see that this interview has greatly distressed you, Rosario," remarked the baronet ; "and, therefore, with the permission of Mr. Manners, you may retire, and endeavour to compose yourself. Of this be assured, at the same time, that in me you shall always find a sincere friend, willing to assist you to the fullest extent of my power ; and I hope that ere long there will be no necessity for the secrecy which you now maintain, and that every cause of sorrow and anxiety will be removed from your mind."

Rosario tried to give utterance to his feelings of gratiude, but could not; and bowing to Evelyn and Sir Laurence with infinite grace and respect, he retired from the room.

"What a mysterious youth is this," said Evelyn, when he was gone; "I feel doubly interested in him since this discovery, and the simplicity and innocence of his manners convince me of his sincerity. I know not how it is, but so powerful is the impression he has made upon me, that my heart yearns towards him with the same feeling of affection as if he were my brother."

"And I," replied the baronet, "can scarcely describe the sensations with which he has inspired me. But I feel as if I could regard him as my own son."

"The extreme delicacy of his appearance, and the modest timidity of his manner, are not his least remarkable characteristics," added Evelyn ; "nay, if he were attired in petticoats, he would really pass admirably for a female."

"He seems to be most devotedly attached to you, Evelyn, and I feel much gratified to think you should have been made the instrument of snatching him from an untimely and dreadful fate ; for I must confess that he has frequently occupied my thoughts, and I have felt a most unconquerable desire to behold him again. You must bring him with you when you visit the mansion."

"Most assuredly I shall," said Evelyn ; "and that pleasure I will do myself tomorrow, if no unfavourable change takes place in the condition of my poor father. Most impatiently do I await a meeting with your sweet niece, the lovely Angela, whose charms have so much improved since last I had the felicity to behold her."

"One precaution, I think," observed Sir Laurence, "it is necessary for us to adopt in respect to the safety of Rosario, although I do not think it probable that the gipsies will again venture into this neighbourhood, especially since his escape, as they will be fearful that he will reveal all he knows; but still it will be as well that they should not know where he is concealed, or they might adopt some secret means to take his life.   Therefore he had better be seen abroad no more than can be helped, and it would be as well for him to retain the name that he assumed when you discovered him."

"I am perfectly of that opinion, Sir Laurence," remarked Evelyn; "and your advice shall be carried out with the greatest caution."

They then separated, and the baronet made his way towards his mansion, deeply absorbed in thought, on the unexpected events of the day.

The form of Rosario was still presented to his vivid imagination in the most interesting colours, while his features haunted him with a force that gave rise to a most powerful and unaccountable feeling in his breast.   The impenetrable mystery that surrounded him, also gave rise to various conflicting and doubtful conjectures in his mind, and he longed more than ever to solve it.

On arriving at Branscombe House, he found Amanda and her daughter seated in the drawing-room, anxiously awaiting his return.

"I have a surprise for you, my dear sister and Angela," said the baronet, after he had been seated for a few minutes.   "Who do you imagine the much-talked-of protege of Evelyn Manners turns out to be?"

"Why, Horace Milton, I presume, Sir Laurence," said Amanda, with a smile.

"True; that is his incognito; but who do you think the said Horace Milton is in *propria personæ?*"

"Now, really, my dear brother, on that subject it is impossible that I should be able to form even the slightest conjecture."

"Then," said the baronet, "I will ease your anxiety and suspense by at once informing you, that the so-called Horace Milton is no other than the long lost Rosario, the gipsy boy."

Angela uttered a faint scream, and turned very pale.

"Why, Angela, my sweet niece," said the baronet, "what is the matter with you?   Sure there is nothing very alarming in the name of the former object of our interest."

Angela blushed to think she had betrayed such emotion, and in a faltering voice replied,—

"Pardon me, dear uncle, for this weakness—but—it was the sudden surprise, and ——"

"Aye," interrupted the baronet; "I do not wonder at it, and you may be sure that I was not less surprised on beholding him."

"And has he then escaped from the gipsies?" asked Amanda.

"He has," answered Sir Laurence; "and Providence threw him into the hands of Evelyn Manners, as has been described to us before."

Angela trembled, and felt a sensation at her heart which she could not resist.

"Poor youth," ejaculated Amanda; "how extraordinary is this.   But where are our inveterate enemies, the gipsies?"

"They were in France when Rosario left them," answered the baronet; "and there is not much fear of their venturing here."

"I know not that," remarked Amanda; "they have such a secret way of carrying their designs into effect that we cannot be too much on our guard against them."

"Very true," coincided Sir Laurence; "but hear me out."

Amanda and her daughter listened attentively, and Sir Laurence then related all the particulars of his interview with Rosario, and expatiated warmly upon his personal appearance, and the urbanity of his manners.

With what emotion did Angela dwell upon every word that her uncle uttered respecting Rosario; and with what secret gratification did she listen to the flattering encomiums he passed upon him; but when he informed them that it was the intention of Evelyn, accompanied by Rosario, to visit the mansion on the following day, if the baronet was no worse, her agitation was so great that she could scarcely conceal it. She dreaded to meet Evelyn, knowing the hopes that he had formed, and that she could never encourage them by any return of his passion; and she longed, yet feared, to see Rosario, lest she should reveal those thoughts which he had, in spite of all her efforts, inspired in her breast.

Angela was glad when the time arrived for them to separate, and when she was alone in her chamber, she gave free indulgence to the thoughts which struggled in her bosom. She could not restrain her tears, when she reflected upon the strange mystery that was connected with Rosario's fate, and the many sufferings he had hitherto endured and was likely to undergo, and she fervently offered up her prayers to Heaven for his protection.

She then called to mind the graces of his person, which had been so vividly described by her uncle, and she sunk into absolute despair when she remembered the difference of their stations, and the impossibility of their ever being united, if even Rosario should imbibe any sentiment of love for her, which, indeed, under all the present circumstances, seemed most improbable.

Angela passed a restless night, and she rose with a sad heart in the morning; but while the family were at breakfast, a messenger arrived from Evelyn Manners to inform them that the baronet, his father, had passed a dreadful night, and that the physicians predicted that his dissolution was rapidly approaching; so that, of course, it would be impossible for him (Evelyn) to visit Branscombe House for the present. Angela was sincerely grieved at the calamity which seemed to be about so soon to attend Evelyn; and not a little regret did she feel at the delay which must take place before she would again behold Rosario; but she endeavoured to console herself with the thought that the time was not far distant when she would be allowed that pleasure; and tried, but in vain, to weaken the influence which Rosario had gained over her mind, well-knowing that it might be fraught with danger to them both, and cause them much future misery.

Evelyn's father expired in the course of the day, deeply lamented by every one, for he was, in fact, a most excellent man, and had taken delight in performing deeds of charity and benevolence; and in him, the poor, especially, had lost a friend and benefactor, who had never turned a deaf ear to their supplications, and was always the first to encourage and assist youthful talent and industry.

His funeral obsequies were performed without pomp or ostentation, and his remains were followed to the tomb by many humble mourners, who had liberally experienced his benevolence and philanthropy while living.

A few days after the interment of his father, Sir Laurence Cleveland and his family paid a visit of condolence to the young baronet, Sir Evelyn Manners, but many a pang and many a fear did Angela feel on that occasion.

She knew, she acknowledged the worth of Evelyn, and she was also aware that he was flattering himself with hopes that he had already won her affections; but she felt that she could never regard him with any other sentiment than esteem, and she would therefore much rather that she did not behold him, as she could not, by her conduct, flatter him to encourage hopes which could never be realized.

But how could she meet Rosario? How could she conceal from the observation of her friends the emotions which the sight of that mysterious and interesting youth would excite in her bosom? She trembled lest she should betray herself, and felt ashamed and confused to think that she should ever have suffered the form of the gipsy boy to gain so powerful an ascendancy over her mind; hopeless as such an union must be, and great as might be the miseries attendant on the encouragement of such a passion. And yet how anxious was she again to see Rosario, especially after what he had suffered, and the improvement which Sir Laurence had described to have taken place in his person.

The meeting between Evelyn and Angela was of the most cordial, yet, so far as regarded her, of the most painful description. She saw the admiration with which the young baronet beheld her, and the thoughts which were passing in his mind; and, when she reflected upon the anguish she would probably inflict upon him, when she undeceived him, she could not help experiencing the deepest regret.

Sir Evelyn had much improved in person since Angela had before seen him, and the manly accomplishments of his mind were now displayed to the fullest advantage. Angela looked upon him, as she had ever done, with the most unqualified admiration and esteem, and lamented that she could make no other return for the sentiments he entertained towards her. To this regret was added the favour with which his suit was viewed by her mother and Sir Laurence, and the certainty that, in rejecting them, she would not only destroy the hopes of a worthy young man, but also, in all probability, incur the displeasure of those who were so dear to her; although she could not believe that they would ever wish her to grant her hand where her heart could not accompany it.

To Evelyn the gentle graces of Angela had never appeared to greater advantage, and he hung with rapture upon every word she uttered; but, at the same time, he could not help noticing, at times, the almost freezing coldness of her manner, and the timidity and confusion with which she received his observations. There was none of that amiable freedom of manner with which she had been wont to delight him in the early years of their friendship, and there were moments when he almost imagined that she viewed his society with distaste, and would have been glad to have escaped from it. And yet did he exert himself more than ever he had done before to render himself agreeable to her, and could not imagine in what way he had ever committed himself so as to forfeit her regard.

It is true that Evelyn had never yet ventured to confess his love, but he had flattered himself with the hope that it met with a return from her, and that it only required a declaration on both sides to make them the happiest of human beings. Surely, absence had not banished him from her regard; or had some other man supplanted him in her affections, if, indeed, she had ever experienced such sentiments towards him? This thought was most torturing, and he strove to banish it from his breast. He resolved, however, at the earliest opportunity, to know his fate from her own lips, and thus at once to dissipate both doubt and suspense.

After about an hour passed in conversation, Sir Evelyn suddenly observed,—

"And now, I presume you will have no objection to be introduced once more to your old acquaintance, Rosario, whom I encountered in so remarkable a manner?"

Angela trembled, and she felt the blushes mantling in her cheeks, so she averted her eyes, and cast them towards the floor.

"Rosario was aware of your intended visit," continued Sir Evelyn; "and he evinced the greatest uneasiness, and, as I could plainly observe, would fain have been excused from seeing you. And yet I cannot penetrate into his reasons."

"Nor I," returned Sir Laurence; "he knows that we have the most friendly feelings towards him; and, therefore, why should he feel any diffidence in our presence?"

"I don't know," said Sir Evelyn; "but so it is. Rosario is certainly a most mysterious youth, and I am at a loss to understand his real character, although I firmly believe him to be strictly virtuous and honest, and I am truly satisfied that he is most fervently devoted to me by the ties of gratitude."

"There can be no doubt of it," said Sir Laurence; "but will you send for him, Sir Evelyn?"

"I will," replied the latter; and he immediately rang the bell and desired the servant to request the attendance of Horace.

Angela's heart fluttered violently, and she fixed her eyes upon the door with mingled feelings of irrepressible emotion and suspense, and she was fearful that her mother and Sir Laurence would notice her. Several minutes elapsed, and the persons present began to think that Rosario was not in the house, when a light and hesitating step was heard upon the stairs, and Sir Evelyn, advancing to the door, opened it, and led Rosario into the room.

The youth seemed overwhelmed with confusion, and the timidity of his demeanour astonished every one who beheld him. But what were the emotions of Angela, as she tremblingly raised her eyes towards him, and they rested on the almost feminine graces of his person, and the delicate beauty of his countenance? Time had, indeed, worked a wonderful alteration in him, and he far surpassed all that she had anticipated of him. She felt so violently agitated that she could with difficulty only conceal it from her friends, and when Rosario advanced, and she heard him speak, in tones so sweet and musical, she felt a mingled sensation of transport and terror steal through her bosom which was almost overpowering.

Rosario, too, seemed to gaze at her with admiration and the greatest respect, and when her glance met his, crimson blushes suffused her cheeks, and her heart fluttered more violently than ever.

Rosario was evidently greatly confused, and very ill at ease, and it might have been observed that when he beheld the attention which Sir Evelyn paid to Angela, that his face crimsoned, and a faint sigh escaped his bosom. It was with evident reluctance that he took his seat with the rest of the company, and not all their endeavours and the kindness which they evinced towards him, could remove this restraint. The observations he made in reply to the questions that were put to him, were delivered in a faltering voice, and at times his mind seemed so bewildered that he did not appear to know what he said.

After about an hour passed in this manner, Rosario was permitted to retire; and although Angela felt more at ease now he was not present, she could not help experiencing a sensation of regret at his departure.

"And what think you now of Rosario?" inquired Sir Evelyn, addressing himself to Amanda—"do you not think that time has worked a wonderful improvement in him?"

Angela felt her emotion increase.

"It certainly has," replied Amanda; "but what can be the reason of his extraordinary timidity, when he must be aware that every one here feels the greatest friendship for him, and the deepest interest in his welfare?"

"It is, indeed, as you say, madam, most extraordinary, and I cannot understand it," said Sir Evelyn. "But probably he imagines that we must view him with some doubt and suspicion, in consequence of his former connection with the gipsies, and the mystery with which he is surrounded."

"It may be so," remarked Sir Laurence; "but surely there is no necessity for it."

"Not the least, that I can see," said Lady Blanche. "But, Angela, my love, how pale you look! Surely the appearance of Rosario cannot have caused this agitation?"

Angela blushed deeply at this unexpected question, and she then endeavoured to smile, while, to add to her confusion, Evelyn fixed upon her a look of such a peculiar description, that she was almost inclined to believe he penetrated her thoughts.

"My dear aunt," she replied at last, "you cannot but suppose that it affords me great pleasure to find that Rosario has escaped from those bad people, the gipsies, and that he is in safety here; but I could not help feeling a momentary sensation of alarm as a thought struck me what might be his fate should they ever at any time discover him."

"Very true, Angela," remarked Sir Laurence; "they would not fail to sacrifice him to their vengeance, should they ever have the opportunity. But still I do not think there is much chance of their being able to do that, as it is not very likely that they will venture again to this country where they are so well known. Besides, under his present disguise, as Horace Milton, they will not very easily discover him."

"I hope not," said Angelina; "but still, when we know the daring of these people, it makes us suspicious."

"Very true, my sweet niece," said Sir Laurence; "but if Rosario only uses proper precaution, and does not venture abroad no more than he can help, he will, I rather think, have nothing to fear."

Sincerely did Angela wish that her uncle's ideas might be realised; but she could not banish all her apprehensions from her mind, and the thought of the real danger in which Rosario was placed, greatly agitated her, and added to the confusion which the sight of him had caused in her breast.

At length, as the evening approached, the company arose to depart, and when Sir Evelyn bade her farewell, and promised to call at Branscombe House in a day or two, Angela trembled so violently that it was impossible for her to conceal her agitation from the object who had excited it. However, it did not cause him much surprise, and he attributed it to a far different cause.

When they had arrived at Branscombe House, and Angela was permitted to retire, she felt the greatest relief, and gave herself up entirely to the many thoughts which crowded on her mind. In vain she tried to banish the image of Rosario from her memory, and the more she reflected upon the graces of his person, and the gentleness of his manners, the more lasting became the impression on her heart. Yes; she could not deny to herself that there already Rosario reigned, and when she thought of the utter hopelessness of that love, and of the anguish which she must inflict upon the noble and generous Sir Evelyn, when she should reject his vows, she could not restrain her tears, and for some time wept bitterly.

But there was something so peculiar in the expression of Rosario's features, that she could not account for the feelings which came over her as she reflected on it, and the longer she did so, the more she became involved in mystery and perplexity. And should the gipsies discover him, which they were, she thought, in spite of all Sir Laurence Cleveland had said, not at all unlikely to do, she shuddered to think what his fate would be; for it was quite evident that they would not pause at the perpetration of any crime for the gratification of their vengeance.

Alas! would it not have been far better for them both had they never seen each other? for even should their sentiments ultimately prove to be mutual, they could never hope to gain the consent of Mrs. Clearmont and Sir Laurence to their union. It would have been preposterous to have imagined such a thing for a moment. Thus, on every side hope was banished, and Angela could not look upon the probable future without a feeling of dread.

That night Angela slept but little; but she endeavoured to conquer the agitation of her manner in the morning, lest it should attract the attention of her friends.

CHAPTER XXIX.

THE PASSION OF ANGELA GAINS STRENGTH.—AN UNEXPECTED CALAMITY.—THE
DEATH OF LADY BLANCHE.

SEVERAL days passed away without any change taking place in the circumstances of the inmates of Branscombe House; but the anguish of Angela increased, especially as Sir Evelyn daily visited them, and his attentions became more earnest and importunate than ever. This the more annoyed and alarmed her, as her mother and Sir Laurence seemed to give every encouragement to him; and they did not appear to doubt for an instant that the sentiments Sir Evelyn so openly displayed for Angela were returned by her with equal ardour. Indeed, they had no reason to think to the contrary, for the attentions of Sir Evelyn had always to them appeared to be most agreeable to the damsel, and they could not for a moment imagine that it was possible she had fixed her affections on any one else, so limited had been the society in which she had mingled. Alas! could they have penetrated her thoughts, how great would have been their astonishment, regret, and emotion.

Angela had never seen Rosario since the day described in the foregoing chapter, and the anxiety she felt once more to be in his society was almost insupportable. Yet did she dread to see him again, for she knew that it would only increase her anguish, and be encouraging hopes which it seemed impossible could ever be realised. Was she not, in fact, acting imprudently by not banishing him from her thoughts altogether? She was satisfied that she was, and yet she found it impossible to do so; for his image was so deeply graven on her heart, that nothing could ever efface it.

They now paid another visit to the Grange, and again Angela and Rosario met; but his conduct was, if possible, more diffident and retiring than before, and he scarcely ever ventured to raise his eyes to Angela, although he seemed to watch the attention which Sir Evelyn paid her with the deepest emotion, and it appeared two or three times, as though he had the greatest difficulty in repressing a sigh. This con-

See p. 355.

duct Angela noticed, but she was at a loss to understand it, and it gave rise to much reflection in her mind.

When Angela returned home, she felt so indisposed through the anxiety of her thoughts, that she almost immediately sought her chamber; but she could not obtain any relief in sleep, and she passed several hours in the greatest state of misery.

Thus elapsed several weeks, and although Sir Evelyn was almost a constant visitor at the mansion, and did not appear to be happy unless he was in the society of Angela, he had not yet made a confession of his love, and a feeling of doubt and foreboding seemed to prevent him from doing so. Angela had frequently seen Rosario, but there was no alteration in his behaviour, and he appeared to be anxious to avoid her society as much as possible.   This added to the melancholy of Angela, and filled her bosom with a variety of conjectures, upon which she could come to no satisfactory conclusion.

But a calamity was about to befall them of such a nature as to absorb every other feeling, and which for some time rendered them all inconsolable.   Lady Blanche, whose health, much to the alarm of Sir Laurence, had been for some time declining, had become so bad that she was unable to leave her chamber, and the physicians at last gave not the slightest hopes of her recovery.

The whole of the family were thrown into a state of utter despair at this sad circumstance, and Sir Laurence was almost mad, and could not be prevailed upon to leave her chamber either day or night; but Lady Blanche bore her sufferings with the most pious resignation, and looked forward to her approaching dissolution with Christian fortitude and hope.   Her earthly career had been a spotless one, and she, therefore, dreaded not that eternity, which to the wretched, dying sinner presents so many terrors.

And great was the grief of Amanda and her amiable and affectionate daughter, at the prospect of so speedily losing that friend and relative whose numerous virtues had so fondly endeared her to them; but they stifled their own sorrow as much as they could, for the purpose of tranquillising, in some measure, the feelings of Sir Laurence, and the Little Emeline.   But almost entirely ineffectual were their efforts in that respect; for both the baronet and his daughter looked upon the calamity as the destruction of all their hopes.

Sir Evelyn Manners continued his visits to Branscombe House; but, of course, while the family were placed in this state of affliction, he could not think of advancing his suit, and Angela was thus relieved from one subject of anxiety and annoyance. But she saw nothing of Rosario, and notwithstanding her intense anguish of mind at the melancholy and hopeless state of her aunt, her thoughts would ever and anon revert to him, and she would calculate, with the most eager impatience, upon the time when she might behold him again.

And now Sir Laurence recalled to his mind, in more vivid colours than ever, all the affectionate attentions of his devoted wife; the risks she had ran for his sake, and the mild forbearance with which she had treated his former errors; and he looked forward to her anticipated loss as one that would to him, and all who were connected with her, be truly irreparable.

Lady Blanche sought to console him, and by her own example to inspire him with fortitude to submit with calmness and resignation to the will of Heaven; and the baronet struggled hard with his feelings; but it was not likely that, under all the circumstances, he should be able to succeed to any extent, although he endeavoured to prepare himself for that final shock, which he now plainly saw was inevitable.

Three days before this melancholy event took place, the poor invalid having sunk into a tranquil slumber, which seemed likely to revive her, the baronet, in order that he might give free vent to the feelings that oppressed and distracted his brain without interruption from any member of his family, left the mansion, and wandered into the woodlands in the vicinity, where, in a most secluded spot, throwing himself upon the green sward, he gave himself up entirely to the agonizing thoughts which rushed upon his fevered brain.

In the intense anguish and despair of his mind, he could not help giving utterance to a wish that the same hour which summoned Blanche to the bosom of her Maker, should also terminate his earthly career. He was aroused from these dismal reflections by hearing a loud and unnatural laugh near him, and raising his head, no language could pourtray his astonishment, disgust, and alarm, on beholding the revolting form of the ancient hag, Madela, standing before him.

The lapse of years seemed to have made but little or no impression upon the constitution of this frightful old crone; but her features were, if possible, more hideous, and her eyes flashed forth an expression of perfectly demoniacal exultation, as she leaned over her staff, and pointed the long bony fingers of one of her hands towards Sir Laurence.

There was nothing at all human in the appearance of this mysterious old woman ; and as she thus stood, uttering strange grating and guttural sounds, she might have been taken for a spirit of darkness, come upon the earth but to triumph over the misery of its unhappy victims.

Sir Laurence was perfectly appalled, and was unable to move or to utter a syllable, but continued to gaze aghast upon the hideous old woman, almost doubting the evidence of his senses. It seemed, indeed, as if she had the power to appear and disappear at any time, and in all places, at pleasure ; and even the person least prone to superstition might have been placed in doubt and bewilderment by her conduct, and the unaccountable manner in which she accomplished her various evil designs.

Again the hag laughed, and swayed her body to and fro as if in the very extacy of fiendish delight; but still she moved not from the spot, standing but a few paces from where the astonished and alarmed Sir Laurence had thrown himself.

" Joy, Laurence Cleveland," said Madela at length, in her usual croaking voice ; " I give thee much joyful congratulation on the prospect of thy speedy deliverance from the danger of being criminally prosecuted as a bigamist. Ho! ho! ho!—and the death of the deluded Blanche Lester should be a happy event to thee, since it may spare thee the fate of a felon; but thinkest thou it would impart much consolation to her in her dying moments, if thou wert to tell her that she never was, and is not now, the lawful wife of Laurence Cleveland—that Lady Clara Cleveland, the deeply injured, the traduced, in spite of all that thou hast asserted, and continue to assert to the contrary, is still living ; also her offspring—thy child—deceiver—murderer, and ——"

" Lying fiend in human form!" exclaimed Sir Laurence, before she could finish the sentence, and starting to his feet, " I will hear no more. I dare thee to the proof, and thus will I drag thee before that tribunal where thou must render a strict explanation of thy conduct. For years have I been endeavouring to discover thee and thine infamous associates, and now that I have found thee, thou shalt not again escape me."

As the infatuated baronet gave utterance to these expressions, he attempted to seize Madela ; but with the utmost ease and composure she grasped him by the throat, and after thus holding him until his countenance became black and distorted, and he was almost strangled, she hurled him from her to the earth, with another demoniacal laugh of exultation and defiance.

" Rash idiot," she cried, glaring upon him ; " hast thou not long before this learnt that thou hast no power over Madela—that she could, if it were her will, crush thee as easily as she could the veriest reptile ? But, no ; thy time is not yet come. One heavy blow is about to fall on thee, and thou shalt live to experience yet greater misery. Remember my promise, recollect my curse, and tremble !"

" Is there no power to release me from this inhuman being ?" cried Sir Laurence, in the most absolute despair and agony; "am I to be thus continually annoyed, mocked at, reviled, defied ?"

"Even so, Laurence Cleveland," returned Madela, with another scornful laugh; "and thou canst not help thyself. I am thy curse—the evil ruler of thy destiny; and will pursue thee to thy final destruction. Oh, but I have rare sport in view— rare sport; and will yet make thee and thine weep tears of blood."

"Base woman, if such indeed thou art," exclaimed Sir Laurence; "I could never so have injured thee, or any one connected with thee, as to give reason for the deadly feeling of hatred and revenge which thou dost evince towards me."

"Liar!" shouted Madela, fiercely; "wouldst know me better? Shall I repeat to thee that tale of horror and crime which I have before rang in thine ears? Shall I tell thee—but no, no; at present it would be to me but a waste of time, and might serve to prevent the full gratification of my wishes were I to do so. Go to thy mansion with the cheerful certainty, that by the time that the sun has arisen twice again, Blanche Lester, she whom thou callest thy wife, will be no more. Ha! ha! ha!"

"God! God!" cried the distracted Sir Laurence; "can I, must I endure all this? Hideous hag! begone,—and dare not again to obtrude thine hateful person upon my presence, lest ——"

"Dare not!" interrupted Madela, and louder and more unnatural was the laugh of defiance to which she gave utterance; "what is there, thinkest thou, poor helpless wretch, that I dare not do? Have I not already proved to thee the power I hold over thee, and that thy very life is at my disposal? Fool! Of what avail is your pretended contempt of me? But I leave thee now to the enjoyment of thy pleasant reflections, with the assurance that we shall meet again before long, and that even in thy greatest misery, I will be present to laugh at and triumph in thy sufferings."

"Stop, mysterious woman; but one word with thee," cried the baronet, worked up to a pitch of the most insupportable agony. But she only turned on him a look of malignant triumph, and immediately vanished from the spot, being quickly hidden from the sight by the thickly clustering trees.

For several moments Sir Laurence remained transfixed to the spot, and gazing vacantly at the place where the old woman had disappeared, completely wrapt in amazement and horror; for the predictions of Madela had an irresistible influence upon his mind, knowing how frequently they had been realised before; but, at length, he moved a few paces from the spot, in the direction of the place whence Madela had vanished, but no object met his eye, and he beat his breast, and groaned in the intensity of his anguish. The dangerous state of Blanche convinced him that there was too much reason to believe that the prognostications of the old hag would be verified; and, as it now seemed evident that the gipsies were not far from the neighbourhood, he had every reason to apprehend the greatest danger from their vengeance. But could it, indeed, be true that Clara was living? He dared not think so, and tried to persuade himself that it was only a scheme of Madela and her colleagues to keep his mind in a constant state of agony and suspense, as they certainly would have brought her forward ere now, when, by so doing, they could so fully have gratified their revenge, and blighted all his prospects.

But what course could he now adopt to protect himself from the evil designs of the gipsies? He knew not; and the more he endeavoured to arrive at some reasonable conclusion, the greater he became bewildered.

Sir Laurence, after some further time passed in this manner, with slow steps, and his bosom oppressed with the deepest melancholy and foreboding, returned to the mansion, and anxiously inquired after the state of Blanche, being in too great a state of agitation to enter her chamber at present, lest his looks should excite her alarm, and she might put such questions to him as might lead him to betray the adventure he had met with. He was somewhat relieved, however, to hear that she was apparently in less pain than she had been for some days before, and a faint ray of hope dawned upon his mind, that she might yet recover. That idea, however, was soon banished when, after having somewhat tranquillised his feelings, he entered her room, and gazed upon her pale and languid countenance, yet still so beautiful even on her rapid passage to the tomb. He saw then, plainly enough, that her hours were numbered, and that the blow which he had prayed so fervently to Heaven to avert would quickly descend upon him, and then the predictions of old Madela returned upon him with redoubled force.

And yet how calm, how patiently, Lady Blanche bore her sufferings; and, when her husband hung over her with uncontrollable anguish, she endeavoured to soothe him, by assuring him that, although for a time they might be separated on earth, they would meet again in Heaven, no more to part; and she begged of him to try to conquer his emotion and regret as much as possible, for the sake of their little Emeline, who would so much more need his parental protection when she was deprived of her.

To Amanda alone, Sir Laurence communicated the particulars of his meeting with Madela, which she was much astonished and alarmed to hear, but advised him immediately to warn Rosario of it, that he might be on his guard, and keep himself as much confined to the Grange as possible, lest he should encounter the gipsies, and fall a sacrifice to their vengeance. This advice the baronet was determined to follow, as he saw how absolutely necessary it was; but still he was greatly in hopes that the gipsies had no suspicion where Rosario was, as Madela had made no allusion to him.

That same day, Sir Evelyn Manners having visited Branscombe House, the baronet drew him aside, and related to him all the particulars, and sought his advice.

"It is most unfortunate, Sir Laurence," returned Evelyn, after a pause; "I had hoped that the gipsies would never again have ventured to this neighbourhood, and that both your family and Rosario would have been safe from their designs in future; but now it appears certain that a portion of the tribe, if not the whole of it, is concealed somewhere close at hand, and that the utmost precautions must be used to thwart their diabolical machinations. As for this old hag, Madela, as you call her, I scarcely know what to make of her, for her actions appear almost to border upon the supernatural."

"They do indeed," returned Sir Laurence; "and although you know I am not over credulous, I can scarcely believe but that she has the gift of prophecy; so many are the predictions that she has uttered respecting me and my family that have been verified. Alas! I fear that her prediction regarding the death of my beloved Blanche, will be too fatally realised."

"Nay, Sir Laurence," said Evelyn, "you must not suffer that impression to remain on your mind. As for Madela's knowledge of the illness of Lady Blanche, there is nothing surprising in that, as it is too well known all over this part of the country."

"And what would you advise me to do, Sir Evelyn?"

" You can do nothing but keep yourself on your guard, and have your servants constantly on the watch. As for Rosario, he must keep himself confined to the house, and in all probability he will then be safe enough, as it does not appear to me that the gipsies have any suspicion of where he is, and no persons but ourselves know him by any other name than that of Horace Milton."

Sir Laurence could not deny the truth of these arguments; and, after some further conversation, they separated, and the baronet, with a disconsolate heart, once more sought the chamber of his wife, where he found his sister, Angela, and Emeline, watching by the side of her couch, and completely overwhelmed with grief.

The following day Lady Blanche was much worse, and it was painfully evident to all, that her end was rapidly approaching. But still, she never for a moment lost her self-possession and resignation, and endeavoured to console her distracted husband and her other relations, and to prevail upon them to submit without murmuring to the irrevocable and all-wise will of the Supreme.

A melancholy day was that to them all, and, in spite of all their efforts, they could not contemplate their approaching bereavement without feelings of the most unbounded awe and poignant anguish.

The third day arrived, and poor Lady Blanche was sinking fast; the physicians assured Sir Laurence that she could not possibly survive many hours, and therefore he had better make up his mind to the worst. Alas! their assertions were too fatally correct, for before the sun had declined in the western horizon, the gentle spirit of Lady Blanche quitted its earthly tenement, and joined its kindred angels in the realms of bliss.

CHAPTER XXX.

THE SORROW OF SIR LAURENCE CLEVELAND AND HIS FAMILY AT THE DEATH OF LADY BLANCHE.—THE ATTEMPT ON THE LIFE OF ROSARIO.

FOR some time after the vital spark had fled from the body of his beloved wife, the all gentle and amiable Blanche, Sir Laurence Cleveland remained in a state of stupefaction, gazing upon the pale cold corse, lovely even in death, with the air of a maniac; then, as the melancholy truth seemed to flash with overwhelming force upon his brain, he uttered a cry of anguish and despair, and sunk in a state of insensibility upon the floor.

In that condition the unfortunate baronet was conveyed to his own chamber, and medical assistance was called in. Nor were the other members of the family scarcely in a better condition; but the youthful Emeline, especially, was in a state bordering on distraction, and was completely deaf to all the efforts which were made to tranquillise her.

She hung over the corpse of her mother with looks of unutterable agony, and it was not without the greatest difficulty that she could be persuaded to leave that chamber of death.

And had it been her own mother, the affectionate Angela could scarcely have felt greater grief, for in Lady Blanche she had lost a fervent and sincere friend, that nothing could ever replace; and when she thought of her many virtues, and recalled to her memory the kind attentions she had paid her, her tears flowed unrestrained.

It was several days before Sir Laurence was able to leave his chamber, and in the meantime the melancholy preparations for the funeral of the late Lady Blanche were proceeded with under the directions of Amanda.

Sir Evelyn Manners had several times visited Branscombe House, to condole with the family on their sad bereavement, and most deeply affected he was to see the melancholy impression it had made upon Angela; at the same time, her gentle sensibility aroused his warmest admiration.

The day before the funeral, Sir Laurence having passed some hours in the chamber of death, and in mourning over the cold remains of his wife, completely exhausted with weeping, and with the vain hope of being able to divert his thoughts from the dismal and heart-rending subject that engrossed them, he left the mansion and wandered towards the scenes to which poor Blanche had been particularly attached. But how sad, how dreary did they now appear to him. He sat himself down beneath the umbrageous branches of a venerable oak, which had been a favourite of Blanche, and where they had often sat together to shelter themselves from the scorching rays of the sun, on a summer's day. Sad and deserted seemed all around, and the breeze, as it gently murmured among the foliage, seemed, to the disordered imagination of Sir Laurence Cleveland to sigh forth the dismal requiem of death.

He recalled to his memory all the events of their life, and when he remembered the devoted affection of Blanche, the Christian fortitude with which she had supported all the many trials to which she had been subjected, and the generous confidence she had reposed in him, even when she had so much reason to doubt him, in spite of all his manly efforts to restrain them, his tears burst forth, and he gave himself up for some time entirely to his anguish, which was even more intense than language can describe.

"And shall I never again listen to thy gentle voice, my beloved Blanche?" he sighed; "shall I no more be gladdened with thy sweet smiles of fondest affection? Oh, God! how can I ever survive this dreadful blow? Better, far better would it be that death should also lay his icy hand on me, since she who shared my whole affections is taken from me."

"But thou shall yet live to endure greater misery, Laurence Cleveland," exclaimed a well-known voice, and looking up, and shuddering with horror, Sir Laurence Cleveland beheld that certain harbinger of evil to him, the frightful hag, old Madela, standing before him, and grinning maliciously upon him.

"Thou hast found the predictions of Madela came true, Laurence Cleveland," she continued; "Blanche Lester, thy paramour, she who weakly believed herself to be thy lawful wife, now lies a breathless corse; and the curse of her spirit will hover over thee. Oh, this revenge, this triumph over thee is glorious; and many more times shall I have reason to exult over thy misery."

"Cursed fiend! for such, indeed, thou must be," cried the baronet, in accents of the most powerful and uncontrollable emotion; "will nothing appease thy deadly malice? Why dost thou again disgust me with thine hated presence?"

"To feast mine eyes in the contemplation of thy anguish," returned Madela; "and to predict the sufferings that are yet in store for thee. Oh, thou hast not yet endured half the torture which thou art doomed to experience; but the time is coming—the time is coming; and then will I again come to congratulate thee on the cheerful aspect of thine affairs."

As the old woman gave utterance to those words, her looks became perfectly demoniacal, and Sir Laurence could not meet her malicious eye without a shudder of horror.

"Leave me, unnatural woman," he ejaculated; "leave me to my misery, and be satisfied with the anguish thou hast already inflicted. Begone, I say, or I will call assistance, and deliver thee over to the hands of justice."

"Ha, ha, ha," laughed Madela, scornfully; "thinkest thou to alarm me by thy threats? Fool! have I not often before shown thee that I set them at defiance? —But, oh, thou art most truly brave to need assistance against an old woman; marvellously brave, indeed. But, behold, I came not unprepared; raise thou thy voice but to create an alarm, and I will lodge the contents of this pistol in thine heart."

As Madela said this, she produced a pistol from beneath her cloak, and levelled it at the breast of Sir Laurence, with a look of determination. He shrunk back alarmed, and knew not what to do, although, for the moment, he thought of rushing upon the old woman, and at all hazards securing her; but she seemed to read his thoughts, and again laughing aloud, she did not offer to move from the spot.

"Why dost thou not call for aid, Laurence Cleveland?" she said, sarcastically; "surely the threats of an old woman cannot so soon have daunted thy manly courage. Thou wouldst deliver me over to the hands of justice, eh! Why dost thou not attempt it?—Oh, thou art most bold, indeed."

"Foul hag, will nothing satisfy thy malice?—Begone, and no longer shock mine ears with thy savage taunts."

"Then it does torture thee to hear them," said Madela. "Thou art not proof against my reproaches, though thou wouldst fain endeavour to appear so. This is indeed a triumph to me; and many more times yet will I come to enjoy it. I leave thee for the present to the enjoyment of thine own thoughts."

Having said this, she waved her hand in a menacing manner towards Sir Laurence, and retreated from his sight.

The baronet stood for a few minutes wrapped in amazement and agony; and then, with a sad heart, he turned from the spot, and retraced his steps to the mansion.

If anything could have added to the anguish of his mind, it would have been this adventure, for the observations which old Madela had made use of had struck deep to his heart, and filled his bosom with numerous doubts and apprehensions. Many were the reflections it gave rise to; and it was some time before Sir Laurence could recover from its effects; but at length he did become somewhat more tranquil, and supplicated the mercy of Heaven in this his severe trial.

And now the day of the funeral came, and universal gloom presided over the neighbourhood of Branscombe House. Labour was suspended for that day, and the inhabitants assembled near the mansion at an early hour, resolved to follow the remains of Lady Blanche to their resting-place. It was a melancholy sight to see the young and the old vying with each other in the expression of their grief, and their reverence for the memory of the departed lady, who had been to them so kind a friend; and had ever been ready to stretch forth her hand to relieve them in the time of need.

When the coffin was placed in the vaults, and the last mournful ceremony was over, the prayers and sobs of the numerous persons present might be plainly heard, and they then slowly dispersed, and left the principal mourners to return to the mansion.

Emeline supported this sad trial with much more fortitude than could have been anticipated; but when the baronet saw the tomb close on all he valued most on earth, for ever, he was unable to restrain the power of his anguish, and had it not been for the support of Sir Evelyn, he must have fallen to the earth.

Just as they had reached Branscombe House, the form of a woman sprung from the porch, and immediately crossing the path of Sir Laurence, she fixed her eyes

See p. 363.

upon him with a malicious grin of triumph. It was Madela; every one present recognized her in a moment; but before any one could attempt to seize her, she was out of sight, with a rapidity that was truly astonishing.

Several persons started in pursuit of her, but without any chance of success, and Sir Laurence and the others entered the mansion, deeply affected at the melancholy events of the day.

No. 47.

And now that the remains of Lady Blanche were consigned to the tomb, Sir Laurence did indeed feel himself lonely, wretched, and miserable, and dense was the gloom which for many weeks hung over the mansion; Angela and Emeline feeling the loss they had sustained as severely as the baronet.

But at length resignation came to their aid, and they became more tranquil; but a melancholy had settled upon the mind of Sir Laurence, which he felt convinced that nothing could ever banish. The threats and predictions of Madela also, continually rang in his ears, and it was in vain that he endeavoured to destroy the influence they had obtained over his mind. Although the strictest inquiries had been made to try to discover Madela, and to ascertain whether or not the gipsies were concealed anywhere in the neighbourhood, they had not been able to obtain any information; and they remained in a constant state of dread of some outrage being effected by their secret machinations.

Sir Evelyn Manners visited the mansion almost every day, and he resumed his attentions to Angela with redoubled energy; although he was disappointed to observe the coldness with which she received them, and which plainly showed that her feelings were far from being in unison with his own.

Rosario also frequently accompanied Sir Evelyn to Branscombe House, and the more Angela beheld of him, and his amiable manners, the more dangerous did he become to her peace of mind; and she reproached herself for encouraging sentiments which could never be gratified.

Rosario, too, she often noticed, seemed more melancholy and abstracted than usual when she was present, while he seemed to eye Sir Evelyn with such a strange expression of countenance, that she could not understand.

At length, some months having elapsed since the death of Lady Blanche, and the gloom which that calamity occasioned being in some measure abated, Sir Evelyn determined at once to have his fate decided, and to ascertain whether or not Angela returned his passion. He therefore sought an opportunity of making his sentiments known to her mother, and to request that she would impart them to Angela.

Amanda received Sir Evelyn's acknowledgements with every favour, and assured him that if his love should prove agreeable to Angela, she would gladly accept him for a son-in-law.

With this answer Sir Evelyn was satisfied, but still he had his doubts as to his meeting with any success with Angela, the coldness of whose behaviour of late had greatly damped the ardour of his hopes.

The following day Mrs. Clearmount summoned Angela to her presence, and after a few preliminary observations, she made her acquainted with the confession of Sir Evelyn, and after passing a high eulogium on his merits, she requested to know her sentiments as regarded him.

While her mother was thus speaking, Angela had turned very pale, and trembled violently, and when she had concluded, she threw herself weeping on her bosom, and, in a voice half choked with emotion, she ejaculated,—

" Oh, my dear mother, I beseech you do not urge me on a subject so painful to my feelings. I feel a proper sense of the honour Sir Evelyn intends me, I admire his virtues, I esteem him as a friend; but—but ——"

" You cannot love him," added Mrs. Clearmount, with a somewhat disappointed look; " that is what you would say, is it not?"

" Spare me, my dear mother," said Angela; " I know not what to say. I am too young yet to think of matrimony; and indeed, indeed, I have no wish to change my condition."

"Angela," said her mother, looking at her with a penetrating eye, "tell me candidly, have you seen one whom you think you could love better than Sir Evelyn Manners?"

Deep blushes suffused the cheeks of Angela at this unexpected question, and she trembled more violently than before.

"Oh, my dear mother," she said, "why do you ask me such a question? You know how limited has been the circle of my acquaintance; and who think you is there who could inspire such sentiments in my breast?"

"Then, my dear Angela," returned her mother, "if such is the case, a favourable answer may, at any rate, be returned to Sir Evelyn, and he may be led to hope that in time he may be able to make a favourable impression upon your heart. It is not my wish that you should become the wife of any man whom you could not love; but Sir Evelyn is a gentleman whom I much esteem, and who is equally regarded by your uncle, Sir Laurence, and I should deeply regret that his hopes should be disappointed."

Angela tried to return an answer, but she could not, her heart was too full; and her mother having affectionately embraced her, and tried to console her, left her to her own thoughts.

When she was gone, Angela, no longer placing any restraint upon her feelings, burst into a copious flood of tears, and then sinking on her knees, she supplicated the Almighty to direct her how to act in that emergency. To be the cause of anguish to Evelyn, caused her sincere regret; but still she was convinced that she could never love him, and would it not therefore be cruel and unjust to deceive him with false hopes?

The form of Rosario now arose more forcibly than ever upon her imagination, and she could no longer attempt to deny to herself the ascendancy he had gained over her heart. But, alas! dared she ever to avow such a passion? Would it be returned by the mysterious youth who had inspired it; or if it was, was it at all likely that her mother would ever give her sanction to their vows? It was not; and it was madness, therefore, to encourage such a hope. How much did Angela dread to behold Sir Evelyn again, for she had no doubt that he would then himself reveal the sentiments he entertained towards her, and how should she ever be able to sustain such an interview? She passed a wretched day, and these thoughts crowding upon and racking her brain at night, banished sleep from her pillow.

When Sir Evelyn was made acquainted by Mrs. Clearmount with what had passed between her and her daughter, although he was not disappointed, he felt the most painful regret, for he saw that there was little or no hope for him, and he even hesitated to confess his sentiments to Angela, fearing that he would receive a direct refusal from her lips. But at last he resolved to hazard the worst, and that the following day should decide his fate; for certainty, he considered, was far preferable to suspense.

To Rosario he confided all his thoughts, and when he had made him acquainted with what had passed between Angela and her mother, he was astonished to remark the extraordinary emotion which Rosario exhibited. When he mentioned the name of Angela, he thought he saw a tear trembling in his eye; and when he expatiated upon the ardour of the love with which she had inspired him, he could observe him tremble, while his cheeks became crimsoned, and it was evident that remarkable thoughts and feelings were passing in his mind.

Sir Evelyn looked at him earnestly, and was at a loss to understand the reason of the agitation he evinced ; and Rosario quickly excused himself, and retired from his presence.

The singular behaviour and appearance of Rosario, however, served Sir Evelyn for reflection for some time afterwards, and he was at a loss to account for it in any other way than the deep interest which he felt in his happiness, devoted to him as he was by feelings of the warmest gratitude and esteem.

The following morning Sir Laurence called upon him, in order to consult with him on the subject of his suit, his sister having informed him of all that had taken place between her and Angela, but which had not the least surprised him, as he had expected that Angela would at first exhibit the timidity she had done; but he believed that she would in time conquer the reserve and diffidence she now felt, for he could not but think that she really loved Sir Evelyn, although she was afraid, at present, to acknowledge that sentiment to herself. This opinion he expressed to the young baronet, and encouraged him to press his suit, not doubting but that he would ultimately meet with a favourable reception.

" I need not assure you, Sir Evelyn," continued the baronet, " that there is no man whom I would sooner see become the husband of my niece than yourself; and I feel satisfied that Angela cannot have formed an attachment for any other person, for she has been but little, as you are aware, in society, and has therefore had no opportunity of seeing any one on whom she could place her affections. Take courage, then, and I feel convinced that your most sanguine hopes will all be gratified."

" Heaven grant that your predictions may be realised, Sir Laurence," returned Sir Evelyn; " for I feel that on gaining the love of the charming Angela, my future happiness alone depends. No other damsel can ever engage my affections; but yet, after the observations she made use of to her mother, I cannot help fearing that I have not created that interest in her bosom which I flattered myself I had done."

" Do not despair, my young friend," remarked Sir Laurence; " Angela is yet young, and you know not what time and perseverance may effect in your favour."

" True; but if I find that my addresses are repugnant to the feelings and wishes of Angela, however painful the trial may be to me to be compelled to abandon my hopes, I will no longer urge my suit. I would win the love of your fair niece, Sir Laurence; and if I cannot do that, I must endeavour to resign myself to my fate; for sooner would I perish than cause her one moment's uneasiness by pressing those vows which her heart could not respond to."

" Nobly spoken, Sir Evelyn; but indeed I do not think that you will be put to any such a trial. However, you must urge your suit to the damsel yourself, and then you will be in a condition to know whether you have reason to hope or despair."

" I will do so this very day," replied Sir Evelyn, " for I cannot endure to remain any longer in this state of doubt and suspense."

After some farther conversation, Sir Evelyn and Sir Laurence both left the Grange together, and made their way to Branscombe House.

Angela was still in a violent state of agitation, anticipating the arrival of Sir Evelyn. Fain would she have excused herself from being present in the family circle that day, but she could not do so with any good grace; and, at the same time, it would be treating Sir Evelyn with a coldness and disrespect which he did not merit. No; she was determined, should Sir Evelyn seek another interview with her, to act with candour, and not to deceive and flatter him with false hopes; and she was satisfied, that when he knew her sentiments, that he was too honourable and generous to urge his suit, but that he would try to conquer his passion, and seek to gain the affections of some other maiden who was equally as worthy of him as herself.

But she found it impossible to conceal her emotion and confusion when Sir Evelyn made his appearance, and she trembled so evidently, that she could not without difficulty support herself. The young baronet noticed her agitation, and while he felt for her, he was convinced, from her manner, that he had indeed nothing hope.

About an hour after Evelyn's arrival, Sir Laurence and his sister purposely retired from the room, and left him and Angela together. She sank back in her chair, and averting her face, her bosom throbbed so violently, that it almost overpowered her. Sir Evelyn looked at her earnestly for a few minutes, and was unable to speak; but at length he ventured to repeat her name in a voice of ineffable tenderness. She looked timidly up, and then, covering her blushing cheeks with her hands, she sighed deeply.

Sir Evelyn could contain himself no longer; his heart was ready to burst from his side with impatience, and throwing himself at her feet, he poured forth the sentiments of his soul, with a fervour and eloquence which was sufficient to make an impression upon even the most insensible heart.

It was several moments before Angela could return any answer, for sobs completely choked her utterance.

"I—I feel flattered, honoured, Sir Evelyn," she at length said, in a tremulous voice, "by the sentiments you have expressed towards me. I need not, I am sure, tell you that I esteem you as a friend, and must ever do so; but truth and candour compel me to say that I cannot return the passion you have so ardently expressed."

"Alas, then, beauteous Angela!" sighed Sir Evelyn; "I am most unfortunate, and I fear that happiness can never more be my lot. Without the love of Angela, the world for me can possess no charms, and better would it have been for me had I never been born. But you will not leave me to entire despair; oh! say that at some future period I may hope to gain your affections, and I will be satisfied."

"I beseech you, Sir Evelyn," said Angela, "not to urge me further. Believe me, I am not insensible to your merits; I honour your virtues; but it would be cruel and unjust to hold out to you any such promises which could never be realised. That you may meet with some other damsel who is more worthy of you than I am, is my most fervent wish."

"Oh, that is impossible," said Evelyn; "never can I love any other woman than Angela Clearmount, and neither time nor distance can banish her from my memory. But I will no longer offend your ears, sweet damsel, by my importunities. Farewell! and may Heaven shower down upon your head every blessing, though I must be miserable for ever!"

Angela looked compassionately upon him, and tears trembled in her eyes. She would have spoken, and endeavoured to impart some consolation to him, but she could not; and extending her hand to him, he pressed it vehemently to his lips; then rising to his feet he fixed upon her one look of unutterable anguish, and, with a burst of emotion, he rushed from her presence.

Angela sank back in her chair, and gave free vent to her feelings in a copious flood of tears. The trial was past, and she felt somewhat relieved; but how sincerely did she regret the misery she had been compelled to inflict on Evelyn, and the despair to which he would be driven.

But paramount beyond every other object, Rosario arose to her thoughts, and the more she reflected upon him, the greater did her anguish of mind become.

She was aroused from these meditations by the entrance of her mother, and she looked up in her face timidly, for she expected to see her angry; but instead of that, she looked upon her with an expression of compassion, not unmingled with regret.

"My dear child," she said, "think not that I come to reproach you; no, Heaven forbid that I should wish to persuade you to do that which might plunge you in future misery; but still I lament that Sir Evelyn Manners has been unable to win your affections, for he is good, honourable, and accomplished. I fear that this disappointment will be the means of blighting all his future prospects in life. He has left the house in the utmost agony of mind, from which, I am afraid, he will not easily be able to recover."

"Oh, my beloved mother," returned Angela, "how sincerely grieved am I to hear this. Sir Evelyn Manners is indeed all you have described him, and, as a dear friend, he must always possess my warmest esteem. I do trust that he will be enabled to forget me in any other character."

"Oh, no, my love, that I am certain he will never be able to do," said Mrs. Clearmount; "so firmly has he fixed his affections upon you. But still I cannot help entertaining a hope that you will alter your sentiments towards him."

"I shall always regard Evelyn as if he were my own brother," replied the damsel; "but in any other character, indeed, I am convinced I can never think of him."

"And yet your heart is not engaged to any other person, Angela?" said her mother, fixing upon her a penetrating look.

Angela blushed and trembled, and scarcely knew how to answer.

"Oh, my dear mother," she said at length, "why do you put such a question to me? What has there been in my conduct to cause you to suspect such a thing?"

"Be not agitated, my Angela, for I am satisfied that you will never place your affections on an unworthy object. But I will press you no further on this subject for the present."

"You are not angry with me, are you, mother?"

"Angry with you; no, child, I cannot be angry with you for having spoken with candour and truth; although I cannot but deeply commiserate with Evelyn Manners, on his disappointment."

"And my dear uncle?" eagerly added Angela.

"He feels the same as myself," answered Mrs. Clearmount; "he deeply regrets that Evelyn has been unable to win your heart; but still he cannot reproach you for having acted as you have done. It is furthest from the wishes of Sir Laurence, as well as myself, that you should make any sacrifice of your feelings, or bestow your hand on him who cannot also possess your heart."

Angela threw herself on her mother's bosom, and gave free indulgence to her emotion.

Mrs. Clearmount did not offer to interrupt her; and, after having embraced her tenderly, she quitted the room, and once more left her to her own meditations.

The trial which Angela had so long dreaded was now over; but still she could not help thinking that there was more trouble in store for her, and she deeply lamented the sorrow she had been compelled to inflict upon Sir Evelyn, who had evidently flattered himself all along that he possessed her love, although she had taken such pains to convince him of the contrary.

Sir Evelyn returned to the Grange in a state of mind which needs no description; although Sir Laurence and Amanda had exerted themselves to the utmost to console him. All his hopes were annihilated by Angela's rejection of his suit, and he cared not now what became of him; for that he would ever love any other woman, he did not think was possible. He could no longer think of remaining in the neighbourhood, for to behold Angela, would only be to add to his hopeless passion, and to inflict additional misery on them both.

Rosario seemed to feel much for his benefactor's distress, and there was a peculiarity in the manner in which he endeavoured to console him, which forcibly struck Sir Evelyn, and created an unaccountable sensation in his breast.

Sir Evelyn now determined to return to the Continent, and to seek in far distant climes to dissipate his anguish, and to banish Angela from his memory; though that, he feared, would be a fruitless task. He made every preparation for his departure, and on his visiting Branscombe House, a day or two afterwards, he made Sir Laurence and his sister acquainted with his intention; and although they applauded the prudence of his conduct, they could not but regret the loss of his society, which had become so agreeable to them.

When this was communicated to Angela, she felt the deepest anguish of mind; but little did her mother and Sir Laurence imagine the source from whence it sprung.

Rosario would, of course, accompany Sir Evelyn, and something seemed to convince Angela that she would never behold him again; and now the full strength of the passion she had imbibed for that mysterious youth was made the more apparent to her; and she looked forward to the time of his departure with the greatest anguish.

It now wanted but two days to the time fixed on by Sir Evelyn Manners to leave England, and, accompanied by Rosario, he paid his last visit to Branscombe House, to bid them farewell, not knowing when, or if ever, he might return. It was a sad meeting for all of them, and Angela could not disguise the intense anguish of mind she was enduring. Rosario, however, appeared to be the most composed of them all, and more than once Angela was certain that she even beheld a smile of pleasure on his countenance, when Sir Evelyn alluded to his departure. Alas! thought the damsel, could he have formed any idea of what was passing in her mind, how different would have been his feelings.

Rosario, after having passed some time in their company, excused himself, and quitted the room, and they understood shortly afterwards, from one of the servants, that he had left the mansion, probably to take a walk in the adjoining fields.

The time passed quickly away, and the evening approached; still Rosario did not return, and Sir Evelyn and the others began to feel somewhat surprised and alarmed, lest any accident had befallen him.

They were about to despatch a servant in search of him, when they were all startled by hearing the report of a pistol, which seemed to proceed from the grounds attached to the mansion.

They immediately started to their feet, and rushed from the house, and stretched bleeding and insensible on the earth they beheld Rosario. Angela no sooner beheld him, than she uttered a loud scream of terror, and sunk senseless in the arms of her mother.

Rosario had wandered farther from the mansion than he had intended to do, and was hastily returning, when he heard the footsteps of some person behind him, as if in pursuit of him ; and, turning round, his astonishment and terror may readily be conceived, when he beheld the gipsy Harold close behind him, who in a fierce voice commanded him to stop.

Rosario, however, increased his speed, and arriving at the mansion, and finding the garden gate open, he rushed in, and was quickly followed by Harold, who having again commanded him to stop, he discharged the contents of a pistol at him, and then made his escape, no doubt supposing that he had murdered him.

———

CHAPTER XXXI.

THE EXTRAORDINARY DISCOVERY.—WHO IS ROSARIO, THE SUPPOSED GIPSY BOY ?

NOTHING could equal the consternation of every one on this fearful discovery, and the distress of Sir Evelyn was extreme, not only at the calamity which had befallen Rosario, but also at the situation of Angela. They were both conveyed into the mansion without delay, and surgical assistance procured ; but it was some time ere Angela recovered, and she then eagerly inquired after Rosario, with an expression of countenance which fully betrayed the feelings that were passing in her mind, and, for the first time, revealed to her mother and the distracted Sir Evelyn that Rosario was the object of her affections. But a discovery was about to take place of even a more extraordinary description.

The surgeon who had been sent for had attended upon Rosario to dress his wound, when he suddenly entered the apartment in which Sir Laurence and the others were all anxiously awaiting him, and his countenance betrayed the utmost astonishment and excitement.

"Now, my dear sir," demanded Sir Laurence, impatiently, "how is the unfortunate wounded youth ?"

"The wounded *youth !*" repeated the surgeon, laying great emphasis on the last word.

"Yes, yes," said Sir Evelyn ; "tell us, is the wound of a dangerous character ?"

"I have a surprise of a most extraordinary nature for you all," said the surgeon. "The being whom you have hitherto known as Horace Milton *is a lovely woman !*"

It would really be totally impossible to pourtray the amazement of all present on this announcement ; Angela shrieked ; her face became ghastly pale, and her whole demeanour betrayed the extraordinary emotion she was enduring. It was not without the greatest difficulty that she could save herself from fainting. As for Sir Evelyn Manners, his agitation almost equalled that she was enduring.

"A woman !" they all repeated in a breath.

"On my honour, a beauteous woman," replied the surgeon.

"Gracious Heaven!" ejaculated Sir Laurence, "how wonderful are thy ways. A woman, and so like to ——"

He checked himself, and his countenance showed the extraordinary thoughts and feelings that were passing in his mind.

See p. 368.

"Good God!" exclaimed Mrs. Clearmount, "I can scarcely believe the evidence of my senses; and yet the delicacy of manners always evinced by the supposed Rosario, the gentle and effeminate features, the light and graceful figure, all serve to confirm the truth of this remarkable discovery. What a strange fate must this poor unfortunate's have been, to compel her to assume a character that must have been so repulsive to her sense of delicacy."

Angela clasped her burning temples, and her brain seemed whirling round. In a moment the whole truth flashed across her mind. The devotion of the supposed Rosario to Sir Evelyn, and the melancholy of her demeanour, convinced her that the young baronet had won the poor unknown's heart.

"But the wound?" remarked Sir Laurence, eagerly.

"It fortunately is not dangerous," remarked the surgeon.

"Thank Heaven!" ejaculated the baronet; and nameless feelings throbbed in his bosom. "The mystery which has so long surrounded this singular being, will probably then at last be solved."

"The poor girl, however, when I left her, was still in a state of unconsciousness," said the surgeon; "and knows not of the discovery that has been made."

"Oh, what will be her emotion when she becomes aware of it?" said Mrs. Clearmount; "but let us hasten to her chamber; come, my love," she added, addressing herself to Angela; "will you not accompany me?"

"I will," answered Angela, in a faltering voice, for she felt at that moment the most extraordinary sensation stealing into her bosom, which she found it impossible to control.

"And let us know, as soon as you can, how the mysterious unfortunate is," said Sir Laurence. "My mind is filled with wonder, and I am all impatience until this extraordinary adventure is fully elucidated."

Mrs. Clearmount and her daughter, accompanied by the surgeon, then left the apartment, and repaired to the chamber of the wounded female; and Sir Laurence gave instructions to his servants to go in pursuit of the attempted assassin, he having no doubt, from the appearance of Madela in the neighbourhood lately, that it was one of the gipsies.

"I am completely lost in amazement at this occurrence," remarked Sir Evelyn Manners.

"And so am I," returned Sir Laurence Cleveland; "the whole affair bears more the character of romance than reality. Who can this mysterious female be, and what can have been the reason for her assuming such a disguise?"

"It is altogether inexplicable," said Sir Evelyn Manners; "I can scarcely believe the evidence of my senses. And then the devoted attachment she has ever evinced towards me. Can she have encouraged a sentiment warmer than esteem for me? And yet why should I encourage an idea so preposterous?"

"And why preposterous?" demanded Sir Laurence. "There is nothing unreasonable in the supposition. I have myself noticed the peculiar attention which the supposed Rosario paid you; but, of course, could never at that time attribute it to any other feeling than that of gratitude. But oh, Sir Evelyn, you can form no conception of my feelings, when I recal to my memory the features of this remarkable being."

"Do they resemble those of any one with whom you are or have been connected, Sir Laurence?" asked Evelyn.

The baronet sighed.

"Alas! they do," ejaculated he; "they are the very counterpart of the misguided woman, my first wife."

"Most remarkable!" observed Sir Evelyn; "should it prove that she is in any way related to her."

"Oh, I cannot believe it; and yet, when I take all the circumstances into my consideration, I scarcely know what to think."

"Had the unfortunate Lady Clara any offspring at the time she abandoned you, Sir Laurence?" inquired his companion.

"She had not," replied the baronet, with some emotion, which he could not repress; "but at the time she was *enceinte*. But even should that child survive, I can never believe otherwise than that it is the offspring of her illicit connection with her guilty paramour."

"Still, should that be the case, and the supposed Rosario should prove to be that child, surely you would not despise her for the faults of her parents?"

"Oh, no," replied Sir Laurence, "I should rather pity her; but still, methinks I could not bear to look upon her, for it would bring the sense of my shame too strongly to my feelings."

"And yet, after all, Lady Clara might have been innocent," remarked Sir Evelyn.

"Innocent!" repeated Sir Laurence; "oh, it would be madness to imagine so for a moment. Was not the proof I had of her guilt too convincing? Did not her flight afterwards fully confirm it?"

"It certainly does look most suspicious," returned Sir Evelyn.

"Suspicious! oh, that is by far too mild a term to give it. But let us drop that subject. I wish the doctor would return, and inform us how the mysterious damsel is."

He had scarcely uttered these words when the surgeon did enter the room.

"Now, my dear sir," impatiently demanded Sir Laurence, "how fares this unfortunate female?"

"She has just recovered her senses, and is progressing as favourably as can be expected in so short a time," answered the surgeon; "but, of course, she has exhibited much emotion on finding that her real sex is discovered. Oh, Sir Laurence, my eyes never beheld a more lovely and delicate creature."

"And you think there is no danger from the wound she has received?" eagerly asked the young baronet.

"Not the least," replied the surgeon; "fortunately the bullet has only lacerated the flesh, without entering the body, and I have not the least doubt but that in the course of a very few days she will be perfectly restored to convalescence. She says that the wound was inflicted by Harold the gipsy."

"Ah!" exclaimed Sir Laurence Cleveland, "my surmises then are correct. The wretches are concealed somewhere in the neighbourhood, and must be discovered. The time is evidently approaching when all these mysteries will be unravelled. But did you not hear her mention her name?"

"I did not, Sir Laurence; but I left her in earnest conference with Mrs. Clearmount, and I dare say she will enter into a full explanation with them."

"How anxious am I to learn all the particulars," said Sir Laurence.

"And so am I," returned Sir Evelyn; "but still we must wait with patience, and no doubt our curiosity and anxiety will be gratified to the fullest extent; but at present the wounded damsel cannot be in a very fit condition to enter into particulars."

To this opinion Sir Laurence and the doctor agreed, and the former endeavoured to await the time when the long hidden secret should be disclosed with patience; but it afforded him and Sir Evelyn much food for conversation and speculation. But we must now return to Angela and her mother, who, on entering the chamber of the wounded damsel, found her, as has been before stated, in a state of insensibility; but, oh! how struck were they with the beauty and innocence of the fair countenance they gazed upon, while the most painful feelings of emotion shot through the frame of Angela, and she felt that she could love the beauteous and mysterious unknown as fondly as if she were her own sister. The only thing that surprised her and her mother was, that they had never before, from the peculiar delicacy, modesty, and gentleness of her manners, the softness of her features, and the sweetness of her voice, suspected her real sex. Her silken hair, which was now unconfined, flowed in luxuriant tresses over her snowy neck, and her whole appearance, as she lay in that insensible state, might have created admiration in the most insensible breast.

For some time they watched her in silence, and waited with impatience her restoration to sensibility; but the doctor had quieted their fears by assuring them that the wound was only slight, and that the damsel was merely insensible from loss of blood. He would fain have persuaded them to leave the chamber, lest, on her recovery, and finding that her sex was discovered, she might be too much excited on beholding them; but so great was their anxiety, that they could not be prevailed upon to comply with this request, and they still sat by the side of the couch, eagerly watching the poor girl's restoration to consciousness, and marvelling what would be the strange disclosure they might have to listen to.

"Poor girl," remarked Mrs. Clearmount, "how beauteous and innocent is her countenance, although worn with sorrow. Surely such a face as that cannot be the index of a guilty mind."

"Oh, no," returned Angela, warmly and tears trembled in her eyes; "I am certain we should be doing the fair unknown an injustice by harbouring such a thought. But what can have been the cause of her assuming such a disguise, and how is it possible that she has been enabled to escape detection for such a number of years?"

"In vain I endeavour to form the least conjecture, my love," said her mother; "but it is evident that she must have experienced great trouble, and has suffered much from the persecution of her enemies, and that she has been compelled to assume the disguise to answer their guilty designs. Certainly, her fate has been a most extraordinary one, and I long for the moment when the mystery will, in all probability, be unravelled. But you are weeping, Angela; what is it that so deeply affects you?"

"Oh, my dear mother," replied Angela, hiding her blushing face in her bosom, "will you not reproach me for concealment when I now confess to you that when I knew this insensible female only as Rosario, the gipsy youth, I loved her?"

"Oh, my poor girl," said Mrs. Clearmount, affectionately, "I see it all now, and marvel not that the graces and accomplishments of the supposed Rosario should have captivated your young heart. I wonder not that, entertaining such feelings as those you have just acknowledged, you should have rejected the suit of Sir Evelyn Manners. But I feel convinced that you may still contrive to love this unfortunate damsel as a dear friend, as a sister, and trust that Sir Evelyn will henceforth be received with greater favour in your eyes."

"Sir Evelyn Manners will always be esteemed by me as a friend, my dear mother," replied Angela; "but I feel satisfied that I can never love him as my husband, and I trust that he will not urge his suit, but will endeavour to fix his affections upon some other maiden who is equally worthy of him."

"That, Angela, I am afraid he will never be able to do," said her mother. "But we will talk no more upon this subject for the present; we have now other business to occupy our minds."

The doctor, who, while this discourse was taking place between Mrs. Clearmount and her daughter, had withdrawn to another part of the room, now advanced towards the bed, and, after having watched the countenance of the wounded damsel narrowly, he said,—

"She breathes more freely; she will recover in a few minutes."

He had scarcely spoken these words, when she breathed a gentle sigh, and immediately afterwards she opened her eyes, and gazed with a strange and vacant expression around her. Mrs. Clearmount and her daughter drew nearer towards her, and waited to hear her speak with the greatest anxiety, while they could not but admire the beautiful expression of her sparkling but melancholy eyes. It was not long ere they were gratified.

"Where am I?" she ejaculated; "have I been dreaming? Where is the murderer, Harold? Ah, Angela and Mrs. Clearmount here, and these tresses left to flow unconfined! Then the truth is but too apparent; my painful, my long hidden secret is discovered."

"Compose yourself, my poor girl," said Mrs. Clearmount, in her gentlest accents; "you have nothing to fear; you are amongst friends who will protect you from all danger."

"Oh, pardon—pity me, for this deception," sighed the unfortunate girl, her head sinking upon Mrs. Clearmount's shoulder, and her eyes streaming with tears; "I may appear culpable, guilty, but do not judge too harshly of me."

"Indeed we will not," said Angela; "but what could have induced you [to assume such a disguise? Surely it could not have been of your own free-will?"

"Oh, no," returned the fair unknown; "indeed it was not; and Heaven knows the bitter anguish of mind I have for so many years endured. It was my enemies, the gipsy Harold and Madela, that compelled me to assume a character that was repulsive to my feelings, for what motive I know not; and they bound me by a terrible oath not to reveal myself to any one without their permission; but accident has discovered the secret; the villain Harold has sought my life, and why should I therefore, hesitate to reveal all I know?"

"Certainly not, my good girl," said Mrs. Clearmount; "you have nothing to fear; and rest assured that it is not mere idle curiosity that prompts us, but an anxious wish to serve you, and to protect you from your enemies. Tell me what is your real name?"

"Eugenia," replied the poor girl.

"But your surname?"

"Alas, I know not; it has ever been kept a profound secret from me. I am only told that my mother also was called Eugenia."

"Most strange!" said Mrs. Clearmount; "and know you nothing of your mother's history?"

"No more than I have already told you and Sir Laurence Cleveland, madam," replied Eugenia. "But would that I could meet with Azrah, who took so great an interest in my fate; I do believe that he knows all connected with me, and that he would no longer hesitate to communicate it to me now that my real sex is discovered."

"He must be found, if possible," said Mrs. Clearmount.

"Alas," returned Eugenia, with a sigh, and a melancholy shake of the head; "much I fear that will be a fruitless task. It is more than probable that he has been sacrificed by the gipsies to prevent his divulging their secrets. Poor Azrah, I never think on him without experiencing feelings which I find it impossible to describe."

"The wretches surely would not dare to commit so atrocious a deed?" said Mrs. Clearmount.

"Ah, madam," said Eugenia, "what is there think you that they would scruple to do, after this attempt upon my life?"

"Alas, no," sighed Angela; "it is quite evident that the miscreants are capable of anything."

"But where is my benefactor, Sir Evelyn Manners?" asked Eugenia; and as she spoke the deepest blushes suffused her cheeks, and her bosom seemed to heave with the most powerful emotion. "Ah, what must he think of the deception I have practised? Sir Laurence Cleveland, too, from whom I have experienced so many favours—oh, how shall I ever be able to meet them again?"

"Make yourself perfectly easy on that point, Eugenia," said Mrs. Clearmount; "both Sir Evelyn and Sir Laurence will rather pity you for your misfortunes; they cannot reproach you for the disguise you have so long assumed, as you acted from compulsion and intimidation, and not from free-will."

"Heaven knows that you do me justice, madam," said Eugenia, "by entertaining that belief. What hours of shame and sorrow has it cost me, and oh, how often have I been half tempted to brave the worst, and to throw aside my disguise; but an unconquerable dread prevented me, and thus I continued the victim of shame and anguish."

Eugenia was now faint with the fatigue of talking, and the doctor, who returned to the chamber at that moment, advised Mrs. Clearmount and her daughter to retire from the room for a while, so that she might endeavour to recover herself.

Angela and her mother both offered some words of consolation to Eugenia, and then complied with the surgeon's request.

CHAPTER XXXII.

THE ASTONISHMENT OF THE PERSONS AT BRANSCOMBE-HOUSE.—THE RECOVERY OF EUGENIA.—ANOTHER ADVENTURE, AND ANOTHER REMARKABLE DISCOVERY.

WHEN Mrs. Clearmount and Angela returned to the apartment in which they had left Sir Evelyn and Sir Laurence, they related to them all that had passed between them and Eugenia, to which they listened with the most profound astonishment, and the deepest interest; and, when they had concluded, they could not help giving expression to their feelings in the most vehement manner; at the same time that they expressed the warmest sympathy in the misfortunes which had befallen that poor girl.

"The miscreant Harold and his infamous associates must be apprehended, and their guilty career be brought to a termination," remarked Sir Laurence. "Still there is a mystery about this maiden's fate which I cannot fathom. What could be the motives of her enemies for compelling her to assume a character which must be so oppressive to her delicacy? And why do they refuse to make her acquainted with the name of her parents?"

"It is altogether inexplicable," said Sir Evelyn; "but it is quite certain that old Madela and the man Harold are goaded on by some particular motives, and the secret connected with the origin of Eugenia is of the most important character. I can never believe that she comes of lowly parents, for there is a nobleness of demeanour, and a refined delicacy of manners about her, which cannot fail to command respect and admiration."

"And who can this singular being, whom she calls Azrah, be ?" said Mrs. Clearmount.

"It is evident from what Eugenia has said," returned Sir Laurence, "that he is her friend, and knows the whole of her history, and that of her parents; but that, being in the power of the gipsies, he is afraid to divulge it. I wonder that he has not endeavoured to escape from them, and to seek the protection of the law from their vengeance. And it was from him also that Eugenia received the miniature; and the features of which pourtrayed therein are so vividly stamped upon my memory. Would that we could behold him, then might the whole of this extraordinary and perplexing mystery be unravelled."

" I trust to Heaven that the fears of Eugenia may not be realized," said Mrs Clearmount; "and that Azrah has not already fallen a victim to the vengeance of the gipsies."

" They must be discovered, and brought to an account for the numerous crimes they have committed," said Sir Laurence. "Eugenia and none of us are safe while they are at large. In spite of all their threats, I am determined to use every exertion in my power to effect that object. And does Eugenia know her two principal enemies by no other names than those of Madela and Harold ?"

" She declares she does not," answered Mrs. Clearmount.

" It is strange," remarked the baronet, " and yet I feel confident that those names are only assumed."

" That is most probable," considered Sir Evelyn. " I am perfectly lost in amazement at this discovery. Poor girl, what bitter anguish of mind must she have suffered in all this long series of years !"

" She must, indeed," returned Mrs. Clearmount; "and it is wonderful how she could ever have found fortitude sufficient to sustain herself under such unparalleled troubles and afflictions."

" But, yet, how fortunate it is that the villain Harold has failed in accomplishing his deadly purpose," observed Sir Laurence; "and that the wound he inflicted is not dangerous. I hope that in a few days she will be sufficiently recovered to leave her chamber, for I am all anxiety until I behold her in her true character. • But, prythee, Amanda, repair again to the room of the patient; she much needs that tender attention which I know you are so willing to bestow."

Mrs. Clearmount and her daughter, who were anxious once more to see Eugenia, and to offer her all the consolation in their power, immediately complied, and nothing could persuade Mrs. Clearmount to quit her chamber during the night, although Eugenia was perfectly calm, and did not appear to be suffering much from the effects of the wound.

When Angela returned to her own apartment for the night, she gave herself up to the variety of thoughts which crowded upon her mind; and so extraordinary was the whole adventure, that she could scarcely convince herself of the reality. How deeply did she sympathize in the misfortunes of the fair Eugenia, and deprecate the cruelty of her enemies; while, at the same time, she felt the most unconquerable curiosity to penetrate the mystery of her origin, and to ascertain who she really was. Those amiable qualities, which, under the assumed character of Rosario, the gipsy youth, had made so powerful an impression on her, had lost none of their influence, and she was still prepared to love Eugenia as a sister; for she felt certain that she could never prove to be unworthy of her affection.

But could this discovery make any difference in her sentiments towards Sir Evelyn Manners? Could she ever regard him in any other character than that of a dear friend, or give any encouragement to his addresses? She felt convinced that she could not; and that conviction caused her much regret, for she honoured the numerous noble qualities of the young baronet, and she lamented that she was thus compelled to disappoint the hopes he had formed.

But now another thought suggested itself to the mind of Angela, which seemed so reasonable, that she could not banish it. She remembered well the devotion of Eugenia to Sir Evelyn, and the uneasiness which she had ever evinced when she knew that they were together, and especially when she became acquainted that Sir Evelyn had urged his suit. Was it possible that her young and prepossessing bene. factor had made an impression on her heart? There was nothing at all unreasonable in the idea; but, if such was the fact, she could not but pity the poor girl, as she feared that her passion was hopeless; Sir Evelyn had declared that he could never love any other damsel but her (Angela), and it was not likely that, notwithstanding her numerous virtues and personal attractions, he would ever give any encouragement to the affections of an unknown, and probably obscure girl.

This idea gained more strength in the mind of Angela, the longer she reflected on it, and she longed for the time to arrive when she might hope that Eugenia would feel no hesitation in making her her confidant, and convincing her whether or not her surmises were correct.

These thoughts occupied the mind of Angela nearly the whole of the night, and she arose at an early hour in the morning, anxious to inquire after the object of her solicitude. She was gratified to find that Eugenia was much better, and that she had had some refreshing sleep; and the surgeon gave it as his opinion, that in a few days she would be restored to convalescence. Angela gave free expression to these feelings, and, as Eugenia listened to her artless observations, her eyes filled with tears of gratitude and esteem.

Eugenia had not failed to remark the impression she had made upon the heart of Angela, when she was known only as Rosario, and often did she regret that her lips were prohibited from revealing to her the whole truth; but, in order that she might endeavour to banish those sentiments from her bosom, and prove no obstacle to the gratification of the hopes of Sir Evelyn, she avoided Angela's presence as much as possible; and thus it was that she excused herself at every opportunity from visiting Branscombe House, in company with the young baronet.

And many a pang had these efforts cost Eugenia, for, from the very first moment that she had beheld Sir Evelyn, an affection sprung up for him in her bosom, which she felt convinced, hopeless though it was, nothing could ever banish.

But now that her real sex was known, Eugenia felt that it would no longer be prudent of her to remain with Sir Evelyn; and the most melancholy thoughts beset her mind as she contemplated a separation from one who was so dear to her.

The acknowledgment of Angela to her mother of the passion which the supposed Rosario had created in her breast, did not at all surprise her; but she was now in hopes that the remarkable discovery which had been made would prove favourable to Sir Evelyn's suit; for she could not but imagine that the attentions he would continue to pay to her would in time strengthen the sentiments of ardent friendship she now acknowledged for him into love, and that she should yet have the extreme happiness and satisfaction of seeing her united to a man who was every way so worthy of her, and an alliance with whom would confer an honour upon any family, however distinguished.

Mrs. Clearmount took an early opportunity to inform Sir Laurence what had taken place between her and Angela, and he communicated the same to Sir Evelyn, who

See p. 376.

was delighted to hear it; and, fresh hope springing up in his bosom, he abandoned his intention of leaving the country, for the present, at any rate, and determined, the first chance that presented itself, to renew the avowal of his passion, with a full hope that his wishes would ultimately be crowned with success.

In this manner more than a week passed away, and Eugenia progressed so rapidly towards convalescence, that she was enabled to leave her couch, and at length to fix upon a time when she would pay her respects to Sir Laurence Cleveland and Sir Evelyn Manners. But it was not without the most painful hesitation that Eugenia looked forward to this time, and knew not how she should again encounter the glances of her benefactors, without betraying the feelings that were passing with such tumult through her mind.

She attired herself in a dress belonging to Angela, and now the graces of her person were set off to the greatest advantage, Mrs. Clearmount and her daughter could not help gazing at her with the greatest astonishment and admiration, and could not help thinking that she was formed to captivate the most insensible individual. Her countenance was pale, but nothing could surpass the softness, regularity, and melancholy beauty of her features; and the longer Angela and her mother continued to gaze upon her, the deeper became the interest they felt in her fate.

But what were the emotions of Sir Laurence and Sir Evelyn when they beheld her; they could scarcely believe the evidence of their eyes, so great was the metamorphosis she had undergone, and such were the superlative charms presented to their admiration. But nothing could equal the emotion of Sir Laurence Cleveland; he trembled—his heart beat violently against his side, and for a moment he averted his looks, in order that he might conceal the agitation he was enduring. He could almost imagine that the same female, the very resemblance of the late misguided Lady Clara, which had so frequently crossed his path, again stood before him, only Eugenia was much younger, and far more lovely.

" Good God!" he reflected, " what could be the meaning of this? Was it some supernatural conjuration to torture him?" He knew not what to think, and remained motionless and silent.

Eugenia sunk at the feet of her benefactor and Sir Laurence, but was too much overcome with her emotions to utter a syllable. Sir Evelyn raised her tenderly, and begged her to be composed; but the tones of his voice, and the kindness with which he spoke, only increased her agitation, and it was several minutes before she could in any degree recover herself.

It is needless to attempt to describe the interview which followed. Sir Laurence and Sir Evelyn repeated the same questions which Mrs. Clearmount and her daughter had put to Eugenia, but without eliciting any further particulars, and they were still involved in as much mystery as ever as regarded the origin of Eugenia.

" And you were very young when you and your unfortunate mother were found by the gipsies?" said Sir Laurence.

"Oh, yes," replied Eugenia, with a sigh; " I was such a complete child, that I have only a slight recollection of it. I remember nestling on her bosom on that cold and cheerless night when my poor mother laid her down to die; the gipsies removed her insensible into their encampment, and I never again beheld her until I gazed upon her lifeless corpse."

" Unfortunate girl," said Sir Laurence, much moved by her words; " your sorrows indeed began at an early age. And is it indeed possible that the gipsies always refused to inform you of your mother's name?"

" They said it was Eugenia, but would not tell me her surname," answered Eugenia.

" And they told you you had a father living?" asked Sir Evelyn.

" Oh, yes; but they refused to tell me his name, though they asserted that he possessed rank and wealth; but they commanded me to learn to hate him, to curse him, for that he was the murderer of my mother."

" Impossible," ejaculated Sir Laurence ; " but surely you could never hate the author of your being, Eugenia ?"

" Ah, no," replied Eugenia ; " but surely the bitterest remorse must wring his heart, if he was the indirect cause of my poor mother's misery and untimely death. Would to Heaven that I knew him, surely he would not refuse to acknowledge his unfortunate daughter."

Sir Laurence felt still greater emotion than ever, and looked at Eugenia more earnestly than before.

" And it was Madela and Harold who compelled you to assume the character in which we have only hitherto known you ?" said Sir Laurence.

" It was," returned Eugenia ; " and vain were all my tears and supplications; they threatened that unless I obeyed, they would sacrifice my life, and I knew them too well to doubt that they would put their brutal menaces into effect. But, alas ! what will now become of me ; poor, wretched, unknown as I am. I can no longer think to obtrude upon the benevolence of strangers, and ——"

" Nay, talk not in this manner, Eugenia," said Sir Laurence, interrupting her ; " are we not your friends, and what have you done that we should now discard you ?"

" Never, never !" ejaculated Sir Evelyn, vehemently, and evidently much moved by the words and the manner of the poor girl.

Eugenia again sunk at their feet, and could only give expression to her feelings by tears and sobs. A silence of a few minutes ensued, which no one seemed inclined to interrupt.

" And this Azrah, whom you say was so kind to you," at length observed Sir Laurence ; " he is a man of mystery, is he not ?"

" He is," answered Eugenia ; " but of manners kind and gentle as a female. Would to Heaven I knew what has become of him."

" And did you never know him by any other name than that of Azrah ?" asked the baronet.

" Never," replied the damsel ; " and it was useless for me to question him upon the subject, for it only seemed to give him pain. Oh, I shall never forget the looks he always fixed upon me whenever he met me ; and the tone of compassion and deep feeling with which he ever addressed me."

" You say that you believe him to be acquainted with your whole history ?" remarked Sir Evelyn.

" I do," answered Eugenia.

" And do you not think that if we could find him, he would reveal everything, when he found that your sex was discovered ?" asked Sir Laurence.

" I think it is most likely that he would ; but, alas ! I fear that I shall never see him again, but that he has fallen a victim to the vengeance of the gipsies."

" At any rate, no means must be left untried to ascertain that important fact, and if Azrah is still in existence, which I am inclined to think he is, to release him from the power of these wretches."

The conversation lasted for some time longer, when Eugenia feeling fatigued, they left her to herself, and retired into the drawing-room.

Strange and perplexing thoughts arose to the mind of Sir Laurence after this interview, and the features of Eugenia were continually present to his imagination, and filled his bosom with the most remarkable and uncontrollable emotions. They were so like those of Clara, especially when she was about Eugenia's age, that it caused the most melancholy and unaccountable feelings in his breast.

Nor was Sir Evelyn Manners scarcely less interested in the singular circumstances connected with Eugenia than Sir Laurence. He could not but think her one of the most lovely beings he had ever beheld, while the sweetness of her manners excited his warmest admiration. But he was yet to remain in ignorance of the sentiments which that poor girl had imbibed for him, and which she had kept so long confined to her own breast.

Several days elapsed, and Eugenia was so far recovered as to be able to leave her chamber, and to join the company in the drawing-room. It had been arranged at the request of Eugenia herself, and in compliance with the wishes of Mrs. Clearmount, Angela, and Emeline, that she should remain at Branscombe House, and Angela, in particular, anticipated much pleasure from this addition to the family circle, for the amiable manners of Eugenia were sufficient to endear her to every one.

The bloom had now returned to the damsel's cheek, and added to the beauty of her countenance, and there was an expression in her eyes at times, particularly when Sir Evelyn Manners was present and addressed himself to her, which almost amounted to pleasure. Angela well understood the feelings that were passing in her mind, but could not hope that they would make any impression upon Sir Evelyn's mind; who, she was annoyed and grieved to find, still persisted in paying his attentions to her.

The utmost exertions had been made to discover the retreat of the gipsies, but without success, and Eugenia was kept closely confined to the house, lest another attempt should be made upon her life by the villain Harold, or some of his associates. Some weeks passed away without anything more taking place worthy of notice, and Eugenia was now completely restored to health; but she was seldom free from melancholy when she thought of the mystery of her destiny, and the utter hopelessness of her ever engaging the affections of Sir Evelyn. She would fain have conquered her unfortunate passion, and banished the image of the young baronet from her mind; but, alas, this was no easy task, and the more she endeavoured to accomplish it, the more entangled did her heart become.

In the society of the gentle Angelina she experienced the greatest pleasure and consolation; nor did she at last hesitate to unburthen her thoughts to her, and to seek her advice; and in Angela she found the sympathy of a sister.

Angela tried to inspire her with hope, but Eugenia dared not to encourage it, for she considered that in a poor unknown girl like her, and whose early life had been passed in the woods and the wilds, and amongst the most abandoned of mankind, though she was herself perfectly innocent, it would be presumption to do so.

Sir Evelyn Manners visited Branscombe House almost every day, and exerted himself to the utmost to soften the heart of Angela in his favour; but he saw, to his poignant regret and anguish, that it was all to no purpose, and at last he determined once more to urge his suit, and then, if she again rejected him, he would abandon his suit for ever, and endeavour to resign himself to his fate. He felt assured that he must sacrifice his happiness by giving up his suit; but if he still found that Angela could only regard him as a friend, deference to her feelings would compel him to submit.

Having thus decided in his own mind, Sir Evelyn sought the earliest opportunity of putting his resolution into effect. The result was exactly what he had anticipated; Angela again fervently assured him of her esteem, and of the proper sense she entertained of his great merits, but that she never could feel for him that ardent sentiment which would urge her to become his wife; and she implored him, if he valued his happiness and her own, to endeavour to forget her, and to seek some other damsel who was worthy of the distinguished honour he had offered to her.

"Enough, fair Angela," exclaimed Sir Evelyn; "it is a painful trial, but as I would sooner perish than cause you one moment's unhappiness, I submit, and from this hour I promise you that I will never more urge that love which I find, beyond all doubt, that you cannot return. May you meet with one more deserving of you than the humble individual who now addresses you; and may Heaven ever shower its choicest blessings on your head."

Having thus spoken, she suffered him to raise her hand respectfully to his lips; and he then, with much emotion, retired from her presence.

Angela sincerely regretted that she was thus compelled to annihilate the hopes of one whom, for his numerous virtues, she so greatly esteemed; but she felt the greatest relief after this latter interview, and the assurance of Sir Evelyn that he would never again urge his suit; and sincerely she wished that he might be able to fix his affections upon some damsel who was worthy of him, and would render him happy.

That Eugenia loved him she was convinced, and she felt a hope that, in time, she would be able to win his affections in return, especially when the mystery which enveloped her should be removed. Ardently she hoped that that circumstance would shortly take place, and that the enemies of Eugenia would be brought to justice. She felt for her the same affection as if she had been her own sister, and she was satisfied that she possessed those innate qualities which entitled her to the esteem of all who knew her."

Angela and Eugenia were constantly together, and the amiable qualities of the latter daily became more apparent. To Angela she was most devotedly attached, and being now on the same terms as if they were actually sisters, Eugenia no longer hesitated to confide to her her every thought. It was a sweet solace, a great relief to that poor girl; and to Angela she, therefore, confessed that from the first moment she had beheld Sir Evelyn she had felt the greatest affection towards him. Knowing that his heart was devoted to Angela, and that from the mystery of her origin, and the difference of their stations, she could never hope to win his love, she had endeavoured to stifle the passion in her own bosom; but, alas, she found that that task was in vain; and even now she felt that without the possession of Evelyn's heart, she could never know anything but the most absolute misery.

Angela tried to console her, and to inspire her with hope; but so difficult was the task where all appeared so utterly dismal and unpropitious, that all her arguments failed; and nothing could dissipate the gloomy forebodings which constantly haunted the imagination of Eugenia.

Sir Evelyn was, as may be expected, deeply afflicted at the final destruction of his hopes, and for several days he kept himself confined to the Grange, and gave himself up entirely to the dismal thoughts which distracted his mind. But still he could not help admiring the candour and sincerity of Angela, and ardently he hoped that her numerous virtues would meet with their due reward.

At first he thought of leaving the country, and seeking in foreign climes to banish the image of Angela from his memory; but he knew that would be impossible; and at length he so far triumphed over his feelings as to become calm and resigned; and resolving to adhere to the promise he had made to Angela, he again visited the mansion of Sir Laurence, and met Angela with more composure than might have been expected.

But with what emotion did Eugenia behold him! she would gladly have avoided his presence, for she was fearful that her looks and actions would betray the sentiments which occupied her mind; but, of course, she could not do so without creating surprise in the minds of Sir Laurence Cleveland and her other friends. Sir Evelyn could not but gaze at the glowing charms, and mark the numerous virtues of Eugenia with the most enthusiastic admiration, and deep was the interest which he felt in her fate, and most anxious was he to unravel the mystery connected with her. He listened to her conversation with pleasure, and could not help thinking that she was formed to make any man happy. Gradually these feelings expanded into a warmer sentiment; and he began to love her before he could acknowledge to himself the power which she had gained over him. He took the greatest delight in her company, and his visits to Branscombe became more frequent; nor did he behold Angela with the same emotion he had formerly done. The glowing passion he had previously felt for her, and which made him think that he could never be happy unless he won her heart, calmed down into a sentiment of friendship, of brotherly attachment, and as that feeling gained strength, so did his admiration and appreciation of the amiable qualities of Eugenia increase.

Angela marked this change in the behaviour of Sir Evelyn with much satisfaction; and she had not the least doubt but that in time Eugenia would entirely win his heart. Nor had Eugenia been blind to the marked attentions which Sir Evelyn had paid her lately; but it was with melancholy feelings of satisfaction that she beheld it, as she could not hope, at any rate, while her birth was enshrouded in so much mystery, to become his wife. She would fain have avoided his society, as she feared that it might be injurious to the peace of them both, but what excuse could she form for doing so; and, at the same time, what poignant anguish would it inflict upon herself?

To feel convinced that she had created a tender sensation in his breast, was indeed a source of secret delight to her; and, when alone with Angela, she gave free indulgence to her feelings, knowing how well she might confide in that amiable friend. And when Eugenia would have given way entirely to despair, Angela, by her gentle arguments, inspired her with hope, and persuaded her to believe that the time would yet come when all her wishes would be gratified; when the mystery which enveloped her would be removed, and Sir Evelyn would no longer hesitate to acknowledge his love, and to make her an offer of his hand.

These thoughts were almost too delightful for Eugenia to encourage; but still, in spite of all her efforts, she could not reject them.

Sir Evelyn felt surprised that Eugenia should so suddenly have gained such an influence over him; but it was in vain that he attempted to banish it; and the more he did so, the more it increased in strength. Had he been acquainted with the origin of Eugenia, and been convinced that no disgrace attached to it, even though poor and friendless as she was, he would not have hesitated to make her his wife, if she indeed responded to his passion, which, from her behaviour, he had no doubt which she did. Her manners were so refined and amiable, that she was fit to adorn any station in society; and when it was remembered the wild and wandering life she had from childhood led, and the rude and savage beings with whom she had been associated, it was the more surprising and incredible,

Sir Laurence and his sister also observed the sentiments which had engendered themselves in the bosoms of Sir Evelyn and Eugenia, and they were well satisfied to see it, both for the sake of the young baronet and Angela. They considered that Eugenia was every way worthy of him. They were deeply interested in Eugenia's mysterious fate, and were anxious that the secret of her birth should be discovered, and every day Sir Laurence became more struck with her beauty and the extraordinary resemblance which she bore to Clara. This caused him much uneasiness, and oftentimes when he looked at her, he could almost imagine that that unfortunate and misguided woman stood before him.

Notwithstanding the strictest search had been made in the neighbourhood, nothing could be seen or heard of the gipsies, and Sir Laurence could not help thinking that they had departed from that part of the country. He often reflected upon the account which Eugenia had given of Azrah, and most anxious was he to discover that mysterious being, who, it appeared, was acquainted with all her history, and, no doubt, would not hesitate to reveal it, when he knew that her sex was discovered, and that he himself was in safety. But it seemed too probable that the fears of Eugenia were realized, and that the gipsies had sacrificed Azrah to their vengeance, or their apprehensions of discovery.

Weeks rolled on, without anything worthy of recording occurring, and Sir Evelyn was a daily visitor at Branscombe House. He had at last entirely succeeded in conquering the passion he had previously entertained for Angela; and the more he saw of Eugenia, the more powerfully enamoured he became of her, nor did he take any pains to conceal the sentiments with which that lovely and amiable girl had inspired him.

Eugenia marked his attentions with delight; yet, when she reflected upon the mystery of her fate, and the obstacle that it presented to her happiness, she could not help feeling the most unconquerable melancholy.

To Angela she freely communicated her thoughts, and received from that sincere friend every consolation and advice. She led her to hope that Providence would ere long reveal the secret of her birth, and place her in a position to receive the addresses of Sir Evelyn without hesitation; and the mind of the poor girl at length became more tranquil, and she did indeed look forward to the future with some degree of hope and expectation.

Sir Evelyn's passion at length gained such strength that he could no longer keep it confined to his own breast, and at last resolved to disclose it to Eugenia, and at once to ascertain from her own lips whether he indeed held a favourable place in her affections; which he had long, from her looks and manners, imagined that she had done.

He, therefore, seized the opportunity when they were alone together, and in the most ardent and eloquent terms disclosed the passion with which she had inspired him, and implored her to tell him whether he had any reason to hope that his love would meet with a return from her.

No language can do justice to the feelings of Eugenia as she listened to him. Crimson blushes suffused her cheeks, and her heart palpitated so violently, that she was unable for some time to give utterance to a syllable. But again Sir Evelyn pressed his suit, and at length, in a tremulous voice, she replied,—

"Sir Evelyn Manners, I will not attempt to deny the high opinion and admiration I have entertained of your merits from the first hour I beheld you, and that you must ever hold the warmest place in my esteem, and ——"

"And love, say beauteous Eugenia," added Sir Evelyn, eagerly; "and make me one of the happiest of human beings. I once imagined that no woman could ever possess my heart but Angela; but it was reserved for Eugenia to convince me to the contrary. Do not, then, again disappoint my hopes, which now are fixed on you; but say that you return my passion with equal ardour, and behold me ready and willing to become your slave for ever."

"Alas!" sighed Eugenia, "of what avail would it be to me to confess a love which, although it meet with a return, can never be gratified?"

"And why not, charming Eugenia?"

"Oh, Sir Evelyn, think of the difference of our stations, the mystery with which my fate is enshrouded. I am a poor, friendless girl, a dependant on strangers, and it would be presumption in me to aspire to your heart and hand."

"Perish such a thought," exclaimed Sir Evelyn, "and think not so meanly of me as to imagine that wealth and station can influence my passion. I love you for your virtues alone, and should feel but too happy were I convinced that you did not look upon me with indifference, and that at some future period I might hope to make you my wife. The word, Eugenia—do you love me? Let me know, I entreat, and I will then no further urge you at present, but exert myself to the utmost to unravel the mystery by which you are surrounded, so that there may be no further obstacles to our union."

Eugenia was overpowered; she could not speak; but she suffered the enraptured Sir Evelyn to press her hand to his lips, and her looks expressed much more than language could have done, and all that his most ardent wishes could aspire to.

"Dearest, most amiable of girls," he exclaimed; "your looks are enough, and have made me the most happy of mortals. Fate may at present appear to frown upon our union, but the time will come when all those difficulties will be removed, and I may proudly lead to the altar a bride which even a monarch might envy."

What passed at the remainder of the meeting, we need not attempt to describe; it is sufficient to say, that before they separated, Sir Evelyn had elicited from Eugenia a full acknowledgement of her love, and a promise to become his bride whenever the secret of her birth should be revealed, and if, when it was, Sir Evelyn should find nothing to cause him to repent of his words.

After Sir Evelyn left her, Eugenia immediately sought the presence of Angela, and repeated to her all that had taken place, as well as her emotion would permit her to do. Angela listened to her with no feeling of astonishment, and when she had done, she warmly expressed her pleasure and gratification, and congratulated Eugenia on the conquest she had made, and of which she considered her every way so worthy. She was also well pleased to find that Sir Evelyn had conquered the passion he had formerly entertained for her, and had fixed it on one who could return it, and that with a warmth of feeling equal to her own.

"You will be happy, Eugenia," she said; "as the bride of an amiable man, you must be indeed supremely happy."

"Alas! Angela," said Eugenia, "I cannot be too sanguine on that subject. To know that I possess the love of Sir Evelyn Manners, is, indeed, a source of the most infinite gratification to me; but the secret of my birth may never be revealed, and

See p. 386.

then all my hopes will be annihilated; for, of course, I cannot become the wife of Sir Evelyn."

"But the mystery will be unravelled, I feel convinced," said Angela, "and that before long."

"Ah, Angela," ejaculated Eugenia; "what chance is there of it? Would that I could think that there was, then might I hope to be happy. But my enemies will continue to avoid detection, and poor Azrah, who I am certain knows my whole history, I am fearful I shall never behold again."

"Accident may throw him in your way when you least expect it," said Angela.

"Ah, no," replied Eugenia, "I have too much reason to apprehend that he has fallen beneath the vengeance of the jealous fears of the gipsies. Would that I had been able to see him before I made my escape; he might then have been prevailed upon to reveal to me all that he knew."

"I wonder, as he professed so much friendship for you, that he did not do so before," said Angela.

"He must have had some powerful reasons for not doing so," returned Eugenia. "And he frequently told me that his own life and mine depended on his secrecy for the present; but he led me to hope that the time might come when he need no longer hesitate."

"And you say that this Azrah was of the most gentle manners and handsome features?" said Angela.

"Oh, yes," answered Eugenia; "and his countenance bore the most remarkable resemblance to the miniature of my mother, which he gave to me."

"It is strange; might he not have been related to her, which caused him to take so great an interest in your fate?"

"I have often thought so, and it is not at all improbable."

After some further observations, the conversation terminated, and the friends separated.

From that day Sir Evelyn Manners and Eugenia were seldom apart, and their love increased; while their whole happiness centered in the hope of their being united, which depended entirely upon the mystery connected with the origin of Eugenia being unravelled.

They frequently walked from the house together, and on one of those occasions being suddenly overtaken by a storm, they were forced to seek a shelter in the ruins of an old castle which stood at some little distance from the grounds of Branscombe House.

They had scarcely entered, when they were startled by a low moaning sound, which seemed to proceed from some person in a state of the greatest bodily suffering; and turning their eyes in the direction whence the sounds issued, they beheld, crouched in one corner of the ruins, a human figure, but of what sex, by the dim light which was admitted into the ruins—for the storm had overspread everything with a solemn gloom—they were at first unable to distinguish.

"Unfortunate being," exclaimed Sir Evelyn Manners, advancing towards the distressed object, and Eugenia following close at his side; "who and what are you, and what has brought you to your present miserable condition? Speak, and fear not, for you are with those who can compassionate your sufferings, and who are ready to do all in their power to relieve them."

The wretched being, whom they now discovered to be a man, could return no other answer to this than a groan.

"Miserable stranger," said Eugenia, in her most compassionate accents; "you are ill, very ill; and ——"

The stranger interrupted her with a faint shriek of astonishment, and by an extraordinary exertion raised himself on his hands and knees, and, in a voice of extreme emotion, ejaculated,—

"Ah! that voice, that well-known voice, how it vibrates in mine ears! Come nearer, for the love of Heaven, and let me gaze upon you."

The voice of the stranger struck Eugenia most forcibly; a strange feeling of emotion shot through her bosom, and she walked closer to the sufferer, and stooped over him with the utmost anxiety. At that instant a vivid flash of lightning darted in at the ruins, and revealed at once the haggard features of the sufferer to the gaze of Sir Evelyn and Eugenia. Gracious Heaven! how the latter started.

"Almighty Father!" she cried, "thou hast at last heard my prayers, and Azrah, unfortunate Azrah, do I indeed again behold you? Oh! look up, revive, and speak to Eugenia, who ——"

"Eugenia!" repeated Azrah, with a wild and vacant stare; "child of misfortune—victim of untoward fate—injured innocence, whose early days were—but, but—no, it is impossible—it is only some strange delusion of my fevered brain; and yet—Come nearer, injured girl, and—oh, God!"

Unable to articulate another word, the wretched Azrah, with a groan, sunk into a state of insensibility in the arms which were so willingly extended to receive him; and whilst Sir Evelyn gazed in mute astonishment, his fair companion hung over the emaciated form of the mysterious and unfortunate Azrah, in a state of agony which no language could possibly do adequate justice to.

"Oh! God," she cried, "little did I expect such a meeting as this. It is Azrah, Evelyn—he who holds my fate in his hands, and upon whose words depend my future happiness or everlasting misery. Azrah, Azrah, for the love of Heaven, revive, look up, and speak to me! Alas! alas! he is dying—he will never speak again!"

"Be calm, dear Eugenia," said Sir Evelyn; "he has only fainted with exhaustion, and the overwhelming power of his feelings on again beholding you. Would that we could remove him from these ruins to some place of security; or that we had but some means to revive him!"

Eugenia still gazed with the most intense anguish on the pale countenance of Azrah, and her brain was completely bewildered and distracted, not knowing how to act.

Sir Evelyn walked to the entrance of the castle ruins, almost in the same state of anguish and perplexity as his companion; for on the preservation of the mysterious Azrah their fate seemed to depend. He, it appeared, knew the secret of Eugenia's origin; and, if he died, that must, doubtless, ever remain involved in mystery, and Eugenia could never become his wife. That thought was enough in itself to create the greatest fear and agony in the young baronet's breast.

The storm now raged with the greatest violence; the rain came down in torrents, and Sir Evelyn saw not the least chance of their being able to leave the ruins; and he trembled at the thought of what the consequences were likely to be to the unfortunate Azrah.

Eugenia still hung over the inanimate form of the unfortunate man, and her tears fell fast upon his pale but careworn countenance; but still he only breathed slightly, and evinced no signs of returning sensibility.

Sir Evelyn could not but view the pale features of Azrah with the deepest interest and amazement. There was something so peculiarly delicate about them, and the construction of his form was so light and graceful, that it seemed completely out of character with his sex.

But one circumstance more than all astonished Sir Evelyn, and bewildered his mind, and that was, the extraordinary likeness that existed between him and Eugenia. The expression of the features, although worn with care, were the same; and it was only the difference of their ages, or they might have passed very well for brother and sister.

Sir Evelyn was so forcibly struck by this circumstance, that he could scarcely re-move his eyes from them; but, finding that Azrah still remained in a state of un-consciousness, and apprehensive of the consequences, he once more walked to the entrance of the ruins, and looked out, with the hope of beholding some individual who might render them assistance, or procure the attendance of a medical man.

It was not long before he beheld a labouring man approaching, and he imme-diately hailed him.

The man knew the young baronet, for he dwelt on his estate, and, bowing respect-fully to him, he awaited his commands. Sir Evelyn desired him to hasten with all possible dispatch to the town, and request Doctor Edmonds to attend him as quickly as he could, for that on his promptitude, probably, depended the life of a fellow-creature.

The man obeyed, and, heedless of the storm, he precipitately made his way to the town, to deliver the message of Sir Evelyn Manners to Doctor Edmonds.

During the interval that elapsed prior to the good doctor's arrival, the anxiety and emotion of Sir Evelyn and Eugenia, particularly the latter, were most intense. But, at length, to their unspeakable satisfaction, Azrah evinced some signs of returning life, and, in a few moments, he heaved a deep sigh, and, once more opening his eyes, he fixed them with an indescribable expression upon the countenance of Eugenia, who was still hanging over him in the greatest state of agitation.

"Ah!" he exclaimed, in a voice which made Sir Evelyn start with astonishment, "it was not then a delusion? I do, indeed, once more gaze upon thee, unfortunate girl, child of sorrow and mystery. But who is this that accompanies you? Ah! your sex is discovered, and I ——"

Before he could finish the sentence, his extraordinary agitation overpowered him; his eyes again closed, and he once more became insensible.

"Unfortunate man!" said Eugenia. "I fear that he will never revive suffi-ciently to reveal the extraordinary mystery of my fate. Oh, would that the worthy doctor would arrive, and that we had some means to convey him to Branscombe House."

Eugenia had scarcely given utterance to these words, when the sound of carriage wheels smote their ears, and the next moment the vehicle containing Doctor Edmonds stopped at the ruins.

"Poor fellow," said the good doctor, when he beheld Azrah; "he is, indeed, very ill, probably from long fasting, and anxiety of mind. He had better be removed as speedily as possible. Have you any knowledge of him, Sir Evelyn?"

"Oh, yes—yes," eagerly answered Eugenia; "I knew him well; and probably on his recovery depend my future happiness or misery. For mercy's sake, sir, do what you can to restore him."

"Compose yourself, my dear young lady," said Doctor Edmonds; "you may de-pend upon it that nothing which skill and exertion can effect, shall be wanting to save him. But there is no time to be lost; here, George, assist me to remove the unfor-tunate man to my carriage. Shall he be conveyed to the Grange, or Branscombe House, Sir Evelyn?"

"To the latter, my dear sir," replied the baronet.

Mr. Edmonds bowed, and then, with the assistance of his coachman, Azrah was lifted into the vehicle. The doctor, Sir Evelyn, and Eugenia followed, and they were driven off with the greatest rapidity to Branscombe House; Azrah still exhibiting no signs of returning sensibility, and Eugenia being in a state of the most insupportable anxiety and apprehension, while Sir Evelyn in vain endeavoured to tranquillize her feelings.

CHAPTER XXXIII.

MORE ASTONISHMENT IN STORE FOR EUGENIA AND HER FRIENDS.—THE LONG HIDDEN SECRET DISCLOSED.—THE ANGUISH OF SIR LAURENCE.

SIR LAURENCE CLEVELAND, and his sister, together with Angela, had been most anxiously awaiting the return of Sir Evelyn and Eugenia, and they were not a little astonished and alarmed when they saw the carriage of Doctor Edmonds draw up to the door; for they were afraid that some accident had happened, and they immediately went down to the hall to ascertain at once the whole particulars.

Sir Evelyn Manners was the first who alighted from the vehicle, and was quickly followed by Eugenia, who rushing up to Sir Laurence, in a voice of extreme agitation, exclaimed,—

"Oh, my dear Sir Laurence, we have found him at last. He is here; he is with us; but alas, alas, I fear that he is dying."

"Whom, child?" eagerly inquired Sir Laurence; "of whom do you speak? And why do you evince this terrible emotion?"

"Azrah," returned Eugenia; "we found him in the old castle ruins. But see, he is here. Oh, he will die—he will die; and the mystery with which my origin is enshrouded, will never be unravelled."

The insensible form of Azrah was now lifted out of the vehicle, and Sir Laurence, as soon as he gazed on his pallid and careworn features, felt a pang shoot through his heart such as he had seldom before experienced. Mrs. Clearmount and her daughter were equally interested, but they endeavoured to console Eugenia, who was almost sinking with the excess of her feelings.

"Gracious Heaven!" muttered Sir Laurence, to himself, "that remarkable likeness—what can it mean?—Unfortunate, mysterious man! Let him be immediately conveyed to a chamber, and pray, my dear sir," he added, addressing himself to Doctor Edmonds, "do your best to restore him."

"You may depend on me, Sir Laurence," replied Mr. Edmonds. "I am in hopes that a warm bed, and such remedies as I shall apply, will revive him, although he is certainly very much reduced."

Azrah was then borne to a chamber; and Sir Laurence led Eugenia, followed by Sir Evelyn and the others, into another apartment, where Evelyn related all that had taken place, and their unexpected meeting with the unfortunate object of their solicitude.

"Poor fellow," ejaculated Sir Laurence, "he must have suffered a great deal; but, thank Heaven, he has escaped from his enemies, the gipsies, and should he recover, which I trust to Providence he will, the painful mystery which has so long enshrouded the fate of Eugenia will be unfolded."

"Oh, God, preserve him!" cried Eugenia, energetically.

"The likeness which he bears to Eugenia, is most extraordinary," said Sir Laurence; "and the longer I reflect on it, the more am I lost in amazement and bewilderment."

With the greatest anxiety did they all await to hear whether any favourable change had taken place in Azrah; and Sir Laurence and Sir Evelyn were about to go to the chamber to which he had been conveyed, when the doctor entered the room in a great hurry, and, with an expression of countenance which showed he had something particular to communicate, he requested that Sir Laurence and Sir Evelyn would allow him to speak to them in another room.

Eugenia became alarmed at this, and, in an eager voice, she ejaculated,—

"Ah! what is the meaning of this?—Your looks express emotion, Mr. Edmonds. Oh, tell me, I beseech you, is the unfortunate Azrah worse?—Or are my worst fears realized, and is he no more?"

"Do not alarm yourself, miss," replied the doctor, "for I assure you that your present apprehensions are unfounded; but I would rather break the intelligence I have to communicate, which is of a most extraordinary nature, to your friends."

"For Heaven's sake, sir," cried Eugenia, "do not keep me in suspense; I am prepared for everything. Oh, tell me, then, what it is you have to reveal?"

"Indeed, miss," said Doctor Edmonds, "you cannot be prepared for the extraordinary information I have to impart. Had you not better suffer me to speak with your friends first?"

"Oh, no—no," exclaimed Eugenia, impatiently; "do not, oh, do not refuse me; this anxiety is worse than the most terrible certainty. Tell me, is Azrah restored to his senses?"

"Yes. But have I your permission, Sir Laurence and Sir Evelyn?" demanded the doctor.

"Yes," replied the two gentlemen in a breath; "the communication is doubtless of that nature which cannot long be withheld from Eugenia, and perhaps the sooner she is made acquainted with it the better."

"Well," said Mr. Edmonds, "since it is your wish, I will comply. This Azrah, then, whom you have hitherto known as the gipsy, is ——"

The doctor hesitated.

"What?" demanded Eugenia, Sir Laurence, and all the others, impatiently.

"A woman!" answered the doctor.

Eugenia gave utterance to a scream, and immediately fainted in the arms of her lover.

"A woman!" gasped forth Sir Laurence; and a mysterious and dreadful feeling came over him.

"Yes," returned the doctor; "and has once been beautiful; though she is now worn with long suffering, both in body and mind."

"Good God!" exclaimed Sir Laurence, clasping his hands, and staggering to a chair. "What fresh wonders are in store for us? A woman, and those features so like —— Ah! I dare not trust myself to repeat the name. This, then, is she who has so frequently crossed my path. Gracious heaven! what strange thoughts are these which rush upon my brain? Who is she? Tell me, and do not keep me in this state of lingering suspense, or I shall go mad with the tumultuous feelings that oppress my bosom."

"I know not, Sir Laurence," answered the doctor; "for she refused to tell me, or to impart anything until she has seen Eugenia."

"Unexpected discovery!" ejaculated Sir Laurence; "what dreadful apprehensions are these that torture my bosom? Amanda, Angela; for heaven's sake hasten to the chamber of this mysterious individual, and try to elicit from her the important truth."

"We will do so, my brother," said Mrs. Clearmount; "and in the meantime, pray endeavour to compose yourself; for that which this woman may have to reveal may contribute to the happiness of yourself and Eugenia, instead of misery."

"Oh, no! oh, no!" sighed Sir Laurence; "I cannot entertain such a thought. But I beseech you to do as I desire, Amanda; and I will endeavour to await here with patience your return."

Mrs. Clearmount and her daughter, filled with the most unmistakeable astonishment, and their curiosity excited to an extraordinary degree, quitted the apartment, and left Eugenia to the care of the doctor, Sir Laurence, and Sir Evelyn.

On entering the chamber of the invalid, they found her perfectly sensible, and sitting up in the bed, propped up by pillows. But her face was ghastly pale; there was a strange unnatural brightness in her eyes; and it was no difficult matter to perceive that she was enduring the greatest mental and bodily suffering. She had the appearance of a woman about fifty years of age, though probably she was many years younger; for grief had indeed made sad ravages in her form and features, and had left but the wreck of what she had been.

When she beheld Mrs. Clearmount and her daughter enter the apartment, she cast her eyes towards the door, as though she expected some one else to follow, and when she perceived that they were unattended, an expression of disappointment passed over her countenance.

Mrs. Clearmount and Angela kindly approached her, and, as they did so, she shuddered, and averted her face, as if with a sense of agony and shame.

"My good woman," said Mrs. Clearmount, "we come to you with the best intentions, and the deepest sympathy for those misfortunes which you have doubtless encountered. Hesitate not then, I beg, to inform us who you really are, and the motives which could induce you to assume this extraordinary disguise; and if it is in the power of us to ameliorate your sufferings, and to serve you in any other respect, rest assured that we shall feel no greater pleasure than in doing so."

The woman fixed upon Mrs. Clearmount and her daughter an earnest look of emotion, as she replied,—

"You are the sister of Sir Laurence Cleveland, lady; I know you well, and esteem you and your lovely daughter for your virtues. You ask me who I am. I am a poor, wretched, heartbroken outcast; a mother, like yourself, and equally widowed by fate, though not in reality. You ask me who I am; but oh, lady, were you to hear my name, even you, gentle as I know you to be, would turn from me with disgust and prejudice."

"Oh, no," returned Mrs. Clearmount, much moved; "think not so unjustly of me. Whatever your faults may have been, I am prepared to regard you with mercy and compassion."

"But that poor girl—the victim of a cruel destiny; her whom you know only as Eugenia—oh, where is she? Not a word in explanation shall pass my lips, until I behold her."

At that moment the chamber door was thrown suddenly open, and Eugenia, pale and violently agitated, entered, and rushed towards the couch of the sufferer, who no sooner beheld her face than her lips quivered, and had it not been for the support of Mrs. Clearmount and her daughter, she must have sunk back on the pillow.

Eugenia threw herself on her knees by the side of the couch, and seizing the suffering woman's emaciated hand, she bathed it with her tears, as she ejaculated,—

"Mysterious being—arbitress of my fate, to whom my warmest regard has ever been devoted, do I at last behold you in your real character? Oh, tell me who and what you are; reveal to me all that you know of me; for the time has now arrived when secrecy surely is no longer necessary; and on your word depends my future happiness or misery."

"Oh, God!" cried the agonised woman, clasping her hands vehemently together, and her whole frame trembling, "what a moment of trial is this! How can my lips ever reveal the painful truth? But it must be. Justice demands it, and my bursting heart can no longer resist the temptation. You have asked me who you are; prepare, then, to hear that which should strike you dumb with astonishment. Child of sorrow, hear at once the secret which has so long been hidden from you. The wretched being who gave you birth still lives; it is she who for years has been almost constantly by your side, but unknown to you; it is she who now addresses you. Know, Eugenia, that you are my child, and the legitimate daughter of Sir Laurence Cleveland!"

Eugenia stood for a few moments, and gazed with stupified amazement and incredulity upon her who had called her her daughter; then uttering a piercing shriek, she sunk insensible on the bed, and was clasped by the distracted Clara (for she indeed the so long supposed Azrah was) to her bosom.

What words could pourtray the emotion of Angela and her mother at this unexpected declaration? It would be a fruitless task to attempt to do so. They looked towards Clara, and then removed their glances towards Eugenia; and the striking likeness that existed between them fully corroborated the assertion. But what would be the anguish and astonishment of Sir Laurence Cleveland, when he heard of the discovery, and found, alas, that his union with the late amiable Blanche had never been a legal one? They shuddered at the thought, and looked with mingled feelings of pity, reproach, and doubt, at Clara, who was sobbing hysterically as she still clasped Eugenia in her arms, until, worn out with the excitement she had experienced, she gradually relaxed her hold, and once more became unconscious of all around her.

The doctor at that moment entered the chamber, and Mrs. Clearmount and Angela, leaving Clara to his care, without saying a word to him in explanation, they with difficulty removed Eugenia to another apartment, where Mrs. Clearmount left her daughter to watch the poor girl, while she herself, with a faltering heart, sought the presence of Sir Laurence Cleveland, to impart to him, as well as she could, the astounding news.

She found him and Sir Evelyn together, impatiently waiting her return, and on her entrance they both hastily arose to meet her; and it was quite evident to them, from the emotion she betrayed, that she had something of a most extraordinary and exciting character to communicate.

"Now, my dear sister," said Sir Laurence, hurriedly, "what have you to reveal? How is the unfortunate woman, and where is Eugenia?"

"Be calm, brother," replied Mrs. Clearmount, "for you will stand in need of all the fortitude and self-possession that belongs to your character, to hear that which I am about to disclose to you. Eugenia has been removed to her own chamber, for she is overcome by that which she has heard."

"My God!" exclaimed Sir Laurence, "how my heart trembles. Quick, Amanda; if you love me, and regard my happiness, you will not keep me in suspense."

Mrs. Clearmount then related all that had passed between them and the unfortunate woman, and to which both Sir Laurence and Sir Evelyn, particularly the
former, listened with the most unbounded emotion; but before they could give full
expression to their feelings, a servant entered the apartment, and said that the patient
most earnestly requested to behold Sir Laurence Cleveland, his sister, and Eugenia,
as she had something to communicate of the most vital importance; and if the least

delay was made, it might be too late.   Doctor Edmonds had also intimated, through
the servant, that the interview he believed might take place without any immediate
danger to the patient, and might, in fact, be productive of the most beneficial results,
as she seemed most anxious to reveal something which appeared to press heavily on
her mind.

Sir Laurence Cleveland arose from his seat; but his heart trembled; and anxious as he was to hear what the unfortunate woman had to communicate, he almost feared to comply; lest the subject should be of a nature which he was not prepared to listen to.

Mrs. Clearmount saw his hesitation, and attempted to rouse him into firmness, as she felt well convinced that what the long supposed Azrah had to relate, would be of the utmost importance to her brother's and Eugenia's future happiness.

"I am ready," said the baronet, mustering up all his fortitude; "but what can be the meaning of the fearful forebodings that cross my mind? I feel that some revelation is about to be made of the most painful nature, and one that my imagination scarcely dares to entertain. Come, Amanda, we will go immediately to the chamber of the invalid, and let Eugenia be summoned to attend there also."

The servant was despatched to Eugenia with this message accordingly, and then Sir Laurence and Mrs. Clearmount, with throbbing and anxious hearts, left the room, and repaired to the chamber of the unfortunate woman. Sir Evelyn Manners was left in the utmost state of suspense, and would fain have accompanied them to the chamber of the sufferer; for he felt certain that the nature of the information she had to communicate, involved the future happiness of his beloved Eugenia, and that the mystery which had so long enveloped her fate, was about to be, after so long a time, unravelled.

With agitated steps he traversed the room, and awaited their return, and never before had the time to him seemed so long and so tedious.

"Dear Eugenia," he ejaculated, "and shall I at last discover who you really are, and the only obstacle to our union be removed? Oh, that thought imparts to me a feeling of bliss almost insupportable. Whatever may be the nature of the discovery, even if you should be found to be the offspring of the lowest and most depraved (which my heart assures me that you are not); nothing whatever can alter my sentiments towards you. No, dearest girl, I love you for your own transcendent virtues alone; and under any circumstances whatever, nothing shall induce me to forfeit my claim upon your hand and heart. No other maiden can ever supplant you in my bosom. Oh, what transport will it be for me to clasp you to my bosom, and to know that there are no longer any impediments to the consummation of our happiness. And Eugenia will no longer hesitate; oh, no, she will not surely suffer any discovery she may make to alter her sentiments, or to induce her to abandon the solemn promise she has made to me to become my bride, if my affections remained the same, when the mystery which enshrouds her fate should be removed. And can my sentiments ever be changed by time or circumstance? I should feel myself unworthy of the love of that amiable girl; and of the name of man, if I thought they could. But no, away with such ideas; they cannot be. Dear Eugenia, my heart is firmly, immoveably devoted to you, let whatever may occur."

He walked to the door as he spoke, and was half determined to venture to the chamber of the invalid, and to have at once his suspense removed. His impatience exceeded all bounds; and that of Angela almost equalled his own.

On that day—on that very hour—the future destiny of Eugenia seemed to hang; and no wonder, therefore, that Sir Evelyn, in particular, should feel such uncontrollable suspense.

But while Sir Evelyn and Angela were thus agitated by anxiety and impatience, and forming all sorts of conjectures without being able to come to any satisfactory conclusion, what a remarkable and exciting scene was taking place in the chamber of the suffering woman.

On their way to the apartment of the invalid, Sir Laurence and his sister encountered Eugenia, who had just emerged from her room. Her agitation was extreme, and she trembled violently when she beheld Sir Laurence, and could scarcely support herself. He kindly took her hand, and encouraged her by a look to composure and firmness.

She moved towards the chamber, and on arriving at the door, the doctor met them, and in a whisper requested them to enter as silently as they could, and to exhibit no more emotion than was possible; for that the patient was in that precarious state that the least excitement might produce serious consequences; and he almost doubted whether, at present, the interview ought to take place.

With faltering steps they advanced into the room, but although they used the utmost precaution, so that they might not unnecessarily disturb her, the sound of their footsteps instantly caught her ears, and she raised her head from the pillow on which it had been reclining. But, gracious Heaven! how Sir Laurence Cleveland started at the countenance which was then revealed to him. A deathlike chill fixed itself on his heart, and his limbs trembled as if he had been afflicted with the palsy. He staggered nearer towards the couch, and had he not succeeded in catching hold of the back of a chair, he must have fallen, so powerful were the emotions which convulsed him.

The agitation of the unhappy woman was, if possible, greater than his own; her bloodless lips quivered; her bosom heaved violently, and her countenance was as ghastly pale as that of a corpse.

"Good God!" gasped forth Sir Laurence, "is this some fearful vision conjured up to torture me, and rack my brain to madness? or do my agonized eyes indeed behold the wretched, guilty, and treacherous Clara?"

"It is no vision, Sir Laurence Cleveland," returned the unfortunate being; "but her whom you once felt proud to call your wife, and whom you have so long supposed to be no more. Oh, turn not away from me with that look of horror and disgust; for I feel that the hand of death is upon me, and that the silent grave will soon close over my sorrows and my errors. But, before my mortal career is closed for ever, I have much to say; and if you would not sacrifice your own peace of mind, and the future happiness of an innocent being who should be as dear to you as your own life, you will not refuse to listen to me, calmly, patiently."

"Great Heaven give me fortitude to support this overwhelming discovery!" groaned Sir Laurence, clasping his burning temples in a perfect frenzy of anguish; while the unhappy Clara was so overpowered by the various feelings which crowded upon her bosom, that she sunk back upon the pillow, and gasping for breath, could only fix a look of melancholy and impressive supplication upon the distracted and agonised baronet.

Mrs. Clearmount and Eugenia were overwhelmed with astonishment and agitation, and awaited, with breathless anxiety and impatience, to hear the result of this extraordinary interview.

Eugenia felt that something of the deepest interest and importance to her was about to be disclosed; and she looked at Sir Laurence with a fearful foreboding of the nature of the coming revelation.

"The miscreants, the gipsies, then spoke the truth," groaned the baronet; "and my poor, my beloved, my confiding Blanche was never my lawful wife. Oh, horror! horror! Cruel woman, was it not enough that you should so shamefully deceive me, but that you should take so terrible a means of avenging yourself as this? I shall go mad; let me leave the room, for as I gaze upon you, wretched, heartless woman, my bosom fills with disgust and horror, and even in your dying moments I may be tempted to invoke a curse upon your head."

"No, for the love of Heaven, be calm, my brother," ejaculated Mrs. Clearmount, laying her hand upon his arm. "Unhappy woman!" she added, turning a mingled look of pity and reproach upon the suffering Clara. "Oh, why did you not before reveal yourself? Why did you suffer my unfortunate brother to do that, the reflection of which must ever cause him the most bitter anguish?"

"Lady," replied Clara, in a faint, but solemn voice; "as I hope for mercy from that Almighty judge, in whose dread presence I feel that I must shortly appear, I solemnly declare that it was my most anxious wish to do so; but I was held in the power of those whom I dared not to disobey; had I done so, my own life, his life, and that of one fair innocent being who should be dear to us both, would have been assuredly sacrificed to their vengeance."

Eugenia's emotion increased, and she looked in the pale countenance of Clara, and listened to every word she uttered with the most breathless attention. Sir Laurence Cleveland groaned again with the intensity of his agony, and beat his breast in a frenzied manner.

"Oh! Sir Laurence," gasped forth the wretched woman, fixing upon him a look which might have moved the sternest heart to compassion, "do not gaze upon me with those looks of hatred and disgust! Oh, God! what I have for years suffered no one but myself and Heaven can know. I am dying, Laurence; but a short time, and my eyes will be closed for ever in death. Do not, then, I beseech you, do not suffer me to descend to the grave with your curse upon my head. Remember that I yielded everything to you and love. Remember that I am still your wife—your lawful wife, although we have been for so many years separated—and say that you forgive me."

"Forgive you!" repeated the baronet, in a voice half choked by emotion; "wretched, misguided woman! how can you hope for me to forgive you, guilty as you have been? Implore pardon of Heaven, for against its sacred laws you have most offended."

"And so I do," faltered out Lady Clara, in accents of almost overpowering agony; "God knows how constantly my prayers, for many, many years past, have ascended to Him. I have erred, Laurence, deeply erred; but, by all my hope, I solemnly declare not to the extent you imagine. It was not until I suffered neglect and suspicion from you that I suffered myself to become the victim of the seducer. He had dared to make unlawful overtures to me on the occasion when you surprised us, which I rejected with horror and disgust, although I had every reason to believe that you no longer loved me, but that my cousin Mirah had estranged your affections from me. You would not listen to my explanation; you abandoned me; you scorned my letters of exoneration; and it was then, and not till then, that I yielded to the voice of the tempter, and with him fled from your roof. But I then bore in my womb the lawful offspring of our mutual affection."

"Do not drive me to madness with agony!" exclaimed Sir Laurence, his heart beating so violently against his side that it seemed as if it would burst its tenement.

" Remember that you are on the verge of eternity, and tell me whether you speak the truth ?"

" May God so judge me as I do !" solemnly answered Lady Clara, raising her hands and eyes towards heaven as she spoke. " I became not guilty until I imagined that you had abandoned me for ever. But—but search the pockets of the clothes I lately wore, and you will find there a written confession of all. I—I find that I shall not have strength to repeat it, and my time is short. Oh, that pang ! Laurence, Laurence, whom I was once permitted to call my beloved husband, will you refuse to pardon me in my dying moments ?"

" Almighty Father, teach me how to act !" cried the distracted baronet. " Oh ! Blanche, Blanche—poor, deceived, beloved, confiding woman, had you lived to witness this scene ! And my child—my Emeline, she, then, is the offspring of an illicit union ! Oh, torture unspeakable ! Alas ! alas ! how can I think of this, and look upon you, unhappy woman, with mercy and forgiveness ?"

" Oh, for the love of God, do not turn a deaf ear to my dying supplications !" gasped forth Lady Clara. " Think of the years of suffering I have endured; remember that I am the mother of your child !"

" My child ! I have none but my poor innocent Emeline."

" You have—you have !" ejaculated Lady Clara, struggling for breath, and her eyes wandering to Eugenia, who, in a moment, was kneeling weeping by her side, and awaiting the remainder of the unfortunate woman's disclosure with the most intense anxiety.

" Speak—speak, for Heaven's sake ! and do not keep me in suspense," implored the baronet, whilst nameless and almost overwhelming feelings struggled in his breast. " Can what you have asserted be true ?"

" It is, Sir Laurence," answered Lady Clara ; " and again I appeal to the Almighty to attest its truth ! When I quitted that place which I had a right to consider my home, I wanted but two months of my confinement. Laurence, I had then been constant and faithful to you. At the time expected I was safely delivered of a female child, and ——."

" It died—it died ?" eagerly interrupted the agitated Sir Laurence.

" It did not," returned Lady Clara, and her voice assumed a more thrilling tone of emotion than before—" it lived—it still lives, in beauty and innocence !"

" Lives !" re-echoed the baronet. " Oh, where—where ?"

" Here !" replied Lady Clara, extending her emaciated arms towards Eugenia. " It is even the lovely being I now clasp to my bosom, and, with almost my last words, implore the blessings of Heaven upon her head."

" Eugenia my child !" cried the astonished baronet. " Great God of heaven ! can this be ?"

" She is our child, Laurence—the offspring of love and honour," cried Lady Clara ; and, overcome by the extraordinary exertions she had undergone, she sunk back on the pillow, and fainted.

" Mother ! father !" shrieked Eugenia, as she raised her eyes towards the countenance of Sir Laurence. " Oh ! have I indeed those whom I may call by those beloved titles ? Great God, I ——."

She could not finish the sentence; the tumultuous tide of feelings that rushed upon her brain, was more than her strength could bear, and she sunk insensible upon the bosom of her unfortunate mother.

CHAPTER XXXIV.

THE DEATH.—THE CONFESSION.

NEED we attempt to describe the scene which followed? We are certain that we need not; for the reader may readily imagine it. Mrs. Clearmount was thunder-struck; and for a short time Sir Laurence stood apparently in a state of complete unconsciousness.

At length he clasped his forehead, and, in spite of all his manly efforts to prevent them, his tears gushed forth, and fell over the fair face of Eugenia, as he snatched her insensible form to his bosom, and imprinted fervent kisses upon her beauteous cheeks.

"My child! my daughter!" he ejaculated. "Oh, God! and may I honestly call her by those beloved names? Oh, yes! there is a feeling here throbbing at my heart, that assures me that this unfortunate woman has spoken the truth. My child —my Eugenia! oh, may Heaven forgive your wretched mother the errors of which she has been guilty; and may the spirit of the sainted Blanche look down with mercy and compassion on this scene!"

He could say no more, for anguish choked his utterance; and Doctor Edmonds, who was anxious to see to the recovery of Lady Clara, and was fearful of the conse-quences of the excitement which might follow, should they be present when she did so, advised Sir Laurence and his sister to leave the chamber, and to take Eugenia with them for a short time. The baronet and Mrs. Clearmount obeyed; Eugenia was conveyed to her chamber, and left in the care of a female attendant; and the baronet and his sister, in a state of mind which no language can properly pourtray, returned to the apartment in which Sir Evelyn Manners and Angela were so anxi-ously and impatiently awaiting them.

Here the baronet gave free vent to the powerful and all-absorbing emotions which struggled in his breast; and it devolved entirely upon Mrs. Clearmount to describe the extraordinary discovery which had been made; and to delineate by any force of language the feelings of astonishment and emotion with which Sir Evelyn and Angela listened to the remarkable disclosure, would be an arduous and fruitless task.

"God of Heaven, I thank thee!" fervently exclaimed Sir Evelyn, first recovering himself; "the painful mystery is removed, and Eugenia will be restored to every happiness. But to discover that she is the daughter of my dearest friend; oh, this is indeed a pleasure which I had never anticipated! Oh, Sir Laurence, what a sweet consolation ought it to be to you under all your afflictions to know that you are the father of so lovely, so amiable, and virtuous a being as Eugenia."

Sir Laurence sighed, and shook his head.

"But, my beloved Blanche," he cried; "oh, can I ever cease to think of the man-ner in which she was deceived without the most poignant anguish?"

"She is a saint in Heaven," replied Sir Evelyn, "and is spared the misery that this discovery would have caused her. You were neither of you to blame, and, therefore, my dear Sir Laurence, why should you so bitterly reproach yourself? But Eugenia; she is insensible, you say; oh, she will much need the voice of consolation when she recovers."

"I will hasten to her," said Angela; and she immediately quitted the apartment.

Sir Laurence Cleveland threw himself disconsolately in a chair, and his mind became completely absorbed by the various and bewildering thoughts which crowded upon it.

So extraordinary, so unexpected were the events which had taken place, that he could scarcely persuade himself of their reality. Eugenia his daughter—his lawful daughter; it seemed scarcely possible; and yet he could not doubt the solemn assertions of the wretched Clara, and made, too, at the time when her dissolution was rapidly approaching.

But there was one circumstance which was still involved in mystery; and that was the fact which Eugenia had stated of the unfortunate woman whom she had supposed to have been her mother, having died soon after they were found by the gipsies. Who could that really have been, and by what means had Eugenia fallen into her hands? Of course Eugenia was too young at the time to be able now to form the least idea upon the subject. In spite of all the errors of which Lady Clara had herself admitted she had been guilty, the baronet could not help feeling the greatest compassion for her, and sincerely did he pray that Heaven in its infinite mercy would pardon her likewise. Alas! it was a melancholy consolation to him that poor Blanche did not live to witness this strange and painful discovery; for what would have been her shame and agony had she done so?

As for Sir Evelyn, he was completely lost in amazement at all that had taken place; but the discovery of Eugenia's origin filled him no less with delight, for now every obstacle to their union seemed at once to be removed, and, in a short time, he flattered himself their happiness would be rendered complete. Oh, how he longed to embrace her, and to express to her the feelings which now struggled in his bosom. Nor was he long kept in suspense. Eugenia, by the attentions and exertions of the affectionate Angela, soon recovered her senses, and acquired sufficient resolution to enter the apartment in which Sir Laurence and the others were. With faltering steps, the poor girl approached her father, and sinking at his feet, and clasping his knees, she looked up in his face with the most indescribable affection and emotion.

The baronet raised her tenderly, and pressing her to his bosom, in tones which spoke the sincerity and ardour of his feelings, he ejaculated,—

"My child—my deeply-injured child, kind Heaven has preserved you under all the dangers with which you have from childhood been surrounded, and my heart throbs with feelings of the most unbounded gratitude for the unexpected gift. Oh, may every future blessing descend upon your head."

"My father!" ejaculated Eugenia, in accents which no language can convey an adequate idea of; "oh, may I call you by that beloved name? Will you, indeed, acknowledge me, and suffer me to look up to you with love and reverence?"

"Yes, yes, my Eugenia," replied Sir Laurence, embracing her fervently and affectionately; "you are mine, my own sweet girl; nature's voice assures me that you are, and fondly my heart welcomes your restoration. Henceforth you shall share my affection equally with my gentle Emeline, your—your sister."

The scene which followed was of the most affecting character. Sir Laurence again embraced Eugenia, and the delighted Sir Evelyn equally shared in their transports; and looked on the extraordinary events of the day as a fair augury of future happiness.

"But my unfortunate mother," sighed Eugenia. "Alas! alas! she will never recover. Oh, let us hasten again to her chamber, and endeavour to soothe her last sad moments with words of comfort and of hope. Father, you do forgive her the errors of which she has been guilty? When you take into consideration all the bitter sufferings she has for so many years endured, I am satisfied you will."

"May the Almighty God forgive me as I sincerely pardon her," said Sir Laurence, solemnly. Eugenia threw herself on his bosom, and sobbed forth her feelings of gratitude. They were interrupted by the entrance of a messenger from Doctor Edmonds, stating that Lady Clara was much worse, and he feared that her end was fast approaching; and that it was, therefore, necessary, if they wished to communicate with her before her death, that they should return to the chamber immediately, especially as the dying woman had expressed the most earnest wishes to see them again.

The anguish of the baronet and Eugenia was almost insupportable, and it was several minutes before they could in any degree recover themselves, or muster fortitude to encounter the solemn and final interview; but at length they succeeded, and Eugenia, leaning on the arm of her father, left the apartment, accompanied by Mrs. Clearmount and Angela; who thought it most likely that their presence would be required at the melancholy and trying scene.

Sir Evelyn threw himself on a seat, and gave himself up entirely to the mingled feelings of astonishment and pleasure which the unexpected discovery had created in his breast.

That Eugenia should prove to be the daughter of Sir Laurence Cleveland was a source of gratification he had never, for a moment, anticipated; and he could not, for an instant, doubt the legitimacy of her birth, after the solemn declaration of the dying Lady Clara; and with what pride and honour, therefore, could he make her his wife; for he could not believe that Eugenia would alter her sentiments, or that Sir Laurence would refuse his consent to their nuptials, when the mutual friendship that subsisted between them was taken into consideration.

With faltering steps and foreboding hearts, Sir Laurence, Eugenia, and the others, entered the chamber of the suffering Lady Clara. She was propped up in the bed, and the ghastly hue of death had already overspread her features, and gave warning of its rapid approach in the unearthly expression of her eyes.

Eugenia and her father approached her, and the former, sinking on her knees, looked up in her pale face with the most unbounded affection; but so powerful and varied were the emotions which struggled in her bosom, that she could not give utterance to a syllable.

A faint smile overspread the countenance of Clara, and she gazed at her daughter and her husband with an expression that might have moved the stoutest heart to commiseration. Convulsive sobs escaped the bosom of Eugenia, and she pressed the thin, cold, clammy hand of her mother to her lips, and bathed it with her tears.

"The time allowed me on this earth I feel is short," said Lady Clara, in a faint voice; "but I cannot feel the least regret at leaving a world in which I have experienced such bitter misery. But, oh! Sir Laurence—husband—surely you will not suffer me to die without the assurance of your forgiveness. We have both erred, and Heaven knows that it was not until I experienced your hatred and neglect that I listened to the voice of the tempter, or harboured a thought derogatory to your honour, although I had too much reason to believe that the love I thought you once bore me was transferred to Mirah. But—but—let that pass;—my time grows short —Laurence, tell me, I beseech you, will you—oh, tell me—will you pardon the un-

fortunate, dying Clara, who, whatever her faults may have been, has long since re.
pented of them ?"

"Clara," replied the baronet, in a voice nearly stifled with emotion, "as I hope
for mercy from above, so do I pardon you all the faults of which you may have been
guilty, and fervently pray that the Almighty may extend the same mercy to you."

A sweet smile irradiated the features of Lady Clara, and she extended her hands
over the heads of Sir Laurence and Eugenia, as if invoking blessings.

"Oh, thanks—thanks !" she cried. "That assurance has made me happy, and
now I can die in peace."

"Mother, beloved mother," sobbed Eugenia, "must you, indeed, be snatched away from me so soon after my discovering you?   Oh! God, I humbly beseech you to avert this calamity, and suffer my parent to live many years to impart happiness to her husband and her poor child."

"My sweet girl," returned Lady Clara, with a melancholy look of inexpressible affection, "it will not be.   The hand of death is upon me—my eyes grow dim; but it is the will of Heaven, and who shall presume to murmur at it?   But a few years, and we shall meet again in Heaven, no more to part, and where sorrow can never reach us.   Bless you, bless you, my child; bless you, my husband; pray for me; and let my errors be buried with me in the silent tomb."

Sir Laurence and Eugenia embraced the poor sufferer with fervent sincerity; but their anguish was too great for utterance.   A dismal pause ensued; and the strength of Lady Clara rapidly declined, and it was quite evident that the fatal moment was close at hand.

Eugenia's heart was nearly bursting, and she watched the fast changing countenance of her mother with the most indescribable anguish.   Nor were the feelings of Sir Laurence less torturing, although, for the sake of Eugenia, he endeavoured to subdue them, and to appear calm and resigned.

"God's will be done!" he solemnly ejaculated; "but, tell me, Clara, who was the unfortunate woman that Eugenia believed to be her mother, and who, it is said, died soon after her discovery by the gipsies?"

"Mirah," answered Lady Clara, in a voice which was scarcely articulate.

"Mirah!" repeated the astonished baronet; and a nameless sensation of horror and self-reproach shot through his heart.   "Oh! how came she in possession of Eugenia?"

"My breath grows short, and I cannot repeat the tale," said the dying woman; "but—but the confession will explain everything."

"And who are really the villain Harold and Madela?" eagerly asked the baronet.

"Walter Alston and his mother."

"Good God! is it possible?   Then is their hatred and revenge fully accounted for."

"Yes, yes," faltered Lady Clara; "he escaped from transportation, and—but I am faint.   I—I ——"

She closed her eyes as she thus spoke, and sunk back in the bed, and Eugenia uttered a shriek of horror and agony, for she imagined that the vital spark had already fled—so ghastly pale, and so inanimate did the sufferer appear.

Sir Laurence gently removed his daughter from the form of her mother, and the doctor motioned them to silence; for he feared that any violent display of excitement would disturb his patient in her last moments, and he saw plainly that the fatal time was fast approaching.

Once more Lady Clara opened her eyes, and smiled serenely upon her husband and Eugenia.   Her lips moved, but she in vain tried to speak, for her strength was now quite exhausted, and her breathing every instant became more difficult.

Sir Laurence and Eugenia knelt beside her, and each held a hand in theirs, which they pressed to their heart with a feeling of anguish and despair, such as those only who have experienced it can imagine.

Mrs. Clearmount and her daughter raised their eyes towards heaven, and breathed a silent prayer; and so silent was everything in that chamber of sorrow that nothing could be heard save the short and heavy breathings of the dying woman, and the ticking of the watches of the baronet and Doctor Edmonds.

Again Lady Clara gently raised her head from the pillow, and tried to speak; but the power was denied her; a convulsive shudder passed through her frame—her eyes closed; one gentle sigh escaped her bosom, and the once beauteous Lady Clara Cleveland lay a breathless corpse before the distracted eyes of her husband and her daughter.

*   *   *   *   *   *   *

In a state of utter insensibility, Eugenia was borne away from the chamber of death, and the baronet was scarcely less moved at the melancholy scene of which he had been a spectator, and which he had been so little prepared to encounter. He secluded himself in his own apartment for some time, and there gave free vent to the powerful emotions which distracted his brain. Fervently he offered up his prayers to Heaven for the repose of his unfortunate wife's spirit, and many were the tears he shed over the recollection of the sorrows which she had endured, and of which he could not help accusing himself of being indirectly the cause. But what tenfold misery would he have experienced had Blanche been living to become acquainted with all the painful particulars! The thought drove him to utter despair, and it was some time ere he could acquire anything like a degree of composure.

Mrs. Clearmount and Angela were in constant attendance upon Eugenia, and did all that they could to reconcile her to the mournful loss she had sustained; but they found that to be a task not very easy of accomplishment, and they were fearful that it would continue for some time to have the most melancholy effect upon her spirits.

Sir Evelyn, as soon as he could obtrude himself upon her sorrows, sought an interview with her, and tried all that affection could suggest to console her; and he at length had the satisfaction to find that his efforts were not unavailing, for Eugenia became more calm, and endeavoured to submit with fortitude to the stern will of Heaven.

In due time the remains of Lady Clara were consigned to the tomb as privately as possible, but with all the respect due to her memory; and many were the tears which Eugenia shed, when this last melancholy duty was performed. But the affectionate attentions of Sir Laurence, and the assurances of his parental regard, in some measure restored her, and she tried to look forward to the future with renewed hope.

Sir Evelyn continued to visit Branscombe House daily, and in the assurances of his constancy and love, and the approbation which Sir Laurence was pleased to bestow upon their suit, Eugenia found her principal source of consolation. Every obstacle to their union was now removed, and they both looked forward to the completion of their happiness, with impatience, and the most sanguine anticipations.

Sir Laurence had secured the manuscripts alluded to by the Lady Clara, but anxious as he was to become acquainted with their contents, for some time he postponed the perusal of them, for he was fearful that Eugenia had not yet gained sufficient composure of mind to listen to them.

However, time wore away the violence of grief, and Eugenia having declared her anxiety to become acquainted with all the melancholy particulars of her mother's history, and to have an explanation of the extraordinary circumstances which were still involved in mystery, Sir Laurence appointed the following day for the reading of the manuscript; and it was arranged that Sir Evelyn, Mrs. Clearmount, and Angela should be presént, as their interest and curiosity were naturally greatly excited on the subject.

The day arrived, and the friends being all assembled, Sir Laurence began his task.

THE CONFESSION.

WITH a trembling hand, the wretched Clara sits down to write these lines in explanation of all the sorrows and the errors of her past life; and with the humble hope that mercy and forgiveness may be extended to her by those who now view her with prejudice and suspicion. To my husband (if I may still venture so to call Sir Laurence Cleveland) I address myself, and implore him not entirely to condemn the wretched Clara, who, at the time he peruses these sad memorials, will probably be mouldering in the silent grave. And oh, my Eugenia, should these painful particulars ever reach your knowledge, shed a tear to the memory of your unhappy mother, and view her faults with a lenient eye.

I will not dwell upon my early life, for you, Laurence, are well acquainted with all its particulars. Oh, I was good and innocent when you first beheld me, and happy in the affections of my excellent uncle, and the love of Walter Alston, who then, at any rate, was an honest and worthy young man.

Oh, why was this dream of happiness ever disturbed?—Why did Providence ordain that ever we should meet, Sir Laurence?—From that fatal moment must I date all the calamities which have befallen us both; but for that occurrence, we might neither of us ever have known what sorrow was.

From the very instant that we first encountered each other, my heart was estranged from Walter Alston, and became insensibly yours. I flattered myself that you beheld me with admiration, and I felt the most unbounded transport at the thought. During the time that you remained away from our residence, I was dull and unhappy, and I began to feel a restraint in the society of Walter, which I had never experienced before.

In vain I struggled with my feelings, and reproached myself for encouraging such sentiments, seeing the improbability of their ever being gratified, and knowing how solemnly I was plighted to Walter Alston, and that my uncle would never consent to my breaking a compact so solemnly entered into, even if you should make any offer of your hand to me, which the disparity of our circumstances, it was more than likely, would always prevent you from doing.

But why should I dwell upon these particulars, the remembrance of which must be so painful to us both?—Let it suffice, that the more I endeavoured to conquer my unfortunate passion, and to view Walter with the same sentiments that I had ever before done, the more it gained strength in my bosom, until at length I resigned myself entirely to its influence, and determined, in my own mind, that, if I could not become yours, I would never bestow my hand upon any other man. Fatal infatuation! of what numerous evils was it the cause.

What feelings of delight were mine, as I noticed the impression which I had made upon you; and how anxiously did I anticipate your visits; never were you for an instant absent from my thoughts; and every day I began to feel more uneasy in the society of Walter Alston. But I will pass over all these facts, and come at once to the period when I abandoned the home of my kind uncle, and resigned my fate entirely into your hands.

Oh, Laurence, confident as I was in the possession of your love, even though I had brought down upon my head the eternal displeasure of my benefactor, whose will I had never ventured to disobey before, I felt myself one of the happiest and proudest of human beings; and would not have changed my situation on any consideration.

Alas! little did I expect that all my hopes would ultimately be so cruelly blighted.

I date the principal of my misfortunes from the time when Mirah also abandoned the home of our excellent guardian, arrived at our house, and was received under our protection. I imagined, from that time, that your attentions towards me became less warm and less ardent; and I could not but notice the emotion which Mirah ever evinced in your company; and by degrees the terrible idea that she had imbibed a fatal passion for you, and to which you were not indifferent, began to take possession of my brain and rendered me as truly wretched as I had before been happy. And was I mistaken? Alas, no; time shewed too fatally, too clearly, that I was not. Indeed, had not passion completely blinded me, from the first moment that we met, I might have perceived that Mirah's affections were devoted to you, and that her company to you was dangerous. But I am not going to reproach you, Laurence. No; I firmly believe that at first you were blind to the fascinations of Mirah, and that the sentiments you avowed for me were sincere.

But, alas! I know not how it was; it must have been from some fault of my own, that the change I fancied came over you; and yet I examined my past and present conduct narrowly, without being able to discover in what way I had committed myself.

Several times I was on the point of banishing the suspense I was then enduring, by throwing myself at your feet, and imploring you to confirm or to contradict my terrible suspicions; but something prevented me; my courage failed me, and I remained in the same agonising state of mind; daily observing how the fatal passion which Mirah had imbibed for you, gained strength, and to imagine that she was gradually gaining an ascendency over that heart which I had once imagined to be wholly mine.

Oh, Laurence, blame me though you may, even at this distant period, yet you cannot help feeling for me some degree of pity, for the sufferings I then endured. Wretched became my days; sleepless my nights; although I struggled hard to conquer my feelings, and to appear happy.

I felt the utmost pain and restraint in the company of Mirah, and yet I could not help regarding her with the same affection that had ever marked my conduct towards her; in fact, I could not but pity her in having become the victim of a fatal passion; while, at the same time, I considered that you were greatly to blame for giving the least encouragement (which I believed you did) to those sentiments.

Often I was on the point of revealing my thoughts and suspicions to Mirah; but something, a feeling of dread and repugnance, over which I had no control, prevented me; and thus the evil daily, hourly, increased, until I was precipitated entirely into the dark abyss of ruin and misery.

It was these torturing feelings—these maddening suspicions which wrought the change in my conduct, and which you, Laurence, must have observed. I feared to trust myself in your presence and that of Mirah, and kept myself as much secluded in my own apartment as possible, where I brooded over my sorrows, endured all the pangs of jealousy, and lamented that fate should ever have brought us together.

I could not but consider it a judgment, a heavy judgment on me for having so cruelly deceived Walter Alston, and been the means of plunging him into vice, and disobeying the will of my kind uncle and benefactor. I will pass over the horror of my feelings at the fate which afterwards befel Walter and his father, a horror that was increased by your being instrumental to it; but still I could not, after the fearful evidence that was adduced on their trial, believe them otherwise than guilty.

It was about this time that the tempter was introduced to us. Fatal hour! Alas! what horrors, what miseries was it not the prelude to!

The conversation and personal manners of Leonard were gay, intelligent, and charming; and I soon found that they served in a great measure to alleviate the care which had taken possession of my mind. I hailed his visits to the mansion with pleasure, but heaven knows that I never for a moment harboured a thought respecting him which I should have blushed to own; nor did I remark anything in his behaviour which was calculated to excite my suspicion, or I should have avoided him with abhorrence, and immediately have exposed him to your just indignation and chastisement.

Fatal delusion! The hypocrite succeeded but too well, and the veil was not removed from before my eyes until it was too late; and then the unhappy prejudice which had taken possession of my bosom left me without hope.

CHAPTER XXXV.

THE CONFESSION CONTINUED.

I WILL pass hastily over this, the most painful part of my narrative; for even now I cannot but look back upon it with feelings of the most inexpressible horror. Even then I thought not that you viewed the conduct of Leonard with suspicion, nor did I believe that you had any cause to do so; for I firmly believed that the attentions of Leonard were prompted alone by his friendship, and the natural gaiety and generosity of his disposition. Little did I imagine the demon that lurked beneath that specious mask. But the truth was soon about to be revealed to me.

Business, Sir Laurence, called you away from home, and during your absence Leonard visited me; but he was not accompanied by his friends, a circumstance which surprised me not, and I received him with my usual feelings of pleasure.

We passed some time in conversation together, Mirah all the time being present; and I noticed nothing in the behaviour of Leonard of the least objectionable description. At length he took his leave, and in order to imbibe the air, I shortly afterwards walked into the garden, and finally seated myself in the summer-house, which of late had been a favourite retreat of mine. I had not been there many minutes when I was aroused from a reverie into which I had fallen by hearing a footstep approaching.

Imagining that it was Mirah, I went to the door, but you may guess my astonishment and alarm when I beheld Leonard.

A fearful foreboding now came over me, for I could see that his countenance was inflamed, and suspicion for the first time rushed upon my mind. I was about immediately to leave the place, but he prevented me, and closing the door, he sunk upon his knees, and with all the eloquence of which he was such a consummate master, he poured forth his guilty passion in my ears. He painted the feelings with which I had inspired him in the most glowing colours, and declared that nothing but the certainty that you, Sir Laurence, was unfaithful to me, that you loved me no longer, but that you bestowed all your affections upon my cousin, could have induced him to confess his sentiments; and he finally concluded by imploring me not to view his passion with scorn or indifference, but resigning myself to his protection, obtain that happiness which I could never in future hope to experience with him to whom I had unfortunately given my hand. He even dared to assert that my union with you was not a lawful one, and that you only sought an opportunity to discard me altogether.

"The villain! the base, perfidious villain!" exclaimed the deeply excited baronet; "alas! unfortunate Clara, how subtle was the snare that was laid to entrap you."

Eugenia sighed deeply, and tears started to her eyes. It was some minutes ere Sir Laurence could sufficiently recover from his emotion to resume the narrative, but at length he did so in the following words:—

How shall I seek to pourtray the astonishment, horror, and disgust, with which I listened to him? Indignation, and shame for some moments choked my utterance, and I could only gaze at him with looks of the bitterest reproach. All the friendly feelings, the favourable opinions I had formerly entertained of him vanished in an instant; and in a voice of the deepest resentment I commanded him to begone, at the same time I threatened him with immediate exposure if he should still persist in polluting my ears with his odious sentiments.

This had no other effect on him than to make him more urgent in his importunities, and I was about to call for assistance, when the door of the summer-house was thrown open, and you, Sir Laurence, appeared.

I need not attempt to describe the scene which followed. Oh, God, it will never be erased from my memory; nor the insupportable horrors that I felt on recovering my senses, and discovering that you had left me, and with the terrible impression on your mind that I was guilty. I wonder that madness did not seize upon my brain. It was then that I confessed to Mirah the suspicions which I entertained of the sentiments she felt towards you. She did not deny it; declared that she had loved you from the first moment she had seen you; but solemnly asserted that you had never given the smallest encouragement to her fatal passion by word or deed; promised to try and stifle the unlawful feelings in her breast, and if she could not succeed in doing so, she would at once leave the mansion, and never more return there until she could do so with honour and safety.

But, alas! the fatal blow was struck; you were lost to me for ever; for your letters assured me that you would never behold me again, or acknowledge me as your wife. Nothing but despair surrounded me whichever way I turned my eyes, and sincerely did I lament that ever I had been born.

Oh, Sir Laurence, surely your conduct towards me was too severe. Had you but listened with patience and indulgence to my explanation, what years of shame and misery might have been spared us both. But fate ordained it otherwise, and it is useless now to murmur.

You rejected all my supplications; you returned my letters unread; you remained away from the mansion, and it was too fatally apparent that you had abandoned me for ever, and my wretched fate was sealed. At times I was driven to such a state of frenzy that I was almost induced to put an end to my miserable existence. But suddenly very different feelings took possession of my mind. I thought that you treated me with an unnatural severity, and I began to suspect that what Leonard had stated was not altogether without foundation, and that you were only glad of the plea which had arisen for you to get rid of me, in order that you might indulge the lawless passion with which Mirah had inspired you.

A feeling of revenge took possession of my breast, and I began to think of Leonard without prejudice, and to entertain a wish to behold him again.

It was not long before that wish was gratified, for the villain had not quitted the neighbourhood, nor abandoned his designs, but only watched his opportunity to put them into effect; for, notwithstanding all that had happened, he flattered himself that he should still meet with success; and the result of his nefarious plans proved that he was not mistaken.

When I was able to leave my chamber, I frequently wandered from the mansion, taking the most lonely and solitary walks, so that I might indulge in the sorrows that afflicted my bosom without fear of interruption. It was a melancholy source of pleasure to me; and oftentimes my mind was wrought to such a pitch, that I hesitated to return home, and almost resolved to abandon it for ever. Home! it no longer appeared so to me, since all that I had valued on earth was now lost to me for ever.

On one of these occasions I had rambled further than was my usual custom, and the shadows of evening had began to descend upon the earth before I thought of returning.

I had not proceeded far on my way back, when I heard hasty footsteps behind me, and, turning round, you may imagine my feelings of emotion when I beheld Leonard advancing rapidly towards me.

Overcome with mingled feelings of astonishment and alarm, I could not move a step, and Leonard coming up to me sunk on one knee, and taking my unresisting hand in his, he implored me to pardon him for a step to which he was driven by despair; and then he once more poured forth his passion in my ears, and urged me to resign myself to his honour, and to abandon a man who could never have loved me, otherwise he could not have behaved to me with the severity and inhumanity he was now doing. He pointed out to me the pleasures we might find together in a foreign land, and far away from the scene of my present troubles, and declared himself ready to suffer anything—even death itself, to render me happy.

Wretched woman that I was, I now listened but too readily to the villain's arguments and persuasions, and, perceiving the advantages that he had gained, he did not fail to follow it up; I threw myself into his arms, and resigned my future fate into his hands.

The following night I agreed to elope with him from the mansion, and he promised to have everything in readiness for our departure to France.

This, then, was my first commencement of crime, and had you not refused to listen to my explanation, Laurence, I might still have remained as innocent as when you first knew me, and the plans of the guilty tempter would have been rendered abortive. Great was my agitation on parting from Leonard, and returning home. I quickly retired to my chamber, lest the extraordinary emotion I evinced should attract the attention and excite the suspicions of Mirah; and here, when I was alone, I gave free vent to the various and tumultuous feelings which crowded upon my bosom. Several times I shuddered with horror at the step I was about to take, and was half inclined to abandon it; especially when I reflected on the delicate situation in which I then was; and thought of the future fate of the poor innocent being I carried in my womb, deprived as it would be of a father's love and protection. But when I remembered the hopelessness of my present position, and the feeling which

See p. 431.

you now entertained towards me, my mind again became firm in its desperate purposes, and I endeavoured to banish from my bosom every feeling of repugnance.

I did not retire to my couch until a late hour, but occupied my time in making such preparations as were necessary for my elopement. These were not many, and I awaited the hour of my departure with trembling impatience.

The next day I pleaded indisposition, and remained in my chamber, for I was fearful of beholding Mirah, lest my emotion should cause her to put such questions to me as would lead to a discovery of my intentions.

No. 53.

Many were the wandering thoughts which crowded upon my brain during that day.   Many were the tears I shed, the prayers I uttered; and fervently did I implore the forgiveness of the Almighty for the desperate course I was about to pursue.   I invoked blessings on your head, Laurence, and sincerely did I pardon you for the severity with which you had treated me, and earnestly hoped that you might be happier than I could ever hope to be.

Alas! that I should ever have been so blind, so infatuated, as to listen to the voice of the betrayer; but he had now gained complete ascendancy over me, and I was fully determined, whatever might happen to me, to resign my fate into his hands.   I thought that, at any rate, I could not be any more miserable than I was at present. Blind madness! too soon was I undeceived; what else could I expect, when I was thus about to plunge myself into vice? Tediously that never-to-be-forgotten day vanished, and night arrived.   I had seen Mirah, and, with more composure than I thought I could have mustered, I bade her good night, and she left me, under the impression that I was about immediately to retire to rest.   Oh, had she known the thoughts which were then passing in my mind, what would have been her feelings!

The fatal hour came at last; the mansion was wrapped in silence, for all the inmates had retired to rest, and now was the moment when all my firmness and resolution were called into requisition.

Again I sunk on my knees and supplicated the forgiveness of Heaven; then I arose, and gently opening the door, with trembling but noiseless steps I emerged froom the room, and proceeded down the stairs.   I reached the hall; I cautiously unbarred the door; and the next moment I was in the open air.

And here I paused, even on the threshold, and my heart beat violently against my side.   The full solemnity of the desperate course I had taken, and the danger into which I was about to plunge, at once rushed upon my brain, and I was half inclined to return, and to abandon my determination altogether; but that idea soon fled, and wrapping my cloak around me, I walked across the garden; opened the gate, and then pursued my way towards the spot where Leonard had appointed to meet me.   I gained it, and found him there waiting with a vehicle to bear me away.   My feelings now overpowered me, and I fainted in his arms.

When I again recovered, I found that we were proceeding at a rapid rate, and had already got a considerable distance from the mansion.

CHAPTER XXXVI.

THE CONFESSION CONCLUDED.

NOTHING could equal the rapture which Leonard felt and expressed, now that he had got me in his power; he uttered every argument he could make use of to alleviate my emotions, and to justify the step which I had taken; and to my shame, I acknowledge that he succeeded but too well; and I was persuaded, Sir Laurence, that on your head rested all the blame.

Numerous were the vows of constancy and unutterable affection which the deceiver uttered, and I lent but too ready an ear to his asseverations and protestations.

After travelling for about two hours, we stopped at an inn for the remainder of the night, intending to resume our journey at an early hour on the following morning, and to make our way to the nearest sea-port, where we could embark for France.

I will not dwell upon the night of agony which I suffered; for well may those who shall peruse these lines imagine it.

As soon as it was daylight the following morning, we departed from the inn, and pursued our way with all possible speed, lest we should be pursued; and, by the afternoon, we arrived at the place of our destination, and having procured our passports without much difficulty, we discharged the chaise, and embarked for France.

I now endeavoured to reconcile myself to my fate, for there was no retracing my steps; and Leonard was so attentive to me, and exerted himself so much to console me, that he at last succeeded, and I became by far more calm than could have been anticipated.

Unhappy woman! I was now, indeed, lost for ever. But did I feel no pangs of regret at leaving you, Sir Laurence? did I feel no remorse at the step which I had taken? Oh! yes; Heaven knows how severely, at times, I suffered, in spite of all the exertions of my betrayer to comfort me, and to persuade me that I was fully justified in the course I had taken, after the stern severity of my husband's behaviour, and the infidelity of his conduct. Alas! the villain too well played his part, and completely triumphed over my scruples. I learned to view you, Sir Laurence, with sentiments of abhorrence and revenge; to believe that you had cruelly deceived me from the first; and, by the time we had arrived in France, I had become, in a manner of speaking, reconciled to my fate, and determined to place my whole confidence in the man to whom I had sacrificed myself.

Before our elopement from England, Leonard had entrusted a friend with the secret of his guilty amour, and made arrangements with him to forward us every information respecting what took place at the mansion, and the conduct of the baronet after my disappearance; and the first account he forwarded us confirmed me in the opinion I had formed of your treachery, Sir Laurence. (Oh! pardon the harsh expression, but my feelings overcome me, as retrospection brings to my memory the misery of the past.) From that communication we learnt that you had betrayed little or no emotion or regret at my flight; that you had scarcely instituted any inquiries after me, and, moreover, that Mirah had followed you to Branscombe House, and that it had become notorious that an intimacy of a most guilty description existed between you.

On the first receipt of this intelligence, my anguish was almost insupportable; to think that I should be so shamefully deceived by that man on whom I had lavished all my woman's fondness—for whom I had sacrificed home, the love of my uncle, and destroyed the hopes of Walter Alston, plunging him into crime and shame. In the frenzy of the moment, I breathed a curse upon your head, and vowed never again to think of you but with detestation and disgust. In these fearful feelings, Leonard insidiously encouraged me; and the crafty villain had gained so powerful a hold on my mind, that he succeeded but too well.

Oh! Sir Laurence, well can I imagine, should these papers ever meet your eyes, the horror and disgust you must feel at the weakness, the blind infatuation I betrayed. And you, my poor child, whom, from your earliest days of childhood, I have watched, unknown to you, with such anxiety, such feelings of uncontrollable anguish, what will be the sentiments which this my painful confession must inspire you with, gentle, and amiable, and virtuous as I know your disposition to be? Will you not feel the bitterest pangs of regret that you had not died in your infancy, or that the errors of your unfortunate, misguided mother should ever become known to you?

But no; I dare not think that you, my Eugenia, at least, will ever reproach my memory; you must pity, though you cannot help condemning, in some respects, your wretched parent.

     *   *   *   *   *   *

Sir Laurence paused at this melancholy part of the narrative, to give free vent to the feelings which rushed tumultuously to his bosom, and the tears of Eugenia flowed afresh.

The baronet clasped his lovely and innocent daughter to his bosom, and, in a voice half stifled by the intensity of his emotion, ejaculated,—

"Let us ever invoke the blessing of Heaven, my dear child, on your mother's departed spirit; be her errors entirely forgotten in the numerous virtues she possessed. Alas! I am myself equally, perhaps, more to blame than her; for had I listened to the voice of truth and reason, Clara would have been rescued from the power of the heartless miscreant who worked her ruin, and might still have been living and happy."

"Oh, my poor mother!" sighed Eugenia; "how much, how deeply are you to be pitied; and never can I cease to remember you with the fondest affection and the deepest reverence."

Sir Laurence again embraced her affectionately, and then, after another brief pause, in order to collect himself, he went on with the manuscript as follows, his auditors listening to him with the most profound interest and attention:—

Leonard continued to profess the most unbounded affection towards me; and seemed anxious to anticipate my every wish. He was never absent from my society, and appeared only to know happiness when in my presence. Gradually I became more calm, confident in the sincerity of his attachment, and tried to banish you, Sir Laurence, from my memory, or to think of you only with contempt and abhorrence; but cruelly as I believed you to have treated me even, I found that a task far too painful and difficult for me entirely to accomplish. In spite of everything, your image was still too closely interwoven with my heart, for anything ever to remove it.

And now quickly approached that important and critical time, when I must become a mother—the mother of a fatherless babe, the offspring of a man who would never acknowledge it, and who would be looked upon by the ungenerous world with an eye of reproach and scorn, and probably have to bear the stigma of a wretched mother's shame. Oh, Eugenia, what maddening pangs of anguish did your hapless mother endure!

As the period of my accouchement approached, Leonard redoubled his attentions to me, and seemed to wait the event with the greatest anxiety and apprehension. I could not but feel grateful to him, and my confidence in him increased.

The day arrived, and you, my Eugenia, first saw the light of Heaven. Oh, how I caressed you with all the fond transport and affection which a mother must ever feel for her first-born; and how many were the tears of mingled regret and delight which I shed upon your innocent cherub face. But alas! I reflected, what had I to rejoice at? Ought I not rather to lament you did not die in your birth, rather than that you should afterwards run the risk of experiencing those misfortunes which have fallen to your wretched mother's share?

Leonard affected to hail the birth of my infant with as much pleasure as if it had been his own, and vowed that he would ever behave to it with the affection of a father. And for some time I had no reason to suspect that he would fail to fulfil his promise, for he was ever lavish in the fond attentions he bestowed upon the infant. It required time to show the wily and treacherous part he was playing.

Months flew on, and my child daily increased in beauty; and all that a mother's fondest transport could bestow, I lavished upon it. Many were the tears I shed; many were the pangs which crowded my heart, while I held the little innocent to my bosom, or watched it in its tranquil slumbers. How I endeavoured to trace, in its half-formed features, some resemblance to my husband; and pictured to myself what I thought he must feel should he ever behold it, and know it. Surely his heart must relent, and though he might think of its unfortunate mother only with feelings of hatred, he could not close his ears to the voice of nature, which must appeal, in its beauteous features, to his affection. He would not, he could not reject it; he could never carry his cruel suspicions and prejudices so far as not to acknowledge it to be his own offspring.

These, and other ideas of a similar nature, constantly haunted my imagination, and many were the sleepless nights I passed; many were the weary hours I racked my brain with thoughts, which, at times, were almost enough to drive me to madness.

Leonard's friend constantly corresponded with us, and forwarded us all the news we were so anxious to hear; but I fear that his accounts were too frequently much exaggerated, though, unfortunately, at that time, I was far too ready to believe them, and to be prejudiced by them.

From these communications we learnt that Mirah was shamelessly living as the mistress of my husband. How my bosom swelled with indignation, and how thoroughly was I now convinced of the deceitful part which that man, to whom I had given my hand, in the full confidence of his affection, had acted towards me. Frequently I was half resolved to write to him and my cousin letters of the bitterest reproach; but Leonard prevented me, and, by the most insidious arts, encouraged me to hate and despise those whom I had such reason to believe had so deeply injured me.

We went under an assumed name, and no one had the least reason to suspect that we were other than man and wife. In order the better to conceal ourselves, and to mislead Sir Laurence, we got Leonard's friend to get inserted in one of the English papers the account of my death, and which we soon found had the effect which we desired it to have. But how were my feelings of disgust increased towards you, Sir Laurence, when I found the indifference with which you treated my fate, and the little pains you took to ascertain whether the account was authentic or not. It was evident to me that you could never have loved me, and I reproached myself for having been the weak and confiding fool to have been deceived by your professions.

The attentions of Leonard, and the manner in which he seemed constantly to study to promote my happiness, now really made me regard him with something like affection, and I endeavoured to resign myself to my fate, and to devote my whole thoughts and attention to him and my innocent child. But, oh! how fruitless was that task; in spite of all my efforts, the dreadful retrospection of the past would arise to my memory, and dash the cup of happiness from my lips. Was I not living a life of shame? Had I not broken through all the rules of virtue and integrity? And must I not, in future, be excluded from all respectable society—at least, where my errors were known? These painful, these overwhelming truths, were too apparent to be denied; and I shrunk aghast in the true sense of my shame and degradation.

And my poor child, too! What would, in future, become of her, when I might be no more, and she would be thrust friendless, unprotected, on the wide world? Who would assist her, or guard her from the vices of mankind, and the crafty designs of the wicked? Would her father ever acknowledge her? No! It would have been preposterous, I considered, to encourage such an idea; and how could I ever form the resolution to make her acquainted with the particulars of her origin? I could not; my heart would revolt at the task; and better, I thought, it would be for her to remain in ignorance of the melancholy and painful secret.

We frequently entered into company, and sometimes I found in it a temporary respite from the torturing cares which oppressed my mind, and entered into the spirit of the scene with more avidity and vivacity than could have been expected; but this abstraction from my sorrows lasted not long, and when I returned home, and sought my couch, racking thoughts returned with tenfold force, and all the horrors of despair kindled afresh in my brain.

About this time we received a letter from our correspondent in England, in which he informed us that a quarrel had taken place between Sir Laurence and Mirah; that they had separated, and it was unknown whither the unfortunate Mirah was gone, now that she was abandoned by him, to whom she had sacrificed her honour.

This intelligence increased my emotion, and added to the feelings of disgust which I had long entertained towards my misguided husband. I could not but view him as a heartless villain, and at first could not help invoking the curses of heaven upon his head.   *   *   *   *   *

Sir Laurence was again compelled to pause; his bosom heaved with the violence of his feelings, and, covering his face with his hands, he sighed deeply.

Eugenia went towards him, and laying her hand affectionately upon his arm, endeavoured to arouse him from his sorrows.

"Alas!" he sighed, looking up with a melancholy expression of countenance; "too keenly do I feel the justice of these reproaches, my Eugenia. I can never cease to look back upon my past conduct with shame and remorse. Poor Mirah! great as were her errors, I feel that I was more to blame than her. She could not help the fatal passion she had imbibed for me; but it was my duty to advise and protect her, and not to have suffered myself to have been made the instrument of plunging her into ruin. But what became of her afterwards? I am most anxious to know, and by what means you fell into her hands, Eugenia."

"It is indeed most extraordinary," said Eugenia; "and I am all anxiety until I hear it explained."

Sir Laurence made a powerful effort to conquer his feelings, and, having succeeded, he once more resumed the eventful narrative of the late unfortunate Lady Clara.

I felt the deepest sympathy for the misfortunes of my cousin (the manuscript went on to say), notwithstanding the guilty intercourse which had taken place between her and my husband; and most glad should I have been to know what had become of her; but I had no means of ascertaining, and I could not but apprehend the worst, knowing the complete friendless state of Mirah, and the despair to which she must be reduced. I could freely have forgiven her for all that had happened, and would have received her with compassion; for, guilty although I knew she had been, I considered that Sir Laurence was by far more deserving of condemnation; for, had he been sincere in the professions he made to me, he would have firmly resisted any allurements she held out, and, by proper advice, have saved her from straying from the paths of virtue. But now his cruel abandonment of the poor girl, showed him in the character of a confirmed libertine and sensualist; and, as I then thought, sufficiently proved that he was capable of anything that would tend to the gratification of his own vicious propensities; he cared not whether those ends were accomplished by the sacrifice of every virtuous and honourable feeling.

Sir Laurence Cleveland, should these manuscripts ever fall into your hands, which I sincerely hope they will, I am sure you will pardon the expression of my feelings, engendered in a moment of horrible excitement, and under the most painful circumstances. What other construction could I put upon your conduct at that time? Oh, may I live to see the day when I shall be satisfied that I judged you too severely, and when you may be convinced that your unfortunate wife is not altogether the guilty being you have imagined her to be.

This circumstance greatly tortured my mind for some time, and I implored Leonard's friend in the letter we sent him in answer to the communication we had received from him, to endeavour, if possible, to ascertain the fate of Mirah, and to learn whither the wretched girl had directed her steps; for I could form no idea of the course she would take, entirely without friends as she was; and I feared that in the frenzy of her despair she might be tempted to lay violent hands on herself.

How ready was I to forgive her all that had passed, and to take her under my protection, poor and questionable as it was; and Leonard expressed the same feelings, and he prepossessed me more than ever in his favour by the generous sympathy he evinced in Mirah's misfortunes. Designing miscreant! too well did he know how to play the hypocrite, and to conceal the blackest vices under the most specious mask!

All the inquiries of our correspondent to discover whither Mirah had gone, proved unavailing, for not the least clue could be obtained to her, and I more than ever suspected that she had rushed upon an untimely death.

Many were the tears I shed to her memory, and with what bitter pangs of remorse and regret did I recall the happy days of our youth to my recollection, when we were both innocent and happy, and the pride and solace, under every care, of our generous, our excellent, and affectionate benefactor!

Oh, why was that dream of halcyon bliss ever disturbed? Why had cruel fate ever introduced the too fascinating young baronet to us, and thus at once to bring about our misery and destruction?

Dreadful thoughts, poignant remorse! how fearfully did they continue to rack my brain!

How lovely did my little Eugenia every day become, and I endeavoured, in the contemplation of her beauty and innocence, but in vain, to drown the agony of my feelings. Horrible thoughts, painful anticipations, would crowd upon my brain, and at times drive me almost to madness. I thought upon what would be the future fate of that sweet child when she should haply be deprived of me. Would Sir Laurence protect her? would he act the part of a father towards her? I could not be without my misgivings, and it was not many months ere they were most fatally realized, and I was made fully aware of the character of the villain with whom I had associated myself.

Alas! how blind and infatuated I must have been not to have discovered it before! How easily had I suffered myself to be misled, deceived, by his apparent affection! I now heard that my husband had quitted Branscombe House, and it was supposed that he had gone on the Continent. This caused me some alarm, for I was fearful that accident might lead him to discover me, or that he and Leonard might encounter each other; in which case, I had every reason to apprehend the worst consequences.

I was in a constant state of uneasiness, and declined going into company any more than I could help.

Leonard endeavoured to banish my fears, but he succeeded only indifferently; and every day I looked forward to, with a feeling of dread, which I found it utterly impossible to conquer.

Leonard, however, did not relax in his pleasures, although he was unaccompanied be me; and I soon perceived a change in his behaviour to me, which caused me considerable alarm.

He became far less kind in his manners, neglected to pay the little Eugenia the attentions he had formerly done, and was more morose and reserved in his habits than I had ever before known him to be.

I questioned my own conduct, and tried to find a reason for this remarkable and painful alteration in his behaviour towards me; but to no purpose; and still I hesitated to demand an explanation from him.

As this change every day became more and more apparent, I felt truly wretched, and yet redoubled my efforts to please him, but without success. He rejected all my overtures of kindness, and seemed as uneasy in my company as he had before affected to be happy.

He would frequently leave home at an early hour in the morning, and not return till midnight, and then he would retire to bed without so much as exchanging a word with me, or bestowing one look of kindness on my poor child.

Had he then become tired of me—did he no longer love me?—Did he wish to rid himself of what he now seemed to think an incumbrance? These were the torturing questions I put to myself; and I could only arrive at the most fearful solutions. Dreadful was the agony which now settled upon my heart, and I could see that the crisis of my fate was approaching.

And what would become of me, should I be banished from his protection? I had not a friend in the world. I had no means of procuring a subsistence for myself and my child, and I must therefore become a wretched wandering outcast upon society. The thought was dreadful, and it was wonderful that my reason did not sink under such an accumulation of cares and anxieties.

And now for the first time I perceived the sin and madness I had been guilty of in throwing myself into the arms of the tempter, even surrounded as I at the time was with misery and despair. Surely this was a just punishment for me, and I had no doubt that I was yet fated to endure still more horrible sufferings.

Frequently i rayed to Heaven to release me and my innocent offspring from our troubles, an' ، were moments even when I was on the point of precipitating my fate. But some inscrutable power withheld me from the completion of my deadly purpose, and reserved me for trials far more severe than any I had hitherto undergone, great although they had certainly been.

Oh! Sir Laurence, could you then have seen your unfortunate wife, and entered fully into her feelings, I cannot but believe that you would have pitied her, though you might have shrunk with disgust from the bare idea of again taking her to your bosom.

No; I had, since my connection with the villain, Leonard, dishonoured you, and

nothing would ever have induced me to become again the partner of your bosom, had you been willing to make me so.

For many week did I endure this horrible state of agony and suspense, but without murmuring; nor could I make up my mind to seek an explanation from my guilty companion, whose conduct every day became more alarming.

Sometimes I half made up my mind to fly from him, and to leave him at once unrestrained and at liberty. I could not bear the idea of becoming a burthen to the man, who, I was convinced, no longer, if he ever, loved me; but, alas, whither could I direct my steps—where go—what was to become of me? I was lost, entirely lost, and nothing but the most abject despair opened upon my vision of the future.

It would have been a consolation to me, my poor Eugenia, had it then pleased Heaven to take you to itself, for I could not contemplate the probable wretchedness of your future fate without the most indescribable horror.   But the troubles of us both had only just began.

Leonard frequently returned home flushed with wine, and then his conduct was such as to fill me with disgust and terror.

I feared to speak to him, or even to remonstrate with him in the most gentle way; for his passions were naturally violent, and at such times they were even more alarming than usual.

I knew that he was a constant frequenter of the gambling table, and I was inclined to think that he had of late met with some heavy losses which had soured his temper; but this idea added to my fears, for I felt convinced that his unhappy propensity must lead to his ultimate ruin, and then, what indeed would become of us both, when we were left upon the wide world without resources?

Keenly indeed did I now feel my degraded situation, left entirely dependent on an abandoned profligate, who, I was now convinced, viewed me with no other feelings than those of hatred, and as a burthen that he would gladly release himself from as soon as he could.

What would I not have given could I have escaped from such a life of misery and shame; and hourly did I pray to Heaven to pardon me for the sins I had committed, and, for the sake of my poor innocent child, to interpose to save me.

But my fate was approaching to a climax.

One night I had been sitting by the side of the little cot in which my child tranquilly slumbered, watching for the return of my guilty paramour. Maddening thoughts distracted my fevered brain, and scalding tears chased each other rapidly down my cheeks, when I thought of my deplorable situation, and the little hope there was of a change for the better taking place.

To add to the gloom and misery of my mind, a violent storm had been raging all the evening, and now it had increased in fury, every clap of deafening thunder seeming to carry with it the curse of Heaven.

The hour of midnight was long past, and still Leonard came not. The most dreadful forebodings and apprehensions haunted my mind;—had something fatal befallen Leonard; or had he abandoned me altogether? The latter idea gained the most powerful ascendancy in my mind, and already the horrors of my wretched and deserted state presented themselves most vividly and irresistibly to my imagination.

I walked to the window and looked up the street, which was involved in complete darkness, for the lights had all been extinguished; but I could see nothing of him, nor hear the least sound of footsteps, for the streets were entirely deserted; and every person had sought the shelter of their own dwelling from the raging of the tempest.

I returned to the cradle of my infant, whom the battling of the elements did not disturb in the least, and again sat down in a state of the most insupportable suspense, and every moment increased the terror of the ideas which arose to my imagination.

"He will not come," I exclaimed; "oh, what has become of him?   Cruel man! surely he can never have had the heart to desert me in this manner.   If he wishes to get rid of me—to separate from me, oh, why not at once disclose his mind, and no longer keep me in this state of doubt and terror?   My poor babe!   Alas! how soon will you and your unhappy mother probably become houseless?—how soon exposed to all the horrors of the storm, without one pitying friend to afford them shelter or relief?"

My tears flowed fast, and I beat my breast in the intense agony of my feelings.

Another dismal, weary hour passed away, and still Leonard did not return. The storm had somewhat abated in fury, but the rain continued to descend smartly, and the thunder at intervals murmured in the distance.

Notwithstanding the misery of the night, I was several times inclined to venture forth in search of my guilty paramour; but I was afraid to leave my child, and I continued to pace the room in that state of anguish which only those can form an adequate idea of who have been placed in a similar situation.

Every minute appeared an hour, and I listened to the clocks with a feeling of increased despair. Two o'clock struck, and still was Leonard absent.

"I shall never behold him again," I ejaculated; and that idea, unkind as he had latterly become to me, imparted a shuddering sensation to my veins. To be left alone, in the midst of all my misery, without one friend in the world to assist me, or whom I might consult, was too dreadful even for contemplation, and once more I beat my breast in the agony of my excited feelings.

"Ah! is not that the sound of a hasty footstep in the street? It is, and it certainly is approaching the house."

Again I advanced to the window and looked out, but could perceive nothing, and all was silent.

Once more my heart sank within my bosom with a sickly feeling of despair, and I was compelled to lean against the back of a chair to support my trembling limbs.

A hasty knock at the street-door aroused me, and, with a palpitating heart, I again thrust my head out of the window, and in a tremulous voice demanded,—

"Is that you, Leonard?"

"Yes," was the stern and laconic reply; "open the door, and quickly."

Breathing a prayer to Heaven, I descended the stairs, and opening the door, gave admittance to Leonard. His face was flushed, but his lips were pale, and his eyes had such a strange and wild expression, that it terrified me to look at them.

He hurried past me without saying a word, and darting up stairs, he threw himself in a chair, and covered his face with his hands.

"Why have you tarried so long, Leonard?" I inquired, in an affectionate voice; "I have been suffering the greatest alarm, lest something should have happened to you."

"I dare say you have," he replied, in a stern voice; "no doubt you were greatly anxious about me."

"And why should you doubt that I was not so, Leonard?" I returned in gentle but reproachful accents. "But, I see you are excited. What has occurred to disturb you thus?"

"Excited!" he repeated: "yes, I am. All the devils in hell are worrying at my heart, and torturing my brain. But, to bed—to bed, and let me try to snatch a few hours of forgetfulness."

"Oh! Leonard," I ejaculated, "pray do not keep me in this dreadful state of suspense, but tell me what it is that thus agitates you?"

"To bed, I say," he cried, in fiercer tones; "this is not the time for explanation. You will know everything soon enough. To-morrow, to-morrow, but not now. D——n! I say, do not irritate me."

My heart sank within me at the ambiguity and fury of his manner, and I trembled excessively, but I feared to disobey him, and we retired to bed.

But sleep came not to my eyelids; no, it was impossible that I could sleep with such dreadful thoughts upon my mind. I almost feared that Leonard contemplated some dreadful crime; perhaps the murder of myself and child; and I lay and waited for the approach of day, in a state of mind which far surpassed anything I had before suffered.

Notwithstanding the violence of his agitation, Leonard was soon asleep; but he frequently started, and muttered some incoherent expressions, from which I was not enabled to gather anything.

I foreboded the worst, and looked forward to the approaching morning as the crisis of my fate, for I felt certain from his manner that Leonard had some horrible disclosure to make.

I lay and imagined all kinds of fearful things; sometimes I thought that Leonard had committed murder; and that idea gained such ascendancy over me, that I almost shrunk appalled from his side.

How fervently did I implore the Almighty to avert the dangers and evils which I apprehended were impending over me and my innocent child, and at once to release us from the misery by which we were now surrounded.

Never, in the whole course of my wretched life, had I passed a few hours of such dreadful agony as those I now endured. But I fear that I shall become tedious, and will therefore hasten to reveal the awful and revolting sequel to this one of the most important events connected with my unhappy fate.

The morning at length dawned, and we arose, and while I prepared the breakfast, Leonard quitted the room without saying a word to me, and entered an adjoining apartment, which I could hear him traversing with hasty and disordered steps, and talking wildly and incoherently to himself.

I awaited with the utmost impatience his return, and, when he did so, his demeanour was more calm, but still there was a certain expression in his countenance that convinced me that the storm of his infuriated passions had not abated in his bosom.

He took a chair, and for a few moments remained silent, and with his eyes fixed earnestly upon me. I fixed upon him a supplicating look, and was about to speak, which he perceiving, waved his hand authoritatively, and said,—

"No questions, Clara, for I am not in a humour to answer any such as you would doubtless put to me. My business is soon explained; the fact is, that cursed jilt, Fortune, has at length turned round upon me in real earnest, and I am ruined."

"Ruined, Leonard!"

"Aye, beggared. Last night completed the business for me. I know very well that, like the rest of your sex, you would like to read me a severe lecture on my folly and improvidence, but I am not disposed to listen to it; so you may as well save yourself the trouble, and me the annoyance."

"Alas! Leonard!" I sighed, "you have indeed been much to blame; but—but I am not your wife, and probably, therefore, have no right to reproach you. But oh, consider what I have sacrificed at your advice and for your sake, and surely you will grant me the privilege to speak. Oh, God! what is to become of us now?"

"Whining and lamentation, at any rate, will not do us a morsel of good," he replied; "and consequently we may as well not give way to any such weaknesses.

The whole of it is, it's done, and we must endeavour to make the best of it, that's all."

"There is nothing but misery before us," I ejaculated; "oh, would that me and my poor child were in our graves."

"Psha!" cried Leonard; "are you disposed to listen to reason?"

"I will listen to anything, abide by anything that reason and virtue shall approve."

"Virtue!—bah! that word comes not well from your lips."

"Oh, Leonard, and has it indeed come to this? Have I lived to be taunted by the very man for whom I sacrificed virtue and every hope?"

"Well, well," he returned, in milder accents, "perhaps I have been wrong. I did not mean to taunt you, Clara; but this is nothing to the point; it is in your power to save us from ruin?"

"Mine! mine!" I eagerly demanded.

"Yours, I tell you; it requires but another sacrifice on your part to restore me to fortune."

I looked at him with amazement, but was unable to form even the most remote idea of his meaning; but a nameless dread of something which I could not imagine came over me. He seemed to grow impatient, and eyed me with penetrating looks.

"I do not understand you, Leonard," I said at length; "you speak in problems; pray be more explicit, and do not keep me in this suspense. What sacrifice would you now have me make?"

Still he hesitated; and, rising from his seat, he took two or three hasty strides across the room.

My mind was prepared to hear something important, and yet I dreaded to listen to that which he had to propose.

Again he resumed his seat, and after looking at me stedfastly for two or three minutes, he said, in a faltering voice,—

"I will be plain, then, Clara, since you demand it; indeed, the nature of the business, and the desperate character of our present circumstances, will not admit of any equivocation. I need not remind you that my ruin must involve your own, and that of your child."

"Alas! alas!"

"That without I have the means of protecting you, you must become a wretched, houseless wanderer."

"Oh, God, it is too true—miserable being that I am; but why, oh, why remind me of this at such a time?"

"Because it is absolutely necessary to impress you with the importance of that which I am about to propose to you. Nay, I know not but that the sacrifice that I shall be compelled to make will be greater than your own."

"Why torture me thus, Leonard? For the love of Heaven, at once let me know all."

"Well, then, listen to me," he said, in a firmer voice; "and patiently too; do not attempt to interrupt me."

"Go on, go on," I ejaculated; "I am all attention."

"You know the Marquess de Chauteris, who has frequently visited us?"

"Yes, yes; what of him?"

"Curses light on him!"

"Ah! what has he done to create your displeasure?"

"Everything to inspire me with the most deadly hatred," replied Leonard; "and yet I would have you view him with a friendly eye, Clara."

"I do not understand you."

"A few words, and you will, no doubt. It is the Marquess de Chauteris who has thus effected my ruin."

"And yet you would have me view him with a favourable eye. Your words are inexplicable."

"It is the only way by which we can release ourselves from our present difficulties. To be brief, the marquess has conceived a passion for your person, Clara; and on your receiving him with favour, depends the restoration of the money which he has won from me. Do you understand me now?"

God of Heaven! how the blood froze in my veins, at this horrible, this brutal proposal; the look I fixed upon the wretch was enough to sink him into shame and degradation, had he not been totally insensible to every proper feeling. I staggered to a chair; my heart beat quick, and my face glowed with the feelings of shame and indignation.   *   *   *   *

"The inhuman, the black hearted scoundrel!" exclaimed Sir Laurence; "oh surely the words should have choked him before he could have given utterance to them. Unfortunate wife, what a terrible fate was your's, to become the victim of such a monster!"

Eugenia clasped her hands together, and could not speak for the sobs which escaped her bosom. The other persons present were deeply affected, and a pause of some minutes ensued ere Sir Laurence again found himself in a condition to take up the manuscript; which went on in the following words :—

The miscreant looked at me unmoved, and finding that I was unable to speak, he said,—

"I was fully prepared for this display of astonishment and indignation, madam; but perhaps it may be unnecessary to assure you that it will have not the least effect on me. The whole of it is, here is an offer to save us both from beggary; and, if you have the affection you pretend to have for your child, you will not reject it."

Oh, God! how shall I pourtray the horror, disgust, and indignation which swelled my bosom at this brutal explanation? Those who peruse these sad and revolting memorials will, I trust, know fully how to appreciate my feelings. For some moments I could not speak, for such were the contending passions of varied power that struggled in my breast, that they completely choked my utterance. I could scarcely believe that any being, especially one who aspired to the name of man, and who had pretended to be my protector—to love me, could have the utter heartlessness to make such a monstrous, such an inhuman proposition. But my betrayer was not the least affected by my emotion; he had evidently, as he had stated, fully prepared himself for it, and he therefore looked upon me for some minutes with the utmost indifference and nonchalance, until his patience seemed to be exhausted, and he said,—

"Come, come, Clara, these heroics are only a waste of time, and will have no effect upon me. The question is one of beggary or wealth—life or death; the sacrifice will be as great or greater on my side than your own. But, in moments of desperation like the present, we must not stand upon any particular niceties. The whole of it is, we are, as I said before, reduced to poverty; the marquess offers the means of rescuing ourselves from misery; will you, then, rather prefer that yourself and child should become wretched, wandering outcasts, or ——"

"Monster! miscreant! hold!" I interrupted, and my brain burnt with the fever of madness, shame, and disgust; "man you cannot be; fiend you are in human shape, or never could you dare to disgust my ears by such a hideous proposal. Oh, God! what a poor deluded wretch have I been to suffer myself to be betrayed by such an atrocious villain as you are. No wonder that offended Heaven should visit me and my poor unfortunate offspring with its severest wrath. Begone to your base associates, for your sight is now hateful to me, and I feel appalled while I gaze upon you. Misery the most abject—death the most horrible, will I encounter, rather than thus at once sacrifice my soul to your dreadful wishes."

"Woman!" he exclaimed, fiercely grasping my arm, and his features frightfully distorted with the inhuman passions which raged within his bosom, "I stand on the verge of a precipice, and have no time to deliberate. My fate is in your hands, and if I fall, you must also sink with me. The word at once; will you comply or not?"

"Never!" I cried determinedly, and my eyes flashed with the resentment and horror of my feelings; "by all my hopes, never!"

"Reflect, reflect; remember the consequences."

"I will brave them all."

"But your child?"

"Sooner could I sacrifice it in its innocence; sooner with my own hands could I sacrifice that life which is far dearer to me than my own, than suffer it to live to become aware of its wretched mother's shame."

"Your decided answer—quick."

"I have given it, villain!" I replied, in a voice half stifled with emotion.

"Obstinate fool! you shall dearly repent this!" cried the ruffian, and he struck me a heavy blow, which immediately felled me senseless to the floor. *   *   *

"Oh! my unfortunate, ill-fated mother," at this passage ejaculated Eugenia, unable to control the intense agony of her feelings any longer; "to what horrible sufferings were you subjected! Wonderful it is that you had strength to support such dreadful trials."

"My deeply injured wife!" said Sir Laurence, and the most torturing pangs shot through his heart; "oh! why did not Providence reveal to me the awful truth? How quickly would I then have rescued you from your miserable fate, and have taken you once more to my bosom, if you would have pardoned me that injustice I was led into the committal of through fatal error."

"Never before did I hear of such a miscreant as this Leonard," said Sir Evelyn Manners, who had listened to the extraordinary narrative with the most profound attention, and the deepest sympathy in the unparalleled misfortunes of the ill-fated Clara. "Surely the retribution of Heaven pursued him for his monstrous villany?"

"It must—it must," ejaculated Sir Laurence; "but is he still living? If so, never will I rest until I have discovered him, and wreaked my vengeance on his head. The inhuman scoundrel! my blood boils with disgust and indignation, when I think of his name!"

Amanda and her daughter expressed the same feelings, and the baronet, having in some measure regained his composure, went on with the melancholy confession in the following words:—

Happy would it have been for me if I had never recovered my senses again; for how many years of dreadful suffering should I then have been saved! but, alas! fate ordained it otherwise; I was reserved for many more painful trials."

But when I was restored to sensibility, how terrible was my anguish! I should fail were I to attempt to give anything like an adequate description of it.

My betrayer was gone, and my mind felt some relief that l was no longer appalled and disgusted by his presence. My child still slept; I went to it, kissed it frantically, and shed scalding tears of agony upon its innocent countenance. For a moment, a dreadful thought flashed upon my brain, and when I reflected on the horrible fate to which both it and myself were now exposed, I was almost tempted to end at once our wretched existence. But an all-wise Providence arrested my hand, and, sinking on my knees, I fervently implored its mercy and assistance.

But what was to become of me? Could I ever again look upon the guilty wretch who was the principal author of all my misfortunes? If I remained where I was, in spite of all my resistance, I might fall a victim to the brutal passions of the marquis. There was no misery that I might encounter which would not be preferable to such a fate. My mind was in an instant made up; I determined to abandon my guilty paramour; to escape from him while I had the power, and to brave at once the fate which might in future befall me.

I hastened to the room-door, and, gently opening it, listened attentively; but I heard not a sound, and I, therefore, concluded that there was no one in the house.

Now was the time for action; such an opportunity might never occur to me again. I returned to the room, and hastily packed up all the jewellery and money I possessed, and which was sufficient to support me for some time, and then dressed my little Eugenia, who had awoke, and was smiling upon me. I once more breathed a fervent prayer to the Almighty, and, snatching the infant to my bosom, I quitted the room, and, with trembling, but cautious footsteps, I descended the stairs, fearing every moment that I should encounter Leonard, who might not have left the house, and would thus have frustrated my design.

I soon gained the street, and, finding the coast clear, I hurried away as fast as my trembling limbs could carry me, and did not venture to stop to gain breath until I had reached the barriers of the city.

And now the most torturing thoughts crowded upon my brain. Whither could I go? Where seek a shelter or protection? The full weight of my misery rushed with overwhelming force upon my imagination, and I felt myself indeed a poor, wretched, destitute being.

I was in a strange country, with no one to assist me; nay, if I should venture to reveal my real circumstances, and the life I had been leading, what could I expect to meet with but obloquy and contempt?

I shuddered at the idea, and such was my despair, that I earnestly prayed to Heaven to release me and my child by death from our sufferings; and there were moments in which I was almost driven by frenzy to commit suicide.

But the terror of again beholding Leonard, and falling into his power, withheld me from my desperate purpose, and aroused me into action; and, in an instant, I formed the resolution to quit France altogether.

"Yes," I reflected to myself, "I will return to my native land, if it be only there to perish."

I own, too, that a thought crossed my mind which, in spite of everything, I could not help encouraging; it was, that I should again behold my husband, and that probably he would take compassion on me, and pardon me, and acknowledge his child, though he might never more consent to take me again under his protection; nor could I, after what had occurred on both sides, ever submit to become again his partner, even if he were willing.

And I was also anxious to ascertain the fate of my unfortunate, but misguided cousin, Mirah. If she were living, who were more fit to mingle their sorrows together, and to offer up to Heaven our prayers of penitence and remorse, than her and

me? I was ready to forgive her all the wrong she had done me; for, indeed, I could not but consider that my husband had been more to blame than her; for it was his duty to have sought to stifle her fatal and unlawful passion in its infancy, and not to have encouraged it, and finally yielded to its influences. And then the cruel manner in which he had abandoned her, and left her to misery and shame, was more

No. 55.

than a sufficient punishment for all the errors of which she had been undoubtedly guilty.

As these thoughts crossed my brain, I became more firm in my purpose, and committing myself to the care and mercy of Omnipotence, and pressing my poor unconscious child closer to my bosom, I made my way to the place where I could procure my passport.

This task accomplished, I walked some little distance further, and, in a retired part, where it was not likely that I should be known, I entered a *restaurateur's* to procure some refreshment, and to give myself time to compose my feelings, and collect my thoughts, so as to be able to perform the task I had allotted to myself with prudence.

It was a wonder that my agitated manner, and the tears I could not help shedding, did not attract the attention and excite the curiosity of the persons present; but they took no notice of me; and, after some time passed in this manner, I left the house, with a firmer resolution, and, having taken my seat in the diligence, was soon on my way to Calais.

It was a miserable journey to me; for how maddening were the thoughts which crowded upon my bosom; but still, when I reflected on the dreadful and revolting fate from which I had escaped, I felt somewhat more composed and resigned. I imagined to myself the fury and disappointment of Leonard, on finding my escape; and I thought the time particularly tedious until I was fairly beyond the reach of pursuit; although I did not imagine that he would take much trouble about me, fearing that he might get himself into some trouble by so doing.

In due time I arrived at Calais, and procured a passage to England without delay. It would be tedious in me to dwell upon my voyage, during which nothing worthy of noticing occurred to me, and at length, wretched and lonely, I once more trod the shores of my native land.

And now the full misery of my situation, and the wretchedness of my future prospects, rushed upon my brain with overwhelming force, and many and bitter were the tears which I shed, and desperate were the thoughts and half formed resolutions that occurred to me.

I looked around me with a despairing eye, and knew not where to go. All places were now, in fact, alike to me; for was I not a miserable, wandering outcast? Where could I turn to find assistance or compassion? I shrunk from the gaze of mankind, for I fancied that every one looked upon me with suspicion and contempt.

Oh, Sir Laurence, could you but then have beheld me, surely your heart must have been moved to pity towards me and my poor child.

I took the earliest opportunity of converting my jewels into cash; but that must soon be exhausted, and then what was to become of me? The thought was dreadful, and I almost sunk beneath the weight of it.

For two days I stopped at the place where I had landed, and endeavoured to come to some conclusion as to the course it would be best for me to pursue; but it was to very little purpose that I did so; and again I wished that the Almighty would release me and my little Eugenia from our sufferings. But, great as my troubles had hitherto been, they were comparatively trifling to those I was yet destined to undergo.

Sometimes I was half tempted to try and seek out my husband, and, throwing myself at his feet, implore his compassion for me and my child. But when I remembered the circumstances under which we had parted, and what had subsequently taken place, my heart shrunk appalled from the bare contemplation of such a step, and I resolved rather to perish of want, with my hapless babe, than to venture on such a step, confident as I felt of only encountering the hatred, reproaches, and disgust of Sir Laurence Cleveland.

At length I left the place where I had been stopping, and bent my course I know not, and cared not, whither. Three days I travelled on in this manner, living only sparingly, and stopping to rest my weary limbs at night, at the most obscure inns; and at length I found myself, to my astonishment, within only a few miles of my native place, to which my wandering footsteps had unconsciously directed me.

I hesitated, and conflicting, and almost insupportable were the feelings which rushed into my bosom, as the many events of the past vividly presented themselves to my recollection. But some powerful impulse urged me to travel on, and I did so, until I arrived in the very village where I was born.

With trembling footsteps I traversed each well-known spot, and seduously concealed my face from observation, for I was fearful of being seen by any one who might know me. But I met no one with whom I was acquainted. The place seemed entirely deserted by its former inhabitants, and the most sickening sensation of sorrow fell upon my heart.

I reached the well-known house, my native home, where I had passed so many years of happiness and innocence; what a melancholy change had come over it; I could scarcely persuade myself that it was the same place. Fresh persons, strangers to me, now inhabited it, and deep (at least to my distempered fancy) was the aspect of gloom which characterised it.

Again my tears fell fast, and I paused and rested myself against the trunk of an ancient tree, in the back of which I had, many years before, carved my name.

What numerous painful remembrances did the contemplation of this create in my bosom. That name I was now ashamed to acknowledge; and I prayed that the recollection of it might be blotted out for ever.

I wandered to the old churchyard; I sought out the tomb of my lamented uncle, and kneeling before it, implored his spirit to look down upon me with mercy and forgiveness.

I remained there until darkness began to envelope the earth, and then rambled from the village, and proceeded a distance of about three miles, lest I should be known before I ventured to put up for the night.

I racked my brain for some time in vain before I was able to come to any conclusion upon what course to pursue, as my money would soon be exhausted, and then what was to become of me and my child?

But at length I resolved to go to London. There I hoped to be able to procure some employment; and I cared not how menial it might be, so long as it enabled me to obtain an honest subsistence for me and my tender offspring.

The next morning I procured a place in a waggon that was going to the metropolis, for the coach was too expensive for my limited means, and I was very soon on my journey, with the most melancholy thoughts, for I was about to enter, as it were, upon a new world, and should be surrounded by strangers, who, probably, instead of viewing me with compassion, would look upon me with suspicion and distrust.

The waggon, on its route, passed near the mansion of Sir Laurence, and the reader may judge of my agonising emotions on again beholding it. My heart throbbed violently against my side, and I strained my eyes in the direction of the building, almost expecting, but dreading to behold my husband. And would he not pity me, I reflected, did he but know my present situation? Surely he could not refuse to acknowledge me, guilty although I had been, but still not more guilty than himself? But no; Fate had issued its stern decree, and we must never meet again; we must, if possible, cease to remember each other, only as the most perfect strangers.

The waggon passed on, and the mansion of my husband slowly faded from my sight, and then I gave up my thoughts entirely to the deepest melancholy and despair.

The journey to London was a tedious one; but, at length, I arrived there, and alighted from the waggon, and knew not whither to direct my steps.

Alas! how discordant was the gaiety and bustle, which on every side surrounded me, to my feelings. My heart sickened at the disagreeable contrast.

I was walking slowly from the coach office, when I perceived a gentleman just entering the mail; and, as he did so, something fell from his pocket, which was not observed by any one but me. I would have hastened to the gentleman, and apprised him of the circumstance, but, before I could do so, the coach was driven off, and was soon rattling over the stones with the greatest speed.

With a palpitating heart I advanced to the spot where the coach had started from, and, to my astonishment, beheld a purse lying on the pavement. I first looked around to see whether any one was noticing me, and then picked it up. The coach was now out of sight. The purse felt heavy; I hastily thrust it into my bosom, and then hurried away from the place.

When I had got into a remote corner, where there was no person near, I took the purse from my bosom, and eagerly examined its contents. You may judge of my amazement and agitation, when I discovered that it contained no less a sum than forty guineas, besides a considerable quantity of silver.

I clasped my hands together, and returned my fervent thanks to the Almighty, for it seemed that He had not deserted me in the hour of need; and my bosom felt re- lieved of a considerable portion of its weight of care.

I walked on some distance further, and then went into a small huxter's shop, per- ceiving a decent-looking elderly woman standing behind the counter, and asked her if she could inform me where I might obtain a lodging, as I had only just arrived from the country, and was a complete stranger to London. The woman could per- ceive, no doubt, from my manner, that I was not attempting to deceive her, and she, therefore, replied to me with much kindness, but expressed a little more curiosity than was agreeable to me. She said that London was a terrible place for a good- looking young woman to be in without protection, and then inquired whether my husband had not left the country.

I felt greatly confused at this question, and, for a moment or two, knew not what answer to make. I thought that the woman looked upon me with an eye of suspicion, and feelings of shame and conscious guilt swelled in my bosom.

My heart revolted at the idea of being compelled to speak an untruth, and to act the part of hypocrisy; but stern necessity has no law, and I, therefore, informed the woman, in reply to her interrogatory, that my husband was, unfortunately, no more, and that, being without friends or relations in the country, and being skilful at my needle, I had come to London with the hope of being able to procure sufficient employment for the support of myself and my child.

My appearance and manners had evidently made a favourable impression upon Mrs. Bingley, for that I afterwards discovered was the woman's name, and she, therefore, politely invited me into her little parlour, and requested me to be seated.

"Poor thing!" she said, "you are very young to be left alone in the world, without friends or relations, and with a child to support. I am myself a widow, and have been so for more than ten years, and a hard struggle I have had of it, I can assure you, what with an extravagant son, and one thing or another. I can sincerely feel for you, for you appear to have seen better days. Ah! my poor child, London is a sad wicked place, and poor people have a hard matter to make a living at all, especially females, the price of whose labour is miserably low. It may be some time before you are able to obtain employment."

"All these things I have considered, madam," I observed; "but I must trust to Providence, who, I hope, will not forsake me. I am not without a little money to support me until I may obtain employment, and, therefore, I have every reason to hope for the best. But can you inform me of any place where I may obtain a decent lodging?"

"Why," answered Mrs. Bingley, "I have a comfortable little furnished room myself to let, and if, after looking at it, you approve of it, as you seem to be a respectable young woman, I should be most happy to receive you as a lodger."

I warmly thanked the good woman, and felt extremely happy to think I should have been so fortunate as to meet with an asylum so soon.

Mrs. Bingley immediately conducted me up the stairs to the room, which pleased me much from its cleanly appearance, and, suffice it to say, that the bargain was immediately sealed, and I became her lodger from that hour. At the request of the good woman, I then joined her at her frugal repast; and, after some time passed in conversation, as I felt fatigued with travelling, I excused myself, and retired to my room.

There I fell on my knees, and with clasped hands, and tears in my eyes, poured forth my gratitude to the Supreme for the protection I had already received, and fervently supplicated His aid for the future.

Alas! I needed all the fortitude I could muster to support me in a life that was so new to me, and in which I should, no doubt, have to encounter so many struggles, in order that I might be enabled to support myself and my tender offspring with decency.

I once more examined the contents of the purse I had found, and rejoiced at my good fortune. It was indeed a treasure to me under my present circumstances, and left me no occasion to be under any apprehensions of present want, and I therefore endeavoured to look forward to the future with some degree of hope. This was, however, a task not very easy of accomplishment, and I passed many hours of the greatest melancholy and agonizing thought. I felt myself a poor, lonely, and deserted creature, shrinking from the world's scorn and reproach; and I feared what would be the future fate of my child, should fate deprive her of my protection.

Frequently were my thoughts fixed upon my husband, and many were the bitter tears those thoughts cost me. In my heart I sincerely pardoned him for the injustice with which he had treated me, and the errors of which he had subsequently been guilty; and often I was half resolved to address an epistle to him, informing him of all the unfortunate events which had befallen me since our separation, and throwing myself upon his mercy and forgiveness; but something withheld me—it was either a feeling of pride or fear, and perhaps a mixture of both.

Mrs. Bingley behaved to me with the greatest kindness; she saw that I was labouring under some secret sorrow, but she never annoyed me by impertinent questions, and I soon became as much at home with her as if we had been acquainted for a number of years.

Mrs. Bingley exerted herself very kindly and promptly in my favour, and she soon procured me some employment, and I can safely say that I never in my whole life had felt more happy than in the receipt of my poor wages, earned by my own honest labour.

In this manner several months passed away, and I began to feel more contented and happy; but vain were all my efforts to forget the past. I seldom ventured to leave the house, and as Mrs. Bingley had but few visitors, except her customers, my life was as secluded as, under the circumstances, I could desire.

Mrs. Bingley had an only son, who was a wild and dissipated young man, who had been the cause of much trouble to his mother, frequently visiting her, and compelling her by threats to contribute io his extravagant wants. I had seen him two or three times, but, disgusted with his appearance and manners, I always avoided his presence as much as possible.

It happened one evening that Mrs. Bingley, having lent me a newspaper which she had borrowed, almost the first paragraph that my eyes fell upon, was the account of a fearful duel which had been fought in France, and in which both the combatants had fallen. The reader may judge of my emotion and astonishment, when I discovered that the victims were Leonard and the Marquis De Chanteris!

Notwithstanding all his vices, and his brutal conduct towards me, I could not help feeling some degree of pity for his untimely fate; and I prayed that the Almighty would forgive him for the many sins he had committed.

" The villain !" exclaimed Sir Laurence, " had he met with an ignominious death upon the scaffold, it would have been no more than his crimes merited."

  *   *   *   *   *   *

It was some time (the manuscript went on to say) ere this event was banished from my memory; but a circumstance was about to take place, which entirely superseded every other thought.

I was seated one cold and dreary winter's afternoon in my little room, at work, when I was suddenly arroused by hearing a confused noise in the room below, and soon afterwards, by Mrs. Bingley herself, calling loudly upon my name.

I immediately hurried down stairs, and was surprised, on entering the shop, to behold Mrs. Bingley supporting in her arms the wretchedly clad form of an insensible woman, who she hastily informed me had entered the shop apparently with the intention of asking relief, and had immediately fainted away, no doubt from exhaustion.

" Poor thing, poor thing," ejaculated the compassionate woman; " how thin and wretched she looks. She must be suffering dreadfully from the effect of cold and hunger. Alas! it is a sad time for the unfortunate and destitute poor. Pray help me to take the wretched woman into the parlour."

I immediately complied with Mrs. Bingley's request, and we placed the unfortunate creature in the old arm chair before the fire. Her form was horribly wasted, and it was quite evident that want had done its work, and it seemed doubtful whether she would ever recover to sensibility again.   We immediately sent one of the neighbours for a doctor, and I then proceeded to remove her long hair from her face, over which it had fallen ; but no sooner did I behold her features, than I uttered a loud scream, and became as insensible as herself.

It was my unfortunate cousin, Mirah !

I must pass hastily over what followed.   The shame, astonishment, and horror of poor Mirah on recovering and beholding me.   She threw herself frantically at my feet, and, with a bursting heart, implored me to forgive her.   I embraced her, and could only reply by convulsive sobs and tears.

The amazement of Mrs. Bingley, on this discovery, as may be expected, was very great ; but I satisfied her by a brief account of Mirah's misfortunes, carefully concealing such facts as might tend to prejudice Mrs. Bingley against her, and likewise reveal the most painful circumstances of my own history ; and the good woman expressed the deepest commiseration ; and the satisfaction she experienced that an All-wise Providence had directed her footsteps to her own relation.

Mirah was immediately conveyed to a warm bed, and the medical man administered to her wants, but he said that her constitution was so reduced by long privation and mental suffering, that her recovery must be a work of time, and even then it would require the greatest care to restore her to convalescence.

With what anxiety and affectionate solicitude did I watch by the couch of the hapless Mirah ; and a thousand times did I thank the Almighty for making me the instrument of saving her from a horrible fate.   Sincerely did I forgive her for all the injuries she had done me ; for I was satisfied from her wretched appearance that she had already been most dreadfully punished for her offence ; and that we had both been the victims of an untoward fate, over which we had not the least possible control.

For several weeks poor Mirah remained in a most precarious state, and the doctor would not allow her to fatigue herself with talking any more than could be helped ; but my unremitting attentions, and the commisseration of Mrs. Bingley, tended more than anything to restore her, and at length she was enabled to leave her bed, and the medical man declared that all danger was past.

How fearful was the narrative we now have to relate to each other.   How bitterly did Mirah weep over my misfortunes, and reproach herself for the guilty manner in which she had contributed towards them ; but I again endeavoured to console her by an assurance of my forgiveness, and I at last succeeded better than   could have anticipated.

The story of Mirah was a dreadful one.   After she had been abandoned by S ir Laurence, she had wandered to London, where she continued to reside in a state o comparative seclusion while the money she had in her possession lasted, and had in vain tried to procure a situation, or to get some employment; and then she was, indeed, reduced to a state of the greatest misery and distress.

Her situation was most awful ; she was alone, without money, in a strange place, and without a friend to whom she could apply for aid or council; and it was therefore not wonderful that she should have taken the deplorable and shameful course she adopted.   She became the victim of a fashionable and unprincipled *roue*, who had accidentally met her, and for some time she lived under his *protection*, and endeavoured to drown the agony of thought in the artificial pleasures which her companion provided for her; but ineffectual were all her efforts; and every succeeding day made her more miserable than ever.

She was thoroughly disgusted with the life she was leading, and yet she knew not how to escape from it. She sometimes was driven to such a state of despair that she was upon the point of laying violent hands on herself, and thus at once terminating her wretched existence, but Providence arrested her hand, and reserved her to endure trials yet more severe than any she had before encountered.

Some months elapsed without any change in the situation of Mirah, when her paramour was suddenly seized with a severe illness, which entirely baffled all the skill of his medical attendants, and in little more than a week, from the time of his attack, he was a corpse.

To describe the misery and despair of Mirah, now that she was again left alone in the world, would be a fruitless task. She was once more sent forth destitute, without a home or shelter. What could she do under these dreadful circumstances?—what was to become of her?—At first she thought of seeking the baronet, and imploring his pity and assistance; but on more mature consideration, she shrunk from such a course with repugnance; her pride revolted against it, and she resolved to suffer any misery, any shame and degredation rather than submit to such humiliation, especially when she firmly believed that Sir Laurence would reject her with scorn and opprobrium. Let me pass over the career of horror into which the poor deserted girl was precipitated. The silent grave has many, many years closed over her sorsows; and, oh, may her sins be forgotten, and forgiven by that Almighty Judge, before whose awful tribunal we must all some day appear.

At length even that wretched resource failed; sickness came upon her, and after remaining for some weeks the inmate of an hospital, during which time she constantly prayed that death might terminate her wretched existence, she was once more driven homeless and penniless upon the cheerless streets.

Once she attempted suicide in the frenzy of her despair; but she was arrested in her deadly purpose, and first conveyed to a prison, and then to a workhouse; but there they refused to let her remain only a few days, and heartlessly thrust her forth to obtain her living in the best way she could.

For some time she wandered about, existing only from the scanty charity of strangers, until chance directed her footsteps to that residence where I had for so many months found a peaceful asylum.

*　　*　　*　　*　　*　　*　　*

Sir Laurence was here again obliged to pause to give vent to the powerful emotions created in his bosom, by the melancholy recital of Mirah's sufferings; and in which all his auditors so warmly participated. He could not but severely reproach himself for his past conduct, which had been productive of so much misery; and he would have given the world, had it been in his possession, could he but have recalled the fatal actions of former years. But, alas! it was useless to torture himself upon the subject, and it was only by the sincere penitence, which he now felt, that he could hope to make atonement. He again proceeded with the eventful and melancholy narrative.

When poor Mirah had concluded her sad recital, we both for some time wept our tears of commiseration upon each other's bosom; and it was a long while ere we were restored to anything like composure.

In a few weeks Mirah became resigned, if not happy; happiness, alas! under any

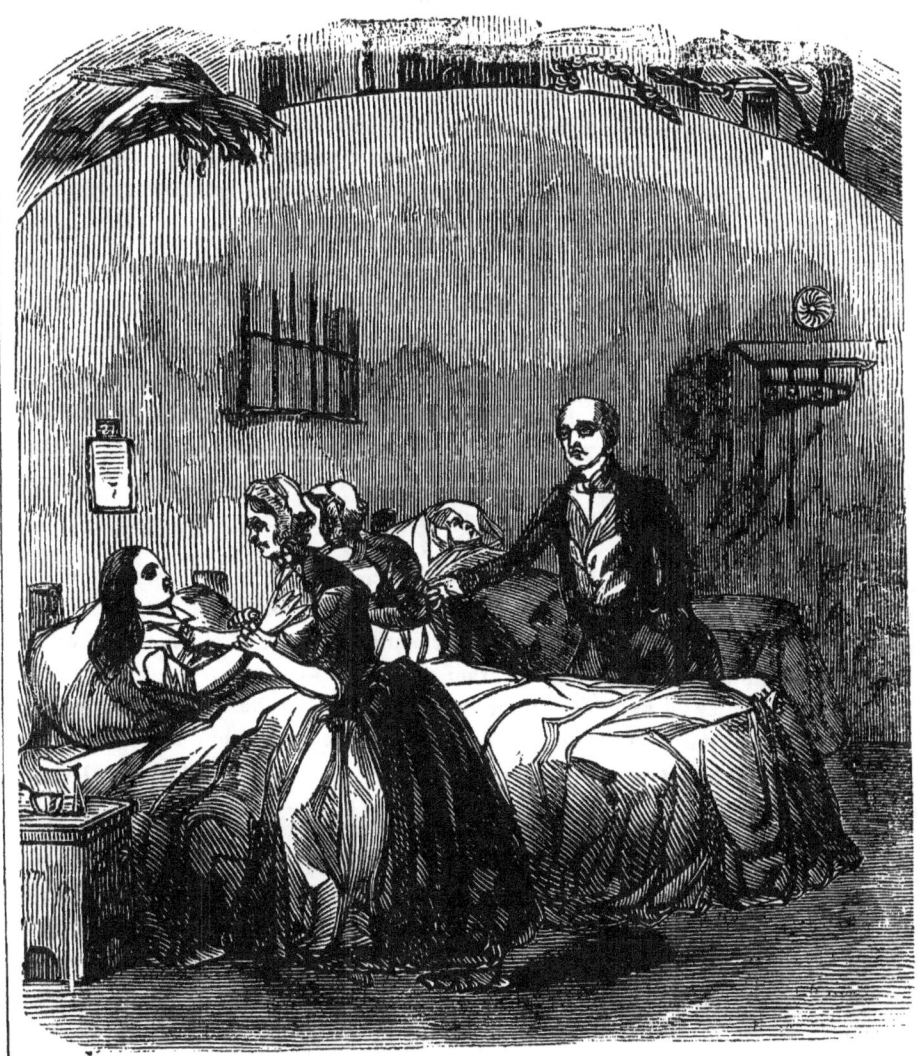

See p. 446.

circumstances, it was impossible should ever again be hers; but, for my sake, she endeavoured to appear as contented as she could.

I had enough employment for us both, and it was fortunate that I had; for the money I had had by me was entirely exhausted by the long illness of my cousin, and we had nothing but the fruits of our own exertions left to support us. We, however, gave not way to despair, and for some time nothing occurred to disturb us.

But another, and as severe a trial as any we had hitherto undergone, was in store for us.

The winter again set in, and the work we had hitherto obtained, fell off, until at last we were left entirely without anything to do.

No. 56.

And now the most terrible fears took possession of us. We had but a few shillings in the world, and when they were gone, what would become of us we knew not. We dreaded even to think; and many were the wretched days and sleepless nights we passed together, and in vain endeavours to think of some plan for the future.

Mrs. Bingley never abated her kindness towards us, and tried to inspire us with the hope that fortune would take a turn in our favour; but she was a poor woman, and unable to render us any assistance, if even she had been under any obligation to do so. We were also in arrears of rent to her, and it grieved us much to know the inconvenience that circumstance must put her to.

We were already under the heaviest obligations to her, which we were unable to repay, and therefore our present hopeless situation tortured us the more.

Mrs. Bingley also exerted herself to the utmost to procure employment for us, but without no better success than ourselves, and we therefore saw nothing but misery and actual starvation staring us in the face; and were often driven to that state of anguish as to be half tempted to abandon the house altogether.

Oh, Sir Laurence Cleveland, what must have been your feelings, in spite of the prejudice you entertained towards us, had you known the horrors we were then enduring? But our misery was not yet half complete.

Mrs. Bingley was taken seriously ill, and the doctor pronounced her life to be in the most imminent danger. This added to our alarm, and we were constantly in attendance upon her; for although we were now completely penniless, and depended entirely upon her kindness for our support, we could not think of abandoning her in her present alarming and deplorable situation.

Young Mr. Bingley visited his mother several times, but he evinced no feeling towards her, and it was even evident that he looked forward to her death with unnatural satisfaction and impatience, with the hope of becoming master of the trifling property the poor old woman was possessed of.

We also noticed that he viewed us with jealousy and suspicion; and he frequently threw out hints which fully prepared us for his future conduct.

Mrs. Bingley lingered for little more than a month, and death then deprived us of the only earthly friend we had left.

The breath was scarcely out of his amiable parent's body, when Mr. Bingley took possession of the house and his mother's property, and abruptly told us, that unless we were prepared to pay to him immediately the money we owed, we must depart; for that he did not think it prudent to lodge, rent-free, a parcel of lazy women.

What could we do? We deigned not even to reply to the heartless and brutal ruffian, but packing up what few trifling articles we possessed, we left the house, unknowing where we should again find a shelter, or how to procure a meal's victuals.

We wandered about for some time in silence and despair; for we were both of us too much oppressed with anguish of mind at our dreadful situation, to make use of any observations towards each other, or to offer any suggestion for the future.

The air was piercingly cold, and, although I wrapped my little Eugenia as closely as I could in my shawl and cloak, I could not shield her from its intensity, and for some time the poor child rent the air with her cries.

My God! I cannot even now look back at that time without a sensation of the most indescribable horror; my brain whirled round with the insupportable burthen of my cares, and fervently I wished that me and my poor child were in the cold and silent grave. Surely an all wise Providence watched over us, even in that dreadful hour of trial, and prevented us, in our despair, from rushing unsummoned into the presence of our Maker.

Mirah's agony was most horrible I knew, although she endeavoured to conceal it as much as possible, because she was fearful of imparting to me more anguish than that I was at the time enduring.

Still we rambled on, cold, silent, and despairing, until we had got some distance from the residence of the late Mrs. Bingley, when, worn out and weary, we sat ourselves down on the step of a door, and then for the first time myself and Mirah gave vent to the agony of our feelings in a copious flood of tears.

This in a trifling manner relieved us, and we endeavoured to turn our thoughts towards adopting some plan to pursue in our desperate and forlorn situation. Several persons who passed stopped to look at us, but we could see that it was only curiosity that prompted them to do so, and not from any feeling of sympathy in our evident distress and misery.

But night was approaching, and then what was to become of us? We could not remain exposed to the open air in the cheerless streets; and yet how were we to procure shelter?

Unacquainted as I was with London, and having never before been placed in such an emergency, still I had heard of such places as pawnbrokers' shops, and casting my eyes up the street, I beheld the well-known sign of one of those ruinous resorts for the wretched victims of poverty.

I had two or three articles of jewellery, of trifling value, but still they might procure us a few shillings, and I therefore conquered my repugnance, and leaving my little Eugenia in the care of Mirah, I walked towards the shop, which I entered with a timid air, and placed the articles I wished to pledge on the counter, without naming any sum as the loan which I wished to be advanced upon them.

The man looked upon me with suspicion, eyed me narrowly, and put innumerable questions to me, which, although I naturally felt greatly confused, I answered so artlessly, that his doubts at length seemed to be removed, and after examining the articles I offered minutely, he lent me much more on them than I had expected, and I quitted the shop.

My mind felt a temporary relief, now that I knew I had the means of present support and shelter, and on rejoining Mirah, we both, with tears in our eyes, offered up our humble but fervent prayers to the Almighty, and supplicated His mercy for the future.

Having walked on some distance farther, we entered a coffeeshop, where we requested to be supplied with such refreshments as we required, which was immediately served us by a clean and affable-looking woman, and the warmth of a blazing and cheerful fire imparted the greatest comfort to our shivering limbs.

It was now night, and having partaken of the refreshment, we inquired of the mistress of the shop whether she could accommodate us with a bed; and, without putting any impertinent questions to us, which would have been most annoying to us under our present circumstances, she replied in the affirmative, and having expressed a wish to retire, she immediately showed us up stairs into a comfortable bed-room, and wishing us good night, retired.

I placed Eugenia in the bed, for she had fallen asleep, and then me and my cousin sunk upon our knees, and once more poured forth our supplications to the Supreme. We then retired to bed, with a hope of gaining a short respite from our cares in sleep.

But it was not until two or three hours afterwards that our wishes in that respect were gratified.

We lay thinking upon our deplorable situation, and mingling our sorrows together. Nothing could surely be more forlorn than the difficulties we were at present placed in. Whichever way we turned our thoughts, they were met alone by misery and despair. Without friends, without advisers, to what dangers might we not be exposed? Whither could we direct our steps? The money which we now had was so small in amount that it would soon be exhausted, and then what indeed but death from want could await us?

The prospect was indeed most horrible, and might have appalled even stouter hearts than ours.

The morning found us in the same state of uncertainty and misery, and we arose with sad and bursting hearts from our bed, little refreshed.

We descended into the coffee-room, where we partook of breakfast, and the worthy hostess behaved to us with much kindness, and seemed conscious that we were the victims of some great trouble.

This idea emboldened us to speak, and at length I briefly stated to her the destitute situation we were placed in, and begged her to inform us whether she was aware of any place where we might find employment.

The good woman shook her head, and looked upon us with increased pity as she answered,—

"Alas! poor things, yours is indeed a most melancholy case, and I am sincerely sorry for you; but I know of nothing whatever, for business altogether is in a most depressed state at present in London; and it is quite dreadful to hear of the different cases of misery and destitution. Have you no friend to whom you could apply, in this, your emergency?"

I shook my head and sighed deeply, and then replied in the negative. The poor woman expressed her regret on hearing it, and after we had remained there about an hour longer, we took our departure, the kind-hearted woman not only refusing to accept anything for the lodging and refreshment we had had, but thrusting a shilling into my hand as we left the door. Many years have passed since that occurrence, but never have I ceased to remember the benevolence of that generous-hearted woman with feelings of the warmest gratitude and esteem.

Another wretched day we passed, and without being able to come to any decision; and sometimes we were wrought up to such a pitch of distraction, that we were almost induced to put an end to our earthly sorrow, by at once terminating our wretched existence; but fate ordained that a different destiny should attend us.

We had been totally regardless of the way we proceeded, and towards the evening found ourselves in a small suburban village a few miles from the metropolis.

It was very cold and cheerless, and we were tired and sick at heart with walking and thinking, and therefore resolved to seek some asylum for the night.

Observing a small, homely looking ale-house at the further end of the village, we advanced towards it, and observing the host and hostess (a comely looking couple) standing at the door, we requested to be accommodated with some refreshment and a bed.

The landlord and his wife immediately complied, and invited us into the house, where the refreshments we required were promptly placed before us. We then sat for a short time longer in conversation, and to deliberate our plans, but without being able to come to any satisfactory conclusion, and at length retired to the humble chamber allotted to us. Thus passed the second day of our dreary and miserable wanderings. That night, worn out with fatigue, we did obtain a few hours' repose; if, indeed, it could be so called, for our minds were haunted by the most frightful and torturing dreams, such as never fail to distract the imagination of the afflicted.

In the morning we again arose with sad and heavily oppressed hearts, and having partaken of breakfast, we once more left the house, but without being able to decide whither to go.

We were indeed now wretched outcasts, and it seemed of little consequence to us whither we wandered. There was nothing but the prospect of an awful and lingering death before us; why, therefore, should we continue to suffer such torture and suspense?

Leaving the village, we entered on the high north road, and then for the first time a thought occurred to me. It was that we would return to our native place, where we might still find some acquaintances or friends who would take compassion on us, and endeavour to assist us to some employment; and if not, we could but resign ourselves to our fate, lay ourselves down and die, and it would be better to perish among those who knew us, and might drop the tear of pity over our remains, than amongst strangers.

These were melancholy thoughts, but I encouraged them, and even felt a yearning anxiety to proceed on the journey as quickly as possible. Mirah, too, approved of the proposal; in fact, her bosom was entirely the abode of despair, and it was now a matter of indifference to her to what part we directed our footsteps.

It was a bold step, and nothing but the desperate urgency of our circumstances could have urged us to undertake it. Our means were indeed most limited, and the distance we were from our native place, was very great. We could not afford to ride, and it would take us several days to accomplish the journey, and our money would, in most probability, be exhausted, if even our strength did not fail us. It was a wonder that we had the courage to undertake it, but it could only have been the utter helpless and destitute state in which we were placed that could have urged us on.

And we had every difficulty to encounter with; my poor child could only walk short distances, when I and Mirah took it by turns to carry her, so that we could proceed but slowly; and that, of course, rendered the prospects of our success the more gloomy and cheerless.

It is impossible for me to do adequate justice to the almost unparalleled suffering we endured on that miserable journey. I recall it now to my mind with the greatest horror.

We were compelled to be most economical in the outlay of the scanty sum we possessed, or our money would have been expended even before we had proceeded many miles on our journey. Our meals were made in the most frugal manner, and of the coarsest kind, and at last we could not afford to pay even the paltry sum for our night's lodging, but were obliged to seek shelter in such barns or outhouses as we happened to meet on the road.

The weather was piercingly cold, and we were overtaken by several violent storms, when we were obliged to seek refuge in such places as we could find, for, to proceed through them was utterly impossible; so that all this protracted our journey to a most dreary length.

Both myself and Mirah became sick and exhausted, so that the most dreadful fears began to beset our minds, lest we should not be able to proceed much farther.

For our own parts, we could have met death with resignation, and even with pleasure, as a happy release from our sufferings; but the little innocent Eugenia! the thought of her distracted us, and made us cling to life; for what was to become of her when deprived even of our miserable protection?

Alas! it would have been a fortunate thing had it pleased Providence to have taken us all at that time, for what horrible sufferings would it have saved us!

And you, my poor child, shall I ever behold you again? Shall I ever know your fate? or will you ever peruse these melancholy lines, penned by your unfortunate mother? If so, knowing your gentle nature, which, with a bursting heart, I have watched for so many years, how copiously must your tears of anguish flow over the harrowing recital.

We had now been five days on our dreary journey, and still, so many were the difficulties we encountered in our way, that we had yet many miles to travel. It must take us many days to accomplish it, if even our strength did not sink under the task, which was not improbable, for we were now nearly exhausted.

And what prospect was there before us, even if we should reach the place of our destination? It was so long since we had left our home, that it was not improbable that we should not now find any one who knew us, or would be willing to assist us. I recalled to my memory the day when I had revisited the place after leaving Cyril Percy; all were then strangers to me; even the spot itself was so altered, that I scarcely knew it, and what, therefore, could I expect it to be now?

As these thoughts recurred to me, I own I felt greatly disheartened, and could almost have been tempted to abandon my design altogether, though we had advanced so far, that it would seem almost like madness to recede.

"At any rate," I reflected, "they cannot refuse us an asylum in the parish workhouse; they will not allow us to lie down and perish in the streets; and I will submit to any degradation to save my poor child."

Still we proceeded on our way, weary and footsore, until we found ourselves reduced to our last sixpence! My God! what a horrible moment was this. I shudder even now as I reflect on it. We had been journeying over a wild tract of country for some hours, and the night was one of the most miserable and cheerless description, until, arriving at an old ruined barn, which could only afford a partial shelter from the inclemency of the weather, I could proceed no farther, and Mirah was also very ill, and her pallid countenance plainly showed that she was suffering much more than she chose to acknowledge.

We crept into the barn, and I threw myself with my child, exhausted, on a heap of straw, which we found in one corner.

The wind howled fearfully without, and we were all perishing with the intense cold, and I felt as if I were dying, though, for the sake of my child, I struggled against my sufferings as much as possible, and Mirah lost all care about herself in her anxiety for me and my Eugenia.

At length nature could hold out no longer, and I became insensible. Would to Heaven that that insensibility had been but the prelude to death. Would that I had never awakened again to the horrors which awaited me.

On opening my eyes I looked around me in amazement and confusion; for the scene was so different that I could not understand the meaning of it.

I found myself reclining on a mattress, in a strange room, and with two old women seated on either side of me, watching me. I asked franticly for Mirah, for my child, but they only stared at me with stupefied astonishment, no doubt imagining that I was mad. I repeated my questions with more frenzied haste and impatience than before; and they then informed me that they knew nothing of the persons whom I mentioned; that I had been found alone and in a state of insensibility in the old barn, the night before, and that I was then in the workhouse.

To attempt to describe my horror and distraction would be a fruitless task; I raved like a maniac, and attempted to rise from the bed, but was forcibly held down, and again my senses left me.

It was not until some days afterwards that I learned the cause of Mirah's disappearance with Eugenia. On using all the means in her power to restore me, without avail, and fearing that I was dying, she had determined to make a desperate effort to find some human habitation where she might procure some assistance; but fearing to leave Eugenia alone with me, she had wrapped her in her cloak, to shield her as well as she could from the weather, and taken her with her; hoping to be able to return shortly.

Long she wandered, losing her way in the darkness of the night, and without meeting with any signs of a house or a human being, and her horror and alarm exceeded description.

And now she felt her strength gradually failing her, and a deathly faintness came over her, the awful harbinger of her approaching fate, when lights glimmering at a distance suddenly met her sight.

This rekindled the sparks of hope in her breast, and she exerted all her little remaining strength, and she made a desperate effort to move towards the spot from whence the lights proceeded. Even sick, weak, exhausted, dying, she urged on her way to some considerable distance; but nature could no longer struggle against her sufferings, and clasping the tender form of my poor Eugenia to her bosom, she sunk down on the cold earth, where she was afterwards found by Harold and the rest of the gipsies. But I am anticipating the events of my sad narrative.   *   *

"That part of the painful mystery then, is explained, my child," said Sir Laurence, at this part of the dismal recital, with much emotion. "That unfortunate woman whom you were led to suppose was your mother, and who perished, was the ill-fated Mirah. How wonderful are the ways of Providence, and by what miraculous measures are they brought about!"

"They are, indeed," ejaculated our heroine, deeply affected. "Poor Mirah, her's was a sad fate, and next to my mother never shall I cease to revere her memory."

Sir Laurence pressed her hand in silence, and he then read on, as follows:—

For three days I remained in a most precarious state, and hourly prayed for death, though I received every attention and commiseration from the authorities of the workhouse.

I entertained a strong opinion that Mirah had been plunged, by the agency of her despair, into the perpetration of a frightful crime, namely, the destruction of herself and Eugenia; and if such was the horrible fact, life to me would in future be a dreadful curse, a perfect hell, and the sooner I were rid of it the better.

As soon as I could find sufficient composure to do so, I made the master of the workhouse acquainted with the particulars of the disappearance of Mirah and my child, and he lost no time in taking all proper means to discover what had become of them, but without success, and my despair and agony became so great that it was thought impossible I could recover, so reduced as my frame was from my long and accumulated sufferings. But Providence reserved me for another fate. I did recover sufficiently to leave my bed, and I then insisted that I should be permitted to leave the workhouse, that I might go in search of Mirah and my child.

For some days they forcibly detained me, and endeavoured to tranquillize my feelings; but, alas, what effect could all their arguments have upon the distracted mind of a bereaved mother? The more they sought to control me, the greater became the frenzy of my fevered brain; and it is, indeed, a wonder that madness did not seize upon me altogether.

Oh, picture to yourselves—ye who may peruse these papers—what must have been my feelings at this time!

Search had been made for miles around the neighbourhood, and even a reward offered to any one who could furnish such information as might lead to the discovery of Mirah and my child; but not the least traces of them could be found, and the authorities of the workhouse began to doubt the truth of my statement, or, at least, putting the most charitable construction upon it, that my mind was certainly deranged.

I saw what their feelings and opinions were, and it added to the poignant anguish of my mind. Mirah and my little innocent, Eugenia, I reflected, were no more; and should I rest until I had satisfactorily ascertained their fate? Nature revolted at the bare idea, and again I demanded to be set at liberty.

The determination of my manner prevailed, and, after supplying me with a small sum of money, they allowed me to depart.

Never shall I forget the frantic agony of my emotions on leaving the workhouse. I rushed wildly to and fro, not knowing whither I went; I called loudly on the name of Mirah—of Eugenia; in fact, I acted the part entirely of a mad woman; and, no doubt, I created much astonishment and alarm in the bosoms of many of the persons who beheld me.

At length I found my way to the old barn in which we had sought a shelter from the inclemency of the weather, as though, even after the lapse of so many days, I should be likely to discover them there. I beat my breast and tore my hair at its lonely and deserted appearance; and then I sunk down on my knees, and, with clasped hands, and a voice hoarse with the agony of my feelings, I implored the mercy of the Supreme, and supplicated the restoration of my child, or that immediate death should overtake me.

Then I again wandered on, venting my sorrows on the open air.

In this manner I continued rambling wildly about, and scarcely ever stopping to rest myself during the whole of that wretched day. But my mind was so disordered that I took no direct course, and merely made a circuit of the neighbourhood of the old barn.

Often was I on the point of laying violent hands on myself, but some inscrutable power withheld my hand, and saved me from adding another crime to my other offences.

The darkness of night overspread the earth, and I then found myself in a wild part of the country, with no signs of a human habitation near.

I now paused, and looking around me, for the first time began seriously to consider what I had better do. Mirah and my child seemed lost to me for ever, and such was

the weight of despair upon my heart, that I could willingly have laid myself down and died; but such was not to be my fate at present.

Once more I resumed my dreary ramblings, reckless whither I went, and occasionally, in the bitter anguish of my feelings, venting curses on my hard fate, and deprecating the dispensations of Providence.

All kinds of frightful conjectures tortured my brain. That Mirah should have deserted me, and taken my child with her, in such an hour, was a circumstance I could not in any way account for; and sometimes I denounced her as cruel and deceitful, and invoked the heaviest maledictions upon her head; but in my calmer moments I reproached myself for it, and endeavoured to persuade myself that she had acted from the best of motives, but that some fatal accident had befallen her and Eugenia, and that they had both perished,

But it is useless for me to attempt to describe all the agonising and conflicting thoughts which racked my fevered brain, and which continued to gain strength as I proceeded.

Still I went on, and the aspect of the country remained as cheerless as before, and it appeared to me as if I had wandered into some wild and uncultivated spot, where human foot had never before trod. I cared not, for all places were alike to me now.

Suddenly, while I was absorbed in these dismal reflections, I beheld lights glimmering at a distance, and I then supposed that I was approaching the abodes of humanity. And, at that moment, a powerful feeling of hope sprung up in my hitherto lonely and wretched bosom. It seemed to whisper to me that some important revelation was at hand. I quickened my pace, and the broad glare of what appeared to be fires, was now revealed to me more distinctly.

This cheered me on; and now the features of the country were changed, and, in place of wild and uncultivated nature, whose very aspect was enough to inspire the mind with gloom and horror, under any circumstances, I found myself surrounded by scenery of the most romantic and picturesque description.

At last, I found myself on the borders of a valley, from which the glare of lights I had first perceived proceeded, and a gipsy encampment met my view.

I hesitated to proceed, for I apprehended that I should meet with little hospitality from these rude and lawless people, and, probably, I thought that I might be subjected to some outrage; but my limbs trembled beneath me with fatigue; I required rest, and I, therefore, determined to run every risk, and to implore the pity and assistance of the wandering tribe.

I began to descend into the valley, when my head became giddy; my limbs tottered under me, and, sinking on the earth, all consciousness left me.

On recovering my senses, what was my unspeakable astonishment on beholding Harold and Madela (in whom I immediately recognised Walter Alston and his mother) bending over me! I must leave the reader to imagine the tumult of emotions which rushed through my bosom.

Madela and her son scowled upon me, and I could perceive too plainly that I had little to expect from their pity and mercy. My mind was filled with dread, and, clasping my hands vehemently together, I tried to give utterance to my feelings, but my tongue refused its office.

"So, deceiver," exclaimed Walter, in a hoarse, unfeeling voice, "fate has at length placed you in the power of him whom you deserted to become the bride of the villain who made me what I am, and consigned my aged father to an ignominious death? Oh! but this is a gratification to my revenge which I have long hunted for in vain, and it shall be my fault if I do not take advantage of it."

"Spare me—spare me, Walter!—mercy—mercy!" I cried, sinking on my knees.

"Mercy!" shrieked the old woman, and her eyes glared with the intensity of her feeling; "wretch!—abandoned prostitute! what mercy can you expect from us? Had it not been for you, should we not now have been comfortable, happy, and respectable, instead of the despised and wretched wandering outcasts that we now are? Oh! I could wreak my vengeance in your blood, but that we have years of torture— of shame, and degradation, in store for you!"

" For the love of God, do not reproach me thus !" I rantically exclaimed. " Oh, you know not what a miserable wretch I am, or surely you—even you—would pity me. Suffer me, I beseech you, to depart, and ——"

" Depart!" interrupted Walter, with a fiendish grin; "fool! think you we are mad, to part so easily with that which we have long been so anxious to get in our power ?—Suffer you to depart, to betray me into the hands of justice, and consign me to the hands of the hangman? Never—never! We have you now, and you leave us not again."

" Oh, Walter! surely you cannot have become so entirely lost to every feeling of humanity?" I ejaculated, still remaining on my knees, and looking up imploringly in his face; " I will never betray you—I will never reveal to any one that I have seen you, or that I know you are still in existence. Put any oath, however horrible, to me—I am ready to swear I will not."

" I dare say you are," returned the ruffian, with a malicious smile; " but we happen to know you before to-day, and will, therefore, take good care to make security doubly secure."

" Heaven preserve me !" I frantically cried. " You will not surely do as you say ?"

" You will soon have good reason not to doubt our promise," returned Madela.

" Monsters !" I screamed, starting from my knees with the air of a mad woman ; and, indeed, delirium had partly seized upon my brain; " you shall not—you dare not detain me! you shall not prevent me from going in search of my poor lost child !"

" That child, the detested offspring of Sir Laurence Cleveland, is at our mercy," said Walter, with a look which I can never forget.

" No, no, no !" I exclaimed, and I fixed my eye full upon him, as if I would penetrate to his very soul; " you can have no power over my poor innocent; she is lost —lost, and therefore has, at least, escaped your murderous hands."

" Ha, ha, ha !" laughed the savage villain; " how greatly are you mistaken; even now, this very moment, if we were so disposed, could we embrue our hands in the blood of your bantling."

" How--how ?" I gasped forth, and my heart palpitated so violently against my side, that it seemed as if it would burst its tenement. " Many days ago Mirah deserted me, taking my child with her, and it was in going in search of them that I fell into your power."

" And what if we tell you that Mirah is dead ?" demanded Madela.

" Dead—dead! How know you that? But it is false! You only make these statements to torture me."

" Would you have proof that we do not ?" demanded Walter, whom I will henceforth call by his assumed name Harold.

" Yes, yes," I answered, eagerly ; " but you cannot give them me."

" But three days since, Mirah breathed her last."

" My God—my God! is it possible? But—but how know you this !"

" She died in our presence."

" 'Tis false!"

" Fool"

" Where are your proofs ?"

" She lies buried even near this spot."

"For the love of Heaven!" I gasped forth, in a voice almost stifled with emotion, "tell me, do you speak the truth?"

"We do."

"And my child! my child!"

"Lives."

"Lives—lives! Almighty God, I thank thee! But where?"

"Behold her!" cried Madela, who had retired to another tent which communicated with the one we were in, and the next instant my child, my little Eugenia, was clasped to my throbbing bosom. The surprise was too much for me; I covered the face of the child with my kisses, and then, with an hysterical laugh, I fell insensible upon the earth.

I had remained in a state of unconsciousness for several days, for, on my recovery, I found that the gipsies had left the valley, and had now taken up their abode in the old abbey ruins.

I was confined in one of the apartments which had fallen the least into decay, and, on regaining my senses, found myself attended by one of the female gipsies.

At first I had but a shadowy recollection of what had happened, but at length the whole important truth flashed upon my memory with the speed of lightning, and, starting up wildly from the rude pallet on which I found myself reclining, I hastily demanded where they had taken my child, and invoked the heaviest curses upon their heads, if they longer detained her from me.

The woman quitted the room immediately, without returning me any answer, and shortly afterwards Madela and Harold entered.

"My child!" I cried, in frantic accents, and I could feel the blood boiling within my veins, while I fancied myself at the time imbued with more than human strength. "Where is my child? Monsters! you dare not—shall not keep her from me!"

"Come, come," returned Harold, coolly, "these heroics are all in vain, and therefore you might as well spare yourself the trouble of giving utterance to them."

"My child!" I repeated, in more frenzied tones than before—"give me back my child, or may the curses of outraged Heaven descend upon ye!"

"Beware!" said Madeline; "lest you provoke that dreadful revenge it is in our power to take."

"Wretches! ye have murdered it. Oh, could not even its innocence stay your cruel hands?"

"Bah!" cried Harold; "what a headstrong fool [is this. She seems resolved to provoke her own fate, and that of her hated brat. We will leave you, madam, until you have become more cool, and learned a little wisdom."

"No, no," I ejaculated, alarmed by his manner; "oh, if you have but one spark of humanity left within your breasts, have mercy upon me. Keep me not in suspense, I beseech you, but tell me, where is my poor innocent babe?"

"The brat is safe enough," replied Harold; "but, on your uncomplaining submission to our will, depends its life."

"What mean you? You will suffer me to depart with my offspring?"

"Never! Henceforth you must never leave us, but bind yourself by oath to keep our secret, to reveal not to Eugenia that you are her mother without our permission and to aid us in our plans of vengeance against the detested Laurence Cleveland. The child already, as well as its age will allow it to comprehend, believes you dead, and you must never more behold each other in your present character."

"Oh, spare me! spare me!"

" We think we show you much more mercy than you deserve, or have a right to expect," returned Madela.

" There is only one condition on which you and your child will be again permitted to see each other."

" Name it," I eagerly demanded; my mind at the same time worked up to a pitch of almost insupportable anxiety.

"It is," replied Harold, "that you both assume male attire, and know each other only as Azrah and Rosario."

" Oh, God!" I exclaimed, "my heart is revolting at the bare idea! What a monstrous, what an unnatural proposition is this."

"It may be so, in your idea," remarked Harold, coolly; " but you must submit to it, nay, bind yourself by oath to comply with it, and never to reveal yourself to any one, without our permission, for on that alone depends the life of your child."

"Oh, for pity's sake!"

"Nay, you have heard our determination; are you ready to comply with it?"

" Are there no other conditions?" I asked, in despair.

"None. Quick! the word! We are not disposed to parley."

"Heaven help me!"

"There! enough of preaching. Do you consent? or will you rather behold your offspring sacrificed?"

"Oh, you dare not commit so hideous a crime!"

"Indeed! you had better not brave us to it."

"Recollect its innocence."

"Bah! The word at once, without any more of this nonsense."

" Reflect—reflect!"

"It requires no reflection; our minds are made up, and you know the consequences of disobedience; if you do not avail yourself of the offer which is now made you, the blood of your child, whom you profess to love with such maternal affection, will be upon your head."

" Oh, monstrous!"

" Will you submit?"

What was I to do? Any person who reads these lines, must, I am certain, commiserate the horrors of my situation. I knew well, from their observations and their manners, that they would not fail to put their threats into execution; I saw that there were no means of escaping from them, and of saving my poor child, and, therefore, the only alternative left me, fearful as it was, was obedience. The pangs which shot through my heart in those few moments which I paused to reflect, I cannot describe; while Madela and Harold stood by and watched me with the greatest impatience.

" But when shall I see my child?" I at last inquired.

" As soon as you are sufficiently recovered and collected to do so," was the answer; " but only in the disguise we have mentioned, nor must you ever, at any future period, give her reason to suspect your real character. Remember, that her death would most immediately and inevitably follow."

" For the love of God, relent."

" Pshaw! we have nothing at all to do now with that Power to which you appeal. At once decide; we have already delayed too long."

"And will you swear that no harm shall come to Eugenia if I consent?" I demanded.

"We will promise; and that is enough," answered Harold; "we have more to gain by her living than her death."

"What mean you?"

"Vengeance!"

"Against whom?"

"Sir Laurence Cleveland."

"Ah! to what lengths may your dark passions tempt you?"

"Would you spare him? Do you not curse him?"

"No, no; deeply as he has wronged me even, I cannot."

"Idiot! but we waste time; the oath! are you ready to take it?"

"And I shall see my child?"

"Yes, yes; we have told you so."

"You will not separate me from her?"

"Not while you act in obedience to our will."

"And," I added, in a hesitating voice, and the crimson blushes mantled in my cheeks, while I gave utterance to the words so revolting to my feelings; "and you, Walter, will you promise me not to take any brutal advantage of your having me in your power? That—that you will not remember the former passion that existed between us?"

"Between us!" repeated Harold, with a savage frown, and biting his lips; "but, no matter, I will remember it only with hatred. No, no; time and circumstances have entirely changed the current of my feelings. I live only for revenge. In respect to that to which you have alluded, you will have nothing whatever to fear from me."

"But, I and my child will be deprived of our liberty," I said.

"Liberty!" repeated Harold; "what greater liberty can there be than that which you will find in the gipsy's life?"

"But the disguise you would have me and my poor Eugenia assume—oh, my heart revolts from it."

"Bah!" cried the ruffian, impatiently, "I am sick of this hesitation. You ought to be grateful to me for the mercy I show you."

"Mercy!" I sighed.

"Aye; can you call my leniency by any other name? Had I suffered my most deadly vengeance to prevail, I should have sacrificed your brat, the offspring of that hated individual, from whom I have experienced the greatest injury and injustice, the moment it fell into my hands."

"Oh, dreadful!" I ejaculated; "you surely could not have been so lost to every feeling of humanity as to sacrifice the life of that innocent being, who certainly has never done you any injury."

"Humanity! what have I now to do with the feeling? Have not your deceit, and the villany of that man to whom you gave your hand after it was solemnly pledged to me, entirely estranged me from it? Am I not a poor, proscribed, despised, wandering wretch, with the stigma of a murderer resting upon my name? And all this has been your doing, and that of the miscreant, Sir Laurence Cleveland."

"Oh, Walter," I cried; "I own that I have wronged you; but I was myself deceived. Think how severely I have been punished."

"Punished! Oh, not one-half so severely as you deserve to be. But again I say, this is a waste of time—the oath."

"Ay, the oath," ejaculated old Madela; "no more of this idle twaddle; but let her decide at once, or the child perishes."

"Give me, I implore ye both, some little time to reflect."

"Not an hour," was the reply; "our minds are made up, and you know the consequences. If you regard your bantling, as you profess to do, you will not hesitate a moment."

"And must I then be compelled not to acknowledge my own sufferings?" I cried.

"You must not."

"And she must be compelled to assume a character, which, when she arrives at years of knowledge, must be so repugnant to her feelings?"

"Even so."

"And to be brought up in the midst of vice, to have her mind corrupted, and probably to be made a disgrace and alien from society, when she might otherwise have been an ornament to it."

"If you will have it so," answered Harold, with a look of malicious triumph.

"Fearful idea! Is there no way of saving her from so dreadful a fate?"

"None."

"Oh, God! that cruel fate should place us in your power. Better would it have been for us had we both died."

"Ah, but fate reserved ye both to gratify my vengeance."

"Alas! alas."

"Do you still hesitate?"

"Heaven have mercy on me, and teach me how to act," I exclaimed.

"No more of this whining cant. You have heard our will. Nothing can move us from it, and you must submit to it, or take the consequences."

"Indeed!" I sighed; "I see that it is useless to appeal to you, for you have now become insensible to every feeling of pity."

"Pity! Why should we pity one who has so deeply wronged us — who has plunged us into crime, and rendered us what we are?"

"Deeply do I repent my behaviour towards you, Walter."

"And of what avail is your penitence?" demanded the ruffian, fiercely. "Can it recall the past? Can it replace me in that society which I never disgraced, until you and Sir Laurence Cleveland, by your base treachery, blasted all my hopes for ever, and drove me to desperation? Can it restore to life that aged man, my father, who perished on the scaffold, for a crime of which he was innocent? Talk not to me of pity and compassion, lest you excite me to greater severity. I offer to show you more mercy than you deserve. Beware how you reject it, for, by every power of darkness, the consequences will be even more horrible than you can now form the least conception of. Again I command you to take the oath, or before the sun sets this evening, you shall behold the mangled corpse of your child, and even then you shall not escape from our power, but shall be subjected to still greater punishment than that we now intend you, for your obstinacy."

I clasped my hands together in agony and despair, and for a few moments I was so overpowered by my emotions that I could not return any answer. Useless I saw it was for me to attempt to persuade the wretches to relent, and yet how my heart revolted at the idea of binding myself by oath to such a course! Still there might be some opportunity present itself of my escaping with my child from their power, and that hope stimulated me to accept the painful alternative.

"Come, decide at once," passionately demanded Harold; "do not attempt to trifle with us, for you will find that we are resolute."

"Alas!" I returned, "I have too much reason to believe you."

"Then it requires not a moment's consideration on your part to decide in which manner it will be most prudent for you to act."

"But once more I implore you to tell me whether it is your intention to separate me from my child?"

"It is not, if your conduct does not urge us to it."

"And must I not indeed acknowledge her?"

"We have told you so."

"Oh, have you no regard for a wretched mother's feelings?"

"None for the discarded wife of the detested Sir Laurence Cleveland. We show you more mercy than you merit, by permitting you to be near your child."

"It is a dreadful alternative," I said, after a pause; "but Providence, I trust, will not entirely desert me, and—and I submit."

"'Tis well for you that you do," said Harold.

They then administered to me a horrible oath, which I repeated after them, with trembling lips. The excitement of the moment was too much for me, and I had no sooner given utterance to the words than I fainted away.

When I was restored to sensibility, I found myself alone; but the fearful and torturing recollection of all that had taken place immediately flashed upon my brain, and I groaned in the anguish of my feelings. I lay for some time, in this wretched state, but at length I struggled with my emotions, and arose from my bed, but found to my dismay, that my own clothes were removed and replaced by male apparel. What disgust and indignation swelled my bosom at this discovery, and how bitterly did I weep when I reflected on the misery and utter hopelessness of my situation, and it was some time before I could form the resolution to assume the revolting disguise. But I saw it was useless to struggle against my fate, and the thought of again beholding my child urged me on. I dressed myself, and covering my face with my hands, I sat myself down, and gave way to the torturing feelings which distracted my bosom.

At length I somewhat aroused myself, and hastened to the door, with the determination of venturing into the presence of the gipsies, and again endeavouring to behold my Eugenia. But the door was locked, and I could, therefore, only endeavour to wait with patience until my cruel enemies should choose to release me.

I once more threw myself in a chair, and gave unrestrained indulgence to my agonized feelings. I now felt myself truly wretched and degraded, and thought that it would have been much better for both myself and my unfortunate offspring had we perished, rather than to become subjected to our present awful fate.

At length I heard footsteps approaching the room in which I was confined, and my heart leaped within my bosom. Immediately afterwards the door was opened, and Harold once more stood before me.

He eyed me with a savage expression of triumph, and, covered with shame, disgust, and confusion, I averted my face, and the most convulsive sobs escaped my bosom. It was evident my misery afforded the heartless ruffian the greatest gratification, and he continued to gaze upon me with the dark malice of a fiend.

See p. 678.

Oh, what an alteration had time and circumstances effected in that man, on whom I had once placed my affections. It was scarcely possible to imagine that he was the same individual; surely I had myself principally to blame for this melancholy alteration. Had I remained faithful to him; had I never suffered Cleveland to seduce my affections from him, he might still have been the same honest and worthy being that he was when I first knew him. And I did indeed reproach myself bitterly for my past conduct, and would have given the value of worlds, had I it in my power, to have recalled it. But it was too late, and nothing could excuse the brutality with which Harold and his mother now acted towards me.

"Admirable!" exclaimed my tormentor with a savage grin, and still surveying me with rude and vulgar boldness; "you have but to stain your complexion, and get rid of some of these flowing tresses, and then you will look the character you have assumed to perfection. Ha, ha, ha! Who would ever have thought to have seen the once beautiful, modest, and delicate Clara Roseburn in such a disguise?"

"Hard hearted man," I ejaculated, tears starting to my eyes; "is it not enough for you that you have me in your power, and have made me submit to your villanous plans, but that you must mock me thus? Oh, Walter, whatever may have been my conduct towards you, I have deserved not this."

"Not deserve it!" he repeated; "oh, but you have, and more, much more. You now, I hope, experience some of the torture, the shame, and the self-degredation that you and Sir Laurence Cleveland have inflicted upon me."

"Almighty God!" I exclaimed; "have mercy on me, and rescue me and my child from the power of this monster."

"Beware what you say, or I will invent such additional tortures for you, that you can now little anticipate. As for your escaping, it is useless for you to entertain any such idea. You are as secure with us, as if you were buried deep in the bowels of the earth."

"Alas, alas! that it should be so," I sighed. "But be satisfied, I implore you, Walter, with what you have already done, and ——"

"Satisfied!" he fiercely interrupted; "oh, no; this is but a commencement to the business; never shall I be satisfied, until I have fully gratified my vengeance, not only against you, but Laurence Cleveland. Oh, I will hunt him down as I would a ravenous wolf, and invent such tortures for him as the imagination can little conceive. He shall learn to feel and dread the power of the outcast Walter Alston, whom he now supposes to be lingering out a life of slavery and ignominy in a foreign land."

"Cruel man, will nothing move you to relent?"

"Nothing. My soul thirsts alone for revenge—deadly, implacable revenge; and I will not hesitate at the perpetration of any crime to obtain it."

"But my child," I cried; "oh, let me once more behold and embrace my innocent offspring."

"Not so fast," said the ruffian, coolly; "all in good time, all in good time."

"Oh, God! you surely will not be worse than your word? You cannot surely take delight in torturing me thus?"

"It will be as well for you not to be too impatient," returned Harold, "for it will have no effect upon me. You must await my pleasure."

"Miscreant! you have deceived me!"

"And if I have, it is only fair retaliation," he replied, with a malicious grin.

"Oh, Heaven, give me patience!" I cried, wringing my hands. "Monster, let me hasten to my child; you shall not, dare not keep me from her."

"Dare not! Ha! ha!"

"You still mock me! Fool that I am to be thus betrayed."

"And how could you help yourself?"

"Mercy! mercy! Walter!" I once more ejaculated, sinking on my knees, and looking up in his face with an expression which might have moved the most inflexible heart to compassion; but he eyed me only with a look of triumph.

"You may as well compose yourself," said Harold, at length; "for until you have done so, I shall not permit you to see Eugenia."

"Oh, I will be tranquil," I replied; "I will not say a word, or do anything that can offnd you; but keep me not in this horrible state of anguish and suspense, or I shall go mad."

"Then I will leave you for a day or two to cool yourself," said the heartless villain; "and perhaps by that time you may find yourself more at home in your new character."

"Oh, no; you cannot be so entirely lost to all feeling."

"I do not pretend to possess any," he answered."

"Ah! you have deceived me—cruelly deceived me. Idiot that I was to trust to you; I could expect nothing less. You have murdered my poor innocent child. Your words convince me that you have, and may the curses of Heaven descend upon your guilty head."

"Restrain your curses," replied Harold, "for they are useless. Your brat still lives, but it depends upon your own conduct when, or if ever, you shall behold her again."

"I will do all—I will do everything you require; but do not keep me from her. Oh, why should you do so, since I have acceded to your will, and have promised not to reveal myself to her until I have your permission so to do?"

"To-morrow, if I find you more collected, I will suffer you to do so," answered Harold; "but everything depends on that."

"To-morow!" I screamed; "oh, no, I cannot wait till then; drive me not entirely to distraction."

But he heeded not my agony; he only mocked my supplications to scorn, and thrusting me aside, he quitted the apartment, and fastened the door after him.

My mind was now more distracted than ever. I could not contain myself within the bounds of anything like reason. I threw myself on the floor, and rolled about in the very agony of despair, then I rent the place with my cries, and acted altogether the part of a maniac. It might have melted the sternest heart to pity to have seen me.

Never can I forget the horrors of that day and night. It was a wonder that my strength did not sink under the weight of such accumulated sufferings. To sleep was impossible, and I continued to traverse the apartment the whole of the night, calling upon the Almighty to look down with pity upon me, and not to try me beyond the strength of human nature to endure. Oftentimes I threw myself against the door to try to burst it open, but what would have been the use of that, even if I had succeeded? It was not likely that I should have been able to have seen my child, and it was only more than likely that I should incurred the most deadly vengeance of Harold.

The next morning came at last, and found me in the same state of distraction, or notwithstanding the promises of Harold, hope had failed to enter my bosom; and the thought then occurred to me that I was only retarding the gratification of my wishes by thus giving way to my emotions, and I made an effort to compose my feelings, but with little oa no effect.

Eagerly I watched the appearance of Harold; but two hours elapsed, and no one came near me, and thus was my anguish increased to an almost insupportable degree At length, however, I heard footsteps ascending the ruinous stairs which led to my apartment, and my heart palpitated with hope and expectation. But, alas! how soon was I doomed to be disappointed. The door opened, and instead of him

I

expected to see, one of the gipsy women made her appearance, bringing with her some refreshments, which she placed before me, and was then about to retire without saying a word, but I sprang towards her, and grasping her arm, in a frantic voice implored her to have pity on me, and to tell me where Harold was, and what had become of my child.

The woman viewed me with perfect indifference, and was not about to return me any answer, only I renewed my questions with tenfold vehemence and distraction of demeanour, and she then merely said that Harold was in the ruins, but, as regarded the child, she was not permitted to answer any questions respecting it.

In vain I supplicated her, with tears in my eyes, and frenzy in my manner; she was insensible to pity, and tearing herself away from me, she hurried from the room, and shut and fastened the door after her.

I threw myself on my knees, and for some minutes I became completely lost in the horror of my feelings.

Had I had the means at hand, I should undoubtedly, in the distraction of that moment, have committed suicide; but it was not to be; and great, indeed, as were my sufferings at that time, I was reserved to endure others, if possible, still far more severe.

The next morning dawned, and I awaited with the utmost impatience and anxiety the result.

The woman did not appear as I had expected she would have done, and as hour after hour elapsed without any one coming near me, I began to think that I was abandoned altogether.

I listened with breathless attention to catch every sound, but all was perfectly still in the ruins, and therefore I supposed that the gipsies were away.

I walked to the casement of my gloomy chamber, and looked out; the scenery commanded from it was romantic and picturesque in the extreme, and, under any other circumstances, would have excited my warmest and most enthusiastic admiration; but all now appeared dreary and cheerless to my jaundiced eye.

I continued at the window for some time, entirely lost in the torturing perplexity of my own thoughts, and gazing with a vacant eye upon all that it encountered. But at length my attention was arrested by an approaching object. It was Harold.

I threw myself on my knees, and fervently I supplicated the Almighty to move his stubborn heart to compassion towards me.

I was still in this posture, when I was aroused by hearing footsteps ascending the stairs which led to the apartment in which I was confined.

My heart throbbed with expectation; I started to my feet, and tried to assume as much composure as I could, in case it should be Harold. My expectations were not disappointed, for immediately afterwards the door was opened, and the ruffian presented himself.

He gazed at me steadfastly for a few moments, and a grin of malicious satisfaction overspread his now forbidding features.

"Well, Azrah," he said in sarcastic tones: "I am glad to see you looking the masculine character so well. Ha! ha! ha! who would imagine that the individual now standing before me was the once fair and seducing Clara Roseburn, the scornful beauty who presumed to think that the honest Walter Alston was unworthy of her hand?"

"Mock me not, Walter," I replied, my bosom swelling with indignation; "have you not already tortured me enough?"

"No," he returned; "there are no tortures that I can invent, that would be sufficient to punish you for your conduct towards me. But I triumph; I have you and your brat in my power, and that, at any rate, is some satisfaction to my feelings of revenge."

"Oh, Walter," I cried, clasping my hands vehemently together in anguish; "I implore you not to keep me in suspense, but to suffer me again to behold my child, and I will pardon you everything."

"Pardon me! ha! ha! ha!" laughed the villain; "most gracious truly. However, I am inclined to yield to your request, since you have taken the oath which binds you to my will. Remember, if you do not faithfully adhere to that you have pledged yourself to, the life of your Eugenia will be immediately sacrificed. It will be madness for you to contemplate any disobedience to my will, and I therefore warn you in time."

"Oh, Walter," I returned, "hard and cruel as the promise is you have extorted from me, I will faithfully adhere to it, if you do not deprive me of the consolation of at least beholding my poor child."

"I have promised you, on certain conditions," replied the villain; "and, although you merit it not, I will not fail to keep my word. Banish your emotion, and follow me."

I did, indeed, make a powerful effort to conquer my emotions; but my heart was ready to burst.

Harold led the way to another room, in which was Madeline and my child; but, oh, how metamorphosed, how pale and wan were her cheeks; she gazed at me, but she knew me not.

Yes; I again beheld my child; but I was not permitted to embrace her or to speak to her. Heaven only knows how I withstood the anguish of that meeting; but still I felt grateful that her life was preserved, and, when I was ordered to withdraw, I returned to my own apartment, and, throwing myself in a chair, endeavoured to reconcile myself to my fate.   *   *   *   *   *   *

Years flew by, and Sir Laurence Cleveland returned to England, and then I hear, of his intended marriage with Blanche Lester. Need I attempt to describe the anguish of my feelings? I had long since pardoned my husband in my heart, and I pitied and esteemed Blanche Lester; for I knew she was amiable, and I shuddered at the misery in which she would be plunged by her union with a man on whom she could have no lawful claim. I implored Harold to suffer me to save her, but he threatened me with the most dreadful vengeance if I attempted to betray the secret; and the union was suffered to take place, and my oppressors exulted in their triumph.

I have but a few words to add to my dismal narrative. The events which transpired will be generally known; the escape of Eugenia at last determined me to run every risk, and, searching out Sir Laurence Cleveland, to throw myself at his feet and reveal everything. God of Heaven! give me strength to accomplish my object, and let me again behold my beloved Eugenia, ere I close my eyes for ever in death.

Here the manuscript abruptly terminated, and the emotions of Eugenia and her father found vent in tears. It was some time before they were restored to composure and then they fondly embraced, and Emmeline was introduced to Eugenia as an affectionate sister whom she must ever love and revere.

CHAPTER

THE MARRIAGE.—THE DEATH OF HAROLD.—CONCLUSION.

It was a lovely morning, about three months after these events, that the village bells sent forth their merriest peals, and all was life, and gaiety, and joyous expectation, in the neighbourhood of the Grange and Branscombe House. The peasants were all attired in their holiday gear, and splendid equipages were rattling into the town every minute. It was the morning on which the delighted Sir Evelyn Manners was destined to lead the beauteous Eugenia Cleveland to the hymeneal altar.

For several days past, the most extensive preparations had been made at both mansions, and it was intended to celebrate the auspicious event with the greatest taste and magnificence.

The ceremony is over; the bridal party had quitted the altar, and were emerging from the church, when the loud report of a pistol was heard, and so close to Sir Laurence, that all imagined he was shot, until they beheld one of the attendants sinking, bleeding, to the earth, and all eyes were immediately directed in search of the assassin.

It was Harold!

"D——n!" cried the miscreant; "I have missed my aim!"

Several persons made a rush towards him; but in a moment he snatched another pistol from his bosom, and, presenting it at his head, he cried,—

"Harold, the gipsy, will never die upon the gallows; thus he prevents it. My dying curse light upon ye all!"

With these words, he discharged the contents of the pistol, and sunk a frightful corse upon the earth.

*   *   *   *   *   *

Old Madela had died some weeks before these events took place, and the tribe being abandoned by Harold, and apprehensive of detection, had dispersed, and were no more seen.

We have little more to add. The union of Eugenia and Sir Evelyn Manners was blest with every happiness that their numerous virtues entitled them to; and Sir Laurence Cleveland lived several years to witness their felicity, and to offer up his gratitude to the Supreme for the blessings he had bestowed upon him after his numerous errors.

Angela and Emmeline, in due course of time, were both married to distinguished and amiable noblemen, and are living at the present time, honoured by all who know them.

THE END.